ECHOES
of
GLORY

Books by Robert Flynn

Fiction:
In the House of the Lord
North to Yesterday
The Devil's Tiger
The Last Klick
The Sounds of Rescue, The Signs of Hope
Tie-Fast Country
Wanderer Springs

Short Stories:
Living with the Hyenas
Seasonal Rain and Other Stories
Slouching toward Zion and More Lies

Non-fiction:
A Personal War in Vietnam
Growing up a Sullen Baptist
Paul Baker and the Integration of Abilities
When I Was Just Your Age
Burying the Farm

ECHOES *of* GLORY

Robert Flynn

TCU Press

Fort Worth, Texas

Library of Congress Cataloging-in-Publication Data

Flynn, Robert, 1932-
Echoes of glory / Robert Flynn.
p. cm.
ISBN 978-0-87565-389-1 (pbk. : alk. paper)
1. Heroes—Fiction. 2. College teachers—Fiction. 3. Political campaigns—Fiction. 4.
Playwriting—Fiction. 5. Texas—Fiction. I. Title.
PS3556.L9E36 2009
813'.54—dc22
2008036756

TCU Press
P. O. Box 298300
Fort Worth, Texas 76129
817.257.7822
http://www.prs.tcu.edu

To order books: 800.826.8911

Cover illustration by Deirdre Flynn Bass

Designed by Vicki Whistler

Dedicated to

Reverend James Emmett Flynn

CHAPTER
ONE

⸙

Sheriff Timpson Smith lumbered through the dim, drafty Mills County courthouse, his boot heels gunshots on the wooden floor. The courthouse—a stone breadbox with a metal birdcage for a bell tower—was not designed for grace or beauty but for the assertion of authority. Five Mills was a facsimile of thousands of rural towns that had a sole reason to exist—the courthouse. It was the center of gravity, and it weighed heavy in the county.

Despite his years in office the sheriff had never grown accustomed to the dank smell of limestone, sweat, fear, perfume accented with the ammonia and disinfectant from the public toilets in the basement that had once been the sheriff's office. Without a glance he walked past the display of rusty tools, pistols, and rifles left by the five Mills brothers who had become out of place in their place. The case was as familiar as the face of his wife that he seldom studied any more. He howdied the mayor, district attorney, developer, clerk, lawyer, cronies, supplicants, court flies, he alone in boots, hat and without a tie.

"There goes Timpson Smith. We won't see his like again," someone said, loud enough for him to hear. "And maybe that's a good thing." They chuckled without derision. He was an emblem like the display case, the monument, the pistol on his belt. When he was gone the county would have to invent another.

The sheriff had been a tare extending his roots until he was tangled with the "courthouse crew" so that none could be uprooted without disturbing the others. They weren't friends, but teammates with privilege by association. They had exchanged glances, touches, confidences, as thick as high schoolers in a huddle, but he was quitting the team. They didn't fear him any more or need his sanction. He had announced his retirement with something akin to guilt; remembering the boy he had killed, the lies he had told, the little crimes of the law. They had accepted his announcement with relief.

The sheriff focused on the stairs. Damn, they got steeper every year. And louder. There was a lawsuit to force the county to put in an elevator for a paralyzed veteran who wanted to serve on a jury but couldn't climb the stairs. Ronald Reagan and the sheriff would be out of office. And maybe the vet would be dead before the issue was resolved and the elevator installed.

He climbed to the drafty second floor with its one courtroom, jury room, conference room, and judge's office. One of the sheriff's duties was to provide courtroom security, and he stepped in the side door to survey those present, a visible threat to anyone who troubled the decorum of the building. The only big trial in years had been of a coward who had tortured and killed a young girl but those who wanted to draw and quarter him had been tamed by church and state, and he was a frightened child who cried for his mother in his cell. "I didn't go to do it," he said. The scenes that usually required the sheriff's glare had been property, divorce, and child custody cases.

A half-dozen people were scattered down the courthouse pews. They glanced at him and looked away. After the implicit warning and the judge's nod he stepped back into the hall that was lined with locked filing cabinets. The building seemed poised to explode papers and folders over the town of Five Mills even after they had moved the tax collector, county clerk, agriculture extension, road commissioner, and indigent care to the old jail. His department had expanded to occupy the third floor—space for more files, more deputies, more reports, more everything. Martha was right; the job had become too complex for him with its intricate relationships between social mores, business ethics, and usage of the law. He didn't want to think about that. If the calendar didn't require an election he would happily remain in office. But he had given his word to Martha.

Reaching the third floor, he stopped for a moment to catch his breath. Every year in office he had added a pound and, although too young to retire, some days he was troubled by old wounds and two knees that no longer communicated with each other or the rest of his body. Voters liked heft in a sheriff the way they liked mass in a court-house, and he had obliged them.

The words of his mother came to him every time he saw his name on the sheriff's office door. "Fools' names and fools' faces are often found in public places." His fool name and face had been public too long. He knew they would have his retirement, disability check from the VA, Martha's inheritance from the sale of her father's store, but he was too young to do nothing. He didn't want to return again to those aimless days before Korea. But who would he be other than the face on the statue?

He hadn't intended to be sheriff. Nothing in his life had happened intentionally, not since leaving for Korea. He had done what he could for people who had never doubted his goodness and only once had doubted his judgment. But their faith had become a burden. "Holding public office is like sucking bear tits," Ross Fulcher, the DA, warned him. "Hang on too long and you become the meal."

Every year he arrested people who would be ashamed to do some of the things that corporations and politicians did every day. His job was to enforce the law and protect the people, and those from whom they needed protection were those who wrote the law and those who rewarded them for writing it.

Early on he had found satisfaction in the job. Before the nearby city of Advantage in Doss County had become a commercial center with a state university. Before the Able Company Expressway linking Five Mills to Advantage had shrunk the distance to twenty minutes of competitive driving, sucking high school diplomas out of Mills County and turning Five Mills into a bedroom 'burb and fraternity playhouse. Former mayor Bob Silver said, "The three worst things that ever happened to Five Mills were the railroad going to Advantage, the college going to Advantage, and the Able Company Expressway linking Five Mills to Advantage." The university had been courtesy of Senator Prince Pritchard and the expressway courtesy of Senator Billy Pritchard, but that statement cost the mayor an election because people said he had forgotten Second Platoon.

The sheriff opened the door into what looked more like a bunk-house than a cop shop. The desks, chairs, walls were covered with photographs, maps, boxes, folders, clothing, pieces of weapons, cars, and radios—things around so long no one remembered whose they were or what purpose they had once served. "Let Larry clean it up," he thought.

He nodded at Mrs. Stutz, whose first husband Sarge Lewis called him "slacker" because of his deferment at the end of World War Two as sole support of his mother. Sarge had died with Second Platoon. She had fled Five Mills, worked at the air base in Fort Worth, had a man in her apartment most nights, and spent most weekends in someone else's. When she learned of plans for the monument in Five Mills, she returned to buy a tableau for Sarge. Timp had hired her as secretary-dispatcher when he became sheriff, and she sat prim, frail, and stalwart outside his private office like an old and ill-used parrot. The older she got, the bigger the lips she painted, the brighter and more ruffled her plumage. It was noon, and he had already had several conversations with her by radio and telephone.

"Bryan Frazier called about the parade. He wants to know whether you think it's better to add blacks in the tableaux that are not on the monument or to add black actors to the tableaux that are on the monument regardless of the color of the man represented."

"Other than providing security I have nothing to do with the parade."

"Babbs Morrison, Larry's campaign manager, wants you to endorse Larry."

"Larry's running unopposed. Why does he need my endorsement? Or a campaign manager?" the sheriff asked.

She looked a "duh" at him over wire-rim glasses. The sheriff walked into his office and the allegory of his life: the Congressional Medal of Honor, Purple Heart, United Nations, and Republic of Korea medals, a photograph of the crowd at the high school grandstand where he was honored by the county, the key to Five Mills presented by the mayor, the proclamation from the governor, the photograph of him with Audie Murphy and a starlet. And the *Life* magazine aerial photograph of Five Mills with a US flag over the house of every family that lost a relative in Second Platoon. Except for the aerial photograph, the story was so familiar that the sheriff no longer noticed but worried what to do with it when he vacated the office. The photograph he had memorized as though it were a map to a private country.

T. J. Munday, the mayor who had recruited him for sheriff, had insisted on the display in his office after the election. "Politically necessary," Munday said. "You can't do the job unless you get reelected." Timpson Smith's own little shrine.

As though being sheriff were more than shuffle papers, make speeches, and hire deputies. At least it had been—back in the days when his duties were checking alarms and locks on stores downtown, when a heavy case-load consisted of cows on the highway, a stolen horse or dog, and maybe kids joy-riding in a pickup left running with the keys in it. That was before the Able Company Expressway. Now loose livestock meant a possible seventy mile-per-hour collision. Once a suspicious car parked on a country road could mean kids with a bottle swiped from a liquor cabinet, or some boy pressuring a girl to pleasure him; now it could mean date rape or kids blowing grass. Once fraternity initiations were attempts to dig up the grave of a homeless woman under the guise that she was a witch with golden earrings; now they meant a night at the TripleS X Theater.

The jail had been closed; prisoners were transported to Advantage but still the paper work grew. Five Mills had no police force; the sheriff's department provided security for the town, the suburbs, and the farmers and ranchers of Mills County. The sheriff had spent the morning at an elementary school telling the children about a "child call" program staffed by volunteers and organized by his wife after a boy claimed another boy had touched his social parts. What are social parts? his teacher had asked. Where you get social diseases, he said. Some children reported they had broken a dish or asked the definition of a word, most just wanted to talk to an adult. Declining income had forced mothers into jobs to support the family.

They were the children of parents who worked in offices, shops, bowling alleys, restaurants, and taverns in Advantage, leaving home before the kids left for school, and sometimes coming home after the kids had gone to bed; parents who paid teachers to nurture their children and police to protect them. They were good kids who saw adults as incidental. They scarcely knew aunts, uncles, or grandparents but clubbed together for "family." In a few years they would be in middle school and some in gangs.

Before he left the school the sheriff had gotten a call that Wally Sech was on the Able Company Expressway waving a flag and yelling obscenities. The story that might have been a warning to the town was used to recruit another Mills County platoon, the Timpson Smith Platoon. Wally had enlisted to avenge his brother but the war ended and Second Platoon was no longer exclusively Mills County. Wally came home on leave, went to Captain Billy Pritchard's home in uniform and accused Pritchard and the Marines from Advantage of cowardice. Wally, who had been described as "intense" in elementary school and "fractious" in high school, was discharged with a personality disorder.

Wally took over his father's dry cleaning service, was almost bankrupted by polyester fashions and the dry cleaning store behind Timp's house that took garments to Advantage for return the next day. Most of the workers were undocumented, but they came and went so rapidly Advantage police overlooked them. The border was too far and Border Patrol too busy to investigate. Wally was oblivious to such portents of change, obsessed with revising the past. He stood on the edge of the expressway with a flag and a sign, "Second Platoon bled, Able Company fled."

"You can go home or to work or I'll have you taken to the state hospital. Which do you want?"

Wally got in the back. "How many Commies did my brother kill?"

"Seven or eight maybe," the sheriff hedged.

"Eight. He killed eight commies. He died for something. I told everyone in the state hospital what happened to Second Platoon."

The sheriff had taken Wally to the dry cleaning store, the flag fluttering out the window. He picked up the overnight reports on his desk. Family disturbance in Sleepy Hollow—husband and wife argued; he hit her. Family disturbance in Country Place—a man and his mother went to ex-wife's home to return child; mother argued with ex-wife and slapped her. Such things had happened when he first took the job, but they were family secrets not public complaints, and the women bore their scars in silence.

Hood ornament stolen from Dr. Baines' Mercedes. Exercise bike, stereo and speakers, suitcase containing man's suit and other clothes, two pairs of boots stolen from front yard in Advantage. Suspect believed to be in Mills County. Ed Harkins, a salesman with a family in Five Mills, and Rowena Tooley, a young, single mother in Advantage with expectations. She had thrown out his belongings and someone had taken them.

Mrs. Lubitsch locked herself in her car again and couldn't remember how to get out. Two hitchhikers taken to expressway to Advantage and told not to come back. Disturbance at the Heavenly Gates Modeling Studio but no arrests. Unlawful carrying—kids playing with guns.

Mrs. Stutz buzzed him. "We have a 10–15." Civil disturbance. She loved the argot. "It's Harley Kruger and When and How."

Wynn Mills and his Vietnamese wife, Hao. Before "When and How" it had been "Win and Lose," for Wynn's father and mother, Horace Wynn and Lucy Mills. The legendary Mills family had become threadbare reality. One Mills had died at the Alamo, one at Goliad, three had fought at San Jacinto. After San Jacinto the three had marched into the heart of Texas to build a plain but sturdy limestone house on a little rise they could defend against Indians. According to tradition, they had planted oaks from acorns taken at the San Jacinto battlefield, arrow distance from the house, an oak for each defender who died at the Alamo.

"John responded to a 10–54," Mrs. Stutz said. Livestock on the expressway. "He must be out of his car. I haven't been able to get Larry either."

Riding the range, the sheriff thought. Larry Maddin spent more time on the pistol range than anyone. "Let's see if Wynn and Kruger can work this one out themselves." In Texas, land disputes often led to feuds that resulted in violence, and the sheriff did not want this to be another one.

The Mills family had an outdated code of honor that made them seem combative. They required honesty that some found intimidating. Quick to laugh, they were fierce when threatened, and sensitivity to menace had passed from father to child. The Mills required a lot of space.

"Why did you build your house so close to the Mills house?" Timp had asked Kruger. The Kruger house was tucked into the corner of his property closest to the Mills house.

"It's across the road from the Mills house," said Kruger who had always lived in the city where distance was measured by doors. His house was surrounded by a stone wall, and the only gate was on a side away from the Mills house.

Harley Kruger had dreamed of a fortune made in the halls of Congress and the canyons of Wall Street. Instead he had retired from the Air Force as a lieutenant colonel after a career of writing government contracts and was hired to write contracts for a defense corporation. He worked methodically, spending longer hours than anyone, ignoring irregularities after the CEO suggested he do so, and devising his cover through a maze of underlings who didn't have the imagination to understand the subterfuge. There was money in it if you could endure the untidiness, the stress, the words and numbers that were as slippery as lies. Kruger had announced his retirement and quietly retired to Mills County. He disliked disorganization, and life in the corporation had become chaotic with spin-off companies, subsidiaries, offshore offices.

Harley and his wife bought two hundred acres from Wynn Mills to whom selling family land was akin to treason. Wynn made the decision to rescue his wife from Vietnam and because Kruger agreed that none of the land would be developed and none of the Alamo oaks would be cut. Oaks were scattered across the ranch but there were three motts regarded as the Alamo oaks. Kruger's property enclosed one of the motts and part of another. When Kruger wanted to cut trees for a street and lots for his children's future homes, he had offered Wynn a job cutting the oaks.

Wynn explained to Kruger that generations of Mills County folks had climbed, picnicked, held camp meetings and weddings in the oaks; cutting them was sacrilege. Wynn didn't say that in order to intimidate Union sympathizers a Mills boy had been lynched from one of the oaks his father planted; the Mills had fought for the Union because of loyalty to Sam Houston. The Mills women had cut some of the oaks because bushwhackers hid behind them to shoot at the house. Wynn had been denied unemployment benefits because he had refused a job cutting the oaks.

"Nothing belongs to everyone," Kruger said. It took money to insulate oneself from the desperation of others, the disorder and din of the wretched city life he had escaped, and Kruger had built a splendid house with a stone wall around three acres with gardens, furnishings, fountains, a pool. But income was slower than outgo, so Kruger sold the land, except for his three acres, to a corporation owned by himself, Mayor Claiborne Williams, and developer Glen Timberlake, with Dr. Baines as a silent partner.

Timberlake bulldozed oaks for a street. Wynn didn't have the money to fight him. "Does having money give you rights that other people don't have?" Wynn had asked.

"You have to accept that no matter how hard you fight, some things are not going to be right. And some people are going to benefit because of it," the sheriff had told him.

The Kruger-Mills dispute shifted from trees to water. Kruger turned a tap and there it was. He had a deep well and a powerful pump for fountains, a swimming pool, palm trees, a tropical garden with fish ponds and bamboo, and water for the lots he hoped to sell. The Mills' well went dry, leaving Wynn no water for his family, his house or his livestock. Wynn couldn't afford a deeper well and a pump to replace his windmill.

The sheriff mediated. Kruger agreed to curtail his water use until Wynn's well recovered. "Hell, I'll pump water into his well free of charge. Deadbeat couldn't pay for it anyway. I offered him a job and he refused it."

Until he could afford a long hose that would not be cut by traffic on the road, Wynn and Hao pumped water from Kruger's well to barrels in their pickup, carried water from the barrels to their house and to the barn for their cows. The sheriff shook his head at how hard it was for people to be neighbors.

Two hibiscus and bougainvillea stolen from driveway. Five steers stolen from the Rocker T ranch. Woman using the restroom in the Advantage mall heard someone enter the stall next to her. Red shoes, high heels, painted toenails pointing at the toilet. Suspect believed to be in Mills County.

Mrs. Stutz called. "I still haven't been able to reach John or Larry."

Sheriff Smith called Kruger. Two pit bulls kept inside the Kruger fence had escaped the day before, and they killed the Mills' mutt. Wynn shot Kruger's dogs. Kruger told Wynn he would have to pay for his registered and trained guard dogs. Wynn said he killed the dogs to protect his children.

There wouldn't be trouble because there was no reason for it. "Just calm down," the sheriff said. Kruger lived in a stone house with a six-foot stone wall topped with metal spikes. All he lacked was a moat. "I'll talk to Wynn."

The Advantage newspaper, radio and TV had resorted to "crazed vet" shorthand when Wynn had thrown two professors out of a beer joint several years earlier.

By a quirk of Texas morality, Five Mills was dry, but Mills County was wet. Some church members served alcohol in their homes but frowned on men and women mixing in a tavern. Others wanted an upright image, but they also wanted pleasure and profit, so there were road houses, liquor stores, the TripleS X Theater, Soft Stroke massage parlor, Wild Rose and Heavenly Gates Modeling studios outside the city limits but on the road to hell where they attracted college kids with fake ID cards. There were occasional outbursts of moral outrage. An old-timer wrote that the places on the expressway were "God sins to the lonely." The paper did not correct his spelling and the name stuck.

Wynn had been drinking in one of the joints, and a couple of male professors with coeds made remarks about Vietnam. Wynn pulled one of them out of a chair by his belt and shirt collar and shoved him out the door. The other ran behind the bar. The bartender called the sheriff. The sheriff and Wynn sat in the cruiser and talked.

"You can't stop me from fighting for what I believe in," Wynn said.

"There's justice, there's law, and there's what is," Sheriff Smith said. "This is what is. You can fight it all your life like your father did." Horace had died in the Advantage jail while Wynn was in Vietnam; someone had called his boy a "baby killer." It took four cops to wrestle him into a police car and then into a cell. "But you have to fight with the law not against it."

He told Mrs. Stutz to call the Mills. People fought with the weapons they had or could buy, and Wynn could not afford the law. Wynn's telephone had been disconnected for lack of payment.

Smith rarely responded to a call, but everyone had a how-some-ever and Wynn Mills was his. He put on his hat because a sheriff had to wear a hat when on call just as he had to wear boots to look bigger.

"Tell Kruger I'm on my way," he said as he left.

He walked out into the sunny fall day, slid into the cruiser, made a note of the mileage and the section he would be in, and rolled down the windows. Odor gave up some crime and some criminals. The county was divided into sections plus a hot zone around the Able Company Expressway and town that everyone patrolled. He drove past the smiling face of Larry Maddin on campaign posters. Larry ran unopposed, but he ran scared.

Mills County was Timpson Smith's county. He knew its back doors, back streets, back roads, back-stabbers better than anyone. Near empty square except for Timberlake's office, Wally's dry-cleaning business, *The Grist* newspaper, the county library that was to be named for a writer who had lived in Five Mills while writing the saga of the Mills brothers. The writer had died in an airplane crash during a storm; they found his manuscript, but the rain had ruined it. The library board changed the name to honor Glen Timberlake who had given the vacant building to the library and might give money.

Vacant buildings that tempted the idle young, near-empty stores that listed toward the road to hell—All-Night Laundromat that attracted vagrants and nickel and dime thieves; Overnight Dry Cleaning; the barber shop where black men congregated to tell their anger; Motley Drugs that offered dusty, out-of-date patent medicines, stale candy, cheap sandals, plastic purses, and school supplies; Rent-All that sold used clothing, tools, and sports equipment of suspicious origin; Payroll Loans, only $20 cash; Grabbit N Grin for bread, milk, aspirin, condoms, soft drinks, gas, magazines, and used paperbacks; Drop By drive in that offered warm coffee, stale pastries, and watered drinks. Everything was cheaper, fresher, better at cut-rate stores in Advantage if you had a reason, a car, and gasoline.

Once-splendid homes in the central district restored by young professionals who wanted safe streets and low taxes, and three houses converted to apartments for college students who curtained windows with Confederate, American, or Texas flags, drank beer and dried clothing on the porch and parked cars on the lawn. The sheriff smelled nothing suspicious.

Pink granite monument emblazoned "Second to None," with heroic tableaux around the base and the bronze courageous wounded Marine who loomed over him as a constant reminder of debt, duty, and shame. Timpson Smith belonged to it just as he belonged to the county. Peace had no monuments. Not in Mills County. Peace had no heroes. Peace had martyrs. During the Vietnam War when students from the college had announced plans to desecrate the "symbol of aggression," it had been his job to protect it, he who hated the statue more than any of them could.

Solid Rock Church, bigger, weightier than the courthouse, with a spire that could be seen from any place in town and expensive electronic equipment that required extra protection. Every school day, Sunday, Wednesday night, and special occasion at the church or church school, cars spilled out of the massive parking lots and from in front of the crooked shades, stained roofs, broken sidewalks of what had once been proud middle class houses on Main Street. Every week there were complaints to the sheriff's office about cars that blocked residents' driveways and every month letters to the editor of *The Grist* about taxed houses on taxed property that had been destroyed to make room for the church, school and parking lots that were tax-exempt.

A state highway separated Five Mills from Sleepy Hollow, commonly called "Dogpatch," the instant slum of shabby houses without driveways or sidewalks that he had once helped Timberlake sell. Three times it had been his duty to present eviction notices to those to whom he had sold houses because they refused to pay for roofs that leaked, plumbing that failed, doors that couldn't be closed.

Downhill from Sleepy Hollow was Freetown, a community established by former slaves who had not been allowed to live in Five Mills. Clapboard houses, littered dirt streets, abandoned cars rusting in yards. Brown weeds choked the dry creek that drained floodwaters from Sleepy Hollow through Freetown. There was only one exit from Freetown and a traffic jam every morning for those who worked, went to school, or shopped. There had been frequent wrecks and two traffic deaths but there were no visible crimes he could cite or prevent.

Bordering Freetown was the new golf course being built to please Timberlake and the retirees who had lived and worked in Advantage but wanted a house on the golf course in Five Mills where property was cheaper. They also wanted a traffic light, and the mayor had promised it.

Beyond the golf course the land was empty, devoid of the rural communities that once had huddled around school, church, store, gin or grain elevator. The government extolled family values, but the economy forced women out of the home and into jobs. Country houses had disappeared until the advent of Country Place, a gated community designed for discriminating homeowners who lived in houses designed to please others, the streets segregated by the size and expense of the houses.

Why did a town so small need suburbs? he had asked even while selling houses in Sleepy Hollow. Moving farther into the countryside. Homogenized not by race, interests, or education but by income and the degree of detachment required with the most expensive suburbs the farthest from the stores, schools, churches where neighbors gathered, but with quickest access to the courthouse. The accidental death of a child, the triumph of a public school team, the scandal of a family were a curiosity, no more than that.

It was his county and he would give his life for it but it would be Larry's soon. Larry wanted his endorsement; well, there was a way he could get it. Babbs, his campaign manager, could get Wynn a job at the college. Groundskeeper, carpenter, electrician, Wynn could do it; he had to do everything on the ranch. He could take night classes, run a few cows, keep a garden, and have a steady income. While the boys were in school, Hao could take classes, blend into the goulash that was Mills County. The Yankee wife never did and the Mills family that had been singular became outlandish. Wynn would never leave Mills County, never sell all the land no matter how desperate. As long as he lived next door to Kruger, who believed he could do what he wanted with his property, there would be trouble.

There were no clear lakes, clean pastures, snow-smacked peaks, but it was warm in the sun, and the countryside smelled of trees, cattle, fallow fields. Even when it was brown and dry like today he liked seeing the gently rolling land interrupted only by a creek with pecan, cedar, and cypress trees or the bare, stark branches of mesquite.

"Chief, Kruger says Wynn came to his house and threw food inside his gate upsetting the dogs," Mrs. Stutz reported over the radio. Kruger had already replaced his dogs. "Kruger threatened to shoot Wynn if he didn't leave. Wynn told him not to miss because he wouldn't."

"Did Wynn leave?"

"Yes," she said.

"Tell Kruger to stay in his house and wait for me. Turning on Yanky Road," he reported, closing the windows and speeding up after pulling onto the blacktop. The trail to the Mills place had been called Yankee Road in derision. By the time the county got around to building the road "Yankee" was no longer pejorative but the spelling was changed so as not to give honor to the Mills' Union sympathies. As further insult the county decided the best route for the road was through one of the oak motts and close to the back of the Mills house. It was damn stupid to threaten Wynn Mills.

***

Without taking his eyes off her, Larry Maddin took the money, folded it and placed it in the pocket of his western twill shirt that was as close as he could get to the look of the Texas Rangers.

She was larger than he liked, not flabby but tired and a little bored. That always turned him on. He liked to excite them, see their eyes light up, and their bodies tense with desire. He liked to watch their faces go slack as their senses gathered around their core, their moans when he filled their emptiness, giving voice to their void. He hitched up his gunbelt, stretched toward six feet, lifted his Stetson, brushed back his straight dark hair and dropped his hand to rest loosely on the butt of his pistol. "The next time you entertain your girlfriends, invite them here. Don't write hot checks at Dick's Last Chance. If you want to go dancing, I'll dance with you. Hell, I'll pick up the tab."

She looked at the shrub planted to hide the metal garbage can, then back at him. "I'll remember that," she said evenly. P.J. the d.j. nattered about taxes on a radio somewhere in the doublewide that smelled of stale coffee and warm body. P. J.believed people cared what he thought.

Larry waited, hoping P.J. would play something seductive. The idea that a man wanted them excited women—the knowledge that he was armed and dangerous and he wanted her right then. Women liked to be a little afraid of a man until they realized that 'til the end of time meant until the end of their time. He still had plenty of time left. "I'm sorry we had to meet this way, but I'm glad we cleared this up," he said, tipping his Stetson and then turned on the AstroTurf that served as porch and walked away to let her know that he was under control; he wasn't harmless, but he could be trusted. P.J. was still talking.

"Nice meeting you," she said before closing the door.

It wasn't an invitation, but it contained a hint of interest. He'd give her a couple of days to think it over and then at the end of his patrol he'd stop by to see how she was doing, maybe bring something extravagant. Women liked that. Roses. A bottle of wine. A couple of steaks. She looked like she could tear into red meat. And afterwards, so would he.

He had left the cruiser at the entrance to the treeless trailer park, decorated only by cheap cars and garbage cans. Half the people there had reason to fear him—dead-beat fathers, mothers writing hot checks expecting child support to cover them, pot heads, owners of cars with overdue payments or expired inspection stickers—let them all sweat.

He looked at his watch. Time to make a swing by the God sins, the touchy-feelie Wild Rose, Heavenly Gates, Soft Stroke side by side in a weedy field that had been a drive-in movie; customers could park in back behind the wooden fence and slip from one to the next. Sometimes the girls met at the fence to smoke cigarettes and sip gin, sometimes screamed at each other and pulled hair, sometimes wrestled with men in fear, passion, or commerce.

Too early for much business, but the girls would be there, especially those looking for work. He liked to meet them, make sure they weren't runaways, then drop by at closing time, see if anybody wanted an escort. If they'd had trouble with a client, and most of them did, at some time, they liked an escort. If they lived alone, he escorted them inside to be sure no one lurked in their closet and once he was inside what were they going to do, call a cop? Sometimes all he got was a grope and a promise, but he kept going back until they gave in or moved on.

Usually they let him slip his pistol in their holster as the cost of doing business and a few led him straight to bed. Those were scary because when you pulled back the covers you never knew what you were getting into. Once he went to bed with a dancer who had accidentally on purpose sat on his lap. There was something sexy about a tomboy girl until he found a third leg. He gave the guy an LA beating—not enough for a hospital record but enough to keep his mouth shut.

Babbs thought he shouldn't be seen with a lot of women before an election, but a man associated with violence was attractive to women, and there were so many women, and they all wanted to be mothers. Children were the mirror in which women reflected their ego. He had paid for a couple of abortions and supported a child out of wedlock. He was not irresponsible; he was a free spirit. Women liked that. Even the kind who were desperate to nest liked that he was a handful.

You didn't have to marry for sex, but you did for home cooking. Home cooking was overrated; he preferred the envy of other men. "That damn Larry has screwed every woman in two counties." He remembered the bachelor's blessing, "May you marry an interesting woman," and he didn't want to go into a joint and find his wife there or have her dry up because she heard things she wasn't supposed to know. Martha Smith was willing to be Mrs. Sheriff but he didn't know any women like that. Better to be feared than loved; they tried harder.

Larry heard the dispatcher calling. The old bitch must be seventy, judged everyone by whether they bought a tableau. Larry was going to replace her when he became high sheriff. His first day as deputy Mrs. Stutz reported a green pickup westbound on east expressway. "What's the problem?" he had responded. She paused a beat then replied, "Wrong way." She had never let him forget it, sometimes called him "wrong way."

He hurried to the car. "Ten-one," he responded. Unable to copy. Let her think it was the radio. "What's burning your bloomers?"

"Please keep communication official, Larry," she said in the tight-ass dismissive way she had. Laaaaary. Making it sound like an insult. He hated Larry and tried to use Monte as a nickname. Monte Maddin. They'd respect that. The nickname had never caught on. Sheriff Maddin would.

"Harley Kruger reported a 10–15 and a 10–32." Civil disturbance and man with a gun.

Damn professioners, Larry thought, *worked and shopped in Advantage but complained in Five Mills*—Water and Sanitation, Tax Appraisal, Housing and Street Commission, above all the sheriff's department. Ask a neighbor about property lines, to look at a child's cut foot, for a ride to town, something you would ask any neighbor, and you got a bill or a bird. Drop a cigarette butt in the street and they called the sheriff. Larry thought being a deputy made him an insider but it didn't.

***

Advantage, a soulless town, was the creation of Doss, Pritchard, and Babbs who had come to Mills County after the Civil War to despoil the defeated. Doss had railroad interests, Pritchard was a banker and land speculator, Babbs opened a general store, post office, stable, hotel, and newspaper. The newspaper championed Pritchard for mayor. Voters could elect a carpetbagger or a freed slave from Freetown and even former Rebels voted for a carpetbagger.

Advantage had a heart of business, a history of commerce, and some professors at the university discovered the quaint town of Five Mills and moved there seeking bargain homes and country values. Old timers called newcomers "professor." Lawyers, doctors and other professionals followed and the name was enlarged to "professioners" to include them all. Babbs said they were Larry's base but he didn't need a base. He was unopposed.

Harley Kruger was part of the third wave, outsiders who made a fortune in Pittsburgh or some place and retired to the country life only a city man could afford. To discover that he lived next door to the most dangerous man in the county. "When and How?" he asked.

"John is working a 10–54. I couldn't get you so the chief took it."

Damn, he had been collecting hot checks and the sheriff was going to the Mills place alone. A couple of cows on the road to hell could keep John busy for hours. "Ten-seventy-nine," he said. On his way.

"Make it a 10–40," she said. Silent run.

He was a baby when Timp was in Korea but he had spent hours studying the monument with a wounded, defiant Timpson Smith on top and the legend on the back, "utter disregard of personal danger, gallant display of heroic action, no thought of their own survival, honor words cannot express." When he played war games with other kids he was always Smith, fighting alone with his dead comrades around him, too tough to surrender or die. He had memorized some of the words from the story. "Grizzled veterans of Tarawa and Iwo Jima viewed the scene of the ferocious fight in openmouthed awe; some wept, others prayed." Timp was the reason he went into law enforcement. The day Timp welcomed him to the department had been the proudest day of his life.

Larry tried to coax speed out of the old clunker, having to treat it like a girlfriend instead of a wife. He liked to use the lights and siren when going this fast but he didn't want to warn Wynn. Wynn was a trained killer and flashing lights or a siren might send him back to the 'Nam. Larry had seen Wynn and the other vets huddled in bars, talking about zapping and fragging and killing gooks. Treating him as an outsider. He often imagined himself in Saigon during Tet, keeping gooks out of the Embassy, fighting on with everyone around him dead, coming home a hero, offered a movie career. He could be an actor, too, if he were given that kind of break. He was tall and wiry like a Texas Ranger. He wore long sideburns to make his face look thinner, more mature, more like Clint Eastwood, and he did a good imitation of John Wayne. Babbs said anyone could act like Wayne but they didn't look like Wayne. Neither did John Wesley Hardin, Billy the Kid, L.H. McNelly. Maybe if they had looked like John Wayne they wouldn't have had to kill so many people. He squinted to crease his baby smooth face.

Larry envied Wynn that cold, killer look. Like Timp, Wynn could walk into a beer joint and have everyone quail. Larry had a badge and pistol but some people didn't take him seriously. His biggest fear was that there would be a disturbance and no one would listen to him. It was a frequent nightmare; bedlam and him unable to get control even when he fired his pistol.

Wynn carried his killings like a badge. Looking down on him because he had never shot anyone. Larry touched the gun strapped to his ankle. John Banks kidded him about carrying two pistols but he feared being alone and unarmed. People didn't understand the terror of stopping a car on a deserted road. Walking into a dark building and not knowing who was inside or how armed. Like Timp had done. Bullets flying past him. Taking deliberate aim and putting a bullet right through the kid's heart. Damn.

Mrs. Stutz called a 10–20, asking his location; Timp was on the scene. Larry was turning on Yanky Road and stated his ETA as five minutes.

Still without lights or siren, Larry pushed a little harder on the accelerator, coming to the rescue, like Timp must have felt when he landed in Korea, preventing the Reds from driving US and UN forces into the sea. Wouldn't it be something if he rescued Kruger? If he rescued Timp? He had let Timp down when Scott Baines was killed. Timp never said anything but he knew. Walk up to Wynn and demand his pistol. "Either you give it to me or I take it and fire it up your ass." Stand up to Wynn the way Timp stood up to the mob that was going to destroy his statue, single-handedly defending the monument as no one else could have done.

So caught up was Larry in his drama that he almost turned on the lights and siren for the proper effect. He imagined a television crew arriving as he did, filming him disarming a crazed Wynn. Thousands of people seeing it. Ensuring his election as a sheriff everyone feared and admired. Until Hollywood called him to play tough guy roles.

***

Instinctively the sheriff looked for new trash in the illegal dump called Timberlake Park. Paints and chemicals had contaminated the soil and seeped into a creek. He had been unable to find the drivers or contractors responsible, the state was unable to find the owner, and contaminants continued to poison the creek.

He rolled down his window and sniffed for foreign odors but there were no car tracks or signs of recent activity around the old barn where Scott Baines had died. Until then his life had seemed blessed. Martha wanted him to retire after Scott's death but he needed that election. He promised if she would help him it would be his last. He had squeaked out a victory because of old friends and loyalties but he had strained them.

Mrs. Stutz reported that Kruger had heard shots from the Mills house. "Kruger's scared. I can't keep him on the phone."

Wynn had been expelled from high school for assaulting the coach. His mother had worked beside Horace in the field, picked and canned other people's corn or peas on the halves to feed her family, cleaned other women's houses, took in washing and ironing. One day the coach said a ragged football play was as "sorry as my washer woman." Slow to forget the beating Wynn gave the coach, quick to forget the Navy Cross and two Purple Hearts, people regarded Wynn as though he had been in the penitentiary rather than Vietnam. No one offered him a job. The sheriff was unable to hire him because of his arrest for assault and battery.

Above the brown of the fields rose the green of the Alamo oaks, the idiosyncratic live oak trees that held their leaves all winter and shed them when other trees turned green. Mrs. Stutz reported that Kruger said Wynn had killed Hao and their two boys and was coming after him. "I'm still working on backup."

Timp believed Kruger was overwrought and that he could best handle Wynn alone, but he liked the security of a backup. "Tell John to come easy." He saw square-headed, crew cut Kruger and his petite, skin-so-tight-it-shined wife in their dark blue Mercedes waving him to a stop. He pulled up and lowered the window. "He's gone crazy," Kruger said. "He's killing everyone." Mrs. Kruger's round eyes were made rounder by fright. The farther professioners moved into the countryside for peace and quiet the scareder they got.

"What happened?"

As usual Hao had cleaned house for the Krugers that morning but Kruger told her he would keep her wages until Wynn paid for his dogs. He did give her leftover food. "Wynn threw the food in our yard and went home to get a gun," Harley said. "She tried to stop him and he beat her up. We could hear her screaming. Then we heard a shot and the screams stopped. He killed her and the children and was coming after us."

"Did you see Wynn shoot anyone?"

"Oh, he shot her all right," Kruger said. "And the boys too."

The sheriff closed the window, drove past the Kruger mansion, turned into a dirt lane, scattering chickens and feathers, to the front of the house that faced away from the road. The Mills house remained much as when first built except for a bathroom attached to the back and a porch added to the front.

He sat for a moment in the car with the engine running to see if Wynn had replaced his dog, then called 10–23, he was on the scene. The rose bushes along the house had been neatly pruned and the garden lay plowed and fallow waiting for spring and rain. No cows were visible beyond the fence. He got out of the car, slamming the door as loud as he could. He didn't want to surprise Wynn or a dog. He stood beside the car and called.

"What do you want, Timp?" Wynn called from inside the house.

"We've had a complaint. Come outside so we can talk."

"You're armed."

That damn pistol. When first elected he didn't carry a pistol although people grumbled about it. Guns made them feel secure as they were more familiar with guns than laws, and guns more rarely misfired. His old battalion gave him the Colt .45 with the Marine Corps emblem engraved on one side and the monument on the other; US and UN flags were embedded in the grip. He wore it to honor the dead and to please the voters. Wearing it had become part of dressing. "Come out in the yard where we can talk. I think I have a job for you. Your wife and your kids, too. It involves them."

"They're not coming out."

The hair on his neck prickled. He had to be certain the family was okay. Gathering his body around him and drawing breath he walked toward the house.

"Don't come any closer. I'm not going to jail and I can't take this shit any more." Wynn's voice cracked. "Is he going to pay for my dog, my chickens?"

"I think I can get you a job at the college, a steady income with benefits. Your wife would be part of the deal. Tell her to come out so we can talk."

Out of the corner of his eye, the sheriff saw a cruiser stop beside the Kruger car. *Please God, let John come easy*, he prayed. The car rolled past the Kruger house and stopped on the county road behind Wynn's house. Larry Maddin got out of the car to sneak up on the house. *Damn fool, what was he doing?* The sheriff feared if he called to Larry, Wynn would think he was surrounded and start shooting. He flexed the fingers of his right hand to wave off Larry knowing that Wynn might think he was preparing to reach for his pistol.

He had to get Wynn outside and disarmed before Larry showed himself. He raised his right hand, pushed back his hat and rubbed his brow, shielding his eyes so he could look for Larry. Larry was back in the car. Maybe he'd stay there. "If I put the gun on the porch will you come out and talk?"

Wynn slowly pushed the screen door open with the barrel of a shotgun. "Put your gun on the ground, back up, and I'll put the shotgun and your pistol in the swing."

Wynn would be between him and the guns but the sheriff decided to risk it.

"Larry wants a favor and I think I can get one from Babbs Morrison in return."

Slowly, he pulled out the pistol and placed it on the ground, then backed up, his hands still away from his sides.

***

"Kruger reported a 10–78," Mrs. Stutz said. Officer in danger.

Larry's celluloid fantasy melted in the reality of an armed and dangerous Wynn Mills. Involuntarily Larry slowed. Realizing what he had done, he picked up speed again but not too fast. Timp wanted him to sneak up on Wynn, catch him off-guard. He slowed when he saw Kruger in the middle of the road waving. Kruger stood beside his car, visibly scared.

"Wynn has gone berserk," Kruger said. "He killed his wife and kids and the only thing stopping him from killing us is the sheriff."

"Where is the sheriff?"

"He drove up in front of Wynn's house. You'd better hurry."

Larry drove slowly down Yanky Road. He could see Timp's car in the yard and Timp standing away from it. Timp's hands hung away from his sides like Wynn had a gun on him. Holy crap.

He pulled the car off the road and behind an oak tree where he was not directly in front of any window and left the engine running. He got out of the car then turned back to report he was on the scene. He couldn't see Wynn but he saw Timp flexing his fingers preparing for a quick draw. Slowly he approached the house. Wynn had a gun on Timp. He backed up behind the tree, leaned against the tree to take a shuddering breath, wondering if he should make a run for the car and call the Highway Patrol.

There wasn't time. Taking a deep breath he pulled his pistol, bent low and raced for the protection of the house. There was a loophole in the wall and he raised to take a quick look. It was blocked. He took a longer look. It was permanently blocked with concrete. Staying below the small, shoulder-high windows he crept around the solid limestone house that smelled of generations of Mills pissing in the yard. He slid along the wall, quickly turning the corner, startling chickens whose yelps unnerved him and alerted Wynn. He slipped along the wall, stepping around a stack of firewood and ducking under a window, until only the corner of the house was between him and sight of Timp. Taking a deep breath he peeked around the corner of the house until he could see Timp. Jesus, Timp's pistol was gone.

Positioning the gun beside his right ear, Larry stepped far enough around the corner to clear one eye and the pistol. He saw Wynn's back with the butt of a shotgun on one side and the end of the barrel on the other. "Stop or I'll shoot," he yelled, his voice sounding strange in his own ears, harsh, loud, frightened.

Startled, Wynn turned.

"No," Timp yelled, his voice lost in the screams, shouts, bedlam.

CHAPTER
TWO

⚜

Wynn turned, quick as a snake. Larry fired, as fast as he could pull the trigger. When he stopped Wynn was on the ground in a cloud of dust. Larry sagged, gagging at the sharp stench of gunpowder. He reeled from the screaming, wailing, and above it all, his own voice, thin, high-pitched, "Are you all right, Timp?" And Timp's voice. "What happened?"

Larry leaned against the stone wall, gasping for breath, holding the pistol on Wynn who was covered by his wife, sons and the sheriff kneeling over him. The sheriff got up, walked down the barrel of Larry's pistol, took it from his hand, and put it in his holster. "Go to the car and call for an ambulance."

Larry started for the sheriff's car. The sheriff caught him by the arm. "Go to your car. Call a 10–79." Larry started for his car. "Wait." The sheriff picked up the pistol and shotgun and put them in his arms. "Take these with you. Get back to the office and make a report."

Larry stumbled past the house. Someone grabbed at him and he jerked away almost dropping the guns reaching for his pistol. It was a tree branch. Larry put the guns in the back seat, got in the car and spun around in a shower of grass and debris, oblivious to Kruger who tried to wave him down. He was on his way to town before he remembered to call. "Code eight," he said. "Mills place. Wynn has been shot."

He slammed on the brakes, barely making a curve. Jesus, if he didn't slow down he was going to kill himself. Wynn had almost killed him and here he was trying to kill himself. He took his foot off the accelerator again, unable to control his speed. Jesus, he had killed Wynn Mills in a face-to-face showdown. Scared as he was. Man, was he scared.

Larry chuckled to himself. All his life he feared being a coward. For the first time he could confess that he was scared because he had proved his courage. Brave as Timpson Smith; that was his ticket to the office.

"State his condition. What is Wynn's condition?"

"Unknown." He was so befuddled he ran off the road and had to jerk the cruiser back on the blacktop. "I shot him," he said, and forced his foot off the accelerator. "Call the coroner." He had killed a man. He wondered how it felt. His legs trembled.

"Is the chief okay?"

What if there was someone else in the house? What if after he left something happened to the sheriff? The sheriff told him to leave. He put his foot on the brake, slowed the car, and pulled off the road. He took a deep breath and put his head between his arms on the steering wheel. Timp told him to call an ambulance. He had called an ambulance. Notify the coroner. Get back to the office. Make a report.

     ***

    The sheriff was stunned, his senses recoiling from the gunshots, gasps, groans, wails, Wynn's body shuddering, a boot-heel scarring the ground. No movement, no sound. Wynn Mills, a hero in a war where no one wanted heroes, dead on his own land. He had done nothing to prevent it. "What happened?" Timp asked, his voice lost in the ringing in his ears.

"I got him Timp I got him Timp I got him."

The sheriff kneeled beside Wynn, feeling for a pulse, having to reach past the woman to do it.

Timp already knew, knew beyond faith that Wynn was dead. He looked at the woman wondering what he could do. *Get Larry off the scene.* He didn't want the woman to have to look at Larry. He didn't want to have to look at him either.

Larry held the pistol in both hands pointing at them.

"Go back to the car," Timp choked.

Larry's eyes were wide but unseeing, his mouth open, his hands trembling.

Timp tried to swallow bile. "Call a 10–79." He couldn't bring himself to say body wagon or coroner although Hao knew as well as he.

Keeping himself between Larry and the woman and children, the sheriff took the pistol, put it in Larry's holster, and took him by both shoulders. "Go to your car. Make the calls. Go to the office and write a report."

Then, he tugged the shotgun from beneath Wynn's back. It was an antiquated double-barreled shotgun with two thumb-buster hammers; neither had been cocked. He broke the breech, took out two shells, and gave Larry his pistol, too; he didn't want to look at them. If he hadn't been wearing the pistol Wynn would have put down the shotgun before Larry got there. If he had left it in the car. If he had thrown it on the ground. *The hammers hadn't been cocked.*

He returned to the woman and children. He didn't know whether she wanted to cry on his shoulder or scream in his face. He put his hand on her shoulder. She flinched from fear or anger and refused to face him. "I'm sorry," he said. He sat beside her, too close to the body. Over the dark, musky stench of the blood-soaked ground was the faint smell of Hao's sweat and the pine of cleaning oil. Timp patted the youngest boy, Tien, who was shaking and poking at the blood-stiffened ground with a stick. Timp couldn't reach the other boy without touching her.

He went into the house, ignoring the onion, fish sauce, puppy dog, wash day smells and cleaned his hands of the blood from the shotgun. He found a blanket and covered Wynn, having to pull the woman away to do it. The woman and her two sons threw themselves on the blanket. She had left everything that was familiar to follow a dream of love and freedom. What did she think of America now?

He returned to the house, got a towel and wiped the blood from the hands and faces of the boys. He reached for the woman's hand and when she did not resist, he cleaned her face too.

Where the hell was the body wagon? He wanted to get them away from death in the yard, away from the cameras that were coming. He had to ask her questions, fill out papers. God, he hated the job some- times. He sat beside her, realizing for the first time that the ground was cold; crows, startled out of the oaks by the gunshots, settled back on the branches. Chickens returned to the yard, cocking an eye at the body on the ground. She still cried but softly now, like an American. Not that wailing. He hadn't heard wailing like that since his mother learned of his father's death. She had shrieked, wanting her throat to hurt, until she fainted. He thought she had died.

He was surprised at how small Hao was, thin, but tough, familiar with dead bodies in the yard. Pretty, with the full cheeks, short nose and dark, serious eyes of a child. There were good people in the county. They would help her. They had sustained him all his life.

Larry pulled into the department parking lot beside the court-house. He saw Jimmy Vines who had bought the local paper, *The Grist*, and turned it into a daily. Jimmy had a photographer with him. Larry didn't want to see anyone. He wanted to sit in a quiet place sur-rounded by people who ignored him. He took the microphone and reported his mileage, picked up the briefcase he carried as part of his image and pawed through the contents—spare handcuffs, telescope, magnifying glass, extra flashlight, county map, town map, chalk, law books, rubber gloves, hand sanitizer. He cleaned his hands of the blood from the shotgun and dabbed where it had streaked his shirt. A van from the Advantage TV station screeched to a stop. Two men jumped out and unloaded equipment. He wiped unsuccessfully at his shirt. What the hell, he had been in a battle. The TV camera forced him out of the car.

"There was a disturbance at the Mills ranch," he began hoping to tell his story without questions. "Timp took the call. I backed him up. When I got there, Wynn had a shotgun on Timp and when I told him to drop it—"

"What time was this?"

Larry looked at his watch but came up with no numbers. "It was . . . it just happened." They looked as though he hadn't answered the question.

"Was Wynn alive when you left?"

Their questions made no sense. The sheriff said to call a 10–79. "Wynn was dead."

"Where was Wynn hit?"

The picture flashed before him, the dust, the blood. He must have shot him everywhere. "Wynn was holding his wife and children hostage."

"How long had the sheriff been there when you arrived?"

He couldn't look derelict. "I responded as soon as I heard the call."

"Was there anything unusual about the call?"

"Wynn Mills can be violent."

"Was he considered dangerous?"

The questions came fast; they were in a hurry to get to the scene for pictures of Wynn. Larry was trying to answer the next question while remembering how incompletely he had answered the last.

"If you had gotten the call would you have waited for a backup?"

Larry wanted to appear in charge without making the sheriff look bad. "That's why I favor a volunteer posse. We're shorthanded but we don't want to ask taxpayers for more money." That would sound good to voters who wanted security but didn't want to pay for it.

"Let's get a shot of you as you approached the suspect. In front of that tree? I don't want the courthouse in the background." Larry assumed the approved movie model, feet braced, gun hand extended, left hand gripping wrist. "Can you spread you legs a little more? The other way."

"Is that Wynn's shotgun?" Jimmy Vines asked, hunched like a vulture looking in the car. "Hold it up so we can get a picture." Larry gingerly picked up the bloody shotgun. "Show us how Wynn held the shotgun."

"He had it cradled in one arm kind of like—" He cradled the shotgun streaking his shirt with dried blood. "He had a pistol in the other hand."

"Let's get a shot of that."

Larry got Timp's pistol but had no memory of how Wynn looked. "Try to point both of them at me. Crouch a little. Turn like Wynn did when you told him to drop the guns. Try it again and point the guns directly at the camera. You're holding the pistol with the barrel pointing down. Great."

"Isn't that Timp's gun?" Vines asked. "Did Wynn have Timp's gun?"

"No." He looked at the commemorative pistol without belief. Timpson Smith's courage was dogma requiring no evidence. They looked at him as though he had lied. Did they think Timp had backed down? The thought sickened him. He pulled out a handkerchief and began cleaning the pistol of dirt and blood. "When somebody has a shotgun you back off. And reach for a rifle." They chuckled and made notes. "We should be glad Timp's going to be around to retire."

"So you saved Timpson Smith's life?"

Saved Timp's life. The way he had dreamed. He couldn't believe it. "Timp would have done the same for me," he said, magnanimously. The TV crew hurried to their van and left for the Mills place. Vines watched them go then posed Larry by the cruiser, one hand holding Wynn's shotgun, the other holding Timp's pistol just above his own holstered pistol. "You can use this for a campaign photograph," Vines said.

***

Deputy Cecil Smart led the pick-up crew to the scene. Larry believed Cecil was too old to learn modern police work but he was off-duty and had come to help. Cecil would investigate the scene and be unresponsive to media. "Came as soon as I heard," he said.

"Don't let the media trample the scene. I'll get back as soon as I can."

Hao and the boys tried to go with Wynn's body but the driver said no. The sheriff put them in his car, carefully avoiding the bloodied ground. "We go with Wynn," she said.

"When he's ready. Right now I want to get out of here." They were lucky the cameras hadn't beaten Cecil to the scene. They must have intercepted Larry. He almost smiled at that. Larry was going to be sheriff so let him deal with the reporters.

The sheriff did not follow the ambulance but took the back roads he knew. He told Mrs. Stutz that Wynn's body had been picked up and reported 10–7, out of service. The media would get their photographs; they would get their stories. What they wouldn't get were pictures of Hao and the children clinging to Wynn's riddled body. He didn't have to appease them any more.

He remembered 'Round Back Chili, a country beer joint where farmers and ranchers drank to avoid the college crowd at the express-way taverns and God sins. He pulled the cruiser behind the paintless wooden shed that posed as a roadhouse and seemed to be held to-gether by rusting metal signs. Beer bottle caps served for paving. A single red neon sign that flashed BEER day or night, open or closed was its only identification. 'Round Back Chili was what others called it. He led Hao and the boys past the plastic tables and chairs scattered under a tree. Inside, the children, half-blind in the dimness that smelled of sour beer and cigarette stubs, looked wide eyed at the boars' heads, antlers, bobcats, mountain lion, Confederate flag, blinking beer signs that illuminated photographs of seminude women on the walls that weren't covered with old license plates. Hao seemed in shock, obvious to time or place. A farmer sitting at the bar stared at their blood-streaked clothes. "Been in a wreck?"

Timp answered him with a glare and said to Harold, "I need food for these folks, whatever you have." The farmer returned his attention to his beer. Anyone who sold alcohol had to get along with the sheriff, and Harold always had something to worry about—selling beer after hours, selling beer or cigarettes to minors, using illegals to clean and wash dishes.

"This ain't no restaurant," Harold said in his whiny, insolent voice. Harold was thin as a rake with spaced teeth to match. A down-turned

mouth covered the spaces in steady disapproval. The chili around
back was take-out and regulars helped themselves, putting it on their
bar tab. "Is the county going to pay for this?" he asked.

"I'm going to pay for this," Timp said and Harold left grumbling.

Timp seated Hao and the boys at a back booth where he could
see anyone approaching them. Harold and the farmer had their heads
together at the bar. The woman wept quietly. Sitting between her two
sons, Hao looked like a child herself. The boys wept too but sneaked
looks at the nuts and pickled quail eggs on the table. Reaganmuffins in
a land with the richest makers of the deadliest weapons the world had
ever known.

The sheriff remembered that hunger. When his father died women
came, held his mother, rubbed her wrists and bathed her face with
perfumed handkerchiefs. He hid in his room not knowing who to be
until they coaxed him out with fried chicken, mashed potatoes, pickled
peaches, cakes, pies, more riches than he had ever imagined. He had
never eaten so well.

Harold brought them chili, tamales, crackers, catsup and pop. "Stay
here until I come get you," Timp told the woman. He turned to Harold,
"Give them peanut patties, chewing gum, anything you have that they
want. If anyone bothers them, tell them I said they will be charged with
witness tampering." Harold's lip curled to show the sheriff he didn't like
being talked to like the sheriff owned the place but he would do what
he was told.

Smith returned to the car and reported 10–8, back in service. "They
are plenty mad," Mrs. Stutz said. "They talked to Larry then went to the
Mills place and talked to Kruger. They aren't happy that you moved the
body."

The sheriff allowed himself a smile. He wasn't a candidate and he
didn't need their good will. "Where are they now?"

"They're waiting at the courthouse for you and watching the
funeral home for the widow and children."

***

Cecil had drawn a rough sketch of the scene and taken photographs. "I didn't say nothing to the reporters but 'keep back,'" Cecil
said. "Wynn had an old rifle and pistol in the attic out of reach of the
boys." He showed Timp a hog's leg and a Springfield '03 that had belonged to Wynn's grandfather. In the evidence bag was an expended

shotgun shell.

"Birdshot. Like the ones I took from Wynn's shotgun," Timp said adding his two shells to the bag. He searched in a pattern the reverse of the one Cecil had done. Larry used a revolver so there were no shells and little evidence. Larry said the average homicide required 200 pieces of evidence. This was no homicide and Timp knew the manner and cause of death and the coroner would make it official. He stopped and studied the ground clearly marked where Wynn had turned and where the guns hit the ground. He looked at Cecil who was watching him. Cecil had seen it too.

"I got pictures," Cecil said.

***

Larry slumped against the cruiser watching Vines and the photographer disappear like his cover. He had always pretended to be as brave as Timp while standing behind him; now he had to be as brave as Timp every day. A few curious souls had been drawn by the cameras. "Our next sheriff is going to be as big a hero as the last," one of them said. At his side a young girl made love to an ice cream cone. Some day his name would be on a glass case of photographs and honors alongside that of Timpson Smith. And the Mills brothers. He straightened and walked into the courthouse nodding at endorsement.

"Timp called," Mrs. Stutz said in the disapproving way she had. "Wynn is dead." Damn, shot him through the heart. Scared as he was. "How was Timp taking it?" she asked. "Wynn was a friend of his."

"He came close as a clinch to being killed by a friend." She looked at him like he smelled bad. He held out his arms to show his bloody shirt. "It got hairy before the dust settled." She was unimpressed. "Wynn had Timp's pistol."

"Where were you when I tried to get you?" Bitch was going to be the first thing he took care of when he was sworn in. "You're supposed to be close to the telephone." No matter what he did she withheld approval the way women did even when you had them panting and moaning.

Without responding he went into the bunkhouse and sat down. In the beginning the sheriff's office had been a desk in the jail. Deputies were whatever idle men the sheriff could find when he needed them and if they had to spend the night they hung their pistol belts on pegs in the wall and slept in the empty cell. Eventually a night deputy was hired and a cot added. Later the department was moved to the basement of the courthouse with an office for the sheriff and records and a room called the bunkhouse with chairs, cots and pegs for the deputies. Even after the department took over the third floor and deputies were given their own desks the place looked like a bunkhouse with coffee cups and half-eaten sandwiches on the desks, the trashcans overflowing. That shit would change when he was sheriff.

Larry knew he should call Babbs Morrison. Babbs had told him never to speak to the media without conferring with him first but he had no chance. Babbs, a political science professor, had offered to manage his campaign for sheriff to get a promotion or something at the college. He no longer needed Babbs to tell voters who he was. After today they knew.

He picked up the report form. Case number. Offense. Initially it had been Civil Disturbance but had escalated to . . . Attempted Murder, Assault With a Deadly Weapon. He wrote in Timp and himself as victims and Wynn Mills as suspect. Address, race, sex, date of birth, description, driver's license number, Social Security number, he would leave for Mrs. Stutz.

He didn't want to write where he was when Timp took the call. "Above date, time and location, I was dispatched to the Mills place to back-up Sheriff Smith. Wynn Mills had shot at Harley Kruger and his wife and was holding his own wife and children hostage. Upon arrival—"

He was interrupted by the telephone. "This is P.J. the d.j. Can you confirm that Larry Maddin killed Wynn Mills?"

Why the hell was a disc-jockey calling him? "That's affirmative. I—"

When Larry replaced the receiver it immediately rang again. *The Grist.* "I'm working on the Mills story and want to clear up a few details."

After hanging up, he began again. " . . . approached the house under cover. Observing Sheriff Smith in danger, I ordered Mills to drop—"

Damn. His thoughts were interrupted by the arrival of John Banks, unprofessional as usual in jeans, T-shirt, and battered field jacket. When he was sheriff he would tell John that a black deputy had to look at least as official as white ones, and if John wanted to call that prejudice, let him try.

"Hey, man, I hear you got into some heavy shit," John said, sipping coffee and showering Larry's desk with powdered sugar from a doughnut.

Larry displayed his bloody shirt. "Wynn was threatening to kill

Timp. I shot him through the heart at fifteen, twenty yards."

"Not bad shooting when you're scared."

"He would have killed Timp." John pursed his lips. "Just ask—" He almost said ask the reporters. "Ask Timp." John grunted, maybe in admiration but blacks had their own code. "Timp gave up his pistol."

"Bullshit. Timp didn't go to shoot anybody. Wynn wasn't dangerous."

"The hell he wasn't." John thought he should be sheriff but John was too jaunty, too . . . black. "He tried to shoot me."

"Man, Wynn wasn't going to kill anybody." John left dusting his hands after leaving his coffee cup on Larry's desk.

John was going to be the first deputy to go after the election. And John knew it. Unprofessional. Larry returned to his typing. "Despite my warnings Mills refused to drop his weapons. Believing my life and that of—"

The DA came in, placed one haunch on the desk and folded his arms across his chest. Larry rolled back in his chair. To lawyers everything was "reasonable doubt" or "inadmissible evidence." Ross Fulcher looked bigger than his average height, soft overhung middle, and sallow for his fifty years. But he had the eyes of a policeman who had seen everything, the confidence of a public official who knew anything he did to you could be lost or misfiled and anything you did in defense would be used against you, and the arrogance of a lawyer who knew no matter how right you were he could get you on a technicality.

Fulcher didn't say anything but Larry knew he had noted the bloody shirt. "Give me the facts," Fulcher said in his drowsy voice.

Larry knew the less he said the harder it would be for Fulcher to trip him. Wynn threatened Kruger, took his own family hostage, disarmed Timp, and turned the weapons on Larry. "I had to shoot him."

"Why did Timp take the call?" Fulcher asked in the unnerving way he had of asking dangerous questions as though the answer didn't matter. Larry shrugged and tried to appear puzzled. "I'm glad you were there."

Larry nodded modestly. "Every one of the Mills was tough."

"Wynn's got two boys." It wasn't exactly a question.

The widow had all that land and Kruger had plans for a private kingdom for the select. She was pretty for a gook. Larry wondered if he should drop in as her protector, see how she and the kids were doing.

"I'll talk to the justice of the peace; we support our officers."

Larry nodded his thanks. He needed the DA and the mayor for the party's approval. Sometimes it was Republican sometimes Democratic but the same people ran it, changing parties as easily as they changed suits, always for a high moral purpose. Whatever the name or platform the goal was the same—privileges for people like themselves, restraint for others, and the authority to make it so. "What will the mayor say?"

Mayor Claiborne Williams was a squirrel to DA Fulcher's basset hound. Fulcher was most dangerous when he appeared half-asleep. Clay was fluent in numbers, but tried to look important, and only looked insecure; politics was messy and he was afraid to make mistakes. Williams was mayor because his older brother, the one you could count on, died with Second Platoon and because voters didn't like certainty in public office. Except for sheriff. There, certainty was important and if the sheriff said someone was guilty they probably were or they wouldn't have been arrested. Trials were for show like weddings of couples who had been living together for years.

"Clay'll piss and moan about bad publicity but there's no one in the county he'd rather see dead. Timp will back up everything you say." It was almost a question.

"I backed him up." Timp damn well better back him up. Fulcher rapped his knuckles on the desk to signal the end of the meeting.

Larry turned back to the report. Maybe he would get a medal or commendation from the state for saving Timp's life. He read over the report, then retyped it. "Observing Sheriff Smith with his hands in the air, I ordered the heavily armed Mills to drop his weapons. Despite my warning, Mills turned the weapons on me. Seeing my life and that of Sheriff Smith in danger, I shot Mills, attempting to disable him. Mills continued to aim his weapons at me until it became necessary to kill him."

He read the report with satisfaction. Running unopposed was a liability, Babbs said. Without opposition it was difficult to gain the respect of the voters. But he had become the gun. He pulled his pistol but had no audience.

With Wynn gone all Larry had to do was ride herd on kids like Scott Baines. Timp had been the best, but the Wild West was over. The old-timers liked having a gun so tough he scared hoods, hustlers, hippies, and homos out of town. Timp was the "before sundown" sheriff they wanted and would vote for as long as he ran. The professioners didn't like Timp humiliating their kids.

When Timp caught teenagers drinking, dragging, or smoking dope, he had a one-foot-in-the-jail talk with them. Then he talked to their parents but professioners stuck up for their kids. And some of the pot came from home.

Larry was what the professioners wanted—a sheriff trained in law enforcement, who had studied criminal investigation, who knew the difference between criminals and citizens who made a mistake. They didn't want handcuffs on their kids or a record because they had too much to drink, slapped their wife, pinched an employee's ass, or roughed up a girl at the Heavenly Gates. They didn't want Timpson Smith as sheriff, not after he killed Scott Baines. And more of them moved to Mills County every year.

   ***

Cecil returned to the courthouse while the sheriff drove the path that Hao had walked to serve the Krugers, down Yanky Road through the Alamo oaks, another battle the Mills had lost, turning into the private road on Kruger's property and then down the flower lined driveway. Kruger's expansive yard was devoid of live oaks because they shed their leaves in the spring littering the swimming pool where no one ever swam but Mrs. Kruger sunbathed. And because Kruger wanted to live in a garden, not a forest. Flowers bloomed inside the wall where the stone house hunkered for protection. Once it had been a meadow with scattered oaks and banks of bluebonnets, Indian paintbrush, Indian blanket, wild verbena, Mexican hat.

Kruger couldn't see Wynn's house because of his wall but Wynn had seen Kruger's wall every time he looked out a back window. Timp honked and waited for Kruger to unlock the gate. When Kruger came outside Timp was halfway out of the car ready to shoot the new dogs and force his way into the house. Kruger, in a silk guyabera and cashmere slacks, was a little stooped by rich living. Although an avid golfer, financial success had gone to his stomach. He carried authority the way he carried the drink in his hand. He tempted the dogs inside a pen with treats and closed the gate on them. He opened his own gate and walked to Timp's car and handed him a sack with a plastic food pack and a soft drink. When Timp didn't take it, Kruger dropped it in his lap. "You probably missed lunch," he said.

"Wynn is dead," Timp said although Kruger already knew. He wanted Kruger's head filled with Wynn's death, a death that began when Kruger bought some of the Mills Ranch, when powers in the county agreed to merchandise Kruger's new property removing most of the Alamo oaks. But Kruger could no more understand Wynn's death than a cow could understand how chewing its cud resulted in butter.

"Why didn't you come when I called?" Kruger had faced a congressional committee; he didn't flinch before a country sheriff.

After moving to Mills County Kruger had been summoned by Congress regarding contracts to his previous employer. He was accompanied by Pastor Murphy, and their prayer on the steps of the capitol was perhaps accidentally captured by cameras. At the hearing congressmen alternated between praising the corporation for protecting America and asking about cost overruns, falsified tests and defective products. Kruger's patriotism and moral standards were lauded, his loss of memory scoffed. Murphy told the media of Kruger's charity that included a mission trip to the Holy Land.

A reporter received an anonymous tip that Kruger's successor, a married man, had had a homosexual relationship with a military officer. The media turned on Kruger's successor, and Kruger, and the CEO whose mistress lived in an apartment owned by the corporation and flew to trysts on the corporation airplane, were forgotten. Kruger returned home and the pastor denounced secular politicians who persecuted Christian patriots while pampering addicts, perverts, and women with children but no husband. "My wife obeys me and there are no divorces, no battered women, no homosexuals, and no single parents in my family." That was before his daughter's marriage.

"Wynn wasn't going to shoot you," Timp said. He had failed Wynn and he wanted Wynn's death to jam Kruger's throat the way it did his.

"I had no way to know his intentions," Kruger said evenly. "I called for help and it didn't come. I've called before and you did nothing."

Like pharmaceutical companies, Kruger was immune to the pain of others. "I need you to tell me what happened."

"Our dogs are not pets. They are trained guard dogs. His mongrel runs loose and chases anything that goes down the road. When our dogs escaped and his dog chased my car what did he expect? We didn't know that he had shot our dogs until we returned home. Those were expensive dogs."

"Did you talk to Wynn?"

"Their telephone doesn't work and I wasn't going to go over there. He came over here and demanded money. When I told him we were holding her money to pay for the dogs he went crazy. Is she okay?"

"She wasn't shot," he said. He didn't want to suggest she was okay.

"I've always opposed soldiers bringing foreign women home like souvenirs. No American woman is going to let him sit on that land and make her clean house for others. If he sold me another hundred acres she would never have to work again. If he had done that none of this would have happened." He dismissed the sheriff, wanting him to take the stench of Wynn's death with him.

The sheriff watched Kruger enter his fortress believing he was comfortable with profiting from someone else's tragedy but Kruger had compromised his plan to save a dream in which Wynn was not even a conceit.

***

When Timp returned to 'Round Back Chili the boys had eaten. Hao had neatly stacked tamale shucks on a napkin. Horace had dumped half a bottle of catsup in his bowl and was dipping crackers in it. Horace Wynn Mills, in the second grade, was named after his father, and Tien Mills, in the first grade, was named after hers. Already they were known as Horse and Ten. Horace, big and fair, looked like his father. Tien, delicate and dark, looked like his mother. They were the last of the legendary Mills family.

Fighting with the Yankees had marked the Mills with the sour scent of other that later fights could not suppress. The Mills family never missed a war—the absence, injury, or death of each male diminishing the family and its prominence in the county. Three Mills brothers and two of their sons rode north to the war. Only a son returned and he brought a Yankee wife with him, Trudy Wynn, which further alienated folks who snickered at "the Wynn-Mills." Some claimed the woman was African, others that she was Indian. The Mills retaliated by naming one male in each generation Wynn Mills.

Those, like the Mills, who lived by a code that prescribed violence in the name of honor were surpassed by the Pritchards, Dosses, Babbs, who lived by a code that justified violence in the name of profit. Horace Wynn Mills, the one Timp knew best, had dropped out of school to help his father scratch out a living with outdated equipment and worn out land; his father had been maimed at Belleau Wood.

"You never knew your Grandfather Horace," he said to Hao's boys. Horace was found dead in the Advantage jail. Timp found no evidence of police brutality. "He liked mules. Do you like mules?" The boys who had never seen a mule looked at their mother wondering what their response was supposed to be. Horace held a catsup-soaked cracker halfway to his mouth.

Country folks had no money for tractors and Horace believed in the honesty of mules. "Every man gets mule fever once in his life," Horace said, while they laughed, those who had never had mule fever, woman fever, gold fever, or yearned for a name. The mules and Horace were a match—stubborn, humorless, prosaic.

One of the mules declined to yield the right of way to a lawyer in a car. The mule was killed, the car destroyed and the lawyer wanted to be paid for his car. "It's a public road and my mule has got as much right to it as a car," Horace said, while folks slapped their knees and elbowed one another.

Tien was learning to snap his fingers and he snapped them until his mother took his hand between both of hers.

The lawyer took the fight to the courthouse where the odds were better. "The judge said I should have a lawyer represent my rights. I thought the law represented me. What the hell have I been pay-ing taxes for all these years if I have to buy a lawyer to represent my rights?" Folks laughed at such innocence. Horace was fined; refused to pay and went to jail.

Timp wanted to tell that story to Hao and the boys but lacked the ability to make them understand the caprice of the law. "Did your father tell you about his pet rooster?" They glanced at each other and nodded.

As a deputy Timp had to confront Horace with a bad check. Farmers were so poor that a chunk of salt pork was passed from house to house to flavor beans or soup and folks joked that if there were a wild critter in sight the Mills ate it or married it. Horace didn't have enough money to cover the check. Lucy unknotted the handkerchief where she kept her egg money and Wynn broke his piggy bank. They were fifty-seven cents short.

"Wynn, take your rooster to the Posey's and see if they'll give you fifty-seven cents for it."

"Pa, they'll eat it." The rooster became Wynn's pet when the other chickens pecked its wing off; the mules, cows, dogs meant work not play.

"Son, if they buy it, they got a right to do what they want with it."

Timp bought the rooster. "I better not carry it in the county car," he said. "Would you keep it for me until I can get it?" He never went back for the rooster and they never ate it because it didn't belong to them. Timp didn't know the moral of the story Wynn had told them. They sat in silence until he looked at Hao. Hao pulled her long, dark hair away from the nape of her slender neck, raised her head, and opened her eyes on him.

"You are Wynn's friend," she said. She had eaten nothing. Her eyes were red and swollen and she dabbed at them with a napkin. "Why do you shoot him? He do nothing wrong."

"I'm very sorry," he said. "I was his friend. No one wanted him to—" Wanted him to die? Too brutal. Wanted him to be hurt? Too trivial. "Can you tell me what happened?"

Hao had cleaned the Kruger's house but they didn't pay her. Wynn told her to go back and ask Harley to pay her for her work and for the boys' dog and the chickens Harley's dogs had killed. Harley gave her food scraps. Wynn took the food back and asked for money. While she talked Hao picked at a place on her open hand made rough from housework and gardening. "We are being without money. Wynn need money for water hose. Kruger say bad things to Wynn. Wynn throw food in his gate."

"Why did he get the gun?" Timp asked.

"People listen when he have gun. In Vietnam everyone listen. With gun they don't slam door on his face. He shoot at sky. Wynn very pissed."

"Did Wynn threaten you or the children?"

"No," she said, her eyes fierce. "Wynn trying to protect."

"Why didn't he let you come to me?"

"If you got us you got Wynn. He do anything for us."

"Did he ever hit you or hurt you or the boys?"

Her eyes were like razors. "Wynn save me," she said, daring him to disbelieve it. Her chin trembled but she refused to cry.

Timp wanted the boys to feel the security of a full belly and bought them peanuts, another soft drink and gave them the plastic food pack that he wanted to throw at Kruger's gate to excite his dogs. "Did Wynn have any insurance?"

"Mr. Meador sell insurance."

***

Larry sorted papers and organized his desk. He couldn't concentrate, flashing to that moment when he and Wynn Mills shot it out. He pounded a fist into his hand. Damn, he was going to have a hard time sleeping tonight. He'd run by the trailer park and take hot-check hottie dancing. Let her grind off the edge. He pounded his fist again. He should have taken the call. Thank God he got there in time.

Cecil walked in with evidence bags. Even with the leather bomber jacket, that Larry had advised, in khaki pants and shirt Cecil looked too old, too soft to be a lawman. He ignored Larry and began his report. "So you did the investigation?" Larry asked. "Did you talk to Kruger?"

"Timp talked to Kruger. Did you contaminate the scene?"

Larry was the only trained investigator in the department and when he was high sheriff Cecil was out. Instead of answering he looked at the useless pack of protoplasm with contempt. If Cecil didn't need a place to hang his hairy, scaly, oversized ears he'd have no use for a head.

"There were no weapons at the scene," Cecil said.

"Timp told me to bring them, Wynn's shotgun and Timp's pistol. Did he tell you I killed Wynn Mills?" he asked, wanting to tell the story again.

"Timp didn't say anything. He did his own investigation. I need your weapon too."

"What did you say to the media?"

"I didn't say anything to them. I'm not going to until Timp tells me to."

Cecil was old and ignorant but Larry knew he could be useful. "I've got my report here if you want to read it." He wanted everyone to read his report. Complete but understated like a hero's report should be.

"Timp likes everyone to write his own report."

Larry shrugged. "That's what Timp likes," he said accenting Timp. Timp wouldn't be sheriff much longer and Cecil knew it. He pushed his report toward Cecil. Cecil picked it up.

***

Timp reported he was returning to the courthouse to draw the cameras there and took back roads to town. Hao sat between the boys in the back looking at her lap. A jackrabbit darted in front of the car and all three of them winced at the thump the tire made. He avoided a terrapin and Horace Wynn looked back, apprehensive of its future. Timp stopped, carried the terrapin across the road and drove away. In his rearview mirror he saw it turn and start back across the road from which he had saved it.

He drove past the funeral home. Seeing no reporters, he ushered Hao and the boys in the back door of the extension to what had once been a gabled, turreted home and into the office of the funeral director, a short, pudgy, cheerful man who smiled at people every day and with a gesture of his limp, white hand bade them welcome, sit here. Timp told him that he wanted Wynn to get whatever the VA provided for veterans—a man who disposed of the county indigent had to get along with the sheriff—and he wanted the media kept away from them. The director lost his smile. He had to be on good terms with the media, too.

Leaving them there, he went into the back to talk to the coroner from Advantage. Wynn had been shot two or three times. "It looks like the bullet that hit Wynn in the side first penetrated his arm. I'll know more later"

Timp thought of calling Martha and asking her to come to the funeral home to be with Hao; she had done it before. Instead, he drove to the place he had turned to when he came home from Korea, the clapboard building with benches for pews and venetian blinds in the windows, lacking a sign or a cross to grace its presence. A sign or a cross would draw attention to the building rather than to the church that met there.

It wasn't the Colt that tamed the frontier; it was the Bible, iron-skirted women, and poor, uneducated Bible punchers preaching a stern God who expected his followers to work hard, to act with mercy and humility, and to expect nothing from this world. Not power, not riches, least of all justice. "The Lord will repay," they proclaimed. The frontier had passed and with it those inclined to wait on the Lord. Folks gravitated to churches like Pastor Murphy's Solid Rock where a benevolent God required only a little earnest money before pouring out his blessings on his chosen. God repaid donors to Murphy's church and school tenfold what they had given, dollars for dollars to those who needed dollars, dollars for days to those who needed days. "That's a better deal," folks agreed, even in Mills County where God previously repaid good deeds and charity in the hereafter.

Before Korea Timp had believed in God, believed in America; they were almost synonymous. He didn't require divine intervention to save Second Platoon in order to believe but had prayed for it. His faith raveled when the truth he found in Korea was unacceptable in Mills and his story beyond his control.

He had gone to church not for redemption but forbearance. He found it, not in confession but in communion. They befriended him, made him sheriff, supported him in faith when they had no understanding but he couldn't accept their love, their honors, their loyalty because they didn't know who he really was, and if they knew they would despise him.

As their sheriff he tried to keep kids out of trouble, rescue troubled marriages, runaway wives, errant husbands, defend them from the abuses of power, safeguard their private sins and errors. As sheriff, he knew too much of Saturday night and they showed him Sunday morning, living as best they could, most of them. They reared children who respected him and would never confront the law, most of them. They were his people, and in church, scrubbed, in their best attitude, they seemed at home in their souls as they struggled to awaken to the glory of Sunday after a week of playing dead.

He parked at the edge of the dirt street that had no curb and got out. A garden hose snaked across the dirt yard, ending at a scrawny tree that looked beyond salvation. Timp remembered painting the wooden frame building but couldn't remember a time when the church looked as if it *didn't* need paint. The front door was unlocked and he stepped into the dim sanctuary and walked down the single bare board aisle, his boot-heels echoing off the walls. The choir room was on one side of the pulpit and the pastor's office on the other. Both doors were open but even in the gloom he saw no one until Brother Jonas stood up with a screwdriver in his hand. "Had to replace a wall plug," he said. "Let me turn the power on and I'll shake your hand."

Brother Jonas was a fundamentalist in the old dispensation; belief in a just, omnipotent God who loved mercy, forgave the unforgivable and required more of the faithful than of unbelievers. He had never asked why bad things happened to good people; salvation was not a rabbit's foot and he didn't need the threat of everlasting punishment to believe. Why good people did bad things to others in the name of goodness he pondered every day.

In addition to being pastor, Brother Jonas was a farmer. He was not seminary-trained; he knew more about caring for his people than he did about entertaining the congregation, preaching convention, and selling happiness. He tended the property, cleaned the church, preached on Sunday, visited the sick and elderly and officiated at more funerals than weddings and baptisms combined. Wynn was one of his flock and they had accepted Hao, maybe befriended her.

Timp told Brother Jonas of Wynn's death and asked if some women from the church could go to the funeral home to be with Hao and to take her home and stay with her as long as she wanted. "Do you know where their truck is?"

"It's in the shop. Wynn hasn't been able to pay for it but a neighbor loaned him a truck to haul hay and helped him move cows to his pasture until they can buy a water hose," said Brother Jonas in an earnest but untrained voice. Farming was a profession that required a clear eye for evaluating land, men, and their worth.

"I'll help pay for the truck. She'll need it," the sheriff said. He offered the preacher money and asked that the women buy food for the family. "And some one to cover up the blood in the yard."

Brother Jonas refused the money and as for the yard, "I'll do it myself," he said. His rough hands and broad shoulders showed he was capable of such effort. "Before the women take her home. And the church will furnish the food. Later I'll take her to Advantage and help her get what the government offers. They automatically reject people the first time because some people are too sick or too poor to put up a fight. I don't blame the clerks though; they're just trying to follow the law."

Brother Jonas and every able bodied man in his church had been in the military, serving their country, not its government. They weren't slackers and would no more be deadbeat patriots than they would be deadbeat parents. They paid taxes to their country because the Bible commanded it but they believed the government distributed power and money to those who bowed before it and Brother Jonas and his followers refused to bow.

"I try to enforce the law; I don't write it," Timp said, defensively.

"We don't either," said Brother Jonas who was wroth that his country had become a den of thieves. There were few rich people in his heaven and fewer CEOs. He promised to call Meador about Wynn's insurance.

***

It was a short drive to the courthouse and Timp had to get his story together. He didn't want to damage Larry's campaign; however, after Larry had time to deal with his guilt for Wynn's death, they had to review the shooting so that nothing like that ever happened again.

He drove into the department parking lot, reported his mileage, then walked around to the front of the courthouse. It would please the

TV crew because they would have better light and a more dramatic setting but he did it because it made it easier for him to leave. They could follow him inside with their questions but they couldn't follow him into his office without invitation.

He had made that mistake earlier and they had focused their cameras on the Medal of Honor, the commemorative pistol, the Second Platoon monument visible from his window. He had wanted to explain coherently rather than giving incomplete answers to random questions. They interrupted his statement with questions whose answers he believed should have been evident. His answer that Scott was in a dark building and had shot at him brought more questions. Did he identify himself? Did he shoot to kill? Did he have a grudge against the boy? Had the boy broken in? Had he stolen anything? Did he know how young the boy was?

They accused him of using them, hanging on after the questions became repetitive, wanting a picture of an angry sheriff throwing them out. What they got was a photograph of him pointing a finger at the camera over a caption, "Sheriff declares teenage killing necessary."

Dr. Baines, who had never forgiven Timp for telling him they had to scrape his brother's melted body from truck metal, blamed Scott's death on the brutality of a frontier sheriff. He recruited a deputy to run against Timp and sued the county. The sheriff and the county won but the mayor was unhappy about the expense and bad publicity.

***

Questions about where he had been, remarks about deadlines, job to do, wasting taxpayers' money greeted Timp as he reached the steps at the front of the courthouse. "It's a good thing I'm not running for office," he said and they laughed. "The death of Wynn Mills is a tragedy. He was a hero and he should be buried with full military honors."

"Why did you take the call?" the questions began.

"We're a man short of a full roster." He used part-time deputies who were cheap, furnished their own cars and were okay for expressway duty but they couldn't investigate and he didn't know how they would react to a crisis. "John was busy, Larry responded."

"Harley Kruger said that Wynn went berserk, took his family hostage, and shot at Kruger's house."

Timp saw them jockeying for an angle. Thank God he wasn't running for office because he intended to kneecap that rumor before it grew legs. "There were no hostages. It was the last of a lot of little things."

"Are you saying that Mr. and Mrs. Kruger were in no danger?"

Not with birdshot in a gun that wasn't cocked. He had been infected by Kruger's fear. "No one was in danger." He didn't understand their excitement. "I was scared," he admitted.

"Didn't Wynn threaten to kill you with your own pistol?"

He wished they had never given him that damn pistol. "Wynn agreed to put down his shotgun if I put down the pistol. Larry didn't know the situation and in the confusion Wynn was killed."

"Are you saying Larry was at fault in the death of Mills?"

Having immobilized the crazed vet story he wanted to protect Larry. "Things happen quickly and when guns are present mistakes are tragic."

"How do you explain the discrepancies between your stories?"

"Law enforcement has taught me that no two people see an event the same way. That's why I require every officer on the scene to write a separate report. And perceptions change with time. Tomorrow this will all look a little different. Now I've got to get to work." He made his way through them, ignoring their shouted questions.

CHAPTER THREE

&

Alone on the stairs to his office, the sheriff decided he had done all right. It was too complex to be compressed into a bark. He would be quoted out of context but he didn't think he said anything that would dishonor Wynn or damage Larry.

Mrs. Stutz looked relieved to see him. "You okay, Chief? It took me a long time to get Larry on the radio."

She had been with the department so long she considered herself an officer. He wished she hadn't called Larry but she had followed procedure. "I'll speak to him," he said, accenting his authority. "Do you have his report?"

"Not yet."

Ross Fulcher disliked Timp's policy of every officer on the scene writing a report because there were discrepancies that had to be explained in court. Nevertheless, plural reports were more likely to include important details, and Timp believed they were more accurate and objective if each officer understood at least one other officer was writing a report.

The sheriff wrote that he had arrived on the scene to find Wynn Mills inside and had persuaded Wynn to come outside by disarming himself. The untimely arrival of deputy Maddin led to the accidental death of Mills.

Mrs. Stutz buzzed him. "Rufus Moore and he is irate," she said.

Rufus was always irate, even before his stroke. "I'll take it, then tell Larry I want to see him." The school had made Rufus' children go to the gym, wash their hair, and take a bath. Timp knew the boys got up early, fed the hogs, milked the cows, and came to school in the same clothes. "Ruf, tell the boys to wear rubber boots and overalls when doing chores before school and don't lean their heads on the cows while milking." Cows had lice. Ruf didn't like it but he would do it.

***

At the buzzer Larry picked up the phone. "The sheriff wants to see you," Mrs. Stutz said.

"I'm on my way," he said, winking at Cecil who was finishing his report. Timp wanted to thank him, maybe recommend him for a medal or citation. From now on he was going to be one damn scary guy. He walked into the sheriff's office the way Timp walked—heavy but not overbearing. "Sorry I was late, Jefe. I'm just glad I got there in time." He shifted his gunbelt.

Timp did not smile, stand, or shake his hand. "I know you were excited, and this is not a good time to talk about it but don't ever again walk into a scene and start shooting. Didn't you see me motion you to clear out?"

Larry sank into a chair. "I saw you preparing to draw."

"I was afraid you would startle Wynn or make him suspicious."

"Suspicious?" Larry asked in disbelief. "He assaulted his neighbors. He held his family hostage."

"They weren't hostages and he shot in the air. I talked to his wife."

"She'll say anything now that he's dead and she'll get the ranch." If Timpson Smith said it was snowing in August you had better wear a coat; that was his reputation for honesty and Larry's faith in it. Why was he taking a gook's word over his? A cold needle inserted itself in Larry's brain. Timp was going to run again. "I did what you would have done." He didn't say *if you had been younger and quicker* but Timp heard it and almost rose out of his chair. For a moment Larry thought if Timp had his pistol he would pull it.

"If you had been five seconds later he would have been unarmed. That's what I didn't want, for you to show up like we had tricked him." Timp took a deep breath. "I can understand how it happened, and I'll stand by you."

A spanking was what it sounded like to Larry. "Timpson Smith can't retire with a second mark on his record, is that it?"

"The shotgun wasn't cocked. It was loaded with number nines."

Number nines would blow your face off if you were close enough. "He had your gun, too. Your gun sure as hell would have killed both of us."

"It was a neighborhood argument. Wynn didn't have to die."

Larry wanted the sheriff to accept him as an equal but Timpson

Smith wanted to be the only hero. "I'm not going to give up my shot for sheriff just because you gave up your pistol. That was your decision, and one that some people are going to consider dumb." This wasn't Korea. This was Timpson Smith's own county and he had . . . Maybe a lot of men would have but that didn't make it right. "I stood by you when you shot Scott Baines and I would stand by you now if you were running for sheriff. I'm going to go home and put on a clean shirt."

Timp nodded. "Turn in your report before you leave." He knew two kinds of lawmen: those who liked rules and those who liked being around rule breakers. He picked up the ringing telephone. Martha had just heard the news. "All you all right?

In high school someone had decided who was pretty and who was popular. Martha had been class secretary, organizer of parties, proms, and contests while others took credit. She was never class favorite or football queen, the things that counted, but men envied Timp because Martha cared more for her posture than her dress, still closed her eyes when she danced with him, and was equal to any crowd. The more expected of the sheriff, the more required of her and she surprised everyone, not least herself.

"I'm okay," he responded. "I'll tell you when I get home."

"Is there anything I can do for Larry? For Wynn's family?"

"Their church is looking after Wynn's family."

"It's just so awful. P.J. called Larry 'the man who killed Wynn Mills.'"

What a terrible thing to say, thought the sheriff who had been called "the man who killed Dr. Baines' boy." "That will destroy Larry. I'll warn him." He considered calling a staff meeting the next day to clarify what had happened but there had already been the monthly meeting and the special meeting the previous week to explain that until Larry was elected he was another deputy. There had been complaints that Larry was getting bosshead.

Timp walked into the bunkhouse to warn Larry what people had heard on the radio but it was empty. After five o'clock, calls were routed to the deputy on duty through the dispatcher in Advantage. He went to Mrs. Stutz's desk and picked up Cecil's and Larry's reports and carried them into his office. He scanned Cecil's report, focusing on Wynn's antiquated rifle and pistol and partial box of corroded ammunition for each, plus a box of number twos and one of number nines for the shotgun. He read Larry's report then read it again.

Larry still misjudged the situation. Timp recalled how befuddled he had been in Korea. "Are you Second Platoon?" Later, "Are you the hero?" Even now he doubted his memory. But Wynn's death wasn't Korea; it was the death of Scott Baines. No matter how many times he dreamed of Scott's face, his vacant eyes, dead mouth accusing, "You killed me," he had no doubt that in a similar situation he would act the same.

He dialed Larry's home number but Larry didn't answer. Should he leave a message for Larry to rewrite his report? Let Larry sleep on what he had done, order his memory. Tomorrow would be soon enough.

   ***

Larry met Babbs at the Lazy Lizard on the expressway. They sat behind Larry's Lone Star and Babbs' chablis, a substitute for Perrier when the barkeep said, "We don't sell that shit here." A terrier and a toad, they sat at a back booth to attract less attention. Larry was packed and wound because of weight training and topped by a big hat. Babbs was stubby, with sallow skin that rose high on his bald head. Larry liked women; Babbs liked power. Larry thought Babbs smart but not savvy, plugged in but not tuned in. Babbs thought Larry elemental but adjustable like a pair of pliers.

Babbs ignored the chablis. "I told you not to talk to the media without talking to me first. Did you talk to anyone else?"

Larry raised his bottle, signaling for another beer. "Ross Fulcher. Said he would take care of everything. Timp. He's pissed because I made him look bad. P.J. He's a disc jockey and instead of playing music he spreads rumors."

"He has the biggest audience in Mills County," said Babbs who supplied P.J. with gossip. "He called you 'the man who killed Wynn Mills.'"

Larry pumped a fist. "That's my campaign slogan."

"I don't know," Babbs said. "The Mills are a legend in Mills County."

"That's what I want to be, a legend. Killing Wynn Mills will get me more votes than computers in the bunkhouse that no one cares about except me. Hell, most people in Mills County don't know what a computer looks like."

"You'd have to rewrite the story."

"Then by damn let's do it." Babbs didn't respond. Babbs didn't like any ideas but his own. "Hell, everyone in the department was scared of Wynn except Timp. Timp was his friend. That's why he gave Wynn his pistol."

"'The Man Who Killed Wynn Mills.' It might work. I almost wish you had an opponent. I'd like to see if they could come up with something better. I'll get started on Wynn's reputation," Babbs said.

***

Timp turned from the report on his desk and looked out the window. Why did they put the damn statue where he had to see it every time he looked outside? More familiar than his face, it was his face. It represented him in a way nothing else did—not his badge, his name, his wife. His pistol. Those who had seen the statue believed they knew who he was.

Most of the Marine Reserve Company had been from Advantage. Mills County demanded and got its own platoon, its own monument. Timp wanted a tableau of fighting Marines but family survivors said Doss County would claim it also represented their Marines. Second Platoon was always treated differently or there were complaints about the senator's son, Captain Billy Pritchard. That's why there was a monument, why their names were on the monument and his face was on the statue. Why he had been given medals.

Mayor T. J. Munday had announced that Timp now belonged to the town. "As long as you live, you are father, brother, son, husband to all." He had endured the ceremony believing he had outlasted the occasion.

He had joined the reserves because he was ashamed of his deferment during the war. The orders calling the reserves to active duty had been as sudden and unexpected as death by sniper. Excitement matched fear, possibility and tensions were high at the Advantage train station when they left. He couldn't look at Martha clinging to Rocky but she kissed Timp's cheek after Rocky boarded. Everyone was unnerved by Corporal Meador and his wife who had a vicious argument. Walter Clemmons and Rick Adams weren't speaking to each other. Aaron Grinstaff avoided his girlfriend who held a baby.

Against his better judgment he picked up the ringing phone. "Are you okay?" Vic asked. Vic Holloway had been in Able Company and they had met again visiting their mothers at the nursing home. "I know you don't need help because heroes can't need help." Vic was in a wheelchair.

"We're buddies telling war stories," Timp said.

"Without romance."

"Those that are true aren't believed and those that are believed aren't true. I thought by putting down my pistol I could save Wynn."

"You tried so you're a hero."

"They decide," Timp said.

"Who?"

"They. The media. Whoever."

"God loves you, the church hasn't decided, the crowd listens to a disc-jockey. Do you know what your problem is?"

Of course he knew. He knew so well the words were slick on his tongue. "I lived. They died. I must have been spared for a reason."

"What do you think the reason is?"

He had tried to be what the county had lost but every year they lost more farms, more ranches, more of downtown, more of their heritage to monster stores owned by aliens who didn't know who the Mills were or what they represented. Slowly and inevitably as sundown. "So I can save them."

"Who? Who can you save?"

He hadn't saved anyone. He hadn't saved anything but the statue.

He was almost to the door when the telephone rang again. Glen Timberlake wanted him to check out a Mexican who wanted to buy a lot in Alamo Acres for himself and maybe others for his children but he wanted the security gate up first. Kruger was afraid he was hiding something or hiding from something. "Drugs?" Timp asked.

"I don't think so," Timberlake said. "He's in the government."

Mordida, Timp thought, the little bite for doing favors. Probably his money was in US banks and if there was a political change he wanted a refuge from those he had injured. "I'll see if he has any records here."

    ***

Professor Bryan Frazier felt like Picasso working as a house painter. How could he serve God in this place? He needed a stage that could reach people. He had something to give if he had a chance. Instead, he marked student papers on Restoration drama at a degree factory for wannabe CEOs.

The TV was on and Bryan also listened for his voice because he applied the talent God had given him to the opportunities God provided. If that meant commercials for a car dealer he did them believing that if he were faithful in little things God would give him bigger roles. All he needed was for someone at the top of the noise to give him a nod. That's all he needed, that touch. It had been promised—the next project, next occasion, next story. If ever there was a profession in which chance or God played a major role it was acting.

Bryan studied the commercials to improve his performance because he was taking any street out of Advantage and the university that regarded the arts as frivolous. He had the looks—tall and lithe like a tennis player, a broad, smiling, blue-eyed face with swept back blond hair. He could play a surfer, athlete, rock star, the sweet-faced soldier who was first to die, a romantic lead in a comedy. Casting directors, who chose a professional athlete or rock star instead of him, told him he had talent. He had the desire. He had a place in this world and all he wanted was to fulfill the purpose he believed God had for him.

Although it tested his faith, God's purpose included directing a parade in Five Mills and the ridicule of his colleagues. "Hey, Bryan, seen any good parades lately?" To them he was a failure and a failed actor was lower than an adjunct professor. A losing coach received more respect.

When the dean asked him to direct the parade in Five Mills using student actors to portray the heroic tableaux Bryan saw it as expression of the administration's contempt. The school wasn't interested in creative work or original thought but in styles and fads of thinking. History of theater, his least favorite class, was his only class the administration considered legitimate and directing a parade was as meritorious as directing *Death of a Salesman* that everyone had seen on the screen.

Bryan's best chance had been to play a cursing, woman-abusing addict. The part was given to Rich Lee, a minor actor who was best known for the starlets he claimed to have creamed. Before the film was released he was sued by an underage girl for filming his seduction of her. He had received blistering reviews and the film was DOA. Rich turned to Jesus, and in addition to forgiveness found himself in celeb magazines, megachurches, and on religious TV telling how his faith in Jesus had turned him from addiction to sex and drugs to a serious actor who had committed his talent to God. Solid Rock had paid Rich to perform at the church and the college paid him to speak to the drama department. The dean introduced Bryan to him as "directing a parade in Five Mills."

Second Platoon wasn't Thermopylae or the Alamo. The platoon got lost, blundered into the North Korean army and was shot to pieces. A desperate little town appointed the sole survivor sheriff for life and appropriated the deaths of forty men as its excuse for being. Bryan couldn't refuse to direct its parade because the university needed the help of Senator Billy Pritchard to get a government contract for a research project and the senator had been commanding officer of Able Company, to which the platoon belonged. Only Bryan's religious faith prevented him from regarding the pathetic attempt of Five Mills to catch a glare with contempt equal to that of the dean toward him.

The parade should have been simple—flags, marching bands, patriotic floats, but Five Mills demanded floats portraying the tableaux around the monument and the school required equal opportunity, at least publicly; there were no black professors. None of the tableaux included blacks. The sheriff who had described the tableaux for the sculptor refused to return his calls because he was an unknown actor, but the sheriff was an unknown hero. That's why they had the statue, why they wanted a parade. If Audie Murphy hadn't been an actor no one would remember what he had done in the war. Deeds were forgotten unless they were immortalized by monuments or words. Who would remember Richard the Third if not for Shakespeare?

Bryan had read the newspaper clippings—"gallant band of warriors." The sheriff had been sent home as "a banner around which a thousand men could be recruited." Timp's humble public servant act failed to persuade Bryan although it made him even more heroic to Mills County.

When Bryan heard " . . . sheriff of Mills County" he turned his attention to the screen and watched commercials featuring women in low cut dresses and short skirts. "Vietnam veteran terrorizes his family and threatens neighbors," the anchor said. "That story next." Followed by a commercial in which Bryan stood by "America's most envied car" and told viewers that driving the car would make them a god like himself. Bryan hoped what his students saw was his understated confidence and not the vanity he was paid to portray.

Bryan was replaced on the screen by a man whose thoughts had been scattered by a bus. "Deputy Larry Maddin received a call that Mills County Sheriff, local hero Timpson Smith, was in danger."

"Wynn Mills has a reputation for violence. He had threatened the Krugers, taken his family hostage, and was threatening to kill Sheriff Smith," the deputy said. "When I told him to drop the guns he pointed them at me."

The grave-voiced announcer returned to the screen. "Sheriff Smith told a different story."

"There were no hostages, I wasn't in any danger." The camera zoomed in on his empty holster. "It was a regrettable accident caused by confusion."

The sheriff disappeared from the screen to be replaced by the anchor. "The coroner is attempting to determine what part drugs and alcohol may have played in the deadly encounter."

Timpson Smith appeared less heroic on TV than on the statue. Bryan hoped that embarrassment would lead to cancelation of the parade that was already a joke.

***

Martha snapped off the TV and went to the kitchen to find something to do although dinner was in the crockpot. Timp was the bravest man she knew but why did he want to be sheriff? Hadn't he seen enough death and ugliness? She hadn't understood even in the beginning when there weren't drugs, gangs, horrible crimes against women and children. She wanted to save him from that as she had saved him from the madness of Korea.

Martha never expected to be more than a wife and mother after a sensible wedding and to inherit her father's store. She didn't deserve a man like Timpson Smith. What a strange, compelling boy he had been in high school in patched but clean clothes and dandruff from washing his hair with homemade soap. "Snow head," some had called him. She had tried to befriend him but she was coy and he was bashful; she was a butterfly and he was not a collector.

He had come home a hero on a crutch, his arm in a sling, a last dispatch from those who didn't return. She was in awe at what he had become, a warrior god. She hoped he would come to see her, lied that it was because she wanted to hear about Rocky. When he went to Hollywood where fame, flesh, and misfortune could be his future she thought she would never see him again. He returned to sell houses in Dogpatch and screw the widows and sisters of his platoon buddies. When he came to her she held him to her breast while he told her of Rocky's love for her, embraced him almost as her dead husband. And she let him—no—nothing so passive, she threw herself on him like a slut, abandoned herself like Piggy. And he had made love to her the way Rocky had. She had been confused, frightened by her passion and he had made it so familiar that she had been swept away by intimacy. She cried and told him she loved him. She wanted to be his friend, she wanted to take him into her life, she wanted to absorb him with her body, she wanted to be furious with him. She wanted to please him the way he pleased her.

After he left she was overcome with shame. What contempt he must feel for her; what shame he must feel for Rocky. What stories he must be telling Glen Timberlake. She was surprised that he returned, stunned that he could want her. When he said he loved her she was happier than she had ever been. Something she once had was hers again, only now she knew how precious and precarious it was. She had feared she would spend the rest of her life alone. She thought she would never again know that touch, see that look that Rocky had when he wanted her, never again sleep beside someone in intimacy and know confidence in his love.

She had been curious about the most commonplace thing he did, confused that he was so much like Rocky. She wished he could be the sweet boy she remembered before he went to Korea but it was a secret she swore she would keep as she tried to be worthy of the man he had become. She had addressed meetings, answered questions, told voters what her husband could do for them, and asked for their support. She didn't like doing it but Timp needed her and she hoped it made up for the children she couldn't give him. She had never wanted to be president or nurse or teacher. She wanted to be a mother, to hold life in a manageable form, to make her children's clothes, read to them, teach them to cook and swim and dance. She wanted to fill her husband's stomach, and heart and bed.

Hearing screams, Martha ran to the backyard, but it was teenagers flirting on their way home from an after-school program. "Damn," she said although she rarely swore and only when she was alone or with her husband.

***

The sheriff drove to Shady Acres studying his run-down neighborhood as carefully as he had the others. Whether a bicycle in the street meant an abducted child, a careless one or an accident. Whether a strange car in the neighborhood meant a visitor or a burglary. Burglars drove big cars, often stolen, and usually left a driver in the car for a quick get-away.

The once fresh and green ornamental trees that had come with the houses had died, blown down or grown gray and shapeless. The once pastel houses were sun-faded white. His own ranch-style house was an ell with two bathrooms, two small bedrooms and one large one. Men bought things because they liked them, women because of possibilities. Martha had ripped up carpet and put down tile, changed the color of the rooms, put up paneling in the den and wallpaper in the living room and bathroom. There was a patio in the back and a chain link fence that offered no seclusion but suggested a wilderness with a thin veneer of trees beyond. Vines grew on the fence and flowers beside it.

Like his neighbors he and Martha bought the house because of the natural greenbelt beyond their backyard. The land would be a park for children they had been assured, hiking and biking trails, picnic tables. The property was rezoned and the city punched Timpson Smith Street through it to link up with the expressway and lined it with "only $20 cash" stores, street lights, and boomboxes. The city had provided no sidewalks, and children on their way to school had to walk in the street. Timp prayed every day that no harm would come to children who took shortcuts through the brush or to teenagers who sometimes lingered there.

Martha often sat on the patio watching children on their way to or from school and sometimes in the evening he joined her. They were unable to see stars because of the streetlights but able to see the lighted spire of Solid Rock Church. The department had given him a large barbecue grill but he never grilled meat or allowed it of Martha. When she seared a roast he left the house.

Martha had reached the age where elderly men followed her in grocery stores but at home she wore simple house-dresses. Timp didn't like flowery dresses, so before he came home she had changed into a green one. Perhaps Timp wouldn't have noticed even if it were flowery but when she met him at the door he did note the look on her face. It was a look he had seen before, concern with a pinch of anger that he had subjected her to it. She had been agitated by the disc-jockey version of the news.

"They said drugs or alcohol might be involved," she said.

"Bastards," Timp said, so agitated he slammed his fist into his hand. "It'll be days before anyone knows." The media had predisposed people to believe in drunk or drugged veterans holding their families hostage. Parents told their children Santa Claus was real, then told them he was not real but the media treated Santa with the same legitimacy as Jesus Christ.

"They're trying to make Larry into a younger Timpson Smith."

"Larry is not fit—" He stopped. Not fit to be him? To be sheriff?

"Had you rather had someone else support you?"

He would have been safer alone but he couldn't tell her; she would believe he took risks. "It was a mistake." The word could not suggest the enormity. He went into the bedroom to strip off the suit stiff with dried blood and to shower, put on jeans and a T shirt.

"Bryan Frazier called about the tableaux," Martha said.

Laying a wreath at the monument, reading the names of the dead, speeches of "noble sacrifice, unremitting courage, rich red blood of youth" had been enough until Bryan, a publicity-hungry professor, wanted a parade with floats depicting the tableaux at the base of the monument. Rocky's family bought a tableau of Rocky and on one float would be a kneeling student with a flag in one hand and a pistol in the other. Parents with little money, widows with no income, African Americans in minimum wage jobs were unable to buy a tableau and once again they would be unrepresented and angry. On the final float Bryan wanted Timp reenacting the pose on the statue, followed by college students pretending to be widows, orphans, parents, siblings dressed in mourning. Second Platoon was a nightmare that grew more terrible every year.

"I'm not talking to Bryan Frazier." He had talked to the designer. "We didn't have a flag. You can't hold a machine gun in one hand and fire it with the other." She doodled on her pad and decided flag in one hand and pistol in the other. "Rocky didn't carry a pistol." She said she wasn't picturing what happened; she was illustrating what it meant, like Custer's Last Stand. "Someone is going to hold a flag; is it going to be you or someone else?"

"Bryan's trying to save the platoon," Martha said. He turned away so she couldn't see his agitation that Second Platoon had become the glorious dead who gave hope to the town. "You'll have to tell him the story sometime."

"No, I don't." As a child while fulfilling his farmyard chores he had come upon a dead rat and for some boyish reason stamped it with his bare foot. The rat, swollen with the gases of decomposition, exploded pus, guts, milky gobbets over his foot, the stench and sight sickening him. He ran as far from the smell as he could before losing the contents of his stomach. He swished his foot in the cows' water tank unwilling to touch it with his hands, then rubbed sand over his foot until his skin was raw. For a time he could not eat but his mother made him come to the table where he had to face the rat's image in the gray meat and milky rice on his plate. At night he was awakened from dreams by a sickness in his stomach. His mother asked what was wrong but he couldn't tell her without making the memory more awful by putting it in words.

"Do you want to invite Larry over for dinner?" Martha asked, going into the kitchen. She knew not to put the finishing touches to dinner until he was inside the house even if he called to say he was on his way. "I made enough."

"I don't want to see Larry right now."

"Timp, you can't leave him alone. He just killed someone. You've killed more people than he has. How did you feel?"

He had felt disembodied. In a world inhabited only by himself, filled with empty eyes and gaping mouths screaming "You killed me."

When Larry didn't answer the telephone Timp was relieved but wondered where Larry was—the shooting range? People who swallowed too much of the world at one gulp took different ways to digest it. He hoped Larry wasn't at the radio station confronting the d.j. who called him a killer.

He left a message inviting Larry to drop by for dinner or coffee and dessert, a drink if he wanted one, although Timp wasn't sure there was liquor in the house. Other than an occasional beer with supporters during campaigns Timp seldom drank unless on vacation. Emergency calls at night were rare but he wanted to be able to respond with a clear head.

He had to regain his trust in the Larry who had offered to tell Dr. Baines and his wife that their son was dead. It was a job Timp had to do. The drive to Eddie's house after Scott died had been the longest and shortest of his life. Too long to endure and not long enough to invent what to say.

Timp and Eddie had gone to school together but weren't friends. Timp was shy and didn't join others without invitation; Eddie thought he was stuck-up. Eddie had only two sets of overalls and shirts and unable to bathe regularly spoke mostly to teachers. Timp thought Eddie believed only teachers were smart enough for his conversation. Both were thought standoffish. Eddie's brother, Clyde, died with Second Platoon and their father asked Timp what they should do with Clyde's GI Insurance. Their father was a sharecropper and worked odd jobs when he could get one. They had never had a home. Timp said Clyde wanted Eddie, who clerked at the drugstore, to have the money for his education.

He had been to the Baines house after students at Solid Rock School had food-poisoning. Food preparation at the school was done by the same Hands of God volunteers that prepared Wednesday night Hour of Power Suppers, Abraham and Isaac Barbecues, By Our Fruits Monthly Dinners that recognized accomplishments, Moms and Daughters Banquets, Ananias and Sapphira Budget Campaigns, Thanksgiving and Christmas feasts, opening of school bashes and all-church picnics. He and Baines were members of Solid Rock and he had asked Baines to speak to Pastor Murphy about food safety since the school was outside state regulation. Baines declined.

After Scott was arrested in Advantage for selling his father's prescription pads, Timp had taken him home but his warning was stopped at the door. When he went to tell them of Scott's death both parents answered the door as though waiting for him yet believed he had no right to be there. Eddie, who borrowed a coat for high school graduation, wore a dark blue silk suit and pale blue silk shirt. BeverLee, whose skin looked shrink wrapped over fine bones, wore tight faux snakeskin pants and a stretch silk shirt that Timp tried not to look at. The entranceway was graced with signed photographs of Richard Nixon and Ronald Reagan.

Old-timers joked that when Dr. Baines returned to Five Mills a former classmate described his symptoms and asked, "What does that sound like?" The doctor said it sounded like a gold mine to him. They called his third wife a monetary marriage because BeverLee required a gift every time he made her unhappy, and the house was littered with memorials to her displeasure. Some eggs were hand-painted, some contained jeweled chariots, bouquets of rubies, garnets, and sapphires; trees with jade trunks, emerald leaves, and ruby fruit. One opened to a miniature of the monument. Folks said Eddie was better at diagnosis than at dialog.

BeverLee was a shopper not only for herself, Scott, Dr. Baines, friends, but for people whose looks pleased her or whose needs distressed her. She bought anything attractive, amusing, or imaginative then looked for someone to give it to. She did not give money to church or charity. If she gave it, she bought it. Eddie preferred writing checks, and had financed two of Pastor Murphy's trips to the Holy Land. He also worked the Saturday night knife and gun club in the emergency room of the Advantage hospital.

They had led him into the living room but nothing looked comfortable. After rolling in the barn, with Scott's blood on his trousers, Timp was reluctant to sit on the Baines' expensive furniture that did not seem intended for human encounter. He sat stiffly on the edge of a chair of silk brocade in a room BeverLee had selected as their stage suddenly bereft of comforting props—cathedral ceiling, Persian rugs on a marble floor, sculptures of slender Eves, Delilahs, and Bathshebas teasing robust Adams, Samsons, and Davids and paintings of similar subjects on the walls. They sat side by side, each a star in its own galaxy, Eddie upright, his face impassive as if he were giving a death message rather than receiving one. He held a crystal egg in his hands. BeverLee perched beside him her hands folded in her lap and grimly tried to look lovely while hearing horror. She took the egg from her husband and threw it at the marble fireplace where it shattered. Despite himself, despite the strength of her fingers that glittered with rings, the honesty of her tears, he had thought the gesture theatrical.

"If you've said everything you came to say get out," Eddie said.

***

Timp sat in his Naugahyde easy chair in a living room decorated with paintings that Martha had bought from the Ten Talents Art Classes at Solid Rock Church, pretty pictures of snow on the rooftop and a lighted Christmas tree in the picture window, fields of blue bonnets and Indian blanket, deer browsing peacefully in a glade with a cabin in the distance.

He idly flipped through *Guns and Grits*, a gift subscription to the quintessential magazine of southern life. If Larry didn't replace him, who would? It was hard getting taxes from patriots who had the voice of an endangered turtle with a government tuned to the feeding cries of predators. A low budget county like Mills couldn't afford trained deputies but relied on discards from cities. They knew the county; except for Larry and Chad Norvell they knew the people. They knew their duty but were unsuited for leadership. Ernie Klemp was the most experienced deputy but had a cleft palate. P.J. called him "Ernie Clap" and so did P.J.'s listeners. Howard Goss followed orders but had the eyes of an elephant and the memory of a hawk. Fooled by a prank call about a poisonous snake he not only shot the rubber snake out of a tree he had held his pistol to his face to take aim, the recoil breaking his nose. When some boys said they had a rabid dog penned in a yard Howard shot the mayor's dog in the mayor's backyard.

Cecil Smart was old and slow and had been embarrassed by a TV reporter from Advantage assigned to do a story on Mills County outlawing fireworks on the Fourth of July because of a drought. The reporter gave firecrackers to children who gleefully threw them at each other and at huffing, cursing Cecil who tried to catch the "little bastards" while the reporter filmed his story. Professioners were sensitive to Mills County being portrayed as bumpkinville. Chad Norvell was inexperienced and his ambition was a job with the Advantage police. Clarence Page was conscientious but thought analyze meant narrate. John Banks was the one he would have chosen for backup, the one he would have chosen for sheriff.

Martha called him to the table. Their meals were simpler now. Martha knew he ate lunch whenever and wherever he could so at home meals were healthy. Tonight a green salad, crockpot stew, and coarse bread. Iced tea was perennial. Their meals were quiet. He knew things that he could not tell; the husband of a woman in Martha's Daughters of Eve Fitness Center was cheating. Pastor Murphy advised her to make herself more appealing to him.

Martha had lived in Five Mills all her life, had worked in her father's clothing store. She knew everyone except the professioners and she had met many of them through God's Blessing Fashion Club, Mary and Martha Bible and Cooking Class, Ruth's Readers Book Club, the Widow's Mite Investment Club that bought stock in Enron, Tyco, HealthSouth, Lincoln, and Silverado savings and loans because of their Christian leadership. She didn't like the books that the pastor's wife selected and disagreed with the pastor's son who led the Bible study but Martha had not gone to college and Solid Rock was her sorority. Timp refused to join the Sons of Gideon Gun Club but his church membership inspired the stained glass window of a soldier kneeling in prayer with his Bible in one hand and his rifle in the other.

"I saw your mother today," Martha said.

In the beginning Martha had spent long hours in the nursing home adjacent to the Advantage hospital, holding his mother's hand, stroking her face, talking to her. Now she talked to the charge nurse and examined her mother-in-law's gown and bed linen. He found excuses in work. For women family was a vocation, for men it was moonlighting. "How was she?"

"The same. I don't think she knew I was there. Poor thing."

He didn't want to think of his mother's estrangement from the habits of her body, the shared experiences of others, the certainty of her mind. It was too similar to his hospital time in Korea, Japan, hospital ship. He had known nothing of what happened to him outside his room. She knew nothing of what happened outside her body, perhaps not that. He preferred death to the "life" that she had, for himself but also for her.

He smiled remembering how she had looked a warning at him when he found Peggy walking near the farm and took her home. "I wish your father were here," his mother said when he returned home, "to tell you about girls like that" went unsaid. His mother thought he knew nothing about sex because she had told him nothing but he knew a carload of boys had called her "Piggy" and dumped her on a country road to soften her up for sex. "Why are they mean to me?" Peggy asked. "I try to be nice to them." She had cried on his shoulder.

Martha looked at him expectantly but she did not like him to talk about Peggy to whom he had been counterfeit Doug and they lapsed again into silence.

"Do you think what happened might be because Larry wants to be like you?" she asked.

"Larry is nothing like me."

"Don't be so angry," she said.

"I'm not angry," he said, trying not to look angry.

After dinner Martha watched television. He sat at the formica table with stainless steel chairs pretending to be reconciling the bank statement and wishing for a cup of coffee. Martha wanted to replace the breakfast set but he liked the utility and familiarity of it. The older he got the more he gave up. Cigarettes, fat, sugar, and now caffeine. He limited himself to three cups of coffee a day and he was well beyond that.

Walter Clemons' father called to say he didn't believe Timp surrendered his pistol, not the one the battalion gave him. He had been drinking and his speech was slurred. "My boy was a hunter like you. Trained him myself. Wanted to be a sniper, go after them Commies the way he stalked deer. Shoot them from so far away they died before they heard the shot. See the look on the faces of the others when their buddy drops dead and they don't know where the bullet came from or who would be next. He was a good shot, maybe as good as you."

"He was the best in the company," said Timp who had never been a hunter and wasn't an expert rifleman.

"How many of them yellow bastards do you think he killed? Picking them off long range until they closed in on him? A dozen? Two dozen? At least a dozen, right?"

"It was an ambush," Timp said.

"I know he died quickly but they had to get close to do it. Picking them off one by one. Did he die quickly?"

"He never knew what happened."

"I don't believe you surrendered your pistol and anybody who says you did is a lying son of a bitch," he said before hanging up.

Timp shook his head, caught between amusement and despair. Walter's father had seen the monument and thought he knew what had happened. Timp hadn't wanted to go to the battalion reunion to receive the pistol. They said, "Remember when we ran out of water and our rifles got so hot we pissed on them?" "Remember when it was so cold our rifles jammed and our boots froze to our feet?" "Remember when we were cut off, no food, running out of ammo and a ROK truck drove through a roadblock bigger than shit and all it carried was mattresses?" He didn't remember. One Marine said, "I don't think you was ever in Korea." Another said, "Are you kidding? He knows more about Korea than anyone." Both were equally true and false.

"The news is about to come on," Martha said. It had been their nightly ritual, the news, then going to bed, making love and forgetting the county. Now they spent more time side by side than face to face. "Mills County deputy kills berserk veteran to save sheriff's life. That story next." The TV screen was filled with a patrol car, lights flashing, siren blaring, swerving down a dirt road at high speed, imperiling farmers and chickens.

He sat down beside Martha taking her hand to reassure her. She smiled at him, then turned her attention to the screen where a policeman stood in the middle of a window exchanging shots with a killer with a rifle behind a shed. Even a fool was smart enough not to stand in a window when he was being shot at. Timp didn't watch cop shows because of the distortions that corrupted the public's perception of chaos and order. What wasn't advertising sold illusions.

The only television station for those without a satellite dish was the station in Advantage, and the only incidents in Mills County to receive attention were bizarre, scandalous or bloody. Fraternity boys had mutilated a cow and one Mills resident said it was the work of aliens. Although Timp caught the boys, the Advantage TV station reported a UFO panic in Five Mills that made national tabloids, embarrassing the town.

"We never get fair reporting from Advantage," Martha said.

Because they didn't have the size, wealth or political power of Doss County, Mills County boasted of the five Mills brothers. Because of Second

Platoon Mills County was more patriotic; some called the men of Doss County cowards. The senators Pritchard were from an old Doss County family and *The Grist* questioned their trustworthiness but the media in Advantage didn't lose advertisers if Wally Sech or Ernie Clapp represented Mills County in the news. P.J. discovered that jokes about Five Mills boosted his ratings. "Slow as Main Street in Five Mills. How far is it across Mills County? Too far to stop." Mills citizens listened to his show so they could complain.

After the usual Advantage fires, car wrecks, shootings, and ribbon cuttings, a grave voice announced, "Deputy's quick action saves life of Mills County sheriff. Stay tuned for this and other stories." After commercials the anchor announced that Marine hero Wynn Mills was dead. Harley Kruger told how Wynn shot at the Kruger house and held his own family hostage while the screen showed the Mills' house and the bloodstained ground, then Larry holding Wynn's shotgun and Timp's pistol. "Wynn was threatening to kill Timp; I had to shoot him. Timp did the best he could. That's why he isn't running for reelection; he realizes his limitations."

"Wynn would have gotten a fine at most," Timp said, returning to the living room. The station had time to organize the interviews to frame the event, cutting and splicing answers with questions that weren't asked on the scene. If the story was news tomorrow it would become more pointed as the station made it their story. They would decide what had happened.

He called the station. "Are you saying that Wynn Mills was not on drugs?" he was asked.

"I'm saying that we won't know until the tests have been done."

"The radio has been reporting since this afternoon that Wynn Mills may have been on drugs. We're reporting that's what they said. If you say that he was not on drugs or alcohol we'll report that's what you said."

Martha sat down beside him and wrapped his arm in hers. "They have to make it news," she said.

'It wasn't news." He didn't know a name for it. "I let Wynn die."

"Timp, you're alive. That's what matters. Larry's alive. That woman and her children are alive. That's what matters."

"Wynn is dead. That's what matters."

"I'm going to get ready for bed," Martha said. "Don't sit here and brood. When you retire we'll be free of this sickness every time someone is arrested or gets hurt. We won't have to live like this any more."

He nodded but didn't move and she left. He was enraged at the imprecision of the media, the smug acceptance of it by citizens who heard or read about an event and believed they knew the story. They worshiped information and distrusted revelation. They preferred gossip about the private lives of public figures scarcely better than themselves to insight into how the latest legislation altered the legal environment that defined citizen and the rights thereof. They were tempted by the fabulous the way Christians were tempted by the literal.

The media would define Larry the way they had forged him—a football star, although he wasn't on the team, a hunter, a dead shot. He came home to those who knew it wasn't true but believed it. The media would define Wynn, the meaning of Wynn's death, the character of Five Mills. They would fashion the people Wynn's widow and children would be, as sure as God. He couldn't even prevent that. He could prevent Bryan Frazier defining Second Platoon.

The Grist had occasional stories of early days in Mills County but those glimpses of births, deaths, picnics, church meetings did nothing to define Mills County as East Texas or West Texas, a philosophical rather than geographical distinction. East Texas was closer to the plow than to the horse, closer to Gettysburg than Little Big Horn, closer to plantation than to reservation. West Texans favored wild over tame, believed that God's gifts to men were guns, dogs, women, and pickups evolved from horses; more inclined to drygulching than lynching, to fighting than reasoning. Mills County was in the center whether you said branch or bayou, arroyo or gully.

Five Mills had been a prosperous farm and ranch community and Mayor Pritchard sold them on a bond issue to bring a railroad to the county so they could ship produce to markets. Doss was connected to a railroad building west, Babbs needed a railroad to haul goods to his store, Pritchard needed a train to bring men hungry for land and loans to buy it.

There were no eligible mates like them so the Doss, Babbs, Pritchard children married each other. It was a good arrangement. They established a town in the less fertile part of the county. Pritchard, who had become a representative, encouraged the state to give land to the railroad and Doss persuaded the railroad to come to the new town called "Fruitful, Texas, where a farmer can live like a king."

Pritchard's son and his wife, a Babbs, began a newspaper in Fruitful and discovered that creative advertising was a highly valued skill. The newspaper promised cheap land, free seed, and a glorious future and the railroad brought immigrants and Civil War veterans who believed their future was in their callused hands. Rain follows the plow the paper said. Opening the ground opened clouds. But the clouds didn't open, the seed was mostly weeds, taxes were increased to pay off the bond that brought the railroad that gouged them for shipping produce, Pritchard's bank foreclosed on loans. At least three children died of malnutrition before their broken families accepted that they had been duped by promises and dreams.

Pritchard, supported by two newspapers in two towns, was elected governor and persuaded the state to divide oversized Mills County into two, creating Doss County, and Fruitful changed its name to Advantage. For years the only paved road in Mills County led to Advantage where farmers delivered their produce and bought supplies. During World War Two the government built an air base near Advantage on land owned by Babbs. After the base was closed the state placed a university there.

Politicians proclaimed their everlasting debt to Mills County that gave its sons for liberty and Five Mills believed the college would be payment of that debt. The mayor explained it to Timp. "Five Mills lost its chance when your friends died in Korea. We lost our most productive men in their most productive years. They give soldiers medals; they give slackers contracts. Soldiers leave widows and orphans, slackers leave heirs." It was one of those secrets public servants had to bear.

Martha wanted him to retire among the people he had served. They were good people but he knew their secret shames as they knew his public face. Martha's friend, stopped for drunken driving, who said she had eaten too much marinated steak. The neighbor who put her broken leg in a wagon and hopped down the alley to care for the man she loved but couldn't marry because she would lose her pension. The teenagers whose bodies were recovered from a car after a flood, their clothes around their knees but the water could have done that. A deacon who had been a Night Crawler. The new family in town with a credit card from an exclusive clothing store in Advantage. Before payday he questioned them about trading new clothes for food; clothing was the only thing they could buy. The man whose granddaughter was believed to also be his daughter. The man who drank to kill his sex drive because Solid Rock would not accept gays. The neighbor who gave up boots for soft soled shoes after he came home late, pulled off his boots and slept on the couch. He was awakened by his wife hitting him on the head with one of the hard-heeled boots.

Timp had been sheriff a long time and he had enemies, and friends, who feared what he knew. Just as he feared what they didn't know about him.

***

Martha put down the book selected by the pastor's wife who made all the selections, a book that told her how she could become the wife her husband dreamed of. What about her dreams?

She knew she wouldn't sleep until Timp was beside her and feared he would be up half the night brooding. When Dr. Baines' son was killed, he didn't sleep or eat for two days. He had awful nightmares, calling Rocky's name or her name. She knew he too grieved Rocky and she had held him tightly until he became quiet and she lightly fingered the scars on his back, arms, and leg thinking how close she had come to losing him before he was hers.

She didn't like sleeping alone. "Don't sleep on your stomach," her mother had said when she was a girl. "That's the devil's position. The devil will get into your hands and they'll get under you." When Rocky didn't come home, sometimes in her loneliness, they did.

"Who will I be if Rocky doesn't marry me?" she had wailed to her mother.

"You'll be yourself."

"I don't want to be myself. I want to be Rocky's wife." Her life, the life of the town, had been changed forever by Korea. And every day people drove past the monument without sight. She supposed it was necessary to forget. Yet she sometimes wondered who she would be if Rocky had not died—the silly bride who had taken to the store the biggest fish Rocky caught to buy a pan that fit it.

A lot of people were surprised when she married Rocky who was two years older than she and Timp. He had been drafted during World War II, but never left the states. Rocky was loud and bold, saying things he ought not say to girls.

"Are you marrying Rocky so you can be his cheerleader?" Eddie Baines had asked her. Her father, who thought Rocky was a brown-nose for not having seen combat in the Pacific, was pleased that he joined the reserve company of World War Two retreads who wanted the extra money and younger men who had missed the glory of the Good War. Her father had fought the Japanese and the house had been filled with his hatred of them, her childhood scarred by his stories of killing them.

Rocky said he had joined the reserves because of the contacts, especially Captain Billy Pritchard.

As Rocky's wife she had been a wide-eyed, awestruck audience for his friends and associates. If he had lived he would run her father's store and be president of the Chamber of Commerce, the Lion's Club, the city council. At social events she would hug and kiss the women like they were friends, gasp at the men's accomplishments, and giggle at their jokes and innuendoes like she was interested. Her opinions would be dictated by P.J. the d.j. and Pastor Murphy, her conversation, recreational flirtation. It seemed unfair that her identity was so entangled with that of another. "What if I had married someone else?" she asked her mother.

"Then you would be someone else," her mother said. She didn't want to be someone else. She didn't want to be herself by herself. She wanted to be who she was with Timp. She had cried herself to sleep wondering what she would do if he didn't marry her. He said first there was something he had to tell her. She thought it was about all the widows and girlfriends he had slept with. They were lonely, he was a hero, intimate with the one they loved. She could understand it but she wanted what she felt to be unique.

He wanted to tell her about Korea. By the time he came home everyone knew the story. One love she had lost, another she had nearly lost. She didn't want to know how fragile her identity was. How capriciously death had taken one man to give her another. She had laid Rocky to rest, first in the ground and then in her heart. She didn't want to keep digging him up to grieve.

"Did you tell Peggy the lower part of Rocky's face was shot off. He couldn't scream, he couldn't swallow—"

"I confused him with Doug."

"Did you and Rocky talk about me? When he was dying?"

"He was calling your name."

"Stop," she screamed. "I don't want to know. Rocky died quickly."

"I had to stop him."

"No, stop. Stop. I don't want to hear any more."

"I killed your husband."

"Rocky was a hero," she said. She knew he was hollowed by guilt because he had not been able to save Rocky or the others, but stories of how close she came to losing both of them made her mind sick as well as her stomach. She made him promise he would never tell her how Rocky died. She wouldn't have cared if he had come home a deserter. Which one? That's where she became confused. She barely remembered Rocky and if he had come home she would never have known Timp.

***

Timp slipped quietly into bed with Martha. He feared when he closed his eyes he would see Wynn, Hao, the boys, or dream of voices calling someone to save them, corpsman, Jesus, Mama. He focused on Martha, not a picture but a montage. The bubbly, popular girl he had loved in high school; even then he knew she would be Rocky's show pony but that she could step into the traces beside him and pull half the load. Rocky's bride, so beautiful, so hopeful in her bridal photograph he could not watch her take her vows. Rocky's chocolates, flowers, and giggles wife.

Trapped on the farm with Martha married to Rocky life seemed without promise but to replicate days of labor. There was no other woman who could give his life meaning. Sometimes he saw Peggy and they went to Advantage for a milk shake but until he played Doug they had never been intimate. He thought the call-up for Korea was liberation.

Martha became the widow who received him as fulfillment while making love to Rocky. He watched the sculptor turn his face into an image that was not him as the woman he loved fell in love with a man who wasn't him either.

He rarely studied his relationship with the efficient Martha who managed his home and his campaigns, a relationship as obvious as the statue, and he belonged to it the same way. What had once been desire had been replaced by devotion, and passion had become compassion. It was a good trade. He didn't want to wake Martha but placed his arm around her and shaped himself to her back. He knew her body as he knew his own, knew its curves and creases, yet he wondered if he had ever known it as Rocky had.

Rocky had talked about the way she breathed when she slept, the way she curled around his hand. How she liked her hair messed with, her throat stroked and kissed, especially the soft spot just below the edge of her jaw, the nape of her neck, tiny wet kisses at the small of her back. Rocky let her wear short nightgowns but no panties. If he was married to it he wanted to be able to touch it when he wanted. How she smelled. How she whimpered before orgasm and purred like a kitten afterwards. "I pin her to the bed so she can't move and tease her. She goes crazy when I do that."

"You know just the way to touch me," she said, trapping him in Rocky's dream. Sometimes, with Martha asleep beside him, he thought how strange that he knew her before he knew her—that soft breathing sound, the way she snuggled her back against him to be certain he was there, took his hand and pulled it to her breast. How fortunate it was for him that Rocky had died. It seemed sacrilege to thank God for Rocky's death but if he had lived Rocky would be married to Martha and what and where would he be? Not a hero. Not the sheriff. Not Martha's husband. He had been the sole beneficiary of a disaster. Nothing in his philosophy could account for that.

"War causes us to give up many things," the colonel said when Timp returned to the states. "For your buddies it was their lives. For their families it's a loved one. For you, one of those things may be the notion that there is only one way to see an event. Do you understand?"

"No, sir," Timp said.

"There is more than one way to be a hero. One is to die, the other is to serve. You can serve your buddies, their loved ones, your country. You're going to get the Congressional Medal of Honor."

"I don't deserve a medal."

"Second Platoon does and you're Second Platoon. People are going to ask questions but nobody's going to understand. Nobody. Do not pretend that only your sacrifice counts. Do not destroy what your buddies mean to their families and friends. They gave their lives for their country. Your country asks you to be the messenger of hope. Can you do that?"

The Marines had landed at Inchon, UN forces pushed toward the Yalu River, the platoon had been forgotten, and Truman was meeting with MacArthur to prevent war with China. The medal was awarded by Senator Prince Pritchard whose son was still in Korea with the rest of the company. "Tell the press that the real heroes are those who died and you accept the medal for Second Platoon," the senator said on the way to the football field.

"I didn't plan to say anything."

"We must play our role as the platoon played theirs," the senator said.

He had played his role. Peggy showed him the baby that some said wasn't Doug's. He told her that Doug had spoken kindly of her. "I don't think he liked my breasts," she said.

"He loved your breasts. He said they were nice handfuls."

"Oh," she said, placing his hands on her breasts. "Oh, he liked . . . he liked to squeeze them, just like that, and . . . um . . . then he would blow on them . . . softly pinch the nipples and . . . roll them between his fingers . . . harder . . . and then bite them . . . until I mashed them in his face."

He had followed her directions so well that she forgot and called him Doug. "Spank me, Doug, and call me a slut."

Afterwards, she asked, "Did Doug die well? Was he disfigured?"

"The lower part of his face was blown off. He couldn't swallow, probably drowned in his own blood," he said seizing the moment like salvation.

She lay so still, so rigid he thought she had stopped breathing. Then she curled in pain. "No, please, no."

"He died like the others," Timp said.

"Doug was as brave as you."

"Yes. He was as brave as I."

"You lied to see if I loved Doug even if he weren't a hero."

He had told Martha how Peggy wanted him to play Doug so he could explain that Rocky taught him how to please her but she thought Peggy represented all the widows and didn't want to hear. When he tried to be himself, she thought it was something he had learned with another woman. He didn't want to play Rocky in her dreams but what would she think if she knew he had seduced her by pretending to be Rocky?

The first time they made love he had struggled with feelings that gained power by their newness. He loved Martha and that love filled him with shame and fear. Shame because he had taken advantage of his knowledge of her. Fear that she recognized how he had used her dead husband.

He tried to talk to her about the Rocky he knew. Tried to tell her the Timp he had been. Because the more he believed she loved him, the more unworthy of her love he felt. "I had to stop him from calling your name."

"Shut up," she screamed. "I won't hear any more lies. Why do you have to destroy him? You're destroying yourself."

Beside him in the dark was the person he loved most in the world, yet he was alone in a memory she could not understand. Children would have been a comfort but Martha was barren. He never mentioned it, hoping that his grace would translate into forbearance on her part when the mirage vanished and he was revealed.

CHAPTER
FOUR

❦

"'I shot him through the heart,' deputy says," was the headline of *The Grist* with a photograph of Larry beside his patrol car, one hand holding Wynn's shotgun, the other holding Timp's pistol. "Sheriff says deputy confused" was accompanied by a file photograph of Timp before the monument, his image towering over him. He looked shrunken, pale pretender to the face above, the small screen representation of an exaggeration.

On the front page was an editorial. "In light of the contradictory statements by the two law officers on the scene it is difficult to know what happened. Nevertheless, Sheriff Smith, in his one-ranger style, went to the scene without backup. Smith has served Mills County well but he has recognized that it is time to step aside for someone younger and more capable. Sadly, his retirement may be one life too late."

There was a letter to the editor from an old timer who wanted the professioners to go back where they came from and to take their ill-bred children with them, and one from a professioner who wanted deputies protecting the suburbs rather than giving tickets on the expressway and for the sheriff to teach old-timers how to drive.

A back page reported war on the set of a TV series as a blast of bad publicity targeted cast members. The actors muttered "betrayal" as they battled to survive.

The shooting made the front page of the *Advantage Advertiser* with a photograph of Hao and her children cowering behind the door. For those who read the story the photograph illustrated their fear of Wynn but Timp knew it was the camera they hid from. There was a stick figure diagram of the event that began with Mills shooting at his neighbor's house and terrorizing his family and ended with the wife and children embracing Larry. Both papers portrayed Wynn as troubled and dangerous, Timp as ineffective, Hao and her boys as hostages, Larry as their savior. Both stated that Wynn was reported to be on drugs and that he had a hidden arms cache.

An inside page screamed "Athlete embattled over contract dispute refused to surrender," "Bloody slaughter as three shows dropped from next year's TV schedule," "Starlet explodes bombshell, announces prominent politician father of her child." Timp stared at the cereal box. If he finished it within a year he would have eaten it at its best.

"What are you going to say to Larry?" Martha asked, anticipating his thoughts. They had been married so long they thought alike.

"I don't know. I have to call a special meeting." He got up from the table to get his pistol but it was at the office. Particularly today he didn't want to wear it but particularly today he needed to show he had it. The hell with what they thought; he wasn't running for reelection.

Timp worried over going to Larry's trailer to clarify his report but Larry wouldn't have slept much and it would be better if they met in his office with the report in front of them. He called the office. Howard Goss reported overnight a minor accident, coyote in Shady Acres, deer in garden in Country Place, caller denied permission to shoot it. Professioners moved to the country so their children could enjoy nature until a raccoon scattered their garbage, a deer ate their daisies, a skunk invaded their garage, or coyotes ate their cat. Then they wanted wildlife disappeared. Old timers liked to watch the deer and coons, listen to the coyotes, and they endured hawks and owls that sometimes fed on pets. The deer belonged to the state but Timp had the coyotes trapped and relocated.

Mrs. Lubitsch had fallen into a shrub outside her door and couldn't get up. She had fallen into the shrub so many times she had crushed it into a nest. A neighbor helped her up but noticed she was not properly dressed. Goss told her again about the nursing home in Advantage but she said she had never lived in Advantage and she had no intention of dying there. Her daughter-in-law would come see about her.

Harvin Knight was living in his former store that had lost its lease and was without utilities. Harvin's brother, corpsman Doc Knight, had died with Second Platoon. Before Harvin lost his business selling and repairing clocks and watches because of cheap electronic imports he bought a tableau of Doc holding a dying Marine and looking toward heaven. Man urinating behind building. College woman screaming in an apartment house, thought she was paralyzed because her cat was lying on her hair and she couldn't raise her head. The usual noncusto-dial stops—driver's license checks, vehicle registration checks, failure to display proper vehicle lights.

The Advantage dispatcher reported that Wally Sech was outside the radio station daring P.J. to come out. P.J. would arrive at noon and the station feared an altercation if Wally was still there. "I'd like to punch P.J. myself," the dispatcher said, "but we're going to lock your guy up if you don't come get him."

Wally was happy to see him. "If he doesn't apologize I'm going to take him to truth city, turn his lying lips into a toilet seat. Saying you crawfished. Those pinkies from Advantage watched the platoon die." Wally shook his head, his eyes wild, his hair ungroomed. "I would have charged down the middle of the road, not crawled into a hole and let my brother and you other guys die."

"You can get in your car and leave or you can lock it up and get in the cruiser," the sheriff said. "You're going home."

Wally had his chest up. "Anyone tells me you ducked is going to get a hare lip," Wally said, getting in his car. "And you can't arrest me because I'm carrying a flag."

Since he was in Advantage Timp stopped to tell Devin Deason that Hao and her children didn't embrace Larry and that they weren't afraid of Wynn. He feared even after a retraction the images would remain.

He had known Devin since the long, skinny sixteen-year-old reported for his father's newspaper. Called "Scoop" because he was an incurious reporter, Devin took mail-order cartoon classes. After the medal ceremony he had interviewed Timp. Timp had tried to clarify facts that the press had gotten wrong and denied that he was a hero. "Wouldn't you like to go back to Korea and kill more of the people who killed your buddies?"

"No," Timp said.

"There is no doubt that he remains the same simple, straight-shooter who left here only weeks ago and has seen horrors most of us cannot imagine. But he survived and who knows what greatness is in store for this humble man from Mills County who said there were good men in Doss and Mills counties and they would avenge his buddies," Devin wrote.

Devin had drawn cartoons for an Austin newspaper while in college. Failing to get syndication as a cartoonist he returned to Advantage as publisher and became a successful, self-aware Chamber of Commerce businessman and a connoisseur of fried foods, cheap wine, and ambitious friends. A little bent and no longer thin, he remained publisher when a corporation bought the newspaper but lost choice of wire services and syndicated columnists.

Heads came up when the sheriff walked into the building and Scoop waved him into his private office. Timp laid out the story of the shooting in detail and how offensive the stick figures would be to the widow and children.

"I did those myself," Scoop said, his cheeks red but they had been red when Timp appeared. "They illustrate the sequence of events."

Timp argued that the figures showed the widow and children embracing Larry and the photograph suggested they were hiding from Wynn.

"Carl may have been aggressive but he'll get an award for that shot. The woman and children were clearly frightened and the photograph shows that. I'm rather proud of the stick figures." The red rose into his thin, pale hair.

"I've never seen or heard of Wynn on drugs," Timp tried again.

"The coroner is checking for them," Scoop said.

"That's routine." Timp restrained himself. "Wynn kept in the attic an old pistol and rifle that belonged to his grandfather the way most people do."

"In other words, a hidden arms cache," Claiborne said.

"It's not the same." It was Easter and the Easter parade.

"It's the story radio is telling, TV is telling. Do you think we're going to change that to tell your story?"

"It's not my story. It's what we do to people who stumble into the spotlight."

"This newspaper is owned by a corporation that doesn't care what happens in Mills County. Seventy-five percent of our income is from advertising. How much of that comes from Mills County? Less than 5 percent and that's from Glen Timberlake. We carry news about Mills County as a public service but it doesn't make the front page unless it's something that Advantage readers want to read. We've done that story and we likely won't mention it again."

"Don't make Wynn Mills a criminal."

"This paper doesn't care who the bad guy is but it has to be Wynn or Larry and there's no money on Wynn."

"I beg you not to describe Larry as the man who killed Wynn Mills."

Scoop stared at his desk for a moment, his face glowing, then looked at Timp. "You have a reputation for trying to make yourself bigger by destroying those around you. Your monument isn't high enough?"

The sheriff fought anger and humiliation past the billboard advertising a Gun and Blade Show, the billboard of a larger-than-life Pastor Ryland Murphy holding a Bible in one hand and pointing a finger at all who passed by. "I ask nothing but your attention" the sign said. Murphy's first attention came from ridiculing feminism, women's eternal desire to be superior, their pride that goeth before a fall. Notoriety had made Murphy the voice of the church when the media wanted a quote, an attitude or an opinion.

Timp drove past Guns-Rugs-Ammo and other warehouses that posed as discount stores, dwarfing the God sins housed in mobile homes so they could be moved across the county line when Pastor Murphy targeted them.

The distance between the hawk and the dove was the dollar, Timp fumed as he parked in front of *The Grist*. Scoop had never been in a war but knew what to write about Korea. He had never seen violent death but had chosen the story his paper would tell before Wynn's blood had jellied.

Jimmy Vines had turned *The Grist* into a daily "dedicated to progress." In contrast to sturdy Scoop Deason, Jimmy was slender and kept his head down so that with his tuft of dark hair and pinched shoulders he resembled a vulture. "I didn't really know Mills," Vines said, looking over his glasses. "I kind of admired him. But this is a small newspaper in a small town up against the corporate media in a city. That damned P.J. is all over the radio telling how Wynn killed women and children in Vietnam and threatened people back home, his own family. The story is out there. The *Advertiser* reported it. We couldn't ignore it. I lowered the volume as much as I could."

"Can you say that it was a tragedy, an accident?"

"Larry is running for office, you aren't," Vines said. "Hell, Timp, this paper has given you headlines for years."

When Timp stood to leave he saw a stack of posters with Larry's picture over "The Man Who Killed Wynn Mills." The man who caused Wynn Mills' death is who Larry was, he thought, but he was also blameworthy.

"They're all over town," Vines said. "Babbs Morrison has outlined his campaign budget with us. Tomorrow's paper is going to be about Wynn beating that coach, killing people in Vietnam, and shooting Kruger's guard dogs leaving Kruger unprotected. It's all over the radio."

Maybe it wasn't the photographer Wynn's family was hiding from, Timp thought. Maybe it was the disk jockey and his microphone.

Timp drove down weedy Timpson Smith Boulevard in Sleepy Hollow, checked the broken streets and sagging porches. He had been present when a carpenter yelled, "Hey, the sides don't fit." "Do they touch?" the contractor asked. "Nail it." Timberlake had needed quick sales to avoid bankruptcy.

Timp crossed the highway to the unpaved streets of Freetown that was suspicious of law officers and watched him warily through dusty blinds and stained curtains. When Sleepy Hollow covered the ground with impervious roofs, streets and foundations runoff from heavy rain flooded houses in Freetown and a girl on her way to school had drowned. Residents of Freetown wanted the county to do something. The county declined. The remedy was a lawsuit but Timberlake would hire lawyers, engineers and keep the case in courts until homeowners ran out of money. As sheriff his weapons were as unserviceable as theirs. The law was like medicine and other businesses—you got less than you paid for but if you paid nothing you got nothing. That resentment still flamed in the barbershop.

He stopped when he saw John Banks in his car. John, whose father had died in Second Platoon, was off-duty.

"Just checking the temperature," John said. "Shooting Wynn unsettled these folks. If that can happen to a white guy named Mills, what can happen here?" He looked at Timp with his round, pleasant face and when Timp didn't respond he looked away. "I read the paper, I heard P.J. on the radio. I was a-nnoyed, b-nnoyed, all the way to p-nnoyed. Anybody who knows you, who knows anything about police work can see through it."

Timp thought of asking John to speak to Scoop, but John wasn't a witness and Scoop would remember it as a political stunt.

"Suspicious character, had his name on his shoes so I took him to the Advantage nursing home. Kid pushing his grandma around; his daddy wouldn't take him so I brought him to the station to chill. Sixteen and there was no problem to which he didn't have the solution. Got him washing squad cars as community service." Timp nodded at the too-familiar stories.

"Trash fire," John said pointedly. John didn't yell, he didn't repeat himself but when he spoke you had better listen.

The new golf course made Freetown valuable property. Once Night Crawlers, including some of the sheriff's posse, drove through Freetown in caravans late at night to remind black citizens of their vulnerability and to discourage political involvement. When Timp became sheriff he put a stop to the Night Crawlers but Freetown had never been incorporated into the city and had no sewers, no city water, no fire protection and no garbage pickup. Racism had died as an institution but had survived in practice.

Timberlake and an expansion company from Dallas vied for property in Freetown adjacent to the golf course. Two vacant houses had burned damaging an occupied house whose owners sold and moved. *The Grist* blamed bad wiring, derelicts, kids playing with matches. John believed the houses were burned to frighten the residents into selling. Mills County had two trained firemen, the rest were volunteers. None was qualified for arson investigation. Timp had his deputies maintain regular patrols.

John fiddled with the cartridges in his belt. "I saw the posters, Timp. I keep swallowing but Wynn's death don't go down. I've never whistled another cop, but Larry, may his retirement be premature, don't score in my 'hood."

"If you have any evidence of wrongdoing I want to see it."

John showed empty hands. "When Larry announced I didn't say nothing, not to you, not to nobody. But that was before Wynn Mills. If you care about this county, you better do some thinking about Larry."

***

When he reached the office he told Mrs. Stutz to call a special meeting of the deputies. "Call Larry last and I'll meet with him before the others." He was sure every time Larry closed his eyes he saw Wynn's torn body, his bloody clothes askew, his wife and children wailing over him, rethinking thoughtless choices—driving faster or slower, approaching from the other side of the house, standing beside Timp with his pistol holstered—that would have saved a life, a family. He wouldn't sleep well and he needed time to see what he had done.

"Chief, don't you think it's time John bought a tableau for his father? He has a job, he has a car," Mrs. Stutz said. "He would be the first black."

Maybe John didn't want to be the first or the only, Timp thought. "You are not to mention the tableaux in this office," he told Mrs. Stutz.

He signed off on the monthly gas bill and wrote another requisition for portable radios. He was short a deputy because politicians believed cutting taxes was an honorable way to buy votes. Portable radios would have saved Wynn's life.

Brother Jonas called. "Mr. Meador says the insurance policy is void because Wynn committed a crime. Can you talk to him?"

Timp telephoned "Milk" Meador. No matter how much time Meador spent in the sun his skin was white with his veins showing blue beneath. "If someone dies as the result of an unlawful act, the policy is void," Meador said. "That is stated in the policy. I saw the news, I read the newspapers, I know what happened."

"They got the story wrong."

"I've supported you a long time, Timp." Meador was party chair. "What you say is what I believe. What the official report says is what the company believes. You show me the report that says Wynn's death was the result of something other than an unlawful act and I'll get her the money."

"I appreciate your support. I ask this as a personal favor." Milk's darker and older brother was Timp's fireteam leader in Second Platoon.

"I don't like being pressured, especially when you ask me to do something that is unethical and probably illegal."

"I'm asking you to see this woman and her children as human beings. They have done nothing wrong. Her husband was a hero." Like Scoop Deason and Jimmy Vines, Meador was a draft dodger. Wynn served in their place.

"When I see the official cause of Wynn's death, she'll get the money."

Timp had dealt with companies before where words in contracts meant something different than they did in church and where an obscure clause was the most important of all. He asked Mrs. Stutz to call Brother Jonas. "His wife is going to get him; he's on the tractor," she said.

When Jonas called back Timp reported his conversation with Meador. "She and the boys are going to need the insurance," Jonas said. "Could you talk to Pastor Murky?"

Pastor Murphy led his followers to discover mysteries in the Bible that had been hidden from Christians for two thousand years to be revealed by him. "I didn't study theology but everything I've found in the Bible is what Christians have known for centuries. We're unable to live up to our Savior's demands so we require obedience to Leviticus. Holy in church, hollow outside it."

Timp imagined Brother Jonas rehearsing or reciting a sermon. Jonas had not forgotten that Murphy's passion extended beyond love for the poor. Murphy had divorced the woman who worked to pay for his education to marry a young woman from a wealthy family. Murphy had one child by his first wife and two by the second, all of them, except his first wife and her child, employed by his church. Cynics scoffed that Murphy was the only one to whom God had returned tenfold. "Hao is not one of his flock but she is a child of God," Jonas said.

"How is she doing?"

"She's grieving as she should but what upsets her is what they are saying about Wynn. I don't know how to protect them from those posters."

Timp called his pastor about the insurance. Murphy was a fundamentalist in the new dispensation; the Kingdom would come by the military might and political power of America, a city on a hill. Greed was good, violence was redemptive, and war on the weak was not only profitable, it was popular. Riches were the measure of God's blessing. Health and security were rewards for goodness. Divorce that Jesus had condemned was forgivable but homosexuality that Jesus had not mentioned was not. Jesus asked his followers not to use God's name for secular purposes, pray or demonstrate piety in public, or do charity for an earthly reward. He commanded his disciples to pay their taxes and love their enemies but Murphy loved least those whose choice of scriptures to ignore was different from his.

"Brother Jonas talked to Milk. I thought perhaps—"

"It is unethical for Brother Jonas to interfere with my church affairs or my church members. God put Harley Kruger in a position to keep America safe and gave him the ability to make money and to use it for good. The stone steps that you pass every time you enter my church are from the sacred land of Israel, steps that Jesus and his disciples walked on. Those steps were given to the church by Harley Kruger. I fear that you are in danger of envy."

Although Murphy said every one was equal at the foot of the cross, one's power was weighed, one's money counted in his church. When Timberlake was juggling income and debt and burdened with Freetown flooding, Pastor Murphy provided spiritual comfort. "Harley feels bad about Wynn's death," Murphy said. "He asked what he could do."

"If he could see a human being through a dollar, that would help."

"Don't permit idealism to make you cynical," Murphy said, "No one but God notices the fall of every sparrow. Men have to choose the sparrows."

Timp called the radio station in Advantage and asked to speak to P.J. "Don't try to intimidate me," P.J. said in the gravelly voice he had perfected. "Don't try to censor me; I don't live in your county and you have no authority here. You may think you're a hero but heroes don't bully people."

Timp had a brief dream of arresting P.J. for some infraction, but called Martha instead. "Larry is running as 'The Man Who Killed Wynn Mills.'"

"Oh, Timp, you can't mean that. Can't you do anything?"

"Larry isn't 'The Man Who Killed Wynn Mills' unless he wants to be."

"I'm trying to help Wynn's widow," he told Kruger. "It would help if you said that you weren't threatened, that you overreacted."

"We are doing what we believe is appropriate," Kruger said, hanging up.

The coroner called to report that Wynn had been shot three times. "One bullet broke his left arm. A separate bullet struck him in the left side, missing his heart but puncturing a lung. The fatal bullet penetrated his heart when he was on the ground."

"Would he have lived if—"

"I don't know why not. The bullet in his left side did not hit his arm. His arm was in a raised position."

Timp had tugged free the shotgun that had fallen behind Wynn's body. "He raised his arms before he turned?"

"He was sideways to the shooter and his arm was in a raised position."

***

Larry had been awake half the night face to face with Wynn Mills. He had gone to the trailer park to take hot-check hottie dancing but she wasn't home. At the Wild Rose he found a college kid trying to pull a chocolate eclair to his car. He slapped the student, shoved him into his car, and watched him leave. She was darker than Larry liked but the pink parts were the same. She said she had a roommate so he had to bring her to the trailer park. He preferred sleeping in someone else's bed. Less cleaning up to do, easier to say goodbye. He almost wished he had gone home alone. He couldn't get his mind off Timp. How many times he had wished he had been old enough to fight beside Timp. When finally they had faced death side by side—The idea that he might get old and soft terrified him. He vowed to keep in shape and when he got too old or shot-up to take calls, stay in the office or quit it. And never, ever back down.

The other half of the night had been filled with nightmares of Wynn slowly turning. Chocolate ass called someone to come get her, frightened by his attempts to scream. If Timp had waited for backup instead of playing Audie Murphy—then Timp sent him to face the media unprepared, giving himself time to get his story together and confuse what happened.

It galled Larry that, dammit, Timp couldn't admit that he needed help. Telling people his life wasn't in danger was a shot in the back, something a pussy would do. People measured him by Timp's scale but that would stop if Timp admitted Larry had saved his life. They would love his ass for that.

Larry was still in the rumpled bed when Milk Meador called. "What's going on?" Meador asked. "Timp said Wynn's death was an accident."

Larry was half asleep and it took him a moment to focus. Meador was president of the Chamber of Commerce, chair of the party. "I haven't seen him since . . ." Larry wanted to say since Timp tried to steal his shine but he didn't know the party's position.

"A couple of hundred thousand's riding on whether Wynn's death was an accident or the result of an unlawful act. Timp wants me to give Wynn's widow the money but insurance isn't charity. There are rules."

"I shot Wynn because he was threatening to shoot me and Timp."

"And that's what the report is going to say?"

"That's what my report says."

"Has Timp asked you to change it? Do you think he might run?"

"Do you want him to run for reelection?" That would be a kick in the mouth; save Timp's life so he could serve another term.

"We want you to run unopposed. I'll talk to Mayor Williams." No matter who was chair of the party it was run from the mayor's office.

Larry lay back on the bed. He had a good bed, expensive sound system, dumbbells and free weights he picked up cheap at the Rent-All under cover outside. Everything else came with the trailer, except for the nudes. Maybe they weren't art but he liked them. Women liked looking at women's bodies too. Turned them on. He prided himself on how little he slept in his own bed and he hated the trailer. It offered seclusion, temporary neighbors; no one cared who came and went. As sheriff he'd have to move to a better place but maybe keep this one too.

Larry needed to ask Babbs about the message from Meador. He shambled to the tiny kitchen and looked in the refrigerator. To hell with it, he'd pick up coffee and doughnuts at the Drop By, tell Babbs about Meador's call, check out the coeds. Larry had taken law enforcement and public relations classes at the college but his father was a plumber in Advantage and the girls weren't impressed without the badge and bullets. One of them had dropped him for a longhair with a paint brush over his ear. Larry had followed him for a while but he never crossed the county line. Good thing for him. The boys thought they were going to be FBI or Texas Rangers. Well, he was going to be sheriff of Mills County.

Outside, Larry picked up the weights and did six curls and six military presses before getting in the car. The battered Plymouth was less than a foot from the trailer where he had skidded to a stop to excite Dustee, that was her name. The manager had spoken to him about it before but Larry had given him a lawman's stare; anyone who ran a trailer park had reason to fear the law. Larry wanted a motorcycle. Until he became sheriff he could use a cruiser only on official business which meant he needed a car for privacy. When he became sheriff he would have to drive a cruiser everywhere and might never own a motorcycle, might never speed down country roads with tits pressed to his back, her hair streaming in the breeze, looking stud.

It vexed him that outside the county he couldn't carry a piece. He had a .45 like Timp's except for the engraving, the revolver he killed Wynn with, a .32 Baretta for a throw-down and he was saving money for a Glock. He had never considered being a fireman, no weapons. He had dreamed of being a soldier and guarding women POWs, tying them down and teasing them until they begged for it, but he didn't want to be stuck in a hellhole without women. He felt smaller, lighter when he took off his pistol belt with the gun and holster, two extra magazines, flashlight and handcuffs. He liked the low center of gravity, the power in his legs the pistol gave him.

He locked the pistol belt in the trunk of his car and his pistol in the glove compartment before starting to Advantage. The throw-down he left strapped to his leg. If nothing worked out at the college he might drop by the God sins to meet the girls and hear what people were saying about him. On the way to the coffee shop he saw one of the new posters. "The Man Who Killed Wynn Mills." He would start a new era of law enforcement in Mills County—as scary as Timpson Smith, as up-to-date as Advantage, giving the old timers and the professioners what each wanted.

***

Timp parked the patrol car off the road, avoiding parking where he had parked before. A house in the country, good family, quiet life. How could he have let it happen? He walked to the house not knowing what to say. Jonas had covered the blood soaked ground but Timp could still smell it.

Hao wore jeans and a faded T-shirt, "Wife of a Marine, the toughest job in the Corps." Her face was pale and puffy and she was startled to see him. "I know it doesn't make it any easier to accept but no one intended it to happen," he said with his hat in his hands.

She let him in. A once large, open room where neighbors forted up during Indian raids—women and children on pallets on the floor, the men standing watch at the loop holes—had been partitioned into smaller rooms. He stepped into a room that served as living, dining room, and kitchen. It was hot with a fire in the large fireplace that had once warmed the whole house. The room smelled of woodsmoke, fried chicken, ham, roast beef with onions, carrots, and potatoes, baked beans with bacon on top, lemon pie. The boys in jeans and T-shirts were stiff, standing like sentinels to sound the alarm. Timp sat in the chair she indicated, Wynn's chair, but she didn't sit down.

On the TV set were glass-fronted boxes of flags presented at gravesides by a grateful nation. Had the spoils ever gone to the fighters or their widows? Timp wondered. Perhaps in some other century. On the wall was a calendar with a photograph of the Iwo Jima flag-raising, a plaque with Wynn's name, the Marine emblem, the name of his unit; a shadow box containing Wynn's US and Vietnamese medals, the bargain family portrait that had appeared in the paper after Wynn's death, and a faded photograph of the Union survivor in his Yankee uniform, surrounded by his children. His Yankee wife was absent from the picture because she had ruined her only good dress fighting the attempt of neighbors to burn them out. It was her absence and the photographer's remark that she was "all black" that began the legend that she was Indian or African American and the Mills were tainted with her blood.

Hao served him tea and placed a piece of chocolate pie before him. The women from her church had been generous but soon their attention would turn to others in need. A bouquet and an unopened plastic wrapped basket of food, still bearing the delivery tag, was on the table. Timp knew without asking that it had been sent by the Krugers.

He asked her to sit down. "Bad people come. They just are pushing into house. I tell them stop but they don't hear. They make pictures and shout to us," she said, polishing the table with a cloth. Even sitting down she remained in motion. She smelled faintly of cedar.

He nodded his sympathy hoping she understood he could not interfere with the media. "They won't be back." But they would be at Wynn's funeral. The boys stood beside her at the table and Hao straightened their clothing and smoothed their hair. "How did you meet Wynn?" he asked.

A squad of fifteen Marines and a Navy corpsman lived in her hamlet, patrolled the trails, set up night ambushes and trained the men to protect their families. Wynn, a sergeant, led the Marines. Her father was "honcho," Wynn's Vietnamese equivalent. The Vietnamese platoon fought beside the Marines against the Viet Cong. "Wynn was wanting to be like you," Hao said.

When her father was killed, Wynn extended for a year so that he could protect her family. He went home because of the death of his father and looked for work to pay for his return to his wife. Seeing South Vietnam collapsing he sold land to Kruger and returned to rescue his wife and her family but there was resentment that turned raw when Kruger sold the land to a corporation to merchandise.

Tien was learning to whistle and Hao took his face in both her hands. She had never lost faith that Wynn would return. "One day he walk into village. My heart stop."

"What happened to your family?"

Her grandparents wouldn't leave, her mother, aunts, and uncles wouldn't leave without them, siblings wouldn't leave without their mother. "Wynn write boo coo forms. They never come. Maybe dead, maybe Thailand. I think I make God very angry."

"What did Wynn shoot Kruger's dogs with?"

She went to the trashcan—garbage was kept separately and went to the pigs—and retrieved two shotgun shells. Number Twos, good for geese, a fox in the hen house or chicken-killing dogs. "Where does he keep them?" She unlocked a cabinet and showed him a box of number twos and a box of number nines. Wynn had no intention of shooting anyone. Timp asked if she would like Martha to stay with her but she and the boys needed to be alone.

When he told her she might not get Wynn's insurance she stopped moving, her mouth open in disbelief. "Wynn pay every month."

He said Brother Jonas would help her with assistance.

"I cook, I clean, wash, iron, sew, whatever people are wanting. I work in garden. I work like bear and half. We sweat it." It wasn't herself or the boys she was worried about. "Please don't shitcan Wynn. My boys don't understand."

She pulled her sock down and scratched her heel, a gesture so innocent that tenderness rose in him. She was spared the illusions of war by artists and the media, *The Iliad,* Gone With the Wind. She knew war where heroism and horror converged, where horrible men were capable of heroic acts and heroes did ghastly deeds, where everyone died for their country, their God, their home. He had failed Wynn but he would save her. He would endorse Larry and Larry would rewrite his report. Larry had learned that killing was easier than living after killing.

On the way back to town he turned on the car radio. " . . . a violent man," P.J. said. "Enraged by an overheard opinion he didn't agree with he assaulted two professors. It took Sheriff Timpson Smith to restrain him. In high school he assaulted a teacher until deputies restrained him." P.J. failed to mention that the coach was ten years older and twenty pounds larger.

Mrs. Stutz had not been able to contact Larry but a national tabloid had called. A reporter was revisiting old stories—a four-year-old girl who survived three subfreezing nights lost in a forest; when found she said a giant had taken her to his cave, fed her soup and when it stopped snowing carried her to the highway. No sign of his or her tracks were found. "She says she remembers a big man taking her to a cave. She thinks their tracks were ruined by searchers." A woman who won the lottery after promising to light a candle to St. Jude every day now lived in Mexico with servants and private guards and belonged to "one of those hands-in-the-air rapture churches." A woman who was singing the national anthem on TV when her shoulder strap broke exposing a breast and bringing her both a movie and a record contract was now a star in porn films.

"You're the one who wrote about UFOs in Mills County," Timp said.

"Same publication, different writer. I'm the one who wrote 'The Gallant Last Stand of Second Platoon.'" The sheriff knew the story; he had heard it read so many times. "Monstrous attack, vicious and implacable enemy, heroic resolve, utmost personal courage, resolute sacrifice."

"I got great quotes from you. 'Where the hell did the yellow bellies go? Bring 'em back, I want another shot at those bastards. Help me to my feet, give me some ammo and I'll chase them to China.'"

"I never spoke to you," the sheriff said.

"I was a freelancer in Pusan trying to scrabble money to get to Japan if the Reds overran you guys. A major gave me the story—a tenacious platoon blocked a road and despite ferocious human wave attacks, bullet-swept terrain, prevented a breakthrough that could have pushed our troops into the sea."

"That's not what happened."

"I gave readers what they needed. MacArthur wanted to be president and the North Koreans were kicking his ass, McCarthy screamed that Truman was losing the war because of Reds in his administration—people needed glory. It was the biggest story I ever wrote, 'Tough, stalwart Leathernecks burnishing their Devil Dog image,' big for a week. You were in a restricted area in the hospital. So, what has that story done for you?"

The sheriff closed the connection.

***

The Dosses moved to South Texas to take over a railroad. The Pritchards moved to Austin to pursue politics. The Babbs were addicted to riches, not money, but riches that made money both desired and despised. The more of it they had the less it meant to them. They operated stores, granaries, gins in two counties, paying too little and charging too much until farmers formed a co-op and built their own gin and granaries.

Babbs Morrison had learned in school that flag-waving was the best refuge for a coward and in church that religion was the best excuse for the abuse of power: God told me to do it. He had learned from the Pritchard side of the family that the purpose of government was to keep the money in the right hands and to protect the powerful from those who would replace them. From the Babbs side of the family he discovered that education was to teach students that they deserved whatever they could get and they were not responsible for consequences to those less powerful or less privileged. That understanding of how things worked made him a good professor. He didn't just teach from the textbook; he gave students family insights into the powers that controlled their lives. However, teaching counted for nothing without publication.

Babbs didn't complain. He had learned as a child to manipulate the system. He discovered a man who published his own books to certify his expertise as a financial adviser and printed books for others who paid for them. It was an easier but more expensive way to gain tenure and promotion. Babbs had volunteered to manage Larry's campaign to get material for the book but he had no decisions to make, no strategy to plan, just printing posters and arranging speeches to the Rotary Club. He wished he had a better candidate. His biggest problem was keeping Larry out of the story.

He was neither surprised nor pleased to see Larry; Larry sometimes sat in on his classes to meet women. "You seen Morgan Murphy?" Larry asked. Babbs didn't know who Morgan Murphy was. "The DA let me look at her films." Larry whistled. "I want to meet that woman."

Babbs wanted a wife and family and he dreamed that some day it would happen but he didn't have time to bird-dog women like Larry or preserve thirty-year-old cherries like God's prosecutor Bryan Frazier, defender of the gentle gender. Bryan complained about sex jokes and adult language unless it was on the stage and lectured colleagues about their conduct toward black and women students, particularly black women students. Babbs preferred to listen and store until needed. Forbidden fruit was the shortcut to ruin in sex-obsessed places like Advantage and Five Mills—you did it, you did it to the wrong person, or you did it to the wrong gender. He warned Larry that the third rail in small town politics was a songbird sex partner.

While Larry fretted that Meador might not give him the party's or the chamber's endorsement, Babbs pretended to study his bookshelves crammed with books he would never read sent by publishers who scalped textbooks. Larry had gone into law enforcement believing a gun demanded respect and using a gun had given him respect. Larry was down to earth but tried too hard to appear down to earth. Rather than change him Babbs would make him the sheriff a guy had rather have stop him for speeding after a couple of beers, the sheriff a mother had rather have catch her son with a joint.

Babbs toyed with a ceramic male figurine, a present from a coach. After P.J. reported rumors of homosexuality in the athletic department the coaches no longer called Babbs "pecker breath" in the faculty club but presented him with the figurine that had a peppermint stick for a penis. It was the hairy soap kind of gag jocks liked. He kept it the way warriors kept the sword of the defeated. "Will the other deputies support your views?" he asked.

"Cecil will but what if Timp changes his story for the endorsement?"

Babbs was delighted that Timp might run. If the sheriff contradicted what he told the media and the party endorsed him to save Meador some bucks the print prophets and micro-phonies would hound him out of office. Babbs bit off a piece of peppermint. It was the defiant gesture Babbs loved. "I'll talk to Meador," he said. He didn't want Larry loitering in his office.

"Want to meet for lunch?" Larry asked.

Babbs gestured at his desk cluttered with things he didn't want to discard or to file. "I'll let you know what I find out," he said.

If Timpson Smith ran for reelection Babbs had a David with a slingshot against the Goliath of a hero incumbent and Babbs would have to find the smooth stones. Win or lose he could get a book out of that. Some voters were still angry because the death of Dr. Baines' son raised taxes. Smith had enemies like Dr. Baines who would throw money at Larry to defeat the sheriff, and Babbs could plan strategy, make decisions, analyze what worked, what didn't and why in his book. And he could ask Smith-haters for more money every time he suggested Smith was winning.

Babbs believed he could goad Smith into running for reelection by suggesting his retirement was because his nerve failed him but it had to be without the party's endorsement. He puffed his chipmunk cheeks, ran his hand up his bald head and called Meador. "Larry says the sheriff may change his report to get the party's endorsement for reelection. If he contradicts his statements to the media and you endorse him that may be gold in your pocket but it will smell like roadkill politics when it hits the air."

"Are you sure Timp wants to run?"

"That's what P.J. says. Why else would Timp change his report?"

Babbs could almost hear Meador counting the money but Meador, who believed Babbs and P.J. were like twins who always wore the same colors, was counting the things the county had done for Smith. "What about a retirement dinner with media coverage?" Babbs suggested. "If you don't want the party split, talk to the mayor." Clay Williams was

Babbs' cousin. The Babbs had squandered their money on ill-chosen marriages and ill-mannered divorces but everyone thought they were rich, which was almost as good.

The mayor, always rumpled with an undisciplined mustache and a toothbrush in his shirt pocket, handled his parents' affairs, provided their care and was restoring the family fortune but his parents considered him their lesser son. The one you could count on died with Second Platoon. Clay's every conversation regarding his family, office, bank, church involved numbers in which he was eloquent. Voters' bank accounts were correct, their loan payments exact, but unlike totals, ideas did not always reconcile.

Babbs knew his cousin would tell Milk the cost of a retirement dinner and who could underwrite it. He called P.J. "There's a rumor that Sheriff Smith is going to run again." Pete Johnson, bushy-headed muppet, disliked authority. In high school he discovered his only weapon against bullies was wit and the mouth to go with it. He almost became a radio preacher because he wanted the platform but a d.j. had a wider audience. "He's going to change his report of Wynn Mills' death to gain the party's support." P.J. loved intrigue and controversy. When people argued they quoted him and he became the center of the story. "Can you confirm whether he has officially announced?" Babbs asked before calling the *Advertiser*, *The Grist* and the TV station.

***

Bryan was surprised to receive a call from the mayor of Five Mills whom he had never met. He agreed to recite Timp's welcome home speech to Able Company at Timp's retirement dinner. "Some of us carried heavier packs, some carried bigger weapons, some suffered more pain, some suffered more terror, some climbed steeper hills, some trod deeper snow but we all served together. America is better today because we served together in Korea. America will be better tomorrow if we work together at home.'"

The mayor had a fallback position if the dinner weren't enough. "Milk Mcador suggested a pageant instead of a parade. P.J. has offered to narrate it. Of course, we'd want you to direct it."

A pageant would resolve the problem of including everyone from the platoon but a pageant? P.J.? Bryan had made sacrifices for principle before believing God would reward him for it. "The tableaux couldn't be static," he said. "It would require space. And cost more money."

"Send me an estimate, what you would need, what it would cost. The chamber might be willing to sponsor it."

Bryan tried to envision the pageant with P.J. making asinine comments while actors struck poses, shouted heroic phrases, fired blank ammunition. It depressed him. He had prayed for the train to tomorrow in a town where the train didn't stop any more and God had given him a pageant. Then Bryan had a vision. A play and he would be writer, director, and lead.

Bryan knew acting was his place in life when he had played John Proctor in *The Crucible* and had seen the effect on the audience. It wasn't the applause; he had revealed the image of God in a flawed man. Hamlet had enlightened more souls, crossed more cultural barriers than Leviticus.

He had been man with bags, waiter, ticket agent with speaking part, "Where to?" A critic mentioned his hairstyle. His friends laughed at his pretension but told others they knew a Hollywood actor who had been in three films. He got a minor but continuing role in "Hogan's Heroes." With that promise he married his college sweetheart and they moved to California. He could clearly see God at work in his life.

Then came the draft. Deferments were no easier for minor actors than minor athletes. His wife moved back home and he went to the army. The army assigned him to Special Service escorting USO tours in Vietnam. He did everything they asked that he could morally accept—no drugs, no women. He played straight man to Bob Hope in the Christmas Show, a five-minute scene in Saigon, Da Nang, Quang Tri, Pleiku, twenty seconds on TV. They promised to remember him. He returned to Hollywood but his contacts were always busy or out of town. His wife refused to give up her job and move to the coast.

Her family, like his, associated acting with divorce, debauchery, and deceit. If he wanted to give others sorrow, joy, guilt, grief, catharsis he should be a preacher, they said. They were dismayed that he appeared in plays with murder, adultery, obscenities. None of their friends in business, medicine, or law saw contradictions between their careers and their ethics, and the church smiled upon their pecuniary motives. He felt like Joseph sold into slavery by his brothers. Then a gift from God, he was offered a supporting role in a feature film. He called his wife and she seemed pleased for both of them.

"It's an actor's dream," his agent said. "Big name producer and director. They're going for an X rating for the publicity then cut it to get an R." Featured was a child actress in her first sex role with him as seducer. A woman whose bare breast was seen on network TV was given a character role.

Bryan reasoned that he could be the drug addicted, abusive pimp because the pimp was someone God loved and he could reveal the emptiness in his selfish, materialistic life. He could play the seducer of an underage girl and expose the degradation of sex without love. That most of his lines included "Jesus Christ" was the cockcrow in his dream. He could not use his Lord's name as a curse. He talked to his wife, his friends, former pastors, fellow actors. He called the woman who was given a character role.

"It was my agent's idea to get exposure, pardon the pun. There are so many singers and it worked. It got me publicity for a record contract that I never got a dime from and publicity for a movie contract, a couple of minor roles in lousy films that did more harm than good. This will be the third time I've played a whore and if the film does well I may have five more years before I play madams."

"Did you ever go back home?"

"I can't get hired if my past comes up. I tried working in an office, in a store, a proposition came with the job. Everyone thinks they know what I am but they don't even known who I am. The lottery was rigged but I'd do it again and hope to handle it better." He heard the click of her cigarette lighter. "Blasphemy doesn't seem that big a deal. I mean, everybody does it. You're a man. Promiscuous? You're a romantic. Alcohol and drugs? Daring. Rape, murder? People get over it. If you're gay, keep it a secret and no one will care."

That was no help at all. He wasn't gay and getting away with it didn't fit into his dream of who he was, what he could do.

He was offered a teaching job in Texas and a lead role in a pilot about renegade elements in the government running terror projects for profit. He accepted the college offer to save his marriage but he was one disappointment too late; she had moved on, she said. He believed she had moved on to someone else.

Bryan's mind was in overtime, refusing him sleep, rest, prayer, but he struggled on to find God's way at a school that was run like a business, taught students who had no interest in theater but thought it was a fun major, and made TV commercials for people who believed it was a good commercial if the equipment worked. He compromised who he was every day. Sometimes it seemed that God wanted him to fail.

He had done dramatic readings at Solid Rock Church without pay but happy for the opportunity—The Creation, The Nativity, I Corinthians 13, and had been invited to the Brides and Bridegrooms of Christ Singles Club. He wasn't ready for dating but he wanted female companionship. He met Morgan Murphy; she too was divorced. When seemly he would invite her to a concert at the college.

His spirits lifted. The pilot never found a sponsor, but a play . . . He knew that war was often senseless, always brutal, that men died because of foul-ups, because of strategy and politics but if he could show that God used even war, the sacrifice of the few for the good of the many . . . It troubled Bryan that Pastor Murphy searched the Bible for scriptures he could use to condemn others but the pastor believed in him.

***

Deputy Goss reported a truancy violation and an elderly woman who couldn't remember where she lived. "Emily Lubitsch, 1215 Oak," the sheriff said. A man who didn't give his name said his wife died in the emergency room while waiting for her insurance company's approval. Homer Hartley who had a left eye that drifted and claimed three appendectomies. Most folks believed any doctor worth his stockbroker could perform two. "The hospital is in Doss County," Timp explained.

"The police said they couldn't do anything. If I had done that it would be murder. How can a corporation do it and get away with it? I pay taxes like . . ."

The sheriff wanted to say that where greed was a virtue it excused any vice. Instead, he laid the telephone on his desk and ignored it until beeping signaled that he was no longer connected. Miss Abernathy, who refused to be seduced by men or Ms, had not forgiven God for creating sex and would be buried out of wedlock, wanted the sheriff to look for her white puff of a dog that had escaped when she went outside to throw rocks at a squirrel.

John Banks called to say that Pastor Murphy asked for more church protection because they picketed the Women's Clinic and feared reprisals. "I asked him what they worshipped at his church. If you're poor that's where you go for a pap smear, mammogram, or cancer screening." John spoke his mind regardless of consequences. The sheriff wished he had done the same.

Brother Jonas reported that the Veteran's Administration would furnish a coffin, a grave marker, and a flag. He would take Hao to Public Welfare in Advantage after the funeral to arrange for food stamps and aid for dependent children. "Jesus died for those people but the government won't feed, clothe, or care for them unless they're worthy. If I can prove Hao and the boys are worthy they'll help her with a budget."

"What about the truck and the water hose?" Timp asked.

"There are a couple of men in the church who are working on it. I'll tell them to contact you if they need help."

There was an anonymous report of a disturbance at the TripleS X. "I'll take it," Timp said to escape the office until time for the called meeting. The TripleS X caused no problems; sorority pledges were the only women ever present, and there was no alcohol, but there were more complaints about it than the lingerie models or unlicensed masseuses. Films of Pastor Murphy's daughter appeared in dorms at the college and were traced to TripleS X.

Morgan Murphy had the wedding of the decade at her father's church where he pointed out the biblical requirement that a wife be submissive to her husband. Her husband, poster boy of machismo, required her submission to sexual practices that some regarded as abusive. He filmed her undressing, bathing, begging him to wait as he deflowered her.

Unaware of the filmmaking but horrified by his use of her, Morgan had run home to discover everyone knew her story except her. She wanted to hide from jokes about submissive women, MM & SM. Her father required her to greet the congregation at each service, welcome visitors, and say a prayer. Some became ashamed of the films and destroyed them but there were rumors of a club that met at the TripleS X to share them.

When Timp came home from Korea he wanted to hide but his mother had been unable to save the farm and had bought a small house in Five Mills. The county that had lost so many young men looked to him for salvation. Working at the gas station was unthinkable. The chamber could think of no way to replicate his heroism but on the silver screen. He didn't see how that saved anyone but they raised funds to push him to Hollywood and Senator Prince Pritchard arranged for Audie Murphy to introduce him to a producer. By then battalions had been lost, regiments destroyed, divisions mangled, and Second Platoon was no more than a footnote in the battalion history.

He met with Audie Murphy, a starlet who was bait, and a producer. "Are you the hero?" the producer asked. "Can you sing? dance? You're not pretty enough for a lead, not big enough for a heavy. Show me how you looked when you killed all those gooks."

Timp looked at him in horror.

"Can you do mean? Look, kid, you have nothing to sell."

The starlet attracted the attention of two young drunks who mocked Timp to get her notice.

"Let's go some place else," the producer said.

"We can't walk away," Murphy said.

"Sure you can," the producer said. "And there won't be any mothers crying because of you."

"Maybe we should let them beat us up, be heroes," Timp said.

"They'd start a fight with someone else and get killed," Murphy said. He told the two drunks, "We're leaving and if you say something I'll kill you."

The producer and starlet left and he and Murphy went to another bar. They talked about Texas, how hard life had been when a child. "But I slept at night," Murphy said. "Why do you want to be an actor?"

"People back home need me to be somebody."

"I enlisted in the National Guard expecting to be sent to Korea," Audie said. "War was the realist I have ever been."

"My whole platoon was killed. What did they die for?"

"What did I die for? Hitler and Tojo were replaced by Stalin and Mao. You and your buddies prepared the way for whatever calamity people do to each other next. You died, too, Kid. You don't know it yet."

When he returned home in failure folks suggested the clergy. People would come to hear how the Lord preserved him. The chamber said if he couldn't be a celebrity then he must be a commercial success. He could sell but it had to be something respectable like real estate or insurance.

Glen Timberlake's grandfather was a Mills County sharecropper; his father, a handsome man with the confidence of an athlete, had married the prettiest girl in Advantage, who gave him a son on Pearl Harbor day. He enlisted the next day and died on Guadalcanal. His mother moved to Dallas to work and married her boss who gave Glen his name signifying riches and the attendant power and a financial settlement with the understanding that he was not part of the Timberlake family or fortune. Glen moved to Advantage and sank the money in a piece of Mills County land and a dream called Sleepy Hollow—a community of inexpensive houses close to town. Small towns, like ugly bachelors, were so excited by a new possibility that they showered them with promises.

"You and I can save this place, keep young people here by giving them a house and a job," Timberlake told Timp, his face smooth, his eyes fierce with conviction, his smile constant. For four years there had been no construction in Five Mills. The lumber yard had moved to Advantage, the hardware store was on the verge of closing, carpenters, plumbers, electricians worked in Advantage if they worked at all. "You have to see the family survivors," Timberlake said. "I'm not asking you to sell anything. I'd like you and your medals in the model home. Give them a brochure, answer their questions, explain how they can use the GI insurance to purchase a home as an investment." The houses sold, the lumberyard reopened, the hardware store prospered, trucks and workers made citizens believe Five Mills had a future.

The family survivors wanted answers. Ten elderly black men had met every day to pray for John Banks' father. Did their prayers make no difference? They wanted consolation. "Did my son die quickly?" Affirmation. "Did he fight to the last?" Pardon. "Did he forgive me for kissing my old boyfriend?" They wanted consent. "Did he agree that I should move out of his mother's house and go back to Paint Rock?" "Did he say he wanted my son to take his name?" "Did he say I should keep his car?" They wanted validation. "Did he call my name when he was dying?" "Did he die a Christian?"

They wanted to know what the platoon died for. "They died for you because you sent them." "Skip died for us that we might be better," Skip's sister pleaded. "Yes," he said and watched his pious fraud inspire a father who had succumbed to failure and give direction to an aimless brother. He wondered how far he could go, how much they could take before the platoon was lost. The platoon fought heroically, died instantly, no one was mutilated, no-one was burned.

The women invited him to dinner to talk about their son's, brother's, husband's, sweetheart's last goodbye, last letter, last wish. "Thank you," they said. "I couldn't go on if you hadn't told me." Some wanted him to hold them and he did briefly before backing away, afraid of losing more of himself.

The men took him hunting or fishing to drink beer and talk about their son or brother and the things they had done together. After dark and hard liquor they told stories the women didn't know—how his son hoped to sink his bayonet in the belly of a Commie, to see his face when he died. "A bayonet never misfires," he said. "I bet he fought with his bayonet and the butt of his rifle if he ran out of ammo. Slash, parry, thrust, parry, butt stroke. Damn, that boy was something."

They wanted him to know things he couldn't know. "Did he believe it was his kid? I know he got in there because I know my son. I don't know if he was the only one."

They wanted him to remember things he tried to forget, the crunch of a bayonet felt as much as heard, the click when it hit button or bone, the sharp intake of breath when it went home, the hot outrush of breath when death came, the smell of boiling blood, burning hair, searing flesh, flaming tires.

When live lobsters first came to Five Mills, his mother bought one. She was told to drop it in boiling water but the pan was too small and the lobster clawed at the sides trying to escape, its antennae signaling horror.

When Timp could take it no more Martha's mother invited him to take over the store but a hero couldn't measure another man for trousers. Mayor T. J. Munday appointed him as his driver and special deputy. "You'll meet the right people so you can run for sheriff." The special deputy had special duties. "Tell the artist the heroic stand of each man who has a tableau."

"You're the face on the statue," the sculptor said. "Shake your fist at the enemy. This isn't reality; it represents reality. The reality is courage. Hold your rifle in one hand and shake your fist with the other."

"I'm not asking you to make a speech or nothing; I just want you on that platform with me wearing your uniform and medals," the mayor said. "As a tribute to all them boys that died with you. I mean, that was with you when they died. Lead the audience in the pledge of allegiance. It would mean so much to everybody. As mayor I represent the town politically but you represent the town's spirit. Next election we'll run side by side."

A child on her way to school had been swept into a flooded creek because of new development and as deputy he went to search for her. Tawny Green appeared to be asleep under a cedar tree, her head resting on an outstretched arm, giving Timp hope although he knew it was false, hanging on to that lie until he touched her cold face and looked into her hollow eyes.

He wanted Timberlake to share his grief, his guilt, but Glen had a bigger problem. He was broke. He had explained his situation to his stepfather, asked for a loan and was rejected. His failure proved he was not worthy of his name. He had to borrow money for a new project to finish Shady Acres. "I'll help that girl's family when I can but if I take responsibility I'll be ruined." No one from Freetown had ever sued; the court was the white man's way of maintaining control. "I can't fail, Timp," Timberlake said. "No matter what it costs."

It cost the life of Tawny Green and Five Mills as Timp had known it.

***

As expected, Timp found two cars behind the TripleS X. He went into the dim trailer made dimmer from coming out of sunlight. "Hey, it's the hero," a voice said. Timp made out Vic seated in the darkness. "Anything you want is on the house. Semper Fi."

"Are you working here now?"

"I been here four days. Hard to get a job with these," he said, patting his legs. "Perfect job for a man dead from the waist down. Ramp to the door, toilet down the hall, all the screen pussy I want to watch. Everything a man could want."

Timp asked about the sex club that met there. "First I heard of it but I have the films," Vic said. "Sold one to your deputy." Timp didn't ask which deputy. Vic's hair was long and his beard matted. His stomach bulged over shrunken legs. "Two guys in room A if you want to check. No club because there's no room here big enough for more than three. No chairs except this one." He patted his wheelchair.

He had a styrofoam cup in one hand and Timp wondered if it held liquor, which was illegal. Vic leaned forward and spat tobacco juice in it. "A lot of guys hated you. You were home and we were freezing our asses at Frozen Chosin fighting for the ridges. All we heard from home was Second Platoon. I don't even remember that. I remember Inchon. We had to wait eight hours after Third Battalion landed, eight hours for the gooks to get ready for us, and then we had to climb ladders to get over the seawall with them waiting. I may forgive MacArthur for that screwup but I'll never forgive him for sending us into Frozen Chosin. Every officer we had was screaming 'trap, trap, there's Chinese everywhere, they're surrounding us' but MacArthur wanted to be president and licking the Chinese would do it. They kicked our ass. Mountains, high winds, blowing snow, twenty-below zero, companies climbing the ridges to drive off the Chinese and never coming back, rifles froze, artillery shells fell short, corpsmen carried morphine syringes in their mouth to keep it from turning to ice. We crapped in our pants to keep our asses from freezing when we dropped them. But we fought our way out."

Vic spat in the cup again. "I did everything by the book, every patrol, every firefight. My buddies carried me down from the ridge, moved a dead guy and laid me on the hood of a truck to keep me warm. There were four or five of us on it and when someone died there was a waiting line of wounded. I told them to leave me in the snow. Let me freeze. My love life was gone forever."

Vic tried to work up another spit but his mouth was dry. "You were the hero. I was the old dog that pisses in his bed, craps on the floor, too crippled to run off, too young to die. My wife hung on until I had to knock her loose because I couldn't look at her anymore. Folks I had known all my life were ashamed of me. My own folks."

"They were ashamed of themselves because duty, honor, flag— you're what the words mean," Timp said.

"There are truths that can't be lived with. War is one of them, what you ask of people you don't know and hope never to see. You and me, we're the end product. They need one of you for every one of me. You had to replace a whole platoon. Man, that's a bear and a half."

Down the hall a door opened, a man stepped out, saw him, pushed his friend back and closed the door.

"When I heard that Captain Billy had given money for your statue I put a pistol in my lap, covered it with a blanket, rolled up to him and asked him why and if he gave the wrong answer I was going to kill him and then myself. You don't need an enemy; all you need is a target. He said Doss County offered to help pay for the monument and that you asked that the monument be for the whole company, but Mills said no. They had to be better than us. I go asiatic every time I see that statue in the paper or on TV but I don't hate you any more. I do my job, you do yours. Semper Fi."

"Semper Fi," Timp replied, wondering if he could carry Vic's pack.

When he returned to his office the phone was ringing, there was a note from Mrs. Stutz that she had been unable to contact Larry and a message from Martha. "*The Grist* asked if you were running for reelection." He didn't answer the telephone.

CHAPTER
FIVE

Timp read the reports again. No matter how imperfect his own recollection, Larry's report was wrong. He had tugged the shotgun from under Wynn's back. Cecil's report didn't contradict his but it didn't contradict Larry's either.

Cecil's crude diagram showed where Timp and Larry were and the position of Wynn's body on the ground but no indication where the weapons were. The photographs were not with the report and he looked for them on his desk and then Mrs. Stutz's desk and files. He had hoped to talk to Cecil before the meeting but the deputies trooped in together, impatient to get it over.

"The media are reporting a split in this department," he began. "There is no split. Larry and I were on the scene yesterday; Cecil investigated it. There are differences in interpreting the scene and they will be straightened out. You weren't there, you didn't read the reports so I don't want you talking to the media or anyone else about what someone says happened. This department is going to do its job of protecting and assisting the public and that's all we're going to do. There will be no politics in this department."

There were no questions and he wondered why he had called the meeting. He asked Cecil into his office. "Have you seen Larry's report?"

"He wanted me to read it before I made my report." That wasn't the procedure and Timp waited. "I've got almost two years before I can retire."

Cecil was honest but Larry would probably replace him anyway. "Have you talked to the media or anyone else?"

"Not until you tell me to. I know you didn't surrender your pistol."

Did Cecil think this was about his pistol? "Where are the photos?"

"They didn't turn out."

"I'll see if someone else can process them." Photographs would show the blood pooled around objects under Wynn's body.

"I'm not good with technical stuff." Cecil had lost the shell casings from Timp's pistol during the Scott Baines shooting and the media had erroneously reported that Timp fired only one shot. Timp testified that he had fired seven times but Dr. Baines focused on the lost casings claiming a coverup. When Cecil found the missing shells after the inquest it made matters worse. "You can take it out of my salary," Cecil said hopefully. "Maybe I could take the photos again." Brother Jonas had covered the bloody ground.

"You saw the marks of the weapons under Wynn's body."

"The weapons were gone when I reached the scene."

Timp studied Cecil's troubled eyes. He, Hao, the boys, the pickup crew had tracked over the scene. "When they picked up Wynn's body didn't you see where the blood had pooled around objects that had been removed?"

"When I got there things were messed up," Cecil said, not exactly accusing him but it would sound like that in the courtroom or the media. Charges of tampering with evidence would ruin Cecil and probably Larry and Timp doubted he could prove anything beyond incompetence. "Did Larry tell you to destroy the photographs?"

"Not exactly. I know you can fire me. Two more years. After that I'll say what you want me to say. You screwed up too, Timp," Cecil pleaded.

Timp called Larry and when he didn't get an answer, he went to the trailer park. He was relieved that Larry wasn't home.

***

Martha had spent the day cleaning the house after snapping off the radio at P.J.'s comment between records. "When Larry Maddin got a call that drug-crazed Wynn Mills had taken his wife and children hostage and disarmed Sheriff Smith, Larry knew he was in for the fight of his life."

Now she was cleaning the bathroom, the job she disliked the most, the one that received most of her fear. She had been afraid since the first call asking confirmation that Timp was going to run. She told the caller to ask Timp but the questions came because Timp had not returned their calls.

When you were a hero everyone had expectations. He had been pushed into a place where he had no training or experience but he learned. Every vacation he visited other sheriffs while she went sight-seeing or shopping alone. They went to dinner at a nice restaurant, he had two drinks and she drove back to the motel. On the weekend they opened a bottle of wine and talked about the sheriffs, their staffs and procedures, then finished the bottle after making love.

And he became who they wanted him to be. That there might be other ways to help the family survivors of Second Platoon and the citizens of Mills County had not occurred to him. He wasn't a loner but had become one because his office put him outside the circle of those who wouldn't cheat a stranger at cards but would take advantage of a friend's ignorance or trust and consider it a triumph.

They expected her to be Mrs. Sheriff and accepted her with caution. Friends stopped stories after a glance at her. Conversations ended when she walked into a room. She had found women she could confide in at Solid Rock, women from Advantage disinterested in Mills County. They gossiped about those who attended Bible Cure to discover what the Bible said about your diet, your illness, your finances, your family relationships, your vote, and joked about how fat, how well, how wealthy they were.

The women drove from Advantage because, like Martha, they wanted to join the Daughters of Eve Fitness Center that was restricted to church members and there was no competition because it was tax exempt. Their husbands liked the pastor's sermons on individual responsibility although there was less of it every year. Mom and pop stores had disappeared, the Advantage hospital was owned by a corporation that only the business office could talk to, insurance company claims were handled by anonymous people in anonymous places, and neither corporations nor elected officials were accountable for unintended consequences. Her friends loved rugged individualism in books or on the screen but not in their husbands or children, and women and minorities need not apply.

Martha attended bingo and casino nights for Solid Rock School. The more one's life depended on chance the easier it was to believe that God controlled it. Timp didn't go because Murphy and his family were the only employees with health care and retirement benefits, and the school, bingo, and casino nights were unregulated, but eight-liner gaming machines were illegal. Timp said when he retired they could move someplace where they weren't known but she didn't want to leave the town that had raised and formed her as her parents had, and likely wherever they went would be much the same. She couldn't rob the town of their hero. And that's what they would say.

"Where have you been?" she asked when Timp came home, meaning why didn't you take the calls. "Everyone in two counties wants to know if you are going to run. That's for you," she said when the telephone rang.

"I'm not taking calls."

"I suppose that means you're not running," Martha said.

"It means I have to talk to Larry first." Although he rarely revealed office details he told her about Cecil's report and the photographs. "I should have taken the photographs myself," he admitted. "But I was involved in the scene and I wanted to get the widow and children away from it. If Larry forced Cecil to change his report I can't let him be sheriff."

Like war, finishing the job was a fatal attraction. "Are you sure?"

"Wynn had dropped the weapons and had his hands in the air. Keep that quiet until it becomes public."

"What are you going to do?"

"I'm going to talk to the party."

"Call Clay. Tell him you want to meet with them tonight."

Clay said that they would meet with Timp after the offices closed the next day. Martha knew what that meant. There was a time when Timp told the party faithful when to meet. It also meant the following day would be a long one with more questions from the media.

They talked little at dinner, each trapped in separate fears. On the late news Advantage TV reported rumors that Sheriff Timpson Smith was running for reelection. "However, Mayor Claiborne Williams announced today that Five Mills is honoring Smith with a retirement banquet. Proceeds from the banquet will be used to help finance a parade honoring Smith for his heroism in Korea."

"Those mills must pump something other than water," the weatherman said. "And speaking of water, we have a chance for rain tomorrow."

***

Larry had no success at the university but at Heavenly Gates Mikki was afraid of a man who had fingered bills into the panties she modeled. Larry took her to her apartment in Advantage where she had a roommate. They each took a chair leaving him the couch. A box labeled Small Conversational Hearts was on the table. He reached to open it but the roommate put her hand on it. "You need to give us some privacy," he said.

"You need to leave," the roommate said. "I'm fixing to call a cop."

"I am a cop."

"Not here you're not."

"I'm a cop where you work." Larry practiced interrogation. Women thought he was interested in them, spilled their drawers. Men required more time. If you showed interest in them they clammed up. "Why do you work in a place like that?"

"We work there because we can earn more in one night than we can in a week working on campus. Now leave and don't come back."

"We don't want women like you in Mills County," he said, automatically placing his hand where the butt of his pistol should have been.

"If I tell you of something illegal in Mills County will you leave us alone?" Mikki asked. Killing a bad man and solving a crime in the same week meant more front page. He nodded. "The Rose has eight-liners."

Only sin sniffers like Pastor Murphy cared; to everyone else it was harmless fun, like Wild Rose and TripleS X, but he should tell Timp. "Okay."

On his way to The Wild Rose Larry reasoned that if he reported the eight-liners Timp would call the media, make the bust in front of cameras and Larry would be back in the bunkhouse until a future election. Unless Timp replaced him the way he was going to replace John, and Cecil who was just hanging on, and Ernie Clapp who was an embarrassment. He stopped at the Rose, opened the trunk, and strapped on his pistol.

Inside the doublewide was a room with tables. The models in high heels and lingerie threaded their way through arms, legs, kissing sounds, lapping tongues, proposals, and tables. At one end was a narrow hall with dressing rooms on one side and a locked door on the other. He ordered the proprietor to open the door. The proprietor was surprised to find illegal machines, players, and money. Larry checked the IDs of the men, warned them they were violating the law and let them go. They could express their gratitude on election day.

The cashier was too old and plump for him. Too much vibrato. "Did you ever notice how fat women have dirty toenails?" he asked her boss. He told her to give him the money and get out and the proprietor nodded.

"Gambling is illegal in Mills County," he said after everyone but the proprietor had left. "If I report this, they're going to smash your machines, confiscate this money and put you in for a pokey. I'm not going to do that. I'm going to make campaign funding so expensive that either you or your patrons move on." Larry stripped bills from the stack. "I'll be back in say a week to see if I have made it expensive enough."

***

Timpson Smith trudged through the courthouse disregarding the smells of limestone and ammonia and the cronies until they spoke to him. "Clay, Ross," he responded to the mayor and DA. He nodded to the others who congregated in the lobby to share views and information inappropriate in an office. "Ole Timp is back in the news," one said, the others chuckled.

Mrs. Stutz said the media were asking if he was going to run for reelection and that Scoop was on the line. If he denied the rumors he would seem dishonest; if he refused to confirm them he would seem ambivalent, which he was. "Tell them I have no comment."

In his office, Timp faced his own questions: Larry with most of his body behind the wall, Wynn's body that seemed shrunken on the ground. He had tugged the shotgun free, the hammers uncocked. The memory warted like a sty. Still he was grateful for the concreteness of the autopsy.

He looked at the overnight reports. A runaway believed to be in Mills County. Three people reported cars coming to a stop, honking and blinking lights in an alley close to a student apartment house suggesting prostitution or drugs; a garage was using the alley to check brakes and lights. Woman arrested for soliciting claimed she was paid to dance for men not with them. Clerk at the Grabbit N Grin asked customer for ID for cigarettes and man threatened her and left without paying. A teacher reported a student said his mother spanked him with her girdle and all the straps hit him; mother said she caught her son wearing her underwear and swatted him with a girdle. Traffic hazard, driving while license invalid.

He turned to the budget. Larry wanted newer weapons but guns were mostly symbols of authority and sometimes a gun on the scene incited rather than impeded violence. Larry wanted to replace one of the cruisers but Timp's priority was another deputy. Flashlights. Flares. Cost of living raises; there was never money for more than that. The safer they were the more security they wanted and the less willing they were to pay for it.

Mrs. Stutz buzzed. "Larry is here," she said.

***

Larry slept alone but he slept better and he was in a buoyant mood when he bounded up the stairs two at a time and burst into the office wafting youth and vigor. Before he could close the door Stutz hammered him. "Why didn't you call in yesterday? I left messages a dozen times."

"I was off duty and outside the county investigating." It was a Get-Out-of-Jail-Free he could redeem if needed.

"The sheriff wants to see you," she said looking at him over her glasses. "As soon as you come in, Wrong Way."

"And I want to see him." He leaned over and kissed the top of her head. Fire her ass, he thought. Hire someone young, accommodating.

He walked into Timp's office and sat down, not as though it was soon to be his but as a man who had something to say. "Jefe, I'm upset about what happened with the media." Larry knew the media had to present Timp as a hero because damn it he was and they owed him for all the years he was sheriff. One—he struggled for a word—slip like making an exception for a friend should not distort a lifetime of hero-ism. Best to give him a chance to explain.

"So am I. We have to put that behind us and deal with the situation as it is now." Timp put his elbows on his desk and leaned forward to show he was willing to meet Larry halfway. "It was a disturbance call and you misinterpreted the scene."

Larry didn't try to hide his surprise. The old bastard was going to make it look like he shot Wynn because he was scared? No way. He saw the stubborn look Timp had on the statue. A banzai charge wasn't going to work. "I'm sorry for Wynn's widow but our job is to protect business."

"Our job is to protect citizens."

"Hell, Jefe, it's business that pays the bills, prints the posters, buys the ads, gets out the vote. If you depended on citizens you'd never get elected. We can't change the story for all of them."

"You've already changed the story, you and Cecil."

"You corrupted the crime scene when you gave me the guns."

"And that's in my report. You asked Cecil to change his report."

"Aren't you asking me to change my report?"

"I don't think you have the maturity to be sheriff."

That was a fart in the face. "You're the one with experience and you tried to play buddy with Wynn. I saved your life."

"You needlessly took a life. That happens sometimes even with seasoned officers but I haven't seen anything in your attitude that suggests it couldn't happen again. You want to be known as a killer."

Just like Timp was. "Jefe, you've always backed your deputies." Unless the complaint was from half the town related to someone in Second Platoon.

"Larry, the guns were on the ground beneath Wynn's back. The coroner said Wynn's arm was raised when he was shot in the side."

"He was pointing the shotgun at me."

"He was on the ground when you shot him through the heart. If you hadn't he would still be alive. You fired three shots that missed."

Larry placed his head in his hands. If he had known his pistol was empty he would have reached for the deuce.

"I want the report to reflect that Wynn's death was a mistake but that you were not personally responsible for the mistake."

Shooting Wynn was a mistake but it wasn't his mistake? "You sound like you're running for office." Timp's expression didn't change. "I wouldn't have run if you had said you were." The old fart was going to stand and die. "You're a tough hombre to follow. I need your endorsement to say I'm the same kind of man you are."

"You're not the same kind of man and I'll endorse you when I believe you're ready to be sheriff. You can start by changing your report."

Larry didn't notice the smirk on Mrs. Stutz face when he left, his creed torn. Timp had failed him. Timp had done what a bunch of hippies could not do—defaced his image.

***

Timp stared at the door after Larry left. There was a difference between him asking Larry to correct his report and Larry asking Cecil to change his but it was too complicated for TV.

He left to meet Martha at the church for Wynn's funeral. Wally had beaten him there attracted by Marine reserves from Advantage as honor guard. He stood across the street with a flag and a sign, "Second Platoon Died, Able Company Lied." "If you create a disturbance you're leaving," Timp said.

"I just want folks to know," Wally said.

Cecil and Ernie Klemp were already there. Larry wanted a volunteer posse for funeral escort, give them a chance to wear a badge and pistol and pick up extra money. Ernie liked funeral duty; Cecil needed the extra pay. When they saw him, they went inside. He thought they were on duty but they had come to show the department's respect.

Timp joined Martha inside the church. For two days Martha had eaten jello, salad, and jello salad so she could wear the pricey but elegant five-year-old dark suit she bought for funerals, including her own. She wore black shoes with wedge heels for walking in the rough cemetery. Those inside were church members, nearer his age than Hao's. They tried not to meet his eyes as though embarrassed that he was there.

Jonas' church believed in serving the living rather than decorating the dead but there were a few potted flowers from patios and porches and an enormous spray with a ribbon, NEIGHBOR.

Rather than platitudes about pearly gates Brother Jonas talked about farming and the process of birth, death, rebirth, "this world and one more decentable. Some go to seed before their time," he said, "but when they are planted in the ground they spring to life again in a new earth without the sorrow, without the pain they have given and the pain and sorrow they bear."

At the conclusion Brother Jonas invited Wynn's family to come together around Wynn's body to celebrate the life they had known and the life he had left in them. Hao and the boys stood stiff and small before the coffin with Brother Jonas, she in white shirt and black pants, black jacket; her boys dressed the same, the clothes from Rent-All.

Brother Jonas invited friends to come together around Wynn's body to celebrate the life he had shared and the memories he had left with them. Cecil and Ernie joined the group, all of them on the opposite side from Hao and the boys. Timp looked for a way to leave without appearing to escape and thought he saw the backs of the Krugers.

Brother Jonas invited all to meet in love as children of the God to whom Wynn had returned and grieve the life they had lost. Timp did not want to intrude on those gathered before the coffin but Martha took his arm and they stood at the edge of the group until Brother Jonas placed Timp between himself and Hao. After a prayer calling all God's children together in love, the three of them and the boys followed the coffin to the cemetery behind the church. Outside, Timp saw four Stetsons bent over an open hood trying to start the hearse.

There was no funeral awning, no chairs and no attempt to disguise the hole that lay open like a plowed field. The grave smelled of old dirt, not a freshly tilled garden. The Marines fired a rifle salute and handed Hao the flag that had covered his coffin, token of a grateful nation. Hao took Timp's arm and held it as the others withdrew until only the two of them stood before the grave.

"I kill Wynn," she said.

"No, Hao. No."

She had been afraid, trying to keep the boys behind cover. She heard the startled chickens, looked out the window, saw Larry and screamed, causing Wynn to turn, resulting in his death. "Hao, I'm not sure exactly what happened but I am certain that it wasn't your fault. It was an accident."

Without looking up she put her arm around him and placed her head on his chest. Timp looked down at her in surprise and began to put his arm around her but stopped not knowing whether to pat her or hug her.

***

Timp watched Martha leave, Wally still in silent rebuke, then returned to the church. He didn't remember hearing Hao scream. Could Hao's scream have caused Wynn to turn with the shotgun raised to defend her? With birdshot? The hammers uncocked? The shotgun was beneath his back.

He thanked Brother Jonas for the service. "Every day belongs to the Lord," Jonas said. "Some days I farm, some days I preach. Who knows which is most important?"

"Larry thinks that Wynn was killed in an unlawful act."

"People sometimes tell me they made an important decision because of something I said that I am certain I never said and don't believe."

That wasn't an answer Timp could use. "If I endorse Larry for sheriff he might agree that Wynn's death was an accident and Hao could get the insurance. But it might not be best for the county."

"You can't go wrong if you tell the truth."

"What if Larry and I both believe we're telling the truth?"

"Then do what you know is right."

Truth and right always seemed simple to preachers. Like him, they knew secrets that could do nothing but harm; they knew truths too painful for some to bear. The seed in the ground was a pretty metaphor to hide the gaping hole in the earth. Why did they pretend otherwise?

A biblical scholar lecturing at the college stated that the Hebrews crossed the Reed Sea, a marsh, not the Red Sea. Pastor Murphy interrupted the lecture to denounce the professor as an ignorant atheist and blasphemer and led an exodus from the lecture hall. Timp pondered whether his life was a restless sea that might pause once in its impatience or a river that pursued the easiest path or a swamp of dangerous secrets and hidden perils. As a child he had loved the image of God parting a sea so the favored could walk on dry land. But God had parted no seas for him and as an adult he preferred the story of God leading people an often winding, sometimes torturous path through a swamp because that's how his life had been.

When Timp returned to his office Mrs. Stutz said Fulcher wanted to know when the reports about the Mills shooting would be filed. "Tell him the reports will be ready when I say they are."

Although he thought it was probably a mistake, when he saw Larry alone at his desk in the bunkhouse he pulled up a chair and sat beside him. "Did you hear anything before you told Wynn to drop the weapons?"

"You didn't tell me to back off," Larry said.

"Not me necessarily, did you hear anything? Did you hear chickens?"

"I was worried about a dog. Why would I hear chickens?"

"Did you hear her scream?"

"God, yes, I don't think I'll ever forget her screaming."

"When did you first hear her scream?"

"What's going on?" Larry asked. "What do you want?"

"Never mind," Timp said.

***

Timp read the reports again, examining every word, beginning with Larry's and ending with his. There was nothing in his report he could change and nothing except the coroner's report to support his view. Taking the folder, he walked downstairs to the DA's office. He put the folder on Fulcher's desk and sat down. Ross read them and looked up with the sad, disappointed expression he usually saved for witnesses who had lied to him. "Are you running for reelection?" he asked.

"Larry misunderstood the situation and mistakenly shot Wynn Mills."

"There's nothing like that in these other two reports."

"The guns were under Wynn's body and he was on his back. The coroner's report shows he was shot in the left side and his left arm was raised. The photos would have shown that objects under his body were removed."

"Where are the photographs?"

"Cecil ruined them."

Ross looked at him sharply. "Are you charging him with something?"
"At this time, no."
"The commissioners are plugged into Larry's account," Fulcher said.
Timp left knowing the party had abandoned him.

***

Babbs had students waiting to see him but he had a message to call Larry. "Timp asked me to change my report. Maybe he'll endorse me then."
"If you change your report you'll lose the voters."
Larry feared opposing a hero but the public had turned against Sam Houston, the biggest hero Texas had, when he opposed secession and Sam had died a hero turned embarrassment. Babbs had to turn the public against Timp. He started to call P.J. then called Milk Meador instead. "Timp has threatened that if Larry doesn't change his report he is going to run against him. That's unethical. There should be an investigation of the sheriff, pressuring deputies to change reports. I'd call the media but they'd see it as a campaign trick and you know they've always sided with Timp."
"I can call the media."
"That's not a bad idea. Who will his campaign manager be?"
"Probably his wife. She's always done it," Milk said.
The easiest way to destroy a campaign was to drive a wedge between the manager who got blamed for everything and the candidate who floundered from a thoughtless remark to a careless apology. Managers and candidates had to spend too much time together and with a husband and wife team persistent stress would be highlighted by casual blunders and neither could escape. A wife was constitutionally defensive about her husband and would look like a crab if he kept her complaining to the media.

***

Timp went downstairs to the mayor's office when it closed for the day and was greeted by the political power of the county who had met before he arrived—Milk, Clay, Fulcher, Timberlake and Pastor Murphy. Clay Williams' and Milk Meador's brothers had died in Second Platoon. The sheriff was a daily reminder of what they had lost and gained.
They sat around an oval table with Claiborne at one end and Timp at the other. The room smelled of cigar smoke from earlier pre- and post-

official meetings, the musty cellar scent of bound volumes of rules, ordi-
nances, tax and census records and the sharp, brassy smell of spittoons.
Fulcher rapped his knuckles on the table to open the meeting. "We have
two reports that corroborate a justifiable shooting and an inconclusive
coroner's report."

Wynn's widow couldn't afford an outside investigator and the party
had embraced Larry's story with relief. "There was no reason for Wynn
to die," Timp said. "Larry misjudged the situation. How do you know
he wouldn't again?"

"We have a solid ticket," Clay said. He pulled a toothbrush from
his shirt pocket and brushed his mustache briefly into order. "Me for
mayor, Ross for DA, Larry for sheriff."

"You have a gun without a safety for sheriff," Timp said.

"We supported you in the last election," Clay said passing out a
report of how much the election cost the party and another of how
much it cost the county to win the wrongful death lawsuit by Dr.
Baines. "You said it would be your last. Voters are still angry about
your lawsuit."

The more officials waved the standard of justice the less willing
they were to ask voters to pay for it. "It wasn't my lawsuit."

"It was made necessary by your action," said Fulcher who had chosen an attorney from Austin to defend the county. "Are you going to
stand by your word not to run?"

"I can't recommend Larry."

"Do you have someone else in mind?"

"John Banks."

Fulcher stared at Timp. Clay fluttered like a buzzard driven from
its meal. Milk's head snapped around the room as though looking for
someone who wasn't there. Pastor Murphy's head tilted to one side like
a saint in a Renaissance painting. "It wouldn't be fair to John," he said.
"He would always be judged against the statue." Fulcher pointed out
that voters wouldn't replace a hero with a black man. Milk said everyone
would know the party endorsed him only because he was black. Clay
said no one wanted to be stopped by a black man with a gun, especially
not a woman. "Who would believe what he wrote in a report?"

A schoolyard ditty came to Timp's mind. Red and yellow, black
and blue, each will get his Christian due, Jesus loves the little children
of the world.

"Some in the media and many in the county would say that you asked Larry to change his report so that you didn't look cowardly," Murphy said as a concerned pastor. "That story would destroy your reputation after all your years of faithful service. None of us wants that."

"I asked Larry to change his report because it was wrong."

"Are you absolutely sure of what you saw," asked Fulcher who knew no one was absolutely sure of what they saw.

"I'm sure Larry is not ready to be sheriff."

Clay fidgeted as long as he could and told Timp about the pageant that would be an authentic reenactment of the platoon's battle. "It'll cost a lot of money," he passed around an estimate, "but the chamber has offered support and perhaps Solid Rock. You will be the star, standing alone, shaking your fist at the enemy while the lights fade."

But he couldn't go back to that time before Korea when every day was a loss. "I want the party's endorsement."

"You were a good soldier," said Timberlake, smiling. "It's time to be a good soldier again."

"If I don't run in the primary will you stop Larry smearing Wynn Mills?"

Clay wrote numbers on a pad and nodded. "I'll tell Larry when the meeting is over," he said but he meant his cousin Babbs. "We're not asking you to fade away, you will always be the town's hero."

It wasn't the fading of the bloom that frightened Timp but fear that the petals would shatter. "We'll see," he said and left the meeting.

"What do you think that means?" Meador asked.

"He'll run as an independent in the general election," Fulcher said.

Pastor Murphy, who pointed out mistakes before his parishioners knew they were mistakes and challenged their thinking until they stopped, huffed after Timp to check him before he drove away. The pastor was short and corpulent, his plump face cut with a slice of mouth that easily turned up or down to show his yes or no and eyes that glittered menace behind his glasses. "Stop, Timp. Wait," he called breathlessly. Timp got in his car and waited. The pastor got in and sat down. He smelled of success and expensive cologne. "God saved you for a reason," he puffed.

When he joined Solid Rock, God had saved him to teach duty to God and country in Murphy's school, telling the story of Second Platoon. "How can you expect patriotism when public schools teach that apes are man's ancestors, that Travis didn't draw a line in the sand, Columbus didn't discover America, Americans committed genocide against the

Indians, Dresden and Hiroshima were war crimes? That's not what they teach at my school," Murphy had said.

"They crossed a line at the Alamo whether it was real or figurative," Timp replied. "Every man who stayed crossed a line."

"Exactly. Sometimes it's necessary to draw a picture, perhaps embellish it a bit for moral clarity. Imagine if Fannin had reached the Alamo and Travis had been the only survivor. What a role model he would have been. Texas might still be a nation instead of a state. Think what you can do with your story."

But he hadn't had the story Murphy wanted to hear. Now, God had saved him for a different reason. "When you see wrong you arrest the wrong-doers. When I see sin I point it out. Who is to say that in the eyes of God my job is holier than yours? But we must do something about the moral decline of Mills County."

"If you mean the God sins I can't do anything about them until a woman solicits or an underage boy slips in." Timp saw the deliberate seduction of the young by advertising and entertainment, turning girls into sex bait and boys into bullet bait, both into retard discards but there was nothing he could do about it.

"If you're referring to the films of your daughter, I confiscated them," Timp said. He gave them to Fulcher who said they showed bondage, oral and anal sex, doggie style and a wedding night that resembled rape. "TripleS X sued and got them back."

"Abortion and homosexuality also tear the sacred fabric of family. The Bible says women were created to bear children; to be barren is a curse. A woman who refuses to bear children curses God and her husband."

He and Martha had heard that often at Solid Rock and had seen women burst into tears. Timp could remember when it was divorce that tore the fabric of family and divorcees hung their heads in shame. It didn't seem to apply to men. "Your wife supports abortion," Pastor Murphy said.

Martha questioned why God made some women so fertile that the smell of semen impregnated them and others so barren that modern science couldn't help. Nevertheless, she believed a woman's uterus was her property, at least as much as a mortgaged house. "Martha gives financial support to the clinic because they give breast exams, information, birth control, pregnancy tests to women who can't afford them." She didn't do volunteer work to avoid embarrassing him. "If you know of any illegal activity at the clinic I will investigate," he said.

"The public schools permit homosexuals to teach their accursed lifestyle. The gay agenda to destroy marriage and family will bring God's curse on us."

"If there is a complaint I will investigate it." He believed the boy who touched another's social parts had been abused by his mother's live-in but rather than protecting her son she had defended her boyfriend.

"I haven't told the church yet," Murphy confided. A man wanted to market Murphy by broadcasting his church services on a religious network, perhaps a weekly interview to sell Murphy's books. "Perhaps God saved you to be the military/law enforcement expert on defending Israel and our way of life and checking Satanic perversion. Our books can be ghostwritten."

"I'm not an expert."

Murphy gave him the cold look he cast on his congregation. "Your office can be a pulpit for moral clarity," he said with the clarity of a clergyman blessed with a tax-free income. Lesser folks had to parse tolerance and find a course between bad behavior and incorrect opinion.

Timp needed Murphy's support if he ran as an independent in the general election. He watched Murphy leave wondering what he had to do to get it.

When Murphy's former church had fired him for adultery, Murphy found a role model in Ronald Reagan who divorced his wife to marry a pregnant mistress. Church leaders who wanted Reagan to be president overlooked divorce and forgave adultery, relieved that he wasn't the Hollywood pretty-boy they feared. As with Eve, it was the woman's fault, not his partner in adultery but the bitch-mother of his nancy son. A good woman had rescued him from that and the churchmen's rage turned on women who competed with men and expected special rights. And on their gay allies determined to feminize the warrior-spirit of America.

Murphy came to Five Mills with his new wife and in a vacant store on the square preached with the charisma of those who never doubt their goodness or the riches that God owes them because of it. God also owed those who contributed to his ministry, Murphy preached, telling of a poor woman who gave the house payment and won the lottery. A man who lost his job gave his last paycheck and a week later a forgotten relative died leaving him a farm. The lottery was for $2,000 rather than the millions listeners imagined and the farm was twenty rundown, worthless acres. Murphy wasn't greedy but ambitious and prosperity was the only way to prove that he and his ministry had God's blessing.

The church was meeting in the high school auditorium when Murphy said evolution was man's puny attempt to explain away the power of God. "I confess I am almost convinced that Betty Friedan is related to apes." Even the women laughed but there were complaints that sexist remarks were made in a public building. Murphy said he was under attack for preaching the Bible. A member of the ministerial alliance told the media that Murphy's chauvinism was unbecoming in a Christian but Murphy didn't meet with them because they had nothing to say that he cared to hear.

A woman professor said Murphy was an ignorant bigot. Murphy disliked the university because it infected the community with liberal ideas. A professor who had been to Russia said that the US had nothing to fear; the Soviet Union was collapsing. Only Reagan could save us and Murphy denounced the professor as a Communist but the slander wasn't as useful as in the past. Murphy was particularly incensed that the professor who called him ignorant wanted the school to provide her female companion the same medical benefits as a man with a wife. "God didn't make woman to be a man," said Murphy who loved women as he loved all who were not enemies of God.

Preachers from out of town, out of state, wrote or called thanking him for his courage. He received letters, some containing money, and invitations to speak to obscure groups that weren't social or religious but were interested in his subject. A religious TV program invited him to make a statement regarding the gay agenda. He didn't know what the gay agenda was and realized he had missed a chance to speak to the nation. He knew that Jesus said nothing about homosexuality but did condemn riches, greed, building bigger barns and living off investments but he also knew that like other religions Christianity called few beyond the culture into which they were born.

White teenagers pulled down the pants of a young black boy. The newspapers decried the racist act but Murphy said it wasn't racist; it was homosexual, and homosexuals were the number one threat to America. He announced plans for a school where boys wouldn't be turned into girls but into men who would defend their country, where students were allowed to pray and the Bible was read every day. To his surprise he received money for the school from businessmen and corporations. Money for the school paid for the parking lots and the foundation of Solid Rock Church.

Murphy's school had busts of MacArthur, Reagan and Robert E. Lee in the foyer and US, Texas, Confederate, and Christian flags. Students

recited pledges of allegiance to the flag and the Bible. In the classrooms
they learned that America was founded as a Christian nation but that
the intention of its founders had been perverted by gays and liberals.
All its wars were just. Capitalism was ordained by God, consumerism
was an extension of Christianity, and God blessed those nations that
blessed Israel.

The school paid little to anyone unless you were a member of
Murphy's family and few teachers were certified. The school principal
was replaced by the pastor's son who had no training or experience
in education. The fired principal, an early and faithful member of the
church, had given up benefits and better pay as principal of a public
school because Murphy believed God's will was that he be principal
of the church school. When the man sued for wrongful termination,
the school said he was fired for improper conduct with students. He
asked Timp to clear his name, but Murphy refused to cooperate, his
voice rising to god-shouting heights explaining that the government
had no business in his church and they would handle such matters
as they saw fit. Fulcher said there was nothing he could do. Murphy
complained to the party that Timp had interfered in a church personnel
matter although he was not on the church's school board. Murphy was
supported by Dr. Baines, chair of the church board and Murphy's first
big conquest. Baines joined Solid Rock because the Advantage church
he belonged to had rejected him as a deacon because of divorce. With
Baines as a trustee, Solid Rock became solid.

***

The sheriff parked in front of the nursing center that had, with some
effort, been made to look warm and inviting with trimmed shrubbery
between the parking lot and the entrance and Christmas lights sparkling
inside. He always dreaded going in. They seemed so hopeless, those inside, disabled veterans of a thousand lost battles with inanimate objects,
medical neglect, casual disappointment, a distant and indifferent government, unchallenging jobs, patiently waiting for their last appointment.

He put on a smile and greeted those waiting by the door in wheel-
chairs eager to see a new face, hoping it was one that knew them, reaching
for a human touch. A scarred hand gripped his wrist as though it were a
saddle-horn, trying to hang on to a horse that had disappeared beneath
him. The man's face strained with a story he was desperate to tell, his eyes
bulged with effort, his tongue moved in and out of his mouth unable to

form words. An apologetic daughter tugged Timp's arm free. The staff were apprehensive; he was a law officer and could make trouble.

Along the corridor were happy family scenes, children gathered around a father who carved them a whistle, a child on tiptoes watching a mother nurse her baby, a happy, well-fed, well-dressed family rapt at the carving of a Thanksgiving turkey.

He walked under limp balloons left from some party, forlorn in their attempt to look festive. Laughter and screams of excitement echoed from televisions placed in each room so the residents would not have to die beyond the sounds of gunshots and ecstasy, substituting color TV for memories that came in shades of gray.

The sound was muted on his mother's TV but the screen jumped with the game show frenzy usually associated with insanity. He looked in, almost guiltily. This was the only privacy remaining to her and he intruded with reluctance. He ducked under the tinsel icicles and touched her hand but could not tell if she were conscious. Her eyes were almost closed, her mouth agape, her breath shallow, gently sucking at her lips. He found it hard to believe that once she had marked the longitudes and latitudes of his world. Once she was all he needed. Once he had feared she might marry again and he wouldn't know who he was. "You'll be my son," she teased him.

Who was her son? he wondered. Larry once told him, "A woman can't be a wife and a mother." He had thought it was macho crap but now he understood. Some women defined themselves as wife until they had children, then they were first a mother. Father was a role, a function, an expression of personality; it was not a definition. He wasn't a father, so what was he? A sheriff but not a savior. A survivor but not a hero. An actor who played his role. He had no definition that had not been given him by others.

He sat in a chair as solitary as he had ever been. Gently he took her hand, the only remaining connection between them, aware that he was waiting for her to die, betrayed by her constant heart that continued long after she could have wished. Waiting while life became the enemy as Rocky's life had once been.

After his father was killed, he had a childhood dream of saving his country, saving Five Mills by killing a German spy. The dream died after Hiroshima. The only way he could imagine saving his country was by exploding an enemy airplane carrying atomic bombs but he couldn't think of a way to destroy the bomber without blowing himself up with it.

"Mother, I don't know what to do," he said, his words hollow in his ear. "I can retire and Martha and I can live in peace." But only if they moved away, and Martha said they were too old to make new friends, begin a new life. He wouldn't be at peace if Larry fired John or corrupted Cecil or failed to save . . ."I can't leave the county without . . ." Without what?

Others talked to him of lives without purpose and he scarcely knew what they meant. Since Korea he had lived the most purposeful life he knew. Someone else's purpose. There was no answer, no sign that she had heard.

He kissed her on the forehead and left. Vic was outside in his wheelchair. "I see you every time I come here," Timp said.

"Who else am I going to hang with?" Vic asked. "I'm as good as any of these folks. You have to be better than everyone." He lighted a cigarette.

"Those things will kill you," Timp said.

"I'm counting on it. We all try to choose the first nail; I figure this is my third."

"What was the first?"

"Dying before I ended up like this. What was your first?"

"Dying before ending up like this."

"You have legs, you have a wife, you're a hero. There are a million guys like me who wish they could be like you. What do you want?"

"To be an ordinary guy in an ordinary life." He sat on a planter box near Vic. "I should have died with the platoon."

"You didn't, so what do you want now?"

"To save them. Tell their story."

"I thought you did that."

"I didn't do it right. They didn't believe me." He had allowed the platoon's story to become a lie. He tried to be what their families wanted him to be but he was a moon pretending to be their sun.

"Haven't you saved them the only way they can be saved?"

"How can I save anyone with a lie?"

"It's a lie they want to hear and they love you for it. What do you think would have happened if they had believed you?"

"They would know the truth." If there was no truth how could there be meaning?

"What if they don't want to know the truth?"

"But they will. Someday they will."

CHAPTER
SIX

⌘

Martha waited anxiously to hear the party's decision. Why didn't he call? Unable to sit idle she ironed his shirts, which was almost like caressing him. But dull. TV was even duller so she listened to music on the radio for distraction. Between records P. J. the d.j. said the sheriff of Mills County had threatened to run for reelection if his deputies didn't change their reports of the Wynn Mills shooting. "He'll run because he doesn't want to be remembered for surrendering his pistol while Larry Maddin bravely confronted the gunman."

She turned off the radio and the oven where a roast awaited dinner. When the news came on she turned on the TV, which also reported that the sheriff had asked deputies to rewrite an official report. DA Fulcher stated that the procedure was that each officer on the scene write a separate report. Deputies Cecil Smart and Ernest Klemp confirmed that reports were not rewritten to remove discrepancies. Now if he didn't run they would say it was because he was caught trying to change the facts about Wynn's death.

She didn't want him to run. He wasn't a good campaigner, and he would face serious opposition from a younger man who didn't carry the weight of old grievances that Timp did. Martha had managed his first campaign. "Mills County Needs His Courage, His Honesty." Glen Timberlake had paid for his only radio ad—Peggy saying, "I trusted him to defend my country, I believed him when he sold me my first home, I know he can protect Mills County." He was easily elected, winning a majority in Sleepy Hollow as though a salesman were not responsible for the product he sold. He was their man in ways she had only begun to understand.

Timp could retire with honor. Now that was threatened by a young man who wanted to know the madness Timp had known, to be the Timp that Timp had escaped.

"They're not going to endorse me," Timp said when he came home. "If he can't admit that he made a mistake and learn from it, then he shouldn't be sheriff."

Martha knew what that meant. He was unwilling to turn the job over to a lesser man but everyone in the county was a lesser man. "If the party doesn't endorse you the Chamber of Commerce won't."

"And Pastor Murphy. And Glen Timberlake."

"Were they there?" He nodded.

"The money was in the room asking you not to run. You have no money, no campaign plans, no organization."

"We've never had an organization," Timp said.

"Because the party endorsed you; they're the organization." The party put his name on the ballot, raised money for the party's candidates, organized volunteers to distribute posters, walk blocks, and telephone voters.

"They offered to change the parade to a pageant." To an ordinary person that would be good news but Timp always saw things differently.

"They want to honor you for what you have meant to this county." She instantly regretted using past tense. "When you—" she didn't want to say die—"are gone it will be like removing the monument. Do you have to do this, Timp? Haven't we earned the right to live for ourselves?"

"I'm not going to run in the primary. I may run in the general election as an independent."

"How would you explain changing your mind?"

"I said I didn't plan to run but I didn't pledge I wouldn't."

"That's not what Larry will say."

"It's a bad time to retire."

"He'll say you were sheriff of a bad time."

"Five Mills needs an experienced man as sheriff."

"He'll say your age and experience are what allowed Wynn to disarm you."

"Martha, if I decide to run I'll have to have your help."

There were twelve windows in the house and she liked to be able to see through them and she couldn't do that and run a campaign. Had she reminded Timp to mention someone's name, praise some cause, stop one sentence short? After the campaign she remembered the mistakes even though he won. What would she remember if he lost? "Ask me when you get there," she said.

The late news from Advantage had a brief film of Hao being presented a flag beside Wynn's grave. "In Mills County a one-time hero was laid to rest today and his widow embraced the man he tried to kill," the anchor said.

The weatherman quipped, "Could it have anything to do with her husband's life insurance?"

"The Mills County sitcom continues. Sheriff Smith has offered to endorse deputy Larry Maddin for sheriff if Maddin changes his report regarding Mills' death. That would make Mills' widow eligible for his insurance."

Followed by an ad for a dentist who outlawed embarrassing dentures, the story of a curse on the cast of a sitcom where the latest manifestation was a miscarriage by the star, and how women recreated themselves with breast augmentation.

Martha and Timp went to bed with stones for pillows. Timp's stone was Scott Baines. When Scott died Timp wanted to get out of law enforcement but he needed an election to get past that horror. It was an ugly, brutal contest. Eddie financed an opponent who called him a killer, accused him of murdering a boy who tried to surrender, claimed Scott was shot for trespassing on his father's property, and charged cover-up after Cecil lost evidence and Larry's report was identical to Timp's. Timp's and Fulcher's argument regarding officers on the scene writing separate reports was leaked to the media. At Scott's funeral Pastor Murphy preached on the temptation to violence when persuasion was more effective. "Those who live by the sword die by the sword but those who live in love live forever." Timp had squeezed out a victory but no one believed he had to kill Scott.

Larry could have followed his two brothers in their father's prosperous plumbing company in Advantage but he chose law enforcement. Timp respected him for that. After Scott Baines' death, after offering to tell Scott's parents, Larry had returned to the office and prepared the staff to support him. No one had supported him more vigorously in the media firestorm.

When Timp turned the body over, Scott's sour breath reached Timp's nostrils. He had crashed out of the barn, hitting the wall with his shoulder, to gag and urinate at the same time, seeking denial, reversal, oblivion. Behind him he heard Larry's voice. "You shot Dr. Baines' kid. Damn, right through the heart."

Without Larry he could not have gone back inside, could not have followed routine—preserve, search, collect, starting with the outer perimeter, then in reverse. Determine facts of crime, identify criminal, write a report. He had never gotten Scott's face out of his dreams. And he had not forgotten how much he had needed Larry.

Martha's stone was campaigning as an independent if Timp decided to run. She would have thirty days after the primary to collect 500 signatures of those who did not vote in the primary to put his name on the ballot. That shouldn't be a problem as the major candidates were unopposed. The bigger rock was funding. In the beginning Timp was invited to speak at clubs, lodges, churches, and he addressed crowds from the courthouse steps, patted heads and backs when he was on patrol that he increased in election years. But Babbs was trying to redefine Timpson Smith. She would have to fight that.

The county was no longer homogeneous, many of the platoon's survivors had died or moved away, few voters remembered Korea or the story that brought national attention. They preferred images of a triumphant America crowing over emasculated Germany and Japan. Timp was a relic, the monument as archaic as a Confederate flag in a schoolroom.

Martha was awakened by the smell of coffee. Timp was shaking cereal into his bowl when she walked into the kitchen. On the table was *The Grist* with the banner, "Timp Temporizes." A story quoted Larry, "I wouldn't have announced my candidacy if Timp hadn't given me his word that he wasn't running," followed by an editorial, "Is the hard-to-kill sheriff playing hard to get?" "Hard to kill" wasn't pejorative but it was a few firefights from "hero." A box below the fold announced that the retirement banquet honoring Sheriff Smith had been canceled. An inside story revealed the agony of an actress torn to shreds by critics' salvos.

The *Advantage Advertiser* had only a brief notice of Wynn's funeral and a photograph of a guilty Timp being embraced by a passionate Hao while Martha glowered in the background. Inside stories revealed the anguish of a rock star that a groupie might abort the child he had planted in her and how divorce rescued an actress from desperation.

***

Timpson Smith marched into the Mills County courthouse nodding at the hangers-on. They respected Larry for killing Wynn but didn't like him flaunting it. They wanted to forget the shooting and shake their heads at the decline of the founding family of the county. New posters had appeared with a new slogan, "The Man Who Saved Timpson Smith."

They watched as he purposefully climbed the stairs and showed each other raised eyebrows.

The inquest was perfunctory. Mills had been killed by Deputy Maddin, his death an "unavoidable conclusion," no evidence of alcohol or drugs. Fulcher sealed the records. The *Advertiser* did not report the inquest, *The Grist* reported only the conclusion.

"John Banks is on the telephone," Mrs. Stutz said as he entered the office. "There's a man on the floor at the Grabbit N Grin."

"I need a Spanish speaker," Banks said. "I don't know whether he's drunk, on drugs or had a stroke. I understood only twenty percent of what he said."

"That's pretty good," Timp said.

"That was his English."

"Call an ambulance and let the hospital figure it out."

"Chief, have you seen the Baines tableau?" Mrs. Stutz asked. "I cleaned Sarge's but I don't think Dr. Baines ever looks at his brother's." Dr. Baines bought a tableau of his brother defending a fallen Marine. "I thought if you told him—"

Mrs. Stutz' first husband, "Sarge" Lewis, had enlisted in the Army after Pearl Harbor. After the war he joined the Marine reserves for the extra money and died in Second Platoon. Sarge said while he fought in Italy Captain Billy Pritchard held down a stateside recruiting office. Sarge had only one war story. Patrol, spread out, dusk, most Germans had pulled out. A sniper fired two shots and vanished. Walking through a cemetery he saw a girl hiding, young girl, fifteen, sixteen. Not frightened exactly, sullen but also resigned. He pushed her back on a marble tombstone, pulled her dress up, and took her. She turned her face away, pushed at his shoulders, cried but she didn't scream. More like she expected it. Germans had already done it to her he figured. It wasn't rape, not in Italy. Them people, especially the women, was used to it. You could trade cigarettes or candy for sex. Stockings would get you a real woman. Sarge talked of the pussy he was going to get in Korea. "You're the conquerer or you're the savior—either way they got to give you what you want."

"The Grimsruds want you to talk to their grandson," Mrs. Stutz said.

The Grimsruds were one of the reasons he wanted to retire. Their daughter had been killed by her husband, a Vietnam veteran, and their young grandson had witnessed the brutal murder. They had gained custody of the boy and brought him to Mills County where he could forget what he had seen. When the murderer became eligible for parole they returned their grandson to Missouri to beg the board not to free his father. Timp had written a letter, at their request, asking the same. The boy, now eighteen, wanted to know his father. Timp told him he was old enough to decide for himself.

He looked at the overnight reports. Miss Abernathy claimed harassment by college students who threw a dead squirrel in her yard and her dog was still missing. Deputy Goss believed the squirrel had electrocuted itself on a power line. Man with blood on his face lying on sidewalk in Oak Meadows. Man said his wife hit him. She said he was drunk and fell down.

Bryan was on the telephone with a question about the platoon and Peggy Betts wanted to see him. He heard the disapproval in Mr. Stutz voice as clearly as Peggy must have. He had time for Peggy.

The town had formed its opinion of her as a young teen, and, like the face on the statue, it was cast in bronze. In high school they had snickered because she wore her hospital bracelet until it broke. They thought she had no shame but she wore it because it was all she had left of what she believed was her baby. She had used Timp to make love to Doug, but before Doug, before Korea, she loved Timp because he defended her, and he had loved her as purely as he loved anyone because she was abused.

Few called her Piggy anymore, but her status had not improved. To many, her relationship with Doug seemed less a marriage than an exchange of services. "She got a license and his life insurance," folks said. "They didn't have time to get a ring." After Doug died Peggy married Riley Betts, a veteran of World War Two. The town disapproved, saying she married him for his disability check. Riley's wounds meant they would never escape Dogpatch. In America's medical apartheid illness guaranteed poverty. Illness and poverty sometimes guaranteed abuse. Timp had seen Peggy with bruises. He could tell from her shame that it was no accident, although she said it was. He told her that no one had the right to hit her but she was relieved when he let it drop.

"I shouldn't have come here," she began.

She thought he was embarrassed to have her for a friend but he was ashamed of his role as a surrogate Doug. "Oh, I need you, Doug," she had said. "Come home. Come home, Doug." Timp tried to look friendly but official. "You're a taxpayer. How's Riley?" He had never heard her say an unkind verb to him; her expectations had never been high.

"Riley's real sick and I don't have anyone else to turn to. Mrs. Stutz hates me because I used Doug's insurance to buy a home for myself instead of a tableau for him. No one had heard of a tableau when I bought the house. I've been trying ever since to save enough money."

"Doug doesn't need a tableau. Everyone knows what he did." He had told them.

Tears dripped from her chin. "Larry has been hassling me about a hot check. You know what our house is like. There's always something that needs fixing. I paid a contractor to repair the roof and he still hasn't done it." She laid a paper on his desk.

Timp did know what her house was like, cheap to buy but expensive to own. Because homeowners in Sleepy Hollow were poor and the houses shoddy, contractors required payment in full and then delayed the job to build new houses. "I'll talk to him but he's going to say he gave you a special rate for prepayment and that he had a previous contract."

She nodded resignation. "I could pay my bills if the people who owed me paid theirs. Riley went to Eddie, Dr. Baines, for tests because the VA said it would be six months before they could do it. Riley had to give him a $300 deposit in case the VA didn't pay. They paid all but $38." She pulled papers from her purse and laid them on his desk. "I asked Eddie to return the deposit a month ago but I still haven't gotten it.

"We had to have food, Riley had to have medicine, so I wrote a check. I told Larry to get my money back and I would pick up the hot check. He said I was a deadbeat. He called me Piggy. Riley got so upset I had to take off work. I can't afford to take him to the doctor and he can't keep anything on his stomach. We get behind but we've always paid our bills."

"I can loan you some money."

"No." She put the papers back in her purse and closed it. "Things aren't going well for us right now, Timp. I'm working as a teacher's aide and I don't need Larry coming to school or parking his police car in front of the house. I know younger women who screwed him to get him off their back." She ducked her head at the careless image.

It was easy for a woman to accuse an officer of harassment but hard to prove. He had heard rumors but he had never had an official complaint against Larry. "File a complaint and I'll investigate," he told Peggy.

"I came to you because we're old . . . we've known each other a long time. I can't afford to make an enemy of Larry. He's going to be sheriff."

In middle school Peggy, plump in a young voluptuous way, was called Piggy because Rocky said she squealed like a pig every time he stuck it in her. "Slap her, show her that you don't like her and she'll do anything." Once Rocky had pinched her nipple in the school hallway to amuse his friends. "Name it or lose it," he said while she cried. Timp told him to leave her alone and Rocky shoved him against a locker. He told her to tell the principal. Peggy had never been the smartest in her class but she knew even then that people in power like the principal kept their power by sucking up to those with power. "This school looks out for Rocky and people like him," she said. "Rocky and his friends will just be meaner."

A man was foolish to think he could save a woman from anything. Spinsterhood, but nobody feared that any more. Loneliness, until they discovered they could be alone with you in the same room, the same bed. Childlessness, but with conception your laureate was gone. "I'll talk to Larry," he promised. He would call the contractor and Dr. Baines' office but they were in Doss County.

Peggy left defeated, too abject to show her anger at the impotence of office.

    ***

Brother Jonas had taken Hao to Advantage and gotten her what help he could but Donna, the case worker in Five Mills, was rude to him and ruder to Hao. "Sometimes I think the government is the way the rich take vengeance on the poor for not providing them with enough luxury," Jonas said.

Timp knew Donna because he directed indigents to her office. Her husband had left her with three small children and she had groveled to feed them and toiled long hours for her education and position. Now with a little power and hardened by experience she scorned those like Hao who had left their native land for an easier life and those like Hao who had been given a house and land, things she would never have. Timp said he would take her because he hadn't been able to help her get Wynn's insurance.

It was morning in America at the old jail that still smelled of despair,

126

the sour odor of poverty that made soap expensive, hot water extravagant, fresh clothing a dream. Welfare queens who drove Cadillacs filled the hall waiting to beg for a job, food for their hungry children, help for their elderly parents, medicine to help them through another work day. Bad teeth, bad hair, carrying greasy sacks, Styrofoam boxes of food snatched from garbage cans and bags of discarded clothing, they were abandoned with dedicated indifference by their government. Veterans restless with dreams of madness, mothers and children deserted first by husbands and fathers too honest to steal, too loving to watch them go hungry; the mentally wounded, under or over qualified workers troubled more by useless hands than empty stomachs.

In Mills County, "welfare queen driving Cadillac" meant Freetown, and blacks waited with heads down, eyes on the floor. A woman with long, tangled hair, a torn and faded dress, run-over shoes that left her heels touching the floor, clutched a soiled, stuffed rabbit like a Baptist clutching a Bible. Beside her, maybe with her, was a young girl so busy growing up that she hadn't had time to grow pretty.

Timp saw Harvin, Doc Knight's brother, waiting in line. Doc, corpsman, had acted older brother to Timp. "I thought you dropped dead," Timp said.

"I did twice. I come back up but the doctors thought I was gone. You have any watches or clocks you need cleaned? For free."

"Where are you staying?"

"I don't have a place right now."

"Can you mop, sweep? I'll call the Advantage police and see if they have a vacant cell." He walked past the barrier that held the needy at bay. Harvin and Hao followed. He used Donna's phone to call, gave Harvin some money and told him to hitchhike to Advantage, get something to eat and go to the jail.

"What can I do for you, Sheriff?" asked Donna who was blessed with plenitude rather than pulchritude. Her smile showed too much gum on a puffy face and her ankles were swollen.

"We'll wait," he said.

"You're already here."

He told her he wanted Wynn Mills' widow and children to receive the assistance they were entitled to.

"Larry doesn't like foreigners, criminals, and deadbeats getting handouts from working people," Donna said.

"Larry has nothing to do with county welfare," Timp said.

"He will when he's sheriff."

"If you embarrass this woman or anyone else, I'll report you to the regional and state directors."

***

Larry was at his desk when Timp waved him into his office. "Do you know Donna in the aid office?"

"She's a mistake I once made."

"Have you harassed anyone coming to that office?"

"I said before we give them what they want, they should give us what we want. Snitches know the perps; they're neighbors. Maybe someone overheard."

"And maybe someone gave us bad information because of it. This office has never politicized county services and I want it to stay that way." Larry didn't reply. "I've received a complaint."

Larry recognized the oldest trick in criminal investigation, Interrogation 101; suggest there was a complaint and wait for the accused to say what it was. "Can I see it?"

"It's not a written complaint."

Larry shrugged. "Then it's not a complaint."

"I'm investigating a complaint that you ask sexual favors."

"Hell, John calls for backup on speeding tickets because he's afraid some white woman will accuse him of rape. Do you think he lives in Freetown because of the scenery? It's so he can run outside in his boxers and pick up the paper before daylight and not have a complaint from a white bread neighbor." And because that's where the poontang was. "I'd like to see a woman look me in the eye and accuse me." He would expose her ass.

"It's a preliminary investigation. You won't see her."

"If you do your job there are always complaints." The old bastard was punishing him for saving his life. "Every time I confront someone I make an enemy." And he knew who they were. "Probably Piggy. I'd go to jail before I'd stick my harpoon in that whale."

"I don't think you'll ever have the maturity to be sheriff."

The son of a bitch had the stand-and-die look he had on the statue. "The party is going to endorse me," Larry said. The expression didn't change.

***

Timp told Martha about Peggy's complaint without mentioning her name and of Larry's belief that charity should be a bribe. "I have to oppose that."

"What are you going to use as a campaign slogan? How about 'Dependable, experienced, a man you know.'"

"That sounds good," he said wanting to avoid confrontation.

"That's why Babbs is using it. He has trumped your best qualities."

"I have to have your help," he said. He didn't find it easy to ask.

She no longer had the energy, the enthusiasm for the kind of fight this would be, but, being a woman, she was accustomed to having her hands in shit. "Call the media," she said. "Tell them you will run as an independent." In an off-year election it was easy for folks to vote the way they always had, pulling one lever in the primary and ignoring the general election. She had to change that.

The early news did not mention the inquest or that Sheriff Smith was going to run for reelection, but showed a clip of Pastor Murphy warning the God sins on the road to hell to get out of Mills County.

***

Along with those seeking land or work, the railroad brought an estranged religious group, refugees from whiskey soaked factories, coalmines and railroad camps, seeking seclusion. Only the men ever came to town, except to vote, and it was always the same men. They sold fresh and canned meat, fruits, vegetables, and handcrafts such as embroidery, hand-sewn clothing, wooden furniture. They had a school for their children only, to teach what they wanted them to know. No science, little math, but Bible history and the bloody line of martyrs that ended at their doorstep. Their secrecy was a source of curiosity and attendant gossip. They stole babies, although none were missing in the county. The men had many wives and fathered their own grandchildren. They approved slavery except slavery to alcohol. Their votes drove liquor out of Mills County and inspired the forming of Doss County where Babbs opened liquor stores.

Drought, prosperity, the infiltration of contagious ideas split the sect. Some moved on but others remained holding peculiar notions of the purposes and uses of religion. Some of those notions were still honored in Mills County.

***

When Babbs heard about the pageant he was caught between a flood and a fire. A pageant portraying Timp's heroism gave him a reason not to run and if he did run it would glorify him during a political campaign. But Timp running was what Babbs had prayed for and he shifted into low gear. Politicians didn't really believe that Communism was so seductive that people would be unable to resist it if given a choice, or that it was so efficient it would take massive corporate welfare to compete with it, but it was easy to frighten voters into believing it. He would co-opt religion the same way—exploit the fear that homosexuality was so attractive that children would be unable to resist it, inflame xenophobia with stories of immigrant crimes, infectious ideas, inferior culture and religion that would subvert undefined traditional values and democratic ideals.

He needed to get voters to the primary to show support for Larry and to keep Timp on the defensive. Babbs called P. J. to start a rumor that Timp had given Larry his endorsement. Listeners would assume Larry had changed his report but when Timp announced his candidacy they would believe Larry had refused on principle. Then he started a letter campaign and called the "micro-chimps" to propel rumors.

***

"The only thing Mills County has that Doss County doesn't is a genuine hero instead of Senator Billy Pritchard, a coward who failed his own men. Timpson Smith would no more surrender his weapon than Davy Crockett would," wrote Wally Sech in a letter to the Advertiser. A professor at the college replied that Crockett had surrendered at the Alamo. People rose to defend the Alamo again, like Travis unable to abandon it

Martha knew the argument was Babb's work, since Timp was always brought into it. Letters from those offended that Crockett didn't die the way he did in the movies brought responses that Five Mills' hero surrendered to Wynn Mills, who was drunk or stoned. Those letters brought replies that when Timp surrendered his pistol he was old and slow and knew he would be saved by his deputy. Others revived charges that the men from Advantage had sacrificed the platoon to save themselves. That brought responses that Timp had exonerated the company and countercharges that he had covered up for them.

A columnist for the *Advertiser* called. Did Timp believe Crockett surrendered at the Alamo? Timp replied that even with automatic weapons not all soldiers died instantly. At the Alamo many must have been shot, stabbed, bludgeoned, but not dead. Why would anyone be surprised there were POWs? Still he lost the support of those who believed their illusions were their ideals.

Martha complained to Scoop Deason about the letters but Timp wasn't a candidate in Doss County and the newspaper enjoyed the reader interest. *The Grist* said the Op/Ed page was for public opinion. The Advantage radio station told her they would air her husband's response to P.J.'s comments. She could hear how shrill her voice was as she warned they were being used. "Aren't you trying to use us, Mrs. Smith?" Always Mrs. Smith the candidate's wife, never Martha the campaign manager.

***

Harold Ford told *The Grist* that the sheriff had brought Wynn's widow to 'Round Back Chili "with Wynn's blood still on her" and made him serve her at county expense. P. J. reported that the sheriff had pushed a foreigner ahead of a long line of Americans and quoted Donna. "He didn't exactly threaten me but I knew what he meant—his lady friend got special consideration."

During a political campaign rumors were news. The more Timp denied the stories, the louder they became. Professioners were more open-minded toward non-native citizens but the rumors resonated with old-timers—carpetbaggers taking over the county.

Martha turned to friends, supporters, her church clubs asking them not to vote in the primary so they could sign Timp's petition. At the Daughters of Eve a woman asked if she worried about Timp seeing so much of Wynn's widow. At the Widow's Mite she was asked how well she knew Hao by a woman who wanted to be buried next to her ex-husband so that when he was resurrected she could watch him march off to hell aflame. "I told you so, you bastard," would be the last Christian words he would hear.

Martha slammed down the receiver, furious with herself. Why did she always sound like a nagging wife? Reporters assigned her that role and she played it as though she had memorized the script. When they asked about "that Vietnamese woman" she wanted to tell them they had been city-slickered but she was the one caught off-guard. She thought all she had to do was tell them Timp needed their names on a petition and they would skip the primary. He had been their morning star but she feared they saw the deaths of Scott Baines and Wynn Mills as twilight. Babbs contrasted Timp the candidate with Timp the statue, like celebrities who looked less real in person than they did on the screen.

She knew Timp had cut a swath through the widows, girlfriends. Worry of running or retiring had put him under stress and a young woman might allow him to reassert himself. A young widow who needed him. With children who adored him. Martha recalled her desperation when she feared he would not marry her. Now, for the first time since marriage she feared losing him.

She heard Timp come in and, despite her wishes, she was the bitch-wife everyone thought she was. She didn't like what she had become, and she resented Timp for it. When Timp slumped in a chair looking old and tired, she was exasperated. "Have you heard the rumors about you and Hao?" she asked grilling Timp about rumors she had confidently denied.

"I can't stop rumors."

She expected him to be angry, resentful, anything but resigned. "You can tell me they're not true."

"They're so ridiculous they don't require denying."

His response was as reassuring as a summons. She remembered Hao embracing him but it wasn't her she feared most; it was her children. Could Timp become so attached to someone's children that he would leave her?

"She doesn't have any friends, Martha. I've tried to help her."

Timp's precision troubled her. He was too calm, too guarded. She would have preferred he yelled at her. "Do you love her?"

She could scarcely breathe waiting for his response as Timp, always careful about honesty, searched for an answer. But his denial brought her more comfort than a reflexive response could have.

"I love you," he said. "I've never loved anyone else."

"We know who started the rumors and why. How do we stop them?" The rumors were effective because denying them gave them currency. "I'll help her. That will keep you out of it and I'll start a backfire by taking her shopping and to church clubs."

Martha bought eggs from Hao and sold some to neighbors. She took Hao with her when she encouraged voters to skip the primary so they could sign Timp's petition. She took Hao to Ruth's Readers Book Club. The pastor's daughter-in-law reviewed a book explaining why America must protect itself against foreign philosophies and cultures incompatible with a Christian nation. The pastor's wife pointed out that colleges, including the one in Advantage, taught classes in Asian languages, cultures, and literature.

Babbs had planned to spring rumors of a sexual relationship between Timp and Hao after Timp got on the ballot but P. J. had revealed it prematurely and Martha had stifled it before it had a chance to breathe. Rumors of infidelity stopped and rumors of misjudgment began. P. J. said what happened to Timp in Korea would drive any man crazy. "No one can be brave all the time," he said. Others noted that Timp did not seem himself. He would never have put an outsider before those who had always supported him.

P. J. reminded listeners that Timp pretended Wynn Mills' death was an accident so his widow could get his insurance but the image of her hiding from her husband and embracing Larry as their savior was so implanted that the story cost Timp credibility. He lost more credibility when he had to deny that he threatened to fire Larry if Larry did not change his report.

***

Milk Meador wanted a referendum on a bond issue for a civic restoration project to remove the vacant buildings on the east side of the courthouse and replace them with five oversized, decorative windmills. Beneath the windmills would be a strip of boutique stores catering to professioners and those from Advantage who attended Solid Rock and might stop for Sunday dinner and some shopping before returning home. The shops, branches of larger Advantage stores, would promote the Windmills Project and promise local employment. A bond issue would turn out the voters whether they favored it to boost the economy or opposed it to keep taxes low.

Larry feared that the project would glorify the Mills but Babbs assured him the Windmills Project would not add to the stature of the Mills family. Babbs' fear was that so many would vote for the referendum that Timp would be unable to get on the ballot. He was more alarmed when in exchange for the party's referendum on vice, including the Women's Clinic, Pastor Murphy told his congregation that a vote for the Windmills Project was a vote for the heritage and history of Mills County. Most voters knew the vice referendum was non-binding and would have no effect on their business or pleasure but wanted to appear righteous by voting against evil.

Babbs called Murphy to warn that so close an identification between the church and the party could cause the church to lose its tax-exemption. Murphy claimed the right to preach whatever he wanted to preach in his church and warned the government not to interfere. Babbs called Milk Meador and warned that association with Solid Rock could turn those who resented the church's wealth and power against the party. Meador said he had no control over the pastor. Babbs feared he was losing control of Larry's campaign.

***

Although P. J. made Martha curse to herself, ignoring him was hearing footsteps behind her in the dark and not turning around. "Larry Maddin didn't change his report as the sheriff demanded but the sheriff gave his endorsement to Maddin in gratitude for saving his life," P. J. said. "What else could he do?"

If Timp denied he endorsed Larry he lost credibility. If he didn't deny it he gave supporters his okay to vote on the Mills Project or the vice referendum making them ineligible to sign his petition. Babbs was blowing Timp away before he had a chance to campaign.

Because he wasn't running in the primary the sheriff wasn't asked to respond when Babbs told the media, "Wynn Mills wasn't a bad guy." The more dangerous Wynn looked the more understandable that Timp gave up his pistol. "Some want to appease troubled men like Mills and advocate loving lawbreakers into law-abiders but maybe a firmer hand from the sheriff would have straightened him out." The contradiction to his previous statements didn't seem to bother the media.

Babbs had stolen a march on her but there was nothing she could do until after the primary except encourage supporters not to vote.

***

Babbs worked on Larry's image; brave as Timp but not as rigid. Tough on crime but pranks and practical jokes that caused minor damage or injury were understandable. Ready to share a drink or a laugh but quick to defend a woman or her honor. He advised Larry to avoid public statements about the vice referendum but privately pledge to drive prostitutes, pornography, and pedophiles out of the county. "If you ever plan to get married, now would be the time to do it. Women love weddings. Next best thing, engaged but it has to be someone you can be seen with in public, preferably in church."

Larry had been thinking of making a run by the clubs, maybe see Dustee. His nightmares had kept her awake but she liked him being a little scary. And damn she could screw, agile as a squirrel, and she went after him teeth and nails. He should get married? At least engaged? He remembered the bachelor's blessing, may you marry an interesting woman.

He had almost gotten married once. Cassie was smart, ambitious, independent, communications major, interested in TV broadcasting, looked good, sounded good, presented herself well but nowadays women could lose their hearts while holding on to their pocketbooks as good as men. He had to listen to women's rights regarding employment, reproduction, finances, politics. Would she shut up during a campaign? During breakfast? He broke off the engagement and she did the worst thing a woman could do to a man. She told him she couldn't live without him and then did.

Joyce was pretty and built like a jail. Solid, unadorned, impenetrable. She used the N-word when he was rounding second base. He'd like to see her mouth pop when he shoved it in her but wouldn't marry her for the privilege.

He could be seen in public with Denise, maybe engaged until after the election. She had a kid, nice kid but someone else's. She was quick into bed and quick out of it; he liked that. Adventurous but not ambitious; he liked that too. In the morning she looked like someone had stolen her Tampax but at night she looked at him like she wanted him, like she loved him. If there was a difference, he hadn't learned to recognize it, and he didn't want her looking at someone else the same way. He liked dogs, he really did, but she used his electric shaver to trim her dog's butt.

He wanted a good-looking wife but not so good-looking she drew attention from other men. A good body, he wanted that, but he didn't want her in pools or athletic clubs where guys could see daylight. Smart, but not eager to express opinions. Being wanted was better than being loved because sex was enough. Being loved meant crap like gifts, guilt, reporting in. Instead of getting married he would date only in Advantage. Not screw any of the women at the clubs. Escort them home, the perfect gentleman, then after the election collect.

The woman he would like to date was too dangerous during a campaign but maybe when he was sheriff. Stuck in his head was the film of Morgan Murphy on her wedding night. "No, wait, please, stop, please wait." He'd like to play that scene with her but he'd have to marry her or be arrested. Would a wedding night like that be worth it? She was broken in now, maybe ruined. Still she was one sexy bitch.

He couldn't tell her that he had bought the film but he could tell Pastor Murphy that he would track down and destroy the films of his daughter, ask to personally apologize to her because the department had not responded more quickly. Tell her he wanted to know more about her father's faith, ask if he could take her to church on Sunday. She greeted the visitors, made announcements but if, when she was through, she sat beside him during the service, he would have the voters in his bed.

The pastor lived in a large house, the only one remaining from the block of houses that had become the church parking lot. Murphy was at the church, his wife, son, and daughter-in-law at the school; Morgan opened the door.

"I'm sorry about what happened to you and I promise you I am doing everything I can to round up those, uh, items and destroy them and punish everyone involved in this and guarantee that it will never happen again," he gushed. She blushed, which pleased him. "I'd like to talk to you about church sometime. I don't really belong to a church right now but I watch Solid Rock services on TV." He did mostly to see her greet people and make the announcements. She invited him in, a lost sheep returning to the fold.

When Babbs learned that Larry had sat beside Morgan at her father's church he called immediately full of warnings. "If you sit with her many times you'll to have to join the church. Eye flirting is okay. No off-color jokes, no innuendoes, talk about religion, values, family, things like that." Larry did, hoping to discover the path to her passion.

***

Babbs discovered that the owner of the TripleS X was part owner of a unisex shop, part of the Windmills Project and passed the information to P. J. who had learned in high school to leverage those in power by mocking those who opposed them. He had learned as a newspaper reporter that there were stories he could not report. He turned to radio where smartass remarks about public faces brought laughs rather than rebukes. His show had gone from a music format to music with innuendo so that listeners didn't miss the commercials, to music with gossip, to provocative commentary with music. He liked it when those in power struck back because it made him look important. Advertisers took note of people talking about him and wanted more commentary on select subjects. Citizens of Mills County worked in Advantage, used Advantage services, but didn't pay taxes in Advantage. The only thing they did for Doss County was increase the crime rate.

There were also subjects that were verboten. Billy Pritchard was instrumental in getting the monument in Five Mills but when he replaced his father as senator he aided Doss County and, more importantly, the corporation that owned the station and the corporations the station depended on for advertising. Only obliquely could he attack the senator, and that meant through Five Mills and Timpson Smith.

He thought Pastor Murphy could countenance any shame other than being ignored, privately he called members of Solid Rock the sincere but misguided, but when he made a suggestive remark about By Our Fruits, Solid Rock's monthly dinner honoring those who had received recognition or had done a good deed he discovered there was no profit and a lot of peril in attacking popular religion. Not only did church members call the station, they called the sponsors of his program.

P. J. didn't mention on the air Murphy's support of a unisex store owned by a pornographer but the religious TV network that wanted to market Murphy dropped him from future plans. Murphy turned against the Windmills Project unless it excluded the unisex store and told listeners why. The party dropped its support for the referendum against sin.

Both referendums passed and Larry won by a larger vote than Timp had received in the previous election. If Martha collected enough petitions to get Timp on the ballot before the general election Timp would have to convince citizens they had been wrong to vote for Larry in the primary. Babbs had rolled a stone across the tomb and it would take a miracle to resurrect Timp's chances.

Martha saw Larry parked in his personal car on the road outside Hao's house. Hao said she and the boys were afraid to go outside. Larry said he was moonlighting for Timberlake.

CHAPTER
SEVEN

✤

Babbs' plan had worked. There were enough people who didn't vote in the primary that Martha could collect the petitions but she would have no time for campaigning. More than five hundred signatures were required because some who had voted in the primary signed as a token of friendship and the party would disqualify them. She and Hao went door to door, driving county roads, coping with gates, chickens, dogs. A man in Shady Acres said they had voted in the primary but wouldn't look at her when he said it. A woman in Country Place invited her in and signed the petition beside the plastic windmill the chamber had given to supporters of the project. On Main Street the emotionally and diversity challenged didn't invite Martha in with Hao beside her but asked, "Why is she here?" At the barbershop a black man asked, "Is she your driver?" Involving Hao was a mistake so Martha also took the boys to show voters their Americanness.

Sometimes they saw Larry parked where he could watch Hao's house. Timp believed he was trying to scare Hao into selling. "I think he's courting her," Timberlake said.

Babbs believed he again had control of the campaign. His aggressive tactics made Timp seem defensive. Larry wanted technology for data storage and retrieval, providing instant communication with other law enforcement agencies. Timp wanted another deputy and portable radios. Larry wanted a constable responsible for the town, answerable to the mayor, and each deputy patrolling a single area so he knew it well. Timp wanted deputies patrolling different areas plus everyone patrolling downtown and the expressway to avoid favoritism and because Freetown would be outside the jurisdiction of a constable and on the fringe of a patrol area.

Larry wanted deputies to wear uniforms on duty. Timp believed the deputies' dress should be similar to that of those they served. Larry wanted a jail that would provide prestige, jobs, and revenue for housing convicts when there was no room in state pens. Timp admitted a new jail would be required in the future but presently it was cheaper to pay Advantage to hold prisoners.

Larry wanted an unpaid sheriff's posse for private property accidents or minor thefts, hubcaps and lawnmowers, where a report was required for insurance purposes but an officer with the power of arrest was not necessary, and to transport prisoners to Advantage. "Forty percent of crime originates from 10 percent of county addresses," Larry said. "I want my deputies watching those 10 percent." Most voters believed that 10 percent lived in Freetown and Sleepy Hollow.

Timp had inherited a "posse" composed of cronies who were permitted to carry guns, park in no parking zones, shoot deer inside city limits, commit minor traffic infractions and other noncustodial offenses. Some were Night Crawlers who were too decent to join the Ku Klux Klan but insisted that peace required segregation. He had disbanded the posse, making enemies of those in it and those who hoped to be. He did not want the posse revived but his statement that law enforcement was best done by trained officers underlined Babbs' charges that he was untrained in law enforcement, and P. J. said his request for another deputy meant more taxes, appealing to patriots who believed someone else should pay for roads, schools, courts, and crime-free streets.

Larry had taken courses in personnel management, civil liability, organized crime, and criminal investigation. Timp countered that most investigation was done by the State Department of Public Safety and eighty percent of county crimes were solved by information coming from people who knew and trusted the sheriff. Mills County knew and trusted him.

Babbs coached Larry in pithy, deceptive, but easy to remember slogans. The old print boys had loved Timp's yarn-spinning but on television the yarns were unusable. Martha had supplied him with hollow but snappy responses but he preferred talking about the country he knew as a boy when guns were for hunting or heirlooms. When drugs meant aspirin, milk shakes and comic books. When patriotism meant voting, serving, paying taxes and keeping the neighborhood clean. The first sign of old age was fearing the future and revering the past. Martha had failed to save him from that trap.

Babbs had defined the campaign—a young, sharp professional against a battered vestige of the "wild west" who didn't know when to step aside and was incapable of dealing with modern crimes. "Timp is not a certified peace officer as required by most states," Babbs said. "A sheriff's most valuable asset is experience backed by common sense," Martha responded.

Five Mills had annexed suburbs and paid for it with a sales tax that fell disproportionately on the old-timers as the professioners shopped in Advantage. Merchants in Five Mills went out of business. Larry's position was that growth was good, taxation was bad. Timp's explanation that the sheriff's office had nothing to do with annexation or taxation but that suburbs did require more patrolling was too long for attention.

Men admired Timp but his closest friend was a disreputable cripple; women were drawn to his strength but he saw them as victims or voters. Larry was casual and fun, a boy they could train to be their man. Martha understood why Timp didn't want Larry to be sheriff; despite training or experience he would always be a shirt that needed ironing.

***

A homeowner in Sleepy Hollow complained to *The Grist* of his house's crumbling foundation. Although he had bought the home after Timp had been involved *The Grist* mentioned the partnership of Smith and Timberlake in the development of Sleepy Hollow. "You'd better talk to your friend in Dogpatch," Martha said.

He protected residents of Sleepy Hollow whenever he could but it was hard to ask them for support, and seeing the houses he had helped to sell fired him with shame. He parked his car in the crumbling street and followed the gravel sidewalk to the porch that sagged at the same angle as the screen door. Beneath the flag given to her by a grateful nation he had mimed Doug's role, knowing he had lost not only himself but also the truth about himself, only the lie could be loved.

She had been the only one, except Martha. After Martha he avoided her. Because Peggy interpreted his avoidance as disgust she was happy each time he came to ask for her help. "Nobody in Sleepy Hollow voted for Larry. The guy who wrote the letter, he didn't even know you," she said. "I can ask him to call *The Grist*."

He shook his head. "I know you're busy with work and Riley but could you ask your neighbors to sign a petition. I need every name I can get."

"I'll get every name in the Hollow," she promised.

He crossed the highway to Freetown and stopped before the house where John Banks was born. John's mother watched warily from a window as he approached. She knew her son considered him a friend but the badge and pistol that brought security to Country Place brought fear to Freetown. "John's not here," she said from behind the door, only her face showing. "If you come to ask about your petition I already got everybody in Freetown signed up."

"Thank you."

"I didn't do it for you. I did it for them."

He took the dirt road along the brushy fork of Flat Rock Creek to talk to Zeek Bivins. He hadn't been to the ramshackle ranch since he had gone as a deputy because Zeek missed a jury summons. When no one answered the door he went to the barn, followed by barking dogs, and walked into a shotgun held by the son who had just returned from juvenile detention. "You're trespassing," the kid said.

"I have a jury summons for your father. This is his property."

"It ain't done it. You're trespassing and I got a right to shoot you."

"Has your father died?" There had been no death notice.

"He's dying and he ain't serving on no jury. It's my place now and you can back off or crawl off after I gut-shoot you. I ain't fooling."

"I have to deliver the summons," Timp said. He had to know if Zeek was okay.

"I'm warning you," the kid said but Timp raised his arms and went to the house. Zeek was ill but wanted to be left alone.

This time there were no dogs and Zeek came to the door, a wreck with a long hair caught in the zipper of his stained fly, but Timp had never seen him look young. He signed the petition and wrote a check to Timp's campaign. "I don't need it no more," he said. "My boy was killed in a holdup. I thank you for letting him live as long as he did."

***

Timp dreamed of the farm his mother lost while he was in the hospital. It didn't look like the farm but he knew that it was. His father said, "It's not the way it used to be," and it was a terrible condemnation. He wanted to apologize but when he opened his mouth he said, "It never has been." He moped through breakfast hoping for a problem he could solve but it was Sunday. Timberlake called and asked to meet with him. Timp had planned to go to church; it was important to be seen in church although his years of membership there had been eclipsed by Larry sitting with Morgan. Martha thought he should meet with Timberlake who might offer funding. Timberlake had prospered and, despite the running sore of Dogpatch, had supported Timp's campaigns.

In the reception room of Timberlake Enterprises opposite the courthouse in what had once been the bank Timp was confronted by a framed photograph of him receiving the Medal of Honor and another standing in front of a Timberlake sign with Sleepy Hollow as a backdrop. On a desk was a scale model of Alamo Acres. To Timp it looked like a military cemetery, the lots laid out in neat rows, trees uniformly placed.

"We started out together," Timberlake said warmly. "We have both been successful and you made it possible. Five Mills is becoming a town of professional people who look to the future. Alamo Acres is the future. We're going to bring homeowners, taxpayers, money for schools, streets, county assistance, law enforcement."

"There are no sidewalks."

"Sidewalks look middle class; there are secluded walkways behind the houses. America prospers when people drive."

"Trees?"

"Kruger doesn't like oaks. They're dark, rough, grown without pruning, children warping them until no two are alike. We'll plant decorative fast growing trees. Kruger hates disorder. That's what drove him to the military, to business, to Mills County where he can live out his days in serenity. This is Kruger's dream, a secure, self contained community of select clientele. Uniform green lawns, flower gardens, elegant homes, happy children playing in designed playgrounds. No rowdy children running through the streets, no children soliciting on Halloween. Fine restaurants, shops, a movie theater, secured by a wall with an armed guard at the gate. On the Fourth of July an American flag will fly in every yard, and at Christmas lights will decorate every house. A school bus will pick up and deliver kids at the security gate until we have our own school."

Uniform except that Kruger's house would have its own security wall inside the security wall. "How did you get involved with Kruger?"

They had met at a convention. Kruger disliked government because it was messy with none of the quick decisions, the clear line of authority in the military where the colonel told the major, "You take care of that or I will get someone who can," and the major told the captain and the captain told the lieutenant and the lieutenant told the sergeant who took care of it. And if it didn't meet muster the sergeant misunderstood the order. Same in business.

"The Mills place fell into our laps. We need someone to train and supervise the officers. We think you're going to be sheriff but you may want to keep us in mind. No worries about voters, we'd give you a lot, help you finance your house. You belong here with us and some day you're going to want to be here, enjoy the retirement you have earned. We can be your dream but we need each other whether you're sheriff or not."

"Does this have anything to do with the Mexican you asked me to check out?" The Mexican was nothing out of the ordinary for Mexico or sometimes the US when defense contractor was the polite term for corporation on the dole and kickbacks were called campaign funding.

"We've always been straight with each other," Timberlake said. Theoretically that was true, practically, no. "Buying the land was only the first expense. Before we sell a lot we have to put in streets, power lines, water, and sanitation. We're sitting on an underground lake of pure water and enough of it for fountains, flower gardens, a swimming pool for every home, but we need money for drilling, pumping, streets, curbs, walkways. Harley, Eddie Baines, some other partners and I, own part of a savings and loan. Right now it's a black hole. We're paying 10 percent on loans and getting 6 percent on investments. We could lose everything but a few sales and we're out of the swamp."

Timberlake's smile was that of Mary when Jesus suckled her breast. "We have contracts ready to be signed, lots for Pastor Murphy, his son, and his daughter. If he signs, Dr. Baines and two lawyers from Advantage will buy lots and the pastor promises he can sell more, but one of the contracts is to the owner of TripleS X. He has a right to buy whatever he can afford but Murphy doesn't want him as a neighbor and Solid Rock is a silent partner. We want to put him and the Mexican and other incompatibles inside their own fence on separate property.

"The Mills place is the logical place for a neighborhood across the road and we will pay a fair price for what she is willing to sell. We'll provide her with water; it would cost her a fortune for a well deep enough to reach the aquifer. We'll connect her to the sanitation plant, give her a contract to clean the houses before buyers move in, hire her own crew if she wants. When the shops are ready she can have a produce shop rent free for two years. The only gardens will be flower gardens. You can explain to her what we can offer. As chief of security you can look out for her, see that she's treated fairly."

"So you need quick sales of property you don't own?"

"And a long-term loan to buy the land for cash flow."

"Why do you need me?"

"Mrs. Mills trusts you. You support us, we support you."

"And the Alamo oaks?"

"How many oaks do you need to preserve a legend? A professor says none of the oaks are as old as the Alamo, most are your age. The Mills who was lynched there? Records show he was shot elsewhere and his body left in the oaks. I wanted to let you know our plans and your place in them. We want you to have a home there when you're ready to be security chief."

Timp had not given up the dream of beginning anew and he drove away with no more worries about what he would do if he lost the election. It wasn't the office Timp minded giving up but work itself. Hanging around the courthouse like some of the old pols wasn't his future. He could hire John Banks when Larry fired him. Larry promised to give the staff a fair chance before any personnel changes but a sheriff could get deputies to leave whether they wanted to or not.

Martha would be angry if he withdrew from the race after all she had done trying to get him on the ballot but she might be agreeable when he told her about the free lot, new house and a job. The Alamo oaks were in the way of progress and if progress didn't get them then age, drought or disease would. Mills County didn't have history; all it had were legends. George Washington planted the trees or chopped one down.

When he turned into his neighborhood it looked shabbier than he had noticed before with more unpleasant changes to come and none of the openness or privacy of Alamo Acres.

He thought Martha would be at church but there was a note on the table. Two bulldozers were attacking the oaks and she and Hao were going to stop them. Bulldozers would accomplish their purpose before Hao could get an injunction to stop them. If Timberlake called the meeting to keep him from a telephone he didn't know Martha. Maybe Timp didn't either. When Martha left the note she knew she was inviting him into a trap. Stopping the bulldozer would cost him votes if he ran, chief of security if he didn't.

***

Kruger was disappointed not to be sole owner of Alamo Acres and he was in danger of losing everything but God and the law worked in mysterious ways. Because he no longer owned the land his agreement to save the oaks might not be valid his attorneys said. They also said bulldozers were cheaper than courts. He blamed Wynn's death on the badge and badger sheriff and his hotheaded deputy but he wouldn't have dared hire bulldozers if Wynn were alive. He had to pay overtime to the drivers and probably a fine because of the fuzzy valentine court but it was cheaper than waiting on the law.

He watched Hao and Martha place themselves between the bulldozers and the trees. Then a dozer sharply veered and struck a tree that shrieked as its roots tore but it didn't fall. Hao darted between the tree and the dozer before it could strike again. Timp drove his cruiser between a bulldozer and Martha. He got out and signaled the other driver to stop. Kruger was enraged. "Do you have any idea what those drivers cost?" he screamed.

"It's against the law to work on Sunday," Timp said. "If there's any more bulldozing today, they're going to jail along with whoever hired them."

"Come back at midnight," Kruger told the drivers. He got in his car and drove back to his house. He saw Martha and Hao enjoy a moment of triumph but he knew they had only temporarily stopped him. Not even Pastor Murphy preferred blue laws over profit.

***

The phone rang when Timp got home and he expected Martha but it was Timberlake. "Harley just called. We're both sorry as hell about what happened to Wynn but we have to protect our investment. It won't help anyone if we fail."

Yes it will, Timp thought. Personal tragedy, national disaster, even scandal was someone's wet dream.

"Senator Pritchard told us to look out for you and we will but stay away from the oaks."

Giving Hao food, work was something Brother Jonas' people could do. Saving the Alamo oaks, if there were any, was a battle they didn't know how to fight. Neither did he. "Are you telling me how to do my job?"

"Harley's mad but he agrees that you're the best man for security chief."

"Are you going to do that again?" he asked when Martha returned.

"Are you going to arrest me if I do?"

"I hope I won't have to."

"What can she do?" Hao was a victim of someone else's progress and she would get all the justice she could afford, perhaps one old, defeated lawyer dumpster diving outside carpeted law offices. "In twenty or thirty years it won't matter who was sheriff but it will matter that the oaks are gone," Martha said.

Asking Martha to drop the campaign was as difficult as asking her to manage it. "Chief of security," he said with enthusiasm. "A free lot and financing for a house. We could say we couldn't get enough petitions."

"I'd rather handle rattlesnakes."

"I could hire John Banks, other deputies who don't want to work for Larry, protect Hao's interests."

"You can protect Hao's interests as sheriff."

But he couldn't. He had never arrested anyone for a white collar crime.

***

Babbs learned of the bulldozers with alarm. He needed Timp on the ballot. He called Larry; Larry knew nothing about it but said Timberlake supported Timp. "Hell, Timp lets him dump construction trash at that illegal dump everyone calls Timberlake Park." Babbs wanted to call P. J. If you needed an echo that was the one you wanted but P. J. was a spigot easier to turn on than turn off. He hoped Martha would call it a dirty political trick and eligible voters would sign Timp's petitions but he had to be prepared to win them back for the general election.

***

Timp strode into the Mills County courthouse, nodded to the mayor, a JP, the DA and their supplicants, leaving silence in his wake. Without moving they seemed to close ranks. He was no longer privy to their conversations.

He checked the crime reports. Wallet stolen from shopping cart in Advantage, perp believed to be in Five Mills. Man stole his sister's gold chain and sold it to Rent All. Woman walking near downtown followed by man in car. Pregnant woman shoplifted crackers and cold cuts at the Grabbit N Grin. Ernie Klemp picked her up and took her back to the store where she paid for the items but left without them. She wanted someone from the sheriff's office to get them for her since she had paid for them. Vandalism, someone had painted "faggot" on door of house rented by two male teachers. Sudden death/natural, Mrs. Lubitsch found dead in her backyard.

Ross Fulcher walked into his office, closed the door, and leaned against it. "The judge thinks a court will be inclined to rule that Kruger can cut down any oaks that aren't 'Alamo oaks.' She could bring in experts to testify that individual oaks are 'Alamo oaks' but you're talking years and dollars."

Saving some of the oaks was like limiting pregnancy to just on one side. "Aren't there laws protecting the environment? Heritage?"

"Heritage and environment can't compete with commerce, you know that. Especially in an election year. Until you judge for breadth rather than height women will never win a pissing contest."

What belonged to everyone, the oaks, air, water, airwaves, flag, Constitution belonged to everyone only so long as everyone was willing to fight those who wanted them for their own profit.

"Does she have any recourse?"

"She could sue the county, use the money to fight for the oaks."

Timp had considered that; sue for wrongful death but not now, not during a campaign. He missed being one of the courthouse gang but he was troubled by Fulcher's suggestion. Was he being drawn into an ambush?

"That's an interesting election you're in," Fulcher said. "But a bitch in heat will wreck a dog race." Timp thought the reference was to Hao but Fulcher meant Morgan Murphy. He closed the door behind him.

Martha called to say that Hao had been to a lawyer and a judge who treated her like someone else's cute child they did not want in their lap—politely refused to understand anything she said, chuckled at how seriously she took men's business, fawned on her when she became upset, and apologized when she left. Martha brought her to the courthouse and Timp took her back to the attorney and judge and got a temporary injunction to stop the bulldozers. He was recognized as her protector and in the presence of her man they treated her like a citizen but Timp knew he would pay a price.

P. J. criticized him for stopping men at work to help out a lady friend who was on welfare and accused him of hurting the economy. "Sheriff Smith doesn't believe in private property and that's Communism."

The *Advertiser* and *The Grist* reported that stopping the bulldozers was a political stunt to grab attention. Looming over the choir on the big screen, his voice in surround sound, Pastor Murphy preached on the virtue of risk and reward as exemplified by capitalism, forgetting that no man can serve two masters. The pastor exited a side door beside his reserved parking place, hurrying to languid satisfaction after rigorous worship. Seeing Timp he scurried to his car, his short arms flapping, but Timp stepped in the open car door, a skill he had mastered. "When I asked you to help Hao were you thinking of your investment in Alamo Acres? The savings and loan?"

"I'm responsible to the Lord for what this church does with its money," Murphy sputtered. "Jesus' parable of the talents shows God wants us to make a profit and the bigger the profit, the greater is God's reward. And if God wants a church and school in Alamo Acres I intend to plant it."

"Is that all Timberlake offered you?"

"I don't need a sheriff advising me on investment," the pastor said, waving Timp out of the way. "My family is waiting for dinner."

***

When Babbs was certain that Martha had enough signatures to put Timp on the ballot he took a bite of peppermint stick and started the campaign in earnest. After Timp became a deputy, Martha and her mother sold the clothing store to Carl Emerson who went broke when the road to hell put Advantage in shopping distance. Emerson told a TV reporter that Timp had insider information about the expressway and that's why they sold the store.

P. J. reported plans for a Cinco de Mayo celebration at the university. The school was an easy target because of its athletic teams, traffic, students, taxes, and professors who said, wrote, assigned, staged, performed, or exhibited something controversial. A TV investigation discovered that some students wanted history professors to teach that the Mexican War was illegal and that the US should return the stolen land to Mexico.

That kicked up an ant bed. A caller said that an illegal alien on drugs in Five Mills was taken to the Advantage hospital at taxpayers' expense where he received better treatment than citizens could afford. "How many of those people can we support?" he asked. "Is Mills County going to pay for that?"

An Advantage businessman who was featured in the *Advertiser* said he had organized a demonstration while in Mills County High School because a beloved teacher had been fired. Sheriff Smith told him he was going home or to jail, his choice. He chose home and the demonstration ended. It hurt Timp with his core supporters but he couldn't explain that the teacher had reached retirement age but lied that she had been fired.

Pastor Murphy discovered a gay/lesbian club at the college. "Folks, your hard-earned dollars are going to limp-wristed professors who support a gay agenda at home and gay-loving Sodoms abroad," he preached.

***

When Timp's petitions were certified putting him on the ballot Martha told him they had leaped the first hurdle but he knew he had cleared it except for one toe. Stopping Kruger's bulldozers had not been reported as vigorous or decisive but as hurting the economy and few things were more sacred than the economy. P. J. reported that not a single deputy had signed his petition. Martha had wanted him to ask them but he refused.

He knew the next battle was fundraising, something he had always left to her because he felt it diminished his office. She was doing her best but the well had dried up. Farmers and ranchers had always supported him by speaking favorably of him and voting for him. The lumber yard and hardware store had put up posters in their windows. He hadn't needed anything more until Scott Baines died. Then he had to go to them, sit on the porch and convince them that he was still the man they knew and that he had shot in self-defense.

"Hell, Timp, I knew you weren't scared. I thought maybe you got tired of all that teenage nonsense and wanted to make an example."

The God sins gave to all candidates because they needed the good will of whoever won and Martha had gotten that money. The family stores had been replaced by big basket, cheap goods warehouses that had their own security, as did the junk yard partially enclosed by a metal fence that took up much of what had once been the most productive farm in the county, and the lot of worn out cars affordable to young boys and out of luck women.

This time he had to ask money from those were trying to save their way to anxious retirement and ask for volunteers when they scarcely had time and energy to tend their gardens. He went to former mom and pop store owners forced out of business by the suppliers of Christmas every day. A long time supporter wanted to help but barely had money to feed his cows. He had to listen to the reasons an elderly woman couldn't help this time before she wrote him a check. A farmer said that he held private property sacred and Timp had no right to stop bulldozers on a man's property. Timp reminded him that he wanted the sheriff to stop a neighbor who could no longer make a living with a cow and calf operation and opened a feed lot. The farmer had complained of the smell. The farmer said, "That was different. It just was."

He could do nothing for the farmer except promise that the stench would become as ordinary as propaganda, as familiar as God sin.

***

Babbs' remaining challenge was defacing Timp's image. To do that he had to change the story of the monument. It didn't glorify the platoon but Timp's egotism. Timp exploited the death of his comrades to go to Hollywood, he used their survivors' money to pay for his statue, he sided with Captain Pritchard against Second Platoon.

The monument had been controversial from the beginning. First planned to memorialize the dead of Able Company, Mills County wanted it in Five Mills. Some wanted special recognition of Second Platoon; others wanted a monument for only Second Platoon. As contention over the monument grew, so did its conceit—a life-size soldier atop the monument with tableaux of the heroes around the base, the names of those who died on the front, their story on the back—bold challenge, depraved enemy, intrepid action, chivalric deeds, determined effort to defend.

As the monument became exclusive Timpson Smith appealed for inclusion of the company. Captain Pritchard contributed, as did other members of the company, birthing rumors that it was payment for Timp covering up the cowardice of those from Advantage. When he ran for sheriff that was one of the charges against him and it was repeated until everyone lost interest. Now it was born again.

P. J. reported that Timp showed his Hollywood values trying to strong-arm him into muting his criticism. The *Advertiser* reminded readers that when Captain Pritchard ran for congress and pledged that he would get a presidential unit citation for Able Company, he received Timp's support. Nothing had come of it but the pledge brought questions of what medals other members of the platoon deserved. The new story brought letters to the editor asking if Timp said no one else deserved a medal. He replied that the medals he received were for the platoon but family survivors wanted their own medal for their hero.

The Grist reminded readers that funding for the monument stalled until Congressman Billy Pritchard gave a large contribution and that county officials withheld information about budget shortages until after a bond issue to build the monument had passed. Letters to the editor asked why the monument wasn't enough. Why did they have to have the statue? Why was it Timpson Smith's face?

***

Martha celebrated getting Timp on the ballot by taking Hao to lunch at the best restaurant in Advantage, the one Pastor Murphy patronized. Murphy had the appetite of those to whom God was in debt, his girth growing as rapidly as his congregation. A door opened and she saw him with Timberlake, Babbs, Dr. Baines, Scoop Deason, and men she didn't know. A waitress was the only female in the room. When they left Timberlake and Baines spoke but Murphy joined them with the blessed assurance that only substance could attain. "We have enough signatures," she told him.

"Congratulations," he said without surprise. "Larry thinks 'community service' might include Solid Rock and its school, washing windows, cleaning the parking lot. Will Timp do that?" he asked, dickering for his endorsement.

"I think community service is for the public," she said. "I hear you're seeing a lot of Larry. I've seen him in church with Morgan."

"Larry is helping us with a family concern. Do you know Vic Holloway? I would be disappointed if Timp associates with such people."

"Timp is sheriff. He associates with all kinds of people." Hate the sin but love the sinner until he commits the sin.

"You volunteer at the abortion mill. I suppose they repaid you."

"I donate to the women's clinic because they help women. Some of their supporters have contributed to Timp's campaign." Most supporters and all the staff were Christians. Murphy's malice was not for those who denied God or hated his church but those who heard God in a different way.

"When you don't recognize evil perhaps it's because of evil within."

"If they break the law I'm sure Timp would want to know."

He turned to Hao with a smile of a televangelist who has just received the widow's last mite. "You've been meeting with some of my church groups," he said. "I have a program for boys like your sons, Joshua's Children." Solid Rock had a program for everyone—Thorn in the Flesh AA group; Sacred Encounter for those planning weddings; Babes in the Bulrushes for preschool children; Timothy's Parents for home schoolers; Fellowship Drivers who picked up children, the ill, the elderly, and anyone else who needed transportation to church; Prayer and Fasting Businessman's Lunch at Garden of Eden, the church's food court. Joshua's Children taught boys manly attitudes with Bible drill, rock climbing wall, camp-fire prayer meetings and weekend paintball shootouts where Biblemen opposed Evildoers. The teams were changed each week because Biblemen always won.

"Please bring them sometime," Pastor Murphy said as he left. "Your boys are going to need some male mentors and there are good men who work with Joshua's Children. The district attorney, the mayor, the sheriff." They did, occasionally, usually before election. "I believe your boys know the sheriff."

Churches were not divided as much by tradition and dogma as by need. Citizens neglected by the government needed to believe they were valued by God. The connected and the desperate needed the promise of financial return for their good deeds. Those comfortable with their holdings needed to believe their clutch was blessed by God; those who feared doubt needed a church that reinforced the confidence of their youth. Young people needed a church where they could meet each other.

Solid Rock was comfortable to professioners who had no extended family or time for friends and to old-timers whose family and friends had died or moved away. If you gave Murphy your money, Solid Rock had balm for your bruise.

Some came to see Rich Lee, born-again actor who told how God had rescued him from drugs and starlets, Miss Texas who modeled her bathing suit and sang her talent song in her competition gown, an Olympic weight-lifter who quoted scriptures about God's power while lifting weights, Bryan Frazier who read Bible stories, and a former POW who escaped to tell the stories Murphy wanted Timp to tell. Others were drawn by near-professional performances by the pastor who said some claimed their ancestors were monkeys and wanted public schools teaching children that theirs were but that he had been shaped by the hands of God. His talented wife, son, and daughter spoke and sang on the wide stage with theatrical lighting, surround sound, opera seats and on the huge screen behind the choir showing close-ups of the performers. Some came to scoff and remained as members. Others brought their faith as another investment in a bond today and a guarantee tomorrow.

Martha had grown bored at the country church Timp preferred and she told him they should consider Solid Rock that was surrounded by parking lots like a moat around a castle. It was easy to be a member; Jesus' way was the American way of life.

Timp remembered when Christians weren't the rich and powerful that Jesus condemned but he hadn't enjoyed comrades since Second Platoon. He spoke to the Sons of Gideon about laws regarding carrying guns in the county. He led the Biblemen in defeating evildoers and had enjoyed playing with the kids. He talked to Ezekiel's Wheels about road safety, Solid Rock's school kids about Child Call and to Prayer and Fasting about his plans for the sheriff's department. They were grateful for anything he did for the church.

"We go with you," Hao told Martha after the pastor left. The church she attended was for burying the dead and caring for the sick and had nothing for children. Martha didn't know how to answer. John Banks said when you accepted Christ as your savior you were a new person but you were still the same color but Hao's ethnicity was not a bar. Solid Rock had black members, Brother Jonas' church did not. Pastor Murphy pointed out the enemy—the indolent, the weak, the sickly, fathers who didn't provide for their families, mothers who worked to buy finer clothes, judges who gave special rights to mothers who killed their unborn babies to continue their debauchery, aliens and perverts who corrupted children, politicians who raised taxes to give money to the undeserving, preachers who coveted his success.

She remembered a sermon in which Murphy said it was sinful pride for women to want to be part of what was not their role and wondered what role Hao would have. Would her boys be accepted at the school where students had their own roles? Boys with fast cars, girls with fashion clothes, kids from Advantage, those who would go to expensive colleges, those who would receive scholarships, those who walked to school at the bottom and athletes who were recruited to bring attention to Solid Rock at the top. There were no physically, mentally, emotionally, or financially challenged students, not even if they were members of the church.

"Brother Jonas's church has been very helpful," Martha replied.

"But you my friend," Hao said. "My boys have no friends."

***

P. J. was the snag in Martha's pantyhose, claiming that white women had abortions in order to save their figures while blacks and illegal aliens bred like germs. "Folks, in your lifetime they are going to outnumber us in parts of Texas. What some of the Beautiful People don't know is that one of the workers at the abortion clinic is a homosexual believed to have AIDs."

"You are no better than the person you listen to," Martha told women in her church clubs and asked them to call the radio station and request more music and less commentary. Those who did were told that P. J. was what the sponsors wanted. Selected listeners had their complaints heard on the air. A woman said she was afraid to walk alone in Five Mills because of perverts and illegal aliens.

Martha called the station to point out that Mills County had less rather than more crime but facts could never trump images. Martha replaced the telephone, silently thinking obscenities she rarely said aloud. She was tired of being the shrew, tired of the way reporters and editors looked at her when she complained they were not fair. She took off her night gown to dust the furniture on the way to the kitchen, dropping the gown in the clothes bin before slipping on a house dress. This was what she disliked most about campaigning—neglect of her house, of herself. She had given up shopping, baking, hair appointments, dropped out of Child Call, and hadn't seen Timp's mother in a couple of weeks. The woman could be dead for all she knew. She had given up Daughter's of Eve, Widow's Mite, Ruth's Readers for fund-raising. Still she was a step behind Babbs.

She feared losing the election more than Timp did. She had disappointed him by not agreeing to adopt. She could love an adopted child as her own but every time she looked at him holding the child she would think someone else had given him something she could not. She would not disappoint him again.

"I've never been in a mess like this," Martha told him. "We went to the party in the wrong dress. The papers have tried to be objective—"

"Objectivity was killed by the dollar," Timp said. "Remember when memory was the only objective reality?"

"That was before first grade," Martha said. "That damn disk jockey is driving the story. He wants to be heard and who has the biggest rain barrel? Every time he shouts you magnify his voice." P. J. attacked those with power. Some day it would be Larry's turn. "Every story about you gives him a bigger audience." Martha fought tears. "I have called the media until they're not even courteous any more. I've asked our friends for money until they avoid me."

At his request she asked the women in her groups their opinion of the church's investment in Alamo Acres and a savings and loan. None knew of it. She screwed up her lip in contempt of church secrets but she saw the rocks in the road. Few were surprised and their concern was the return on their dollar.

***

Nothing angered Pastor Murphy more than government intrusion in church affairs. He had been delighted to welcome the town's hero as a member but the sheriff had been unwilling to be God's voice in his office. He had asked the sheriff to tell the story of Second Platoon to his church and school but Timp said it was many stories.

"The story is bigger than the details," Murphy said. "Did Jesus feed five thousand or was in 4,991? Your message is that the platoon sacrificed themselves to save their comrades and God saved you."

"God didn't save the others." Believing God loved him more than those who died was more of a burden than the sheriff could bear.

"I can't tell everything," Murphy said. "There is only so much people can hear. They want a simple story. What we can do is tell that story."

But the sheriff didn't tell the story. He didn't even control his wife, permitting her to support abortion and stop bulldozers, to tell people of the church's investments, something she had no reason to know. The sheriff had threatened Solid Rock's school after a sleeping child was left on the school bus while everyone in town looked for it, opposed community service for the church and school, and befriended a man who sold sex films of Murphy's daughter. To recover the videos Murphy had sued Morgan's husband who testified that he had a right to photograph his wife. Not only had Murphy lost the lawsuit, the miscreant was quoted as saying Murphy didn't believe that a wife had to submit to her husband.

Every day Murphy searched the Bible for references to current events. He had read enough to know the Bible could be used to justify abortion but a woman's right to choose would give a woman authority over a man even if he were her husband or father. And if Timp couldn't set boundaries on his wife, then he was as weak as Samson no-hair.

Pastor Murphy was incensed that women, some of them mothers, modeled lingerie for men who fingered bills in their bras and panties. His wife commanded a phalanx of women who ran his errands, made his calls, visited in his name, composed the faculty, and scrubbed kids and dishes in his church and school. Women did almost everything except decision-making. But the Bible said a woman was not to have authority over a man and Pastor Murphy could not be a man of God and permit women to control reproduction.

Larry was a lost lamb that the pastor was bringing into the fold and he was grateful to Larry for destroying the films from hell but he was alarmed by Larry's interest in Morgan. He and her mother had talked to Morgan but she said she would see whomever she wished or she would move out of the house. He could hardly wait to get her safely remarried and behind the walls of Alamo Acres. If he no longer had control of his own daughter he still had power over Larry. Larry needed his endorsement and what he needed from Larry, more than community service, protection of his church and school from thieves, vandals and government interference was Larry's help in closing the abortion mill.

He met with Babbs in his favorite restaurant to present his offer. Babbs, whose family sold slaves for Yankee dollars, engaged in gun running and emerged with a fortune, believed he was as ethical as Murphy who thought the purpose of government was to control reproduction, curb the passions of women and queers, and promote churches and schools like his. He also believed he was smarter. He said he would pass information about the clinic to P. J. but Larry could not be involved.

***

The idea of a play had been a drop of fresh water on Bryan's withered faith. The mayor had said "pageant" and "maybe" but it would be a play or nothing. No pageant, no parade. If God would grant him the grace to write the play as he saw it—a message of their faith and their love for the country they left in order to save—it would be his deliverance from Egypt. His Promised Land.

He had foreseen the problem with the play. Too many characters, too many scenes and the crotch shot was the battle. That would be difficult and expensive to stage in a theater but easier and cheaper on the football field. An inspiring outdoor drama might become popular like *Texas* in Palo Duro Canyon that played every summer drawing audiences from around the world. He would play Timpson Smith and dared dream that some day it would become a film, perhaps even a Broadway play and he would ride that glory as far as God would take him.

He had not found the success he coveted in Hollywood but he had learned that a bare breast could be a godsend to ambition. A star arrested for drunken driving would steal the spotlight from thousands of children sickened by chemical waste. He needed something far enough from home plate to capture the tabloids. Wire services, radio, and TV had twenty-four hours to fill and casting grandsons to play the dead heroes was the kind of quirky story they favored. If he could portray Timp as the bravest man in Korea while Timp was accused of caving to Wynn Mills it would be like Davy Crockett surrendering at the Alamo or John Wayne turning yellow on Iwo Jima.

The sheriff didn't want to retire with handing over his pistol the last act; his supporters didn't want him to. Potential revenue would put local media on his side. He was researching the battle with his students. Science profs who worked with students on experiments received credit not only for publication or grants but for working one-on-one with students.

Perhaps educational television would film the production and his future would be as an actor, director, and producer for educational TV. Or religious TV if he could find a religious theme. How often God had used minor actors to effect his will—Joseph sold into slavery by his brothers, Rahab saving Hebrew spies, Ruth becoming ancestor to King David and Jesus Christ.

He told Morgan of his plans for an outdoor drama after church one night leaning against his car in the nearly empty lot outside her home. She thrilled as he told her of his dream for a life in educational or religious TV. She told him a woman in the church had a flame for him. "If you're interested in dating."

"I neglected my wife for what I thought was God's plan. I don't want to make that mistake again. I still think I was born to be an actor. Until I know for sure that's not God's will but my wish I can't ask a woman to be part of it."

"You're a very honest person."

"It's hard to know."

"You should talk to Dad. He knows what God wants everyone to do."

"What does God want you to do?"

"He wanted me to go back to my husband. A wife must be submissive to her husband. I told him I'd kill myself first. It was hard for him. He divorced his first wife because she wasn't submissive. Mom saw some of the . . . those things. I don't know what she told him but he said I could stay but I couldn't hide in his church. I didn't have to confess but I had to face them until they accepted it. That's why I greet everyone before the service and make the announcements."

"What do you think God's will is for you?"

"I hope it's to marry a good man but I'm afraid of making another mistake. You know?" He knew and he would give her time.

"I've never seen the films but when I stand in front of the church I know that's what people see or fancy. Can you imagine how awful that is? To never be myself but images on a film. That's the way I'll always be seen."

She was crying and he held her close. She put her arms around him kissed him and he wanted to make love to her, he believed he could but it wouldn't be right to take advantage of her vulnerability. He called her the next day and invited her to a concert in Advantage but Larry had borrowed a motorcycle and they were riding with the church's Ezekiel's Wheels to give a picnic and a sermon to the homeless in Advantage. Bryan understood how she might be curious about a man like Larry but the pastor wouldn't permit a serious relationship. He went to the church to see the pastor hoping to see Morgan but she wasn't there.

The pastor was enthusiastic when Bryan told him of the outdoor drama that would unite the town, old-timers and professioners working together, teaching the children of Mills County their legacy. They had seen the statue but they didn't know what it meant. He was writing the script while his students researched it. There would be run-throughs on the football field in the summer to organize the scenes and work townspeople into the play, rehearsals when school started in the fall, presentation in October.

"I'll do it myself if I have to, write it, direct it, play Timp. The Marine Reserves can play the North Koreans, relatives can make costumes, find props, raise money, and play the heroes." The play would put Five Mills on tourist programs, draw visitors who would eat and sleep in Advantage. Murphy pledged Solid Rock would help.

***

In war and politics you used the weapons you had. While Babbs looked for smooth stones for his David, Pastor Murphy launched a missile at Goliath.

"It wouldn't be fair to Larry," the mayor said.

158

"Exactly," the pastor replied. "It's what I've been praying for."

Clay nervously brushed his unruly mustache, the expense figures running in his head. "I'll form a committee. You'll be on it, of course. *The Grist, Advertiser* to represent the Senator. P. J. can play Timp. He'll draw a crowd and give us publicity."

While the mayor called the media, the pastor called Martha. "They're asking you to be a hero and withdraw from the race," Martha warned Timp. "For the good of the platoon. Pastor Murphy said you saved their monument and now you must save their play."

"It's a pageant," Timp said.

"It's going to be an outdoor drama to honor you and the platoon and Bryan Frazier will write and direct it to open in October. His students are researching it to make it authentic. Pastor Murphy said it wouldn't be fair to spotlight you so near the election."

If Bryan's students researched the incident the play would not glorify the platoon and retirement would not save him. Having wanted to withdraw earlier he now knew that he couldn't. "I'm not going to withdraw."

"We'll ask that the play be postponed until after the election."

"No."

"Do you want to stop the play?"

"Yes."

"Bryan wants to show their survivors what happened and put the dead to rest."

"They don't want to know what happened. They want a story that will make them feel good."

"Rocky is dead; you are alive. That's what happened. The rest is pain I don't need to resurrect. Sometimes I think I don't know you."

"You don't."

Sometimes she thought that was what bravery was—he had been too stubborn to die. "Sometimes I really think I don't know who you are."

"You don't know who I am. We don't know the truth about anyone. Not even ourselves. We don't want to know."

"But you told them. You told everyone."

***

She had waited for him; she didn't know how long because she could no longer tell day from night. Sometimes she could hardly tell sleep from wake but she struggled against that because there was so much she wanted to tell him. Timpson, her son.

She was a woman made for bearing children. She had dreamed of children at her feet while she worked, feeding them, tucking them in bed. She promised her husband lots of children but he deserted her to serve his country. And her, of course; he was fighting for her. Men always said that when they did what they wanted. She would have remarried, someone who could give her children but she was tied to Timpson and the farm.

She had contented herself with hopes of grandchildren but there had been none. Martha had been good to Timpson; she cherished her for that. It was hard to understand that Martha could not have children while she had been a human incubator and was given one. Adopting a child would have advertised an incompleteness Martha could do nothing about, being less than a whole woman. The expression came to her unbidden from her husband's talk of a whole horse as one that had not lost its male parts.

She heard him when he came in, felt his breath, his lips upon her cheek. She struggled to give some response, prayed for her tongue to tell him how much she loved him. How proud she was of him.

It took him a long time to prepare himself to speak. He told her he had to run for reelection, that he wouldn't be able to see her as much as he had hoped. She wanted to pat his hand, tell him it was okay. That's the way men were, escaping into work whenever possible. A family was like a house, something to come back to, not to live in.

His voice became quiet, grave. "I'm not who you think I am." She wanted to tell him he was her boy and that nothing he did could ever change that. Why did he trouble himself?

He talked of Korea, chaos, unbathed men, hot tarpaulin, rice paddies that smelled like shit, gardens that smelled like shit, ridges that turned legs to fire, footpaths called roads, horror.

She wondered that anyone was surprised. Wasn't it always carnage? Intrepid action, resolute devotion, indomitable spirit—words to cover the gouts of blood, strings of torn flesh. They all died that way, the enemy as well. Her husband would have been valiant to her if he had stayed home and helped her raise children.

Aid station, hospital, hospital ship. Fed to the media. "Are you our man?" they asked. A story they knew but he didn't. The story of the glory of Second Platoon. He had not realized this was another kind of combat, as earnest and deadly as an ambush.

She knew the speech by heart. "Your son-brother-father-husband died for his country. Let that comfort you." She had felt betrayed when her husband left for the Army, and him excited, glad to go. Leaving her behind with women whose sons never left the states, whose husbands were deferred because they were needed at home. Her son thought it was unpatriotic to equate his father's loss with economic loss. Women weren't supposed to think those things. She knew widows who had returned in need to their fathers' homes, widows who escaped into madness, into alcohol, into debauchery; widows who lived half-lives, struggling to save their families; widows who sought companionship at any cost.

"Death before dishonor" was a man's conceit. She would have welcomed home her husband if he had denounced his country and denied God. What greater dishonor was there than to leave a wife and children?

He thought he was saved to be a messenger but they invented their own messages. Skip died that we might be better. They clutched the stories to their breasts, retold them at the dinner table, at family reunions, Fourth of July picnics, Veterans Day parades. *The Grist* published the stories when the monument was dedicated.

She had always believed her son was different, feared that difference would put him outside her protection. The first time she saw him, not much bigger than a puppy, she knew he was special. He had the most serious expression and when he opened his eyes and looked at her, she felt a knife turn inside. He was not what they needed him to be but he posed and they pretended.

For years she had hidden in her heart that secret joy and dread that her son was special until she saw the town's need for him to be something else change him into something that was not her son, something that not even her mother's heart could touch. Her relief that it was her son who survived slowly turned to dismay as she realized what survival cost him.

He stood surrounded by broken limbs, shattered heads, burst torsos to strike a pose. "Set your jaw. Straighten your lips. Bare your teeth. Rifle in one hand the other a fist. You are the face of indomitable courage."

When she learned of the statue she went to the committee and asked them, "Give him back to me." She begged, "Let me have my son again." He was the only thing the world knew of them. They were made in his image.

Sometimes she wished that he were like everyone else, even—to her anguish—that he had died like everyone else, leaving her memory of him certain. The tiny promise she had held in her arms. The boy who clung to her and cried when his father died. The man who hugged her before boarding the train that would take him, that would take all of them to Korea and death. The memories would be intact.

Something had happened to him in Korea that neither she nor anyone else could understand. And on the other side of that gulf had emerged a man who was flesh of her flesh, bone of her bone, and as separate from her as curds and whey.

She wished he had never been celebrated. Yet, she wanted that for him too, wanted him to have everything. She brought him into the world. She gave him to the world. She could not shelter him from the world nor the world from him.

She struggled to say something and he put his ear close to her mouth.

Timp saw her lips open and close over her dry and open mouth. Did she speak? Did she know he was there? He stepped outside the room and spoke to the nurse. "Probably gas or swallowing. Sometimes her eyes flutter," the nurse said.

Timp was not convinced. Did she hear what he said? He went into the nearest restroom and in the mirror tried to imitate the movement of her lips—Be? Me?—her words as vague as those of an oracle.

As in Korea, Timp waited for rescue.

CHAPTER
EIGHT

❧

There had been a bump of excitement when Timp earned a place on the ballot but that had faded and Martha had been unable to stop Scoop Deason's cartoons of him in a battered helmet and threadbare uniform. Timp had never permitted her to champion him as the face on the statue, not wanting to campaign as a killer. Bryan Frazier was going to do it for her.

Bryan invited Morgan to the Brides and Bridegrooms of Christ banquet, but she was going with Larry. Larry was not someone Morgan could want or the pastor could find attractive as a son-in-law. When she saw Bryan in the play Larry would be forgotten.

The parade had been acceptable to the professioners as bucolic burlesque, but the pageant was more expensive, and the play extravagant. Why glorify a past that few of them even knew about? But Bryan had Pastor Murphy's pulpit and when Milk Meador said the chamber would offer financial support Bryan knew his prayers had been answered. Faith wasn't climbing a mountain but living in a monsoon with brief glimpses of the sun. Then Milk said P. J. had agreed to play Timp. Bryan was not going to be pushed aside by an ego-freak with a talent for self-promotion. Bryan envied P. J. because P. J. had a public persona and he didn't; some of his colleagues listened to P. J.'s silly comments. There would be no play unless Bryan played the lead.

"Timp is Second Platoon," Bryan assured Babbs. "If he has to quit the race to save the platoon he'll do it."

"Postpone it until after the election," recommended Babbs.

"I can't postpone it; it involves the whole department and the fall schedule has been set. If it can't be done here I'll move it to Advantage."

Some of Bryan's colleagues saw him as a publicity whore for making commercials for the local TV station, joked that he spent more money on his hair than on books in his field, but Babbs would like to have Bryan for a candidate. He recognized Bryan's capability, and it would be easy to manage someone that sincere. All Bryan needed for a political career was guidance. But Babbs didn't want Timp to withdraw from the election and if it were moved to Advantage the voters would blame Larry.

Before Babbs could conjure a way to keep him in the race, Timp declared, "The election is not about the platoon but the future of the county." It was weak but his supporters stepped up to defend him. The party threatened to withhold support for the play if Bryan did not cancel or postpone it. Bryan said the Advantage chamber would support it.

Murphy had blended piety, prosperity, and patriotism into a weapon but Babbs preferred the classroom, where the right to grade was the power to control, or the press conference, where he could slough or hold information like playing cards. Like other professors, he taught ethics in class but outside the classroom the university was a business—financial management was more important than teaching, research, athletics. Not much different from Solid Rock where it was finances, indoctrination, politics.

Babbs had fretted about the lack of controversy in the election and just when it looked promising it was over without enough politics for a post card. He could blame Timp for stopping the play but changing the meaning of the monument had worked only for Larry's base. He could make Larry a hero by withdrawing until the next election and run unopposed but that would mean no book. He could make Larry a hero by magnanimously agreeing to permit the play despite the unfairness. The grateful voters would forget by sundown. He could make Larry the hero of the play by . . . by playing the hero of the play.

Babbs gasped at his audacity. Larry would be Timp. He had made Larry young Timp; now he would transform Larry into heroic Timp. It was worth an entire chapter—the virtual hero defeating the actual hero through image projection. The idea was so outrageous that even if it didn't work it would get attention; if it worked it would be Robert Montgomery portraying Dwight Eisenhower on the screen and then beating him for president.

There were two minefields, Larry and Bryan. Babbs would have to draw Larry pictures. They would believe Larry was the hero because he would be the hero they wanted—no modest Sergeant York or baby-faced Audie Murphy. Chest beating never lost votes. Bryan would have to make Larry look good so that he looked good.

Bryan would be reluctant to give up a role he was writing for himself, but Bryan was a born-again Christian, a sucker for sacrifice. Babbs couldn't ask him to sacrifice the role to save the play; by design professors were less colleagues than rivals who competed for the favors of the administration. "Five Mills would get the play, Timp would get publicity, the platoon would be glorified, and Larry would get equal time by playing Timp," he explained to Pastor Murphy. Murphy had another and better plan to stop Timp. He agreed to persuade Bryan.

***

"You sacrificed your best chance in films to hallow God's name," Murphy said. "Now when it appears God is rewarding that sacrifice you are asked to take the Isaac of your ambition to the mountaintop and sacrifice it. God's promise that Abraham would be father of many nations was not fulfilled until Abraham surrendered his control over that promise. Perhaps as a test of faith God wants you to sacrifice control over the play."

Bryan had written a speech that was going to be the turning point of the play before the chaotic and climactic scenes as portrayed on the tableaux: Second Platoon surrounded, some wounded some dead. No one was ready to surrender but many had given up hope. Timp stood with his rifle in his hand.

"I'm just a Pfc.," Timp said, "but in this situation the only rank is courage and that means we're all equal. I don't know what you're fighting for but I'm fighting for Mom and the folks back home, Mills County folks, the best I've ever known. Some day people will know what happened here and I want them to be able to say, 'those Mills boys are as brave as any men anywhere—the Alamo, Bastogne or Iwo Jima.' If I die, today I'll stand with those immortal heroes and they'll salute me as an equal. And if I live, I'll go home to tell Mills County folks their boys took the best, the worst the enemy could give them and not a man from Mills faltered in his duty." Then he raised his fist to the enemy, striking the pose on the statue. Bryan knew he could deliver that speech and have every man present standing and cheering and every woman wiping her eyes.

"Timp carries the play. If Larry can't do it I'll have to take it back." And Morgan would see what a fool Larry was.

"Solid Rock will pay for special coaching," Pastor Murphy said.

The newspapers carried the same story as television. The play was unfair because it lionized Sheriff Smith before the election but candidate Larry Maddin believed it would be even more unfair to those who had worked so devotedly on the project to cancel it because Sheriff Smith went back on his word. Maddin agreed that despite the disadvantage to himself, the reenactment to honor the heroes of Second Platoon should proceed as planned.

The next day the big story was that Bryan Frazier, professional actor who was scheduled to play the role of Timpson Smith, had made his own sacrifice to honor Second Platoon. He had gallantly stepped aside to allow Larry Maddin to portray the heroic Smith.

***

Larry sat in his patrol car in front of the Wild Rose modeling studio although the girls didn't like it because it scared away the timid. He told Morgan he wanted voters to see him pressuring the God sins and that he liked seeing the girls arriving fresh from making beds and school lunches before putting on their professional faces. She wanted to sit in the cruiser with him and see it for herself but Babbs said no. She wanted to see where he lived but Larry said no. He wanted to get her alone but he was ashamed of how he lived.

He was tempted by Timberlake's offer of a nice house, not as prestigious as sheriff but it had advantages. Morgan had a sweet face, easy smile, graceful body, and a walk that was home cooking. He didn't know women could be like Morgan. Sweet but smart, too, smarter than he was. And better. He dreamed of what he would do to her when he got her alone, someplace other than his trailer, plow her to get her out of his head.

She asked him to pray with her before every date that they would do the right thing. It was awkward; most of his prayers had been *Please, Lord, let her be as gullible as she is gorgeous.*

When Morgan told him her father was going to make headlines a warning flashed in Larry's mind. When her father asked his schedule and suggested he wanted a friend on duty Larry called Babbs. Babbs told him to let Timp handle anything that brought headlines.

Larry was still furious at Babbs' betrayal. The play would not be canceled but he would win the election if he could convince everyone he was Timpson Smith? What kind of bullshit was that? Babbs had put a hand on his knee and squeezed. He hated it when Babbs did that. Did Babbs know he had dreamed of being a tough guy movie star? Had worked on an exit line for his death scene. "Tell folks to remember me as a man who never ran from a fight."

He wished Morgan's ex would drop by. He'd wipe the dirty pictures out of the slime bucket's head so he'd never think of her again without remembering the beating he got. He wished he had never seen the film, wished she had never known the humiliation of those acts so he could teach them to her himself.

***

After much negotiation an oversight committee was formed. Scoop Deason and Jimmy Vines would be in charge of publicity and share the advertising and *The Grist* would print posters, handbills, programs and commemorative issues. Mayor Williams would serve on the advisory committee chaired by Milk Meador and the finance committee chaired by Glen Timberlake. Pastor Murphy was in charge of a memorial service for the enactors and the family survivors.

Bryan saw it as a simple morality play. Second Platoon sacrificed itself to save others. Only Timpson Smith survived and he would tie the play together by running from one living tableau to the next carrying ammo, bandages, encouraging his comrades with the spotlights following him.

The committee, the party, the chamber, the pastor wanted their hand prints all over it. Scoop demanded a prologue by Captain Pritchard explaining how he had to save the company, Clay insisted the platoon saved the company, Bryan said he would resolve it in the script. Milk wanted none of the faltering, self-effacing speeches of Timpson Smith; Larry would proclaim his patriotism, his belief in a noble cause. Bryan agreed because if Larry couldn't have the crowd on their feet cheering, he could. As chair of the party Milk wanted P. J. as narrator because they needed him on their side. Bryan agreed that P. J. could announce the beginning of the play and introduce celebrities but he intended Timp to make the transitions from scene to scene. All demanded that Timpson Smith be statuesque.

The Grist had editorialized that MacArthur would have won the war if Truman had left him alone and Vines did not want the play to contradict that. Bryan's students had verified that Truman knew the Korean war could not be won because China would not accept an American army on its border and that MacArthur nearly engineered defeat by bringing China into the war. US and UN forces survived because they controlled the air and sea and Korea was a peninsula where Chinese troops could be contained. No one on the committee liked that but no one knew much about Korea. Bryan said the play would be limited to the action of the platoon without political references. "I should have been a lawyer," he thought.

The blacks threatened to boycott the play and appeal to the NAACP if they weren't included. The Reserve Company refused to participate because Bryan could think of no way on a football field to show how they were cut off from the platoon by a mountainside making it appear the company had watched the platoon die and had done nothing. He had started feuds between families because every family wanted their hero to be the last to die. He decided the next to the last scene would not be cluttered with wounded and dying actors, just Timp in the eye of the storm holding the enemy at bay. He could visualize the scene, it was dramatically correct and his students would make it historically correct, but he didn't know how he could do it without pyrotechnics.

The last scene, almost an epilogue, had to be the doctors and nurses, no matter how much Senator Billy protested. The women wanted to do more than raise money and sew costumes. He had included some in flashbacks as the men thought of their wives, mothers, but the women wanted an active role and he needed them to represent compassion and tenderness as he balanced courage and brutality, hope and horror. The nurses searched for living among the dead and one by one returned to say there were no living. Then they would find Timp, help him to his feet and he would strike the pose on the statue, his rifle in one hand, his other raised in a fist.

He worked every day with Larry who had an innate ability to make himself look more important than he was, a presence when he thought people liked him, a vulnerability that Bryan could use to make him appealing, but he required work if he were to avoid people laughing at his open mouth style of acting. Timp was the centerpiece of the play who had to overcome the lack of talent in the rest of the cast. If Larry couldn't, Bryan could.

"These people think high school plays are great because they know the kids in the play," Babbs said. "They're thrilled when everyone remembers their lines and no one throws up on stage. They'll love this play because it's about their families, their neighbors, because their families and neighbors are in it. They'll love Larry playing Timp."

All Bryan wanted was for the play to be good enough for subsequent productions when he would play Timp.

***

Pastor Murphy preached on a rare subject, personal sacrifice, pointing at the stained glass window of a kneeling soldier with his rifle at his side, his helmet before him, offering his deadly piety to the Lord. Beneath the window was a plaque listing the names of those who had died with Second Platoon, but it wasn't clear whether he was preaching about Larry's sacrifice for the play or Timp's sacrifice in the war.

***

There were days when Timp wished he had retired after Scott Baines. It would look like guilt but he had never been able to give Martha much and he could have given her that. Now if he quit she would see it as less of a gift than a betrayal.

Martha wanted Larry to remain a deputy so he had less time for campaigning. Timp wanted him to resign because of time he spent on the play. Larry thought Timp could hardly fire the man who saved his life but worried that he neglected campaigning. Babbs wished Timp would fire Larry so he would look vindictive. He bought a TV ad of two elderly parents whose daughter was murdered by her husband in front of her young son. The murderer was eligible for parole and the sheriff told the killer's son to testify for his father and he was given parole and now he was coming to Mills County, and the sheriff had done nothing to protect them.

One old-timer recalled memories of how clean the town used to be before those God sins on the road to hell that the sheriff did nothing about.

A professioner said she was a Christian and she wanted Christian officials who prayed in their offices, displayed the Ten Commandments, Christmas trees and manger scenes, and weren't afraid to denounce atheists, socialists, and humanists who supported crime. "We can't even pray in schools or the courthouse or other places we pay for."

The windmill bond issue raised taxes and ads quoted Timp as saying tax-complainers loved their country like a woman they could use for free but the ad that damaged most was of a small woman who said, "My daughter was kidnapped, raped, tortured, and murdered. Next year the murderer will be free and I will never see my daughter again."

Timp remembered the small, whiny man/child with bleached blond ringlets around his baby face, who was twenty-four but looked fourteen. He had been sickened with disgust but he had felt more pity than hatred. The girl's mother had asked, "Why didn't God strike him dead before he killed my child?" He had no answer for her as he had no answer for those who asked, "How could God let the whole platoon be killed by godless Communists?" He had pondered that question for a long time; the answer was unacceptable. "I've tried to correct those stories," Timp told Martha. "I've gone to the newspapers, radio, TV; they say they can't take sides in a political campaign."

"Explanations are never as memorable as accusations," Martha warned. They also didn't receive the same headlines.

"People are scared," Martha said. They were afraid of their children, afraid for their children, afraid of what their children might become, afraid the good life had escaped them. They feared changing health and career expectations; they feared a world they no longer understood. They wanted to believe that God intended them to be secure. They wanted to know if God, represented by Pastor Murphy, and the state, represented by Timpson Smith, were adversaries and which one controlled the courts, schools, commerce, government. They wanted assurance that he understood his duty was to protect those in power.

Pastor Murphy preached, "We don't want to create beggars but believers. It is because of their sin that they require charity. They are poor because of bad choices, because of drunkenness, laziness, moral relativism, and the only way to save them from misery is to give them the joy of a Christian life."

***

Everyone knew it would happen someday. Today was not a good day. Mrs. Stutz stepped into his office. "Pastor Murphy is blocking the door of the Women's Clinic." She looked at him over her glasses. Asking the pastor to leave was throwing a rock at the church; ordering the pastor to leave was taking out a stained glass window. "Larry called in sick; John Banks replaced him."

Sending John Banks to stand between angry white men who wanted to please God and white women who wanted health care would be the end of John's career and maybe his life in Mills County. Maybe the other deputies as well. This was a political statement aimed at elected officials who failed to listen to the church's directives.

"It's not an emergency," he said, and Mrs. Stutz went back to her desk.

He called Martha to warn her. "Oh, Timp," she said. "Do you have to do this?" But knew the answer. Men made things bigger than they were. It was a woman's job to make them smaller. "I'll try to think of a response."

Cameras were already on the scene and a small group from the church. He slowly got out of the cruiser, nodded to his fellow church members and crossed the parking lot where three frightened women, none of whom looked pregnant, huddled between their cars. "Jezebels," the pastor yelled at them. "God will not forgive a woman who murders her baby and a man who helps her is in mortal danger. You disgrace the name of woman. You dishonor the name of God." The men from the church took up the cause. "Whores. You'll rot in hell."

The inhumanity of man toward man was matched only by the inhumanity of religion toward women. He would have expected a deputy to do a cursory check for weapons; he didn't think he had to do that. He asked the pastor to step away from the door. "I will not permit this evil," the pastor said loud enough for the microphones to record it. "Larry Maddin has vowed that if elected he will not arrest people for their religious beliefs."

Larry had been attending the Sons of Samson Fitness Club with special dispensation, King's Men Bible Class, and Prayer and Fasting Business Lunch, where the right people got to know the right people. There was a joke that more deals were made in Prayer and Fasting than in Chamber of Commerce. "Larry might not arrest you for your religious beliefs but if he keeps his oath as a law officer he will have to arrest you for trespassing."

"God's law is greater than man's law," the pastor said, still speaking for the microphones and waving an admonishing finger for the cameras.

When the court integrated the school Timp had escorted children from Freetown past indignant citizens, some of them ministers, who believed their God-ordained way of life was threatened. "God's law before man's law," became the slogan of those who talked of reviving the Night Crawlers. Timp learned of a secret meeting and attended it.

"As long as I'm sheriff, God will enforce his laws and I will enforce man's laws," he told them.

"If you do not move from the door I will have to arrest you." The pastor's supporters moved forward and Timp turned to stop them. Murphy slipped a handcuff on Timp's wrist with the other cuff on his own.

"I arrest you in the name of God," he said beaming at the cameras.

"You can unlock the cuff and walk away or I will take you to the courthouse and file charges."

"I don't have the key," the pastor said smugly.

Timp pushed his way through Murphy's supporters with the pastor in tow. The cameras recorded the women slipping into the clinic behind them. When they got to the cruiser a man from the church produced the key and released Timp. "You have dishonored God and God will not permit you to win the election," the pastor said, then got in his car and followed by the others drove to Advantage to solemnize their triumph with a meal.

The reporters had questions. He asked them not to identify the women they saw at the clinic and to obscure their faces. "Everyone is equal before the law," he said. "That applies to the pastor the same as to me."

He returned to the courthouse where Ross Fulcher waited. "Are you trying to lose the election?" he asked.

"I'm trying to do my job."

"That's why you have deputies. Do you want me to file charges?"

Timp had been worrying that since he let the pastor drive away. "Let him puff for a couple of days. If it was a statement he's made it." All were not equal under the law. He discovered that the first time he put on a badge and arrested the mayor's son for drunken driving. Rediscovered it every time he made an arrest, every time he ran for office.

***

P. J. reported that Pastor Murphy had arrested the sheriff for not enforcing God's law. Pastor Murphy said he was disappointed that Timp hadn't stood with him. The pastor did not endorse candidates but for the first time he wished he could. Man should never put himself before God or man's laws before God's laws. P. J. quoted Timp as saying that everyone was equal before the law. "But are all laws equal?" he asked.

The TV station showed Timp leading Murphy away while women sneaked into the clinic. The *Advertiser* had a front page photograph of Timp handcuffed to Murphy over the cutline, "Who is under arrest for breaking whose laws?" There was a back page photograph of a rock star and an actress and the story of his desperate war against drugs and her valiant effort to save their embattled marriage.

An editorial in the *Advertiser* stated that Pastor Murphy had the right to express his religious opinions even at a women's clinic. Timp explained to Scoop that Murphy blocked the door. Scoop said the editorial was the position of the corporation that owned the *Advertiser*. In addition to newspapers, the corporation owned a cruise line, two recreational parks, a sports team, and clothing stores.

"What does a corporation have to do with a women's clinic?"

"The paper isn't regulated by the government but the corporation is."

"The Supreme Court declared abortion legal," Timp said.

"When was the last time the Supreme Court subsidized or wrote laws for corporations?" Scoop asked. "When women have more clout that'll change and we'll change with it."

Although he needed it, Timp had returned the money from the God sins after the media reported he had accepted it. Larry hadn't returned his. "That's old news," Scoop said with a sigh. "Everyone knows that."

Timp had walked into a trap and been unable to use it to his advantage. Martha fielded the calls. Friends from her church groups said Timp should apologize to the pastor, even some who thought the pastor should not have blocked the entrance. Anonymous callers demanded his resignation or said he was soft on criminals but arrested law-abiding citizens like the pastor. There were also supporters. Some resented the church for tearing down houses for parking lots, stopping traffic before and after church and school, blocking streets and driveways. Even some who were opposed to abortion thanked Timp for standing up to the pastor. Frightened by technology beyond comprehension, corporations beyond the law, religion beyond constraint, government beyond citizens' control, they needed to believe he feared nothing.

"They took the first round with that blocking the gates of hell stunt but the second round will be yours," Martha assured Timp. Martha had to beg citizens to sign petitions, beg them for money, beg them to vote but had faith in the play. Bryan would save them.

But Bryan could not save them from P. J. "How much longer can Mills County put up with the embarrassment of a sheriff who has gone from local hero to loco hero?" P. J. asked. "Arresting his own pastor?" He verbally sparred with a caller who said what the sheriff did was legal. "It's legal but is it sane?" P. J. asked.

Another caller said Timp had sworn to uphold man's law. "When he stopped bulldozers working on private property on Sunday was he upholding God's law or man's law?" P. J. responded.

When a caller reminded P. J. of the heroism of Sheriff Smith, P. J. replied that he may have been a hero in Korea but in Mills County he shot a teenager.

***

Scott Baines was a small, contentious kid with a left arm that ended at his elbow with three tiny fingers. Timp was shocked when he took him home to talk to his parents; they were colder than a corpse three days in the morgue, unhappy to see him, unhappy that he had taken Scott from school, unhappy that Scott was accused of stealing prescriptions. Mrs. Dr. Baines complained to the mayor. Timp had tried to befriend Scott but had killed him instead.

A power pole stood in the yard of what was once a house, now a pile of rotting lumber, scraps of clothing, the rusting ruins of a stove. A wire ran from the pole to the deserted barn with a new door and expensive lock. When Timp opened the car door he sniffed a smell he had never noted before—sour, chemical, almost astringent. The barn door was unlocked and when Timp stepped inside he saw a red glow but didn't know what it was. He knew someone was in the barn. Unlike deputies he didn't carry a flashlight on his belt.

He was so scared he could hardly breathe. In the darkness of the barn he could hear his breath, hear his heartbeat, certain that others there could also hear it. He identified himself and ordered them to step outside. A shot whipped past his head and he fell to the ground and scrambled over small canisters trying to find something he could get behind but found nothing. There was another gunshot and he tried to bury himself in the dusty ground. He heard Larry calling outside, "Timp, are you okay?" He was afraid to answer. Afraid to reveal his position. He didn't want to move. He didn't want to be in the barn alone. "Don't come in," he called, his voice shaky, his head in the dust, trying to muster courage to move. He rolled on the ground then emptied his pistol at the flash before rolling again, colliding with the wall.

He reloaded and cocked the .45, the metallic clicks loud in the silence that was worse than the shooting. The gunflashes had come from the same place. He had to know if the shooter was alone. In the close barn there was the stench he had smelled outside, the smell of gunpowder, and that other smell, the one that made him gag washed over him. Had he been shot? He could locate no pain, no wetness. He must have hit someone. Were they waiting for him to reveal himself?

He partially stood and moved to put the wall of the barn at his back, for the first time noticing the moldy smell of old grain and a gurgling. He crawled forward until he could feel a body and checked for a pulse while he groped for the weapon. When he secured it he turned the body over and yelled "Bring a light." He was relieved when Larry opened the barn door; he was no longer alone. Cautiously, holding it away from his body Larry flashed the light around the barn past old metal tables with bottles, canisters, hot plates, moving cautiously toward the lump on the ground that seemed small and shrunken. "My God," Larry said. "It's a kid." But he already knew by the light from the open door. Eddie Baines' kid.

Timp didn't understand the hot plates, the chemical bottles, chemical burns, the inhalers scattered on the ground, until the Highway Patrol arrived to conduct their own investigation. No one believed that a kid, especially a doctor's kid, could or would make drugs. No one believed his story. He was the killer hero they wanted. Nothing went right after that.

***

Martha wanted to find another church but Timp refused. "They're not going to run me out of church," he said and it wasn't only the election. He believed he could effect some change from inside the church but the church was impregnable against outside critics or reformers. He took Martha to Solid Rock Sunday Night with free pizza, soft drinks, and musical entertainment. In a few days the media storm passed and when Larry joked that he wouldn't arrest his pastor he received only embarrassed laughter and scattered applause.

Timp asked for a meeting with Murphy, and the pastor agreed. He was ushered into a conference room where the pastor and the church council waited. Clay Williams, Milk Meador, Harley Kruger, Dr. Baines. Ross Fulcher was a member of the church but saw the council as conflict of interest. Timberlake lived in a penthouse apartment overlooking the college where he walked in the evening. Except for property he held for sale and the car he leased, like his stepfather he owned nothing, not even a wife.

"I took an oath to uphold the law," Timp began.

"That's yesterday's lunch," said Pastor Murphy, who wore small gold handcuff cufflinks given to him by Dr. Baines after a sermon on man handcuffing God's laws. The meeting was interrupted by a church secretary serving shrimp cocktail. Murphy stabbed a fat shrimp and swabbed it in sauce. "What can the sheriff do for us today?"

"Whatever is legal and ethical."

Murphy finished off the shrimp cocktail with a smack and tore into his prime rib. "Christianity is under attack. America is under attack."

You couldn't be dog-catcher, teach in public school, or hold public office unless you were the right kind of Christian. America was the richest and mightiest nation in the world. What were they so afraid of? "You want to put that on a lower shelf?" Timp asked.

"The family is under attack. Pornography seduces children into homosexuality and you have done nothing to stop it." The pastor's jaws shook in righteous anger as he wolfed his lunch.

Two divorced male high school teachers shared a house in Five Mills. They couldn't afford to live alone and would be fired if they lived with a woman. They told him they liked Five Mills, liked the school but would leave if he lost the election. "There are civil rights," Timp told Murphy.

"What's civil about rights?" the pastor thundered. "There's nothing civil or right about homosexuality, bestiality, and other abominations."

What threatened families in Solid Rock was the intertwining of divorce and the economy. Timp knew Jesus had never mentioned homosexuality but did condemn divorce but he didn't want to argue Bible with the pastor. "I have to have reasonable cause to break down doors to see what adults do in private."

"My life has been threatened because I speak out against abomination and you have done nothing to protect me."

Murphy claimed he had received death threats but had destroyed the letters because they were vile, desecrating the church. What was he so afraid of? Murphy accepted his silence as guilt. "You're not going to do anything about homosexuality just as you have done nothing about abortion."

"Larry has paid for abortions."

"He knows he did wrong, he has confessed to me and God has

forgiven him. So we must forgive him too."

Timp looked at Eddie Baines. "I've done abortions," the doctor confessed. "Not any more, and only for prostitutes and girls modeling or massaging. Never college or high school girls."

"I saved him from that," the pastor said, "and he has shown his gratitude to me."

"Tell me what you want that I can do," Timp said, tired of the sparring.

"God wants a church and school for my son," Murphy said.

"In Alamo Acres."

"Plans for Alamo Acres may leave no space for a church and attendant facilities. But nearby. Across the road would be ideal. You were Wynn Mills friend, his widow trusts you. We can help each other."

"I'll ask her to donate a couple of acres for the church."

"As you know, that won't meet our needs."

"You're concerned about investments."

"Dr. Baines, chair of our finance committee, believes this is the right way to go."

"You want her to sell you land for another church, school, more houses. In addition to the church and school will they have their own stores, movie theater? Will you require more land in the future?"

"No one knows the future," Murphy said. "That's why we must plan."

"If Jesus is coming as soon as you say, wouldn't it be better for the church to worship under the oaks? Buying a new shirt could be a sign of doubt."

From the pastor's sharp intake of breath he knew he had hit bone. "There is a homosexual in your department and as a citizen I demand you do something about it." Murphy finished his key lime pie and left. The others followed without looking at Timp and a woman came in to clean up.

Timp wondered who it could be. One of the part-timers?

***

Senator Billy Pritchard asked Timp to meet him and picked him up outside the courthouse. The senator insisted on Billy just as his father had insisted on Prince. A driver took them into the countryside, Timp and the senator in the back sitting stiffly apart. There was little of the captain left. His flesh had lost tension except for his face that was scarred from fund raising and dealmaking and his eyes that had seen greater horror in politics than on the battlefield. "I knew when I enlisted I would be a hero or a coward because my father was a senator. I didn't know I would be both."

"Neither did I."

"You made corporal, right?"

"Yes sir, in the hospital." Timp deferred to Pritchard as captain more than as senator. Sarge was wrong that the captain had been a stateside Marine. "He'll be as scared as you are, sonny boy." Captain Billy had led a rifle platoon on Okinawa and collected a Purple Heart.

Timp's respect made the senator wary. "I hear they're researching the story," the senator said. "What do you think they'll find?"

"Everything." They sat in silence for a few miles, Timp scanning the countryside for anything out of place. "You did the right thing," he said.

"I did what I had to do." The senator turned his attention to a man in a pickup calling up his cows to count them. "I've always wished I could have charged down the road. Everyone in the company wanted to but I couldn't let them. Everyone of us has had one night when he wished we had all died together. I lost the platoon but I held the road."

Pritchard turned to face Timp. "What was it like waiting for us?"

"There wasn't time. Thirty seconds, three minutes?" He held out his hands unable to measure eternity.

"What are you going to do about the play?" Pritchard asked. Timp shook his head. "I can repeat what I said before, you're a hero and as long as you're a hero the platoon was heroic and the rest of us can be proud."

"Thank you, sir, but no."

***

Bryan had used the vacant football field every summer-long evening staging scenes but he was not pleased with his script. The committee had okayed it because he had included the things they wanted—the willingness of Mills County men to fight, their courage in hardship and battle, their love for their country. But there was no unifying theme and surprisingly little drama. All the men were heroes who died without questioning their destiny. He had tried to individualize them but the committee and the families opposed any breaking of ranks, any who were less heroic than others.

Frustrated, Bryan decided that Captain Billy would give orders to the platoon in the middle of the football field. The platoon would get in the trucks. The trucks would circle the stands while Pritchard marched off to command the company that was off-stage. The trucks returned to the football field for the ambush. He needed a dramatic moment when Pritchard ordered Second Platoon into the trucks. "What did he say?" he had asked Timp. "Second Platoon, mount up," Timp said.

He wanted slow motion close ups to make each man important before he died. A tableau when the lights focused on this truck and then that one, tied together by Timp going from truck to truck, scene to scene, man to man, giving them the will to fight on.

He needed at least an hour for the battle. Establish the characters in memories with their wives, girlfriends, mothers before the battle, end the first act with the explosion of the ambush, intermission, then the second act with the scenes following the initial attack in slow motion. Give the audience a chance to say goodbye to them one by one. No stage blood, but there had to be movement, action. Authentic but dramatic, like an illustration in a magazine to make the story vivid. Larry had to be the unifying force who pulled everything together.

But Bryan didn't like the Larry he saw. After walking him through every emotion, the meaning of each line, how to say each speech Larry screamed his lines, overacted his part and threw everyone out of tempo and tone. Scenes of action turned into chaos and actors ranted through scenes of introspection.

He had tried to write the battle scenes as Shakespeare might have written them if he had been writing for television with the commercials as comic relief. Every actor was bigger than life. Every death assumed heroic proportions. Bryan was in despair. How could he have thought the play could save his career? He wanted to walk away from it but he was made of sterner stuff. He feared if he took over the part Larry could gain Morgan's sympathy but not when she saw the fool Larry was on stage.

He quietly told the the actors that this was a reenactment not a deification. Everyone acted as if the platoon were suicidal. "Think how you want to say your lines. You can't yell every one of them. Think through your characterization. Some of you are more reluctant to die than others. You have a young wife, a new baby, an elderly mother."

***

His students hadn't found much news; it was a small but rare success. Most news stories echoed the first sensational report of the death of

Second Platoon, a story that was born one day and died the next except in Mills County. Military records revealed that North Korean infantry attempted to secure a road so that tanks could sweep into the rear, destroy supplies, communication and command, and drive UN forces into the sea. Able Company had blocked them; one platoon was overrun.

Before they left for summer vacation he warned them that the information was private and they were not to talk about it but he had used some of it to add human touches to the characters. Some of it because not all of it was appropriate. Sarge Lewis charged the enemy to give the others time to prepare a defense but one man wrote his brother that Sarge said if you can't get laid in Korea you can't get laid anywhere.

Sergeant Elroy Lubitsch wanted his wife to keep her job and live with his mother. They had argued about it several times but before he died he asked her to quit her job and go back to Paint Rock.

Wally Sech wanted to play his brother who, out of ammo for his BAR, had grabbed the platoon flag that Rocky had stuck in the ground before he died, and attacked the enemy with it. Bryan said Wally was too old to be convincing but he was afraid Wally would be unmanageable.

J. C. Wheat fell on a grenade to save his buddies. Fatally wounded he asked Timp to read an unopened letter from his wife. Inside was a picture of a baby. "You have a son," Timp told him. J. C. was Claiborne William's brother-in-law. The letter was returned to his sister unopened but she believed her husband knew his name lived on in Junior.

Walter Clemmons and Rick Adams were best friends until Walter got drunk, ran off the road and tore up Rick's car. He told Rick he was sorry, having to cry around the stitches in his face, but Rick had shunned him. Walter had shot the enemy at long range until they closed in and overwhelmed him. Rick ran to his rescue with his bayonet until they both fell dead side by side.

The youngest in the platoon, Joel Parsons, whose neck seemed too thin to hold up a helmet, cried of homesickness every night. Out of ammo he fought the Reds with his rifle butt. Before he died, he told Timp he had accepted Jesus as his savior and his last words were a prayer his mother had taught him.

Trent wanted to play his father Aaron Grinstaff, Jr., assistant machine gunner who was hit carrying ammo to the machine gun but Trent didn't like the way Bryan used his father. He wanted to die firing the machine gun as portrayed on the tableau. The machine gunner was black and his family couldn't afford a tableau but wanted him dying at the machine gun in the play. And Aaron Grinstaff wasn't Trent's father. Timp told Trent's mother that Aaron, her boyfriend, wanted her son to have his name.

Corporal Eldon Meador, Milk's brother, had caught his wife with a former boy friend just before the reserves were called up. As the company shipped out he yelled that he was going to divorce her. He attacked the enemy with his entrenching tool but before he died he forgave her. She never remarried.

Eddie Baines brother had been a high school football star, bigger, better liked than Eddie. His father had worked hard all his life but Clyde wanted Eddie to have his GI insurance for his education. When Eddie was in his residency neighbors tried to look after his parents who were no longer able to take care of each other and finally were moved to a state facility where they died alone on separate floors.

Private First Class Timpson Smith had been shot, had numerous shrapnel wounds and a puncture wound from a bayonet that had missed vital organs. The details gave a chance of life to the scenes that were tableaux with limited action. These were real people whose deaths had inspired their families, defined their county. For the first time Bryan felt God's spirit guiding his hand. Yet it didn't work—Timp a mythic god refusing to surrender or die.

There was also the report of an atrocity.

***

With the end of summer came the return of the students. Some worked on the play, some had moved on, one went to P. J. "Did you show this to your professor?" P. J. asked. "What did he say?"

"He said we should keep it to ourselves."

"So no one else knows?"

"Everyone on campus knows. Why did we have a war with Korea anyway? Did they attack us or something?"

P. J. called Mayor Williams. "I have to talk to the reenactment committee," he said.

P. J. called Timp. "I know what happened to Second Platoon. I'm meeting with the committee before breaking the story on the air. You can make a statement on my show or meet with the committee."

Timp declined both invitations. He thought he was relieved. Deliverance had come. His prayers had been answered. The truth was known. The dread was over. He was free. He was miserable.

He wanted to confess because he wanted forgiveness. No matter who he was, what he had done, he was one of them and needed restoration.

CHAPTER
NINE

♗

There wasn't much for P. J. to tell. "They bayoneted the dead and wounded. How did they do that if Timp was still fighting? There was no heroic last stand, no gallant sacrifice, no inhuman resolve. Timp gave them that story. He's a coward. A fraud."

When P. J. left they scuttled without moving waiting for someone to fall on the grenade. Scoop glanced at Clay and Milk who had family in Second Platoon. "I thought he was trying to demean Captain Pritchard and the boys from Advantage." Scoop paused. "I lost respect for him for telling me that."

"He told me how my brother died," Milk Meador said. "Jaw hanging by the skin, mouth and teeth gone, eyes blown out, head bulged like a hemorrhoid. I wish he hadn't told me."

"He told me," Claiborne said, brushing his mustache sprung loose by P. J.'s report. A tableau pictured his brother, Mike, charging the enemy with grenades. "I asked him not to tell my mother."

"He confessed to me," Pastor Murphy said. "A sordid, fruitless story, arms and legs and death told by those who know not the redemptive power of God that gives meaning to futility. That was not the story I wanted the church to hear."

"He did what he had to do to save the town," Timberlake said. "We don't know what would have become of Five Mills if those men had died for nothing."

Jimmy Vines looked at Scoop. "What are you going to do?"

"We've told the story of the platoon. We'll not do it again."

"What do we do about P. J.?" Meador asked.

"Hire him as PR director and his job will be to protect the story rather than to reveal it," Timberlake said.

"What do we do about the play?" Bryan asked, frustrated that everyone was ignoring the pile of dog-doo on the floor.

"Soldier on," Milk said. "They died for their country, for us. We sleep better today because of them."

"It's what everyone believes," Claiborne said.

"It would be best for the county," Jimmy Vines said.

"Present it as planned," Pastor Murphy said, nodding agreement. "It has a message that we all agree with." They examined each other and nodded.

"Before we go I think we need to thank God for this mighty country we live in and pray that God will keep us strong so that we may retain His blessing and uphold the immutable laws that God has writ for everyone, from the highest to the lowest, from the lawmakers to the law enforcers to the law keepers. God's laws, laid down from on high for every soul in Mills County. Let us pray." Pastor Murphy shaped a prayer that told God, and others on the committee, what they were to do to please him.

After legislative handshaking and back-patting the others left but Bryan lingered. Sensing his lack of faith, the pastor stayed with him. "I don't know how to write it," Bryan said. "Everything I have written is a lie."

"This town, this county, these people have tried to be worthy of Second Platoon. That has made them better people. P. J.'s story doesn't make people more patriotic, more God-fearing. Your job is to make that story inspirational."

"But it's not true."

"Your job is to make it true. Is everything you say on stage true?"

"I reveal my character's deceit and the audience is suspicious of what I say but not the meaning of the play. If I write this I'm saying this is what I mean."

"Do you mean everything you say in commercials?"

It was a question that nagged Bryan. He had made a beer commercial selling himself as a perpetually immature adventurer careless about relationships. Consume this product and become me. He had watched John Wayne pretend he was Audie Murphy. He wondered if the two ever met—an actor who pretended to be a hero and a hero who pretended to be an actor. It was clear which the public preferred. "I play a role that corporations pay me to play. I exaggerate, conceal information, lie. It's called advertising. It's capitalism, it's the system the school honors, the church honors."

"The committee will want to see the script when you complete the revision," the pastor said.

***

P. J. returned to the station and told the station manager the story he had and how he wanted to break it. The manager said no, the station would lose every advertiser and listener they had. It was risky but P. J. called corporate headquarters. It's a non-story, they said, outside the reality management was creating. P. J. had gotten too big to turn back when the Pulitzer was in sight. He told Babbs. "It's a story I can't break but you can."

Larry said they had to cancel the play. "The son of a bitch has lied to us for years."

"If he lied about the part he played he lied about the others too," Babbs said, squeezing Larry's knee. "Is that what you want to tell voters? People don't want to give up church-blessed beliefs, especially when it's unpleasant. They'd have to rethink who they are, their memories of the dead, the stories they have been told about their country, about war." He shook his head. "Nobody ever won an election by telling unpleasant truths. Play the hero, take your bows."

P. J. resigned himself to another near miss with glory but Babbs knew the problem was Bryan. How would he rewrite the play?

***

Larry couldn't play Timp if he believed Timp was a coward but he didn't. He had seen Timp face down others, including himself. Hell, Timp had faced down a mob come to desecrate the monument. He shot Scott Baines.

Larry had just gotten out of his car when a bullet came through the wall. He dropped to the ground, terrified. Timp was inside, maybe dead, and if he opened the barn door he would be a silhouette target on the shooting range. Larry crouched behind the car. There was more shooting.

"Don't come in until I'm sure it's okay, then bring a light."

"I called for backup," Larry yelled, hoping that would scare whoever was in the barn. He waited with the car between him and the barn until Timp told him to come in. "Are you sure?" he called. Larry opened the door, fell to the ground, rolled over coming up with his pistol pointed in front of him. "It's okay. Bring a light." Larry flipped on the light. "You killed a kid," he said, seeing Timp kneeling over Scott. Even with Scott dead, Larry didn't want to be in the dark barn alone. Until he shot Wynn Mills, he thought himself a coward. He remembered Timp in the barn—shaken, exhausted, turning to him for support. That was the Timp he needed to portray.

***

Timp had no appetite, had hardly slept since P. J.'s call. He waited for headlines, radio, and TV news breaks to announce his exposure. When they learned the truth they would turn on him as they had turned on Jesus after his triumphant entry into Jerusalem. Beloved one day, despised the next. He was going to the flames and he was taking Martha with him like grease on a skillet.

Why were they waiting? They had to announce that the play had been canceled. He drove to work expecting his campaign photographs to be defaced, "coward" to be spray painted on his office door. He expected with every phone call, every meeting to have some trusted friend call him "hypocrite."

Mrs. Stutz asked if he had seen the newspaper and he said, "No, but I've been expecting it." "It was right here on my desk," she said. One night a TV program was interrupted for a special bulletin. It was a severe weather warning but he had been so unnerved he left the house. Martha, thinking he was checking the sky, said, "They'll call if it's an emergency."

An irate taxpayer called because the school board had levied a fee to improve and enhance the football field and bleachers. "It's not for football; it's for that play and you're the reason they're doing the play," the man yelled before slamming down the phone. Nine dollars of wrath over a two dollar fee.

He had a recurring nightmare where he saw familiar but unrecognizable faces full of gaping mouths. He studied the glances of strangers. What knowledge did they hide behind their greetings? He watched Larry who said "Good morning, Jefe," with a wink and a smile as though they were co-conspirators. He could see a windmill rising outside his window with Wally Sech in lonely protest because it detracted from the monument.

If he withdrew now, interest in him would fade as quickly as the campaign posters. Perhaps the Alamo Acres job was still open. It was the best gift he could give Martha but would she look foolish or dishonest for centering the campaign on his heroism? If he had dropped out of the race to save the play he would be the Timp they loved. He would have saved the lie that pleased everyone, saved the platoon from ignominy, saved his friends from humiliation, saved Martha from knowing the truth about Rocky. He who had saved no one.

He and Martha could take Hao and the boys some place where no one knew them. They could be parents to Hao, grandparents to the boys. He could be himself without the badge, the pistol, the statue. Blameless. Free of impossible expectations. He was surprised at how attractive the dream was. But without the platoon, the office, the statue, who was he? Timp with no past, Timp with no roots; he didn't know who that Timp was.

Sad Sad the bitter whale, he thought remembering the stuffed whale he took to bed with him every night when he was a child, named after words from a hymn. Only later did he realize it was bitter wail.

***

Bryan sat in the stands staring at the vacant football field. He had imagined his dreams coming true in that vapid place. He was amazed at his own naiveté to think this play could have meaning bigger than the football field. The play had been a picture puzzle scattered all over his desk, all over the field with one hero killing Reds here and another killing Reds there.

He had wanted the climactic scene to be abstract—flashing lights, sounds of battle with Larry firing his rifle, confident in his Lord. Clay Williams had balked when he figured the cost of the pyrotechnics but Babbs had persuaded Dr. Baines to provide flashpots, electrical cable, control panel, safety devices, up to two people certified to operate them, with travel expenses from Dallas for three nights. That would give time for news to travel, for the media to respond.

He had written a lull in the battle, Larry frantically searching for others against the coming assault. He had written a moment between Timp and dying Rocky. Larry cradled the fallen man in his arms. Rocky said, "Give me a pistol. I have a few more shots in me." Bryan didn't like "shots"; that suggested drinking, which Rocky was said to have been fond of. It might provoke levity at a crucial moment. He had changed it to "take one more gook with me." He didn't like "gook" because it was racist but it was what Rocky would say. Freed from the compulsory tableau, he had changed "Tell Martha I died with my pistol in my hand" to "Tell Martha I died thinking of her."

Larry looked for others to form a defense but found them dead. "Dead. All of you dead. Why have you forsaken me? Leaving me alone against those who would destroy us." He liked the Free World implication and Larry would like the suggestion that Timp saved the company.

He had written a prayer scene, Larry's Gethsemane. "Lord, I have never begged before." Larry fell to his knees. "I don't ask that you spare my life when my comrades have died. I don't ask that you take away this fear and pain. I beg that you give me the strength to face what comes, the courage to die like a man, the power to save my comrades who await death on the ridge." Then flashes as Larry, shaking his fist at the enemy, disappeared in explosions, smoke, bursts of color, shafts of light.

There was a lie in the heart of the script, the biggest lie the climax of the play. The project that he had prayed for was a fraud. What did he want the play to say? That in war men died for nothing? Did Shakespeare say that? The Bible? Killing Philistines was good no matter what means were used.

He had wanted to believe that the statue represented valor that was stronger than death, that one uncompromising man could make a difference. He had sacrificed the lead role to save the play that was going to say that. He had to cancel the play or the play had to say that Second Platoon was the glorification of a lie. But didn't some art glorify lies? Cowboy and Tarzan movies? War novels? Battle panoramas? Histories?

He could cancel the play and refuse to say why. But that would enhance his reputation as one who sabotaged his chances for success and claimed it was God's will. He could tell the truth and destroy Timp, destroy the county's image of itself, destroy the memories of the dead and inflict pain on their survivors. He began a letter to the chamber, the party, and the dean. "I regret that I can no longer participate in the writing or directing of *Second to None* because doing so would require me to disclothe the truth—"

He stared at his words. He had written disclothe instead of disclose. Was that a message from God not to reveal the naked truth? He had wanted the play to be the dramatic truth. The words came unbidden. There was Timp's version, there was the military report, but there was also the dramatic truth. Did Samson catch 300 foxes? Kill a thousand with the jawbone of an ass? Were Henry V's speeches to his troops in iambic pentameter? The writers were after the dramatic truth. So was every actor who played the role.

People celebrated the death of winter, canoe races on a dry riverbed, the invention of beer. A tribute to a platoon of men who died while serving their country was truer than that.

Second To None wasn't a literal reenactment; it was a dramatic interpretation. He had to make it entertaining and with a moral regardless of the facts, like a movie version of the Alamo. The details, the characters didn't have to be exact. How many times had he taught that? They had to be credible to prove the thesis that Americans would die for freedom, that their deaths were not in vain, that one man could make a difference. Timp, a mythic god, refusing to surrender or die, that was the lie.

"Make me thy messenger," Bryan prayed, and realized that should be Timp's prayer, not that God save him but that God not leave the people of Mills County desolate. "These who died are worthy of remembrance. Many in Mills County have suffered a loss greater than they can bear. Make me your messenger that I may tell the story of the glory of Second Platoon to cover the nakedness of their grief. Let me be Second Platoon's last goodbye that Mills County will know their loved ones died like men who knew their duty to their God, to their country and to their families. Let me be the instrument of Your truth. Help me to tell their story well, to manifest their courage that others may not live in fear."

God saved Timp. That was literally true. God wanted Timp to live to tell the story. What a scene if he could write it the way he saw it. The enemy preparing a final assault, Timp alone crying, "Make me your messenger."

The play hadn't worked because he was trying to deify war and warriors. Bryan was struck with amazement; that had been God's plan from the beginning. If it had not been for P. J. he would not have discovered the truth at the heart of the play. Thank you, God, for P. J., Bryan prayed. Help me make this what you want it to be.

In addition to God, Bryan needed the senator. With the right breaks and the senator's help, Bryan could get network coverage. He might sell the script as a TV movie with him playing the lead. He would play bit parts if that's what God wanted him to do; he just wanted to be of use.

Bryan met with the committee to outline his plan for rewriting the script. "Timp realizes he can't save himself. God has to do it. He prays that God will permit him to return to Mills County as His messenger."

"That's better," Milk Meador said.

"Timp prays in a shaft of light, then pyrotechnics around him and by their light there are glimpses of Timp praying, then darkness on the stage. Curtain."

"What about the doctors and nurses?" Claiborne Williams asked.

"I cut the doctors and nurses looking for survivors."

"That'll make a lot of people unhappy," Claiborne said. Bryan nodded.

"What about the statue?" Milk Meador asked.

"I'm making Timp's prayer the climax and I've changed the name of the play to The *Message of Second Platoon*." He knew Murphy would approve.

"After his prayer, Timp could face the enemy and shake his fist," Milk persisted.

"I don't want triumph over the enemy to be the message."

"He is in God's will and whether he lives or dies is no longer up to him," Murphy said. "He will die for God and country or he will live as God's messenger for Second Platoon. I think the committee will agree to that." The others nodded. "People will want to see the statue pose."

That was the money shot. Bryan agreed to flashing lights showing Larry at prayer, explosions while the lights dimmed, Larry disappearing until all that was seen was the pyrotechnics and then Larry walking out of the smoke in Timp's statue pose as the pyrotechnics faded and the lights rose on a thundering ovation. "I'll need a supertrooper spotlight," Bryan said.

***

"How's the play coming?" John Banks asked Larry, surprised at how much time Larry spent in rehearsal. He had never been that dedicated before.

"Okay. You know they have your father throwing grenades. I thought he carried a Browning Automatic Rifle."

"Yeah, well—"

"There's a rumor about how some of those guys died. Did Timp ever tell you how your father died?"

"He told me my father died instantly but I pushed. 'A bullet to the head? Did it mess up his face? Don't people sometimes live with part of their head shot away? How do you know he didn't suffer?' 'His guts were blown out of his mouth and ass. He didn't feel anything.' I kinda wish he hadn't told me that. It's a hard picture I have to live with."

John turned back to his desk. "Ten old men met every day to pray for my father and he vomited and farted his guts. Anything else you want to tell me about the platoon?"

"I just wondered if you had heard," Larry said.

"Did Cecil tell you how his cousin died? Hanging upside down over the tires, his eyes, ears, nose, lips sliding down his skull and melting in the flames, his teeth browning through the receding gums. Lots of good stories about the platoon."

***

Timp walked into the mayor's office and was surprised to see Bryan, Clay Williams, Milk Meador, Scoop Deason, and Jimmy Vines. Conversation stopped. He apologized and backed from the room.

"Come in, Timp, sit down. We were talking about you," the mayor said. "We're going to tell you what's going to happen."

"Thank you, I'll stand," he said. Maybe they would let him resign.

"Nobody cares about Korea. We need something to get the media interested," Scoop said.

P. J. was placing ads in the Dallas and Houston papers and making public service announcements for area radio and TV stations. On his radio program he interviewed surviving family members including Trent Grinstaff, the youngest actor in the play, Timberlake's foreman, who had the role of his father. "He died firing his machine gun but Professor Fraizer ignored the tableaux," Trent said.

"We'd like you to call the senator," Clay said. "It's about him, too, and if he comes so will the media."

"I know it was only minutes," Bryan said, "but I need two hours counting the intermission to give the actors time to change into their bloody costumes and replace the trucks with papier-mâché ones that are shotup and on fire. It must have seemed hours. That's the way we want the audience to experience it with each man saying their dying words. It must have seemed like the end of the world."

What Bryan said came closer to what he felt than anything he had been able to say. It had been the end of the world he apprehended—a world with certitude, where currency implied substance and symbols were as solid as dollars. His world had changed almost as much as that of those who died.

"When the show is over I want people to believe they experienced it," Bryan said. "You have to give me some dramatic license. We want it to be true in meaning and emotional impact, like a parable."

He had braced for the purifying fire of truth, set free of the posturing, the daily misery of being inadequate for the assigned role, free of the burden of lies. He would have accepted their contempt in return for their recognition; it was war. No matter how important the cause, how heroic the effort or painful the sacrifice, the conclusion was comic book morality. People thought the tragedy of war was the corruption of commerce, politics and religion; the physical, emotional, economic ruin of soldiers and their families. The real corruption was in the mind—the belief that war could be rendered on screen, could be manifested in jingles, commercials and political slogans, could be understood vicariously, could be moralized as heroes and villains, could be honest entertainment, could ennoble, justify, sanctify anything. That it could heal or save or make whole.

"I've added a new scene," Bryan said. "It's something I invented but it's dramatically correct. Realizing that you stand alone, you turn to God, not to save you, but to give you the courage to continue."

How many times had he prayed that prayer? Not in Korea, but in Mills County. Long before P. J. discovered who he was.

"I think it's the best thing I've written," Bryan said. "I call it 'Timp's prayer.' We want to use Larry reading it to advertise the play. It won't be political but I'd like your approval."

"It's fair," Clay said. "It's your prayer but Larry's voice. He's the hero of the play but you're the hero of the platoon."

They wanted to use Larry recording his words as written by Bryan? He agreed, not in relief but defeat.

"You're going to like the way Larry makes you look," Bryan promised.

***

"What are they going to do?" the senator asked.

"Deny they know it. Everyone put it in their own ziplock bag."

"But it changed their opinion of me, of Able Company."

"No."

"Then I'm not going to draw media attention to the play."

"Your father said we each had our role to play," Timp said.

"My father was right."

***

Timp walked warily into the courthouse his bootheels expecting land mines. Those in the courthouse seemed more respectful, not as a colleague but with deference. Clay came out of his office to say hello. Fulcher stopped a conversation to speak to him. When he reached his office Scoop Deason and Jimmy Vines separately called to say that Larry's new campaign ads showed him in the statue pose, the photograph Bryan was using to advertise the play. They both rejected the ad because they thought it unfair.

Pastor Murphy preached that illegal aliens got free abortions at the Women's Clinic, that pornography was the language of Satan and the antecedent of pregnant middle school girls and high school and college girls modeling bras and panties and bathing and rubbing men for pleasure. Fathers and mothers feared for their daughters in Mills County.

Both newspapers warned readers not to expect too much of Larry. He was a lawman, he didn't know acting tricks, he was just a hero. The *Advertiser* suggested readers shouldn't expect much of the play either.

Pastor Murphy invited Timp and Larry separately to the Garden of Eden to meet with the Prayer and Fasting Businessmen's lunch that included many who were not members of the church. The Garden of Eden had plastic palms with dinosaurs, volcanoes, and men and women in animal skins painted on the walls but the waitresses wore white caps and aprons over house dresses, both marked with crosses. It was the only full service restaurant in Mills County.

Larry met with them first. Babbs advised him to talk fear, offer security, and promise God. Murphy reminded listeners that Larry pledged community service for the church and received laughter and applause when he said, "I believe most people know we're part of the community."

Larry admitted he hadn't joined a church but said he had been brought to it by the right woman and received applause for befriending a dishonored female. He talked of underage drinking, empty farmhouses, teenage promiscuity, God sins, the abortion mill, pornography—all somehow linked to a gay agenda—and promised security with modern methods of law enforcement. He pledged to do everything in his power to close the God sins and to keep gays away from children and out of the sheriff's department.

Murphy pronounced a benediction. "Lord, we thank you for this mighty country we live in and pray that You will guide us as we decide who should lead us, to keep us strong that we may uphold Your everlasting laws."

The day Timp appeared Murphy announced plans to tear down the house he and his family lived in to make space for more parking and asked others to pray that he would find the right place to live.

Timp said, "If you don't know me it's because you don't go to church here," and received friendly chuckles. "My record is my platform," he said.

"Why haven't you closed the God sins?"

"As sheriff I try to see that every citizen receives equal protection of the law." It was a pledge he had made many times. Few had seemed pleased.

"Why did God let the Communists kill a whole platoon?"

"That has nothing to do with the sheriff's office," Timp hedged. They insisted. "Questions of good and evil should be addressed to your pastor," he tried again, but they were not appeased. "I asked that for a long time and I didn't like the answer," he said. "I believe God loves all his creation. He doesn't love evil but he tries to bring good from evil. While we were trying to kill each other He was trying to redeem all of us."

They didn't like the answer either. "Why be a Christian if God doesn't love us more than He does our enemies?" "Why be good if God doesn't reward us for it?" "What good is faith if it doesn't protect us?"

"Please, I want to restrict this to the duties of a sheriff."

"If you're a Christian why do you oppose traditional values?"

"If you mean working on the Sabbath, I stopped that," Timp said. He expected a laugh but didn't get it.

"God punishes fornication with pregnancy and you let the women escape to sin again."

"I don't believe motherhood is punishment for sin," Timp said and mercifully the pastor adjourned the meeting with a prayer. Some thanked him for coming, some shook his hand, Timberlake put his arm around Timp's shoulder and walked him out of the meeting. "You did okay," he said. "You stirred them up a bit but they'll settle down to vote."

When he returned to his office he saw Larry and asked if he knew of any gays in the department. "Did someone say something about me?" Larry asked.

"Not you. Have you heard that about anyone? Maybe a part-timer?"

"Which one?"

***

P. J. had lost his heat but he was still the sand in Martha's bloomers. He told bland jokes about Timp that were repeated by listeners until the county was saturated with them. Deputy John Banks asked Timp if he could use the radio in the sheriff's car and Timp said, "Sure, what station do you listen to?" Not recognizing the sheriff, an underage boy asked Timp if he would buy him some cigarettes. The sheriff said no but gave the boy his pistol.

For balance P. J. asked, "Is Mills County's most eligible bachelor, bad boy Larry Maddin, hearing church bells?" "How much does a deputy sheriff make not counting bribes?" "Will a wedding present fix a speeding ticket?" "Is a Mills County Romeo about to get roped, baptized, and hog-tied?" "Having discovered the virtue of monogamy, does a certain political candidate in Mills County now want to protect marriage from gays?"

A calling campaign began, insinuations and innuendoes, "insinuendoes," Martha called them. They were almost worse than accusations that could be countered. Anonymous poll takers asked, "If you knew that the sheriff was going to help a foreign woman sue the county for millions of dollars would you vote for him?" "If you knew the sheriff transported underage girls to an abortion clinic?" "If you knew that the God sins that were infested with homosexuals had donated money to the sheriff's campaign?" "If you knew that gays were tolerated in the sheriff's department?" Truth in an election campaign was as rare as compassion in a money lender.

The Grist reported that two male teachers found "fag" spray-painted on their door, shrubs broken in their yard and potted plants overturned. It was repeat vandalism but the first time they reported it. An inside story asked if an actor outed by a gay group was killed by friendly fire.

***

Larry was not happy with his last scene being the prayer. He wanted to fight off the gooks until rescue and end the play with a line like, "About time you got here. Where the hell is the company?" Or, something heroic and upbeat. "Give me some ammo and I'll chase the gooks to China."

"You have to show that you hear God and understand. Peace comes and you can face the ordeal " Larry didn't need some actor to show him how to be tough. Bryan wouldn't allow him to be himself but he couldn't allow Bryan to take over the part without looking like a loser. And Bryan had the trigger.

"The play is a mistake," he told Babbs. "It's publicity for Timp."

"Nobody loved General Patton; they loved George C. Scott being General Patton." Larry had no idea what Babbs meant. "You're the hero because you're the one they'll see being the hero. They'll forget you're pretending to be Timp because Timp never said things like that."

Larry thought that was Hollywood bullshit but he wouldn't have to crawl to keep his job as deputy; he could have a sweet deal, Chief of Security, inside Alamo Acres with Morgan. Keeping undesirables out. Sometimes that sounded better than sheriff.

He thought a piece of Morgan was all he wanted but when he was with her his schemes to light her up, slip it to her were forgotten. It wasn't just the prayer but the prayers made him closer to her and he feared doing something that would make him look smaller in her eyes.

***

Martha knew it was going to be a good day. Last night Timp had needed her in a way he hadn't for a long time. Not frenzied or self-seeking but with heightened ardor. She had rarely faked orgasms but she had reached an age where she pretended aches and stiffness had disappeared and sometimes they did. Lovemaking was truer now because the physical need no longer overwhelmed the spiritual longing. For her it was more fulfilling.

It was a good day until Timp came home late and she put his dinner on the table and told him to hurry and dress for the memorial service. She wanted him in the photographs that would announce the opening of the play in the morning newspapers. She was already in her black suit; the campaign had kept her thin. He said he wasn't going; he would be out of uniform. She said he had to go, it was for him, and to wear his good suit. He said it was for the dead and he hadn't died; she said it was his platoon but he said he wasn't going to use the platoon for political purposes. It wasn't just political, it was fair; she was going with him to the reenactment. He exploded. It wasn't a reenactment; it was a play with dramatic license; it was Larry in his killer-hero pose. It was a lie.

"Honest to God, I am sick of this," she said. "Every time the platoon is mentioned we have an argument. I have to go to the play with you so I can watch Rocky be a hero. What does Rocky talk about before he dies? His faithful wife back home who jumps into bed with the first man she sees after her husband's death? While the audience snickers. I will go with you to the dramatic license and I am going to the memorial with or without you."

She knew he was preparing himself to relive the horror but why couldn't he sometimes want her for something other than his worshiper? Their arguments were absurd. Worse some of it was in front of Hao who cowered like a child. Martha had asked her to ride with them so Timp could talk to her about Solid Rock. Martha thought they treated her like a mascot and Murphy wanted her to give him land for a church.

They rode to the service in silence, Timp in the clothes he had worn all day. Outside the chainlink fence that surrounded the grandstand and football field Wally Sech stood with a flag and a sign: Second Platoon was willing, Able Company was unAble. Howard Goss stood beside him to prevent disruption.

Boy Scouts marched in from one goal line with the American flag and from the other with the Christian flag. They met in the center with the flags side by side. The mayor led the pledge of allegiance. Pastor Murphy prayed a sermon. "Lord, you have been thrown out of the school house, the courthouse, the public square, but Lord you are welcome here. And this, Lord, is where politics should be. Your people defending the American way of life, of liberty in your name to your glory over all the world. And we pray, Lord, that we will face your enemies and fight your battles without fear of man's law or man's favor."

P. J. read the names of the dead and the actors, in battle rattle, responded "Present." Bryan delivered Timp's speech welcoming the company that was intended to mollify the senator. Larry prayed Timp's prayer and there was a demonstration of the "Gawlleee" special effects to end the service. City and county officials posed for photographs with the actors. Timp refused, disappointing Martha, but she believed he would be different when the play opened the next day.

When they returned home, Timp explained to Hao that Murphy had money to buy land if she wanted to sell it. "It's for church," she said, and a school, parking lots and soon a neighborhood of those not good enough for Alamo Acres he told her. "No," she said. "I give it for God."

They watched the late news; there was nothing about the memorial service, no pictures of Larry posing as Timp, which pleased Martha. The anchor did report that a woman whose gown strap broke on national TV died of a drug overdose. Her life story was the American dream, instant celebrity, star in made for TV and blue films, her biography a paperback best seller. There was also film of Pastor Murphy blessing Dr. Baines' new home in Alamo Acres. Murphy, Baines, Timberlake were Mills County legends, poor kids who had gotten rich investing in America. The new house, sharp angles with windows of different sizes topped with roof cups, was called "an architectural wonder." "Yeah," Martha said. "You wonder why rich people want to live in ugly houses."

Interior shots revealed a cathedral ceiling, Persian rugs and Greek and Roman sculpture on a marble floor, faded paintings of Rome and Venice on the walls, an indoor terrace with fountain leading through large glass doors to an outside terrace lined with nudes to a larger fountain in the center of a swimming pool. Kruger presented Pastor Murphy with the deed to his lot and Timberlake announced plans for a new neighborhood, Country Escape."

***

Bryan felt harried as always on opening night. A thousand details, a thousand questions, and he was the fix-it man. He preferred acting, sitting in the dressing room and concentrating on his role. There were reviewers from five newspapers and a TV crew from Dallas. If the play caught the public imagination the Dallas station could feed the story to the network. Bryan had put his best work into the play. He had prayed earnestly over it. Everything he could control had to be perfect so that if the play failed it would be God's will, not his ineptness.

He inspected the props, costumes, lights. The pyrotechnicians looked professionally bored as they double-checked the switch panels and fail-safe devices. He talked to the stage manager; the cast and crew were present. People talked about stars being hard to work with but amateurs were harder. With nothing to lose they missed rehearsals because of a sick child, forgot lines, missed entrances because their concentration was on backstage gossip.

Larry had a case of jitters. "Every enemy I have will be in the front row laughing. I'm the law. I can't let people ridicule me."

"What does this place have going for it?" Bryan asked. "No college, no airport, almost no business. They have the statue. Tonight, you're going to be the incarnation of the statue. They're going to see you striking that pose with all the sounds and lights and pyrotechnics and forever after when they see that statue, they'll think, 'There's old Larry.' You're going to be great."

There were scattered catcalls at the prologue when Bryan recited Captain Pritchard's speech that as long as Timp was a hero they were all heroes. Bryan expected the razz and took the role because he could handle it. When Larry appeared as Timp the crowd stood applauding. Bryan hoped the reviewers were aware of what was happening as the audience changed from spectators to participants. It was what he had dreamed, people coming together in a giant embrace that could lift him into glory.

***

Timp and Martha slipped into their reserved seats when everyone stood to applaud Larry's entrance. Martha squeezed Timp's arm. She knew he was going to win the election. He made them proud when he won his medals and he was going to do it again. Timp didn't wear a suit unwilling to pose as a celebrity or candidate; he didn't dress casually afraid to look humble or disrespectful. He wore pressed slacks, unstarched shirt, comfortable jacket.

Lights revealed one huddled group after another and hidden microphones lifted their voices as they talked of home, girlfriends, wives, mothers. A woman beside Timp silently wept. Martha jumped when Rocky mentioned her name. People chuckled when Pretend-Rocky asked when they would see UN troops and Larry/Timp said, "When we see flush toilets." There was more laughter when the lieutenant, a high school teacher who had talked to the men like they were his students said, "This is our—"

"Main line of resistance," Larry/Timp answered.

Timp was amazed at the power clichés had, surprised that they loved him as a rustic. When Larry described Captain Pritchard as "mean as a sore-eyed dog" some applauded. Timp looked at Martha who was deep inside herself as though listening to the voice of God or feeling a child growing within. Her cheeks were wet with tears. He looked at Peggy, who sat openmouthed, rapt as though Doug had been reincarnated. He looked at Vic in his wheelchair below the bleachers. After the platoon left in trucks and reappeared the field went dark lighted only by the eruptions of special effects.

The intermission floodlights came on and Timp was besieged with handshakes, pats on the back, whispered and shouted words. "Larry does Timp better than you do," one man laughed. Timp hunched in his seat and watched the technicians place their devices around the paper trucks. "It's going well," Bryan said, suddenly beside him. "Tonight Larry discovered who he was. If they liked the first act, the final act will knock them dead."

When the audience settled into their seats, the football field went dark, to be lighted by explosions and the sparkle of gunfire. The lights came up on a blazing truck as Claiborne Williams' brother organized a defense. A spotlight followed Larry as he ran to a truck, discovered everyone dead, seized the machine gun and ran to Joel Parsons, who died saying a prayer his mother taught him, Doc Knight tended the wounded. Despite the heroics, or perhaps because of them, the play diminished the meanest, most significant moment of his life the way the statue generalized his face and made his life superfluous.

Timp searched the crowd for veterans whose eyes saw things they did not want to remember. Those whose knowledge of war came from movies seemed entranced. The young appeared eager to demonstrate their own courage and immortality as Larry ran from truck to truck, looking for survivors, cradling the dying Rocky in his arms. "Take care of Martha," Rocky said. Martha wept on Timp's shoulder.

A storm had rocked the truck, heat and noise so intense that men flailed like fish in mud. He could feel but not hear their shrieks. His throat burned from his own screams as bodies came unzipped, spilled their contents. "Martha," he heard Rocky moan as bayonets stabbed through cloth, flesh, bone searching for him, jamming the pressing but unresisting bodies against him. "Martha." Blindly his hand pushed through torn, sticky flesh, slick and mealy entrails seeking a wound that did not bleed, a mouth that bubbled breath, stopping speech, stopping death, stopping time.

He heard American voices and thought he had been saved. Rescue that had been a dream was unbearable to lose, impossible to believe. He feared he had been preserved for a moment to discover the full horror—there was no rescue. "This one's alive," they said, looking at him with open curiosity like children, their eyes sharper than bayonets. "Who are you?" they asked.

He was a man who had killed another and married his wife.

"Are you Second Platoon?"

"I'm Second Platoon," he thought. "I'm Second Platoon."

"Hypocrite," Martha hissed and Timp jumped. Larry, wrapped in bloody bandages, had emerged from the smoke and struck the pose on the statue. "I hope people see him for the phony he is. I hate a phony worse than a coward." Around them people rose, applauding, whistling, cheering, stamping their feet, the wooden stands rocked.

***

When Martha discovered Rocky had told Timp to take care of her, she burst into tears with so many emotions she could not encompass them. Bryan had written that scene because Timp told him of his love for Rocky. She cried because she had never seen that tenderness in Timp before and because she was ashamed that she had never realized how much Rocky's death had cost Timp. Hearing her name from the stage embarrassed, yet thrilled her. She felt relief that she had not enticed Timp—he had come to her because of his pledge to Rocky—and uncertainty whether he had married her because he loved her or because of that pledge. But she loved him, never more than when she saw his love for Rocky.

Bryan thought Larry's prayer a bit strident but moving. He breathed a prayer of relief that there were no technical glitches in the climactic scene as Larry emerged alone from fire and storm, one hand holding a rifle, the other a raised fist. Then the lights came up on one group at a time with the actors striking the poses on the tableaux; those not having a tableau took the pose they were given in the play. Then the lights came up on the field and they bowed to the audience, turned and bowed to Larry, then saluted him and marched off. Larry called Bryan forward. Bryan was jubilant as he took his bow. He had given the crowd what they wanted, the rest was up to God.

Bryan held up his hands until silence returned and made a short speech about the real hero, calling Timp to the stage. Those around Timp tugged him to his feet, shaking his hand, patting his back, propelling him to the stage. Without makeup, beside his triumphant image, Timp looked shrunken, washed out. Young, virile Larry beamed. Without doubt or shame he hugged Timp. "I've always admired you but I never knew how great you were until now." Timp, frozen faced, took awkward bows while the audience politely applauded. Stand up straight, Martha wanted to shout at him. Look them in the eye. Martha knew at that moment that they had lost.

Bryan motioned the audience to silence again to invite everyone to greet the cast and crew at a party on the field sponsored by the Chamber of Commerce and Dr. Edward Baines, whose brother had been in Second Platoon. Larry waved both arms in a gesture Timp recognized as the way he waved to his supporters after every election victory. "Please take your seats," Larry said and was surprised that they quietly did so.

"Morgan Murphy would you stand please," Larry asked. "Can you put a spotlight on her? Morgan, will you marry me," he asked.

A chant began, Larry, Larry, Larry. The party that began as soon as the serving tables were set up seemed an engagement party. Martha was relieved that it was over and wanted to be at Timp's side but a woman she scarcely knew turned to her like a confidante and they wept like schoolgirls.

When the blinding spotlight was off him Timp stumbled across the field dazed by incredulity. They believed what they had seen. "That Larry is something, isn't he?" they said as he pushed past them. "It was so real." "The way he took up for folks in Mills County." "I cried when he prayed that prayer." "It was like being in church." "He was the Timp I always wanted."

Martha pushed her way through the crowd toward Timp who made no effort to shake hands or speak to those who patted him on the back. Martha steadied him and kissed his cheek. "I'm sorry I never understood," she said.

Vic caught his hand. "Let me buy you a drink, hero," he said. "You just lost the election."

Martha looked a plea at Timp. Didn't he understand that he had to regain the spotlight?

CHAPTER
TEN

Timp sat on the base of the monument, Vic in his wheelchair facing him. Vic handed Timp a bottle. "Black Jack," Vic said. "That's my church."

"They always wanted Second Platoon to be a World War Two movie," Timp said. "Everyone was a hero. The stars came home to love and happiness."

"In movies you never see the faces of the enemy," Vic said. "In your dreams you never forget them. Wave after wave."

Timp handed the bottle to Vic. "MacArthur called us his fire brigade and sent us wherever the North Koreans broke through." They had barely gotten ashore when there was a breakout. "We didn't know where the hell we were or where the enemy was." Hiking, climbing ridges, digging in, waiting. Getting on trucks, climbing another ridge, waiting, hiking back to the place they had just left. Trucked to block a crossroad, waiting, hiking back.

"Like every day," Vic said.

Like every day followed by a night of bugles, whistles, machine guns, mortars, artillery, flares, the fight on another ridge. "Over here," they yelled. "Here we are. Come and get us." Corsairs came at dawn with rockets and napalm. They were ordered to another fire but there were six-bys for only one platoon and gear. Second Platoon was the first to go. The drivers had just come down the road, a jeep with a mounted machine gun in the lead; they didn't suspect anything.

"We came around a hairpin on that goat track they called a road and the gooks hit us with mines, mortars, machine guns." Six-bys overturned, warped, a mine blew the rear wheels off one and it was down on its haunches like a wounded animal. Men flopping around like fresh froglegs in a hot skillet. "I was the one on the bottom." Timp reached for the bottle and another drink. "They were trying to take the road so tanks could break into our rear."

"I remember the tanks," Vic said. "We held the road, knocked out two tanks to block it and Corsairs took care of the rest."

"You were the real heroes," Timp said.

"Yeah, well, it was a war where heroism didn't matter. No one cared."

He wasn't the only one alive; he was the only one who lived long enough to know he had been rescued. He could hear the chuffing of the burning tires, screams, groans. Then he heard them. Cheerful. Musical. They shot and bayonetted the wounded. He could hardly breathe, mouth, nose covered with blood. "Rocky called his wife's name. My wife's name. I had to stop him."

"You didn't kill him, you saved yourself, that's what you can't accept."

They cleared his mouth and nose of sticky, sweet, salty, applied pressure bandages and laid him on top of a truck until a corpsman could get to him. Flaming trucks, bodies splattered across the road, seared beef burned cheese smell of hair flesh blood, Ka-Bars scraping a melted body from truck metal, flashes that he still saw when he failed to prevent them.

He was as reluctant to believe he was safe as he was earlier to believe he would die. "Take care of this one, he's been through hell," they said, as though hell were something he had escaped.

"I didn't save anyone. I saved the statue."

***

During the Vietnam War students from the college, cynical of heroic statues, announced they were going to deface the monument to militarism. If they had done it quietly the media would have denounced vandalism, he would have filed a report and permitted experience, the sternest judge of all, to exact punishment. But they wanted a confrontation and he could not permit them to openly defile the symbol of the town's grief.

The mayor wanted to call out the Highway Patrol, the Texas Rangers. Timp said he would handle it. A show of force would have given them a legitimate target; young people are busy but they don't have plans. He had a plan. It had been a strange confrontation. He was a travesty of the dead the statue had replaced. The students in costumes of Indians, soldiers, the poor were a caricature of those they had replaced. Timp wondered that all of them had not erupted in hysteria at the absurdity. He saw the granddaughter of a Night Crawler. Grandfathers burned crosses to frighten the powerless; granddaughters effaced icons to defy the powerful. He smiled at them.

"I can't let you deface the monument but I can deface it for you," he said, taking an egg from a carton. "Who's going to arrest me? I could mark that tableau but that's Wally Sech's brother." They all knew Wally Sech. "Is Wally here?" They turned, half expecting him, his flag and placard.

"I could throw an egg at that face," he said. "It's my face." He hit the face with an egg.

They watched in silence as he passed out the cartons. Some threw eggs at the statue. A student threw an egg at Timp and others threw eggs at the student. The protest disintegrated into an egg-fight as they ran laughing back to their cars leaving him to clean up. The next day citizens reported that the statue seemed to shine in a way they had never seen before.

It was a Mills County legend that saved him after he shot Scott Baines. "We always have to defend the monuments we make," Timp said, "Even when they're lies."

"Why didn't they put it on the courthouse lawn?" Vic asked.

"Because it would be overshadowed by the courthouse."

"What are you shaking your fist at?"

"The future? Isn't that what we always resist? The truth? Why do we love the idea of hopeless resistance unto death?"

"We need to believe there's something someone will die for and that we deserve those who will do it," Vic said.

"They died for a lie," Timp said.

"We all die for a lie. Audie Murphy died in a plane crash on a business trip. Did he die for profit?" Vic asked. "I'd rather die in battle."

"We didn't fire a shot. It was slaughter. Did that help our country?"

"Right there before your eyes, Second to None. You saved the myth."

"That's not what I wanted to save."

"That's what you did save."

"I should have destroyed it, the statue, the story of the glory—"

"I'm the anti-myth. Semper fi." Vic saluted with the bottle.

***

The play ran for two more nights and after it closed special requests for "Larry's Prayer" played on the radio. *The Grist* and *Advertiser* published the prayer, and handbills with the prayer under a photograph of Larry as Timp were distributed in the schools and churches and left in mailboxes. Martha complained that Timp should get equal time but the media said it was Timp's prayer so if there was any bias it was in his favor. She and Timp had seen Hal Holbrook's Mark Twain at the college and while watching believed that Holbrook was Twain.

Bryan realized the play needed more pageantry, a band or recorded martial music, maybe the Marine reserve company marching before the play began, more flag waving. The pyrotechnics were impressive for locals but to draw visitors and reviewers he needed a new spectacle. He had hoped that Larry would look foolish but Larry had the arrogance, the bravado of a folk hero and Morgan loved it.

Larry went to the Wild Rose. "Campaign funding is over and so are these machines," he said. He had little faith in the proprietor's ethics but experience had taught him that what restrained most men was fear. "Get rid of them. This is going to be a county Timpson Smith can be proud of."

The last week of the campaign there were charges that Timp had released a child molester. Two years earlier a foreign visitor had stopped at the Grabbit N Grin and was fondling an upset child when Ernie Klemp cuffed him. He spoke no English and was quickly surrounded by his screaming, crying family. Timp took him to the jail in Advantage and called the college for a translator. The professor said that in the man's culture that's what parents did to comfort a child. Timp called Fulcher who talked to the Advantage attorney and they released him. Martha explained what had happened and why but it was too late.

The Grist endorsed Larry, the *Advertiser* ran a cartoon of a young warrior racing past an ancient Don Quixote with windmills or maybe oaks on the distant horizon. The televised morning news showed the predawn silhouette of a man resembling Larry holding a vigil at the monument. "It's election day and in Five Mills a candidate pays a solitary tribute to the men who exemplify bravery in that town, perhaps to seek the courage to face the outcome as bravely as they faced their fate." The statue was in full front silhouette so that Timpson Smith's face was not visible.

Usually on election day Timp stayed late at the office to avoid the long wait for the election returns and to greet well-wishers from the courthouse who stopped by his office. Today none did.

"Bryan Frazier wants to see you," Mrs. Stutz said.

Bryan fell into a chair. "Everything went right but nothing worked." A Dallas critic coming to review the play had been reassigned to interview a visiting movie star as to the paternity of the child she was carrying. A Houston TV station was sending a crew to film parts of the show that might be picked up by the network but a socialite killed her husband and his lover.

"If Larry wins, one of the networks wants to audition him and Babbs for a morning talk show about how they made Larry in your image."

Bryan wanted him to explain the mysterious ways of the media, the worship of gold and notoriety; usually one implied the other. Those who didn't have it envied those who did and emulated them no matter how they had gotten it. Horatio Alger was an entertainer or sold drugs, another form of entertainment. Timp had rather explain the designs of God.

"I would have been you if you had withdrawn from the race."

Maybe God had enough stars. Maybe He needed a better audience. "Maybe you should thank God that He hasn't made you special."

"You're happy being a small town sheriff because you have a statue." He made a helpless gesture. "It's so unfair that after all I did Babbs is the one—You can't earn their attention. They bestow favors like royalty."

Timp had not provided either of them any answers. Neither was happy with where he was or with the decisions that had put him there. Both hoped for one more chance. Bryan disappeared without a goodbye. Timp waited for a reason to go home. It was too early for election returns so he went to Advantage to see his mother. He nodded to Mrs. Stutz as he left. She looked wary, as though befriending him might be dangerous. Regardless of the vote, he would be in the office tomorrow.

Although she didn't know who he was or hear anything he said being with his mother put things in perspective. It had been painful seeing her body fail but as she sank into silence and stillness she seemed more tranquil, as though in transition.

He sat beside her holding her stiff, lifeless hand. "I think I've lost," he said. "I think I'll be be relieved. I've never lost an election and I've never been a winner. Once I was spared.

"When you and Martha stood side by side in the kitchen, there was a space between you that neither of you could cross. There is a space between Martha and me that I can't cross. I can't even be who I am. I thought there was an age when life was simpler." He wished he could see into the mind that had held him the way he could not return to the body that had formed him.

***

She wanted to snort. He thought she didn't understand love and loss? A woman? A mother? She had given her body to her husband, her privacy, her separateness, her person-hood until she was no longer one person but two. She had been what they needed and she had lost them both. In the loneliness of the nights of her life she had ached for their presence, the smell of them when she washed their clothes, the touch of their hand to get her attention, the sound of their voice asking her to sew a button, and she had cried bitter tears. But the memory who came to comfort her was not the husband or the son but the boy who stole her scarf when she was fifteen.

She could not remember his face or his name. He had taken her scarf because that was the way boys flirted, waving the scarf, so that the girl had to beg to get it back, maybe promise a kiss. He was too shy to show he had the scarf and she had pretended not to know. He was found the next morning, not far from her house, killed by a rattlesnake. He could have used her scarf for a tourniquet but he was coming to return it. She knew gallantry.

Timpson thought he wasn't gallant because he wasn't a hero in Korea. She had never forgiven Martha for not recognizing Timp's heroism in replacing the sons and fathers the town had lost, not recognizing Timp's gallantry in becoming her dead husband's double.

***

On election evening friends and supporters usually gathered in the backyard to listen to the returns. None had arrived when Timp got home. "Do you want to eat something?" Martha asked.

"Not now."

He lay down to sleep but was too restless. Voters were deciding the kind of people they wanted to be. He had not saved them from that. They had accepted and been entertained by the death of Wynn Mills. They had gloried in the staged death of the platoon. They watched in silence as Hao and her children tried to prevent the rape of the Alamo oaks. He had been sheriff when those things happened and had changed nothing.

Brother Jonas called to say most of his church members voted for Timp. "I didn't tell them to but they did."

Martha had rented a large TV and placed it on the patio so those sitting on chairs and blankets in the backyard could watch. The TV station focused on returns in Advantage and brief interviews at campaign scenes to suggest excitement and moment. P. J. kept a running tally between tunes and reported Mills County races. Some watched the moving pictures on TV but listened to the radio. There did not seem to be so many people this year. At first the contest was even, then Larry slowly gained a lead as votes from the suburbs came in.

Martha took more cookies outside and returned. "I think you should come out and thank people for coming. It's not over yet," she said.

The crowd in the yard cheered when he came outside but it seemed perfunctory. He walked among them, shaking hands, embarrassed by their concern for him. "The next returns will show you moving ahead." "I have a neighbor who said he was going to vote for Larry because of that prayer." He saw a few unlikely supporters but many former supporters were missing.

Peggy hugged him. She was crying. "Don't leave us, Timp," she begged.

"Take care of each other. Obey the law. If you need me, come see me." He didn't know what he could do to help her, help any of them.

"Even if you aren't in your office any more we'll still have that statue. We can look up to that and remember who we are," another said.

They wanted to believe they were better than others; that courage came with a gun and truth with a flag and that he represented both. He hadn't saved them from that. He went back into the house.

The TV station showed a jubilant crowd in front of Dr. Baines' house in Alamo Acres. Once crowds gathered on the courthouse lawn to listen to the returns on the radio. Winners came to shake hands and work their way up the steps of the courthouse to thank the crowd. Losers came to concede and fade away while the victors celebrated with their supporters. Television had changed that. The TV station had only one camera crew for Mills and it went to the predicted winner with a truck standing by if the voting changed. At the last election, he, Fulcher and the other winners had been invited to the "victory celebration" at the mayor's house.

"People here sense victory," the reporter said into the camera, asking some why they voted for Larry. "He had such character." "I voted for Timp for years but a man's got to know when he's through." "Timp's not himself any more." "We're Christians here and you have to respect that."

A gloating Babbs Morrison appeared on the screen. Yes, he was writing a book about how he won the election. He didn't say the TV network had withdrawn its invitation after his audition or that Larry still waited auditioning. "People think in images so what is the biggest image in Mills County? The statue so I made Larry in the image of the statue."

"Is that false representation?"

"Not if people believe it. In the next election, who knows? In this election, it's the truth."

Martha said that John Banks was at the front door but wouldn't come in. Timp went to the door. "Why don't you come inside?"

"You got a lot of friends here, Timp. I don't want to put myself in front of them." Timp was humbled. "It looks bad," John said, as though giving an official election report. "I'm leaving. Most of the guys are leaving. Larry has already told us we're going to do things his way."

That was his right. Still, it hurt. He had spent his life trying to build a department that met the community's needs. What would he leave behind? Trophies, symbols, symptoms. "I wish you'd stay. The county needs you."

"They need me. They need you. They want Larry."

"I'm sorry I didn't endorse you; I could have given you a chance."

"I know why you did it but you didn't give me a chance to fail. Maybe the next brother would have a better chance because I tried."

Timp watched him leave knowing John was right. It would have been hopeless but it was John's decision and he should have supported it.

Mrs. Stutz came, tears streaming down her face. "I don't want to work for Larry but I don't have a choice."

"You give Larry your best the way you've done with me," he said. Martha hugged her and she left still crying.

"It's time to congratulate Larry," he said and Martha nodded. His supporters were quiet when he reappeared. He thanked them for their support and admitted defeat.

"You've never given up in your life, Timp," one man wailed, wanting Timp to fight on until rescue came. In the front yard Vic in his wheelchair gave Timp a silent salute.

He drove to Dr. Baines' new house in Alamo Acres. Wally Sech stood vigil with tears streaming down his face and a sign, Lies, All Lies. The crowd outside the house parted for him to pass through. Most clapped or shook his hand although a few called, "Goodbye, Timp," "Look for an honest job." BeverLee Baines let him in.

In addition to eggs that seemed to have metastasized into every room the spacious house was crowded with politicians and financial backers, Timberlake, Fulcher, Williams, the Krugers, Pastor Murphy, Bryan. He congratulated Larry. "You have my support as long as you fairly uphold the law." He had intended to think of something memorable while driving to the house but had failed. The TV camera came over and Timp had to do it again.

Larry was gracious. "I'm sheriff, you're hero, we're both winners. This is good for Mills County. I want a case in the courthouse like the Mills have to display your medals, the pictures, and whatever else you will give us. I know you could sell them to a museum but they belong to the county." He wanted to recite Timp's prayer but the TV crew had to return to the station.

"Larry, I'm not a hero." He was the false messiah, the plastic Jesus, the one with the sword. He escaped to the outside terrace, Larry followed.

"That day in your office when you looked me in the eye I knew you didn't back down to Wynn Mills. You never backed down to anybody. I beat the best sheriff and bravest man this county has ever known. I'm proud to take your place and I intend to live up to your image."

"You made them uncomfortable," Babbs said. "They never wanted to be that good but you still have that heroic image and I can sell it for you."

"Alamo Acres' new Chief of Security," Timberlake announced. "We've hired Bryan to do commercials for us, very professional, very slick and we want to start with Security with the focus on you. We'll make you bigger than the statue. Come see me when you're ready and we'll talk about staff."

"Hire John Banks. He's good, he's honest and he'll do a good job."

"You're our man," Kruger said. "The kind of people who live in Alamo Acres aren't going to permit a black man to tell them what to do. Maybe in Country Escape."

"I ordered barriers around some of the oaks to preserve them," Timberlake said. "And Hao will be behind the wall and security gate

in the new development on her side of the road. Think about joining us."

"I want you to provide the security viewpoint on the talk show I'm
planning," Pastor Murphy said. "The Communist threat south of the border, the pornography and perversion threat to us as a Christian nation.
And there's a place for you at the school. Your friends who died can't
change. Their story is all that they have and it can't change either."

Timp congratulated Clay Williams and Ross Fulcher on their reelec-
tions. "I'm going to see there's a plaque on the statue with your name
and a list of your medals," Clay said, "maybe a tableau of you receiving
your medals."

"Bryan, tell Timp what we plan," Milk Meador said. "The committee has decided to do 'The Message' again next year. Bryan is going to
be you."

"P. J. thinks a community project like that will attract national attention," Bryan said. "They may want to make a movie of your life."

***

When Timp returned, his backyard was empty but he found Hao
and her boys inside with Martha. All three had been crying and the
boys were not cheered by his hug or by the cookies and milk Martha
had given them. "I vote for you," Hao said, unable to understand how
in a democracy her interests counted for nothing.

"What a nice family," Martha said when they left. "I know the media
on a first name basis. If I chained myself to one of the Alamo oaks—"

"Martha, I'm still sheriff. I don't want to have to arrest you."

Martha laughed. "You're more afraid of me than you are of Pastor
Murphy?"

"If you want to save the oaks a lot comes with head of security at
Alamo Acres so we could pick one with the most oaks—"

"Or you could be a bank guard in Advantage."

He smiled at a thought. "Maybe the children from Alamo Acres can
escape the designed playgrounds and climb the oaks in Country Escape
the way kids used to."

Timp went into the bedroom and lay down, too tired to take off his
clothes. Martha stretched out beside him. "What did Larry say?"

"He's going to put my stuff in a show case next to that of the Mills
brothers and they're going to put my name on the statue." Then who
would he be? What would he do? They'd find out together.

"You're my hero, not because of killing. I hate what that does to you, but I know you will try to do the right thing even if it's wrong for you." She sat up to look at him. "Do you think I let you down? If I had been more aggressive—"

"I'd have had to send Larry to arrest you." They shared a laugh as they hadn't done for a while. "I think you're the most loyal, hardest working campaign manager anyone every had. I was the candidate. I lost the election. I'm not sure I regret it. Maybe I'll know tomorrow."

"Do you have to be at the office early? I could bring you coffee in bed."

"Only if you come back to bed with me."

"Consider it done," she said snuggling close.

"I have been so afraid."

"I didn't know you were afraid of anything."

"I've always been afraid of losing you," he said. The door bell rang. He didn't move. It rang again. With a groan he got up.

"Don't answer it," Martha said.

"I'm still sheriff." Until Larry was sworn in, he had to answer the door and telephone, respond to emergencies and enforce the law.

An elderly man stood in the door. "I'm Aaron Grinstaff," he said. "My son, Aaron, Jr., was in your platoon in Korea."

Timp invited him into the living room. Grinstaff was in town to visit his grandson who told him about the play. "I was in a war. I know what it's like. History, art tend to make people a little taller than they were. Even the Bible. Anyway, I want to thank you for what you did for my boy. He was in trouble from the time he could walk. If he hadn't gone to Korea he would have gone to jail. But his son is real proud of him. And if he didn't say he was going to come home and marry Trent's mama I don't want to know it."

Timp nodded. Maybe the important truths were already written on the heart.

"I may not be back here again. Would tell me the story again."

Timp moved to the edge of his chair to be close to the old man. "Aaron was as brave a Marine as I ever knew. He did whatever had to be—"

"No," Aaron said, putting his hand on Timp's knee. "Tell me your story."

Timp studied the old man's eyes looking for mockery. He saw only hunger. He took a deep breath. "The explosions rocked the trucks.

I couldn't see through the dust and smoke and then I saw the Reds swarming. I couldn't hear but I could see flashes from the burp guns. I fired as quickly as accuracy allowed. Reds fell like wheat and I knew my buddies were doing the same."

"You were wounded but you went after ammo."

"I was hit but I ran to the truck that carried the gear—"

"It was on fire."

"I covered my face with my helmet. I could smell my hair singeing, but I dragged out the ammo cases before they exploded—"

"And picked up ammo and weapons—"

"I grabbed rifles, cartridge belts, bandoliers, bandages from the dead—"

"And carried them to those still firing—"

"I organized a defensive perimeter and pulled the wounded into the center."

"One by one the others fell around you."

"J. C. fell on a grenade, Rick ran to defend his buddy—"

"To give the others time, Sarge—"

Together they wove a story as immemorial as war, sweet as lies, deadly as truth, trustworthy as demons, fragile as friends, certain as desecration, common as death.

About the Author

Robert Flynn, *professor emeritus*, Trinity University, and a native of Chillicothe, Texas, is the author of twelve books. His seven novels include: *North To Yesterday*; *In the House of the Lord*; *The Sounds of Rescue, The Signs of Hope*; *Wanderer Springs*; *The Last Klick*; *The Devil's Tiger*, co-authored with the late Dan Klepper; and *Tie-Fast Country*. His dramatic adaptation of Faulkner's *As I Lay Dying* was the United States entry at the Theater of Nations in Paris in 1964 and won a Special Jury Award. Flynn is also the author of a two-part documentary, "A Cowboy Legacy" shown on ABC-TV, and a nonfiction narrative, *A Personal War in Vietnam, an oral history*.

Bob Flynn has several collections of stories and essays: *When I Was Just Your Age*; *Seasonal Rain*; *Living with the Hyenas*; and *Growing Up a Sullen Baptist*. He is co-editor with Eugene McKinney of *Paul Baker and the Integration of Abilities*.

Flynn also contributes to *The Door*: "The World's Pretty Much Only Magazine of Religious Satire." *North to Yesterday* received awards from the Texas Institute of Letters and the National Cowboy Hall of Fame, and was named one of the Best Books of the Year by *The New York Times*. *Seasonal Rain* was co-winner of the Texas Literary Festival Award. *Wanderer Springs* received a Spur Award from Western Writers of America. *Living With the Hyenas* received a Western Heritage Award from the National Cowboy Hall of Fame.

Flynn's work has been translated into German, Spanish, Dutch, Afrikaans, Malayalam, Arabic, Tamil, Hindi, Kanada, and Vietnamese. He is a member of The Texas Institute of Letters, The Writers Guild of America, Marine Corps Combat Correspondents, and P.E.N. In 1998, he received the "Distinguished Achievement Award" from the Texas Institute of Letters.

His life and work could be described as "The Search for Morals, Ethics, Religion, or at least a good story in Texas and lesser known parts of the world." Please visit Robert Flynn at his Web site: http://www.robert-flynn.net/index.html

Echoes of Glory
ISBN 978-0-87565-389-1
Paper. $19.95.

ISBN 978-0-87565-389-1

9 780875 653891   5 1 9 9 5

immortal
LOVE STORIES WITH BITE

EDITED BY

P. C. CAST

with Leah Wilson

BenBella Books, Inc.
Dallas TX

Introduction Copyright © 2008 by P. C. Cast
"Haunted Love" Copyright © 2008 by Cynthia Leitich Smith
"Amber Smoke" Copyright © 2008 by Kristin Cast
"Dead Man Stalking" Copyright © 2008 by Roxanne L. Conrad
"Table Manners" Copyright © 2008 by Tanith Lee
"Changed" Copyright © 2008 by Nancy Holder
"Blue Moon" Copyright © 2008 by Richelle Mead
"Free" Copyright © 2008 by Amy Vincent

BenBella

BenBella Books, Inc.
6440 N. Central Expressway, Suite 503
Dallas, TX 75206
www.benbellabooks.com
Send feedback to feedback@benbellabooks.com

Printed in the United States of America
10 9 8 7 6 5 4 3 2

Library of Congress Cataloging-in-Publication Data is available for this title.
ISBN 978-1933771-92-2

Proofreading by Yara Abuata and Emily Brown
Cover design by Laura Watkins
Text design and composition by PerfecType, Nashville, TN
Printed by Bang Printing

Distributed by Perseus Distribution
perseusdistribution.com

To place orders through Perseus Distribution:
Tel: 800-343-4499
Fax: 800-351-5073
E-mail: orderentry@perseusbooks.com

Significant discounts for bulk sales are available. Please contact Glenn Yeffeth at glenn@benbellabooks.com or (214) 750-3628.

Contents

Introduction

P. C. CAST

So . . . just what the hell is it with you teenagers and vampires? Huh? Okay, I have my suspicions. As with any mature, reasoning adult over the age of thirty who is also a parent, my natural inclination is to believe their allure has to do with . . . well . . . sex. I mean, come on! I'll admit to reading *Interview with a Vampire* the year it was released. I won't mention that year so as not to frighten you with my advanced age, but I will say I was sixteen the first time I read the book, and I was definitely tantalized and titillated by the overt sexuality of Anne Rice's vamps.

But while I'm taking this trip way back down Memory Lane, I find that I need to admit to more than just my age. If I'm being honest with myself, and with you, I have to add that the allure of the vampire is much more complex than simple lust. The truth is that vampire appeal goes beyond raging hormones and our baser emotions. I devoured Anne Rice's book and then went on to absorb Bram Stoker's *Dracula* and

Chelsea Quinn Yarbro's amazing Chronicles of Saint Germain not just because they were sexy—that's way too simplistic a reason. I got hooked on vampires as a teenager because I identified with them.

About now my adult readers are shaking their heads and thinking, *Cast has lost it . . . again.*

It does sound bizarre. How could a teenager in the '70s, or the 2000s for that matter, "identify" with vampires? Okay, stay with me here. When I was a teenager I understood vamps deep in my soul because, at the very core of my hormone-filled being, I believed I was immortal too. Actually, it was such an innate belief, one that went so hand-in-hand with zits and driver's ed, boy angst and prom, that it wasn't until I looked back in retrospect that I realized what really drew me to absorb all the vampire mythos I could get my hands on.

Think about it. The sensuality and allure of vampires must go beyond biting and blood. Come on! Neither of those things is particularly enticing, even when you add a hot, brooding guy or a sexy chick to the mix. But sprinkle in the ability to live practically forever and to be frozen physically in time so that you don't have to age, and you have a whole new thing. Vampires rebel against time, and they win! Teenagers get that. Because isn't rebelling against time, whether "time" is represented by wrinkles or a parent's disciplinary hand or death itself, what being a teenager is all about?

Of course it is. Or at least it mostly is.

Hopefully you're nodding and grinning and thinking, *Cast hasn't lost it. She's old, sure, but she hasn't lost it. Yet.*

Is it any wonder *Buffy* became such a phenomenon? On one hand, she personified the immediacy of being a teenager. Everything was so deliciously now with Buffy and the Scooby gang. For them, every day really might have been the end of the world. On the other hand, Buffy seemed invulnerable, even to herself, even after she'd died—twice! And who did she fall in love with? Vampires, of course. Yes, Buffy had mortal boyfriends, but she struggled with the fact that it never seemed to work with a regular guy her own age (and species). The characters of Angel and Spike were old, and admittedly, monsters, but Buffy identified and fell in love with them instead. Why? (I mean, besides the fact that they were both so *fiiiiine*.) As vampires, they symbolized everything that Buffy, as a teenager, believed would always be exclusively hers: immortal youth and the possibility of forever. And it worked! Spike and Angel hooked the audience along with Buffy, and whether we were fifteen or fifty we wanted to be with them too—to share in the allure of attainable immortality and forever love.

It's a theme I play with in my own young adult vampyre series, the House of Night, which I coauthor with my daughter, Kristin. In our books the teenage heroine, Zoey Redbird, is changing lives and worlds—moving from her human existence to enter the world of vampyres, where she will make the Change into an adult vamp, or die. During this Change Zoey struggles to maintain a relationship with her human boyfriend. In that struggle she's really saying that she isn't ready to fully embrace the magic and passion and foreverness vampyres symbolize. At the same time, she's inexorably

drawn to the allure of the vampyre, which is best represented in the characters of Erik Night and James Stark, in whom she glimpses the possibility of forever. In later HoN books, add the presence of the mystical fallen angel, Kalona—who is, indeed, literally immortal—and the teenage angst as well as allure is really cranked up. It's scary for Zoey, but it also attracts her, just as it attracts the books' readers.

I think that's something else about the vampire mythos teenagers can especially identify with—the sense of fear that goes along with the promise of forever. It's much like the bittersweet fear you feel as you contemplate leaving home for the first time. It's something you desire—something you look forward to and dream about—but there's also a frightening sense of take-this-step-and-nothing-will-ever-be-the-same about it. And yet even that fear itself is exciting, compelling. Vampires carry that same sense of excitement about them. Sure, we can all push through our hesitation and reach for immortality, but perhaps only teens are willing to truly embrace it, because you're used to the big question mark that is the future and you still believe forever can be attained—that youth can really conquer death and love can be victorious over age and apathy.

Because that's really the heart of youth, isn't it? It's the magical possibility of forever that opens before all of us as young adults. When you're a teenager you've become old enough to see the promise of adulthood, you can practically touch the allure of freedom and the mystery of imagining what is to come, but you're also still young enough to believe that you can move through that future without changing,

without losing yourself and turning into scary cloned versions of your parents.

And that's what the vampires we fall in love with struggle to do too. No matter the mythos, whether we're lost in the world of Lestat, Edward and Bella, Angel and Buffy, or even my fabulous Zoey Redbird, our immortal enchanters all strive to maintain sense of self and find lasting love over the long stretches of their lives. In these struggles they take us with them and, perhaps, the journey is more magically real for those of you who are still young.

Come with me, will you? Let's pass through the realm of immortals again. I was dazzled by the variety and richness of the stories the wonderful authors in this anthology created. It is always a pleasure to visit Rachel Caine's Morganville, and a familiar joy to be seduced by the magic of Tanith Lee's unique voice and vision. I was a proud mom, smiling at Kristin Cast's world in which vampires were created by the ancient Furies, as well as a satisfied reader. The conclusion of Claudia Gray's pre–Civil War story had me cheering. In "Haunted Love" I was pleasantly surprised by Cynthia Leitich Smith's plot twists and turns. Richelle Mead's "Blue Moon" made me breathless. Nancy Holder's post-apocalyptic vision took me on a wild, scary ride, and Rachel Vincent's vampiric siren was a cool addition to our mythos.

I invite you to join me in reading the magic within these pages. We'll be mesmerized by the allure of the vampire together, and by doing so—even if just temporarily—we'll all attain a measure of immortality.

Haunted Love

CYNTHIA LEITICH SMITH

On my way to work, I pass the worn-out white cottage where I lived as a little kid. The windows are boarded up. So is the door. I expect it'll be put up for auction. I expect it'll go cheap. Nobody's moving to Spirit, Texas.

Every year, the high school grads pack up and leave—one or two for college, the rest for jobs in bigger towns. And every other week, a crowd gathers at the funeral parlor to pay their respects to one of the old folks. Death is the most lucrative business in town.

It seems like everyone dies or leaves. But I'm not going anywhere. Spirit is home. It's the little piece of the world that makes sense to me, which, lately, is saying a lot.

"Cody!" calls a bright, female voice from behind me.

I ignore her. I've never been a talkative kind of guy.

"Cody Stryker!" exclaims the teenage daughter of the new mayor—the one who's going to turn the empty storefronts into antique shops and the abandoned houses into

1

bed-and-breakfasts and offer Spirit a future again, or so he says. "Wait," she pleads. "I need to talk to you."

I pause, turn. Did I say nobody moves here? The girl standing in front of me this evening is an exception to that rule. Last fall, Ginny Augustine and her folks arrived in Spirit after the bank foreclosed on their home in The Woodlands.

Typically, you have to live in town for at least a year before running for office, but nobody else wanted the job, so the city council passed a waiver and Mr. Augustine ran unopposed.

My glare falls to Ginny's hand on my sleeve.

She snatches it back. "I don't believe we've met before. I'm—"

"I know who you are." I begin walking again. Glancing at her sideways, I ask, "What do you want?"

I feel a faint flash of guilt when she blinks, startled.

"Well," Ginny begins again, "someone's cranky. Here's the deal: I'm going to handle ticket sales for you. Cool, huh?" When I don't reply, she adds, "You know, at the theater. Movies? Tickets?"

For the first time in more than fifty years, the Old Love Theater will open tonight at 8 P.M. After Uncle Dean's death, I sold off a third of his cattle, his antique gun, and his fishing boat to make the down payment. None of it was worth much, but neither is the Old Love.

It's reassuring to have somewhere to be on a night-to-night basis, though, to have another purpose beyond satisfying my thirst. To have something else to think about besides the night I faced down my uncle for the last time.

I keep going, trying to ignore how Ginny falls in step by my side.

At sixteen, she's girl-next-door pretty, medium height and curvy. Her teeth are even and pearly white. Long, honey-blonde hair frames her friendly face. What with the powder blue baby T that reads *sassy* in rhinestones and her faded denim cutoffs, Ginny looks like she was born and bred in Spirit, like a real small-town girl.

When we reach the theater, she persists in following me around back.

Ginny leans against the door, coy, as I fish my keys out of my jeans pocket.

"Big night," she observes. "You nervous?"

"No," I lie, unlocking the deadbolt. Once inside, I add, "And I'm not hiring."

"Really?" Ginny asks, shoving a sandal-clad foot in the doorway. "You mean you're going to run the projector, pop the corn, restock the concession stand, ring up food and drinks, vacuum the carpet, change the toilet paper, and do . . . whatever managers do—paperwork and bills—all by your-self? Think about it, cowboy. How do you plan to sell tickets and handle concessions at the same time?"

On one hand, I don't want to encourage her. On the other, I don't need any trouble from her leaving pissed off. I don't need trouble—period. I wish she would just take off. "I'm not opening the concession stand."

"Well, there go your profits! You're charging—what?—three bucks a show? I know people around here are cheap, but do you have any idea what, say, electricity alone is

going to cost? It's summer. It's Texas. Think: air conditioning."

Honestly, I hadn't considered that. It's not like I have an MBA or anything. I just graduated from high school a couple of weeks ago. I used to mow lawns in the summer, but this will be my first real job off the ranch. I may have been overambitious.

"Plus," Ginny goes on, "insurance, taxes, and you might want to advertise the place as a tourist attraction. The founders of Spirit were key players in the early days of the Republic, and historical tourism is becoming—"

"Enough." She's a politician's daughter, all right. Opening the door wider, knowing I'll regret it, I say, "Come in. We'll talk."

Ginny quiets as I lead her through the service hallway. It *is* hot in here. Muggy.

I wonder what, if anything, she knows about the building's tragic history, its lingering reputation. A teenage girl—Sonia Mitchell—was found dead in a storage closet in 1959. Another girl, Katherine something-or-other—Vogel maybe—went missing for good. She was new in town, like Ginny, and her body was never found. Both girls worked at the theater. And again, like Ginny, both girls were sixteen.

Everyone hereabouts has heard the story. Partiers have busted in over the years, too, and every now and then a whole pack would run out hollering about a ghost.

There's no denying that the theater has an eerie quality to it. Over the past week, I've seen the letter "S" written in the dust and wiped it away again and again. Once or twice, I

could've sworn I heard a soft voice coming from somewhere in the building. Enticing, musical, feminine . . . I'm starting to hear it in my dreams.

As Ginny and I enter the lobby, I don't give her the satisfaction of cranking the air conditioner immediately.

Instead, I take in my new business, trying to see it the way tonight's customers will. It's a grand old place with a huge antique crystal chandelier, built when cotton was king. Granted, the gold and crimson wallpaper is faded, and the blood-red carpet is worn. So are the red upholstered seats in the screening room—both on the main floor and up in the balconies. But there's still a romance to the place, a whisper of the past.

Besides, my mom loved it. Every time we passed by, she'd say the Old Love was a ghost of the glory days of Spirit, a reminder of who we'd been and could become again.

"Do you know how to run a register?" I ask Ginny, gesturing.

She's already playing with it. I only have one, set at the ticket counter. It's an older model that I ordered off eBay.

"Hmm," Ginny says, scanning the lobby before brightening. "I know! We can lay out candy and popcorn on the counter, post prices, and provide a box with a slot in it so that people can pay on the honor system. Like at the library for folks with fines on overdue books."

That wouldn't work in most places. In Spirit, it'll do fine.

"There are some boxes in my office," I say, impressed despite myself. After a pause, I add, "Why do you want this job anyway?"

Ginny shrugs. "I could use the money."

That makes two of us. The thing about living forever, I suddenly need a long-term financial plan. And, I realize, so far as Ginny is concerned, there aren't any other jobs within walking distance. I bet she used to have a flashy car. I bet it was repossessed.

I can't help wondering if there's more to her being here than that. Not to be conceited, but I'm fairly good-looking. I've got Mom's blue eyes, and they stand out against my deep brown skin, slick black hair, and the sharp features I inherited from whoever was my dad. I'm wiry but solid enough from working on Uncle Dean's ranch.

Outside Spirit, girls are always flirting, not that I know what to say back.

The locals, on the other hand, they pity me. When my mom died, everyone said what a shame it was for me to be orphaned at only ten. They saw my bruises in the years that followed. And they knew what Uncle Dean was like.

For a long time, I thought sooner or later somebody would report him to social services—a preacher, a teacher, the school nurse—but it never happened.

I guess most folks were as scared of Uncle Dean as I was.

Ginny is looking at me with an oddly knowing smile, and I realize she's waiting for my decision. I can't help thinking she may be useful. I can't help wondering if she has a boyfriend. But spending quality time around that flesh-and-blood girl is intrinsically problematic. The flesh is a problem. The blood is a problem. At any given moment, it's a toss-up which is worse. "Okay," I say. "You're hired."

The chandelier rattles, distracting us both.

"Drafty," Ginny says, glancing around. "But where's it coming from?"

She asks too many questions. "I turned on the air conditioner."

It's a lie.

⌒

After a ridiculous amount of negotiation, I agree to ten cents above minimum wage, send Ginny home to change into a white button-down shirt, black slacks, and black shoes, and tell her to come back in a couple of hours.

Unlocking the door to my cramped office, I'm less than thrilled to realize that I may need to hire a second person. Someone local. Quiet.

Within the next few years, I need to sew up an understanding with the good people of Spirit. They may not know what I am, but they'll figure it out over time. On the off chance that Ginny's daddy's "revitalization" plan works, I'll be here for generations. I need to reassure them that my presence is no more threatening than the fact that Edwina Labarge collects snow globes or that Betty Mueller talks to her dead husband or that Miss Josefina and Miss Abigail have been "roommates" for more than thirty years.

I'll need front people, I realize, so that the customers who drive in from nearby towns don't notice that the "young" owner never seems to age.

Inside the office, I hit the ceiling-fan light, and begin sift-
ing through the old newspapers and boxes, looking for one
that will do for the concession stand.

The headline of a yellowed copy of *The Spirit Sentinel*
from June 13, 1959, catches my eye. It reads "City Mourns
Daughter; New Girl Missing."

I lift it, studying the black and white picture—Sonia's
dimple and laughing eyes. I trace the hairline around her
lovely face. Sixteen forever.

I never want to be the kind of monster that destroys
innocence like that.

Reaching into my small half-fridge, I grab a bottle of
blood, pour a quarter of it into a Texas A&M mug, and pop
that into the microwave on the shelf.

Seconds later, I close my eyes, savoring the taste, pushing back the disgust.

I've been this way for only a few weeks.

It's funny. I used to roll my eyes at all those media stories about the trouble kids get into on the Internet. How every
generation of grown-ups assumes that whatever's new—from
flapper dresses to rock-and-roll to the World Wide Web—is
automatically a sign of the apocalypse. My theory was that par-
enthood triggered amnesia followed by paranoia, though I had
to admit it would've been nice to have someone who cared.

Not long after Uncle Dean cracked one of my ribs, I
heard at school that there was this guy in Athens, Georgia,
selling a "power elixir" on the 'net. I figured it was some kind
of steroid cocktail. Probably risky, but it's not like my life
was all that safe to begin with. Anyway, the guy supposedly

supplied a vat of the stuff to the Varsity football team in El Paso that took state last year.

It was so easy. I "borrowed" Uncle Dean's MasterCard and put in my order. The vial arrived overnight in a box packed with dry ice.

I remember thinking as I unscrewed the cap, *What the hell?*

Nothing could've been more appropriate.

Blinking back the memory, I reach for the bottle to pour myself more blood.

Someone has used a finger to write something in the condensation on the glass. It looks like the letter "S." It wasn't there a moment ago. She's getting bolder, making a bigger play for my attention. It's flattering, I admit. "Sonia?"

⌒⌐

"What do you think?" Ginny asks, straightening the newly poured paper cups on the concession stand counter.

"Not bad." I have to give her credit. In Ginny's make-do theater uniform, complete with ponytail, she looks like the picture of all-American wholesomeness. She also had her mom swing by Wal-Mart (two towns north) and they picked up ice, several two-liter plastic bottles of coke (diet, regular, Dr Pepper, Sprite), and several discounted packages of candy bars. It's quite the display of enthusiasm, of *spirit*, you might say.

She grins and grabs a black marker to write out prices and instructions for paying on the honor system. Ginny

brought the marker and poster board with her too. I set the box from my office on the counter before she got back. It's already been wrapped in bright gold paper, another Wal-Mart purchase.

My gaze lands on the skin over her jugular. Luckily for Ginny, I'm able to buy fresh-shipped "provisions" from the same site that sold me the original dose.

The night I buried my uncle's body behind the barn, I received an e-mail from the vendor, telling me I qualified for "special customer status" and giving me a code to log in for future purchases. What I found was a series of pages within the site that included a long question-and-answer docu-ment about our kind, information on how to mix various blood-wine blends, and from there, an online dating service ("Love That Lasts") extended to all registered members at no additional fee. I admit to clicking through it, despite every-thing amused by the ads for growing your fangs and shrink-ing your thighs and finding your "eternal consort." I have *no* intention of going there.

I may be an easy mark, helping to finance some other fiend's long-term retirement. But I got what I wanted. Now I can defend myself against anyone.

I just had no idea that the price would be so high.

I just had no idea that the price would be so high.

Looking out the theater window onto Main Street, I'm pleased to see a line has already formed—a handful of teen-agers and a county deputy with his wife.

This week, I'm showing *Phantom of the Opera*. I've scheduled *The Haunting* with Vincent Price, *Ghostbusters*, and *Ghost* for the three weeks after that.

I'm taking advantage of the place's spooky rep. I hope Sonia doesn't mind. More and more, whenever I fix a loose board or vacuum the carpet or add Crème Caramel potpourri to the ladies' room, I can't help wondering if Sonia approves. I can't help feeling like I'm trying to impress her.

School has been out for a couple of weeks now. The newness of summer has already worn off. Football players and cheerleaders are in double practices, but they're done by sundown and eager to blow off steam. I should be able to pack in the locals and folks from nearby towns, if only because there's nothing better to do.

"Three minutes," I announce, noticing that the line outside is longer now. Much of it is curiosity, I'm sure. But I can build on that.

"That long?" Ginny exclaims, propping up the sign. "The ice will melt."

"The ice will be all right. You're . . . you're doing fine."

I can stand the sunlight, though it seems to weaken me. Just like Ginny's bright smile. She half skips toward the ticket counter and then, with a "Whoa," goes flailing. Without thinking, I pour on the supernatural speed in time to stop her fall.

Ginny steadies herself with a hand on my shoulder. "Where did *you* come from?"

During life, I didn't have friends my age, not in-person friends anyway, just some people I'd chat with on the Internet.

It never occurred to me that I'd feel pulled toward someone now. I know better than to care. I ask anyway. "Are you okay?"

"I guess." She straightens. "I could've sworn I tripped over something."

We both glance down at the smooth red carpet.

Ginny's doing a bang-up job at the register. She's all "yes'm" and "yes sir" with the grown-ups, amicable with the teens, and a charming reassurance that, despite the "haunted" theater and its murderous history, the ghost-movie theme is tongue-in-cheek. We're all just having fun here.

Meanwhile, I'm serving up another row of cokes. It's great. With the honor pay system, I don't really have to interact with the costumers.

At least not until the deputy shoves a couple of rolled-up dollars into the box and says, "Young Mr. Stryker, isn't it?"

"Yes, sir." I keep my voice level. I've never been in trouble with the law. In fact, I'm known as decent enough—as someone who's had a hard life, but who's respectable, graduated with honors. "Welcome to the Old Love, deputy."

"How's your uncle doin'?" he asks, grabbing a coke and a box of Milk Duds and a package of red licorice. "Some boys at Hank's Roadhouse were askin' about him."

I knew that, sooner or later, the questions would come. It hurts to be reminded that Uncle Dean had buddies, that there was a better side to him, one I only glimpsed on the rare holiday or when he'd score a big buck.

I swallow the lump in my throat, make a show of glancing both ways, and meet the deputy's eyes dead on. Lowering my voice, I amp my drawl to match his. "Between you and me?"

The answering nod is sharp.

"I'm thinkin' he finally pissed off the wrong man. Hightailed it to Matamoros before the guy came after him. Didn't even say goodbye."

The deputy takes that in. "Good riddance," he mutters as he starts to walk off. Then after handing the coke to his wife, he turns back toward me, and adds, "I'm glad to see you makin' something out of yourself. Your mama was a fine woman."

For a while, I pour more drinks and offer a "hey" or "howdy" now and then as customers make their selections and pay. But it's not long before I notice the ruckus at the ticket counter.

"Ben, please," Ginny says, her voice rising, "I've got customers."

Ben Mueller was a year behind me in high school. His older brother plays football for Baylor, his mom teaches at the elementary school, and his dad owns a used car dealership on the highway. His granddaddy, Derek Mueller, died two years ago of a heart attack after serving as sheriff for four decades. Ben himself is popular, a solid all-around athlete, and church-going. I only know him by reputation, but he smirks a lot and looks like one of those fungible blond guys on the CW.

"Problem, Ginny?" I ask, approaching.

Ben laughs, and the sound is angry, bitter. "Are you a freak too?"

Behind him, Tricia, the lady who owns the beauty shop, is whispering with her best friend, Martie. They're the unofficial news hotline. If the Old Love becomes known as a place for "wild young hooligans," it's all over. I've got to deal with this fast and without making a bigger scene.

"Ben, please," Ginny says again. "You have to pay or leave."

"Fine," Ben replies. "But just know that I'm—"

I grab his arm, and I can tell he's surprised by the strength of my grip. I stare him in the eye, realizing I'm a couple of inches taller. According to the FAQ on my blood dealer's site, some of us have the power to enthrall the traumatized or weak-willed. It's worth a try. Keeping my voice steady, I say, "You're going to take off now."

"I'm going to take off now," Ben repeats and pivots on his boot heel to stroll out the front door.

I'm surprised that it worked. Again, I don't know Ben well, but I'd never tag him as weak, and as for trauma, anyone could tell he's led a charmed life.

"My hero!" Ginny exclaims, and there's real appreciation in her voice. Then she beams at the two ladies next in line. "May I help y'all?"

After the last customer settles in, I get *Phantom of the Opera* running from up in the projector room. Then I hear Ginny call my name. She sounds shocked, terrified.

I half fly downstairs and burst through the swinging door into the ladies' room where she's pointing at *GET OUT*, written on the mirror in plum-colored lipstick.

It wasn't there before we opened. I didn't notice anyone walking into the room before the movie started. From the look on her face, I'm pretty sure Ginny didn't do it, but the color of the lettering matches her lips. She grabs the tube from the counter.

"It's mine," she confirms. "It was in my purse."

I'd stashed the purse in my office for her when Ginny returned this evening.

It must have been Sonia. I didn't know she could do that, move objects. In any case, it's starting to look like she wants to keep the place to herself. I don't understand. We're still getting to know each other, but it was going so well.

"A dumb joke," I say to reassure Ginny. "Let's get it cleaned up."

Ginny opens the small storage cabinet to grab a spray bottle of glass cleaner and a roll of paper towels. "What did you do to Ben?" she asks in a measured voice, and I realize how sloppy I've been.

If I want to stay above suspicion, I'm going to have to learn to deal with people—especially run-of-the-mill troublemakers—without using my powers. No more enthralling. For that matter, no more super speed.

I answer the question with a question. "What's going on between *you* and Ben?"

Ginny begins spraying the glass. "Can I trust you?"

It's a bigger question than she realizes. I'm not sure I know the answer. "You can talk to me," I say. "Ask anyone. I'm no gossip." That's true enough.

She goes to peek out the bathroom door to ensure no one is listening. "Well—"

"Wait. Let's go to my office. It has a lock on it. No one can just walk in."

"But what about . . . ?" she gestures to the mirror.

I shrug. "We'll say it was the ghost."

"Ghost?" Ginny asks.

On our way, I fill her in on the history, characterizing the haunting as local folklore. From Ginny's severe expression, I figure she either finds the idea of ghosts offensive or blasphemous or, at the moment, she's invested in a more corporeal issue.

I let us in, take the desk chair, and wait, trying not to let my impatience show. We can't stay in here long with the door closed. She's still a minor after all.

There's something about her, though, some strange connection between us. I've said more words to Ginny today than I probably have to anyone in the last year.

Ginny crosses her arms. "I don't know the people of Spirit that well yet, nowhere nearly as well as they know each other. I didn't know about Ben."

I lean forward to clear newspapers off a crate for her to sit on. "What about him?"

She takes a seat. "I . . . We went to prom together. Ben got a motel room on the highway afterward. I thought it meant one thing. He thought it meant, um—"

"I understand," I say. A lot of guys have expectations about prom. I can't help wondering how badly Ben took "no" for an answer. The fact that he was still hassling Ginny tonight suggests it was an ugly scene.

"I had to crawl out the bathroom window," she adds.

It could've been worse. "You want me to walk you home tonight?"

"Yes," Ginny pauses, standing again. "No. I'm fine. It's just . . . I never meant for things to turn out this way. I never thought going on one lousy date would—"

"Haunt you forever?" I ask.

She visibly shivers. "How did you know?"

My uncle's face flits across my memory. "Call it a hunch."

Once the last happy customer leaves, Ginny skips across the lobby with a large black trash bag. "Let's get this over with and go celebrate!" With that, she flashes that sunshine grin and disappears into the screening room.

Celebrate? I'm going to have to sit her down and explain that we're employee and employer, that we can't ever be anything more. Except . . . she could use a friend right now. "Hang on," I say. "Let me help you."

I grab a bag, and then it dawns on me that I should probably hit the restrooms first. So, I head down the hall, my steps

slowing when I hear the mysterious voice again. "Sonia?" Is that *her* singing? "Sonia!"

I let the plastic bag slip from my fingers onto the red carpet and begin walking faster in the direction of the sound. It's louder, clearer with each step I take.

I've heard the song before. Spirit only gets three radio stations—one in Spanish, one that plays country western, and one that plays golden oldies. It's a 1950s hit, "To Know Him Is to Love Him." It's kind of sweet and kind of insipid and, once you've heard it, it's hard to get out of your head for the rest of the night.

The voice leads me to the door of a dingy break room that, in the push toward the grand re-opening, I decided to worry about later. I'm reaching for my keys when the supposedly locked door opens on its own.

Inside, the temperature is cooler, much cooler than it should be, especially with the vents shut. I'm greeted by the sight of a sink and cabinets, an empty space where a full-size refrigerator used to be, a beat-up table big enough for six, and five metal chairs.

The voice is coming from one of ten rusty half-lockers lined against a wall.

I'd hold my breath, but breathing is optional. "What are you trying to tell me?"

When I open the locker, it's empty. The voice grows louder, the room colder.

From behind, I hear something smack the table. Turning fast, I see the dust still flying up from where the little cloth-bound book landed. I walk over, and the song dissi-

pates with each step I take, ending altogether when I pick up the . . . it's a diary.

I flip through the entries, each signed with the letter "S." I slip out an old photo of a lovely dark-haired girl, the same girl whose photo is on the front page of the 1959 copy of *The Spirit Sentinel* in my office. She's cuddling a tabby kitten.

Amazing. After a lifetime as a loner, I suddenly have two new girls in my life.

Ginny is easy enough to figure out. But Sonia? The singing, the diary, even the mysterious "S" here and there all seem a lot more welcoming than the *GET OUT* in the bathroom. Does she really want me to leave, or is she just playing along with the haunted-theater theme?

A moment later, from across the building, Ginny cries out again.

When I reach the screening room, she's clutching her right forearm. Blood is dripping through her fingers. I can smell it. I can almost taste it. I feel my fangs slide.

I pause to regain control, calling, "Ginny!" like I can't spot her toward the front, bent in the aisle.

"Over here," she says, straightening, her face covered by her honey-colored hair.

I jog to her side. "What happened? Did you cut yourself on a chair?" They're old, and the heavy cushioned seats fold down. She could've torn her skin on a spring.

"No." Ginny lifts her hand from her arm to show me three short, deep scratches. They look like fingernail marks. Sounding mystified, she adds, "It was like being clawed by the wind."

Sonia. I catch myself licking my lips. "You need stitches. Let's—"

"No," Ginny replies. "It's fine. I was just surprised."

"It'll scar," I insist.

"Give me your shirt," she counters.

"Wha—"

"Your shirt. So I can use it to, you know, apply direct pressure."

Embarrassed by the misunderstanding, I'm already unbuttoning by the time she's finished the sentence. I fold the material as best I can and tie it around her arm.

"My hero," Ginny says again. She rises on her toes to kiss my cheek and, losing her balance, her lips land, lingering, on my throat instead. "About that celebration. . . ."

"Go home, Ginny," I say, moving away.

She looks stricken, like the child she is. "But. . . ."

I lighten my tone. "I mean, you'd best be getting home."

I watch her walk up the aisle, fuming, and disappear out the door.

Then a disembodied voice—soft, musical, and furious—whispers in my ear, "Murderer, murderer, murderer."

Later, at my uncle's ranch, I walk to his unmarked grave behind the barn. I buried him deep, wrapped in a Mexican blanket. The ground is bare, packed hard. I try to tell myself it's more fitting that he's here instead of at the old cemetery

in town. Uncle Dean loved this land as much as he was capable of loving anything.

The grave unsettles me, though. No stone, no cross. He may not have been a good man, but he was my mom's big brother.

As dawn approaches, I shake off the guilt and go inside.

Now, I'm surfing the Web at the dining-room table, drinking microwave-heated blood and researching ghosts. Sonia's history does track with what I've learned so far. Her death was traumatic. Her murderer was never caught. In the spirit world, that's textbook "unfinished business." A reason to haunt. And it's clear that Sonia wants me to know who she is—writing her initial and giving me the diary are clear enough hints.

According to the newspaper article, though, Sonia was a sweetheart. She used to teach Sunday school and run errands for her elderly neighbors. A quick skim of the diary—peppered with initials—confirms that she was a good-hearted girl with loopy handwriting and typical teen angst: homework, a boy ("D"), a rival girl ("K"). She adored Elvis ("E"), had a kitten named Peso ("P"), and collected toys at Christmas for the poor.

Maybe Sonia thinks I'm a threat to Ginny, and she wants me to know she's on to me. I'm not sure why she attacked Ginny, though. Maybe in her ghostly state, Sonia's confused. Or maybe she's trying to protect Ginny by scaring her off.

I guess there's always the possibility that the Old Love is home to more than one ghost. Katherine, the girl who went missing, is probably K. According to the diary, she and Sonia

didn't get along in life. But there's no hard evidence of more than one entity, and the singing voice that lead me to Sonia's diary in the break room matched the accusing one that whispered "murderer."

Besides, how many dead people could possibly be hanging around the place?

In any case, I can't overlook the lipstick message or the fact that Ginny was injured. If I can't somehow convince Sonia (or whomever) that I'm not dangerous, I'll need to force her out. Either that or my effort to resurrect the Old Love is over.

The question is, how? I'm in no position to be calling a minister or priest.

Worse, the ghost who spoke is right. I can be lethal. I have killed once before.

I take another swig of blood and notice that my caller ID is blinking. Ben Mueller. He didn't leave a message.

Why would Ben call here? Does he seriously think Ginny came home with me last night? It's not like I've got any kind of rep with girls. Then again, he knows Ginny better than I do, and considering the way she kissed my neck. . . .

Still, calling after the way they fought earlier, that's stalker behavior. Maybe Sonia's right to fret Ginny's safety, only she's worried about the wrong guy.

The following evening, patrolling the theater hallway, I don't hear any singing. I don't step into a cold spot. I don't see a fresh letter "S" written anywhere.

Today I was the one who fetched refreshments. I also made some calls, ordered a regular shipment of candy, popcorn, and coke. Tonight I have to put Sonia to rest.

Ginny comes bounding into the lobby at 7 P.M. sharp. She's wearing a different white shirt, its sleeves down and buttoned at the wrists.

"How's your arm?" I ask from the concession stand.

Ginny shrugs. "It looked worse than it was."

"And Ben?" I press. "Has he bothered you again?"

She glances at the front doors. "Not today."

It's then that I hear Sonia whisper "murderer" in my ear again.

"No!" I exclaim. At Ginny's expression, I add, "Not you." I run a hand through my hair, frustrated. "I'm sorry, but you're going to have to leave. We're not opening tonight. There's. . . . Someone's here. This is going to sound crazy, but she's a—"

"Ghost?" Ginny raises her scratched arm. "Yeah, I already figured out that much. And personally, I say we exorcise the bitch."

Wow. That was the last reaction I would've expected. I can't help admiring Ginny's bravery, though. Maybe we could have a future after all, if we're willing to fight for it.

I glance at my mom's Bible, wrapped in a kitchen towel, on the concession counter. I don't know whether I'll burst into flames if I touch it. I don't know what I'm

doing at all. Even though Sonia lashed out at Ginny, I can't help having mixed feelings about taking her on. After all, I'm no innocent, and by all accounts, she used to be.

"Seriously, let's do it now." Ginny takes a step in my direction, only to be violently shoved back by a whirlwind, a fierce wall of air, separating us.

Candy and cups fly off the counter, splattering coke. A bloody slash appears on Ginny's forehead. The crystal chandelier shakes and sways.

"Sonia!" I shout, trying to reach Ginny. "Sonia, please! Listen to me! You're making a mistake! Don't you see? You're hurting her!"

"Murderer!" returns Sonia's voice, this time louder than mine. "Murderer!"

"I—" Do I have to admit it? Is *that* what it'll take? "I'm. . . ."

Ginny is knocked onto her back. She struggles like she's being choked by invisible hands. She kicks with both legs. Then she's lifted, spun, and dropped again.

I reach back for the Bible, letting go as pain flashes across my fingertips.

I don't understand. Sonia knows that *I'm* the monster. Why target Ginny, not me?

For a split second, I wonder if Sonia is jealous, if the girls are fighting over me. But then Sonia wails "murderer, murderer!" again.

"You're right! Sonia, you're right!" I never intended to kill my uncle, even though sooner or later, he probably would've killed me. I just wanted to become stronger, strong enough to protect myself. I didn't know that the blood lust would

come with that strength. I hadn't gained control of it yet. "Sonia, stop! Please! Punish me!"

I'm resigned to face her judgment when Ben tears into the lobby from the service hallway. He has a battle-axe in one hand and—dear God—the decapitated heads of Ginny's parents, by the hair, in the other.

Ben tosses them onto the red carpet. "Howdy, Ginny!"

Has Sonia possessed him? Has he lost his mind?

Ginny is on her knees, her head bent, her hands covering her face.

She's an easy target.

"Murderer, murderer, murderer!" Sonia charges again.

Ben hesitates, his gaze searching for the speaker.

"Sonia!" I duck a box of Milk Duds that whizzes by. I want to help. I need to, but the supernatural wind is holding me back. "Let her go! He'll *kill* her!"

Ginny looks so small, huddled on the red carpet. We've known each other only a couple of days, but she's brought sunshine into my life and made me feel like I belong in the glow. It's not love. It's the hope of love. But it's the closest I've come to it since I was ten years old. If Ginny wants me, how can I be a monster?

I reach for the Bible again and hold it over my head, ignoring the pain. "In the name of. . . ." I raise my voice, start again. "In the name of the Father, the Son—"

With a roar, Ginny raises her face. Her mask of innocence melts away, and I see her for what she is. Undead. Demonic. Like me, a vampire.

I drop the Bible, clenching my blistered hands. "Ginny?"

Ben looks from her to me, like he's trying to figure out whose side I'm on.

"I was going to tell you," Ginny says, her voice pleading. "When your profile showed up on the system, I thought it was a sign." Her shoulder jerks, struck by the ghost. "I want the kind of love that lasts."

The system. "Love That Lasts." She's talking about the blood dealer's matchmaking service. Ginny must have the same supplier.

"Sonia!" she screams. "Don't you have anything better to do? You were a loser in life, and you're still a loser now. I told you this town would be mine someday!"

"Murderer!" Sonia replies. "Katie, murderer!"

So, Ginny was the one who killed Sonia. Sonia was never trying to scare her off, to protect her from me. When Sonia said "murderer," I wasn't the one she was talking about. Ginny had been Katie, Katherine, the girl whose body was never found.

From her crouched position, Ginny lunges at Ben as a swath of blood appears across her torso, staining the white shirt. She knocks the axe from his hand and kicks his boots out from under him. He's no match for her.

Ginny can't fight Sonia, but she could tear Ben apart.

"Let me help him," I say, and the ghostly force dies as quickly as it rose. I vault over the concession stand, snatch the axe from the carpet, and stand between them.

For a moment, I see the hope in Ginny's eyes. Unlike Ben, she knows that I'm one of her kind. She's already admitted that she wants me. She's already called me her "hero"

twice. I slowly shake my head, leaving no doubt about my intentions.

"You wouldn't," Ginny breathes as reality sinks in. She's been beaten by me, Sonia, and Ben together. Her voice is resigned. Her last words are: "Daddy had such big plans."

I sever her head with the blade and, shaking, drop the axe handle.

After a stunned moment, Ben climbs to his feet and puts a hand on my shoulder. "You okay, man?"

"Better now," I say. "You?"

"She came after me on prom night," he explains. "I've been trying to run her out of our town ever since."

Our town. Ben is Spirit. I'm Spirit. God knows Sonia is Spirit.

Ginny was the new girl again, this time with a new name.

"I tried to warn her off," Ben adds. "I tried to scare her off. I went to my family for help, but nobody believed me. She didn't seem like a vampire, you know?"

"Yeah, I know."

What happened here will stay with Ben for a long time. He isn't the kind of person who can destroy someone else, even something else, without it weighing on him. I know how he feels and then some.

⌒

It's been two weeks since that night, since the last time I noticed any sign of Sonia. I already miss her. I'm sorry for

having doubted her goodness, and I'm glad that the monster who killed her will never hurt anyone again.

Ben and I burned Ginny's and her parents' bodies (heads too) behind my barn. We buried the axe, which he'd taken from the mayor's office, near my uncle.

"Come spring, you might sprinkle some wildflower seed on the graves," he said. "I mean, they were human beings once."

I said I would and made a mental note to sprinkle seeds on Uncle Dean's grave too.

The next day Ben fibbed to his aunt Betty that the Augustines had packed up and left in the middle of the night for some six-figure job that the mayor landed up north. Ben explained that Ginny told him her dad was too embarrassed to own up to running out on the town after all his big promises. He claimed that's what their spat in the ticket line had been about.

Betty repeated the story the next day at the beauty shop, and it's become common knowledge since. The deputy is circulating a petition to put his own name on a mayoral ballot. I signed it last week.

Turns out, Ben's not a bad guy. His granddad, Sheriff Derek Mueller, had been the vampire hunter who originally chased the Augustines out of town back in the day. The sheriff had passed on what he'd seen, what he'd learned, to Ben so Ben would know what to do if the homicidal undead ever swung back through town.

Ben has decided to work at the Old Love and save up for college. Apparently, being a good athlete by Spirit standards isn't necessarily the same as being scholarship material. Facing down the undead has grown him up a lot.

He doesn't know what I am, not yet, but he took it well when I explained about Sonia. I hope that when the day comes, when he realizes I'm not just another home-town boy, he thinks back on what happened and gives me the benefit of the doubt.

Tonight after the Ghostbusters save New York City, I thank Ben for a good night's work, lock the front door behind him, and once again hear Sonia singing "To Know Him Is to Love Him."

When I look toward the voice, I see Sonia herself for the first time. She's taken over one of my jobs, wiping down the concession counter, like it's no big deal.

Sonia is a see-through figure in a uniform not much different than the one Ginny wore, except that Sonia's includes a red vest with a gold patch that reads "Love Theater."

I didn't realize she was still here. I don't get it. With Ginny gone for good, why stick around? "Sonia?"

She raises her face, and I see the dimple, the laughing eyes. "Cody!"

"Sonia," I say in case she didn't understand what happened, "your murderer has been destroyed. It's over. You can move on now. You can, uh, go into the light."

Sonia tilts her head. "It wasn't all about justice." Her voice has a hollow quality to it. "Tell me, Cody. Do you believe in love at first sight?"

Staring at her, God help me, I just might. I read on the Web that the more you believe in a ghost, the stronger your feelings for them, the more substantial they become.

With each passing second, Sonia appears more solid, more alive. And I have to admit, in some ways, we would be perfect for each other. We're both tied to this old theater, we'll both be teenagers forever, and we're both dead. Even better, I don't have to worry about physically hurting her. No flesh. No blood. No problem.

This could become more than the hope of love. It could become the real thing. But there's something she has to be told first. She may not know what happened at my uncle's ranch, but I thought she'd figured out what I am from the bottle of blood in the office mini-fridge. I guess Sonia didn't realize what the liquid was or maybe in her ghostly state, some details are fuzzy.

"Sonia," I begin again as she floats toward me. "There's something you should know. I'm a monster, the same kind of monster—"

Her cool fingertips press against my lips, and in her gaze, I see complete understanding, total acceptance. "No," Sonia says. "You're not."

Amber Smoke

KRISTIN CAST

From their place in the bowels of the Underworld, the Furies, Daughters of Night, summon their son. They are skeletal winged creatures, the black of rotting flesh thinly stretched across their hunched, quivering bodies, not much more than flesh sacks barely able to contain the power of each of their morbid talents.

"Alekossss, come."

He was birthed eons ago from the womb of vengeance, conceived by jealousy, and grown in constant anger. Bred to defend mortals, he was sent from their underground realm to the world above, and there, away from their poison, he learned compassion. At first only so that he could mimic and blend. Later, after centuries, humanity took hold within him, causing the Furies unending confusion with their errant son, this man who grew up and away from them.

Alekos appears, his Herculean body glowing from the descent, the return home. "Yes, my mothers?" He steps down from the ledge he was summoned to, his torn jeans dragging through the souls of the doomed as he strolls toward the three creatures in the dark. He can hear their wings rustling with the excitement of his return. Although he had been there only weeks before, they had not seen him in years. Time ticks by slowly below. As he approaches, they gently grab him and lead him farther into the nothing, farther from the whines of the tortured.

"Ssssit." They command. He sits and puts his feet nonchalantly up on the table.

"The longer you're up there, the more disgusting and human you become." Their throats click and rattle as they speak as one.

He removes his feet and snaps his fingers. Oil lamps flicker on, revealing a cave wet and putrid with chaos and death. The three figures huddle together staring at their son across a crude stone table on which sits a bouquet of night-blooming moon flowers the delicate color of infants' flesh. Slowly they begin to rock back and forth as if they are one and not three. Their eyes are dark and endless, and drip with the blood of the tortured. The snakes in their hair alternate between attacking and caressing one another.

"The Fates have decided. Her cord isss being cut tonight." At first they speak as one, then break apart, finishing each other's thoughts.

"You mussst find her,"

"give her life,"

"sssssave her,"

"sso ssshe can"

"give usss"

"vengeance."

The Furies click with amusement as his mind is flooded with pictures of a beautiful young woman: long chestnut hair, chocolate eyes, olive skin, and a black dress. They have chosen her for him. He blinks and stands. Alekos knows he was only there for this—the gift of his mission. It is now time for him to depart, and for the first time in centuries he feels nervous, excited, alive.

"Thank you, mothers." He turns to leave. "Oh! Furies, mothers." He glances back to see them still swaying. "Where do I find her?"

They close the black holes that served as their eyes, grip each other tightly, and send their too beautiful son to the modern world with the sounds of their shrieks echoing their farewells.

C⁓

Stop and stare. You start to wonder why you're here not there.

Ryan Tedder's melodic voice came booming out of my black cell phone, waking me from a much-needed nap. I groped around my nightstand unsuccessfully for my glasses. Seriously blind as a bat, I quickly gave up on reading the glowing caller ID box. Instead I flipped open the phone.

"Hello?"

"Oh my God, Jenna. Were you sleeping?" The annoyed tone picked me up out of the dream world I was loitering in and threw me back into reality.

"Bridget? No! Sleeping, me? No!" I perkily pretended.

"Good! Well, I was just calling to remind you to bring your camera tonight. We're going to have so much fun at Taylor's hotel party! I can't wait! Being seniors is sooo much fun! What are you wearing?"

"Umm, I think my little black strapless dress with my mom's new gold shoes."

Bridget sucked in air. "No way! Those new strappy heels from Saks? That is so not fair! We're going to look super hott, like always. Ugh, hang on, my mom is yelling at me." She moved the mouth piece of her cell away and I could hear her muffled whines at her mom. "*Okay, Mom.* She wants me to tell you not to forget your cell phone because that gross serial killer guy just killed someone else. Well duh, he's a *serial* killer, jeez. Sorry, she is so protective and weird. But anyway, I have to go finish getting gorgeous. See you at the Ambassador at ten! Love you, and don't forget the digital!"

The line went dead. *How is she always so happy?*

I stood up, stretched, found my glasses laying on the floor next to my nightstand, and looked at the clock: 7:57 P.M. *Crap. No time for a shower.*

As I sleepily wandered the five feet from my bed to my ocean-themed bathroom, I could hear my mom screeching at me from her room down the hall. "Jenna! Do you know where my gold strappy shoes are? I just bought them and

they've already *mysteriously* disappeared." She walked into my room and looked around.

I poked my head out of the bathroom door, my hair falling straight into the toothpaste I had just squeezed onto the brush. "Mom! If you're going to come in here anyway, *why* do you have to yell at me from down the hall?"

"Saves time. Which I don't have much of. Paul's going to be here," she looked down at her watch, "in less than an hour. So?"

"Oh, umm, nope. Haven't seen 'em. Sorry." I hardly ever lie to my mom, she's too good at catching me, but this was different. It was the first party of my senior year of high school, and I had to look the best. And I'm sure Paul had seen them already. She's been with the nerdy mortician for like six months. Besides, gold is hot right now, ask anyone.

"Hmm, well, if you see them let me know." She wasn't looking at me; instead, she continued to take inventory of my room.

"Yeah. Okay." I sighed trying to keep the annoyed *I'm running late too* tone out of my voice. I stuck the toothbrush into my mouth.

She started to leave, and her dark curls bounced around her shoulders, making her suddenly look a lot younger than a forty-something-year-old mom. She paused at the door. "And Jenn, don't forget to take Mr. Pepper. He's in his spot by the front door."

Oh Lord, Mr. Pepper. Ugh. I want to actually be popular this year, not be known as "the girl who carries around pepper spray."

I finished brushing my teeth, put my contacts in, and stood staring in the mirror at my messed-up locks. "Up-do!" I decided.

I began wrapping my fingers around my tangled hair in an attempt to turn it into an intentionally messy low pony when the cute Ryan Tedder again blared through the room. I quickly clipped up my hair and glanced down at the sink where I had set my phone. "Connor!" The picture of his goofy smile, sandy shaggy hair, and gray eyes made my stomach jump.

"Hey." I answered casually, pretending not to be excited.

"Hey. I thought you'd never answer. What are you doin'?"

"Nothin'." I rolled my eyes. *Nothin'? I am so lame.*

"Oh, well, that's cool. I just wanted to see if you're coming to Taylor's thing tonight. There's gonna be a DJ, and his older brother's bringing vodka and beer and stuff, so it should be pretty awesome."

Of course I'm going. It's only like the biggest social event of the semester! "Umm, yeah. I think Bridge and I'll probably make an appearance."

"Good. I'll definitely look for you then."

"Definitely. See ya tonight." I hung up before I could start rambling about my undying love for him. *Oh my God he's so f-ing hot!*

I fought off the urge to call Bridget and babble semi-hysterically about Connor actually calling me, and instead trotted to my closet on a wave of happy he's-almost-my-boyfriend thoughts, where my black Tinkerbell cocktail

dress hung waiting. Then I began digging my mom's cute gold shoes out of hiding from under my dirty clothes.

Sadly, Mom chose that instant to prove her radar wasn't fading with age. Thankfully, she knocked on my open door, giving me a split-second of warning.

I jumped. "Mother!" I tried to plaster on an innocent smile as I jerked around to look at her.

"I'm not yelling this time. Ew." She looked at the wad of clothes I'd grabbed to camouflage her shoes. "Don't tell me you're wearing something dirty to your little get-together thing tonight."

"No, Mom, I'm just looking for my, uh, headband. You almost made me pee on myself."

"Sorry. Anyway, Paul's here so I'm heading out on my *date*. Maybe I'll even have a little sex. Hehe." She made herself giggle and turn red as she left me with that disgusting mental picture.

Oh barf! Is everyone having sex except me? I stood up and thought about Connor. *Wait! It's been an hour already?!* I whipped around to face the clock: 9:03. *Shit.* I frantically dressed myself, found the shoes, and ran into the bathroom to put on my face. Luckily, it only takes a little eyeliner and mascara to bring me back from the dead. I checked my phone: 9:21 P.M. *Okay, shoes, and then the thirty-minute drive to the Ambassador.* The shoes, however gorgeous they may be, took about twenty minutes for me to buckle. I'm not a contortionist; feet aren't supposed to bend like that. Stupid (gorgeous) shoes.

I ran downstairs, grabbed Mr. Pepper and my gold clutch, checked for lip gloss and my ID, and nearly tore the

key hook out of the wall in my efforts to bolt out the front door.

"Please start." I sent out a quiet prayer as I ran down the front sidewalk, crunching autumn leaves on my way. I got in and turned the key to my 1969 cherry-red Mustang. It's a super cute car, it just doesn't always run.

Vrrrrrooomm. "Success!" I took off down the street and got about five miles away from my house before my super cute car died. I dropped my head against the steering wheel, banged it a few times, and felt around the passenger seat for my cell phone. "Of course, you forgot it, Jenna. And the camera! Dammit! Bridget's gonna be pissed!" I slouched down in my seat, smashing the puffiness of my dress, and silently cried for my mommy.

As if my mom had miraculously appeared, her words trickled in through my tears: "Jenn, use your bus pass, you silly girl. I got it for you because your car kind of sucks." *Well, duh.* I stopped crying and checked my eyes in the rearview mirror. Thank God for waterproof eye makeup and close bus stops. My mom's gold shoes were definitely not made for walking.

When I got to the bus stop I chose to stand alone while three other people crammed themselves on a bench made for two. *This would be so much easier and way less gross if I had just remembered my phone. Now I have completely passed being fashionably late and entered the "you think you're too good to actually be here" time. And what if Connor is dancing with someone else?!*

"It's you." A male voice broke through my internal rant. *Great. I haven't been here ten minutes and I'm already getting hit on by a bus person creeper.*

"Well, I'm glad you think so." I crankily angled my back toward him and turned my attention to my clutch and my friend Mr. Pepper. *I have got to get a new car.*

"You don't understand. You're—"

I could feel him getting closer so I shoved my hand into my clutch. "No *bud*, I don't think you understand! If you say another syllable in my general direction," I whipped out the pepper spray so the Mr. Pepper label was clearly visible, "I will spray this right in your—holy hell!"

C—

I sucked in enough air to oxygenate a small country as I shot off of my pillow.

Stop and stare. You start to wonder why you're here not there.

My hands were shaking so badly that I could hardly open the phone. "Hello?"

"Hey Jenna! I was just calling to remind you to bring your camera tonight. We're going to have sooo much fun at Taylor's hotel party! I can't wait! Being seniors is sooo much fun! What are you wearing?"

"My black dress with my mom's new gold shoes?" Huh? What? I rubbed my face, trying to reorient myself.

Bridget gasped. "No way! Those new strappy heels from Saks? That is so not fair! We're going to look super hott, like always."

I interrupted her rambling, "Is this a joke, Bridget?"

"Jenn, you know I take fashion and parties very seriously. Are you okay? You're weren't sleeping, were you?"

"Umm, no, no. I'm fine. Just having a mad case of déjà vu." Thirst burned the back of my throat and my head pounded with confusion. I was *not* okay.

"Creepy. Anyway, try not to go crazy 'til after tonight, k? Ugh, hang on, my mom is yelling at me." Bridget's familiar whines were muffled. "She wants me to tell you not to forget your cell phone because that gross serial killer guy just killed someone else. Well duh, he's a *serial* killer, jeez. Sorry, she is so protective and weird. But anyway, I have to go finish getting gorgeous. See you at the Ambassador at ten! Love you, and don't forget the digital!"

I closed the phone, then dropped it on the floor and fell back onto my fluffy down pillow.

"What in the hell kind of dream was that?" I rolled over and looked at my clock: 7:57 P.M., *weird.*

"Jenna! Do you know where my gold strappy shoes are? I just bought them and they've already *mysteriously* disappeared."

I hesitated, staring at her as she stood in the doorway. She was surrounded by a strange vanilla-colored cloud of mist. I rubbed my eyes and blinked a few times, and it went away. "Mom, what did you say?"

"My shoes. The gold ones. From Saks. Look, Jenna it's okay if you wore them, but I really don't have time for this. Paul's going to be here," she looked down at her watch, "in less than an hour. So?"

"Umm, no, I haven't seen them."

"Hmm, well, if you do let me know." Puzzled, she stared at me with her forehead all scrunched.

"What?"

"Nothing, for a second you just seemed different. Well, have fun tonight. Oh! And Jenn, don't forget to take Mr. Pepper. He's in his spot by the front door."

I sat up in bed, staring out the door. *It was just a dream. A really weird, freaky dream. I bet if I think about it longer I'll have played poker with the beaver and Abe Lincoln like in that insomnia commercial.*

Ow! White light burned through my mind along with a picture and a memory. I had an insanely vivid flash of the guy at the bus stop, and two words screamed through my mind: *"FIND ME!"*

"What the hell!" I lifted up the covers to make sure I was wearing clothes and had all of my limbs. *Completely intact. What is going on?*

I heard from beside me: *You start to wonder why you're here not there.*

Leaning over, I slowly picked up my phone from off the floor. Connor. Just like before. This time I hit the ignore button with shaky fingers and turned the phone on silent. *Maybe I need some water. I'll rehydrate. Wake up.* As I got out of bed, I felt something jab the bottom of my foot. I picked up the frame to my glasses, which I had just smashed. *Wait. I can see? I shouldn't be able to see.* I stuck my finger in my eye. No contacts. *Weird déjà vu dreams curing blind-as-a-bat-ness?*

I stared at myself in the bathroom mirror. *Is this what people look like when they're crazy? What the hell? What the hell? What the hell?* "Jenna, just go get some water and some

extra-strength Tylenol," I told myself, hoping speaking my thoughts out loud would bring some sanity to my mind.

As I walked past my mom's open door on my way downstairs to the kitchen I heard her weirdly familiar words.

"Hey! Paul's here so I'm heading out on my *date*. Maybe I'll even have a little sex. Hehe." I cringed as she flitted past me. *That doesn't get any better the second time around.* I glanced at the clock on the wall: 9:03.

I took comfort in doing something as normal as getting a glass from the cabinet. My cabinet, my normal cabinet. And water from my sink, my normal sink. A cool fall wind blew in through the partially open window, bringing the familiar smell of autumn leaves to me. Just like before. Just like when I was walking to my car. My brain launched itself into another flashback seizure as my mind's eye filled with another painful vision. I dropped my glass and it shattered, raining shards of crystal at my feet.

"*FIND ME!*" The voice, *his* voice, sounded more impatient, and it was coupled with images from the bus stop.

Then I knew. I don't know how, and I don't know why, but I knew he was there waiting.

I didn't even notice anything wrong with my foot until I was upstairs putting on my shoes. I was shocked by the small pieces of glass that had stuck in my heel. Blood was staining my fuzzy green carpet. As I painlessly pulled out the glass, I brought it to my face. Holy crap! My blood wasn't my blood

anymore! It was no longer bright red and penny-smelling. Instead it was dull amber, and the sweet, soothing smell relaxed me and made me feel at home.

I really need to find this guy who's in my head.

My foot was completely healed by the time I put on my Coach tennis shoes and ran down the stairs and out the door. *Am I like that chick off of* Heroes? *The one who heals herself over and over again?*

I hesitated as I reached my car. "Jenna, maybe driving is not such a good idea. Not only are you getting weird voicemails in your head, but today seems to be some sort of twisted repeat, so why would your car work this time?" I find that sometimes talking to myself is the best way to sort through my problems, and I am such a good listener. "Where is a do-gooder neighbor when you need one?" I looked but of course, chivalry is dead, and so was my neighborhood.

"Aaaah! I just want to be at the freaking bus stop, people!" I closed my eyes and threw a mini temper tantrum, stomping my foot like a toddler in a toy store. There was a sudden rush through my body that made me feel like I was falling off a tall building. When I unsquished my face and looked around I realized I was there, at the freaking bus stop! And I was sitting on my butt in the middle of the sidewalk.

"Well, that's not right."

"Hey! Hey! Shit!" yelled a familiar male voice.

"You!" I scrambled backward through a pool of my amber blood, and was amazed when I felt only adrenaline and not one bit of pain from coming into such close contact with the concrete. "I've gone completely insane and it's all your fault! Turn me back!" He reached out and grabbed my flailing hands to pull me up and I was smothered by a rush of calming autumn air. My eyes opened super wide and fixed on him.

"You okay?" He cocked his head to the side and stared back.

"I—I think I'm bleeding." Pressing my hand against the back of my head, I came in contact with damp tangled hair. No wound, no pain, just really nappy wet strands. "Well, I thought—"

His smile was slow and a little sarcastic. Actually it was almost a smirk. He shook his head. "What you thought is not even close to the truth."

"Huh?" I said, brilliant. Okay, the guy was so majorly hot it was making it hard for me to think. Tall and blonde and delicious. A complete Justin Hartley look-alike. *Yummmm.*

"Alek." He stepped back just a little and extended his perfect hand. "My name is Alek, and I need you to trust me."

Not knowing what else to do, and feeling completely, utterly overwhelmed, I stuck out my hand for him to shake, and added my best attempt at a hair flip. "I'm Jenna," I said, while the leaves danced around my feet.

"Jenna, you must come with me." He was looking at me with his incredible green eyes.

"Uh, no, I have to—"

He covered my hand with his. He felt warm and strong and the only real thing that had touched me since I'd fallen into this nightmare.

"You have to come with me," he repeated. "Trust me. I'll tell you everything on the way."

Now, I know the whole "don't go places with strangers" thing, but you have to realize that in the middle of all of this unreality, this guy made sense. I know it sounds bizarre, but he just felt right, and I knew I should trust him. Like I knew that he had been there waiting for me.

All right, yes. I can't say it didn't help that he was so darn sexy.

"Fine, I'll come with you, but only because I'm probably dreaming," I said.

He smiled, then motioned for me to follow him. I scurried to keep up with his long strides while I tried to untangle my hair and watch his cute butt at the same time. *You could bounce a quarter off of that thing! Oh my God. I sound like my mother. Talk about gross.* I almost ran into him when he came to an abrupt halt beside a florescent green car. "What is that?"

"A '76 Chevy Caprice," he said, opening the door for me.

"It looks like a giant green popsicle." I slid in onto the white leather seat, distracted by the vintage-ness of the old muscle car, while he went around and got in on the driver's side. I was just getting ready to open my mouth and tell him I had a thing for old cars too, when he leaned over and grabbed my arm.

Looking into my face, he said, "And you're not dreaming. You're dead."

C⟶

"Dead!" I tried to pull back from him. "What the hell?" My heart felt like it was going to pound out of my chest. Instead of letting me go, Alek pressed his body close to mine and wrapped me in his arms.

"Trust me. Let me show you," he said.

Like his voice was a drug, my body seemed to dissolve into him and I gasped as, still in his arms, I began to float above his Jell-O-colored car. White specks of light surrounded me. I looked up at Alek, who was drifting with me. His eyes glowed the red of a rising autumn moon.

Just like his eyes had been before . . . at the bus stop. Slowly, I began to remember as we floated through time back to the moment we'd first met.

He spoke, his voice whispering in my ear. "I was sent here to save you." His words were like mist. "Look down. Remember. . . ."

I looked below us and saw everything. There I was, dressed in my LBD and my mom's hot but uncomfortable shoes, pouting and sullenly complaining to myself while I waited for the bus. There sat the three people crammed on the tiny bench, and then there was Alek, appearing from nowhere. I glanced questioningly at the Alek who floated with his arms around me. His eyes still burned hunter red, and they stilled the questions on my lips.

Watch . . . remember. . . .

I looked down again and saw myself point Mr. Pepper at Alek's face. At those eyes that were just as red then as they were now. I could see myself yelling something, and at the same time I stepped back. It was then that mom's gorgeous stiletto heel missed the curb, and horrified, I saw my arms windmilling as I fell backward, hitting my head on the concrete with a sickening thud.

And that was it. I didn't move as the people at the bus stop surrounded me, obviously not knowing what to do. Through the middle of them walked Alek, but he was like a shadow in darkness. No one seemed to see him at all as he bent over my still body and whispered, "Your death was a gift, given by the ancients through me. You have been chosen. I am your teacher." Then he bent and covered my dead lips with his.

Okay, it was happening, but it wasn't. People were running around down there—literally walking *through* him while he kissed me. And even though they couldn't see him I could feel him. What he did to my dead body, I could now feel happening in my hovering soul as I drank in the exchange of death with life. I should have been terrified. I should have screamed or passed out or flailed against him. Instead I closed my eyes and let my soul absorb what I had seen. I accepted his gift and knew my world would never be the same.

When I opened my eyes, I was back in the car pressed against
Alek's chest. There were no sounds coming from inside of
his muscular body, no breath, no heart thumping. I pulled
back and stared at him.

"Are you even alive?"

My head felt funny, all kinda hummy and strange.

"I'm as alive as are you," he said. "You've just been
changed. We're different. They used to call us vampires."

"Vampires?" I squeaked. "I have to drink blood?" I almost
gagged just thinking about it.

He laughed softly. "It's not blood we drink—it's energy."

"Oh, God! We suck down electricity?" I frantically tried
to remember who that chick was on old *Angel* reruns who
zapped things with her electrically charged hands.

His strong arms were still around my waist and I wondered how they stayed so warm if he was dead. If *we* were
dead. His smile was still in his eyes when he said, "No, it's
not like that, either. You'll see."

His mouth was close to my ear. *Kiss me . . . kiss me
again. . . .* His smiled widened and I felt my face burn with a
blush. Could he read my mind?

"So we kinda match!" I blurted. *What?* As he chuckled at
my dorkiness I pulled away and positioned myself back on
my side of the car. This was depressing. With all this new
power I could feel inside of me, I was still the same lame
eighteen-year-old with no game.

"What was that?" Still smiling, Alek pulled his keys from
his pocket and turned on the car, but for a moment I could
swear disappointment flashed across his face. *Would he really*

have kissed me again if I hadn't gone all superdork on him and then vaulted to the other side of the car?

"Yeah, umm, we match." I tried to stay as perky as I had been when I ruined the moment. "We're both strong, fearless creatures of night sent here to . . . do . . . stuff. What exactly do we do?"

"We all have different abilities." He cleared his throat in preparation, and I wondered how many times he had had this conversation. "I can affect time. That's how I got you to the bus stop, since you were taking too long getting there on your own, and that's also why you woke up today . . . again. Guess you could call that part a side effect. But, I'm not too sure what your ability is, but you'll figure it out pretty soon. It's the same for each of us, but different. You have to discover your own way. I was sent from below—"

"Hell?" I interrupted. "You came from Hell?"

"No. Or at least not your idea of Hell. Look, I was sent here to help you serve up vengeance on some and to save others."

"Like you saved me?"

"Well, kind of." He sighed and cleared his throat. "There are these ancient monsters whose spirits have been locked in the Underworld, and occasionally they find some way to escape. If they do, their only goals are to find a body and create the same chaos they did centuries ago. I'm the first of my kind, our kind, that were made to find these creatures and send them back. So, we're more like—"

"Monster-slaying superheroes?!" *Holy shit! What am I? A toddler?*

He laughed. "I guess you could call it that. I know where to take you, and we'll just wing it from there." He put the car in gear and started driving down the street.

Wing it? That didn't sound very reassuring.

I stared out the window, trying to make myself teleport or move things with my mind, when I noticed the reflection of my eyes. They were flashing from their normal plain brown to brilliant amber. That was good, right? I kept looking out the window and tried to concentrate. We passed a crowd of people leaving a late night movie when it happened again.

"Oh my God! That's it! I just thought it was part of me going crazy, but really it was my hidden superpower." I giddily turned to Alek, expecting him to know what I was talking about.

"What was your hidden power?"

"I can see stuff." It was just like with my mom, the weird vanilla smoke I'd seen around her. I leaned over Alek and pointed out the window to a cluster of people. "Like, I know that the girl in the pink cardigan and those really cute fuzzy boots is completely and totally in love, because I can see hot pink misty ribbons floating off of her. Oh, oh, and look at him." I pointed to a guy standing on the corner holding a WILL WORK FOR FOOD sign. "The smoke stuff around him is all brown and nasty. Hey! He has cancer." I paused, thinking hard, and suddenly *knew*. "He has lung cancer. He's gonna die. Soon." I shivered, not sure how I felt about my new superpower. Plopping myself back in my seat, I stared out the window and watched rainbows of smoke dance off

people and twist through the autumn air, and *knew* things I simply shouldn't.

"That's good, you're learning already. There'll be more to come, though."

I closed my eyes and drew a long, shaky breath. *You're okay . . . you're okay. . . .*

"We're here." Alek turned off the car, and when I opened my eyes I half-expected to see creepy boat docks or a dark alley. Instead, we were in the middle of suburbia parked in front of a brick house identical to the ones on either side of it.

"You're kidding. This is the monster hideout where I'm supposed to fight crime?" Alek was already out of the car, and I hurried to catch up with him, following his longer legs up the driveway and past a very familiar SUV. "Hey!" He spun around and motioned for me to be quiet.

I lowered my voice, and spoke urgently. "But this is Paul's nerdy old Isuzu. He's dating my mom. Look, it has to be his SUV." I pointed at the window. "He has like fifty tacky evergreen air fresheners hanging from the rearview mirror because he smokes in his car and doesn't want my mom to notice." Obviously Alek didn't care, because he kept walking until he reached the side door and I had to scramble again to keep up.

"We're going in."

"What? Hell no! Didn't you just hear me? This is Paul's house and there's no way I'm going in there. Your monster radar is all wrong. Besides, he's on a date with my mom, and look, the lights aren't even on. They're probably not here, or

worse. Ew. They might be—" Alek pressed one hand over my mouth and used the other to guide mine to the door.

"Can you feel that?" His hand lingered on mine and I wanted him to hold me like he had earlier.

Suddenly, the cold sluggishness of fear crept through the door and made ribbons up my arm. I tried to pull away, but Alek wouldn't let me. Rage and disgust followed. Their hot nails tore at my flesh, though the only marks they left were in my mind—on my soul. Alek let loose my hand and repeated, "We're going in there. Remember, trust me. I'm your protector."

As soon as he finished his sentence we were on the other side of the door. *I really wish he would warn me before he popped us places.* Alek nudged me toward the stairs and back into the reality I was trying unsuccessfully to escape. Like ghosts, we slid noiselessly up to the second floor. With each step the suffocating stench of smoky fear grew stronger. I wanted to vomit. At the top of the steps Alek took the lead. I let out a tiny sigh. Okay, right. He was my protector. Besides his superpower of zapping us places and kissing me into being a weird kind of vampire, he also must be super strong (as well as super hot). With him in front he could beat up any ancient boogey monster things lurking in the dark.

We walked into a room absent of all furniture except a metal table, the kind that morticians put dead bodies on. The cold room stank of bleach and blood, and the mixture became red and white ribbons of smoke that bit at my eyes. I scanned the room, amazed at how easily I could see through the smoke and shadows.

It was in one of those shadows that I saw her curly brown hair. I tore out from behind my protector and flew to her side. "Mom?!" The silence burned my ears. "Mom! Mom!" The soft vanilla I'd seen surrounding her earlier barely lingered within the rust-colored tendrils of hopelessness and panic, blinding me with fear. Tears washed my face, and my throat was hard and dry. "Alek, she's not moving. And I don't know what's wrong!" He was immediately at my side. I scrubbed at my eyes, wiping away tears and blinking through the otherworldly mists. He picked up my mother's limp body. She looked so unnaturally still and helpless it made my stomach roll. Mom was never helpless! She couldn't be!

"She's breathing. I'm sure she'll be fine." Alek began to reassure me, but like a bad horror movie, that was exactly when the predator entered.

"Oh, look. It's a party. Jenna, you didn't tell me you wanted to watch. That could have been arranged. I like an audience."

The man approaching me looked like the Paul I knew only briefly. Then my eyes grew hot and his body wavered, like heat rising from a hot summer road, and his true form was revealed to me. The smoke that swirled in and out of his body was terrible. It made his evil naked, and bared, he was fully exposed to me. I saw the sick creature he truly was. The souls of the people he had murdered shrieked purple ribbons of smoky agony from within him and tried to claw their way out from beneath his gray flesh. His eyes were fixed on me, but they wriggled in sockets swimming with parasites.

Putrid lie-filled glop fell from his scorched lips and ate the ground where it landed.

Thanks to my new superpowers, I knew him for who he was—Alastor. A Greek demon who led others to sin and murder. *He's the serial killer, and he was hunting my mom.*

He had stopped moving toward us, and his body shimmered again, changing back into the Paul my mom had been tricked into caring about. "So, Mommy first, or you and your boyfriend?"

And it hit me. The rest of my new gift became clear. I turned to Alek, and in a commanding voice I barely recognized as my own I ordered, "Alek! Get her out of here! Call 911!"

Then I turned and faced the demon. "How about you start with me, asshole?" As I spoke I threw my arms wide and all of the tendrils of emotion swirling in the room rushed to me, wrapping around me, filling me with an incredible surge of power. I felt the dark emotions that had shimmered around Alastor enter my body and I knew the anger and hatred and awful strength of pure evil.

My mouth grew teeth I didn't know I had and my body began to vibrate with the power of the emotions I'd absorbed. I didn't think. I just felt and acted. I launched myself at the man my mother had trusted, wrapped my hands around his throat, and tried to tear off his suit of flesh. I had never felt so wild and so free. It was good to feel his flesh tear, to see his eyes bug out, to hear his whimper of terror. I was bloated with it, filled with darkness, and I wanted to rip him to pieces.

But before I could, Alek was pulling me from my opponent. He threw me against the wall so hard that, had I been alive, I would have surely died. By the time I shook off the shock and got to my feet, Alek had already finished him. He'd snapped his neck. *Let him off easy.* I threw myself at Alek, knocking him back. My fangs cut into my bottom lip and the amber blood that trickled onto my tongue only made my rage grow as Alek regained his balance. But instead of hitting me back, he calmly wrapped his arms around my anger-bloated body, and held me tightly. The hollow sound of his chest and the autumn air that was his scent surrounded us, and like a cool fall rain following a baking hot summer, his presence washed the anger from me, leaving me so weak that I began to cry.

"You can't let it control you. That's where the horror stories of vampires came from—that's why so many of us have inspired bad B movies and the nightmares of humans. It's what happens to us when we lose control. If we let our powers overwhelm us, then we become the monsters we've been created to hunt." He set his chin on my head and I could feel him inhale the dried amber blood in my hair. "Feeding off him was enough. Don't let him taint you. You have to learn to keep the energy and let the evil go. His soul is back below in a far worse place than you could ever imagine, let that be punishment enough."

I looked up at him and suddenly understood. "You called yourself my protector, but you're not here to protect me from them. You're here to protect me from me."

"Yeah, that's right. Are you better now? Feel more like yourself?"

His voice was so deep, so incredibly gentle, and his eyes so warm that I lost myself in them. And then I saw the mist that surrounded him. It was a bright, brilliant amber—the same color as my blood. It reminded me of a clear and early dawn and new beginnings. The tendrils of gold wrapped around me, around us, and I couldn't help myself. I tiptoed and kissed him gently on the lips.

His blue eyes opened wide in surprise. Then he bent and kissed me back and I sank into him, finding my anchor, my center, my protector.

"Jenna, what's happening?"

At the sound of my mom's weak voice Alek and I sprang apart and I ran to where she lay just outside the room of death. I felt Alek move behind me, shielding her view of what used to be Paul.

"It's okay, Mom. It's gonna be fine," I said, reaching out to hold her and breathing a sigh of relief as I saw the vanilla mist that surrounded her, once more cream-colored and healthy, completely free of the taint of death.

Alek stayed by my side, holding my hand and helping to strengthen me, keeping me from becoming overwhelmed by all of the tendrils of urgency, pain, and fear that surged with the presence of the police and EMTs and the neighbors who had started to mill around the front yard like worried sheep. He guided me to my mom, through the chaos that was invisible to everyone else but that I saw as mist within

fog, so thick and swirling it was overwhelming. Mom was completely conscious, though she had a nasty bump on her head. I was still feeling a little sick with worry until I heard her tell an EMT that if she could just have a few Xanax and a glass of wine she'd be fixed right up and could go on home.

"Miss, you can ride with your mother if you'd like," the EMT called to me, still smiling at my mom's request for drugs and alcohol.

"Yeah, I'm coming," I said, then I turned to Alek. I looked into his blue eyes and saw a future so different than anything I could have dreamed that I suddenly felt shy. "Uh, I'm going to ride with her since, ya know, she's hurt." I giggled nervously. "Well, of course you do, you were—" He pulled me close and kissed my babbling lips. Leaves swept around my feet and wind rushed through my matted hair.

"I know." His breath tickled my nose. "I'll follow. You still have a lot to learn."

I jumped into the back of the ambulance and watched his cute butt as I walked all the way to his car. When he got to the bright green thing he looked back at me and his eyes glowed softly. "Hey," he called. "I think you were right before. I think we do match."

I grinned like a fool as the doors to the ambulance closed and my mom started pestering me with *who is that tall boy?* questions. As I tried to make up believable and not-get-me-in-trouble answers, I watched through the little glass windows while tendrils of caressing amber clung to the ambulance, guiding . . . protecting . . . ushering me into a whole new life.

Dead Man Stalking

A Morganville Vampires Story

RACHEL CAINE

Living in West Texas is sort of like living in Hell, but without the favorable climate and charming people. Living in Morganville, Texas, is all that and a takeout bag of worse. I should know. My name is Shane Collins, and I was born here, left here, came back here—none of which I had much choice about.

So, for you fortunate ones who've never set foot in this place, here's the walking tour of Morganville: It's home to a couple of thousand folks who breathe, and some crazy-ass number of people who don't. Vampires. Can't live with 'em, and in Morganville, you definitely can't live without 'em, because they run the town. Other than that, Morganville's a normal, dusty collection of buildings—the kind the oil boom

of the '60s and '70s rolled by without dropping a dime in the banks. The university in the center of town acts like its own little city, complete with walls and gates.

Oh, and there's a secluded, tightly guarded vampire section of town too. I've been there, in chains. It's nice, if you're not looking forward to a horrible public execution.

I used to want to see this town burned to the ground, and then I had one of those things, what are they called, epiphanies? My epiphany was that one day I woke up and realized that if I lost Morganville and everybody in it . . . I'd have nothing at all. Everything I still cared about was here. Love it or hate it.

Epiphanies suck.

I was having another one of them on this particular day. I was sitting at a table inside Marjo's Diner, watching a dead man walk by the windows outside. Seeing dead men wasn't exactly unusual in Morganville; hell, one of my best friends is dead now, and he still gripes at me about doing the dishes. But there's vampire-dead, which Michael is, and then there's *dead*-dead, which was Jerome Fielder.

Except Jerome, dead or not, was walking by the window outside Marjo's.

"Order up," Marjo snapped, and slung my plate at me like a ground ball to third base; I stopped it from slamming into the wall by putting up my hand as a backstop. The bun of my hamburger slid over and onto the table—mustard side up, for a change.

"There goes your tip," I said. Marjo, already heading off to the next victim, flipped me off.

"Like you'd ever leave one, you cheap-ass punk."

I returned the gesture. "Don't you need to get to your second job?"

That made her pause, just for a second. "What second job?"

"I don't know, grief counselor? You being so sensitive and all."

That earned me another bird, ruder than the first one. Marjo had known me since I was a baby puking up formula. She didn't like me any better now than she had then, but that wasn't personal. Marjo didn't like anybody. Yeah, go figure on her entering the service industry.

"Hey," I said, and leaned over to look at her retreating bubble butt. "Did you just see who walked by outside?"

She turned to glare at me, round tray clutched in sharp red talons. "Screw you, Collins, I'm running a business here, I don't have time to stare out windows. You want something else or not?"

"Yeah. Ketchup."

"Go squeeze a tomato." She hustled off to wait another table—or not, as the mood took her.

I put veggies on my burger, still watching the parking lot outside the window. There were exactly six cars out there; one of them was my housemate Eve's, which I'd borrowed. The gigantic thing was really less a car than an ocean liner, and some days I called it the Queen Mary, and some days I called it Titanic, depending on how it was running. It stood out. Most of the other vehicles in the lot were crappy, sunfaded pickups and decrepit, half-wrecked sedans.

There was no sign of Jerome, or any other definitely dead guy, walking around out there now. I had one of those moments, those *did I really see that?* moments, but I'm not the delusional type. I had zero reason to imagine the guy. I didn't even *like* him, and he'd been dead for at least a year, maybe longer. Killed in a car wreck at the edge of town, which was code for *shot while trying to escape*, or the nearest Morganville equivalent. Maybe he'd pissed off his vampire Protector. Who knew?

Also, who cared? Zombies, vampires, whatever. When you live in Morganville, you learn to roll with the supernatural punches.

I bit into the burger and chewed. This was why I came to Marjo's . . . not the spectacular service, but the best hamburgers I'd ever eaten. Tender, juicy, spicy. Fresh, crisp lettuce and tomato, a little red onion. The only thing missing was. . . .

"Here's your damn ketchup," Marjo said, and slid the bottle at me like a bartender in an old western saloon. I fielded it and saluted with it, but she was already moving on.

As I drizzled red on my burger, I continued to stare out the window. Jerome. That was a puzzle. Not enough to make me stop eating lunch, though.

Which shows you just how weird life in Morganville is, generally.

I was prepared to forget all about Jerome, post-lunch, because not even Marjo's sour attitude could undo the endorphin high of her burger and besides, I had to get home. It was five o'clock. The bottling plant was letting out, and pretty soon the diner would be crowded with adults tired from a hard day's labor, and not many of them liked me any better than Marjo did. Most of them were older than me; at eighteen, I was starting to get the get-a-job-you-punk stares.

I like a good ass-kicking, but the Good Book is right: It's better to give than to receive.

I was unlocking the door to Eve's car when I saw somebody behind me on the window glass, blocking the blazing westerly sun. The reflection was smeared and indistinct, but in the ripples I made out some of the features.

Jerome Fielder. What do you know, I really *had* seen him.

I had exactly enough time to think, *Dude, say something witty*, before Jerome grabbed a handful of my hair and rammed me forehead-first into hot metal and glass. My knees went rubbery, and there was a weird high-pitched whine in my ears. The world went white, then pulsed red, then faded into darkness when he slammed me down again.

Why me? I had time to wonder, as it all went away.

C⁓

I woke up some time later, riding in the backseat of Eve's car and dripping blood all over the upholstery. *Oh, crap, she's gonna kill me for that*, I thought, which was maybe not the

biggest problem I had. My wrists were tied behind my back, and Jerome had done some work on my ankles too. The bonds were so tight I'd lost feeling in both hands and feet, except for a slow, cold throb. I had a gash in my forehead, somewhere near the hairline I thought, and probably some kind of concussion thing, because I felt sick and dizzy.

Jerome was driving Eve's car, and I saw him watching me in the rearview mirror as we rattled along. Wherever we were, it was a rough road, and I bounced like a rag doll as the big tank of a car charged over bumps.

"Hey," I said. "So. Dead much, Jerome?"

He didn't say anything. That might have been because he liked me about as much as Marjo, but I didn't think so; he didn't look exactly *right*. Jerome had been a big guy, back in high school—big in the broad-shouldered sense. He'd been a gym worshipper, a football player, and winner of the biggest neck contest hands down.

Even though he still had all the muscles, it was like the air had been let out of them and now they were ropy and strangely stringy. His face had hollows, and his skin looked old and grainy.

Yep: dead guy. Zombified, which would have been a real mindfreak anywhere but Morganville; even in Morganville, though, it was weird. Vampires? Sure. Zombies? Not so you'd notice.

Jerome decided it was time to prove he still had a working voice box. "Not dead," he said. Just two words, and it didn't exactly prove his case because it sounded hollow and rusty. If I'd had to imagine a dead guy's voice, that would have been it.

"Great," I said. "Good for you. So, this car theft thing is new as a career move, right? And the kidnapping? How's that going for you?"

"Shut up."

He was absolutely right, I needed to do that. I was talking because hey, dead guy driving. It made me just a bit uncomfortable. "Eve's going to hunt you down and dismember you if you ding the car. Remember Eve?"

"Bitch," Jerome said, which meant he did remember. Of course he did. Jerome had been the president of the Jock Club and Eve had been the founder and nearly the only member of the Order of the Goth, Morganville Edition. Those two groups never got along, especially in the hothouse world of high school.

"Remind me to wash your mouth with soap later," I said, and shut my eyes as a particularly brutal bump bounced my head around. Red flashed through my brain, and I thought about things like aneurysms, and death. "Not nice to talk about people behind their backs."

"Go screw yourself."

"Hey, *three* words! You go, boy. Next thing you know, you'll be up to real sentences. . . . Where are we going?"

Jerome's eyes glared at me in the mirror some more. The car smelled like dirt, and something else. Something rotten. Skanky homeless unwashed clothes brewed in a vat of old meat.

I tried not to think about it, because between the smell and the lurching of the car and my aching head, well, you know. Luckily, I didn't have to not-think-about-it for long,

because Jerome made a few turns and then hit the brakes with a little too much force.

I rolled off the bench seat and into the spacious legroom, and *ow*. "Ow," I made it official. "You learn that in Dead Guy Driver's Ed?"

"Shut up."

"You know, I think being dead might have actually given you a bigger vocabulary. You ought to think of suggesting that to the U. Put in an extension course or something."

The car shifted as Jerome got out of the front seat, and then the back door opened as he reached in to grab me under the arms and haul. Dead he might be; skanky, definitely. But still: strong.

Jerome dumped me on the caliche-white road, which was graded and graveled, but not recently, and walked off around the hood of the car. I squirmed and looked around. There was an old house about twenty feet away—the end of the pale road—and it looked weathered and defeated and sagging. Could have been a hundred years old, or five without maintenance. Hard to tell. Two stories, old-fashioned and square. Had one of those runaround porches people used to build to catch the cool breezes, although *cool* out here was relative.

I didn't recognize the place, which was a weird feeling. I'd grown up in Morganville, and I knew every nook and hiding place—survival skills necessary to making it to adulthood. That meant I wasn't *in* Morganville proper anymore. I knew there were some farmhouses outside of the town limits, but those who lived in them didn't come to town much,

and nobody left the city without express vampire permission, unless they were desperate or looking for an easy suicide. So I had no idea who lived here. If anyone but Jerome did, these days.

Maybe he'd eaten all the former residents' brains, and I was his version of takeout. Yeah, that was comforting.

I worked on the ropes, but Jerome tied a damn good knot and my numbed fingers weren't exactly up to the task.

It had been quitting time at the plants when I'd gone out to the parking lot and ended up road kill, but now the big western sun was brushing the edge of the dusty horizon. Sunset was coming, in bands of color layered on top of each other, from red straight up to indigo.

I squirmed and tried to dislocate an elbow in order to get to my front pocket, where my cell phone waited patiently for me to text 911. No luck, and I ran out of time anyway.

Jerome came back around the car, grabbed me by the collar of my T-shirt, and pulled. I grunted and kicked and struggled like a fish on the line, but all that accomplished was to leave a wider drag-path in the dirt. I couldn't see where we were going. The backs of Jerome's fingers felt chilly and dry against my sweaty neck.

Bumpity-bump-bump up a set of steps that felt splinter-sharp even through my clothes, and the sunset got sliced off by a slanting dark roof. The porch was flatter, but no less uncomfortably splintered. I tried struggling again, this time really putting everything into it, but Jerome dropped me and smacked the back of my head into the wood floor. More red and white flashes, like my own personal emergency signal.

When I blinked them away, I was being dragged across a threshold, into the dark.

Shit.

I wasn't up for bravado anymore. I was seriously scared, and I wanted out. My heart was pounding, and I was thinking of a thousand horrible ways I could die here in this stinking, hot, closed-up room. The carpet underneath my back felt stiff and moldy. What furniture there was looked abandoned and dusty, at least the stuff that wasn't in pieces.

Weirdly, there was the sound of a television coming from upstairs. Local news. The vampires' official mouthpieces were reporting safe little stories, world events, nothing too controversial. Talk about morphine for the masses.

The sound clicked off, and Jerome let go of me. I flopped over onto my side, then my face, and inchwormed my way up to my knees while trying not to get a mouthful of dusty carpet. I heard a dry rattle from behind me.

Jerome was laughing.

"Laugh while you can, monkey boy," I muttered, and spat dust. Not likely he'd ever seen *Buckaroo Banzai*, but it was worth a shot.

Footsteps creaked on the stairs from the second floor. I reoriented myself, because I wanted to be looking at whatever evil bastard was coming to the afternoon matinee of my probably gruesome death. . . .

Oh. Oh, *dammit.*

"Hello, son," my dad Frank Collins said. "Sorry about this, but I knew you wouldn't just come on your own."

The ropes came off, once I promised to be a good boy and not rabbit for the car the second I had the chance. My father looked about the same as I'd expected, which meant not good but strong. He'd started out a random pathetic alcoholic; after my sister had died—accident or murder, you take your pick—he'd gone off the deep end. So had my mom. So had I, for that matter.

Sometime in there, my dad had changed from random pathetic drunk to mean, badass vampire-hunting drunk. The vampire-hating component of that had been building up for years, and it had exploded like an ancient batch of TNT when my mother died—by suicide, maybe. I didn't believe it, and neither did my dad. The vampires had been behind it, like they were behind every terrible thing that had ever happened in our lives.

That's what I used to believe, anyway. And what Dad still did.

I could smell the whiskey rising up off of him like the bad-meat smell off of Jerome, who was kicked back in a chair in the corner, reading a book. Funny. Jerome hadn't been much of a reader when he'd been alive.

I sat obligingly on the ancient, dusty couch, mainly because my feet were too numb to stand, and I was trying to work circulation back into my fingers. Dad and I didn't hug. Instead, he paced, raising dust motes that glimmered in the few shafts of light that fought their way through smudged windows.

"You look like crap," Dad said, pausing to stare at me. I resisted the urge, like Marjo, to give him a one-fingered salute, because he'd only beat the crap out of me for it. Seeing him gave me a black, sick feeling in the pit of my stomach. I wanted to love him. I wanted to hit him. I didn't know what I wanted, except that I wanted this whole thing to just go away.

"Gee, thanks, Dad," I said, and deliberately slumped back on the couch, giving him all the teen attitude I could. "I missed you too. I see you brought all your friends with you. Oh, wait."

The last time my dad had rolled into Morganville, he'd done it in a literal kind of way—on a motorcycle, with a bunch of badass motorcycle biker buddies. No sign of them this time. I wondered when they'd finally told him to shove it, and how hard.

Dad didn't answer. He kept staring at me. He was wearing a leather jacket with lots of zippers, faded blue jeans, sturdy boots. Not too different from what I was wearing, minus the jacket, because only a stupid jerk would be in leather in this heat. Looking at *you*, Dad.

"Shane," he said. "You knew I'd come back for you."

"Yeah, that's really sweet. The last time I saw you, you were trying to blow my ass up along with a whole building full of vampires, remember? What's my middle name, Collateral Damage?" He'd have done it too. I knew my dad too well to think anything else. "You also left me to burn alive in a cage, *Dad*. So excuse me if I'm not getting all misty-eyed while the music swells."

His expression—worn into a hard leather mask by wind and sun—didn't change. "It's a war, Shane. We talked about this."

"Funny thing, I don't remember you saying, *If you get caught by the vampires, I'll leave you to burn, dumbass.* But maybe I'm just not remembering all the details of your clever plan." Feeling was coming back into my fingers and toes. Not fun. It felt like I'd dipped them in battery acid and then rolled them in lye. "I can get over that. But you had to go and drag my friends into it."

That was what I hated the most. Sure, he'd screwed me over—more than once, actually. But he was right, we'd kind of agreed that one or the other of us might have to bite it for the cause, back when I believed in his cause.

We hadn't agreed about innocent people, especially my friends, getting thrown on the pile of bodies.

"Your *friends*, right," Dad said, with about a bottle's worth of cheap whiskey emphasis. "A half-vampire, a wannabe morbid freak, and—oh, you mean that girl, don't you? The little skinny one. She melted the brains right out of your head, didn't she? I warned you about that."

Claire. He didn't even remember her name. I closed my eyes for a second, and there she was, smiling up at me with those clear, trusting eyes. She might be small, but she had a kind of strength my dad wouldn't ever understand. She was the first really pure thing that I'd ever known, and I wasn't about to let him take her away. She was waiting for me right now, back at the Glass House, probably studying and chewing a pencil. Or arguing with Eve. Or . . . wondering where the hell I was.

I had to get out of this. I had to get back to Claire.

Painful or not, my feet were functional again. I tested them by standing up. In the corner, Dead Jerome put aside his book. It was a battered, water-stained copy of *The Wizard of Oz*. Who did he think he was? The Cowardly Lion? The Scarecrow? Hell, maybe he thought he was Dorothy.

"Just like I thought, this is all about the girl. You probably think you're some knight in shining armor come to save her." Dad's smile was sharp enough to cut diamonds. "You know how she sees you? A big, dumb idiot she can put on a leash. Her own pet pit bull. Your innocent little schoolgirl, she's wearing the Founder's symbol now. She's working for the vampires. I sure as hell hope she's like a porn star in the sack for you to be betraying your own like this."

This time, I didn't need a knock on the head to see red. I felt my chin going down, my lungs filling, but I held on to my temper. Somehow.

He was trying to make me charge him.

"I love her, Dad," I said. "Don't."

"Love, yeah, right. You don't know the meaning of the word, Shane. She's working for the leeches. She's helping them regain control of Morganville. She has to go, and you know it."

"Over my dead body."

In the corner, Jerome laughed that scratchy, raspy laugh that made me want to tear out his voice box once and for all. "Could be arranged," he croaked.

"Shut up," my dad snapped without taking his eyes off of me. "Shane, listen to me. I've found the answer."

"Wait—let me guess—forty-two?" No use. Dad wasn't anywhere near cool enough to be a Douglas Adams fan. "I don't care what you've found, Dad, and I'm not listening to you anymore. I'm going home. You want to have your pet dead guy stop me?"

His eyes fixed on my wrist, where I was wearing a brace-let. Not one of those things that would have identified me as vamp property—a hospital bracelet, white plastic with a big red cross on it.

"You wounded?" Not, of course, was I sick. I was just another foot soldier, to Dad. You were either wounded, or malingering.

"Whatever. I'm better," I said.

It seemed, for just a second, that he softened. Maybe nobody but me would have noticed. Maybe I imagined it too. "Where were you hurt, boy?"

I shrugged and pointed to my abs, slightly off to one side. The scar still ached and felt hot. "Knife."

He frowned. "How long ago?"

"Long enough." The bracelet would be coming off in the next week. My grace period was nearly over.

He looked into my eyes, and for a second, just a second, I let myself believe he was genuinely concerned.

Sucker.

He always had been able to catch me off guard, no mat-ter how carefully I watched him, and I didn't even see the punch coming until it was too late. It was hard, delivered with surgical precision, and it doubled me over and sent me stumbling back to flop onto the couch again. *Breathe*,

I told my muscles. My solar plexus told me to stuff it, and my insides throbbed, screaming in pain and terror. I heard myself making hard, gasping noises, and hated myself for it. *Next time. Next time I hit the bastard first.*

I knew better, though.

Dad grabbed me by the hair and yanked my head back. He pointed my face in Jerome's direction. "I'm sorry, boy, but I need you to *listen* right now. You see him? *I brought him back, right out of the grave.* I can bring them all back, as many as I need. They'll fight for me, Shane, and they won't quit. It's time. We can take this town back, and we can finally end this nightmare."

My frozen muscles finally unclenched, and I pulled in a whooping, hoarse gasp of air. Dad let go of my hair and stepped away.

He'd always known when to back off too.

"Your definition of—the end of the nightmare—is a little different—from mine," I wheezed. "Mine doesn't include zombies." I swallowed and tried to slow my heart rate. "How'd you do it, Dad? How the hell is he standing here?"

He brushed that aside. Of course. "I'm trying to explain to you that it's time to quit talking about the war, and time to start fighting it. We can win. We can destroy all of them." He paused, and the glow in his eyes was the next best thing to a fanatic with a bomb strapped to his chest. "I need you, son. We can do it together."

That part, he really meant. It was sick and twisted, but he did need me.

And I needed to use that. "First, tell me how you do it," I said. "I need to know what I'm signing up for."

"Later." Dad clapped me on the shoulder. "When you're convinced this is necessary, maybe. For now, all you need to know is that it's possible, I've done it. Jerome's proof."

"No, Dad. Tell me how. Either I'm in it or I'm not. No more secrets."

Nothing I was saying was going to register with him as a lie, because they weren't lies. I was saying what he wanted to hear. First rule of growing up with an abusive father: you cope, you bargain, you learn how to avoid getting hit.

And my father wasn't bright enough to know I'd figured it out.

Still, some instinct warned him; he looked at me with narrowed eyes, a frown wrinkling his forehead. "I'll tell you," he said. "But you need to show me you can be trusted first."

"Fine. Tell me what you need." That translated into, *Tell me who you need me to beat up.* As long as I was willing to do that, he'd believe me.

I was hoping it would be Jerome.

"Of everybody who died in the last couple of years, who was the strongest?"

I blinked, not sure it was a trick question. "Jerome?"

"Besides Jerome."

"I guess—probably Tommy Barnes." Tommy was no teenager; he'd been in his thirties when he'd kicked it, and he'd been a big, mean, tough dude even the other big, mean, tough dudes had given a wide berth. He'd died in a bar fight,

I'd heard. Knifed from behind. He'd have snapped the neck off of anybody who'd tried it to his face.

"Big Tom? Yeah, he'd do." Dad nodded thoughtfully. "All right, then. We're bringing him back."

The last person on Earth I'd want to bring back from the grave would be Big Tommy Barnes. He'd been crazy-badass alive. I could only imagine death wouldn't have improved his temper.

But I nodded. "Show me."

Dad took off his leather jacket, and then stripped off his shirt. In contrast to the sun-weathered skin of his arms, face, and neck, his chest was fish-belly white, and it was covered with tattoos. I remembered some of them, but not all the ink was old.

He'd recently had our family portrait tattooed over his heart.

I forgot to breathe for a second, staring at it. Yeah, it was crude, but those were the lines of Mom's face, and Alyssa's. I didn't realize, until I saw them, that I'd nearly forgotten how they looked.

Dad looked down at the tat. "I needed to remind myself," he said.

My throat was so dry that it clicked when I swallowed. "Yeah." My own face was there, frozen in indigo blue at the age of maybe sixteen. I looked thinner, and even in tattoo form I looked more hopeful. More sure.

Dad held out his right arm, and I realized that there was more new ink.

And this stuff was *moving*.

I took a step back. There were dense, strange symbols on his arm, all in standard tattoo ink, but there was nothing standard about what the tats were doing—namely, they were revolving slowly like a DNA helix up and down the axis of his arm, under the skin. "*Christ,* Dad—"

"Had it done in Mexico," he said. "There was an old priest there, he knew things from the Aztecs. They had a way to bring back the dead, so long as they hadn't been gone for more than two years, and were in decent condition otherwise. They used them as ceremonial warriors." Dad flexed his arm, and the tattoos flexed with him. "This is part of what does it."

I felt sick and cold now. This had moved way past what I knew. I wished wildly that I could show this to Claire; she'd probably be fascinated, full of theories and research.

She'd know what to do about it.

I swallowed hard and said, "And the other part?"

"That's where you come in," Dad said. He pulled his T-shirt on again, hiding the portrait of our family, "I need you to prove you're up for this, Shane. Can you do that?"

I gulped air and finally, convulsively nodded. *Play for time,* I was telling myself. *Play for time, think of something you can do.* Short of chopping off my own father's arm, though. . . .

"This way," Dad said. He went to the back of the room. There was a door there, and he'd added a new, sturdy lock to it that he opened with a key from his jacket.

Jerome gave me that creepy laugh again, and I felt my skin shiver into gooseflesh.

"Right. This might be a shock," Dad said. "But trust me, it's for a good cause."

He swung open the door and flipped on a harsh overhead light.

It was a windowless cell, and inside, chained to the floor with thick silver-plated links, was a vampire.

Not just any vampire. Oh no, that would have been too easy for my father.

It was Michael Glass, my best friend.

Michael looked—white. Paler than pale. I'd never seen him look like that. There were burns on his arms, big raised welts where the silver was touching, and there were cuts. He was leaking slow trickles of blood on the floor.

His eyes were usually blue, but now they were red, bright red. Scary monster red, like nothing human.

But it was still my best friend's voice whispering, "Help."

I couldn't answer him. I backed up and slammed the door.

Jerome was laughing again, so I turned around, picked up a chair, and smashed him in the face with it. I could have hit him with a powder puff, for all the good it did. He grabbed the chair, broke the thick wood with a snap of his hands, and threw it back at me. I stumbled, and would have gone down except for the handy placement of a wall.

"Stop. Don't touch my son," my father said. Jerome froze like he'd run into a brick wall, hands working like he still wanted to rip out my throat.

I turned on my dad and snarled, "That's my friend!"

"No, that's a vampire," he said. "The youngest one. The weakest one. The one most of them won't come running to rescue."

I wanted to scream. I wanted to punch somebody. I felt pressure building up inside, and my hands were shaking. "What the hell are you doing to him?"

I didn't know who he was, this guy in the leather jacket looking at me. He looked like a tired, middle-aged biker, with his straggly graying hair, his sallow, seamed face, his scars and tats. Only his eyes seemed like they belonged to my dad, and even then, only for a second.

"It's a vampire," he said. "It's not your friend, Shane. You need to be real clear about that—your friend is dead, just like Jerome here, and you can't let that get in the way of what needs to be done. When we go to war, we get them all. *All*. No exceptions."

Michael had played at our house. My dad had tossed a ball around with him and pushed his swing and served him cake at birthday parties.

And my dad didn't care about any of that anymore.

"How?" My jaw felt tight. I was grinding my teeth, and my hands were shaking. "How did you do this? What are you doing to him?"

"I'm bleeding it and storing the blood, just like they do us humans," Dad said. "It's a two-part spell—the tattoo, and the blood of a vampire. It's just a creature, Shane. Remember that."

Michael wasn't a creature. Not *just* a creature, anyway; neither was what Dad had pulled out of Jerome's grave, for

that matter. Jerome wasn't just a mindless killing machine. Mindless killing machines didn't fill their spare time with the adventures of Dorothy and Toto. They didn't even know they *had* spare time. I could see it in Jerome's wide, yellowed eyes now. The pain. The terror. The anger.

"Do you want to be here?" I asked him, straight out.

For just that second, Jerome looked like a boy. A scared, angry, hurt little boy. "No," he said. "Hurts."

I wasn't going to let this happen. Not to Michael, oh hell no. And not even to Jerome.

"Don't you go all soft on me, Shane. I've done what needed doing," Dad said. "Same as always. You used to be weak. I thought you'd manned up."

Once, that would have made me try to prove it by fighting something. Jerome, maybe. Or him.

I turned and looked at him and said, "I really would be weak, if I fell for that tired bullshit, Dad." I raised my hands, closed them into fists, and then opened them again and let them fall. "I don't need to prove anything to you. Not anymore."

I walked out the front door, out to the dust-filmed black car. I popped the trunk and took out a crowbar.

Dad watched me from the door, blocking my way back into the house. "What the hell are you doing?"

"Stopping you."

He threw a punch as I walked up the steps toward him. This time, I saw it coming, saw it telegraphed clearly in his face before the impulse ever reached his fist.

I stepped out of the way, grabbed his arm, and shoved him face-first into the wall. "Don't." I held him there, pinned

like a bug on a board, until I felt his muscles stop fighting me. The rest of him never would. "We're done, Dad. Over. This is *over*. Don't make me hurt you, because God, I really want to."

I should have known he wouldn't just give up.

The second I let him go, he twisted, jammed an elbow into my abused stomach, and forced me backward. I knew his moves by now, and sidestepped an attempt to hook my feet out from under me.

"Jerome!" Dad yelled. "Stop my—"

The end of that sentence was going to be *son,* and I couldn't let him put Jerome back in the game or this was over before it started.

So I punched my father full in the face. Hard. With all the rage and resentment that I'd stored up over the years, and all the anguish, and all the fear. The shock rattled every bone in my body, and my whole hand sent up a red flare of distress. My knuckles split open.

Dad hit the floor, eyes rolling back in his head. I stood there for a second, feeling oddly cold and empty, and saw his eyelids flutter.

He wouldn't be out for long.

I moved quickly across the room, past Jerome, who was still frozen in place, and opened the door to the cell. "Michael?" I crouched down across from him, and my friend shook gold hair back from his white face and stared at me with eerie, hungry eyes.

I held up my wrist, showing him the bracelet. "Promise me, man. I get you out of here, no biting. I love you, but no."

Michael laughed hoarsely. "Love you too, bro. Get me the hell out of here."

I set to work with the crowbar, pulling up floorboards and gouging the eyebolts out for each set of chains. I'd been right; my dad was too smart to make chains out of solid silver. Too soft, too easy to break. These were silver-plated— good enough to do the job on Michael, if not one of the older vamps.

I only had to pull up the first two; Michael's vampire strength took care of yanking the others from the floor.

Michael's eyes flared red when I leaned closer, trying to help him up, and before I knew what was happening, he'd wrapped a hand around my throat and slammed me down, on my back, on the floor. I felt the sting of sharp nails in my skin, and saw his eyes fixed on the cut on my head.

"No biting," I said again, faintly. "Right?"

"Right," Michael said, from somewhere out beyond Mars. His eyes were glowing like storm lanterns, and I could feel every muscle in his body trembling. "Better get that cut looked at. Looks bad."

He let me up, and moved with about half his usual vampire speed to the door. Dad might not let Jerome have at me, but he wasn't going to hold back with Michael, and Michael was—at best—half his normal strength right now. Not exactly a fair fight.

"Michael," I said, and put my back against the wall next to him. "We go together, straight to the window. You get out, don't wait for me. The sun should be down far enough that you can make it to the car." I gathered up a handful of

silver chain and wrapped it around my hand. "Don't even think about arguing right now."

He sent me an are-you-kidding look, and nodded.

We moved fast, and together. I got in Jerome's way and delivered a punch straight from the shoulder right between his teeth, reinforced with silver-plated metal.

I only intended to knock him back, but Jerome howled and stumbled, hands up to ward me off. It was like years fell away, and all of a sudden we were back in junior high again—him the most popular bully in school, me finally getting enough size and muscle to stand up to him. Jerome had made that same girly gesture the first time I'd hit back.

It threw me off.

A crossbow bolt fired from the far corner of the living room hissed right over my head and slammed to a vibrating stop in the wooden wall. "Stop!" Dad ordered hoarsely. He was on his knees, but he was up and very, very angry. He was also reloading, and the next shot wouldn't be a warning.

"Get out!" I screamed at Michael, and if he was thinking about staging a reenactment of the gunfight at the OK Corral, he finally saw sense. He jumped through the nearest window in a hail of glass and hit the ground running. I'd been right: The sun was down, or close enough that it wouldn't hurt him too badly.

He made it to the car, opened the driver's side door, and slid inside. I heard the roar as the engine started. "Shane!" he yelled. "Come on!"

"In a second," I yelled back. I stared at my father, and the moving tattoo. He had the crossbow aimed right at my chest. I twirled the crowbar in one hand, the silver chain in the other. "So," I said, watching my father. "Your move, Dad. What now? You want me to do a cage match with Dead Jerome? Would that make you happy?"

My dad was staring not at me, but at Dead Jerome, who was cowering in the corner. I'd hurt him, or the silver had; half his face was burned and rotting, and he was weeping in slow, retching sobs.

I knew the look Dad was giving him. I'd seen it on my father's face more times than I could count. Disappointment.

"My *son*," Dad said in disgust. "You ruin everything."

"I guess Jerome's more your son than I am," I said. I walked toward the front door. I wasn't going to give my father the satisfaction of making me run. I knew he had the crossbow in his hands, and I knew it was loaded.

I knew he was sighting on my back.

I heard the trigger release, and the ripped-silk hiss of wood traveling through air. I didn't have time to be afraid, only—like my dad—bitterly disappointed.

The crossbow bolt didn't hit me. Didn't even miss me.

When I turned, at the door, I saw that he'd put the crossbow bolt, tipped with silver, through Jerome's skull. Jerome slid silently down to the floor. Dead. Finally, mercifully dead.

The *Wizard of Oz* fell face down next to his hand.

"Son," my dad said, and put the crossbow aside. "Please, don't go. I need you. I really do."

I shook my head.

"This thing—it'll only last another few days," he said. "The tattoo. It's already fading. I don't have *time* for this, Shane. It has to be now."

"Then I guess you're out of luck."

He snapped the crossbow up again.

I ducked to the right, into the parlor, jumped the wreckage of a couch, and landed on the cracked, curling floor of the old kitchen. It smelled foul and chemical in here, and I spotted a fish tank on the counter, filled with cloudy liquid. Next to it was a car battery.

DIY silver plating equipment, for the chains.

There was also a 1950s-era round-shouldered fridge, rattling and humming.

I opened it.

Dad had stored Michael's blood in bottles, old dirty milk bottles likely scavenged from the trash heap in the corner. I grabbed all five bottles and threw them one at a time out the window, aiming for a big upthrusting rock next to a tree.

Smash. Smash. Smash. Smash. . . .

"Stop," Dad spat. In my peripheral vision I saw him standing there, aiming his reloaded crossbow at me. "I'll kill you, Shane. I swear I will."

"Yeah? Lucky you've already got me tattooed on your chest, then, with the rest of the dead family." I pulled back for the throw.

"I could bring back your mother," Dad blurted. "Maybe even your sister. Don't."

Oh, *God*. Sick black swam across my vision for a second.

"You throw that bottle," he whispered, "and you're killing their last chance to live."

I remembered Jerome—his sagging muscles, his grainy skin, the panic and fear in his eyes.

Do you want to be here?

No. Hurts.

I threw the last bottle of Michael's blood and watched it sail straight and true, to shatter in a red spray against the rock.

I thought he'd kill me. Maybe *he* thought he'd kill me too. I waited, but he didn't pull the trigger.

"I'm fighting for humanity," he said. His last, best argument. It had always won me over before.

I turned and looked him full in the face. "I think you already lost yours."

I walked out past him, and he didn't stop me.

Michael drove like a maniac, raising contrails of caliche dust about a mile high as we sped back to the main highway. He kept asking me how I was doing. I didn't answer him, just looked out at the gorgeous sunset, and the lonely, broken house fading in the distance.

We blasted past the Morganville city limits sign, and one of the ever-lurking police cars cut us off. Michael slowed, stopped, and turned off the engine. A rattle of desert wind shook the car.

"Shane."

"Yeah."

"He's dangerous."

"I know that."

"I can't just let this go. Did you see—"

"I saw," I said. "I know." *But he's still my father*, some small, frightened kid inside me wailed. *He's all I have.*

"Then what do you want me to say?" Michael's eyes had faded back to blue, now, but he was still white as a ghost, blue-white, scary-white. I'd spilled all his blood out there on the ground. The burns on his hands and wrists made my stomach clench.

"Tell them the truth," I said. If the Morganville vampires got to my dad before he could get the hell out, he'd die horribly, and God knew, he probably deserved it. "But give him five minutes, Michael. Just five."

Michael stared at me, and I couldn't tell what was in his mind at all. I'd known him most of my life, but in that long moment, he was just as much of a stranger as my father had been.

A uniformed Morganville cop tapped on the driver's side window. Michael rolled it down. The cop hadn't been prepared to find a vampire driving, and I could see him amending the harsh words he'd been about to deliver.

"Going a little fast, sir," he finally said. "Something wrong?"

Michael looked at the burns on his wrists, the bloodless slices on his arms. "Yeah," he said. "I need an ambulance."

And then he slumped forward, over the steering wheel. The cop let out a squawk of alarm and got on his radio. I

reached out to ease Michael back. His eyes were shut, but as I stared at him, he murmured, "You wanted five minutes."

"I wasn't looking for a Best Supporting Actor award!" I muttered back.

Michael did his best impression of Vampire in a Coma for about five minutes, and then came to and assured the cop and arriving ambulance attendants he was okay.

Then he told them about my dad.

They found Jerome, still and evermore dead, with a silver-tipped arrow through his head. They found a copy of *The Wizard of Oz* next to him.

There was no sign of Frank Collins.

Later that night—around midnight—Michael and I sat outside on the steps of our house. I had a bottle of most illegal beer; he was guzzling his sixth bottle of blood, which I pretended not to notice. He had his arm around Eve, who had been pelting us both with questions all night in a non-stop machine gun patter; she'd finally run down, and leaned against Michael with sleepy contentment.

Well, she hadn't *quite* run down. "Hey," she said, and looked up at Michael with big, dark-rimmed eyes. "Seriously. You can bring back dead guys with *vampire juice*? That is so wrong."

Michael almost spit out the blood he was swallowing. "*Vampire juice*? Damn, Eve. Thanks for your concern."

She lost her smile. "If I didn't laugh, I'd scream."

He hugged her. "I know. But it's over."

Next to me, Claire had been quiet all night. She wasn't drinking—not that we'd have let her, at sixteen—and she

wasn't saying much, either. She also wasn't looking at me. She was staring out at the Morganville night.

"He's coming back," she finally said. "Your dad's not going to give it up, is he?"

I exchanged a look with Michael. "No," I said. "Probably not. But it'll be a while before he gets his act together again. He expected to have me to help him kick off his war, and like he said, his time was running out. He'll need a brand-new plan."

Claire sighed and linked her arm through mine. "He'll find one."

"He'll have to do it without me." I kissed the soft, warm top of her hair.

"I'm glad," she said. "You deserve better."

"News flash," I said. "I've *got* better. Right here."

Michael and I clinked glasses, and toasted our survival. However long it lasted.

Table Manners

TANITH LEE

The moment I saw him I knew. I suppose any one of us would, by now. We're so used, via movie and novel, to the nature and ways of The Vampire (capital letters intended), we can—or ought to—spot one at two hundred paces. And go grab ourselves a sharpened stake—

Or, of course, not. . . .

I had been sent, that is *persuaded*, to attend the October Ball at the Reconstruct Mansion, by my father, Anthony. He said, and here I quote: "You'll find it interesting, I think."

"Why?" I had demanded. For this wasn't how I wished to spend the first five days of the month.

"Because the world is full of people like the Kokersons. If you like, Lel, put this down as the final part of your education. You'll learn how such people tick."

"Tick in the sense," I said, "of clock or bomb?"

"Either," replied my elegant, lovely, and infuriating father.

October is fall. Time of flaming, *fall*ing leaves, of mists and dreams, before Halloween and winter close in. I'd had my own plans, but there you go. Dad knows it all. (The trouble is, as far as I can tell, he usually does.)

And so I accepted the Kokerson invite and packed my bags and caught the train to Chakhatti Halt, and then took a cab driven by a very sweet guy, who looked and spoke just like a really jolly Tyrannosaurus Rex (I do not lie) in (quasi-) human form.

I call the castle Reconstruct Mansion, did so from the very start, the moment I read in a newspaper that they had imported the edifice, once a huge old castle-type house from someplace in Eastern Europe, and were having it rebuilt stone by stone, in a vast parkland some other place, well outside the small town of Chakhatti. The Kokersons, obviously, are very rich. One of them won a lottery about twenty years back. I had seen photos of them. I really didn't want to go. But go there, Anthony thought I must.

In case this makes my dad sound like a manipulative monster I have to state right here and now that is the very opposite of what he is. As I said, it's just—he seems to know about . . . everything. But then, that's how he is.

My name is Lelystra. It's a family name, only usually I have myself called Lel by those who are my friends. Call me Lel, all right?

"Oh! You should have called—we would have sent a car! And you are Lelystra? What a delicious name! Oh, we wouldn't *dream* of mangling it down to *Lel*!!!"

So they greeted me, the Kokersons. A never-ending family, only lacking a father (had he run away? I might have). Toothy, bronzed sons and toothy, bleached daughters, and boisterous aunts, and an uncle like a dark satanic Bill (his name), and the mother, Mrs. Kokerson, or Ariadne, as I was told to call her. She was sixty going on fifteen. That is, she was sixty, but had somehow stayed fifteen in all the *wrong* ways. I felt an immediate requirement to look after her, steer her away from the cocktails—she was *much* too young to even taste one—and perhaps introduce her to some youthfully elderly male.

I flew upstairs with wings of worry on my feet and leapt into the cover of a bright white bedroom, with a bed the size of a softball field.

I tried to put through a call to Anthony. Cunningly he was in a meeting. I left a message. "Dad, I am going to kill you."

Let me describe the reconstruct castle.

An apparent ascending thousand feet of coal-blue stone, with towers, cupolas, balconies, verandas, staircases inside

and out like static stepped waterfalls, and some of them just as slippery. The window glass is lightly polarized. From outside the windows look like smoky eyeglasses. Inside they color day sky green, and night sky purple, with pink stars. The landscape all around is private and full of trees, lake, and deer. October stags bellowed from the woods all night, waking me regular as a fire alarm roughly every thirty minutes.

It was all a gigantic theme park.

The *theme*, presumably, was the Kokersons, or their fantasy about themselves. The feel of fake antiquity and illusory age was so intense it was quite serious.

And we all had to dress in the clothes they provided, females in flowing gowns, males in gothic tailoring, nothing later than 1880, or earlier than 1694. We were like refugees from a muddled movie set. Even the house was like that.

Two days, two bellowing nights passed.

The day of the ball, everyone (or the Young People, at least) spent all morning and afternoon compulsorily in hot tubs, being massaged, creamed, pedicure-manicured, topped off by shampoo and styling (as if for a cat show). Then came the dressing up in the most extreme clothes yet.

I yawned and yawned, blaming it on the wake-up calls of the noisy stags.

My dress, which Ariadne had chosen me, was white. (Ariadne: "So perfect with your lovely pale hair.") My hair

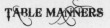

is natural, but somehow the hairdresser had gotten it to go even paler—scared it, maybe. My skin is white too. I like the sun but never take a tan. In the white dress I vanished without meaning to, became a sort of plaster statue figure lacking any features, apart from my eyes which, thank the Lord, are very dark gray.

I thought, *I shall attend, play their silly game, dance a few of the minuets and waltzes* (anything modern was absolutely out)*, and retire graciously soon as I can, later saying I was still there all the while.* I'm good at that sort of thing.

Either that is selfishly self-protective, or my kinder side not wanting to offend or hurt. I have no idea which and I don't care. It works. I escape, others aren't upset.

So I descended the indoor glass-slippery, glass-slipper stair, and entered the ballroom (like the outside of a bridal cake, icing sugar and gilding, with grapevines of chandeliers). I glanced around.

And that was when I saw him. And knew him. Or rather, knew what he *was.*

And all along my spine, rising upward, ran the kind of prickly electricity that on a cat reveals itself as the fur standing on end.

Ariadne sailed by, right on cue.

Me, casually: "Who is that? I *do* like his costume."

"Yes, isn't it glorious? But I'm sure you notice that he's *very* handsome too," she enthused at me.

I answered calmly. "Yes. Quite a good face."

"And *perfect* masculine physique. Strong, like a dancer's. And his hair—"

"Is it really so long or is that a piece?"

"No. It's all his own. It's only that usually Anghel ties it back. How romantic he looks, doesn't he? I'm not surprised you'd pick him out. But I have to warn you, Lelystra, he's cold as snow. Cold as—" She fought for an even more cryogenic noun.

"As very *cold* snow?" I helpfully suggested.

"Well, er, yes. The *coldest* of cold snow. We're all quite crazy over him, and my two daughters are besotted, but he's only ever polite. But then, Anghel has escorted *movie stars*. Always in demand. He only arrived an hour ago."

"Really."

"He's been offered parts himself in so many movies—"

"But always coldly and politely refused," I supplied. I tried to keep all trace of irritation from my voice. *Obviously* he wouldn't take a part in any film. You only had to look at him to see it—this one would never be up at the crack of dawn and out on location in the blazing sun.

He was A Vampire.

Someone called Ariadne then, and she floated off on a sea of people dancing polkas.

Anghel (a name to conjure with) might be any age from twenty to six hundred. Or more. He looked about twenty-two. His hair was black as if he had washed it in the night outside. His eyes were blacker. He was pale, paler no doubt than I was. It wasn't any kind of make-up. He had a handsome—no, a beautiful—and cruel face. It was his mask, evidently, to keep all of us just far enough away—or if near then suitably nervous and/or impressed—while he chose his

victim for that night, maybe for the weekend. It wouldn't be more, because also evidently he hadn't *killed* anyone by drinking their blood. His dates might keep quiet, or be made to "forget" what had gone on, but surely word would have gotten around if none of them ever went home. His quaint costume was that of some European nobleman of the eighteenth century. All black, need I add, and embroidered, the tall black boots flittering with quills of steel and his coat with wild lace cuffs of sheerest snow white (to match his manner, perhaps).

He was unmistakable!

I felt I should have known he'd be here, been *warned*. Maybe I took my ignorance too much to heart.

Yet my—almost *outrage*—made me linger after all. None of the rest of them, it seemed, could figure him out, and put their fascination down only to his looks. I had to assume too that now and then, if only after dark, he had been spotted in everyday garb where, frankly, even if his hair *was* tied back, and he wore jeans and a baseball cap to advertize the Chakhatti Arrows, he would stick out like an eagle in an aviary of pigeons.

I am not ashamed of what I next did. I felt it was my right and duty. If everyone else was blind, I wasn't. Oh, I'm nothing so gallant as a vampire-slayer, not me. Sorry if you hoped that was the next bit. No, I am just a nosy eighteen-year-old woman who sometimes—okay *often* (thank you, Dad)—takes herself a tad too seriously, and who *hates* to be beaten once she wakes up to a challenge. So, well . . . Reader, I *followed* him.

Back on the glacial dance floor a thousand feet pounced, pranced, and stumbled, and the band played and the chandeliers shone.

And I slid like a panther, all right a *white* one, through the mob, spying on wicked Mr. Anghel whose second name no one seemed to know. (I had asked again, here and there, about him.)

First off he danced a waltz with a dazzled girl, who almost swooned and then was non-swooning and dis-dazzled when he abandoned her for another. (Later in the evening I came across knots of unsettled young women fuming or sighing or even sobbing—or plotting how to lure him back.)

He went through about ten girls in ten dances. He was picky, wasn't he? Of course, his partners, did they but know, were better off *not* being the selected maiden for the night's feast.

I did note he could dance stunningly well. Wondered briefly if he'd be as good in a club, decided he would be, as the vampire kind are simply wired to move well, in whatever context. It comes with the territory.

He never actually spotted *me*. I took care he didn't. I've said I'm pretty brilliant at seeming to be there when I'm not. I'm pretty good at doing the reverse too. But now and then he glanced around, looking for a split second slightly uneasy. He was A Vampire. He realized that *someone* was on his track. But I could see too he didn't truly reckon anyone was or could be. His madly *apparent* vampiricness was the

camouflage. He was like an actor in the *rôle* of The Vampire. He *wants* to convince he is exactly that. The true vampire would cut his hair, dress in rags, and keep in the shadows.

All this anyhow, he center stage, me stalking unseen, went on for about two hours.

Then, *he found her.*

I was startled, and then less so. She was completely loud in clothes and make-up, with gold neon for hair. Quite pretty but mainly like a flag. The ideal choice. She thought she was the Star of the Night. She had convinced a lot of other people too that she was. Few therefore would doubt *he* thought so.

The target of some, by now, seventy-odd distracted jealousies, he drew her smoothly off the floor, and next they melted away onto another flight of watery stairs, and so down and out and in between the velvet curtains of the night.

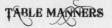

It was rather more challenging hunting them now, in all my white shimmer, for the dark was *dark* even if a half moon was rising on the lake. Yet here too, I could hide. A slant of moonlight through the shrubs, a blond deer slipping from tree to tree—a trick of the eyes. That was me. (I'd better own up. Anthony taught me these skills, though I did have natural talent.)

He and she were fairly unoriginal in their choice of resting place, but then, I suppose, if you have a vast lake like a polished silver tray, and everywhere else the backdrop of

darkness, you simply *have* to perch the edges of both. Which means, presumably, Anghel The Vampire was a romantic? He must have bought into his own legend in a big way.

I watched them a while, as they sat on a bench at the brim of the water. They talked, he speaking low and she . . . well, she had a kind of high and penetrating voice. "Oh, wow!" she kept saying, and, "What did you do then?" I could catch his words too—my hearing is fine—but they sounded like sort of movie dialogue. Quite *good* movie dialogue, but. He was telling her about his harsh life, and the novel he wanted to write, and sometimes he quoted a little poetry (Byron, Keats), and though when most guys do that they come over as truly useless, when he did it, it was quite impressive. But it was all a show, a sham. It was him being The Vampire, in the movie *rôle* he had invented, and for which he'd coined this well-written script.

I wondered if he even made himself sleep, by day, in some sort of *tomb*. If so, probably a really comfortable one, with a crystal goblet of bottled water on the side. . . .

And then, quite abruptly, for somehow—even knowing it had to—I hadn't foreseen exactly when it would happen, he was bending toward her.

I thought, *Is she honestly so dumb she thinks this is just going to be a kiss?*

Sure. The idea of vampires *is* romantic. But not when you actually think about what they do. They bite you. Which, if that wasn't what you wanted, or expected, is an *assault* in anyone's book. And then—they steal your blood. Because again, unless you genuinely desire to nourish them in this

way, it's *theft*. So what do those two procedures demonstrate a vampire to be? Shall I say: A mugger.

When he moved, so did I. I darted forward and burst out on them, white as vanilla ice cream. I made my voice even higher and more piercing than hers—which took some doing.

"Oh, hi! Am I *interrupting*? *Sorry!* But I'm just completely *lost*—and this is such a HUGE place, isn't it? Oh, do you mind if I sit down on your bench? I've been wandering around for over an hour. I mean, where *is* that castle? You wouldn't think, would you, you could lose a place that HUGE, but—" and down I flopped, with the sigh of a woman who just is not going to move for a while.

They were both gaping at me. She looked furious too. He, more as if he had just gotten the answer to a question that had been bothering him for hours. I had no doubt the answer was: *Yes! This plaster-of-Paris person is the one who was following me!*

I let a few moments pass, but neither she nor he spoke. Anyone else but the character I pretended to be would have grasped, however miles-thick they were, that *monsieur et mademoiselle* wished to be *left alone*.

Not I.

"What *ever* do you think of the ball?" I sparkled at them. "Isn't it too divine?"

"Then why," he said, in a low, dark, *awful* tone, "don't you go back to it?"

I'd tempted him from cover.

"I just said, you see," I replied, "I'm lost."

"I doubt that," he said. "If you walk up that path there, the path you just came down, I guess, you can see the house. You can't *miss* the house."

"Oh, really?" I gasped, and right then the neon girl clutched his arm, so for a second he scowled at her. She was in fact too thick herself to realize how terrible this scowl was. She said angrily, "Come on, Ang" (she pronounced that to rhyme with *hang*) "let's just get outta here."

And this was when the stag came shouldering from the woods about twenty feet away along the shore, noiseless and then *extremely* noisy, as branches went rushing and snapping out of the way of its great-antlered head, lit silver by the moonlight. Its eyes flashed electric green—and it bellowed.

That sound, from far off, had been devastating. Being close to it could cause total panic. I'd hoped so anyhow, when I was mentally coaxing the stag—that is, *one* of the stags—to come find us by the lake. This first-class animal had obliged. Neon spurted to her feet. Her eyes—her hair—had gone insane. She shrieked—and *ran*. She left us, him too, and bolted away, around the water and then off into the woods.

He, of course, didn't move.

Nor did I.

The stag though snorted down its gorgeous Roman nose, pawed the grass once as if to say, *You owe me, Lel*, then turned and sauntered back among the shadows.

He spoke once more.

"So you can do that too."

"Excuse me?"

He sighed deeply, stood up, and turned his elegant black velvet back to me. His black hair swung. "This is set in concrete then," he said. "You are to be my downfall."

"Er," I fluted, "my name's Lel."

"Let's not play games. I know you judged me at once, in the house. So, Lel. When do the heavies arrive?"

He had set his baleful eyes on me again. To my annoyance I found I wasn't ready for them. I should have been, shouldn't I. I wasn't a complete dope, like Neon.

"Why don't you sit down," I said.

"And let's talk it over? Very well."

But he stood there. Right next to me. I found too I was uncomfortably over-aware of him, but I should have been able to cope with that, because I already *knew* the power he had, and in my case, prepared as I was, that power really could not and would not be having an effect.

For quite a while then, we stayed, in silence.

The moon silvered the lake, shining it up like an old dollar.

Finally I glanced sidelong at him. He looked magnificently and broodingly sad. Then, just sad. Like a child whose dog died, and he never forgot, even ten years later, the way you *don't* ever forget the ones you love. Things like that.

"Shall I tell you how I came to be—how I got like I am?"

This was what he eventually said. I'd already heard most of what I took to be his "line." Obviously nothing to do with

vampires, but ancient feuds and some curse of his "ancestors" he hadn't believed. He had been born on the borders of France, in a mountain region. His family were aristocrats who had lost everything way back in the 1790s. He had escaped them, and now lived in one room, out here in Chakhatti (the sticks), an impoverished writer who worked nights waiting tables and pumping gas. But of course this mixture of Vampire Angst and modern day necessity was all baloney (as Dad might say).

I hazarded a guess. "Your family is well off, something in big business maybe. They live here and you were born here. You were also well-educated, went to a top grade college—but left on discovering your true . . . how shall I say, vocation? Your family meanwhile still support you financially, because you tell them you are teaching yourself to be a writer."

He threw me a swift glare. "Not bad. Actually I received a legacy—enough money to survive. That was from an aunt of mine. They always thought she was crazy, but she was— what *I* am. She was—"

"A vampire," I said.

"I have to assume," he said, flexing his hands (perhaps practicing how he would strangle me), "you don't believe vampires exist. That is, in the mythic sense. You just imagine I'm dangerous."

"Wrong again. I know true vampires are quite real. And I know, Mr. Anghel, you belong firmly among them."

"Usually people dismiss my *interests* as . . . a fantasy."

I gazed hard at the lake. He was much too distracting.

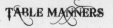

"The only thing that's a fantasy here," I answered, pleased at my own crisp tone, "is your total misunderstanding of what *being* a vampire entails."

"Some secret society—a code known only to the few—" he solemnly said.

"No. Frankly, the opposite," He had turned and I felt him stare at me. It was compelling but I didn't allow myself to react. To the lake alone I added, "You need to talk to someone. If you're as messed up as I think you are, you need some *help*."

He gave a bitter, quite violent laugh.

"Sure. You mean a shrink."

"You need," I continued, "to speak to my father."

"Your—your *what*?"

"Father." I opened the tiny white glitzy evening purse I'd been given, and pulled out one of Anthony's cards, and handed it to him.

He stared at that, now.

"This is some joke, right?"

"No joke, Mr. Anghel—"

"Will you quit that *Mister* stuff—how fucking old do you think I am?"

"You could be a thousand. But no joke. This is for real. If you prefer, I can start you off on the road to redemption by just asking you nine straight questions. All *you* need do is reply, and be honest."

Finally our eyes met.

I thought—well. I thought in one big golden blank. To my relief my voice came out again, not in a husky squeak,

but crisp now as very dry toast. I was at my most business-like, and that was how I asked those nine questions.

⌒

"First question: Do you reflect in mirrors or reflective sur-faces?"

"I don't look anymore. Obviously I don't. I'm undead. My soul—or whatever—that's gone. So, no reflection. The night I realized I threw any mirrors away. And yes, I've learned to shave by touch. I'm good at that, dexterous. It seems to be part of what I am, what I can do, now. The same as I can seem to vanish, even on an empty sidewalk . . . that kind of thing."

"Okay. Second question. Do you go out by day?"

"*You are kidding me.* What do *you* think? Do I look like a case from a burns unit? Yeah, I did once make a mistake. Last winter. I was walking around in broad daylight for one half hour. I was blistered so bad, even inside my clothes, I had to hide for three nights. My *skin*, bits of it, fell off in patches. No. I *don't* go out in sunlight. Sunset is dawn for my kind."

"Question three: How old *are* you?"

"Twenty-two this fall. Next week in fact. I suppose I'll live forever, but I only got started on this *thing* about sixteen months ago."

"Question four—"

"Wait a minute—"

"Question four—" I paused, but he didn't interrupt again. Just looked. With his sorrowful dark eyes. "Do you take and drink human blood? Is that your food?"

"Yes. You know that already. That was what you broke up back there. Me, trying to take and drink and feed on *blood*."

"Question five." (He sighed. Nothing else.) "Do you otherwise eat and drink?"

"No. Oh, water's okay—a glass of wine. Even a beer or a coke. Fluids seem to digest. I don't risk anything else."

"So your last meal was—"

"Sixteen months ago. I threw it right up."

"So blood is your only sustenance. Which leads us to question six: How often do you do this?"

"Once a week. Roughly. I can go a month without, if I have to. But if I don't it's—all I can think of."

"Rather like partying with a so-called recreational drug, yes?"

"I wouldn't know," he said icily. "I never tried those."

"Fine. Question seven: Do you shape-shift? I mean, can you seem to become another thing, an animal say, or even an inanimate object?"

"Yes." (He sounded almost embarrassed, as if he boasted and hadn't wanted to.) "A wolf. Mostly. But once I—I kind of made myself kind of like a phone booth."

I couldn't help it. I burst out laughing. "Did anyone try to—get inside and *make a call*?"

He grinned.

Oh. The grin was beautiful too.

"Yeah. But the door stayed shut."

I pulled us back to grim reality.

"Question eight: Ever killed anyone, Anghel?"

"My God—no. *No.* I don't—I'm careful. It's bad enough being—what I am. I don't want to be a murderer as well."

We were both standing up now. I wasn't sure when I did.

I said, "Question nine, then. And this is the last one. How did you find out you'd become a vampire?"

"How did I—? Look, I'd had suspicions before that we—my family—had the gene for it. I suppose it *is* a gene. Like some families having the gene for red hair, or a particular allergy. . . . I know how it is in books, movies. Someone does it to you, takes your blood and makes you a vampire, just like they are. It didn't happen that way. I said my aunt—I came to realize she was—she was a vampire. She'd just seemed to think she was mad. Everybody put everything weird about her down to that—avoiding sunlight, not eating, that stuff. By the time I connected it all up, she'd been dead two years. And she had left me the legacy. Like she knew I would be the same. So I put it together. I still didn't believe it at first. I said, I want—*wanted* to be a writer. So I started to *write* about it, about my life if I had been, if I *was*, a vampire. I was trying to sort it out.

"Then I met a girl at some party in Manhattan. And she'd read a story of mine, a pretty lurid one, in some magazine and she—she wanted to act it out with me. Scared me. But when I'm scared—then sometimes I have to do it. Prove to myself I can. So, we did. I didn't hurt her. It's important to me you understand that. She loved every minute, and I had a real difficult time putting her off after. But for me—something changed. Something changed when I took the blood. It

was—" he hesitated, looking out at the lake and the moon—
"it was like finding something in your own self, *meeting* who
you really are—and I wasn't who I'd ever thought. And
I was—not better—but I *fit*. And when I went out of the
apartment, everything—the street, the city . . . it was *alive*,
and I was *alive*, in a way it and I had never been, not until
then. Do you begin to see? I can't explain it. I can write with
words, use them, make them work. But with this, I can't *find*
the words. It was like I'd walked out—not of a room, but of
a dark *cave*. My whole world had only *been* a cave—but now
the lights were on and the true world was there all around
me, and inside me, forever.

"So I've answered all your questions, and now I guess
your wonderful father and his men arrive and finish me off.
Right, Lel? That name on the card though, that's a lie, isn't it?
Only one thing puzzles me. Shouldn't it read 'Anthony *Van
Helsing*'?"

I shook my head. "*Oh* no, it surely should not. That name
on the card is a family name. It's mine too."

He looked quizzical. Sad and quizzical and courageous,
all ready to meet some horrible bloodthirsty anti-vampire
end of sharpened stakes and villagers with flaming torches
ready to burn him alive.

It must have been that that made me feel protective, and
want to put my arms around him.

But anyhow that was when he laughed again, a very
different silky, inky laugh—and then he was gone. There
instead stood a great black wolf, the height of a mastiff dog,
with eyes like rubies. The wolf too seemed to be laughing.

But the next second it sprang away, and dove along the lake shore and into the trees.

And *my* next move? I stood there cursing myself.

I knew he wasn't headed for the house, or the town. He had vanished not only from his human shape but out of the life of anyone who'd recently known him. Though everything he said, I was certain, was honest and true, with my artful, smug little plans I'd cornered him, and blown the whole thing. I'd lost him. And worse than that, I had lost him also his own chance of living free and safe in this mad world he had only properly come to see sixteen months before. Oh, Lel. Clever, cunning, know-it-all, stupid, dumb damn Lel.

My father is a physician. He deals with sickness of the psyche and the mind. He has endlessly various patients. He is *good*.

He went into this line of work, as he would be the first to say, because he had already cured both himself, and another member of his family, of a pretty dire life-destructive mental illness. His name, which is real enough, is quite a talking point, but he's found, as I have on the whole, it causes startled amusement rather than giving anything away. It's like that thing about camouflage I mentioned earlier.

Vampirism isn't a disease. It isn't a possession or an evil spell or the devil's work. *It's a way of evolving.* Because the human race did and does evolve. Superman, Batman—they're already around out there. If they keep a low profile, do you *blame* them? A vampire, or what's come to be called

a vampire (the word seems to come from ancient Turkey, and means something like *magician*), is just one more variety of this evolving super-race, the one we watch on screen and read about in books, but which most of us seldom think may just have sat there next to us on the subway.

Vampires are this: They grow up but stay young for a very long while (centuries sometimes). They don't need food or drink, though they *can* eat and drink a little, if they want. Taking another person's blood can bring out awareness of themselves and what they are. But that is only because they have already bought into the idea. That is, they *think* it will, so it does. And in fact where they can come to awareness of the truth *without* assault and robbery, they come to it better and more fully, and with far less damage to themselves. Put it this way: They only go after that blood because they have the notion they are, on some level, vampires. So taking the blood isn't needed. What *is* needed is just facing up to the facts.

Feeding on or drinking blood is—*redundant*. People are *not* the allotted prey, and blood is *not* the essential food. *No vampire on Earth has to have blood.* Just as they don't have to have ordinary food or fluid either. So the Blood Feast made so popular in stories only has value (if that is the right word) in sometimes shocking them into focus for themselves. And believe me, it also hurts them on some deep level too. If you aren't a vampire, though, grabbing blood won't do a darn thing for you. I mean you won't be able to shape-shift or apparently disappear, let alone live to three hundred and forty-nine. Oh, and no vampire can turn anyone else into

one by taking their blood. Unless, of course, they already *were* one to start with.

So, the meaning of blood for vampires is basically a misunderstanding. It has nothing to do with drink or food, with goblets and dishes and the dining table of the world. It is blood*lines*—it's *genes*—as Anghel said. And if you've gotten that gene, you have it. You are a vampire, a Being of the Blood. And one day you'll wake up, and *know*, even if it takes till you're fifty and you look in a mirror (yes, I did say mirror) and think—*I only look twenty-two still. How can this be?*

Because vampires *do* reflect in mirrors, in all reflective surfaces. They cast shadows too. They can even go out all day long in the blazing summer sun. No tan, sure. But the sun won't fry you. Unless, of course, brainwashed by hundreds of years of legendary propaganda, you *believe it will.*

You see, all that stuff is a psychosomatic illness. It *seems* real, so real you'll have the symptoms, as can happen with any major psychosomatic sickness. And in fact a vampire's own abilities can turn against him to reinforce the myth. A vampire *can* seem invisible—so in that looking glass, he *is.* So you come up in blisters too, and seek a big box to sleep in, and hunt down innocent people and mug them for blood. You can even throw up at the smell of garlic, or pass out at a powerful religious symbol. But it isn't for real. It is a kind of *guilt trip.* The vampire knows he is superior. That frightens him. So, unconsciously, he tries to keep himself chained up. No one can be harder on us than we are ourselves, once we've gotten started.

Otherwise, a vampire can live forever, maybe. But you don't need a stake or fire to kill him. You can just shoot a vampire dead, and you won't need a special bullet. Vampires are long-lived, not invulnerable. What they can also do are things like seem to be other creatures, vanish, sometimes fly, and, obviously, call animals to them and ask *them* to do things—like a stag, for example. We don't abuse these gifts. Not when we grasp what we are and why. But then, some of us are lucky. I grew up in a partly vampiric family. I knew by age three what I was, and when I found on my tenth birthday I could turn into a fox, my Dad took a photo of me like that. I still have that picture. Yes, cameras can catch us too.

My father does look remarkably young. He puts it down, to his patients, as the vitamins he takes. And his name—our family name? Draculian. Anthony Draculian. Lelystra Draculian. But no, we're not from that famous branch of our kind (the Romanian one, brought to public attention in the 1800s by clever Mr. Stoker). Though, if you trace bloodlines back far enough, we are related.

And there, you see, these were all the things I should have said to poor handsome unhappy Anghel. And instead I'd been flustered and messed up.

⌒

I had to stay another two days with the Kokersons. I did it and it was hell. But then, there wasn't much point in running back to Dad two days early, howling about my dismal

failure. Anghel was gone. I knew I'd never see him again, I knew I could have helped and instead I only helped make his life worse.

I did put one call through to Dad. But he was with a patient. Oh, let it wait then till I was home. I'd have all the rest of my days after all, to blame myself, and to regret.

C~

Anthony has his office way across town. We live in a big russet brownstone on the corner of Dale and Landry. It's a nice area.

I'd tried to call him again from the cell phone booth on the train, but he was back in another eternal meeting. No one was home.

I dumped my bags and then took the little elevator up to our roof garden. It's only a little garden, a kind of outdoor living room. The last roses were dying on the walls, but the grapevine had big purple grapes. I took some off and ate them, gazing down over the parapet at the sun deciding to sink, as it always does, west of the city.

I had never felt I had to go rob someone of their blood. Lucky in that, I said. Lucky me. I'd had it all very easy. Only when Mom died—I was fifteen then. That had been hard. She wasn't like us, Dad and me, or my uncle. She didn't have the gene. I knew they'd talked about—when she was older, how they would handle that. . . . But it never happened, a truck in town saw to that. It killed her. And we, Dad and me, we wouldn't be immune to that either.

The sky was rose-gold. Birds were flying like scribbles over it. The city made its noises of trains and cabs and people, but I knew the moment my father came back in the house I would sense it, I always did. And then the oddest idea went through my mind. It made me straighten up and hold my breath a moment. This strange thought was—had my father, my clever amazing father who seemed always to know everything—had he known too Anghel was due to be at the Kokerson's weird ball. Had he known I would see what Anghel was—might try to alter things—even think I'd be the one to save Anghel from the dark he'd stumbled into? If that was it, how much more awful it was going to be, telling Anthony that I *hadn't*—

And this was when I picked up what must *be* Dad, that silent step of his I can always hear, just inside the door below. And next the elevator rising.

I was horrified. Not of Dad—of the thing I'd have to say. I braced myself, with the taste of the grapes in my mouth. And out onto the roof he walked. But it wasn't Anthony. It was Anghel.

I froze. Like the biggest fool (the one who wins the Oscar for idiocy), I said, "Whuh?"

And he grinned.

His hair was tied back, a long, long black tail falling down his back. He wore jeans, a shirt, a light leather jacket. Even this way, as I had predicted, you couldn't miss he was something else. Different, astonishing.

He said, "It's okay, Lel. I have a pass for the door. Your father gave it to me. He trusts me. Can you?"

Anthony only ever trusts those who really can be trusted.

But I'd been kidding myself, hadn't I? It wasn't just I felt I'd messed up, let Anghel, a *patient*, down. It was me I was unhappy for. I hadn't been able to stop thinking of him. I thought I had lost him for good. But here he was.

Very coolly I said, "It's early for you to be out, isn't it? I mean, the sun's not down yet, is it."

"He said—Anthony said—take it slow, but try a few new things. So, I do. Just an hour after sunrise, an hour before sunset. And look—" he was close now, holding out his strong, elegant hands. "Not a single burn."

I swallowed. "So you *are* my father's patient."

"Since yesterday. I've made great strides, yes?"

"Yes. Good." Lamely I studied the buttons on his shirt. They were fine, for buttons. It was better than looking up into his eyes.

"Lel," he said quietly, "thank you."

So then I had to look. When I did, those hands reached out and gently took mine. His touch was fiery, but what else? Something in his eyes had altered too. They weren't less overpowering exactly, but—there was something else in them now. I could see—*Anghel*. That is, I think I mean I could see who he truly was. A man not cruel or mean or a robber, never stupid, rich in possibility, brave, yes, *gallant*— only wanting to find his way.

"I apologize for the wolf stuff—the shape-shift," he said to me. "I was—confused. Had to sort it out. As you see, though, I didn't lose the card. And I called Anthony, and I saw him yesterday. He's okay, your father."

"Yes, he is."

He still held my hands. "Lel," he said, and then, very softly, "Lelystra——" And for the first time in my entire life my name sounded wonderful to me, as if I'd never *heard* it before——"Lelystra, you saved my skin. You saved my sanity. You stopped me becoming something I'd never want. And I don't want——I can't make you any promises, or ask for any. Not yet. Not until I *know* I'm really *there*, where I have to be. Where *you* are. But if I make it, then——"

The whole roof was glowing now, the walls, the vines, the grapes, blood-red from the sunfall. And in the blood-red light Anghel leaned forward and kissed my mouth. It was a marvelous kiss, weightless yet profound. As gently as he, I gave it back to him. There in the sunset light as red as blood.

Blue Moon

RICHELLE MEAD

I was trapped.

I'd thought this back door led to freedom. Instead, I found myself in a narrow alley, the only other exit leading back to the main road where cops and others were looking for me. What was I going to do? I hesitated, wondering if the street was safer than going back through the club. Before I could decide, though, I heard a a door close behind me. I spun around.

There was a human standing there. A guy. He looked like he was about my age, maybe a little older. His brown hair was a bit shaggy for my tastes, but his eyes were beautiful. They were a deep, deep green. Like the color emeralds are supposed to be but never are. When I looked at him, the weirdest jolt went through me. He was cute, but it wasn't physical attraction that suddenly gave me pause. It was more like a sense of recognition, as though I'd known him for years. That

made no sense; I'd never seen him before. I shook off the feeling, and, as my eyes swept his body, I saw something else even more beautiful: a purple badge clipped to his belt.

"Get me out of here," I said, mustering as much harshness as I could, given the circumstances. If he worked at this club—and his clothing suggested he did—then he was used to taking orders from vampires. "Take me to your car."

I waited for him to cower, for his eyes to go wide. Maybe he'd gulp or give me a shaky nod. Instead, he frowned and asked, "Why?"

I stared, momentarily at a loss for words. "Because I told you to!"

Those beautiful eyes assessed me the way mine had just done him. "You're afraid," he said, more puzzled than anything else. "Why? Vampires are never afraid."

"I'm *not* afraid—but I'm going to get mad if you don't do what I tell you to do." Desperate, I reached into my purse and pulled out a wad of cash. I didn't bother to count it, but there were some hundreds on top. "Will you stop asking questions if I give you this?"

This time, his eyes did go wide. He hesitated only a moment and then snatched the money from my hand. "Come on."

I followed him back inside the club. I'd entered earlier through its main door, cutting through mobs of people writhing to heavy techno beats. This guy took me down another hall, one that led past a kitchen and some storage rooms. At the hallway's end was another outside door. He

pushed it open, revealing a darkened parking lot surrounded by a wire fence.

He unlocked a rusty Honda Civic, and I scurried in, nervously glancing around me. Aside from the silent cars, the parking lot was empty. For the first time tonight, I allowed myself the brief hope that I might actually get out of this alive.

"What's your name?" I asked.

"Nathan," he said, glancing behind him as he backed out of the parking spot. "You?"

"Lucy." A moment later, I silently cursed myself for giving my real name. What was I thinking? I gave him a sidelong glance, wondering if the name meant anything to him—it had been all over the news, after all—but he appeared to be too preoccupied with driving.

We pulled out onto the main road, and I slouched in my seat. This was a party district. Groups of people were everywhere. Some walked along the street, going from club to club. Some were already in line at the clubs—humans, of course. Vampires rarely had to wait to get in.

I scanned the crowds, looking for any sign of my pursuers and finding none. Not that that meant anything. Bryan had a vast network of agents working for him, men and women who moved with stealth and speed unusual even among vampires.

"Okay, Lucy," said Nathan, still not sounding very respectful. "Where do you want me to drop you off at?"

"Lakemont."

"Lake—what? That's almost two hours away!"

"For the amount of money I gave you, you should drive me somewhere twelve hours away."

"I have to get back to work! I'm on break. I thought I was just dropping you off somewhere."

"You are. Lakemont."

"No way. I can't be gone for four hours. I'll lose my job."

"Get another one."

He scoffed. "Oh, great. That's so typical of you vamps. 'Get another one.' Like it's that easy."

"That money I gave you is more than you make in a week," I snapped. "Probably even a month."

"Yeah, but what about after that?"

"Look," I said. "You don't have a choice here. Either take me to Lakemont, or go ahead and *try* to drop me off somewhere. As soon as you stop the car, I'm going to rip your throat out."

It was an empty threat. I didn't need to feed, nor did I have any intention to when there were so many other things to worry about right now. Still, I hoped I sounded scary and convincing.

Nathan didn't answer. He also didn't stop the car. After several minutes of quiet driving, he said, "We'll never get through the checkpoints."

"You have a purple badge." It was the reason I'd forced him to help me, after all. "You must commute in and out of the city."

"I do. *I* can get through. You could too—technically. But something tells me you don't actually want the patrols to see you."

My stomach sank. I hadn't thought of that. "Maybe I can hide in the trunk."

He laughed, though there was a hint of bitterness in it. Weirdly, something about the sound of his laughter still sent a pleasant tingle down my spine. Too bad I was the one he was laughing at. "You've never had to be stopped and searched at the checkpoints, have you?"

"They'll search the trunk?"

"Sometimes. They do random checks a lot. And if they think there's something suspicious going on, then they'll definitely check."

I turned away and leaned my cheek against the window. The glass was cool against my skin. Hot tears welled up in my eyes, and I blinked rapidly to send them away. No way was I going to cry in front of him.

"Why are you running away?"

"It doesn't matter," I said. Bad enough vampires knew. I couldn't risk letting a human find out.

"Okay, whatever."

"You don't even care. You're just doing this for the money anyway."

"I'm doing it because you threatened to rip my throat out."

"*And* for the money."

He gave a half-shrug, his eyes fixed on the road ahead. "If you're in big enough trouble, maybe I'd get more for turning you in."

I actually had a feeling he would, so I again tried my best to sound fierce. I'd never actually had to force humans to do things for me before. They'd always just kind of . . . done

them. "These people after me are vampires. Not humans. If you think I'm dangerous, wait'll you see them. And if they think you helped me escape—and they will—getting paid is going to be the last thing on your mind."

More silence fell between us, and I realized we were already on the freeway. Maybe I was better at this than I thought.

"You got more money?" he asked.

"Why? Are you raising your rates?"

"Answer the question if you actually want to leave the city."

"Yeah. I have more."

"A lot more?"

"Yes. A lot more. How much do you need?"

His answer was to get off at the next exit and start heading back in the direction we'd come from.

"What are you doing?" I exclaimed.

"Getting you out of the city."

He took us to a part of town I'd rarely been in. Mostly humans lived there, but naturally, vampires ran it. It was dirty and rundown and not a place I'd feel safe walking around if I were a human.

Nathan pulled the car up in front of a shop with a window that said TATTOOS in neon letters.

"Okay. Let's see the rest of your money."

I dug into my purse and handed over my cash. He raised an eyebrow.

"Wow. You weren't kidding." He counted out half of it and then, to my surprise, gave me back the rest. "Hang on to this."

Puzzled but intrigued, I followed him into the tattoo parlor. Loud rock music blared at us. Through an open doorway, I caught a glimpse of a bald man wielding what I assumed were tattooist's needles in a backroom. At the counter, a man with a Mohawk laughed with a heavily pierced girl over some joke. They glanced up at us.

"Nate, you bastard," said the man, still laughing. "Long time no—" His smile faded as he took a good look at me and saw my eyes. The girl visibly paled. Both of them straightened up. The man grabbed a remote control and hastily shut off the loud music, so that the only sound came from a small TV sitting behind them. "Hello, miss. Is there something we can help you with?"

Nathan laughed and—to my complete and utter surprise—threw an arm around me. The smell of his skin and sweat washed over me—and it was delicious. "Relax with the yes-sir-no-sir stuff, Pete. She's with me—doing a little human slumming this weekend."

Some of the tension went out of them, but they were still eyeing me nervously. "Well, good for you, Nate," said Pete, not entirely sounding like he meant it.

"Think you can make her human?" Nathan asked.

Pete smiled and nudged the girl. "Oh, into that, huh? Sure, Donna can do that. Contacts and everything?"

"The works." Nathan's entire posture was relaxed, his smile easy and natural. He was a completely different person than the one who'd been in the car. Of course, I'd threatened to rip his throat out in the car, so the difference was understandable. Meanwhile, I was trying not to think about

how good he smelled. "Something else. . . ." Nathan touched the badge on his belt. "I don't suppose you could make a purple?"

Pete's tension returned. "Whoa, that's a bit out of the norm."

"We can pay."

Pete glanced between the two of us. "It's for *her*? Why does she need it? How far are you taking the role-playing?"

"Nothing like that. I just want to take her home with me—but we can't let anyone know. She's got a jealous boyfriend."

"Sounds like a lot of trouble and money. Easier to just stay in the city."

"Can you do it or not?"

"Yeah . . . take me about an hour or so, and you know it's never as exact as the real thing. You get caught—"

"—and I won't say where I got it," finished Nathan. "I know the drill."

Pete went to the backroom to make our counterfeit badge and told Donna to give me the works. She beckoned me over but I turned back toward Nathan and gripped his shirt, pulling him slightly toward me.

"What's going on?" I hissed. "You guys make it sound like a common thing, vampires dressing up like humans."

"Wow, you really are an innocent, aren't you?" He seemed genuinely amused. "Don't you know any vamps who do it?"

I frowned. "No. Why would they? Like . . . for costume parties?"

"No. Because it's a turn-on for them."

"Ew."

"People are into weird things." He pointed toward Donna. "Go."

Donna was a little older than me—maybe in her twenties—and had obviously bleached-blond hair and too much eye shadow. As she worked, it was clear she was afraid of me. Conversation eventually dropped, except for when Nathan made the occasional remark on our progress.

"What color do you want?" she asked at one point.

"Color what?"

"Contacts. Your eyes."

I didn't know what to say. It was something I'd never even thought about, changing my eye color. My eyes were silver, just like every other vampire's. For a moment, I considered Nathan's beautiful green, but that didn't seem right. Those were *his* eyes.

"How about blue?" said Donna impatiently. "You seem like you could do blue."

"Blue," I repeated weakly.

She retrieved a pack of contacts and spent the next half-hour trying to help me get them into my eyes. I couldn't use a mirror, and I liked neither my own fingers nor hers poking me. Once the contacts were in, she applied a bit more makeup and finished just as Pete returned. He took my picture with a digital camera and then disappeared with Donna into the back to finish the badge.

Nathan walked over and checked me out. "Not bad. You make a cute human. Just don't smile and show your fangs."

"I don't look like Donna, do I? Her makeup's horrible." I realized how that sounded. "Oh, sorry. She's not a friend of yours, is she?"

"Your makeup's fine. And no, I've never met her. Pete's always got a different girlfriend."

"Is he your friend?"

"Kind of. We used to work together at a restaurant when I was in high school. Then he got some money and opened up this place."

"Are you in college now?"

"I should be." I immediately regretted asking him because that easy humor he'd shown since we'd come in disappeared. Bitterness replaced it. "No money. Besides, I spent so much time working in high school that my grades sucked. I'm not good enough to get an academic scholarship and not connected enough to get a vamp endorsement."

I was about to say that I could talk to my father, that he could probably get Nathan an endorsement. It was something vampires did if they wanted favored humans to be trained or educated for a certain position. These humans breezed through the college admissions process and had all their expenses paid for.

I swallowed off the comment, suddenly remembering everything that had happened. I could hardly talk to my father about that. In fact, it was unlikely I'd ever talk to him again. Instead, I told Nathan, "I'm sorry."

"Unbelievable. I've never heard a vampire apologize in my life. And now I've heard you do it twice since we've been—"

The words dropped off as his eyes focused on something behind me. Confused, I turned around . . .

. . . and looked into my own face on the TV.

Seeing my image was always a little surreal. Since vampires cast no reflections, we'd had no way of seeing our own appearances for eons. With the advent of technology like video and photographs, we'd finally gotten a way to see what we looked like.

They'd picked a horrible photo of me. I had dark circles under my eyes that made my skin look whiter than usual. Even on film, the clear silvery-gray of my vampiric eyes showed through. My hair—plain, boring brown—looked like it hadn't been brushed that day. Where *had* they found that picture?

"Ugh," I said. Underneath the image, a perky blond reporter delivered news of my disappearance.

"Today, authorities are looking for Lucy Wade, daughter of Chicago philanthropist and business owner Douglas Wade. Lucy disappeared earlier this evening after a fight with her parents. She is described as a troubled teen, one with a history of drug abuse and stints of running away."

"What?" I exclaimed. "I've never touched drugs in my life!"

"She was last seen on St. Jane Avenue, entering Club Fathom. If anyone has information to offer about Ms. Wade, they should contact the police. Her family says they're anxious to get Lucy the help she needs and are offering a reward for any assistance."

Nathan turned on me. "What the hell? You're Lucy

Wade?" He spoke low enough so the others wouldn't hear, but the anger came through loud and clear.

There was no avoiding it. "Yeah, I guess I am."

He threw up his hands and began pacing the room. "Oh my God. Oh my *God*. I helped hide Douglas Wade's fugitive daughter. Douglas Wade! He owns Fathom. He's like, my boss's boss's boss."

"I know."

"He owns this town!"

"I know!"

"You made it sound like you were some wronged victim, and really, your parents just want to put you back in rehab!"

"No," I said. "That's not true. All of that stuff she just said is a lie."

Nathan spun around, face still angry. "I knew I shouldn't have trusted a vamp. What are you, part of some conspiracy, and they're trying to keep you quiet?"

"You'd be surprised."

"Tell me then."

"I . . . can't. I can't tell anyone. I know something I'm not supposed to, and they want to kill me for it. They *will* kill me, Nathan. My own family."

It was like I hadn't spoken. "Jesus Christ. I'm helping the junkie daughter of one of the most powerful vamps in town. I should just walk away now. If you do kill me, it's no worse than what they're going to do when they find me."

I jumped off my chair and ran up to him. "No. Please. Don't. Look, you don't even have to take me to Lakemont. Just drop me off as soon as we cross the border."

He looked down at me, his eyes like green flames. There was so much rage there, so much frustration. I had the uneasy feeling that when he looked at me, he was seeing years of vampire abuse. A lifetime's worth, really. My kind had come out of hiding and started their occupation of the human world before he was born. Before today, I'd never really thought what it must be like to live under another race's rule—a race that you had almost no hope of defeating. We were stronger, faster, and could only be killed by a stake through the heart—which humans could almost never get close enough for. I had no clue what Nathan had been through.

"Please," I whispered. "You can have all the rest of the money."

He stared at me for several more heavy moments, and as he did, something shifted in that angry expression. I couldn't explain it, but I suddenly knew he'd had that same weird feeling I'd had in the alley. Like there was a connection between us, some longtime familiarity. He sighed. Turning away, he flipped off the TV. "Last thing I need is for Pete to see that. Hopefully, I can get rid of you before anyone realizes I was anywhere near you. He should be just about done."

But after ten miserable minutes of silence passed, Nathan finally eyed the doorway with suspicion. He walked over to it and stuck his head in. "Pete?" No answer came, and Nathan ventured farther in. Thirty seconds later, he came tearing out of the room. He grabbed my arm and jerked me toward the main door. I was so surprised that I stumbled along with him. If I'd wanted to, my strength would have stopped him from even budging me.

"What's going on?" I asked as we stepped back outside.

"They're all gone. There was a TV on back there too. My guess is they saw the story, sold us out, and then took off."

We slid into the car, and he started up the engine. Once we'd pulled away from the curb and were on the road, he handed me the fake badge. They'd apparently finished it and then abandoned it. It said my name was Sara Brown, that I was an eighteen-year-old human, and that I had work clearance to cross out of the city to the suburbs. Most intriguing of all was the picture. Donna had done a good job of diminishing some of my paleness. I wasn't fake-baked or anything, but there was definitely a human-like color to my face. And the eyes . . . the eyes were exquisite. They were a clear, pale blue. I was entranced.

"At least we didn't have to pay for it," I pointed out.

"Not that it does us a lot of good. We can't cross over."

"Why not?"

"Pete would have told the police I was with you. By now, they've pulled up everything there is to know about me— including my car and license plate. Every checkpoint knows we're coming and what we'll be in."

The urge to cry returned, and I again shoved it back. I tried hard to be strong and think of a solution on my own.

"Can we steal a car?"

He cut me a look. "Do you know how to?"

"Well, no."

"Do you think I know how to? You think that's something all lower class humans know how to do? That we're all criminals?"

"Well, no . . . of course not. I mean—"

"But," he interrupted, "you might be on to something." He abruptly pulled over to the curb and opened the car door. "Come on."

I scurried out after him. "What are we doing?"

"Finding other transportation."

We cut through a parking lot and ended up on a street that reminded me of the one Club Fathom was on. Only, much like in the tattoo parlor's neighborhood, everything here was dirtier and plainer. We stood off to the side, and Nathan studied the crowds. People who walked past us didn't give us a second glance. We were both just ordinary humans.

Finally, his eyes landed on two guys walking out of a bar. One held a set of keys and a bit of purple showed near his waist. Nathan took my hand, and we ran up to them. He turned the smile back on.

"Hey, man, are you guys going out of the city?" Nathan flashed them his purple badge.

One of the guys was clearly drunk, and the other (the driver, I hoped) looked like he was in a good mood. "Yeah, out to Evanston."

"Our car broke down," said Nathan. "And there's no way we can get it fixed before curfew. Can we bum a ride with you? Doesn't matter where you drop us off—just get us out, and then I'll call my friends."

The two guys exchanged glances, then looked back at us. "Sure," said the sober one. "No problem." They must have decided we were harmless enough. Little did they know.

Once we were on the road, the two guys talked to each other, practically forgetting we were in the backseat.

"What did you want to study in college?" I asked Nathan, keeping my voice low. "Drama?"

He'd been staring out the window, face stormy, no doubt pondering how I'd ruined his life. "Huh?"

"You're doing a pretty good acting job with everyone," I explained.

He gave me a bitter smile. "When you could potentially be killed by a vamp mob boss, you suddenly get really good at acting. But for the record? You're terrible. I never actually believed you were going to rip my throat out."

"Oh," I said, hearing the disappointment in my own voice.

"You aren't eighteen yet, are you?"

"No."

"How much longer until you are?"

"Less than a year."

A bit of worry crossed his features. "Oh. You could still make a kill now."

"I won't. I'm . . . I'm going to wait."

All vampires had to have their first feeding by the time they turned eighteen, and there were times I felt that desire for blood waking up, even though the thought of actually killing someone in cold blood terrified me. That was why I was in no rush for the kill—that and I had a few other things on my mind, like staying alive. My mom wouldn't get to throw her big first-kill party for me. Of course, if Bryan and the others caught me soon, maybe my parents could just use the decorations and caterers for my funeral.

I moved the subject back. "So, what would you study in college?"

"Mmm. I don't know. Something different. Something with meaning. Something that could change the world." There was an inspired, almost wistful look on his face. A moment later, he seemed to replay his words and grow embarrassed at having admitted something so idealist and vulnerable. His face darkened. "Something that isn't a bartender."

"Well, even if you can't go to college . . . maybe you could do some other kind of work?"

He shook his head, expression darkening once more. "There you go again, Lucy. You still don't see what it's like, not from your position."

"Why is it so hard? You're smart and nice and obviously resourceful. Why can't you do something else?"

He seemed a little surprised at the compliments, but that didn't sidetrack him. "You're a vampire. You're at the top of the food chain. Our master. *You* can do anything you want. You can kill us if you want, and really, there are no consequences."

"The lottery—"

"Oh, come on. Even you can't be naïve enough to believe that the lottery is *always* followed."

To ration our food supply, we'd instituted an annual feeding system. Certain populations of humans—criminals, the poor, other undesirables—were put into a pool and when each vampire's feeding time came, he or she drew a name. It was why the border between the city and the suburbs was so

strictly regulated. It made it easier to track down the "winners." Who got put into the pool was sketchy sometimes, and
as he had pointed out, the system wasn't always followed.
Plenty of vampires indulged in non-regulatory snacks, even if
it was technically illegal. But when humans disappeared, few
people asked questions.

"I can see why you hate us," I said feebly.

He turned back to the window. "No. You really can't."

"Do you hate me?"

"I don't know what I think of you. You've probably
destroyed my life. I should turn you in at the border . . . and
yet. . . ."

"What?"

He sighed. "I don't know. There's something weird about
you. Something . . . well, I can't explain it. It's like I've known
you for a long time. God, that sounds so stupid."

Not entirely stupid. I knew exactly what he meant,
though I still didn't understand it either.

For the rest of the drive, I just sat back and thought. My
whole life had changed. Everything I'd expected to do with
it seemed impossible now. In my mind's eye, I could still see
the disc, that beautiful circle embossed with gold and silver,
covered in swirls and shapes that everyone assumed were
nonsensical designs created by a long-dead vampire artisan.
But when I'd looked at it, the symbols had spoken to me.
Looking at them was like reading a billboard. The message
had come through to me loud and clear—and everyone had
realized it. My father and Bryan had acted quickly, and I'd
barely managed to escape.

"Here we are," said Nathan, interrupting my thoughts.

The car slowed down, and ahead, I recognized the signs of a border checkpoint. Long stretches of cruel, barbed fences. Towering, blinding lamp posts. My heart raced as I recalled what Nathan had said about random checks.

He and I handed our badges to the driver. A moment later, a vampire in a uniform peered through the open window. He looked bored, probably at the end of his shift and tired of inspecting cars. He skimmed through the stack of badges, hardly even looking at them. Hope surged in me. Pete would have tipped the authorities off to my fake badge name, but border security was probably paying a lot more attention to cars with just a guy and a girl. The vampire handed the badges back and then shone a flashlight on all of our faces. It lingered on mine, and suddenly, he looked a little less bored. After a few moments of studying me, the guard said, "Pull through to the holding area." He stepped back, pointing to a spot off to the side of the wooden gate that admitted traffic.

"Damn it," said the guy driving. He didn't sound scared so much as annoyed. "I just want to get home."

I shot Nathan a panicked look. He placed a reassuring hand on mine, seemed surprised, and took it back. "This happens. It's random."

We got out of the car, and a bored-looking uniformed woman searched it. Meanwhile, the guy who'd looked in the window searched us. He had everyone turn out their pockets, and then he felt each of us down. I was the last one he came to. I tensed, fearing recognition, and then suddenly realized that wasn't what I needed to be afraid of.

He pushed me up against the passenger side of the car, standing so close that there was almost no space between us. I felt trapped, suffocated. Then, when his hands began running up and down my body, I thought I would scream. He spent much longer 'searching' me than he had the others, far more interested in my body itself than anything I might be hiding on it. Beyond him, I saw Nathan glowering.

"Will you hurry up?" asked the other guard, clearly annoyed.

"Hang on," said my guard. "She seems dangerous."

I knew I was trembling and hated myself for it, even though it was what a human would probably do. A human girl would stand there, afraid, and take this humiliation. That was all I had to do. It'd be over soon if I could just be patient.

But when his hands slid under my shirt and up to the bottom edge of my bra, I snapped. Anger burst up inside of me. Before he realized what was happening, I lashed out and grabbed him, throwing him as far and as hard as I could into the small brick building that stood at the border. We both had the same vampiric strength and reflexes, but I'd caught him totally unprepared. He hit the wall with a *thwack* and slumped to the ground, unmoving. His face was dazed and blank, but I knew I hadn't killed him. He would heal soon, just like all vampires did.

The woman stood there, stunned for a moment. Then her eyes widened with recognition. "Lucy Wade," she exclaimed, just before leaping out at me.

I blocked her attack as best I could. We were close in size, but she'd been trained to fight, and I hadn't. I hit the

side of the car with a jolt, rattling my teeth. She came at me again while yelling for back-up. I swung at her with a very bad punch. I missed her face but hit her shoulder, which made her stagger a little. Any minute now, reinforcements would show up or the guy I'd thrown was going to get up.

Suddenly, I heard a car door slam. From the driver's side window, I heard Nathan yell, "Lucy, get in!" The engine started up.

I dodged a punch. Eyeing the woman carefully, I waited for her next swing. It came, and I dropped to the ground and scrambled away. I made it to the other side of the car, but she was only footsteps behind. I slid into the backseat on the driver's side. She reached for me, and I slammed the door on her hand. She screamed in pain and jerked back. I shut the door.

She beat on the side of the car, but Nathan hit the gas, heading straight toward the wooden gate. We hit it. The impact pushed my head sharply against the backseat, but we kept on going through a shower of splinters. I suspected the car's front didn't look so good.

I righted myself from my sprawl. "You're insane," I said. Peering around him, I saw that we were going about eighty. I glanced back, half-expecting to see flashing lights. There were none yet, but it could only be a matter of time.

"Me? You're the one who decided to take on the border patrol."

"That guy was a pervert."

"They're all like that," said Nathan. "Well, okay. They're not all the girl-molesting types, but that kind of stuff goes on all the time—and things a lot worse than that too."

"Thanks for another lesson on how terrible vampires are."

I couldn't see his face, but I had a feeling he looked sheepish. "Are . . . are you okay?"

"Yeah. He didn't do much." Something warm swirled in me at the thought that Nathan might actually be worried about me.

The car suddenly swerved off onto an angling road, and I slid to the side, just barely putting my hands out in time to brace myself.

"What are you doing?" I asked.

"You still want to go to Lakemont?"

Did I? *We can help you. We'll protect you.* The words echoed in my mind.

"Yeah."

"Then we can't take the main road. There's going to be an army coming after us."

Even off the freeway, Nathan kept up an aggressive speed. We rode in silence for a long time, and finally, I asked, "What happened?"

"Hmm?"

"Something happened to you. It's why you hate vampires."

"What, you haven't seen enough tonight to figure out why I'd hate you guys?"

Yes, I certainly had. And it was bothering me. I'd played human for less than two hours and learned more than I wanted to about the interactions between our races. And yet, that strange sense I had about Nathan told me there was something more that I needed to hear.

"But I want to know what happened to *you*."

I thought for sure he'd ignore me. Finally, he talked.

"When I was about twelve, there were these vampires who kept giving my brother Adam a hard time. He was, oh, ten, I think. They lived a few streets over—in a much nicer neighborhood—but used to come over to ours to cause trouble. They kept beating him up—never killed him or tried to feed off him. My other brother and I tried to stop them. We were pretty good fighters, but that doesn't matter when you're going up against that kind of strength. They'd just brush us aside. They weren't really interested in us. I think they just liked going after Adam because he was so small. They thought it was funny. Finally, my dad went and complained to their parents."

"And?"

"And, just like that, my dad was blacklisted. He got fired from his job, and no one else would hire him. My mom had to work, but she didn't have it much easier than my dad did. What she was finally able to get hardly earned anything, and so as the rest of us got older, we all started working too." The expression on his face made me think he wasn't even seeing me anymore. He was off in his memories, reliving events from years ago. "The thing is, not long after my dad complained, those guys came back for my brother—and they had a lot more of their friends. They cornered him alone one night and just pummeled him."

"Did they—did he—"

"Die? No. But he was in really bad shape. He had to go to the hospital. Another bill we couldn't afford. They broke

his leg—shattered the bone in some weird way. The doctor technically reset it, but . . . well, it never healed right, and he has a permanent limp."

"'Technically reset it?'"

"Well, yeah. We're pretty sure the doctor, even though he was human, was on a vamp's payroll and told not to treat it properly." He paused. Preparing himself for the next part? "Not long after that, my uncle was taken."

"Taken?"

"For the lottery. He didn't meet the criteria, but . . . well, he ended up in the pool anyway. And one day, he was just gone."

I leaned my head back. "That's horrible. You were right."

"Right about what?"

"Earlier . . . I said I could understand why you hated us, and you said I couldn't. You were right. There's no way I could—no way I probably ever could. You mean it—*really* mean it—when you say you hate vampires. I get that now."

"Yes, Lucy. I hate them. I really hate them. If I had the power to kill every vampire in the world and make things the way they used to be, I would." There was venom in his voice, and even though there was no way he could kill me, I felt afraid.

"I would too," I said.

"Would what?"

"Hate vampires."

Long silence followed. "I never expected to hear a vampire say that."

"Nathan . . . why are you helping me?"

"I don't know," he said, sounding as confused as me. "Maybe it's because other vampires hate you, and by helping you, I'm getting back at them. Maybe it's because I'm trapped in this and have no choice. Maybe it's because I keep saying horrible things about you and your kind, but you're still nice to me. Maybe it's because. . . ."

My breath caught. In the midst of all this chaos tonight, some tiny part of me hoped he'd say something as sweet and simple as, *Because I like you.* "Because?"

"I don't know. I can't explain it, and it's driving me crazy."

The rest of the drive passed uneventfully. No pursuers. Thanks to Nathan's side route, it almost seemed like we might pull this off.

Lakemont arrived much more quickly than expected. I gave Nathan the address I had, and we drove around for a while looking for it. It turned out to be a small house set at the far end of a fancy subdivision overlooking Lake Michigan. The neighborhood was still under construction, so some houses were half-finished and some were simply empty lots. We pulled into the driveway and stared at the house for several moments.

"Now what?" Nathan asked.

"Now we go in. Or, well, I do. You don't have to come with me."

"Is it safe?"

I thought back to the terrified vampire who'd found me just as things were blowing up back home. He'd whispered

that he knew what was going on and that there were others who wanted to help me and keep me safe. He'd given me this address and then disappeared, frightened of discovery. I didn't blame him.

"These people are going to help me," I said. "They know what's going on."

"I'm glad somebody does."

"I'm sorry," I said, meaning it. I got out of the car, and several moments later, Nathan followed. He didn't look very happy.

We rang the bell and waited. An old human woman, a servant presumably, looked out at us in confusion.

"I'm Lucy," I said.

She studied me longer, then laughed shakily. "I didn't recognize you, Miss Wade. The eyes are very clever. Come in. You and your . . . friend. You're safe now."

We stepped inside a very ordinary-looking house. There was no furniture in it yet; it must have just been constructed. There were no lights on either, but vampires wouldn't need them. We followed our guide into the living room, our footsteps echoing on the wood floors.

Ten other people were in the living room, all in suits, and even with my eyes, I couldn't make out their faces very well. Uneasiness started to crawl down my spine. I'd focused so hard on getting here, convincing myself I'd be safe . . . now I wondered if I was as naïve as Nathan kept saying. These vampires could be here to kill me—though it seemed terribly elaborate. The guy who'd given me the address could have just killed me back in Chicago.

"We aren't going to hurt you," said a short woman. "We want to keep you safe, Lucy. My name's Laurel."

"What are you going to do?" I asked.

"Get you out of here. When daylight comes, we'll bundle you up and smuggle you out in a van so that no one can find you."

"Why are you doing this for her?" asked Nathan. "Why do you care?"

"Because we know Lucy's being pursued unfairly," said Laurel. "And you are . . . ?"

"None of your business. And she's not going anywhere with you until we know what's going on." His manner was protective and fierce.

I wanted to tell him there was no need for bravery, except I honestly wasn't sure. Laurel laughed and shifted slightly. A patch of light from outside fell over her face. Her eyes still looked dark. *Dark.* Not silver.

Realizing what I'd discovered, Laurel moved at the same time I did. I locked into a defensive posture, expecting attack, but it was Nathan she grabbed. She put a gun to his head and jerked him toward her. The men with her all pulled out guns of their own and encircled her. I looked from shadowy face to shadowy face, trying to figure out how to get us out of here. This was a strange twist. My father and Bryan had sent humans after me.

"Nathan's not involved with this," I said. "He doesn't know anything."

"Cooperate, and we'll let him go," Laurel said. "You have no real choice."

"I'm not letting you take me back to my parents!"

"Your parents? My dear, we have no intention of taking you back to your people so that they can kill you. We want you alive—we want you very alive."

I understood then. How could I have been so stupid? So naïve? When I'd originally believed these were vampires who wanted to help me, I'd assumed it was because they didn't believe in the prophecy and pitied me. Upon discovering they were humans, I'd believed they'd been sent by my father. Plenty of vampires had humans working for them. The whole time, I'd been blind to one simple fact: The reason all these vampires wanted me to die was the very same reason humans would want me to live. "Yes," she said, no doubt seeing the understanding on my face. "We know. We know about the disc and the blue moon. Come with us, and we'll make sure you stay alive. We want to help you."

"You want to use me." They were some kind of human anti-vampire resistance group, people who were trying to "change the world" and eradicate vampires—just like Nathan wanted to do.

"The way I understand it, you benefit too. Wouldn't that be nice? Being able to go in the sun? Not needing blood?"

"I'm not going to kill my own people!"

"They're trying to kill you," said one of the men.

He was right, and it was something I'd been thinking about all day. I'd said—swore—I'd never fulfill the prophecy. But the more this went on, the more I started to wonder. Why was I trying to save people who wanted me dead? And

yet, as angry as that made me, I knew falling in with Laurel's group wasn't the right course of action. They didn't care what I wanted either. I was only a weapon to them.

"What are you talking about?" said Nathan. "Why would she kill her own people?"

Laurel pressed the barrel closer to his head. "Tell him, Lucy. Tell him the story."

"Let him go," I repeated.

"I told you I would if you cooperated. I want to hear this from your lips. I want you to tell us everything you know."

"Lucy. . . ."

Nathan's eyes were wide with fear and confusion. He was worried about me, I realized, worried about me even with a gun against his own head.

"You don't have to tell them anything, Lucy," he said.

But I had to. His life was on the line—and it was all my fault. I swallowed. "I can kill them. All of them."

"All of who?"

"The vampires."

"Vampires can already kill vampires."

"I can make it so humans can kill vampires." Saying it out loud hurt. It made it more real, and I'd been trying so hard tonight to keep it out of my mind, to deny what I was. What I could do. "There's this prophecy we've always had. No one really believed it. It said one vampire would be born during the blue moon—you know, when a month is long and has an extra full moon in it? That vampire's eighteenth birthday will also occur during a blue moon. That's me. Both birthdays falling on a blue moon."

Nathan was riveted. The other humans were too, no doubt having longed to hear this for some time.

"That could apply to a lot of people," Nathan said hesitantly.

"There's more. We have this thing in a museum—it's thousands of years old. A disc with a bunch of writing on it—but no one can read it. It's gibberish. Except *I* can. I looked at it, and it made perfect sense. It told me how humans can destroy vampires."

"No one's been able to do that. . . ." I could hear the wonder in his voice, and I remembered his words from earlier, talking about how he'd do anything to kill vampires. "But why would anyone think you'd help do it?"

"The prophecy says I have the power to transform humans into vampire killers—people who'd have the same strength and powers as us, maybe more. And that after I create thirteen . . . something will happen to me. I'll still have all my strength and long life but none of the side effects. I'll be able to go out in the daylight. I won't need blood."

"So they think you'd sell them out because of that. They're afraid and want to get you out of the picture, so you don't ruin their rule. And *this* group wants you so that you can bring humans back into power."

"You're one of us, Nathan," said Laurel. "You should see the opportunity here."

"She doesn't want to conquer either race," he retorted. "You should leave her alone."

I'd been sizing the group up the whole time we spoke, looking for any weakness I could use. I'd come up with a

few options when the windows behind them suddenly shattered.

And vampires swooped in.

I couldn't believe I'd ever mistaken these humans for vampires. My people were fast and graceful, instantly spreading out. There were as many of them as the humans, but I knew who would win this fight.

"Hello, Lucy," said a familiar voice. I looked up at Bryan's face. He'd been my family's bodyguard for years, and now he'd been sent to be my assassin. "Nice eyes."

Chaos broke out.

Laurel and her humans turned on the vampires. Guns went off—guns that could hurt vampires but not kill them. Teeth ripped into flesh. It was bloody and terrible. Nathan and I were forgotten as each group tried to establish dominance and claim me as the prize. Free of Laurel, Nathan scurried through the fray and jerked me away toward the front door.

"Come on," he said. "We have to go while they're fighting."

We looked out the front window. Our car was still parked on the street, but it wasn't alone: Four vampires stood watch near it. Bryan wasn't stupid enough to leave us an easy escape.

"What do you think?" Nathan cast an uneasy glance outside.

"I think the two of us might be able to distract one of them."

"You took out two at the border."

"That was luck. I totally caught the one by surprise, and I just barely got in the car before I—"

I screamed as something sharp and biting tore into my leg. My knees buckled, and I sank to the floor before Nathan's arm could catch me. Glancing down, I saw blood on the thigh of my jeans. We both looked over and saw the old housekeeper standing with a gun.

"Mr. Arcangeli told me to make sure you didn't leave."

Mr. Arcangeli. Bryan. Laurel's housekeeper was on Bryan's payroll. That's how he'd been tipped off I was coming. She still had the gun pointed at us, but her hands were shaking. Nathan leapt at her, and she wasn't nearly fast enough to stop him. It was both sad and comical watching him wrestle the old woman, but the pain in my leg made it hard to feel too sorry for her. In the end, he was fairly gentle. Once he had the gun, he shoved her far away from us. Not surprisingly, she didn't make a play to get the gun back. Instead, she turned and ran shrieking into the other room, calling for Bryan.

Holding the gun in one hand, Nathan slid his other arm around me and helped me stand. "I'll be okay," I told him. "I should heal in fifteen minutes or so. Half-hour, tops."

"We don't have that kind of time. Come on."

"The car—"

"We can't get it. Let's just get out of here, and worry about transportation once we're away from this hellhole."

Half-dragging me, Nathan led us down a hall that went out to the kitchen. The kitchen connected to the living room—where the action appeared to be fading, much to

my dismay. I felt pretty confident Bryan's group had won, but there must have been enough loose ends for them to not notice us in the kitchen yet. A small door led out to the backyard.

We stumbled outside, moving at an agonizingly slow pace. On the far side of the lot, we could see a stand of trees that hadn't been clear-cut yet. We aimed for those, hoping we could hide out.

"We can't stay too long," he warned. "The sun'll be up soon."

"Don't worry about me."

"Lucy . . . what are you going to do? About the prophecy?" Nathan's voice was both curious and awed. "I still can't believe it's real."

"Well, somebody does, or else all of that crap wouldn't be going on at the house." I sighed. "I don't know what I'm going to do. I don't want any of it. I don't want anyone to die. I'm scared of my eighteenth birthday. I would give anything to avoid that first kill . . . but at the cost of killing my own people? I don't want either race to dominate the other. I don't want more killing. I wish . . . I wish there could be a balance between us."

We came to a stop at the edge of the trees. Nathan's eyes were alive with excitement. We stood close, my breathing hard because of the extra exertion. "Maybe that's what you're supposed to do. Maybe you aren't supposed to destroy either race. You could bring them—bring us—together."

I shook my head. "I don't know. I don't know."

"I do."

Bryan materialized from the darkness. The housekeeper had apparently reported our escape.

He approached us slowly, smiling. It was still hard to believe this was the same Bryan I'd grown up around. I'd always trusted him, looked to him to defend us from other vampires. I'd watched him kill other vampires too—but I'd never expected to be one of them.

"I'm sorry, Lucy," he said. "I really am. But this is for the greater good. You've always been too squeamish about humans—we can't risk letting you have this power. I'm sorry."

"Stop." A voice cut through the night. Laurel approached from the side, trailed by one of her men. Both were armed, guns pointed at Bryan. She was gasping and bloody, and I couldn't believe she was still upright after what I'd witnessed in the living room. I wondered how many of her cohorts were still alive. She and the man behind her might be it.

"Unbelievable," said Bryan, echoing my thoughts.

He eyed my leg and turned toward the new threat, again neglecting us for a more urgent fight—a fight that I suspected was going to be very, very short from the looks of Laurel and her friend. Nathan touched my arm.

"Come on, while they're distracted. . . ."

"We can't outrun him. Even with a head start."

Bryan flew toward Laurel's counterpart. They fell to the ground, and though I couldn't quite see what was happening, I heard a shriek and wet, ripping noises. I pictured that happening to me and Nathan, imagined my own life—the life I'd wanted to do so many things with—vanishing.

Snuffed out like a candle. Adrenaline burned through me, powering through the bullet's pain, and I took a deep breath. I turned toward Nathan.

"Did you mean it before?" I said quietly. The man had stopped screaming. "About doing something great? Doing something that will change the world?"

Those beautiful, beautiful eyes widened. He understood. He knew exactly what I meant, and that's when I got it. That's why I'd been drawn to him from the beginning—and vice versa. It's why despite every reason he had to hate me, he still couldn't leave me. The disc had said I'd know who I was meant to choose when I created my thirteen.

"You'll be able to kill them," I said. Laurel was screaming now. "But they can still kill you. And they'll try. They'll keep trying to kill both of us."

There was no hesitation, no fear. I thought about the determination I'd witnessed in him all night. Nathan had the capacity to do so many things—he just wanted the chance to prove it. "Do it. Whatever you have to."

I didn't hesitate either. In a flash, I rested my fingers on his head and murmured the words that had burned themselves into my mind when I'd seen the disc.

"By moon and dark, by sun and light, I bind you to me, now and forever, life to life, death to death." I felt something crackle through the air as I spoke.

My mouth moved to his neck, and I let my teeth sink into his skin. The scent that had haunted me all night, his skin and sweat, flooded my nose, just as his blood spilled into my mouth. It was salty and warm and the most wonderful thing

I'd ever tasted. This was why vampires wanted humans. This was why we killed them.

But really, my bite was only a kiss. I pulled back, feeling that power continue to build between us. I had barely stepped away when Bryan came flying toward us, Laurel and the man dead. All vampires were dangerous, but Bryan was one of the most lethal. Few could stop him.

But Nathan did.

I'd never expected to see anyone match Bryan—certainly not a human. For Bryan, it must have been like hitting a brick wall. He staggered back, shocked. Nathan kept coming, beautiful and deadly. He punched Bryan in the face, causing the vampire to stumble again. Bryan came to his senses and pushed forward, taking the offensive.

For a moment, it was a deadlock. Neither could hit the other. Then, Nathan snaked in and grabbed Bryan by the shirt. Nathan slammed him into a tree and punched him—once, twice. Bryan's head hit the tree each time, and when the third blow came, he collapsed. We stared at each other, stunned.

"We have to go," I said. "The others will come. My leg's just about healed."

"Is he dead?"

"He will be soon, once the sun comes up. And so will I. We have to find a place to hide out for the night. Now."

When Nathan didn't move, I realized he was in shock, shock over what he had just done and what he could now do.

"Can you do it?" I asked, suddenly afraid for no reason I could explain. "Can you stay with me?"

I hate them. I really hate them. If I had the power to kill every vampire in the world and make things the way they used to be, I would.

Nathan had made his feelings about vampires clear all night. It was one thing to say, "Sure! Make me a vampire killer!" in the heat of battle—and another thing to accept what it meant afterward. *And* who it had bound you to. Slowly, he seemed to wake out of his daze. He turned toward me.

His hand reached out and rested on the side of my neck. His fingers were warm, yet sent chills through me. My whole body seemed to want his, yet at the same time, I realized what I'd done. I'd created a human who could kill vampires. A human who could kill *me*. And as his hand rested on the side of my neck, I realized that all powers being equal, he was built stronger than me. He could end this now, kill me, and go on a vampire killing spree. No discrimination. No thought for a better world.

Time stood still. Everything rested on him and his choice. The hand on my neck tightened ever so slightly, and then it slid up and cupped the side of my face. He kissed me, and as our lips touched, I felt all the power of that initial bite race back through us. I wrapped my arms around him, our bodies growing warm. I had never experienced anything like this. We broke apart, dizzy and restless.

"That was . . . wow," he said.

I swallowed. "I didn't know that was part of the prophecy."

"That wasn't prophecy," he said, still trailing fingers along my face. "That was us."

"I thought you hated vampires?"

"You don't treat me like vampires do. You don't even treat me like most humans do."

It was probably the highest compliment he could give. My heart fluttered. I wanted him to kiss me again, but dawn was closing in. "What are you going to do?" I had to be sure I could trust him with this power. "Will you stay with me?"

"I'm bound to you, remember?"

"Are you—"

"Bound, Lucy," he said firmly. "Life to life, death to death."

I didn't question him again. "Then let's go. The sun's going to come up."

"And the moon's going down," he murmured. "How long until the next blue one? Until your birthday?"

"Eight months."

"We'd better hurry then."

He caught hold of my hand, and together, we headed off into the night, off to change the world.

Changed

NANCY HOLDER

The vampires invaded New York the night Jilly turned sixteen. She was pacing in front of a club called Watami, waiting for Eli to show, eager to see what he had bought her. He was late, and she knew it was Sean's fault. Sean wouldn't want to come, because it was Jilly's birthday and Sean hated her. But Eli would make him do it, and they would show and she would wonder all over again why Eli couldn't love her like that . . . and how he could love someone who didn't like her.

Then, out of nowhere, the place was swarming with white-faced, bone-haired, blood-eyed monsters. They just started *attacking*, grabbing people and ripping open their throats—dancers, drinkers, bartenders, and her three best straight friends, Torrance, Miles, and Diego.

She still had no idea how she'd gotten out of there, but she called Eli first and then her parents. *No service, no service,*

beepbeepbeep . . . no texting, no net; no one could freakin' communicate.

She was Jilly Stepanek, lately of the Bronx, a semi-slacker who wanted to go to film school at NYU once she got her grades back up. She had been a neo-goth, into Victorian/ Edwardian clothes and pale makeup without the Marilyn Manson vibe, loved steampunk—but now all she was, was another terrified chick on the run from the monsters. Used to be the monsters were in her head; now they were breathing down her neck in real time.

No one stepped forward to represent the vampires or explain why they had taken over the five boroughs like the world's worst gang. There were no demands, no negotiations, just lots of dying. In less than a week, drained corpses—the homeless, first—littered the streets of Manhattan, SoHo, and the Village. As far as Jilly could tell, none of them rose to become vampires themselves. Maybe all the movies weren't true; maybe once they killed you, you were just dead.

The vampires had hunting animals like falcons that dug into their white arms. They were all head and wings, with huge white faces and bloodshot eyes and teeth that clack-clack-clacked like the windup false kind. Blood dripped and splattered onto the ground from the places the bird-suckers gouged their claws into their masters' arms, but—she observed from as far away as possible—either the vampires couldn't feel it or they liked it. Maybe it was their version of cutting.

The bird-suckers swooped and pirouetted across the night clouds, tearing the city pigeons to pieces. A few nights

of slaughter and they owned the skies. A few nights more, and there were no wild dogs on the island of Manhattan.

Three nights after her birthday, a vampire attacked and killed her father; its vampire-bird ran her mother to the ground while they were running out of their house. Jilly screamed for her mom to run faster, run faster, oh, God, but it swooped down on the back of her mother's head and started pecking and tearing. Her mother fell; her eyes were open but she wasn't seeing a thing. Blood from her neck gushed onto the sidewalk beneath a lamp post, and it looked like her shadow was seeping out of her body.

Hiding in the bushes, heaving, Jilly waited it out. Then she ran the other way, in nothing but a black chemise, some petticoats, her boots, and a long black coat she had bought at a garage sale.

She tried to get to Eli's row house but whole blocks exploded right in front of her, and others whooshed up in flames like paper lanterns. Weeping and gasping, she phoned him over and over; she texted with shaking hands. *No service, no service, beepbeepbeep.*

She raced in circles to get past the fires as the smoke boiled up into the dotted clouds of clack-clack-clacking birds.

By four days after her birthday, the streets were a real jungle. The survivors were as vicious as the street dogs the vampires-birds had eaten: hoarding food, and threatening to kill each other over safe places to sleep and water bottles. She had some experience with hostility, from when she had gone drug-mad. Rehab and a lot of love had redeemed her, but the old lessons were not forgotten.

Dodging fiends and madmen, she stole tons of phones—
or maybe she only took them, since there was no one left
alive in the stores to ring up the sales—but there was really,
really, really no service. Trying to find one that worked
became an addiction. At least it gave her something to do—
other than hide, and run.

Her therapist, Dr. Robles, used to caution her to ease up,
not use her busy brain quite so much. He said she had to let
go of loving Eli because people who were gay were gay; there
wasn't going to be a change of heart no matter how much
she wanted one.

She tried to find a cybercafé that the vampires hadn't gut-
ted, but there were none to be found. She broke into office
buildings and tried their computers, but they were fried. She
wondered how the vampires did it. She was sure it was part
of their plot to take over the world.

Just like the vampires, she slept during the day, in the
brightest sunlight she could find, her black coat covering her like a shroud. Even though she had never been a
Catholic, she prayed to the God of the crucifix, because
crucifixes could hold the vampires at bay. She wanted to
pray in St. Patrick's Cathedral but it was too dark and
enclosed; she could almost hear the vampires hissing in
the chapels lining the sanctuary. Her lips were cracked
and chapped. She was filthy. But maybe God would help
her anyway.

*Please, God, please, God, please, God, please, God, please
please please don't let Eli get burned to death or sucked dry by the
demons amen.*

High rises burned down to ash; cars exploded, and the vampires capered on stacks of the dead. And Jilly staggered through it like the last victim of the Apocalypse. No one hooked up with her and she didn't make any effort to take on a sidekick or become one. She had to get to Eli; at least she could die with him.

So she kept skirting the crazily burning buildings in her tattered bad-fairy gear, the indigo in her hair bleached by the sun and coated with dirt. She showed people the photograph of him she always carried in her coat pocket. *No, Jilly, no, Jilly, no, Jilly, no Jilly, no Jilly, no no no sorry, loser.*

She kept waiting for the fires to burn down, burn out. The smoke took a toll on her; the air smelled like someone barbecuing rotten hot dogs; she felt it congealing in her lungs and coating her skin. Five days after her birthday, she was so tired she could hardly breathe anyway, which was a sort of blessing because maybe she would die and then she could stop everything. Escaping the bad was also one of her habits. She was empty, outside and in, just a husk. If a vampire tried to suck her blood, it would probably find nothing but red powder.

She really thought that the time had come for her to die. She thought about her parents, and her friends, but mostly she thought about Eli Stein. He had been her first and only love, before he had realized he was gay. She still loved him; she would always love him, no matter what form his love for her would take. *Brainbrain, go away, obsess again some other day. . . .*

He was crazy-mad for Sean instead and she hoped. . . .

No, she couldn't even think that. If she went anywhere near praying for something to happen to Sean. . . .

You are evil, Jilly, and you deserve to die.

Beneath her coat, she fell asleep and dreamed of Eli, and Sean; because in the summer after tenth grade that was who they were, Eliandsean, like one person, like the person she had hoped to become with him. Once Eli had found his other half, they had come to her house almost every day, because they could hold hands there.

They could brag about their slammin' skillz on their skateboards and video games like any other teenage boys, and they could flirt with each other and sit on the couch with their arms around each other while Jilly's mom brought them sodas and grilled cheese sandwiches. They were amazed and delighted by the acceptance in Jilly's house. Tolerance, in her house, came after a hard struggle, won by determined parents who never let go of Jilly, even after she ran away with a biker, shaved her head, and told her shrink there were no bones in her hands.

It was all crazy in a new way; taggers wrote VAMPIRES SUCK over every surface there was, and people tried to share whatever information they'd learned about them: They were mindless, they were super smart; they had a leader, it was all random. They lured you in with dark sexuality. They attacked you like animals without a plan. It had something to do with global warming; they were terrorists. They were a plague created by the government.

She saw plenty of them. White-faced and leering, they darted down streets and stared out of windows, like terrible Will Smith CGI effects. She didn't know how she hadn't been

killed yet, with all the near misses. One thing she did know, they were more like people than beasts. Just very evil people. Their birds were mindless attackers, but the vampires themselves listened to music and went joyriding on motorcycles and kept the subway people alive so they could go on rides; *it's a dead world after all.*

After another near miss—a vampire turned a corner just ahead of her, and she turned on her heel and ran, hard— she broke down weeping, her thin stomach contracting; and then God must have taken the hint, or felt guilty, or whatever, but He/She/It/They did something miraculous:

It began to rain. Hard. Buckets poured down from heaven like old lady angels washing their doorstoops; gallons and rivers tumbled onto rooftops and treetops like all the tears of all the New Yorkers, like all the blood that had gushed out of the necks of the dead.

And the rain toned down the fires just enough that she soaked her coat and then raced through the fire line, arriving on the other side into some kind of hellish otherworld; everything was covered with gray and white-bone ash: trees, buildings, abandoned cars, rubble. She shuffled through layers of powdery death.

And there it was. *There it was.*

Eli's row house. With the formerly turquoise paint and the American flags and some kid's ash-colored tricycle overturned in a pile of ash like strange granular leaves. Then she thought she saw a shadow move across the window, and she stared at it for a long time, because she had actually made it, and in her heart she'd expected there to be no signs of life.

There were no more shadows and she wondered if she had gone crazy or died and imagined the whole thing. By then, Jilly was certain the dead could be as crazy as the living. She staggered up the stoop stairs, kicking up layers of death that made her gag and choke.

She knocked on the door, but no one answered, and she pushed it open.

Eli and his father faced each other in the living room with the old tapestry of the Jews at Masada hanging over the upright piano. Eli looked taller and thinner, his dark hair long as ever, and he had a semi-beard. He looked like a leftist rabbi in the NYU sweatshirt she had given him. Mr. Stein was still Mr. Stein, in a navy blue sweater and dark trousers.

Mr. Stein was shouting. "You stupid faggot, you're going to die out there."

"Just shut up!" Eli shrieked. "Stop calling me that!"

"Eli," she whispered from the doorway. "Eli, it's me."

They both turned.

"Jilly!"

Eli whooped, gathered her up, and hugged her against himself. She felt as light as a desiccated leaf, unbelievably dizzy, and reeling with happiness. Eli was alive. He was safe. And he was still here, in his old house, living indoors, with his parents.

"Oh my God, are you okay?" he asked; and then, before she could answer, he said, "Have you seen Sean?"

"No," she said, and he deflated. She saw the misery on his face, felt it in the way he nearly crushed her.

In the kitchen, his gaunt, black-haired witchmother was *cooking*, as if nothing had changed. They had electricity, and gas, and as Jilly smelled the hot food—onions, meat—her mouth began to salivate. She burst into tears and he held her tightly, swaddling her in himself. He smelled so good. So clean. Almost virginal.

His father's eyes bulged like an insect's and he stared at Jilly, as if she were an intruder.

"I've been trying to get here," she said. "Everything was on fire. And then the rain came."

"The rain," Mr. Stein said reverently, glancing at the tapestry.

"Now we can look for Sean," Eli said.

"Don't speak that name," Mr. Stein snapped.

For God's sake, what do you care about that now? she wanted to snap back at him. But she took Eli's hand and folded it under her chin. She saw the layer of ash-mud on her hands and wondered what she looked like. A zombie, probably.

"I was just about to leave, to search for him," he said, bringing her knuckles to his mouth. He kissed them, then laid her hand against his cheek. His tears dampened her skin, like more rain. "He called just before it happened, from midtown. I don't know what he was doing there. We had a fight. I was lying down."

Weren't you going to meet me at the club?

Eli searched Jilly's face with his fingers and she felt each brush of his fingertips close a wound the long days and nights had cut into her soul. There was no one she loved more. She would go to her grave loving Eli Stein.

"Of course you're not leaving now. Look at her. She looks like she's dead." Mr. Stein had never liked her. Not only was she formerly a mad slut, she wasn't Jewish, and her family had given Eli and Sean safe harbor to commit their carnal atrocities.

"You need to fix the door," Jilly said. "Or at least to lock it."

"I thought it was locked," Mr. Stein said. He looked at Eli. "Did you unlock it?" He walked to the door to check it, passing close by Jilly so that she had to take a step out of his way. He grabbed the door; she heard a click, and then he turned the knob.

"It's broken." He glared at Eli. "Did you break it?"

"Dad, why would I do that?" Eli asked.

"Maybe vampires tried to get in last night," Jilly ventured. "You need to put up some crucifixes. They really do work."

Mr. Stein crossed his arms over his chest. "Not normal," he muttered.

"Dinner is almost ready," Mrs. Stein announced from the kitchen, smiling weakly. Jilly wondered where on Earth she had found a brisket. In the still-working refrigerator of their house, she supposed.

Eli gave her a look that said, *My parents have lost their minds, obviously.* He had some experience with mental illness, since he was her best friend.

She didn't smile, even though, as usual, they were thinking the same thing. It wasn't funny. She didn't know who was crazy and who wasn't.

"You could take a shower, Jilly," Mrs. Stein continued.

Jilly was too weak and exhausted to take a shower. But Mrs. Stein gave her some mashed potatoes and a piece of cheese and they energized her enough to stagger into the bathroom. For the first time in weeks, she was a few degrees less afraid to be enclosed in a small room; to take off her clothes; to stand vulnerable underneath water . . .

. . . and then Eli was in the bathroom, taking off his clothes too. He climbed into the shower and wrapped his arms around her, sobbing. She started to cry, too, naked with her best friend who did not want her the way she wanted him; they clung to each other and mourned.

"He's out there," he said. "I know he is."

She turned around and leaned her back against his chest. It was so unreal that she was here. To just walk through their door. . . .

"Your parents are probably out there having a fit," she said, her eyes closed as she savored the pleasure of mist, and warmth, and Eli.

"Are you crazy? They're probably dancing in circles. 'He's in there with a girl! He's not gay! He's not a faggot!'" He mimicked his father's voice perfectly. Then he added softly, "What about your parents?"

She raised her chin so the water would sluice over her face. Her silence was all he needed.

"Oh, Jilly. Jilly, God, what happened?"

"I can't talk about it. Don't say anything. I'll never stop crying."

He laid his hand over her forehead. "I'll only say that

they were so good to me. And in Judaism, goodness is a living thing," he whispered.

"Thanks." She licked her stinging lips again.

Head dipped, he turned off the water. Then he toweled her off and retrieved some neatly folded clothes set out by his mother in the hall. A pair of sweat pants swam on her and belled around her ankles. There was a black sweater, no bra. Not that it mattered.

He put back on his clothes, laced his fingers with hers, and took her into his room. There were pictures of her everywhere—at school, at their first Broadway play, holding hands in Central Park. The ones of Sean outnumbered them, though. First there were a lot of pictures of just the two of them, Eli and Sean, the brand-new boyfriends; and then, of Eli, Sean, *and* Jilly, as Eli brought the two "together"—mugging for the camera, practicing for a drama skit, their very silly trip to a book signing at Forbidden Planet. Sean looked pissed off in any picture she was in. Didn't Eli notice?

She stretched out on the blue velour bedspread, feeling as if she had just set down a heavy load of books. It was incredible to her that he had been sleeping on this wonderful bed, in his own room. She didn't even know if her building was still standing. She could go back, get more clothes, get her valuables and money.

Eli would go with her. They could look for Sean on the way.

She dozed. Eli spooned her, holding her; each time she inhaled, he exhaled. It had been that way in the early days, for them. When Sean came along, he added something

new; he was a literal breath of fresh air. Even Jilly had been charmed by the surfer dude who had lived in L.A. and knew movie people who might be able to help her. He talked about working as a stand-in. He hung around stunt men. His uncle had rented out his surf shop as a movie set.

But once he was sure of Eli's love, he changed. She saw it happen. Eli didn't. Maybe changed was the wrong word; around her, he became chilly and disinterested, and she knew he was never going to introduce her to anyone in the industry. But Eli didn't see it.

Sean had actually been a kind of vampire. He sucked up anything he wanted; he drained Eli's friends and class-mates by using them to advance up the social ladder, then blindsided them with his snotty I-am-mean-and-because-I-deserve-to-be-you-must-permit-it attitude. She could almost predict when he'd show his other face. Jilly's mom used to say they should give Sean the benefit of the doubt because he had been through a lot. Any guy who was gay had suf-fered. So they had to be nice to him, even though he was a jerk. She knew what her mom was not saying: *We put up with your bad behavior. Welcome to the real world—the one that does not revolve around you.*

Her mom would never say anything like that, of course.

Because she was dead.

But she had never talked like that, not even when Jilly was the most drug-crazy; she had said Jilly was hurting.

But even when Jilly was at her worst, she still would have done anything to help Eli become more, and more, and more of all the wonderful things Eli was.

"God, I'm glad you're here," he whispered, nuzzling the back of her head. She cried some more, and he held her.

There was a soft knock on the door. Mrs. Stein whispered, "It's dinner time."

Jilly was very hungry, and the smell of food was making her clench and unclench her hands. But Eli had fallen asleep with his arm over her. She tried to figure out a way to slide out from underneath him without waking him up. She couldn't manage it, so she stayed beside him. Her arm began to ache. Her stomach growled.

As she contracted and released her muscles, trying to keep the blood circulating, she heard Mrs. Stein crying. It was a high-pitched, irritating kind of weeping, and it set Jilly on edge.

"No one is helping us!" Mrs. Stein cried. "No one."

Jilly, hungry and despairing and exhausted, listened to the rain, and imagined New York City going up in steam. Then she let herself go fully to sleep for the first time since she had turned sixteen.

The yelling jerked Jilly awake.

"You will die!" Mr. Stein shouted downstairs.

"Stop yelling!" Mrs. Stein was crying again. "You'll drive him away, the way you always have."

"What, drive away? Didn't you hear what he just said? He's leaving anyway!"

Jilly groaned, feeling in the bed for Eli, realizing he'd gotten up. His parents were trying, in their way, to tell him that

they loved him and didn't want him to risk his life by leaving their home. She felt the same way. She didn't want to get out of bed. She knew Eli so well, knew they were going to leave as soon as she emerged from the bedroom—*maybe we can eat first*—and it wasn't going to be a graceful exit.

"It's because they blame you for not fixing me," Eli told her as they left his parents' house. It was still raining; Mrs. Stein had given them parkas with hoods and umbrellas. The rain seemed to have cleared the sky of the vampire birds of prey. Another miracle.

At least they had gotten to have some breakfast first— last night's brisket, and pancakes. And blessed coffee. While she'd been on the street, she'd heard a story that one man had knifed another over the last cup of coffee in a pot in a diner.

She didn't say anything. She couldn't forgive Eli's parents for being so narrow-minded as to pick a fight with their son and his best friend, when they might never see either of them alive again.

She adjusted the heavy backpack, filled with extra clothes, shampoo, toothbrushes, and toothpaste. Eli was carrying the heavier one, packed with food. He had a small satchel over his shoulder too, packed with photographs of Sean, seven of them, as if someone might not recognize him in the first six. Sean was weird-looking, with almond-shaped eyes and a long, hooked nose in a long, narrow face.

So he wasn't handsome, he wasn't nice, and there were other gay guys in their school if Eli wanted a boyfriend. Gay guys who liked Jilly a lot. Unfortunately, Sean was the guy for him.

Eli groaned when they reached the pocket park, site of their first make-out session, after her birthday party in the eighth grade. She'd been so excited and happy she hadn't slept all night.

"Even the trees got burned up," he said. They walked close together, holding hands. She had a strange floating sensation; if he hadn't held on to her, she thought she might have floated away from sheer fear.

They passed dozens of burning buildings, sizzling and steaming in the rain. The subway station split the sidewalk; by mutual unspoken consent, they gave it a wide berth. Darkness and seclusion—perfect vampire territory.

Shadows and shapes moved in the alleyways; they walked down the center of the street, gripping each other's hand. It was strange, but Jilly was more afraid with Eli there than she had been by herself. She didn't think she could stand it if something happened to him. He was so nervous; he was broadcasting "come and get me" to anyone interested in easy pickings.

He pulled a cell phone out of his parka and dialed numbers, listening each time. Finally he grunted and put it back in his pocket, and moved his bangs out of his eyes. Her heart stirred, and she touched his cheek. He smiled distractedly; she knew he was glad she was there, but it was Sean he most wanted to see.

She used to have these long conversations with her girl friends about if Eli would ever come back to her. Eli had been her actual boyfriend for two years. They had made out all the time, but never gone any farther than that. They'd been too young. Then he and Sean had found each other . . . or rather, Sean had found him. Sean had moved to New York and zeroed in on Eli, even before Sean was sure Eli was gay. So Eli had given Jilly the "we can still be friends" speech.

Only in their case, it was true. They were excellent friends. They thought alike, read alike. He thought NYU was a great goal. He talked about going there too. They both hated sports. And Sean, who was a jock, hated that.

He never said a word about it to Eli. As far as Eli was concerned, Sean loved Jilly like a sister. Had used those exact words, in fact, the one time Jilly tried to discuss it with him. But when Eli wasn't paying attention, Sean zinged her out with vast amounts of passive-aggressive BS—veiled threats and lots of snark. He picked fights just before they were supposed to meet her somewhere—like Watami. Being somewhere in midtown when he was supposed to celebrate with her was classic Sean, King of Bitter Homosexuality.

Eli brushed it off, refused to agree to her reality. So she didn't bring it up again, ever. She didn't want to give Sean the ammunition for an "It's either her or me" speech.

As they walked out of the burn zone, the sky began to darken, and a rush of resentment roared through Jilly. Her tired body was aching for Eli's soft, clean bed. She wanted to take another shower, and brush her teeth for a year. She

didn't want to be risking her life, or Eli's, for someone who hated her.

Her mind was trying to figure out what life would be like if they found Sean. And then, before she knew what she was doing, she said, "Watami. The club. Maybe he went there."

He looked at her. "He wasn't going to go. And he'd come to my house first, or try to get to me through our friends." And they did have other friends, gay friends, who envied them for having Jilly's family to hang with.

"Okay, never mind. Maybe he went to school."

Eli raised his brows. "Maybe." He smiled. "It's big. Maybe they're doing like a Red Cross shelter there." He hugged her. "You're a genius, Jilly."

Too smart for my own good, she thought. The old Jilly, pre-rehab—the one without the boundaries—might not have suggested places to look for Sean. But Jilly was a good, nice person now. Maybe that was why he didn't love her. She wasn't edgy enough. She could change. . . .

But he can't. He is gay, she reminded herself.

It was nearly dark. It was so dangerous to be out like this; she'd seen vampires leap from the shadows and drag people away. Sometimes they growled; sometimes they were silent. Jilly had been sleeping next to an old lady in a store one night. In the morning, all that was left of the lady were her shoes. Jilly had no idea why she herself had been left alive. Maybe the old lady had been enough.

They met a man on the street a few blocks from the school named Bo. He staggered when he walked and he

talked very slowly. There was a scar across his face from the slice of vampire fangs.

"They have to feed as soon as they change," he told them. "The vampire who tried to kill me was brand new. There was another one with him, the one who made him into a vampire. He was laughing. My friends staked him. They don't change to dust."

Then he staggered on.

"Wait!" Jilly cried. "Tell us everything you know."

"The new ones are the worst," he said. "They're the most lethal. Just like baby snakes."

Now, as the gloom gathered around them in the rain, they hurried to their old high school. There were lights on and shadows moving in the windows. Neither spoke as they crossed the street and walked past the marquee. The letters had been stolen; there was no school news.

Rose bushes lined the entrance. She couldn't smell their fragrance but the sight of them, drenched by the downpour, gave her a lift. The double doors were painted with crosses; so were the walls and the windows. The taggers had written VAMPIRES SUCK GO TO HELL VAMPIRES on the walls.

There were two guards at the doors—a male teacher named Mr. Vernia and her English teacher, Mary Ann Francis. They hugged both Eli and Jilly hard, asked for news—asked how it was—then ushered them in.

It smelled, and the noise was unbelievable. Students, adults, little kids, and teachers—everyone was milling around; the noise was deafening. People who hated her ran up and hugged her, crying and saying how glad they were

that she was alive. She realized she and Eli should have eaten a good meal before they'd come in. If they opened up their pack now, they would have to share.

Is that so bad, sharing?

"Jilly. Eli," their principal, Ms. Howison, said when she spotted them. There were circles under her eyes and deep lines in her forehead. She looked like a skeleton. "Thank God."

Ms. Howison had tried to keep her from coming back to school after rehab. But crises did strange things to people.

Eli skipped the pleasantries and pulled out all his pictures of Sean. Men and women, computer nerds and cheerleaders, carefully examined each one, even if they knew exactly who Sean was, before passing it on. No one had seen him.

Jilly got too tired to stay awake any longer. Principal Howison promised her that all the doors and windows had been covered with crosses and the ground was dotted with garlic bulbs and communion wafers. Jilly wondered if the rain had dissolved the wafers. How many molecules of holiness did you have to have to keep the monsters at bay?

Bazillions of cots were set up in the gym and sure enough, there were Red Cross volunteers. Eli and Jilly pulled two cots together, stashed their packs underneath, and lay down in their clothes. It was better than what she'd been sleeping on before she found Eli, at least.

Eli touched her face with his hands. "I'm so glad you're here."

"Me too," she said, but what she meant was, *I'm so glad you're with me.*

Eli fell asleep. She looked at the diffused light drifting

across his face, making him glow. She wanted to kiss him but she didn't want to wake him; correction, she didn't want him to wake up and remind her that he didn't love her that way.

Then she heard someone crying. It was muffled, as if they were trying not to make any noise. She raised her head slightly, and realized it was Ms. Howison.

Jilly disentangled herself from Eli slowly. Then she rocked quietly onto her side, planted her feet underneath herself, and sat up. She walked over to where the woman was sitting in a chair, facing the rows and rows of cots. She looked as if she'd just thrown up.

"Hey," Jilly said uncertainly, "Ms. Howison."

"Oh, God," she whispered, lowering her gaze to her hands. "Oh, God. Jilly. You're still here. I was hoping. . . ." She turned her head away.

"What?" Jilly asked.

She took a deep breath and let it out. She was shaking like crazy. "I need you to come with me for a second."

"What's wrong?"

"Just . . . come." The principal wouldn't look at her. Jilly shifted. "Please."

Ms. Howison got up out of her chair and walked out of the gym. The overhead fluorescents were on. Jilly followed her past the coaches' offices and then into the girls' locker room, past the rows upon rows of lockers, and then through another door into the shower area.

Ms. Howison cleared her throat and said, "She's here." Then she stepped back and slammed the door between herself and Jilly.

Jilly tried to bolt.

Sean was there, and he was a vampire. All the color in his long, narrow face was gone. His eyes looked glazed, as if he was on drugs. And she should know.

He grabbed her, wrapping his arms around her like a boyfriend; she smelled his breath, like garbage. He wasn't cold; he was room temperature. She was completely numb. Her heart was skipping beats.

She wet her pants.

"I'm glad to see you too," he said, grinning at her.

She set me up. She gave me to him. That bitch.

He wrapped his hand around her bicep and dragged her forward. She burst into tears and started wailing. He clamped his other dead hand still over her mouth so hard she was afraid her front teeth were going to break off.

"Shut up," he hissed, chuckling. "I've wanted to say that to you forever. Shut up, shut up, shut up."

She kept whimpering. She couldn't stop. Maybe he knew that; he dragged her along with his hand over her mouth. His fingernails dug into her arm and she knew he had broken the skin, but she didn't feel it.

He walked her into a storage room where they kept cleaning supplies—brooms, mops, big jugs of cleaner. She started screaming behind his hand, and he slapped her, hard. Then he slammed her against the wall. With a gasp, she bounced back off and fell on her butt.

He slammed the door, leaving her in darkness. With a sob, she crawled to it and started to pound on it.

"*Don't*," he hissed on the other side.

He's going to get Eli, she thought. *Oh, God, he's going to vampirize him. That's what he's here for.*

Maybe he will let me go.

But why would he? He was the King of Bitter. And she would never leave without Eli.

She fumbled around for a light switch, found one, and turned on the blessed, wonderful light. Her arm was bleeding and it finally began to sting. She didn't know if she wanted to feel anything. She wondered what it would be like when he—

The door burst open, and Sean came back inside. His eyes were glittering. He looked crazy. "Eli says hi."

"No," she begged. "Don't do it. Please, Sean. Don't change him."

Sean blinked at her. Then he laughed. "Honey, that's what love is all about, don't you know?"

She doubled up her fists and bit her knuckles. He lifted a brow.

"I smell fresh bloo-ood," he sang. "Yours. It smells *great*. If you were alone in the ocean, the sharks would come and chew you up. Alone in the forest, it would be the wolves. Alone in the city, and it's us."

Vampires. "How . . . how did this happen to you?"

He ignored her. "I'm going to give you a choice, girl-friend. The choice is this: You can change, or he can change. The other one of you . . . is the blood in the water." He moved his shoulders. "I'll let you pick."

She stared at him. "What are you saying?"

"God, you are so stupid. So incredibly, moronically stupid. I could never figure out why he loved you." He shook his head.

Why did it matter, she wondered, when Eli still loved him more?

"Does it even matter which way I choose?" she said. "You don't even like me." Of course he would change Eli and let her die.

"Maybe it doesn't. Maybe I just want to see what you'd say," he told her. "I'm giving him the same choice."

She stared at him in mute terror.

"I told him that I would change you if he asked me to." He folded his arms across his chest and leaned against the back of the door. He didn't look different at all—he was the same surf-charmer Sean.

"You know I'll say to change him," she said. What did she have to live for, after all? Only Eli. And if he were gone. . . .

"Be right back," he said, turning to go.

"Why are you doing this?" she asked.

He didn't turn back around, just looked at her over his shoulder, as if she was being a nuisance.

"I don't know why he's so loyal to you. He doesn't love you the way he loves me."

"But he loves me," she said, as she realized. "That's why. . . ."

He turned around and stared at her. The expression on his face was the most frightening thing she had ever seen. She took another step back, and another. She bumped into the wall.

He raised his chin, opened the door, and left.

She paced. She thought about drinking the cleaner. She tried to break the mops and brooms to make a wooden stake. She couldn't so much as crack one of them.

She fell to her knees and prayed to He/She/It/Them, *Get us out of here get us out of here come in, God, come in, over. . . .*

The door opened, and Sean came back in, grinning like someone who had finally, really, totally gotten what he wanted. Triumph was written all over his face. He looked taller. Meaner.

Ready to kill her.

"Eli will be changing," he said. "GMTA. You both made the same choice."

She jerked. *No, he wouldn't.*

"And you'll be his first meal. Have you ever seen a newly changed vampire? All they want to do is suck someone's blood. That's all I wanted to do."

"You're lying," she said. "Eli would never. . . ."

But Eli *would*. He hadn't even asked her if she wanted to leave his parents' house to help him look for Sean. He had put her in harm's way, for Sean. He didn't love her the way he loved Sean. Lovers did things differently than friends.

"If it makes you feel any better, he feels terrible about it." Sean sneered at her.

"He's going to hate you for making him do this," she said. "He'll never love you." She was talking to a vampire. To a vampire who was going to kill her. To a gay vampire who was going to turn into a gay vampire.

She felt reality begin to slip away. This wasn't happening. "I'm going to get him now," he said, going for a smile, not quite pulling it off. Irritated, he slammed the door.

She stood as still as one of the mops she couldn't turn into a vampire stake. Her heart hammered in her chest and she had no idea how she could hear all that thumping and pumping because she was

at the door

at the door

at the door

pounding and screaming, begging to be let out.

Ms. Howison was going to have a change of heart and rally all the people in the gym and rescue her.

Sean was going to open the door and take her in his arms, and tell her that he'd been so mean to her because he actually loved *her*, not Eli. That he had only pretended to love Eli so he could stay close to her. And that he wouldn't kill either of them, not if Jilly didn't want him to.

Sean was going to tell her that he was sorry, both of them could be changed, and they would go on as they were, as a trio, only nicer, like Dorothy, the Tin Woodsman, and the Scarecrow.

Sean was going to see some other hot 'y on the way back to Eli and fall in love with him in d, change him, and leave.

Eli was going to escape, and find and they would get out of New York together.

She pounded on the door as remembered the night Eli had confessed that he had someone else . . . a guy

someone else . . . and he had cried because he didn't want to hurt her, his best friend.

"I will always love you totally and forever, I promise," he had said.

The door opened, and she scrambled backward away from it as fast as she could. Her elbow rammed into a container of cleaner. *Throw it at them. Do something. Save yourself.*

Sean and Eli stood close together. Sean had his arm around Eli, and Eli had on his baggy parka. Eli, as far as she could tell, was still human. His bangs were in his eyes.

He was looking at the floor, as if he couldn't stand to look at her.

"No," she whispered. But it must have been yes, he must have told Sean to change him. Sean was going to change him, and then he was going to kill her.

Her heart broke. She was on the verge of going completely crazy, all over again.

Sean took a step toward her. "If it makes you feel any better, it's going to hurt when I change him," he promised her. He sounded bizarrely sincere.

He shut the door. The three of them stood inside the cramped space. She was only two feet away.

Sean placed both hands on Eli's shoulders and turned Eli toward him. Tears were streaming down Eli's cheeks. He looked young and scared.

Sean threw back his head and hissed. Fangs extended from his mouth.

And Eli whipped his hand into the pocket of his parka; pulling out a jagged strip of wood—

—*Yes!*—

—and he glanced at Jilly—

—*Yes!*—

—and as Sean prepared to sing his fangs into Eli's neck, Jilly rammed Sean as hard as she could. He must have seen it coming, must have guessed—but Eli got the stake into him, dead center in his unbeating heart.

Sean stared down at it, and then at Eli, as blood began to pour down the front of him. Then he laughed, once, and blew Eli a kiss.

He looked at Jilly—gargled, "Bitch," his throat full of his own blood—then slid to the floor like a sack of garbage, inert, harmless.

Eli and Jilly stared at him. Neither spoke. She heard Eli panting.

Then Eli gathered her up. Kissed her.

Kissed her.

They clung to each other beside the dead vampire. And Eli threw himself over Sean, holding *him*, kissing *him*.

"Oh, my God, Sean," he keened. "Oh, God, oh, God. *Jilly*." He reached for her hand. She gave it to him, wrapping herself around him as he started to wail.

After he wore himself out, she tried to get up, thinking to see if there were more vampires, to check on Ms. Howison and the others, but he held her too tightly, and she wouldn't have moved away from him for the world.

He held Sean tightly too. "I can't believe it. How evil he was." Eli's voice was hoarse from all the sobbing.

"I know," she said. "He was always—"

"Sean wasn't even in there. When you're changed, the vampirism infects you and steals your soul," Eli went on. "You're not there. You're gone."

Tears clung to the tip of his nose.

"Sean loved you, Jilly. He told me that a million times every day. He was so glad you're my best friend."

She started to say, "No, he hated me," but suddenly she realized: that was going to be his coping mechanism. He was going to believe from now on that the Sean he knew and loved would have never made him kill his best friend.

She put her hand on the crown of his head and found herself thinking of the tapestry of the Jews at Masada in his parents' living room. It was a pivotal moment in Jewish history, when cornered Jewish soldiers chose to leap over a cliff rather than submit to Roman rule. Mr. Stein talked about it now and then, and sometimes Jilly had wondered if what he was saying was that Eli should take his own life, rather than be gay. She couldn't believe that, though, couldn't stand even to suspect it. The rigidity of the adult world was what had made her crazy. The unbelievable insanity of Mr. Stein, who condemned his own son just because Eli couldn't change into a heterosexual Jewish warrior and defy the invading sin of misplaced lust. At least, that was what her therapist had told her.

"You are brilliant, and you're so . . . *much*," Dr. Robles had declared. Dr. Robles, her savior. "People don't change, Jilly. They just see things differently than they used to, and respond according to the way they already are. It's all context. Reality. Is. Context."

Dr. Robles had saved her because he didn't try to change her. So she had never tried to change Eli.

She took a deep breath and thought about her hopeless love for him. And something shifted.

Her love was *not* hopeless. She loved him. It didn't have to break her heart. It didn't have to do anything but be there. Be there.

So she said, "Sean loved you so much." Because that would help him the most.

"Thank you," he whispered. "He loved you too. And I love you, Jilly." He looked up at her, broken and crumpled like a rag—the boy she kissed in the eighth grade, a thousand million times, almost until her lips bled.

"And I love you," she replied. "I love you more than my own life. I always have." It was right to say that now. People didn't change, and love didn't, either. Where Eli was concerned, there was no context.

"Thank you," he said. No embarrassment, no apologies; their love was what it was. Alone in a closet, with a dead vampire, hiding in a school because the rest of the city was overrun by vampires. . . .

She laid her head on his shoulder, and he laced his fingers with hers.

"Happy birthday, sweet sixteen," he whispered. "My Jilly girl."

"Thank you," she whispered. It was the best present ever.

After a while, they opened the door. The sun was out, and for one instant, she thought she heard the trilling of a lark.

Then she realized that it was Eli's cell phone.

Beepbeepbeepbeep. This is God, Jilly. I'm back on the job amen.

Binge

Rachel Vincent

"I need to sing." Andi screwed the lid onto a bottle of dark red fingernail polish. "Come with me?" Her voice was light, intentionally empty, but I heard the underlying desperation. The aching hunger. No one could hear Andi like I heard her.

I went still, staring at the back of the new Disturbed CD's case without really seeing it. "Andi. . . ." After I'd nearly been trampled the last time, she'd said I wouldn't have to tag along anymore. She'd *sworn* she wouldn't ask.

"I really need this, Mallory." Blue eyes pleading with me, she flipped onto her stomach on the mattress, careful not to let her wet toenails brush the bedding. "Look." She shoved long, dark hair back from her face and ran one finger beneath her left eye. "I could fly to China with these bags, and my hands were shaking while I counted down my register drawer yesterday. And you see how limp my hair is? I'm withering. I can feel it."

Did you know a siren can actually starve from silence? It's true. And talking won't help. Neither will standing in the middle of a crowded school hallway, listening to the secrets, the lies, and the general chaos. A siren suffers from her *own* silence, when she goes too long between feedings. And while I loved her voice, in that moment, I would have been grateful for a little quiet from Andi.

"You're not withering. You just hate math, and you stayed up too late last night." And her hair was flawless, as usual. Thick and wavy, with a truly unnatural shine.

She rolled her eyes. "You sound like Ty."

As much as I loved Andi—we'd been inseparable since the first day of fifth grade—I often felt sorry for her brother. Being her best friend was practically a full-time job, so I could only imagine how frustrating it must be for a normal twenty-two-year-old guy trying to rein in a sixteen-year-old siren. Especially considering how quiet and easygoing Ty was. Sometimes I wondered how they could possibly share a mother.

There are no male sirens, and since Ty's dad was human, so was Ty. Andi was a siren, just like her mom, but we had no idea who or what her father was. Her mom had never felt inclined to elaborate beyond the usual, "You're better off without him."

Apparently she was better off without a mother too, because when we were thirteen and Andi's siren appetite began to approach full-strength, her mom had dropped her off at Ty's apartment, and neither of them had heard from her since.

"Look, it won't be like last time, I swear." Andi tucked a lustrous strand of hair behind one ear. "I've been working on my focus. On singling one person out of the crowd. It'll be different this time."

I shoved the CD bin beneath her nightstand and sat cross-legged on the carpet, frowning up at her. "Didn't Ty say he'd take you out this weekend?"

"Yeah, but he said the same thing last weekend. He doesn't understand. And even if he remembers, we'll wind up somewhere really lame, like a honky-tonk talent show. The audience is eighty percent geriatric, all wearing bandanas as a fashion statement."

I rolled my eyes. "If you were really withering, I don't think you'd be so picky." She had to feed to survive. I understood that. But could she really be so hungry again already?

Andi shrugged. "I feel guilty feeding off old people; they're close enough to death on their own. Besides, it'd take three old ladies to equal the energy in one ripe eighteen-year-old body." Her eyes flashed with excitement, and her grin was contagious.

But just because my bruises had faded didn't mean I'd forgotten them. "Last time some jerk shoved me into a sliding glass door trying to get closer to you. I'm not ready to fend off another hoard if you get carried away again."

She frowned. "I told you, I've been practicing." I didn't answer, so she sat up on the bed, crossing arms beneath her breasts. "I'm starving, Mallory. I'll go without you, if I have to, but I could really use some backup."

Which was exactly why I'd always tagged along before:
to keep Andi from making any new friends. Or fans. My
job was to step in and shut her up once she'd had enough,
before she could turn any of the listeners—a.k.a., human
energy drinks—into desperate, fiending addicts or future
mental patients. That moment usually came between the
last notes of the crowd-favorite song and the first notes of
Andi's own personal melody. When a siren starts singing
her own lyrics, it's time to go. Or at least put earmuffs on all
the humans.

I'm particularly well-suited to be her backup because a
siren's song cannot hypnotize most non-humans. I am *leanan
sidhe*, so Andi's singing has no effect on me.

Well, that's not exactly true. Her singing astounds me.
The beauty of her voice makes me ache with longing and
burn with jealousy, all at the same time. But it doesn't flash
boil my brain, or overload my circuits, or whatever it is she
does to make humans fall crazy-in-love with her while she
slowly drains their energy. Andi can't feed off me, and I can't
be hypnotized by her. I'm the only one she can trust to help
her stop before things go too far.

We're a perfect pair. Truly twisted sisters.

"Besides, you know you want to get out of here." She was
grinning again, and I wished I was as immune to her smile
as I was to her voice. "Otherwise we're looking at a bowl of
popcorn, an all-night slasher-fest, and a pizza around midnight, if we're feeling adventurous."

Well, she had a point there. The summer was half over,
and we'd done nothing more exciting than serving fast food

for minimum wage. My mom would be back in a few days, and our month-long sleepover would be over.

Andi read my decision in my eyes, and she was already grinning before I spoke. "I guess we may as well have one last hurrah."

I don't know where Andi heard about the party. Maybe from some guy at work. Maybe from some guy on the street. Maybe from some built-in party guidance system whispering inside her head. All I know is that there's always something going on somewhere, and Andi always knows how to get there, even if we have to drive halfway across Texas.

That's the first rule of survival: Never eat where you live and never hit the same place twice. Eventually someone will notice if people always get sick when you sing to them, especially if there's no hangover to blame it on the next morning. The food poisoning excuse only works once.

"So, this is a private party?" I said when Andi turned off the highway onto a narrow, well-paved road, an hour from our one-horse, dead-end town. "What's the plan? You just gonna climb up on the table and start belting out show tunes?"

Andi laughed and pressed a little harder on the gas as her excitement crested. "Hardly. Though that might work if I get desperate. There's supposed to be a Rock Band tournament."

I pulled down the passenger side visor and touched up my lipstick in the lighted mirror. I wasn't siren-gorgeous; for me, looking good required effort. "Rock Band? Seriously?"

Though she would never have admitted it at school, Andi was pretty good on the plastic guitar; she played against her brother for cash once she depleted her paycheck. Ty wouldn't let her sing, of course, so she played guitar against his drums, and beat him about seventy percent of the time, even with them both playing on expert.

But she was flawless on the mic.

"I think that's it on the left. You ready?"

I nodded, and she slowed to a stop at the end of a line of cars on a dark residential street, her glittery eye shadow sparkling in the flood from a streetlight overhead.

When I got out of the car, I could hear sound leaking into the night from the house ahead: a heavy bass beat with a crunchy guitar riff and angry, staccato lyrics. The clock on the dashboard said it was after eleven, but the night felt new, and suddenly I was high on possibilities, though I hadn't come to feed. Chances were slim that I'd find a satisfying meal at some random party anyway—my skills were harder to define, my appetites much more difficult to satisfy than Andi's. But I shared her excitement. Being with Andi was a rush. Even when she wasn't singing, she exuded confidence and exhaled charisma. People wanted to please her, and I was no exception.

As we clacked our way up the sidewalk toward the well-lit house on the corner, I felt powerful, beautiful in my own right with Andi's arm linked through mine. I'd have a couple of drinks and a couple of dances, and retreat to the back of the room and monitor the show while she fed. Then it'd be just the two of us again, rehashing the play-by-play on the way home.

Andi wouldn't need to drink; she was high on anticipation alone for the moment, and after she sang she'd be stuffed and buzzed on human energy, but physically sober. Why had I resisted in the first place? The plan looked good, and we looked *great*. Everything would be fine. Better than fine.

Andi rang the doorbell. The right half of the double front doors swung open, revealing a guy in a frat T-shirt. He had dark hair, broad shoulders, and a plastic cup of beer. His eyes widened when he took in first Andi, then me. He stepped to one side and gestured for us to come in.

"Don't you want to know who we are?" Andi asked as we brushed past him, and I swear she was half-singing already.

"More than you could possibly imagine." He swung the door shut, and Andi eyed him like a snake about to strike.

"I'm Andi, and this is Mallory."

His eyes narrowed, and he glanced at the closed door. "How old are you?"

"Eighteen last week," Andi lied, then tossed her head toward me. "Her birthday was in April."

That last bit was true, but I'd turned sixteen, not eighteen.

Our host grinned like a hyena. "Ladies, my name's Rick, and you can crash my party any time you want." Rick led us through a large room packed with people dancing, laughing, and drinking, then into the kitchen. "What can I get you to drink?" His wide-armed gesture took in a two-countertop spread of snacks and drinks.

Andi took a soda and I let Rick pour me a beer, then we wandered into the main room just as a new song began to

play. "What's with the toys?" Andi said, eyeing the neglected Rock Band setup in one corner.

"We're having a tournament. Want to play? We can start you off on easy. . . ." Rick angled us toward the set-up while she pretended to think.

She shrugged, as if it didn't really matter. "I might give the guitar a shot. And I sing a little too."

I nearly spit beer all over them both.

"We'll get started as soon as my little brother gets here with the second drum set. So we can duel." Rick mimed smashing the high hat with his empty hand.

"Sign me up?" Andi asked.

Rick nodded like a bobblehead doll, and Andi and I wound our way through the mass of dancing bodies while he scribbled her first name onto the bottom of a list on a yellow legal pad.

"See anything interesting?" I asked, as Andi's gaze roved the room like she was looking over a buffet.

"Him." Andi grabbed my arm. "The one in the cowboy hat and boots, against the wall. He looks *yummy*."

I shrugged and finished my beer, then set the empty cup on an end table. "They say presentation is everything in fine cuisine."

"Exactly."

"I was kidding."

"I wasn't."

As she watched the cowboy in anticipation, I sent up a silent thank-you for the fact that I hadn't been born a siren. I wouldn't die if I didn't feed. But I wouldn't truly

live either. Though my body was nourished, my soul felt half-starved.

"See you when it's over?" she mumbled, eyeing her intended meal like a tiger eyes raw meat. She'd already forgotten I was there, but only because she knew she could trust me to stop her before she drained the poor guy like some kind of mystical vampire. Our system was tried and true, if a little lopsided. I got a night out, a few drinks, and a designated driver. She got an emergency off-switch—someone to keep her from killing everyone in the room if she got carried away.

Which was not beyond the realm of possibility. There was no limit to how much energy a siren could drink, or to how long she could live as a result. Even once she'd gotten what she needed, she could never be glutted, or even pleasantly full. The only thing that stopped a siren from binging was self-control. Unfortunately, Andi hadn't developed much of that yet.

"I'll be here. . . ." I whispered, but Andi was already halfway across the room. She may as well have been halfway across the galaxy.

She'd barely said hi to the walking Slurpee when the front door flew open on her left, revealing a tall, lanky young man with a dark shadow of stubble on his chin and a set of plastic drums under one arm, the foot pedal dragging the ground at his feet.

The crowd broke into applause, shouts of "Evan!" tossed around like confetti at a parade. Rick took the drums from his brother, and someone else handed Evan a beer.

Andi and her prey followed Rick to the corner of the room, where she helped plug in wires and adjust the surround sound settings while the crowd buzzed around them. This was evidently a regular thing for the locals: get drunk and play real songs on fake instruments with two hundred of your closest friends. And they'd accepted Andi like one of their own. It was kind of scary.

And it happened everywhere we went.

"You look like you need a drink."

I jumped and turned to find Evan—he of the plastic drum set—leaning against the wall on my left. I fumbled for a smile and he held out a clear plastic cup half-filled with ice and fizzing soda, but the scent said he was offering me something stronger than Coke.

I had no idea what else was in the cup, but I took it. No matter what this human predator was after with his cheap alcohol and easy grin, Andi was the most dangerous thing in the room, and I was immune to her particular brand of poison—no matter how badly I ached to sink into her song and forget about everything else.

"Thanks." I took a long sip from the cup, and bad vodka scorched a path down my throat. The stuff we snuck from Ty was much smoother, but considering I was underage and crashing someone else's party, I'd take what I could get.

Evan nodded and drank from his own cup, staring out at the room full of writhing bodies like we knew each other well enough to share a comfortable silence.

My next sip went down easier, so I took a third. The trick was to drink enough so that I didn't hate Andi when

she started singing—wasting unfathomable talent on a room
full of humans who could never truly appreciate her—but
not so much that I couldn't stop her before her lyrics became
too dangerous for their fragile psyches.

Usually two drinks was plenty. But as I watched Andi
laughing with her cowboy while she helped Rick adjust the
guitar strap over his shoulder, jealousy scorched a trail up
my spine. Two wouldn't do it this time. Two wouldn't even
come close.

Because no matter what she said, Andi didn't need me
like she needed the cowboy. On our own, we would never
be enough for one another.

I drained my cup, wincing at the fresh burn, and Evan
laughed out loud. "Not new at this, are you?"

Instead of answering, I held out my empty cup.

He set his drink on a nearby end table, where a bottle
of vodka stood next to two sweating cans of Coke. "I didn't
bring ice, but the soda's cold." He popped the tab on the first
one and half-filled my cup.

"I'll take it however I can get it," I said, then flushed
when I realized how that sounded.

Andi's laughter rang from across the room as he poured,
and I tilted the bottle up, giving myself a stronger dose of
liquid patience and tolerance. I was going to need plenty of
both.

But as usual, when Andi started singing a few minutes
later, I forgot how irritated I was. How jealous and . . . forgotten. I got lost in the song. In the beauty of the melody,
the poetry of the lyrics. The perfect shape of her mouth as it

formed each word. The guitarist fumbled, and the "percussionist" sounded like he was trying to beat the drums into submission, but Andi was flawless. Exquisite.

In the middle of the first song, people stopped dancing to listen. To watch her. She sang "Bring Me To Life" better than Amy Lee. Clearer. Cleaner. More visceral. And when the next song started, she moved effortlessly into a lively country shitkicker about revenge on a wife-beating husband.

"You like music?" Evan asked, and I forced my eyes to blink, then focus on him.

Like a fish likes to swim. "Looks like everyone does." All eyes were on Andi. The rest of the fake band practically faded into the background. She could have carried the song all alone.

By the time Pat Benatar started in on her infamous "Heartbreaker"—Andi must have chosen the set list—Evan had gone silent beside me, absently sipping his first drink, tapping his fingers on the wall at his back. The crowd was dancing again, some people singing along, but Andi saw none of them. She watched her living snack like he was the only one on the planet, and he stared back at her like she'd invented sex and promised him the first taste.

She wouldn't sleep with him. She'd come to satisfy a different kind of appetite, and by the time she was done with him, he wouldn't be able to stand up straight. Anything more complicated than that would be impossible for the next couple of days, until he'd regained some energy.

But he'd live.

Andi had to feed to keep from literally wasting away, and she thought it was more humane to take a little bit from

someone different every month or so than to drain some poor soul completely every couple of years. She did love singing for them—she *was* a siren, after all—but she wasn't a killer.

"She's really good." Evan pointed at Andi with his empty cup.

"Yeah, and she knows it."

His brows rose in surprise, and I realized he hadn't known we'd come together. "Do you sing too?"

I flinched, and a cold, hollow ache throbbed deep inside me, so deep no one else could ever see it. No one could ever know how bad I hurt. Except Andi. She knew, but she couldn't fix it.

"Alas, I am completely, tragically talentless." I forced a laugh, like I didn't care that such beautiful music was so far beyond my capabilities that I couldn't even *see* art from where I stood. "I'm just a spectator." A desperately hungry spectator.

"Oh, everyone has a talent," Evan insisted, turning away from Andi to face me fully. "You must be good at something."

He was wrong, on both counts. But he was looking at me rather than at Andi, and that intrigued me, so I answered instead of killing a discussion I would normally never pursue. "No, I am honestly no good at anything that requires creativity. Talent just . . . doesn't run in my blood." I'd never uttered a truer statement, but his grin said he thought I was being humble. Or trying to prolong the conversation.

"Oh, I bet we can find *something* you're good at. . . ."

"Well, I do have my moments." They just don't involve instruments, paints, pens, cameras, clay, or even paper mâché.

Evan's grin deepened, and the look in his eyes could have set off the fire alarm. "Maybe you just need help finding your hidden talents."

"Maybe so. . . ." *Wait.* I took a step back to clear my head and frowned up at him. *Better safe than sorry.* "You don't sing, do you? Or play Rock Band?"

"Nah." He set his empty cup on a shelf to his left. "Those plastic guitars hate me, and I'm not a very strong vocalist."

Relief washed over me, and I felt my smile brighten. "Great. You wanna. . . ."

But that's when Andi's three-song set ended, and the crowd burst into applause. I turned to see her scrolling through a list of songs on the huge, flat screen TV, and nearly choked on my own surprise. Her eyes were glowing— actually pulsing with light—though I was the only one who could see it.

Startled, I went up on my toes, searching the sea of faces for Snack-in-Boots, but he wasn't at the front of the crowd. Or the back of it. He was sitting alone on a couch near the wall, sweaty and pale, still watching Andi like he literally could not tear his gaze from her. He was totally mesmerized, and already suffering, though he didn't seem to realize it.

"Um . . . can you hang on a minute?" I asked Evan, then took off before he could answer, pushing my way toward the front of the crowd. She'd already gone past her safety line, and I'd been too busy flirting to notice. At least she hadn't ditched the band for a solo act yet. That's when the real trouble began.

"Okay, this is a vocalist-only challenge." Andi's crystalline voice carried easily without the mic, and I groaned aloud. "I'm gonna let these guys take a break for a minute and sing one of my personal favorites," she said, beaming at the fake backup band. Because this was her show now.

Crap! She was already flying too high to come down on her own. Andi would turn the microphone way up and the vocals track way down, and within a few bars of the opening notes, she'd be singing her own words without even realizing it. Once that started, it wouldn't end well.

At the front of the crowd, I gestured wildly to get her attention, and all I got for my efforts was a wide Andi-grin, all straight white teeth and hypnotic, glowing eyes. "Andi, you've hogged the mic enough for one night," I said, trying to ignore the stares that turned my way. "Give someone else a chance to sing."

"You want a turn?" Evan called from the back of the room, and I could have died right then.

But Andi just laughed, and the crowd laughed along with her. Not a good sign. She was affecting most of them now, instead of just her snack. "Mallory can't sing!" she cried, then winked at me like she'd just done me a favor. Rescued me from her new too-loyal fans and their glittering adoration.

"Andi. . . ." I began, but she brushed my hand off her arm.

"Just one more song, Mal. I know what I'm doing."

But she had no idea what she was doing. She was flat-out drunk on human energy, because I'd let her go too far. What

happened to focusing on one member of the audience? What about all that miraculous control she'd gained?

Andi clicked a button on the wireless PlayStation controller, then exchanged it for the microphone as music poured from speakers all over the room. She swayed to the rhythm, and the crowd swayed with her.

I glanced around desperately, looking for a plug to jerk from the wall, or a speaker to turn off. But that wouldn't stop Andi. She was just as good a cappella, and if the crowd was too far gone, they wouldn't even notice the missing music. I needed something that would get their attention, because without that, Andi wouldn't sing. There was no point.

I considered "accidentally" bumping the huge TV, but it was a plasma screen—too expensive to replace. The speakers, maybe? No. I wasn't sure that taking out one of them would be enough to stop Andi.

Then I noticed the PS3 whirring on a shelf beneath the television. Perfect. Expensive, but not a whole year of flipping burgers and salting fries. I glanced around until I spotted an unattended drink on an end table, then picked it up casually, as Andi sang the first words of the song. She was sticking to the real lyrics for the moment, but that would soon change. I knew that from experience.

So I edged casually closer to the shelf and accidentally-on-purpose tripped over an area rug. I caught myself with one hand, but spilled someone's warm beer all over the PS3 in the process, making sure liquid splashed into the disk slot.

The television screen flickered, then went black, while the PS3 whirred and smoked.

All eyes turned my way, and Andi's voice trailed into pained silence. Rick shook his head to clear it, then rushed over, face flushed with either alcohol or anger. Or both. "Damn it!"

"I'm sorry!" I sat up unsteadily, faking a couple more drinks than I'd actually had, ignoring the daggers Andi shot my way as the glow in her eyes slowly faded. No one was watching her now. No one was listening.

She hated me right now, but later she would be grateful.

"Are you okay?" A strong hand pulled me up by one arm, and I found myself face to face with Evan, who looked more confused than concerned. He'd seen me rush off, and had probably seen me take someone else's drink off the table. I looked like either a lush or a saboteur.

"Yeah. I'm sorry. I just . . . lost my balance."

"It's trashed," Rick groaned, and the crowd murmured with disappointment. He threw his arms up in disgust.

I swallowed the thrill of success secretly buzzing inside me and was relieved to see anger fading from Andi's expression. She shook her head once, then her focus found me, and her brows rose in question.

I nodded. Yes, I'd sabotaged her song and ruined Rick's PlayStation. All to save her ass. "I'll pay for that," I added softly as Rick unplugged his machine. *With Andi's money.*

The whole thing was her fault. She could cover the damages.

Rick stood with the machine under one arm. "I'm gonna let this dry out and see what happens. So I can either put in

a CD. . . ." His gaze found Evan, and a sly smile stole over his face. "Or I can put my brother on the spot."

"Evan!" someone called from the crowd, and several voices seconded the request. Then someone came forward carrying an acoustic guitar. Evan rolled his eyes like he'd refuse, but took the guitar without hesitation, and I couldn't miss the way his eyes lit up. It was a human glow, not as intense or as scary as Andi's. But it reflected true passion.

"Don't go anywhere," he whispered, trailing one hand down my arm. "I'll just do a couple."

Speechless, I nodded, even as Andi tugged me toward the door. "Let's go," she hissed, glancing from me to Evan, then back to me. I nodded again. We should go while he was tuning, plinking individual notes like the first drops of rain onto a drought-scorched wasteland. I shouldn't risk listening. One near-catastrophe was enough for tonight.

But then he started playing for real, and the notes didn't just plink like drops into a puddle. They flowed, like rivers of sound. They filled my empty heart and echoed in my hollow soul. I ached for that sound. For those notes. For the hands that played them, like they were no big deal, when they were *everything*. My entire world.

I stopped, one hand gripping the doorframe on my way out of the house. Andi pulled on my other arm, but I barely felt it. Barely heard her whisper my name. "I wanna listen. . . ." I murmured, already lost in the sound.

Then Evan began to sing, and Andi simply ceased to matter.

His voice was rough. Gravelly, as if the sound should have hurt coming out. I drank to satisfy desperate thirst, and I'd never tasted anything so wonderful. He'd said he wasn't much of a vocalist, but he was *wrong*. Or else he'd lied. Mere humbleness couldn't account for such an understatement.

His voice was raw emotion, gritty and gorgeous. I wanted to take off my clothes and roll in his voice. Wrap it around me. Wear it. Breathe it. Live it. His song filled me so thoroughly that for the first time in my life, I understood how empty I'd been before. How dull and tedious. I couldn't make sounds like that. Couldn't form notes with my fingers or throat. And I wasn't sure how, now that I'd heard him, I could ever live again without his sound around me. In me. Singing. Making beautiful, aching music, just for me.

"Mallory!" Andi pulled urgently on my arm again.

"Just one song." I dragged her back into the house with me. "I can handle one song. And you owe me." I risked looking away from Evan long enough to glare at her, suddenly sure my own eyes were flashing fiercely. I couldn't compel like a *bean sidhe*, or mesmerize like a siren. But I would do or say whatever it took to get close to Evan. To hear his song.

I needed it. I would die if I couldn't have it. I was sure of it.

"One song. Then I'll drag you out of here by your hair, if I have to," she snapped. Andi was mad. Because someone else was singing, soaking up attention? Or because I wanted to *listen* to someone else singing?

"Fine." Though I wasn't even sure what she said next. I couldn't hear her over. . . .

Evan.

I don't remember winding my way back through the crowd. Don't remember nudging, or pushing, or stepping on toes. But suddenly I was there, and he sat in front of me on a drum stool, a beautiful acoustic guitar on his lap. It sang for him like he sang for me. His fingers slid over the frets, and he plucked the strings without a pick. His head bobbed with a beat he'd created from nothing.

All around me, people danced. They swayed, and bobbed, and clutched one another to the rhythm of his aching melody. I wanted to dance—needed to live out those notes—but I wouldn't ruin his song with my clumsiness.

Then Evan looked up and saw me. He smiled, and his eyes lit up again, brighter than before, and suddenly I was warm inside.

His fingers flew across the strings, and the heartsick, wandering melody deepened, ripened, gaining focus and complexity. His voice teased new words from the air between us. They were his lyrics, but they were mine too. I couldn't have sung them. Couldn't even have written them, but he drew them from me. Gave them to me.

They were ours.

And all at once I understood.

Evan wasn't like the others. Not like the sketch artist in downtown Dallas, or the singing waitress last month. He was more than a temporary fixation. More than a one-night song to scratch my soul-itch. Evan was . . .

genius

The word tasted like a delicacy, but I thought it in a tiny, formless whisper, hardly daring to believe. Was it possible? Was that why Andi had insisted on going out? She couldn't have known, of course, but she didn't need to. Not if this was real, if it was meant to be.

If I was right, Evan and I could give one another everything we'd ever craved. We could make magic together. We could make *music*. I would feed his talent, and he would feed my soul. He would get fame, and fortune, and critical acclaim, and I would get *him*. If he was truly

genius

then I could have him. I could *love* him. And if I was very, very careful, we might live almost a human lifetime together.

My mother once savored a genius for thirty-six years.

I stood frozen, a statue in a room full of motion, thunderstruck and lost in the sound. I could no longer think. Couldn't breathe. I could only lap at his genius like a starving cat with a bowl of milk.

And when he'd finished the last notes, when they hung heavy and lonely in my heart, the cold darkness descended again, and I collapsed. I fell to the floor in a heap of talentless limbs, uncoordinated fingers. And I cried from the emptiness.

"Mallory!" Andi whispered fiercely, trying to pull me up before anyone noticed. But I couldn't move. The silence was too heavy, and I couldn't fight it. How do you slink back to live in darkness after you've been warmed by the light?

Evan set his guitar down and knelt in front of me. "What happened?"

"That was . . . beautiful," I whispered, frustrated and humiliated by my own inadequate, artless vocabulary. He'd given me the most amazing gift I'd ever experienced, and I couldn't even tell him how I felt.

"Thanks." He grinned and pulled me up as new music snaked through the room from several speakers, cool and mechanical after the lifeblood he'd just shed for us. "I never played it like that before." He tugged me gently away from the crowd, his brown eyes lit from within, and I would have followed him anywhere. I barely noticed Andi trailing us. "I think you're good luck."

"Great," Andi mumbled under her breath. "Mallory, we have to go."

"Stay for one dance," Evan said, without even glancing her way. His eyes were all for me. So were his hands, and his mouth, and his *songs*. "Just five minutes."

I wanted to. Desperately. But I would only humiliate myself and embarrass him in front his friends. So I started to shake my head, but Andi beat me to the punch with an ugly laugh.

"Mallory dances worse than she sings."

I glared at her, then glanced apologetically at Evan. "She's right. I can't dance."

When Evan laughed, the sound was melodic. "I'm not asking for a world-class waltz. Just one slow dance." Before either of us could argue, he turned and pushed a button on the stereo, and the speakers went silent. The crowd started

to grumble, but then he pressed one more button and a slow, sultry song slid into the room. The protests melted.

The first notes were just a bass guitar and drums, with a high hat for accent, but the rhythm brought with it images of damp, sweltering nights and little clothing. Evenings when it was too hot to touch anyone else, but you wanted to anyway. I felt the heat in spite of the air conditioned room, because Evan pulled me close and his magical, musical hands were on me. And when the words began, he hummed in my ear, so low that no one else could hear.

I couldn't dance. Not one step. But I could put my arms around him and let him move us both to the music. Guiding me. Playing me like he played his guitar.

I wanted to make music for him, but I couldn't. Art was mine to give, not to make. And it took every ounce of self-control I possessed to keep from giving that song to him as he hummed it. From molding it and making it his. Ours. I forced the urge down. Buried it in the feel of his hands on my back, of his lips as they brushed my ear. I would enjoy him the normal way, if only for a few minutes.

Content in his arms, I closed my eyes, and when I finally opened them, I saw Andi watching us over his shoulder. Watching *me*. Rick stopped at her side, two cups in hand, but she brushed him off without a word, and her hard gaze never left mine.

I closed my eyes again, blocking her out. But a minute later, she pulled me away from Evan before the last notes had even faded around us. "We have to go," she snapped,

glaring at him now. "I have to be home before my brother gets off work."

"Stop it!" I hissed as she pulled me toward the door, but she didn't let go, and I didn't want to cause another scene. "Didn't you hear him?" I whispered desperately, tripping after her. "We're supposed to be together. He's *genius*, Andi! My first."

"You're not ready," she insisted, and I stumbled over the threshold as she dragged me onto the porch.

"Wait. . . ." Evan followed us to the door, but Andi didn't stop, so he jogged down the steps after us.

"How do you know what I'm ready for? You're a siren. You eat people. You don't know a *anything* about true art."

Andi stopped at the curb and whirled on me, her eyes flashing in fury. "You can be pissed if you want, but you saved my ass, and now I'm saving yours. And if you don't get in the damn car, I swear I'll sing to him, and he'll forget he *ever even met you*."

"You're a bitter, jealous bitch," I spat, tears filling my eyes.

For a moment, she looked like I'd slapped her. Then her expression went blank and hard. "I'm all you have. Get in the car."

"What's your name?" Evan stumbled to a stop on the sidewalk. "Can I . . . ? Maybe we could hang out sometime?"

"I don't think so," Andi said, dragging me toward the car, and my heart broke as his expression crumpled.

"Mallory Bennett," I called out, and Andi's grip tightened until it hurt. She opened the passenger door and pushed on my shoulders until I sat, then slammed the door. She raced

around the front of the car, slid into her own seat, and had
the engine started before Evan made it to the curb. And as
we sped away from the party where she'd almost killed and
I'd almost lived, I twisted in my seat to watch Evan fade into
the darkness, fighting back the cold steadily seeping back
into my chest.

I hadn't even gotten his last name.

Andi tried to get me up before she left for work, but I couldn't
look at her without hating her. So I pulled the covers over
my shoulder and stared at the wall. She curled up next to me
and brushed hair back from my forehead. She said she was
sorry. She promised that there would be others like Evan,
later, when I was ready to nurture true genius.

But my readiness wasn't the problem. *She* wasn't ready
to share me.

When I still refused to look at her, she got dressed, and
right before she closed the bedroom door, she swore that the
next time I found a genius, she wouldn't stand in my way.
She would help me.

But I could hardly hear her. I heard Evan in my head,
and in my heart. It was a hollow echo of the live performance, but it was enough to drown out everything else.

I spent the morning in Andi's bed, huddled beneath
her covers, but no matter how many blankets I piled on, I
couldn't get warm. Had Evan's warmth shown me how cold
I truly was? Or was I colder for having lost him?

The sun was high and bright when my phone chirped, signaling a new email. I rolled over and glanced at the clock. Eleven twenty-three. The day was half over. If I could survive another few hours, I'd make Andi take me out again. Anywhere loud enough to block out the echo in my head. She owed me.

The phone chirped with another email. But Andi was more of a texter. . . .

I fumbled on the nightstand, then flipped open my phone and selected the latest email. The sender's name was Evan Taylor. The message read, "Mallory, if this is you, please call me." There was a phone number below the signature.

My heart thumped almost painfully as I dialed, and my pulse shot through the roof when he answered. "Hello?"

"Evan? It's Mallory. How did you get my email address?"

He sighed, and the sound was melodic. "Facebook. Thank goodness you posted a picture. There are four Mallory Bennetts in central Texas."

"I. . . ." I'd lost all words.

He laughed. "Are you busy? You wanna do something? Get some lunch?"

Yes. "No." Even cold and aching for him, for his music, in the light of day, with Evan's song a mere memory, I knew I shouldn't. Not without Andi there as backup. Even if she was wrong and I *was* ready for Evan, I wasn't ready to be alone with him. Not for too long, anyway.

"No?" He sounded so surprised, so heartbroken, my chest hurt.

"Yes." I closed my eyes, ashamed of my weakness. "Absolutely, yes."

"Where are you? I'll come over."

My eyes flew open and I glanced around Andi's wreck of a room. We hadn't done laundry in two weeks, and I didn't even know where Ty kept the vacuum cleaner. So I gave him my address. My mom always cleaned before she left town because she hated coming home to a dirty house.

"I'll be there in an hour."

The phone clicked in my ear, and I flipped it closed, my heart pounding. Then I flipped it back open and emailed Andi. She had to leave her phone in her locker while she was on the clock, so we'd have at least a couple of hours of privacy before she got off work at three, in plenty of time to rescue us if something went wrong.

My precaution in place, I threw back the covers, tugged on the jeans I'd worn the day before, and grabbed my keys. Eight minutes later, I pulled into my own driveway and headed straight for the shower.

I waited for him on the living room couch, staring out the front window. One hour and four minutes after he'd hung up, a dusty gray sedan pulled into my driveway. I raced to the foyer and paused to get my pulse under control. Then I pulled the door open.

Evan stood on my front porch, holding his guitar. He grinned, and his brown eyes flashed in the sunlight. I stepped back to let him in without a word. *I can do this. We don't even have to sing today.* This wouldn't go bad if I didn't let it.

"I couldn't stop thinking about you," he whispered. I leaned against the closed door, and he stepped closer. "Every time I close my eyes, I see you. I dreamed about you."

"What kind of dream?" I breathed, staring up at him, and my pulse became our shared rhythm.

"The best kind." Heat blazed behind his eyes. He kissed me, and his mouth was hot. Scalding. Delicious. He pressed me into the door, and I let him, because kissing wasn't dangerous. And it was almost as good as what I really wanted. What he'd come for.

When my hands found his chest and his found my hair, when we were both breathing hard and craving two different kinds of pleasure, his mouth left mine. His lips trailed over my chin toward my ear, where his warm breath sent shivers through me. "I want to play something for you," he whispered, and I shuddered all over.

"Now?"

"Now. Please."

I could only nod. One song couldn't hurt, and if we didn't make room for a guitar between us, I would wind up making a whole different kind of mistake.

I pulled him down the hall by one hand, and only hesitated a moment in my bedroom doorway. I sat on the bed and he took the desk chair, his fingers moving across the frets before his jeans even touched the upholstery.

"This one's new," he said. "When I was trying to find you, this melody kept playing through my head, and it took me a while to figure out what it is."

"What is it?" I could barely breathe.

"It's your song, Mallory." He smiled, and my heart beat so hard it hurt. "I'm still working on the lyrics, though."

I was right. We're supposed to be together. We're supposed to create together.

This song was different from the one he'd played the night before. More hopeful, but just as passionate. Beautiful. Fresh and captivating. Was that how he saw me?

The notes rang clear, and I could almost feel Evan's voice sliding over me. Resonating within me. Filling me with precious warmth.

Then he felt the song change. Evolve. I was watching his face the moment it happened. At first it was a note here or there. This one extended, that one cut short for emphasis. Depth. Then there were fresh chords, lending a melancholy note to the beautifully simple chorus. Next came new words.

His eyes widened as he tasted the new lyrics. Testing them. Then he smiled and closed his eyes. He leaned back in the chair and kept singing. Kept playing. The notes flowed between us, tempting me. Teasing me. But I forced my eyes to stay open. If I closed them, I'd lose myself in the music. I'd lose us both. So I watched him, reining myself in. Reducing to a mere trickle the flood I wanted to let loose.

He wasn't ready for that. Neither was I.

When that first song ended, he set his guitar down and snatched a blank notepad from my desk and a pen from the jar. For five interminable minutes, he scribbled, and my heart beat to the rhythm of his pen scratching the paper. When he finally grabbed the guitar again, his eyes were bright and eager, but he was sweating in spite of the air conditioning.

That's enough, my head said, while my heart argued otherwise. It would *never* be enough. Evan could sing to me for the next decade, and I would never be satisfied.

Neither would he. Not ever again. We would always want more.

"Are you hungry?" Food would give him energy and distract us both. "I can make some sandwiches," I said, though that delicious warmth inside me faded a bit with each word. I headed for the hall, forcing my feet into motion when they wanted to rebel, but Evan's hand closed around my wrist.

He smiled, but his gaze was piercing. "I feel better than I have in months, Mallory. Like I have something to give. Something to say. Let me play for you. Please."

What was I supposed to say to that? He wanted to play. And I wanted to let him.

"One more," I said, and silently I swore the same thing. *One more, and we'll stop.* We would eat, or watch TV, or I'd find some *other* way to keep him busy, even if that meant diverting one appetite with another.

The next song was pain, raw and exposed. He bled through his notes, and I could almost see his scars. Whoever she was, she'd hurt him, and I wanted to kill her. To draw out whatever she had to offer the world, and drink her dry. Break her for hurting him.

My reaction scared me. How could I be so connected to him already?

He didn't stop to write after that one. Maybe he didn't want to remember. Maybe he knew he couldn't forget. Either

way, he started the next one before I could get up, and I couldn't stop myself. This one was remorse. His greatest regret laid bare, and I was almost ashamed to witness it. I cried with him, then kissed away his tears when his voice cracked, before they could fall on the strings. The vibrant wood.

Comfort kisses became something more, something deeper, but somehow wanting me became wanting to *show* me how much he wanted me—with a new song. I tried to argue, though I wanted the same thing, but his fingers plucked the strings even while we kissed. And when I pulled him up and took the guitar away, he sang without it. We wound up against the wall where his soft, throaty tune roamed as eagerly as his hands. And I didn't want to stop either one. I didn't know *how* to stop us. I was lost in the sound and the feel of him, and the physical element made the musical one so much harder to resist.

When he came up for air, he grabbed the guitar and pulled me onto the floor with him. He sat in front of me, his back pressed into my chest to keep me close, and temptation pulled at me mercilessly. My willpower wavered. I glanced at my alarm clock, and exhaled deeply in relief. Two forty-five. Andi would be on her way soon. I could relax for a little while. Enjoy one more song before she came.

Evan sang about a fractured relationship. About some girl who'd understood him and loved him, but resented his needs. I'd told myself I'd just listen this time. Stay out of the process. But the notes swirled through my head until I couldn't focus on anything else. I got mired in the words,

lost in the emotion, and began doling out new bits for it without even realizing what I was doing. And after that one, I forgot to check the clock.

Next came anger. The notes were violent streaks of red against the backs of my eyelids. The bitter melody scored my heart. But halfway through, something nagged at the back of my mind. Something wasn't quite right. It needed. . . .

I stood and raced into the hall. Cold silence dropped around me like dark curtains and Evan appeared in the doorway as I knelt in front of the back closet. He braced one hand against the doorframe, but I told myself he only looked pale because of the weak lighting. He was fine. He couldn't play so well otherwise.

What I wanted was at the back of the closet, propped carefully on its stand. I stood and offered it to him like sacrifice at an altar. He needed it to get through this song. To get it right. And surely one last song couldn't hurt.

Evan took the vintage Strat and studied it while I dove into the closet again for an amp and the wires. I wasn't supposed to touch the guitar. My mother saved it for special cases. For true

genius

But Evan *was* a special case. My very first. I knew that deep in my soul.

He strummed while I hooked up the wires and the pedal, and his smile was so bright I almost didn't notice the lines around his mouth. The creases in his forehead. It wasn't getting bad yet. He just needed to rest, after one more song. . . .

Evan knew exactly what to do. The crunch and squeal of the electric guitar painted my room with his anger, slashed through pain and into fury so skillfully I couldn't breathe. At some point, my phone rang, and when I considered opening it, I noticed the sun was on the wrong side of the house.

Andi was late, but she'd be there soon. Everything would be fine when she got there. Any minute. . . .

After that, things got fuzzy. My head swam with melodies. Time lost all meaning, and my bedroom began to blur around me. Only the music remained in focus.

Evan became his music, and I knew him through his songs. Every note, every lyrical verse, tugged at my heart; each crunchy riff ripped through my soul. He showed me what he wanted and what he feared. What he loved and what he needed. And I drank it all in. He poured himself into the music, and the music poured into me.

Then, suddenly, he stopped, and there was only panting. Wheezing. His face scrunched in pain, a bitter reflection of the raw emotion he poured into his music. It was the song. It had to be. The song hurt him, but it was better to drain the wound, right? To let it all out, so he could heal. Stopping would be the worst possible thing for us both, right?

"What's that pounding?" The guitar sagged in his grip, as if he'd lost the strength to lift it the moment he stopped playing. But we'd only done a few songs. Right?

I shook my head, trying to clear the fog, but notes bounced around in my skull, obscuring all logic with terrible, unfathomable beauty. I frowned when his dull gaze

finally came into focus. Had his cheekbones always been so sharp?

The pounding came again, and someone shouted my name over and over. "Mallory, open up!" *Andi*. I glanced at the clock. Nine-oh-eight. At night? No wonder it was dark.

I trailed one hand down Evan's arm on my way to the hall, and as I passed the mirror, I saw that my eyes were fully dilated. Literally. The brown in my irises had been swallowed by my pupils, and black bled into the web of red veins.

Oh, shit. No. It couldn't have gone so far already. Everything would be fine. Andi would fix it.

When I opened the door, she gasped, staring at my eyes. Then she brushed past me,. "I left my phone in the car and Carl made me work late. But I've been calling you for *three hours*. I drove by your work and the mall. Hell, I even tried the school."

"Told you where I'd be. . . ." My words came out slurred, and I frowned in confusion. "In the email?"

"No, you just said Evan was coming over. You didn't say where. Mallory, what did you *do*?" But she took off toward the hall without waiting for my answer.

"We're meant for each other, Andi. I took what he had and made it more, and he fed it back to me, and it was *so good*."

Andi turned on me, eyes narrowed in anger. She shoved me into the wall by my shoulders and held me there while the world swirled around me, notes hanging on the air. "You're drunk." Disgust dripped from her voice in thick, bitter drops, but beneath that, there was

envy

I heard it. I know envy like bees know honey. I cultivate it. I drown in it. But not this time. This time I was full of beautiful music, glutted on pure art, and I did it without her. That's why she was really mad. This time *she* was cold, and angry, and forgotten.

"Damn it, Mallory!" She let me go, and I followed her into my room. Her scared little gasp slid into the silence.

Evan sat slumped against the foot of the bed, his thin hands gripping the guitar. His veins stood out all over, like bruises tracing his body. His cheekbones looked like they'd slice his face open, and his eyes had sunk into the dark rings of flesh around them.

"No!" I dropped onto the floor next to him and cradled his face. "Evan? Say something." He groaned, and I turned to Andi. "This isn't possible. It happened too fast. It was just a few songs."

"Does this look like a few songs to you?" she demanded, flinging out both arms to take in the entire room.

Shocked, I stood and looked. For the first time in hours, I really *looked*. There was paper everywhere. On the floor. On the desk. On the bed. Loose sheets of it, notebooks, even Post-its, all scribbled with lines, and words, and slanted, sloppy notes, as if the composer had gone mad.

Tears pooled in my eyes as I glanced at Evan, but even through them, I could see the pencil on the floor near his right hand. It was worn down to a nub.

When had he written them? I'd never left him, yet I hadn't seen the scribbling. I remembered only music. Blissful notes. Painful melodies.

"He's dying," Andi whispered, palms rubbing up and down the sides of her jeans, like she could wipe death off her skin. "You killed him."

"No." I staggered, and caught myself on the bookshelf. "Evan, wake up. . . ." I knelt by him again, and he opened his eyes.

He dragged in another shallow breath, and his chest rose. "What happened?" he whispered, and I closed my eyes.

"Tell him what you did," Andi demanded, and I flinched. But I couldn't speak. So she spoke for me. "She gave you *genius*. But genius is short-lived, right, Mallory?"

My tears fell, scalding against my cheeks. Her words hurt so badly I thought I'd die. But looking at Evan hurt worse.

"What are you?" His dull, colorless eyes accused me silently, his mouth gaping open, lips cracked. He exhaled, one last time. Then his chest was still.

"She's your muse," Andi whispered into the terrible silence.

I sobbed. Tears rolled down my face and dropped to the floor, but they were not musical. They were flat. Empty. That awful chill crawled back into my heart with cold, dead fingers. Even my screech of pain and regret was atonal. Ugly. And now I was empty. Cold. So hollow my heartbeat echoed.

Every drop of warmth Evan's music had spilled into me died with him, chased away by the knowledge of what I'd done. Frozen into a thousand shards of ice, cutting me up from the inside.

I hiccupped and wiped my face, but the tears wouldn't stop. And they couldn't bring Evan back.

"You can't. . . . You *know* you can't do this." Andi turned to me, furious, but with open arms, like she'd yell at me and hug me at the same time. But I pushed her away.

I'd used him up. Wasted a lifetime of talent on one gluttonous binge. And I'd lost him. Lost my chance to inspire love and art in the same breath. Lost a life I was meant to treasure.

I stood and backed toward the wall, wiping tears from my face. Trying to block out the hollow echo in my chest. But there was no more music to cover it.

Andi pulled me forward and her arms wrapped around me. She rocked me, brushing hair down my back. Then she stepped back and made me look at her, and her eyes were the whole world. "You get it now? You and me? We're the only thing that lasts. Everything else is fragile. Fleeting." She gestured with one empty hand to the cooling corpse at her back. "We'll always be the only ones left."

Devastated, I slid to the floor, and she sank with me. We huddled in the corner, shaking. Crying. *Craving.* "I'm so cold, Andi. So empty. Sing to me."

So she sang.

Free

A Story of Evernight

CLAUDIA GRAY

New Orleans
Summer 1841

The house on Royal Street was as refined as any other in New Orleans. Cast-iron scrollwork decorated the gate that enclosed the small garden, where a profusion of hydrangeas bloomed in crimson and violet. No loud parties ever took place within, and the oil lamps always dimmed at a reasonable hour. The honey-colored paint was in good taste, as were the modest, fashionable gowns worn by the ladies who lived there.

Yet it was not a respectable house.

"You mustn't pay those ladies any mind." Althea plaited Patrice's hair as she spoke, her fingers quick and sure. Althea was Patrice's mother, although Patrice was not allowed to call her "Mamma" when anyone else was around. Lately, Patrice had not bothered to call her that in private, either. "Just jealous, every last one of them. What wouldn't they give for a dress made of real Parisian satin? They're poor. You and I—we will never be poor."

"They didn't say we were poor. They said we—that we were bought and paid for."

Althea's hands closed around Patrice's shoulders. The fine cotton of her chemise wrinkled beneath Althea's grip. "We are free women of color," she said quietly. "We will never be slaves. Never."

Patrice had seen slaves working on the levee, without even hats or scarves to shield them from the punishing sun, sweat gleaming on their skin as overseers cursed them to work even harder. She had seen girls years younger than herself scrubbing front stoops on their hands and knees, knuckles ashy and raw from lye. She had seen scars around wrists and ankles, the red ugly welts that showed where shackles had once been. And she knew that cruelties like these took place in other refined houses in the French Quarter, in New Orleans, throughout the South. No, Patrice and Althea were more fortunate than any slaves.

But being a free woman of color did not mean being truly free. This was even more true for Patrice and her mother— who lived in luxury provided by wealthy white men in an "arrangement" that felt as unbreakable as any chain.

Once Patrice's hair had been braided into elaborate buns and loops, Althea treated her like some fragile glass trinket that might shatter before the ball. "Don't you even think about lying down and flattening your hair," Althea said as she loosely tied a lace scarf around Patrice's head. "You can sleep all day before tomorrow's dance if you're tired."

Patrice, who had made other plans during her mother's afternoon naps for months now, simply nodded.

After Althea had left her alone, Patrice watched the clock on the mantel. Mr. Broussard had brought it as a gift after his last trip to Europe—a gift for her, not for her mother. This attention had angered Althea, who had spoken sharply to Patrice for a week afterward. Patrice suspected that was why she was being presented this summer instead of the next, when she would be sixteen.

As if I would want such a monstrosity, Patrice thought as she looked at the bronze nymphs surrounding the clock face. The clock's creator had taken great pains to prominently display all the nymphs' uncovered breasts. *As if I would want any attention from Mr. Broussard.*

Of course, Althea and Patrice both knew that what Patrice wanted didn't matter.

Once twenty minutes had passed, Patrice rose and swiftly put on a simple calico housedress and a pair of slippers. The stairs creaked as she hurried downstairs, but Patrice didn't worry. Althea, like most free residents of New Orleans, was sound asleep. The June heat and humidity were so punishing that free people did not attempt to do

anything at midday except nap. The whole city fell quiet, and it became very easy to avoid being seen.

Patrice tiptoed out the back door toward the shade provided by a magnolia tree's broad, shining leaves. She was still blinking, blinded by the sun, when two hands reached out from that darkness and grabbed her.

"Amos," she whispered, before his mouth closed over hers.

They sank to their knees together, wrapped in each other. Amos's embrace was tight, almost demanding, but after the first few eager kisses, he pulled back. They smiled at each other, giddy as always with their successful escapes.

"Lookin' fancy," he said. With one finger, he lifted the edge of her lace scarf to peek at the complicated hairdo beneath. "Wish I could see you tonight, when you dress up so fine."

"I wish too." Patrice leaned against his broad chest. Blacksmithing had made his muscles as thick as cordwood. He smelled like ashes and horses, like the earthy, dirty real world that she'd been sheltered from throughout her life.

She did not find the smell unpleasant. Amos's clothes carried the scent of his work. This reminded her that, despite his poverty, Amos was freer than she would ever be.

Amos's former master was widely considered to be a soft, foolish person by the finer residents of New Orleans— a subject of ridicule by the proper white ladies who would cross the street to avoid walking near women like Althea. This master had allowed Amos to train as a blacksmith, then

hired him out to people at reasonable wages. Many slave owners did this for various skilled trades. But Amos had been allowed to keep part of his wages. Amos was so skilled at his craft, so very much in demand, that within only a few years he had saved enough to buy his own freedom. And his master had let him! The gossips in town could devise no explanation for such eccentricity.

"This party tonight." Amos said abruptly. "They don't make up their minds right away, do they? It wouldn't happen as soon as that."

Patrice had hidden from this hard truth as long as she could. They had to face it now. "No, probably nobody will pay court to me tonight. But somebody will, Amos, before the season's over. What difference does it make, if it's tonight or two months from now?"

"Two months with you is worth a lot to me. Especially if it's the last two months we ever have." Wearily, Amos leaned back against the trunk of the magnolia tree. "If Althea would've waited one more year, I could've put enough money aside. Enough to get a couple rooms for us. We might have been husband and wife."

"I don't think she would ever have let me marry."

"Let you? *Let* you?" Amos was not angry, only disbelieving. "Your problem is you were never a slave. You don't know what it means, bein' free. If you did, you wouldn't abide her 'letting' you do a thing."

"Amos—"

"Why wouldn't Althea let you marry? Why wouldn't she want somethin' decent for you, instead of—"

He didn't say the rest aloud. That was his way of being kind.

"She wants grandchildren who will have even lighter skin than mine," Patrice said. "She wants to know that there will always be a wealthy white man's name to use if the patrollers stop me—so nobody can ever claim that I'm not free."

Probably Althea also wanted a source of support if Mr. Broussard ever tired of her, but Patrice never spoke of that. She didn't even like thinking about that possibility, because if Althea could someday be abandoned, Patrice could be too.

Amos sighed heavily, his anger exhausted. They always came back to this in the end—to resignation, regret, and yearning for everything they'd been denied. "I imagine it sometimes. You and me. How it might be for us."

"I do too."

In truth, Patrice had no idea whether she could be a good wife to Amos. To be a poor man's wife, she would have to cook and churn butter and scrub clothes on a washboard— chores she'd never had to learn how to do. Althea had never learned either. Slave girls belonging to Mr. Broussard came over each day to take care of such things. Sometimes the slaves' disdainful stares hurt more than those of the white ladies. They would look up from their work, hair hidden under kerchiefs, eyes narrowed, as if to say, *Who do you think you're fooling?*

How they would have laughed, if she had thrown her wealth away to marry Amos. But it would have been worth it, if she and Amos could only have had a chance.

She put her hands on either side of his face, and they kissed again. What began gently soon became more intense. Amos leaned her backward, into the soft carpet of fallen magnolia leaves, and his heavy body covered hers. His homespun shirt was open at the neck, and she could feel the warmth of his skin through her thin dress.

They had never become lovers, because Amos had old-fashioned ideas. Patrice, who could not afford to be old-fashioned, arched her body against his so that he would feel the swell of her breasts, the tautness of her belly.

"If only you were my wife," he whispered against her throat. "How I could love you."

"You could love me now, if you only would."

He pushed her aside, almost roughly, and his face twisted into a grimace. Then he looked at her, his eyes desperate. "Leave with me. Tonight, after the party."

"Amos!"

"We can do it." He clutched at the sleeve of her dress. "A blacksmith can find work anywhere. All we have to do is go."

"We don't have the money." This was no time for foolishness. "We don't know a soul outside New Orleans. If we ran away, we could never call on any of our white folks for help, not ever again. How long do you think we'd stay free? A month? A week?"

Amos's shoulders sagged. The truth had defeated him.

She put her hand upon the open V exposed at the neck of his shirt. "I don't want some white man to be the first to touch me."

"I don't want to do you shame."

"We love each other. There's less shame in that than—than anything else I'll ever have."

They were silent together for a while longer, and she watched Amos's face carefully. In his eyes were his love and desire for her, doing battle with his idea of what was respectable for them both. Patrice had never been respectable, not really, so she couldn't understand why it was so hard for him to choose. When she saw the slight relaxing of the tension in his broad shoulders, she felt she had won.

Patrice whispered, "My room is in the back of the house. The small balcony—you know the one?" Amos nodded. "I'll leave the shutters unlatched. We should be home no later than midnight. Come—maybe an hour later than that. You'll be all right if you have your papers; people know you. All right?"

She still thought he might refuse, out of misguided devotion to her. But he said, "I'll come to you."

C———

Amos departed before the sun had left its zenith. Patrice went inside and took a hasty sponge bath, so that her mother would not smell horses and ashes on her skin. By the time Althea had awakened, Patrice sat demurely on the chaise in the parlor, wearing her silk wrapper and reading Coleridge's *Ballads*.

"You seem to have perked up," Althea said. "About time you realized how lucky you are."

Patrice, half-crazy with anticipation, hid her smile behind her mouth.

As the afternoon cooled and the shadows grew long, they began to prepare for the first quadroon ball of the season. Tonight the young ladies would meet the wealthy scions who wanted a black wife to tide them over until they could take a white one.

Time for a girl to look her best, she thought bitterly.

Patrice dabbed Florida water on her wrists and at her throat, and she tucked verbena sachets into the folds of her gown so that she would smell sweet no matter how warm the crowded room became. Powder would keep her face from becoming shiny and make her skin look even paler.

Althea tied a bit of lace around Patrice's throat and fastened a cameo in front. Then she laced Patrice into her corset; once it was so tight that Patrice felt almost dizzy, Althea proclaimed that she would now fit into her gown.

"Eighteen inches," Althea said proudly as she helped Patrice step into her hoop skirt. "That's as thin as my waist, before I had you."

Struggling for breath, Patrice did not care about any of that—at least, not until she saw herself in the mirror.

The satin of her dress was the palest lilac, and fine lace ruffled at the sleeves and upon the broad, bell-shaped skirt. Her bodice was low enough to show off the new curves of her bosom. Patrice knew there was no girl in New Orleans who could outshine her that night, and for a moment her pride eclipsed her shame.

I wish Amos could see me like this. He'd be amazed.

But he wouldn't see her tonight. Instead, she would be on display to the men who sought to take her as a concubine—including, probably, the one who would take her away from Amos forever.

The thrill of anticipation she felt for tonight, for Amos, could not entirely eclipse the knowledge of her ultimate fate. She and Amos would become lovers soon, but her destiny was still to be a white man's mistress. His plaything. His possession in all but name.

"Pull tighter!" Althea grunted, bringing Patrice back to the here and now, in which she was lacing up her mother's corset in turn. "I swear, I don't know where your mind wanders off to sometimes."

⌒

The carriage called for them just after nightfall. Patrice and Althea rode through the streets to the Salle de Lafayette. Horses' hooves and wagon wheels rattled against the cobblestone streets, and the gaslights on each corner kept the dark at bay.

They swept inside the ballroom side by side, but that was the last moment Patrice would spend with her mother all night. As usual, Althea's friends drew her into a corner for punch and gossip. Patrice might have sought her own friends, who were at least as nervous as she was, but she wasn't in the mood for company.

The band tuned up its instruments as the men began to enter. At first, the arrivals were mostly the older gentlemen,

the ones Patrice already knew—the men who kept company with their mothers. She saw Mr. Broussard staring at her with ill-concealed interest, at least until Althea took his arm and began paying him the sweet compliments he liked so much.

Patrice also glimpsed a tall man with white hair—Laurence Deveraux, whose last name she and her mother kept although he had last visited Althea many years ago. His face reminded Patrice of her own. Although no one had ever dared to call him her father, Patrice knew the truth.

Really, she did not expect Mr. Deveraux to pay attention to her. He never had before. But it would have been nice for him to at least glance her way and see how pretty she looked in her satin dress.

Then the younger men came. One carriage after another emptied out on the walk below, each one filled with boisterous, laughing gentlemen, most of them fresh from university. They strode into the club proudly, their cravats bright against white shirts with high collars. They wore broad smiles and waistcoats of watered silk, and their laughter was too knowing for Patrice's taste.

One of them did not laugh.

He caught Patrice's attention right away. It was only because he was quieter than the others in the room, but he was handsome too. He seemed to be a few years older than some of the other boys, and he held himself with dignity. His chestnut hair was as long as a girl's.

His dark eyes swept through the room, bored and disdainful, as though he hardly expected to see anything that would interest him. Yet when his gaze arrived at her, he paused.

Patrice ought to have behaved like a proper lady, averting her eyes while unfolding her fan. Instead, she lifted her chin and stared back.

I won't play the demure little girl, she swore. *Not for him or for anyone! If I let him see how much I hate him, then he won't court me. I'll have longer to spend with Amos.*

Slowly, he smiled.

Surely he had to be smiling at someone else. Patrice turned her head and started to push through the crowd toward the window. It would be easy enough to lose him in the crush.

Then a hand closed over her shoulder.

She turned to see the man with chestnut hair, who had crossed the busy room with surprising speed. The white kid leather of his glove was soft against her bare skin. "There you are," he said, as though they were old friends, long separated by chance.

Patrice pulled away. "Sir, we have not been introduced."

"I am Julien Larroux."

At first she didn't know how to respond. Unmarried girls and young gentlemen did not introduce themselves to each other; they waited to be introduced by a mutual friend or a chaperon. Julien had been rude to approach her like this, but it seemed ruder to walk away after he had given her his name. "Patrice Deveraux."

"A delight to meet you." Julien's bottle-green eyes focused on her with disconcerting intensity. "Tell me, Miss Deveraux, is this your first dance?"

"Yes, sir, it is." She ought to have fawned on about how elegant the arrangements were, but Patrice did not want to

charm this man. If he desired her, then he was a threat; for the first time, she might be looking into the eyes of the man who would take her from Amos for good.

Her brusque answer seemed to please him. His lips were dark against his alabaster skin; Patrice found the contrast surprisingly sensual—yet not nearly as handsome as Amos's burnished dark features. "You do not flirt like the other girls."

"You flirt just like the other boys. Though less politely, I should say." *There, that will get rid of him.*

Instead, Julien laughed softly. "You don't want to be here, do you?"

"Don't presume to know what I want."

"You have pride. Something most of the women here are sorely lacking. Many of the men too. They crawl. They conform. You—you hold your head high. I believe you have spirit, Miss Deveraux."

Patrice wished she could have slapped him. "If you can't behave properly, I'll have to fetch my chaperon."

"In your heart, I think you don't care very much about proper behavior." Julien's pale eyes seemed to be staring down into her soul, glimpsing her plan to welcome Amos to her bed. Patrice felt the almost irresistible urge to run away from him, as though he were a thief on a darkened road late at night instead of a a gentleman at a party. But fear and confusion kept her frozen in place. He continued, "I shall behave properly—for now. May I have the very great honor of the first dance?"

She could think of no valid excuse to refuse. "You may, sir."

The first dance was the Virginia Reel, a bouncy dance that made everyone laugh and clap their hands. Usually Patrice enjoyed dancing a reel. With so many couples upon the dance floor—three dozen, at least—she should have had more fun than ever.

Not with Julien Larroux.

She told herself that he unnerved her merely because she could not immediately understand him. These other proud, boastful boys—she did not have to meet them to know them. They had no concerns any deeper than the shiny pomade in their hair. Julien danced as well as any of them, never missing a step, and he smiled all the while. But it was not the silly grin the other men wore; it was cool, almost mocking. Worst of all, he seemed to think that Patrice should be in on the joke.

The dance ended, and for a while she escaped to other partners—which was not much escape at all, given their frank appraisal of her charms. But halfway through the night, Julien reclaimed her for a waltz.

"A far superior dance, the waltz." Julien's hand rested upon her back as he led her through the movements. He had thin, bony fingers that made her think of claws. The air was thick with the scent of camellias. "Much more intimate."

"I quite agree."

"Did your mother tell you that?" His eyebrow arched disdainfully. "To agree with anything I say?"

"She did say that, actually. Not that I pay her any mind. I said I agreed with you because I really do. As you should know by now, if you say something foolish, I'll tell you so."

His smile broadened. Julien's teeth were almost unnaturally white. "You don't act like a young lady who's trying to catch a man."

"Perhaps I'm not." She thought of Amos and the way he had kissed her beneath the magnolia tree.

"Why else are you here?"

"I have no other choice," Patrice said flatly.

Such honesty ought to have wiped the smirk from Julien's face. It did not. "You may have more choices than you think."

"I suppose you're referring to yourself?"

"In a manner of speaking."

So soon! Patrice had hoped to have another few months at home before she would have to give herself to some stranger. Yet here was Julien Larroux as much as asking for her already.

"Why me?" she whispered.

"Why not one of your vapid friends?" He nodded toward the corner, where an awkward young girl was valiantly attempting to flirt with chubby Beauregard Wilkins. "Because you wear your satin and lace the way knights once wore armor. I think you see life as a battle—and I like a fighter."

Patrice knew she ought to have been grateful that at least the man who sought her was someone of intelligence and discernment. That, or she should have been terrified of the inner sense she had that something about Julien Larroux was simply *wrong*.

But all she could think was: *He's taking me away from Amos. Taking me soon.*

After the party, during the carriage ride home, Althea was beside herself with glee. "They say that Mr. Larroux is new to the city, but clearly he's of good family, and tremendously rich. He's taken a whole suite in the finest hotel, and he's been asking about a mansion on St. Charles Avenue."

Patrice shrugged. "Has he spoken to Mr. Broussard?"

"Not yet, but I expect he'll pay a call in the morning."

"How can you be so happy?" Patrice whispered. "How can you want this for me?"

The cool, artificial smile never left Althea's lips. "This is all you could ever have," she said. "What else could I want?"

Her implication, clearly, was, *What else could you want?*

Julien Larroux was genteel and handsome. His wealth would buy her a well-appointed house, not unlike the one she'd grown up in, and countless beautiful dresses and bonnets. His slaves would clean her home. She might even have her own horse and carriage.

Those were the sort of prizes that Althea valued. Patrice wanted something else: freedom to make her own choices. As of tonight, any chance of that had been stolen from her forever.

At least I'll be with Amos tonight, she told herself. *They'll never be able to take that away from me.*

As they descended from the carriage, Patrice lifted her skirts to avoid the mud. In the corner of her eye, she caught a bit of movement at the fence beside the house.

Her pulse quickened.

That night, she lay in bed, tremulous with excitement and fear. Her thin cotton nightgown stuck to her sweaty body; the New Orleans heat did not relent, even after midnight.

We'll have to be very quiet, she thought.

Judging from the noises she'd sometimes heard from her mother's room during Mr. Broussard's visits, quiet didn't come easily at such times. But Patrice felt she could acquit herself better than Althea.

Then she thought of Amos's broad, callused hands upon her—without even her nightgown between them—and realized remaining silent might be a challenge.

Patrice sucked on the corner of her sheet, a nervous habit from childhood that she still slipped into from time to time. She did not want to admit that she was nervous, that she could ever be frightened of Amos. Yet her heart raced, beating so hard that her breasts trembled with every thump. Her breathing was fast and shallow.

The shutters over her windows showed thin stripes of moonlight. She watched them, eyes wide, waiting for some shadow or movement.

A sharp squeal outside made her jump, but Patrice almost instantly realized it came from the side gate. No doubt the stray cats were fighting again.

She wondered if Julien Larroux would allow her to keep a cat.

Within a few weeks, Patrice would live in a stranger's house. He would want to touch her, and she would not have the right to say no. She'd grown up knowing that this would be her fate; once, she'd believed that if the man in question

were only young and handsome, all her dreams would come true. How empty those dreams seemed now.

Downstairs, on the back porch, a board creaked.

Amos, she thought. And yet Patrice did not feel her heart leap with gladness. Instead, she clutched her sheet. Her ears pricked, almost painfully, in search of another sound.

It had to be Amos coming to see her. This was what they had planned, the time she had told him. Who else could it be?

Yet Althea had always warned her to keep the shutter doors latched. Otherwise, anyone could get in. Absolutely anyone.

It's Amos. Don't be silly.

The side beam of the porch groaned with new weight, and then she heard the unmistakable sound of someone taking hold of the iron scrollwork that bordered her balcony.

Latch the shutters, Patrice thought. *Wait until Amos says his name. He can whisper without being heard, and you'll be right there. It's him—it has to be him—but just in case—*

At the last possible moment, she leaped out of bed and ran on shaky legs toward the window. The thin slits of moonlight through the shutters suddenly broke into a shadow shaped like a man. Footsteps on the balcony accompanied the shadow getting bigger, getting closer. Patrice reached for the latch—she still had time—

Her longing for Amos overcame her, and she hesitated for only an instant.

The shutters flew open. There stood Julien Larroux.

Patrice sucked in a breath to scream, but his pale hand shot out to clasp her mouth. "Silence," he murmured. He no

longer wore the charming smile he'd used at the ball. His grin now looked more like the bared teeth of a feral beast.

She jerked her head to the side. "You get out," Patrice whispered. Her voice trembled. "Get out this instant or I'll scream."

"Scream?" Julien's angular face lit up, as though she'd suggested a delightful surprise. "Yes, scream for your mother. When she comes in, I'll explain how you left the shutters unlatched for me. How else could I have entered your bedroom? What an—*obliging* girl you are, to have helped me."

"I'll take a caning if it means getting rid of you."

His bottle-green eyes blazed. "When I called you a fighter, I spoke the truth."

"You'll get a fight if you don't leave." Patrice balled her hands into fists. She took some comfort from the fact that Amos would arrive any moment now, and when he saw what Julien was trying to do—

Amos would fight him. He might try to kill Julien Larroux—a white man. And for that, Amos would be hung, either by the law or a lynch mob.

Patrice whispered, "What do I have to do before you'll go away?"

"How unromantic you make it sound."

"Can we just get it over with?" She might have to endure Julien Larroux's touch, but she'd be damned if she'd pretend to enjoy it.

Julien tilted his head, considering. "Only one very simple thing, my fierce Patrice. Allow me to kiss your neck."

". . . what?"

"One kiss upon your throat." Julien's long, pale fingers stroked the line of her jaw, then dipped lower until they rested upon a vein. His eyes darkened, and Patrice knew he was reveling in her quickened pulse. "Allow me that—with no struggle, no cry—and afterward, I shall leave. You and I will not be alone together again until you desire it."

That will be never. Although Patrice doubted this evening's transaction would be so simple or painless, she could not refuse while Amos was at risk.

"Very well." Patrice took a small step forward. "Go ahead."

Julien smiled at her. "Tilt your head backward—yes, like that—and pull at the neck of your nightgown."

Patrice trembled so violently that she thought she might fall, but she shook from suppressed rage as much as fear. Her fingers fumbled at the neck of her gown as she tugged it down, exposing her throat.

Then Julien clasped her shoulders and pulled her close. He smelled—strange, not exactly unfamiliar, but not like anyone else she had ever met. Something metallic had seeped into the air, and the odor reminded her of—of—

Of a butcher shop, her mind supplied.

Patrice's eyes opened wide. Her soul understood something her brain could not yet comprehend. In that instant, she would have screamed—but Julien's teeth sank into her throat.

Then there was only darkness, and pain, yet something sweet within the pain.

Patrice awakened to a scream.

At first, as she pushed herself upright in bed, she thought she must have dreamed the sound. Hadn't she just been having a nightmare? None of the details were clear; like most dreams, they were dissolving in the bright light of day.

Blinking at the brilliant sunshine that flooded through the glass doors to her balcony, Patrice thought that Althea had kept her promise and let her sleep awfully late that day. Yet she still felt exhausted, almost weak. She hoped she wasn't getting sick. This was the time of year when yellow fever often struck.

Patrice frowned. The glass doors were unlatched. Didn't she always remember to latch them?

(*Amos's eyes, soft in the night, shining with love for her. "I'll come to you."*)

Yet he had not come.

Her confusion grew. Surely, if Amos had not come to her, she would have stayed up all night fretting about it, or worrying that he'd been caught out after curfew. Yet she lay in her bed, all tucked in. The only thing out of the ordinary was the open neck of her nightgown.

It seemed as if she were forgetting something—something important. But what?

My mind is clouded, Patrice thought. *Maybe I'm taking sick after all.*

Then she heard the scream again, and this time she knew it was real.

"Mamma?" she cried, as she grabbed her silk wrapper. Her feet, swollen from dancing the night before, jolted with

pain on every step. Slipping into her wrapper as she headed downstairs, she corrected herself. "Althea?"

Patrice flung open the side door and saw that a small group had gathered around the side gate. Althea leaned against a lamp post, half in a swoon, while a small child fanned her with his hand.

"What's happening? Is Althea sick?" Patrice hurried closer, but even as she did so she realized the crowd was not paying attention to her mother, but to something outside the side gate.

Mr. Ebbets, who owned the next house, said heavily, "Child, this is nothing for you to see. Someone has been killed by dogs."

"Dogs?" It seemed too shocking to believe. Or was there some other reason she didn't believe it? Patrice felt herself flashing back to her nightmare—not images or sounds, because she could not remember, and yet there was some kind of connection.

"We've sent for the police," Mr. Ebbets said. "Get your mother inside. Ladies shouldn't be exposed to such as this. That poor boy's throat had been ripped out. Had to be dogs, or some other kind of wild animal."

Patrice slowly said, "But who—the man who died—"

"The blacksmith. That free boy from the Marigny. Didn't he shoe your horse last winter?"

On the ground, amid the feet of curious gawkers, lay a long, well-muscled arm as thick and dark as cordwood.

By the afternoon, the police had taken away what was left of Amos. Althea acted as though nothing had happened.

"You've cried all day," she said crossly, snatching the coverlet off the bed so that Patrice lay uncovered. "Your eyes will bulge as big as a cow's."

"I don't care."

"What are you carrying on for? It's not as if that blacksmith was anyone to us." Althea paused at the foot of the bed. Her looped braids framed her narrow face, the style too girlish for her years. "Was he, Patrice?"

"No," Patrice said, because the time for telling Althea the truth was long past.

Althea took Patrice's pale yellow dress from the closet. "Let me do your hair, and we'll get you dressed. I suppose we'll be late for tonight's dance, but it can't be helped."

Patrice squeezed her eyes tightly shut, willing herself to be somewhere else, or someone else. She rubbed at her neck, where one spot was incredibly tender. Was she imagining that pain, because of what had been done to Amos's throat last night? "The shock—it's too much, Althea. Couldn't I stay home tonight?"

"And run the risk of Julien Larroux setting his cap for another girl? You're crazy. Get out of that bed."

Julien Larroux. Patrice's eyes flew open as memory returned.

(*His teeth in her neck, the metallic smell of blood, the sickening slurp as he swallowed, Patrice struggling against him all the while, unable to fight—*)

She put her hand to her throat again. The skin beneath her fingers felt raw, as though she'd splashed herself with the laundry lye.

Old women told stories about such creatures. Patrice had never listened to those stories—it was just more silliness and superstition, like Marie Laveau's tales about voodoo. Or so she'd always believed.

(*"That poor boy's throat had been ripped out. Had to be dogs, or some other kind of wild animal."*)

Patrice pushed herself upright in the bed.

"That's more like it," Althea said briskly, as she set hairpins out on the vanity table. "I see I only had to mention your beau to get you going."

"Yes," Patrice murmured. "I think I need to see Julien Larroux again."

He looked even more unearthly than he had the night before. His bottle-green eyes flashed with excitement at the

They arrived with the ball already in full swing, pushing into a room already full of laughing young people and the sounds of fiddlers playing. The candles on the walls had half-burned down, leaving ripples of melted tallow on the catch-plates below. Patrice still felt weak, and every sensation was too intense: the body heat of the party's crush, the scratchy lace around her throat, and the scent of the camellias pinned in her hair.

As Althea waved to Mr. Broussard, Patrice stepped away from her. At that moment, Julien's eyes met hers.

He looked even more unearthly than he had the night before. His bottle-green eyes flashed with excitement at the

sight of her, and his long chestnut hair hung free past his shoulders. Julien gave her a dark-lipped smile.

By all rules of propriety, Patrice ought to have waited for him to come to her. Instead, she weeded her way through the party, on the outskirts of the whirling dancers, to find Julien first.

"You look lovely tonight," Julien said. He seemed to be enjoying some private joke. "It doesn't seem as if it's been a whole day since I've seen you. Maybe you've been in my thoughts so much we might as well have been together all night."

"I want to talk to you," Patrice said. "Alone."

Sometimes, when the candlelight caught them just so, Julien's eyes seemed to have no color at all. "Shall we take some fresh air?"

They stepped outside. Clouds covered the moon that night, so the only illumination came from the windows of the Salle de Lafayette, where the dancers were silhouetted. One of the chaperons stepped forward as if to warn them back inside, but Julien gave him a piercing look that seemed to make the old man forget all about the young couple stealing into the back garden alone at night.

"Here we are, my dear Patrice." Julien laid his hands on her bare shoulders, just above the lacy sleeves of her dress. "Did you miss me too?"

Patrice said, "I think you came to my house last night. I think you killed Am—the blacksmith. I think you tried to kill me too."

"An interesting set of assertions." Julien's thumb made little circles against her skin. She felt a strange pull toward

him, as though they were tied together in a way that left her unable to run. His lips were very near her hair. "Why would I want to do any of those things? Besides coming to your house at night, of course. Any man would want to be near you."

"I remember you being there. I remember that you bit me."

She whirled to face him, eager to see him caught off-guard. Instead, Julien smiled, and for once his delight appeared to be genuine. "Extraordinary! Most people can't remember it, unless they're kept awake, and I tucked you in safe and sound. And, if you were curious, quite as much a maid as I found you. Though I was tempted."

"Then it's true." Patrice covered the tender spot at her throat with her fingers. "You're—you're a vampire."

"And I want you to become one too."

Patrice tried to think of a reply to this, but could not. Words and imagination had both failed her. More than anything else, she wanted to run, but she remembered what Althea had told her that time they saw a mad dog on the street with foam flecking his jaws: *Don't run. If you run, that just gives him a reason to chase you.*

She closed her hands around the branch of a nearby tree, as if to steady herself—then quickly snapped off a length of wood, perhaps six inches. "I've heard stories about your kind. I know what to do." With that, Patrice brandished her new stake.

He merely laughed. "You've heard stories. Not the truth. For instance, stakes don't kill us."

Was he lying to save himself? No, Patrice realized. Julien remained completely unafraid of her. She felt small and foolish, and slowly she let the hand with the stake drop to her side.

"Fire, now—fire is dangerous. Beheading too." His silky chestnut hair streamed behind him, caught by a sudden breeze. "I tell you these things because you'll need to know them to be by my side. And also because you have no fire and no blade."

"Oh, God," Patrice whispered. She had always thought she had no choices in life, but she hadn't truly known what it meant to be trapped, not before this instant when she was caught in a vampire's thirsty gaze.

Julien took her hands in his. "I knew the moment I saw you that you had the spark. The strength. Our world is not for the weak, Patrice. Besides, this shallow, empty life of disguised servitude—you hate it. That hatred burns inside you like a bonfire. I want to give you power like you've never imagined. Together, we could make the world our feast."

Power.

In an instant, she knew she had one choice left. She intended to make it.

Patrice tilted her head back. "Drink."

"My beautiful girl." Julien's grin changed as his canine teeth shifted slowly into fangs. Despite a terrible shiver of fear, Patrice did not flee. It occurred to her that if the legends about vampires were true, she was about to die. If Amos had been alive, she could never have surrendered her life so easily. Without him, her path was clearer.

She glanced upward at the moon, silvery and shrouded

with thin clouds. It was strange to think that this was the last thing she would ever see in her life. The moon had never looked so beautiful before.

Then Julien pushed her against the nearby tree, with his hands clamped around her arms like irons, and tore open her throat.

Pain eclipsed everything else, even Julien, even the moon.

Silence.

Patrice had never known that quiet could be so over-powering. She had never realized that she could hear her own heart beating, or that all the sounds she normally heard were filtered through the soft rush of blood in her eardrums. Now that was gone.

Her eyes fluttered open. She lay upon the ground, her pale yellow gown stained with mud. Julien stood above her, watching avidly.

I'm dead, she thought. Something vital in her—something strong, something good—was gone, and she felt hollowed-out. As though every sound she would ever hear from now on would only be an echo, as if everything she touched would be only an imitation of reality. The pure river of constant change that ran through every living being had been stilled in her, forever.

It did not hurt. Even the pain of dying had been better than being dead.

"You won't miss it for long," Julien said. "Not when you see what we can do."

Patrice slowly sat upright. Petals from the crushed camellia she'd been wearing fluttered down onto her dress. She could only think of one thing to say: "I'm hungry."

Julien grinned. "We all awaken hungry. Let's find you a snack, shall we? Ah, look, there's someone now."

Into the garden staggered Beauregard Wilkins, obviously quite drunk. For the first time Patrice realized that she could hear no music or hubbub from the party within; she must have been dead for at least a few hours.

Althea will be wondering where I am.

Beauregard clutched his ample belly, obviously in danger of losing control of himself, but he seemed to forget his own distress when he saw Julien standing above Patrice. "What's this?" he said. "Larroux, old boy, no need to be rough with the ladies."

"You needn't worry about Patrice," Julien said. "She's better than she's ever been. Aren't you, my darling?"

Patrice cocked her head. Somehow, she could hear Beauregard's heart beating. Every single thump was like a drumbeat summoning her. Within Beauregard, blood flowed—hot, living blood—

She pounced at him with strength she had never before possessed. He fell back beneath her, staring at her in horror as her fangs slid forth for the first time. It hurt, and yet it made her shiver with pleasure. It felt right.

This is what I am now.

Then she bit him, tearing into warm flesh to get at what she needed: blood. It flowed into her mouth, rich and hot

and good, and Patrice swallowed eagerly, desperate for the taste of life again. Beauregard struggled for only a moment before he sagged to the ground, unconscious.

"That's good," Julien said. "My savage little Patrice."

When she could drink no more, Patrice sat up. Blood was sticky on her lips. Beauregard still breathed, which surprised her until she realized it shouldn't. "He'll forget he was bitten." Her own voice sounded strange to her now. "Just like I forgot."

"Undoubtedly Mr. Wilkins will awaken tomorrow in the belief that he passed out drunk, as he no doubt would have had you not come along. The scars from your bite will have all but faded by then. No evidence left behind. It all works very well, you see."

"It doesn't kill, then. Our drinking." How strange, to say "our" and mean vampires.

"Not unless we want it to, the way I wanted it to for you."

Julien helped her to her feet and offered her a handkerchief. She dabbed at her lips, staining the white linen red.

"What happens now?" she whispered.

"Now, my dear, we turn New Orleans into our playground. We could live together openly, if you choose. Shock the populace. Or there are other places we can go—places where no living creature could find us. I have so much to show you. So much for you to learn." His fingers traced along the low neckline of her dress, leaving no doubt as to what he wanted her to learn first.

When he offered her his arm, she took it. Her legs were unsteady—not from weakness but from the unexpected power flowing through her.

"Let's walk out the front door," Patrice said. "It's not as if the slaves will dare to say a word."

Julien smiled a slow, hot smile. "Excellent idea."

They walked back into the Salle de Lafayette, which by now was nearly deserted. A few flower petals from ladies' nosegays littered the floor, and half the candles had burned out. An elderly slave woman, her back bent with age and care, tottered around, blowing out the rest. A bucket and rags in the corner testified to the scrubbing she would have to begin soon. It had to be nearly dawn. One lone oil lantern flickered near the front door.

"Where do you want to go next?" Julien said.

"My mother's house."

"You weren't that fond of her, were you? I suppose she's about to get a lesson she'll never forget. I can't wait to see it for myself."

As he opened the door and strode onto the front stoop, Patrice paused in the doorway. "You won't be coming home with me."

"What do you mean?"

She grabbed the oil lantern and threw it at his face.

The glass lantern shattered, mingling the fire with the flammable oil that had splashed all over Julien's body. He screamed—a terrible, animal sound. His entire body was a mass of flame as he staggered backward, then fell onto the walk.

As firelight flickered upon Patrice's face, she thought of Amos and how long and hard he'd worked to be free. She thought of the good strong arms that had held her, and how

Julien had left Amos crumpled in the alley like garbage. She thought of their last kiss.

The old slave woman appeared behind Patrice. When she saw Julien burning, she didn't shout for anyone to come help. She simply watched by Patrice's side.

Once it was over, and the charred thing on the walk would clearly never move again, Patrice said, "I'm Patrice Deveraux. If they need proof it was an accident, you can tell them I saw the whole thing."

"Drunk as those young bucks get, nobody will doubt it."

The two women shared a glance, and then Patrice began the long journey back home.

In her crumpled, muddy dress, Patrice suspected she made quite a sight. Fortunately, the streets were all but empty. Althea would be furious when Patrice got home, thinking that she had been giving Julien Larroux favors that he ought to have paid for. Patrice did not intend to put up with that kind of talk for long. She thought she would finish out the season by pretending to be human, drinking when she wished, learning about her powers. And how lovely she would look in silk and satin, her hair fixed just so. Julien had called her beauty her armor, and she intended never to be without her armor again. When you were beautiful, you could charm the people around you so that they never saw the darker truth.

After a few months, Patrice would know how to handle her new abilities. Then she could set out on her own.

"You there! Girl!"

Patrice stopped walking and turned. A group of lanky white men strolled toward her, half-incredulous, half-gleeful.

They wore shabby overalls and tattered straw hats. She realized they were the patrollers who kept black people from
walking around after curfew—the ones who assumed that
anyone who wasn't white was a slave. "Can I help you?" she
said coolly.

"You don't dress like a colored girl," the leader said with
a snide smile. "You one of them Creole mistresses?" The others snickered lasciviously.

"I'm going home."

"You better answer my questions, gal. Are you slave or
free?"

For the first time, Patrice realized she would never have
to carry her papers with her again. If anyone challenged
her—white or black, living or dead—she had the strength to
tear out their throats.

She thought she might even enjoy it.

Patrice smiled. "I'm free."

About the Authors

Cynthia Leitich Smith is the acclaimed YA author of *Tantalize* (2007), and its companions, *Eternal* (2009) and *Blessed* (forthcoming), all Gothic fantasies from Candlewick Press. She also has written several YA short stories as well as books for younger readers. *Tantalize* was a March 2007 Borders Original Voices selection, honored at the 2007 National Book Festival, and *The Horn Book* called it "an intoxicating romantic thriller." A graphic novel adaptation of *Tantalize* is in the works. Cynthia may be found on the Web at www. cynthialeitichsmith.com. She makes her home in Austin, Texas, with her husband, author Greg Leitich Smith.

New York Times bestselling author **Kristin Cast** is only going to college because she loves education and lives to attend lectures. Okay, not really. Miss Cast currently attends the University of Tulsa and is a communications major. She has won awards for her poetry, as well as served as journalist

for her high school newspaper, *Tiger Tales*, and as editor for her high school magazine, *Tiger Eye*. Miss Cast would like to become so famous people make fountains and/or shrines in her image. You can reach her through www.pccast.net.

⌒

Rachel Caine is the author of more than twenty-five novels, most notably her bestselling Morganville Vampires series and Weather Warden series, as well as being a frequent contributor to BenBella Books's fiction and nonfiction projects. She writes constantly, and frequently gets paid for it, which always surprises and delights her. Visit her Web site at www.rachelcaine.com, and friend her on Livejournal, Facebook, and MySpace!

⌒

Tanith Lee was born in 1947 in the UK. She worked in many jobs until becoming a full-time professional writer in 1975. She has to date written nearly 100 books and more than 260 short stories, four radio plays, and episodes of the cult TV series *Blake's 7*. She has won, or been shortlisted for, numerous awards. She lives in England with her husband, writer and artist John Kaiine, and two permanently hungry Tuxedo cats.

Richelle Mead is the *New York Times* bestselling author of *Vampire Academy* and *Frostbite*. The fourth book in the series, *Blood Promise*, was released in August 2009. A former middle school teacher, Richelle now writes full-time in Seattle. She buys far too many dresses, hasn't seen the surface of her desk in over a year, and rarely gets up before noon. More information can be found at www.richellemead.com.

Nancy Holder is the *USA Today* bestselling author of more than eighty novels and 200 short stories, essays, and articles. She is currently working with co-author Debbie Viguie on *Wicked: Resurrection* for Simon and Schuster. The author of *Pretty Little Devils*, she has contracted with Razorbill for two more YA horror novels. Contact her at www.nancyholder.com.

A recent transplant into the deep south, **Rachel Vincent** has a BA in English and an overactive imagination, and consistently finds the latter to be more practical. She shares her workspace with two black cats (Kaci and Nyx) and her #1 fan. Rachel is older than she looks—seriously—and younger than she feels, but remains convinced that for every day she spends writing, one more day will be added to her lifespan. Find her online at www.RachelVincent.com.

Claudia Gray is the pseudonym of New York–based writer Amy Vincent. She is the author of the Evernight series of vampire novels set in the present day, in which Patrice is a character—now as a 160-year-old vampire. The first book, *Evernight*, came out in May 2008, and the second book in the series, *Stargazer*, was released in March 2009.

CHAPTER 1

IMMIGRANT INTEGRATION AND COMPREHENSIVE IMMIGRATION REFORM: AN OVERVIEW

MICHAEL FIX

This chapter synthesizes the set of papers devoted to integration issues that were initially collected for the Task Force on Immigration and America's Future. The chapter begins by discussing why integration needs to be made more central to debates over immigration reform. It then seeks to define what is meant by the term integration and to draw the broad contours of US integration policy. The chapter proceeds with a review of the evidence of immigrants' integration, examining the second generation's progress, and then focusing more narrowly on trends in education, health, the workforce, and citizenship. The chapter concludes by briefly discussing key elements of a national integration policy, noting several issues raised directly by congressional comprehensive immigration reform proposals. These include health care coverage for temporary workers and legal immigrants and the merits of providing impact aid to state and local governments.

I. IMMIGRANT INTEGRATION: WHY SHOULD WE CARE?

AN AFTERTHOUGHT

There are a number of strong reasons to link discussions of immigration and integration. The integration of immigrants remains an afterthought in immigration policy discussions; in fact, integration remains one of the most overlooked issues in American governance. As a result, there is a mismatch between the nation's immigration policies — which, however broken, are on the whole comparatively generous — and the United States's immigrant integration policies that are ad hoc, under-funded, and skeletal. So today, as it has historically, the integration of newcomers is carried out by families, employers, churches, nongovernmental organizations, and by an increasingly restive set of state and local governments.

There is no national Office for Immigrant and Refugee Integration; this absence stands in contrast to other countries, such as Canada and the Netherlands, which have strong integration offices within their immigration agencies. And an examination of the growing numbers of proposals for comprehensive immigration reform reveals that they pay little if any attention to integration issues.

THE DEMOGRAPHIC IMPERATIVE

There are a number of well-known demographic forces that make the need to focus more directly on integration clear. These include:

- *High sustained flows*. Nearly one in eight people in the United States today is foreign born. One in five children in the United States, and more than one in four low-income children, is the child of an immigrant. Over half of new workers in the 1990s were immigrants, and the foreign born compose very high shares of some occupations, accounting for one in five doctors in the United States, for example. High flows mean that the success of the nation as a whole and of its institutions (schools, the workplace, the military) will increasingly depend on the contributions and integration of immigrants.

- *Dispersal*. It is now broadly recognized that while the immigrant population remains highly concentrated in the six largest receiving states, a work-driven dispersal to new gateway states has been rapid. The migrants in these flows are more recently arrived, poorer, younger, less educated, and more likely to be undocumented than immigrants nationally. Limited community resources, institutional infrastructure, and experience may all present barriers to integration. At the same time, new opportunities and successes may emerge.

- *Shifting legal composition*. A decade ago the unauthorized population constituted about 15 percent of all immigrants. Today it represents almost a third. This trend toward increasing shares of immigrants arriving outside rather than inside the immigration system complicates the politics of developing effective integration policies. It does so by reducing the legitimacy of the immigration system and support for services and benefits that some believe are captured by unauthorized immigrants and their families. While there has been rapid growth in the unauthorized population since the mid-1990s, there has also been a rapid rise in the number and share of the foreign-born population that has naturalized.

■ *Prevalence of mixed-status families*. Policymakers often overlook the fact that three-fourths of the children of immigrants are US-born and are thus citizens; two out of three children with an undocumented parent are citizens living in mixed-status families. Among other things, the mixed legal status of these families has meant that the exclusion of non-citizen parents from services and privileges spills over to their citizen children.

CHANGE IN MEDIATING INSTITUTIONS

The United States has a history of comparatively successful integration. But the past may not be an entirely reliable guide to the future. Mediating institutions that were critical to the integration of earlier immigrants — urban schools, unions, big manufacturing firms, a conscription-based military, and political parties — have all changed in ways that might affect the integration of current and future newcomers. Take, for example, the movement away from precinct-level politics and local party machines. While sometimes corrupt, the machines engaged newcomers and encouraged voting in ways that today's system of primaries and multiple interest groups do not. Moreover, even the most sophisticated social scientists concede that when they examine the evidence, they just do not know what accounts for assimilation's success in the 20th century.[1]

At the same time, there have been important counterweights to these institutional changes. Overt nativism has declined, along with the express official racism embedded in the Chinese Exclusion Acts, the 1907 Gentleman's Agreement with Japan, or the National Origins' legislation of the 1920s.[2] Antidiscrimination norms emerging in the 1960s have had powerful impacts on the workplace. Colleges — particularly community colleges — have evolved into mass education systems as high schools did during the last great wave of immigration in the early 20th century.

PUBLIC POLICIES THAT MAY SLOW INTEGRATION

New policies introduced in 1996 that limit the access of legal immigrants to health, nutrition, cash, and other safety net benefits may undermine integration. The new laws drew brighter lines between citizens and noncitizens, making naturalization the main gateway both to benefits and to protection from deportation.

---

1   R. Alba and V. Nee, *Remaking the American Mainstream, Assimilation and Contemporary Immigration* (Boston: Harvard University Press, 2003).

2   Appendix I of the volume includes a timeline and a brief description of major US immigration legislation.

CONTESTED PROGRESS

Debates about the need for integration policies and the types of policies needed are also muddied by a lack of consensus over the progress of immigrants and their children. Cultural and other critics argue that the new immigration, especially immigration from Mexico, is leading to the formation of a new bottom class that is not integrating socially or economically. As analysis in Chapter 4 indicates, though, the most recent evidence on the second generation (that is, the US-born children of the foreign born) provides a more optimistic view, with all groups including Mexicans progressing from generation to generation. While a "rainbow underclass" may not be at hand, there still are a number of areas for concern — particularly regarding the rates of college attendance and completion of second-generation Mexicans.

THE IMPACTS OF COMPREHENSIVE IMMIGRATION REFORM

The prospect of immigration reform itself raises a number of integration issues, including:

- Will reform emphasize temporary immigration over permanent immigration, thus sidestepping the need for integration policies?

- What implications would the admission of temporary and permanent immigrants with comparatively low skills and English language abilities hold for the nation's workforce development systems? (See Chapter 8)

- Will newcomers be expected to have health insurance? If so, who will pay for it? Or will new immigrants join the already large pool of uninsured people in the United States? (See Chapter 7)

- What fiscal impacts will new immigrant flows have on state and local governments? Will new costs arise, and if so, should the federal government seek to offset some of those costs as it did in 1986, with the last comprehensive reform of immigration? (See Chapter 10)

- Will temporary workers or unauthorized immigrants be required to learn English before they can adjust to legal status (again as in 1986), and, if so, how will that instruction be financed? Does the service infrastructure exist to deliver the educational programs needed? (See Chapter 9)

II. WHAT DO WE MEAN BY INTEGRATION?

The meaning of the term integration — and even the use of the term itself — can be controversial. For the purposes at least of this overview, "integration" is defined as the process of economic mobility and the social inclusion of new-comers. Integration implies a two-way process that involves change on the part not just of immigrants but of members of the receiving community. As Don Kerwin writes in Chapter 5, integration represents a "commitment to shared values and an openness to the myriad contributions of immigrants." Successful integration builds communities that are stronger economically and more inclu-sive socially and culturally. At the same time, integration can also be defined by what it clearly is not — the formation of an ethnically identifiable bottom class made up of immigrant groups or communities of immigrant descent.

III. THE BROAD CONTOURS OF CURRENT US INTEGRATION POLICY

What are some of the key defining elements of US — and in particular federal — integration policy?

ACCESS TO THE LABOR MARKET

The federal government plays a comparatively minimal role in the integration of immigrants. Today, as throughout US history, the integration of immigrants has fallen in large part to the labor market. In sharp contrast to most European countries, the US labor market has been open to immigrants, an openness that is reinforced by the reach and maturity of our antidiscrimination laws. Their combined legacy has resulted in very high levels of immigrant employment, and immigrants are overrepresented in the overall labor market and among recent hires. Indeed, while one in eight US residents is foreign born, one in seven workers and one in five low-wage workers is an immigrant.

BASIC RIGHTS

Beyond open access to the labor market, the United States makes available to all immigrants, largely independent of their legal status, a set of fundamental rights. These include, for example, the right to assemble, to be free of unrea-sonable searches and seizures, and to counsel in criminal matters. These rights can be seen as "a fundamental form of 'integration' into our constitutional sys-tem." (Chapter 5)

Targeted Federal Programs

There are a number of grant and service programs expressly targeted to immigrants and their families or to groups that are largely composed of immigrants (See, generally, Chapter 6). Four major categories include:

- *Refugee placement and settlement programs.* These programs specifically focus on the integration of refugees into new communities. Refugees make up roughly 5 percent of annual legal immigration flows to the United States. Refugees are often fleeing persecution and many arrive in the United States in poor physical and mental health; their departures were in a sense unplanned; and unlike immigrants entering for family reunification or employment, they do not have sponsors.[3]

- *Programs serving migrant workers and their families.* While these programs initially may have been designed to meet the needs of US-born migrant workers in agriculture, today almost four out of five farm workers are foreign born. These programs in the areas of health, Head Start, K-12 education, and job training, then, have been transformed into de facto integration policies serving a largely foreign-born work force and their families.

- *Funding streams set aside for language instruction and the promotion of citizenship.* These funding mechanisms promote English language acquisition among limited English proficient (LEP) children (Title III of the No Child Left Behind Act) and adults (the Adult Basic Education/English as a Second Language (ESL) expenditures). They also support the US Citizenship and Immigration Services (USCIS) Office of Citizenship, which encourages naturalization through public education and outreach.

- *Funding provided to communities to offset immigrants' impacts.* This federal funding helps (a) schools meet the additional costs of teaching recently arrived immigrant students; (b) hospitals offset the costs of unauthorized immigrants' uncompensated care; and (c) state and local governments pay the costs of keeping unauthorized and other immigrants in jail (not included in Table 1).[4] (See, generally, Chapter 10.)

---

3   In the US immigration system, a "sponsor" is the relative or employer who petitions for an immigrant's entry into the United States. Those individuals sponsoring relatives are also required to sign an affidavit of support, which binds them to financially support the immigrant until he or she naturalizes or can show 40 quarters of work in the United States.

4   Table 1 does not include federal reimbursements to state and local governments for the cost of keeping unauthorized immigrants in jail. While these expenditures are immigrant-related, they arguably differ from other targeted spending on immigrants in that they do not further the goal of immigrant integration.

TABLE 1. TARGETED 2004 FEDERAL SPENDING ON IMMIGRANTS, IN MILLIONS OF 2005 DOLLARS

	FY 1999 Spending	FY 2004 Spending	% Change 1999 to 2004
Refugee Resettlement Program	$ 545	$ 429	-21.3%
Migrant Head Start	$ 209	$ 274	31.1%
Migrant Education	$ 421	$ 412	-2.1%
Migrant Education Even Start	$ 5	$ 8	60.0%
Migrant Health	$ 92	$ 139	51.1%
NCLB Language Acquisition State Grants	-	$ 708	-
EIEP (Emergency Immigrant Education Program)	$ 176	-	-
Federal Bilingual Education	$ 273	-	-
Adult Education/ESL	$ 432	$ 630	45.8%
Total	**$ 2,153**	**$ 2,600**	**20.8%**

Source: Julia Gelatt and Michael Fix, "Targeted Federal Spending on the Integration of Immigrant Families," Background Paper prepared for the Independent Task Force on Immigration and America's Future (Washington, DC: Migration Policy Institute, 2006).

Table 1 indicates that the overall spending for these programs remains comparatively low — all told, it even falls well below the $4 billion allocated under the 1986 Immigration Reform and Control Act (IRCA) to reimburse states for the benefits and other costs imposed by immigrants legalizing under that legislation, a small subset of the entire immigrant population. Second, the current funds are primarily directed to two comparatively small — if deserving — populations: (1) refugees (and asylees) and (2) migrant workers and their families. Little is provided for the large number of legal immigrants arriving through the family-based immigration system and working in low-wage jobs or the communities in which they live.

ACCESS TO MAINSTREAM PROGRAMS AND INSTITUTIONS

Spending on immigrants and their family members in targeted programs is dwarfed, however, by spending on mainstream social and education programs like aid programs for economically disadvantaged students (Title I, Part A of the Elementary and Secondary Education Act) or public health insurance for low-income families (Medicaid, e.g.), to which at least some immigrants or their children have access. To illustrate, the Title I, Part A ESEA program's FY 2005 budget was $12.7 billion, while spending under the Title III provisions targeted at LEP students was $673 million.

Among other things, total federal spending on immigrants and their families is driven by the creation of new social welfare programs (the State Child Health Insurance Program, for example); shifts in funding to programs used by immigrants (for example, broad increases in Head Start enrollment over the past decade); and changes in program eligibility that affect all recipients, not just immigrants (shifts in asset limits that determine whether public benefit applicants can own a car, for example).

SOCIAL RIGHTS: IMMIGRANT ACCESS TO PUBLIC BENEFITS

While immigrants' and noncitizens' access to basic constitutional protections is broad, no such right appears to hold for public benefits. Immigrants' eligibility for benefits ranging from those that are means tested (welfare) to social insurance programs (Social Security) has basically been determined by where immigrants fall on what might be termed a "continuum of consent," that is, the degree to which the government has consented to their presence in the United States. Undocumented immigrants are eligible for few benefits beyond emergency Medicaid. Similarly, legal temporary immigrants are eligible for few benefits or services. Legal permanent immigrants' eligibility is determined by the length of their stay in the United States and their participation in the workforce and military. Refugees have been eligible for benefits on more or less the same terms as citizens. Naturalized immigrants have been extended the same rights as citizens.

The 1996 welfare reform law — the Personal Responsibility and Work Opportunity Reconciliation Act (PRWORA) — changed the settled order and represented a major departure in welfare and immigrant integration policy in the United States. Prior to the law's enactment, legal immigrants were eligible for public benefits on more or less the same terms as citizens. Following the law's enactment and subsequent amendments, most legal immigrants arriving *after* 1996 were barred for at least five years from the core federal safety net programs: Medicaid and the State Child Health Insurance Program (SCHIP), Temporary Assistance for Needy Families (TANF), Food Stamps, and the Supplemental Security Income Program (SSI). While reforms to the 1996 law have basically restored benefits to almost all legal permanent residents in the United States before 1996, more than 40 percent of immigrants with green cards arrived after that date. Some states have replaced federal health and other benefits for federally ineligible immigrants by subsidizing service programs with their own funds. Others have not.

CITIZENSHIP POLICY

One byproduct of these restrictions has been that citizenship has become more valuable, if for primarily practical reasons. Citizenship now stands as the gateway to the social safety net and to residential security (that is, the means to protect oneself against deportation). Compared to many countries, citizenship has been comparatively easy to obtain in the United States. It can be secured reasonably quickly (within five years of becoming a lawful permanent resident (LPR), three if married to a citizen or having served in the military). The testing process required to become a citizen has been somewhat arbitrary but not exceedingly difficult; and the English-language requirements to naturalize have been modest.

Changes in the law have meant that citizenship may be shifting as a marker of integration. On the one hand, citizenship can open access to health insurance, basic nutrition, and training programs — benefits that may accelerate integration. On the other hand, decisions to naturalize may derive to a greater extent from practical choices on the part of applicants and less from a sense of belonging and national loyalty. Policies regarding citizenship are in flux as the United States Citizenship and Immigration Service (USCIS) is in the process of administratively redesigning the naturalization test.

IV. HOW ARE WE FARING? TRENDS IN INTEGRATION

Janet Murguía and Cecilia Muñoz have written that immigrant integration in the United States is proceeding comparatively well given the low level of investment made (See Chapter 3). Their contention, echoed by Tamar Jacoby in Chapter 2, is largely supported by results of a new analysis of Census data conducted by Roger Waldinger and Renee Reichl (See Chapter 4). Immigrant integration has long been considered an intergenerational process; Waldinger and Reichl assess broad trends in employment, job quality, and education within the immigrant second generation — all key indicators of integration's success.

GENERATIONAL TRENDS

Waldinger and Reichl compare the first (that is, foreign born) and second (US-born children of immigrants) generations for four groups: (1) Canadians/ Europeans/Australians, (2) Asians, (3) Mexicans, and (4) Other (Central and South) Americans. Comparisons are made with the white and African

American third or later generation (that is, all US-born children born to native parents). Comparisons are also made by gender.

The results indicate that integration is taking place — albeit somewhat unevenly — along historical lines across all groups and along most dimensions. The measures of integration include rates of high school graduation, college completion, labor force participation, income, and job quality as indicated by health care coverage and pension plan enrollment. Highlights include:

- First- and second-generation Asians perform as well or better than whites on most indicators.

- Particularly striking generational progress is being made by Mexican women — especially in labor force participation.

- Despite generational gains, Mexicans lag behind all groups (with the exception of African Americans) on virtually all measures except one that is very important: labor force participation.

- High labor force participation among Mexican males means that generally lower educated Mexicans are finding jobs despite the fact that returns to education are increasing. High Mexican employment levels place the group outside the sociological literature's standard definition of an underclass, which focuses on joblessness.

- As Figure 1 indicates, there has been a sharp rise in the share of Mexican teens aged 16 to 20 enrolled in school full-time, from the very low rate of 35 percent in the first generation to 57 percent in the second generation. Second-generation Mexicans' enrollment rates now approach those of both white (62 percent) and African American (59 percent) children of US natives.

- Mexicans are making particularly strong generational gains in high school completion. Fifty-two percent of first generation Mexicans aged 25-65 had less than a high school degree in 2004, while just 17 percent of the second generation failed to complete high school.

- Rising high school graduation rates among Mexicans do not appear to translate into equivalent levels of college completion (see Figure 2). Only 14 percent of the Mexican second generation aged 25-64 had completed college in 2004 versus 32 percent for whites and 57 percent for Asian second generation.

- On many indicators African American men lag behind all groups except Mexicans. The share of African Americans in the labor force was substantially lower than all other groups and has fallen since 1970.

FIGURE 1. PERCENT TEENAGERS (AGES 16 TO 20) ENROLLED IN SCHOOL FULL TIME, BY NATIONAL ORIGIN AND GENERATION, 2000

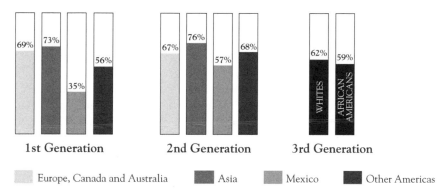

Source: Current Population Survey, March 1997-2003.

FIGURE 2. PERCENT OF ADULTS (AGES 25 TO 64) WITH A COLLEGE DEGREE, BY NATIONAL ORIGIN AND GENERATION, 2004

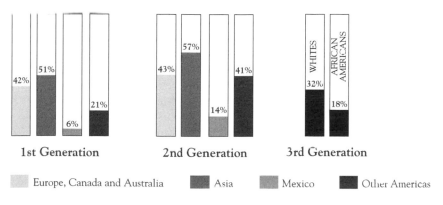

Source: Current Population Survey, March 2004.

While Waldinger and Reichl's findings are in some ways positive, the authors conclude on a note of concern: "If today's second generation adults are struggling to catch up, one also wonders how tomorrow's will manage: after all, these are the children of the immigrant working poor, for whom things have surely not gotten better over the past twenty years."

TRENDS AND POLICY ISSUES IN EDUCATION, HEALTH, WORKFORCE, AND CITIZENSHIP

The chapters on education, health, workforce participation, and citizenship also raise concerns about both the integration of certain immigrant populations and the responsiveness of institutions to their needs.

PRE-KINDERGARTEN TO 12 EDUCATION AND THE NO CHILD LEFT BEHIND ACT

Waldinger's results are consistent with other major studies in the field, most notably those by Portes and Rumbaut that find that children of immigrants as a whole are adapting to the US educational system and in many cases out-performing children of US natives.[5] But the performance of certain foreign-born immigrant subgroups is cause for concern. The Pew Hispanic Center finds that while immigrants aged 15 to 17 make up only 8 percent of their US age cohort, they are 25 percent of all youth dropouts. Seventy percent of immigrants who arrive in the United States as adolescents with interrupted educations in their home countries drop out.[6]

Education policy — and in particular immigrant education policy — is in flux with the enactment, implementation, and pending 2007 reauthorization of the controversial No Child Left Behind Act (NCLB) (See Chapter 9). NCLB — which may represent an important, new de facto integration policy — requires that schools identify, teach, and test limited English proficient students using standardized state academic tests. It requires that their scores be separately reported as a subgroup and that schools be held accountable for the subgroup's performance. Schools failing to meet standards can be subjected to increasingly severe sanctions. In addition, NCLB for the first time imposes a federal requirement that LEP students make progress learning English. The law can be seen as the culmination of a decade of reform that began with schools often leaving immigrant and LEP students overlooked and underserved.

---

5   A. Portes and R. Rumbaut, *Legacies: The Story of the Immigrant Second Generation* (Berkeley, CA: University of California Press, 2001).

6   R. Frey, "Hispanic Youth Dropping Out of US Schools: Measuring the Challenge" (Washington, DC: Pew Hispanic Center, 2003).

FIGURE 3. RATE OF TOTAL K-12 AND LEP ENROLLMENT GROWTH: UNITED STATES, 1993-1994 TO 2003-2004

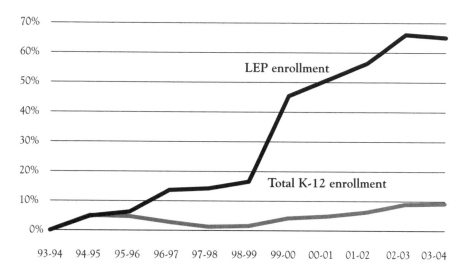

Source: Julie Murray, Jeanne Batalova, and Michael Fix, "Children of Immigrants and New Education Policy and Practice," Background Paper prepared for the Independent Task Force on Immigration and America's Future (Washington, DC: Migration Policy Institute, 2006).

The law's implementation faces a number of immigration-driven challenges that are influencing its success, and to some extent, the resistance it is meeting among state and local policymakers.

First, paralleling larger immigration trends, there has been a rapid rise in the number of children of immigrants and their dispersal to new gateway states. This growth and dispersal comes into particularly sharp focus when examining growth in the limited English proficient (LEP) student population — which rose 65 percent between 1993-94 and 2003-2004. The growth is even more striking in new gateway states such as North Carolina and Nebraska, where the LEP population rose 500 and 340 percent, respectively.

Second, since the late 1990s, the Urban Institute has documented high levels of LEP concentration in a relatively small proportion of schools. A recent study found that 70 percent of LEP elementary students attend just 10 percent of US schools. The study also found that "high LEP" schools were more likely to be urban, to have high concentrations of poor and minority students, to have

Figure 4. More LEP Children are Native than Foreign Born

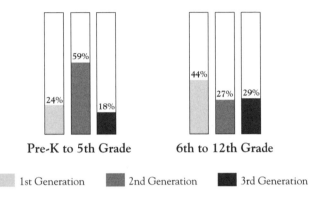

Pre-K to 5th Grade   **6th to 12th Grade**

1st Generation   2nd Generation   3rd Generation

Source: Migration Policy Institute, "The Demography of America's Schools," CUSSW Presentation, November 16, 2005.

larger classroom and school enrollments than "low" or "no" LEP schools, and to have the least experienced teachers and principals.[7] Early results of studies on NCLB implementation suggest that these high LEP schools are disproportionately found to fall short of meeting standards, and are, as a result, subject to the law's sanctions. It remains to be seen, though, whether changes work to the advantage or disadvantage of the LEP and immigrant students in these schools.

Third, the last three decades have also seen a sharp rise in poverty among children of immigrants. In 1970, poverty rates among children of immigrants resembled those of native whites. Today they are much closer to those of African American youth.

Fourth, a recent Urban Institute study found that overall, students master English as they advance in grade.[8] Nonetheless, as Figure 4 indicates, over three-quarters of elementary school students and over half of secondary school students who are LEP are *natives* who were presumably born and educated in US schools. Third-generation children of natives comprise a significant share of LEP students. Plainly, this trend underscores the need for accountability and, perhaps, for expanded access to high quality pre-kindergarten instruction that increases language skills and school readiness.

---

7   C. Cosentino de Cohen, B. Chu Clewell, and N. Deterding, "Who's Left Behind?: Immigrant Children in High and Low LEP Schools" (Washington, DC: The Urban Institute, 2005).

8   R. Capps, M. Fix, J. Murray, et al., "The New Demography of America's Schools: Immigration and the No Child Left Behind Act" (Washington, DC: The Urban Institute, 2005).

Figure 5. Changes in Percentage of Low-income Children (below 200% of Poverty) Who Are Uninsured, 1995 to 2004

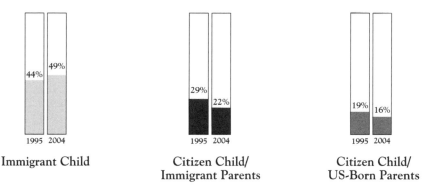

Immigrant Child	Citizen Child/ Immigrant Parents	Citizen Child/ US-Born Parents

Source: L. Ku's analyses of March 1996 and 2005 Current Population Surveys

Finally, it should not be surprising to learn that most parents of LEP students are themselves LEP and that the linguistic isolation that LEP students experience while at school is mirrored in their homes, making academic progress doubly difficult. Their isolation highlights the need for education strategies that involve the entire family. However, funding for the largest federal program that provides family-based literacy, the Even Start Program, was recently halved.

HEALTH CARE AND INSURANCE

The data presented by Ku and Papademetriou (Chapter 7) make clear that many recent immigrants and their children are outside the mainstream in terms of their access to health care. Fifty-six percent of low-income non-citizen immigrants are uninsured as compared to 23 percent of low-income natives. As Figure 5 indicates, between 1995 and 2004 the share of uninsured immigrant children rose from 44 to 49 percent.[9] High rates of uninsurance translate into lower rates of health care use, and apparently, into poorer health outcomes. According to an Urban Institute report, children of immigrants were substantially more likely to be reported to be in fair or poor health than children of natives.[10]

---

9   At the same time, though, the introduction of the State Child Health Insurance Program, coupled with expanded outreach to immigrant and minority communities, and declines in employment-based health insurance led to a rise in the public health care coverage among citizen-children in immigrant families. See R. Capps, G. Kenney, and M. Fix, "Health Insurance Coverage of Children in Mixed-Status Immigrant Families," Snapshot 3 of America's Families, No. 12 (Washington, DC: The Urban Institute, 2003).

10   J. Reardon Anderson, R. Capps, and M. Fix, "The Health and Well-Being of Children in Immigrant Families," Assessing the New Federalism Policy Brief B-52 (Washington, DC: The Urban Institute, 2002).

There are several explanations for immigrants' low insurance rates. Fewer foreign than native-born workers are insured by their employers because they work in the lowest paid segments of the labor market, often as contract workers. Access to public benefits also influences insurance rates. As noted, the 1996 welfare reform barred most legal immigrants entering after 1996 from federal Medicaid and SCHIP coverage for at least five years, transferring the costs of subsidizing coverage to their sponsors. Sponsors may have had a difficult time shouldering this extended burden given the fact that employer-based family insurance coverage can cost $10,000 a year and individual coverage $4,000. Another reason for low levels of coverage is the rise in unauthorized migration and the federal bars that existed both before and after welfare reform to providing public coverage (other than emergency Medicaid) to the unauthorized. Finally, access to health benefits is determined not just by eligibility but by providers' language capacity (the availability of bilingual staff, translators, etc.). Low rates of insurance translate into comparatively high rates of uncompensated care provided by public hospitals, clinics, and charitable organizations.

Ku and Papademetriou argue that a number of persisting myths about immigrants and their health have made informed policy decisions more difficult.

First, contrary to popular belief, immigrants are not the primary reason the number of uninsured is growing. In fact, analysis by the Urban Institute's Health Policy Center found that between 1994 and 2003 most of the increase in the number of uninsured was attributable to native citizens and was driven by declines in private insurance.[11]

Second, the health care costs of immigrants, while often uncompensated to providers, are often overstated. Immigrants are less likely to use emergency rooms than native citizens. Moreover, a recent paper in the *American Journal of Public Health* noted that per capita medical expenditures for immigrants — whether paid for by insurance or out of pocket — were less than half those of native citizens.[12] The findings held even when controlling for the effects of factors like insurance coverage, race/ethnicity, income, age, gender, education, and health status.

---

11 J. Holahan and A. Cook, "Are Immigrants Responsible for Most of the Growth of the Uninsured?" (Washington, DC: Kaiser Commission on Medicaid and the Uninsured, 2005).

12 S. Mohanty, et al., "Health Care Expenditures of Immigrants: A Nationally Representative Analysis," *American Journal of Public Health* 95:8, 2005.

Third, though a topic of much concern to state policymakers, offering health benefits does not create an immigrant magnet. The geographic patterns of dispersal that occurred in the late 1990s reveal substantial migration out of states offering high benefits — most notably California — toward new gateway states in regions that are generally characterized by low taxes and low benefits (the Southeast, the Rocky Mountain states, and the Midwest).

These patterns of health care coverage and the myths that surround them beg the question whether immigrants admitted under comprehensive immigration reform should be allowed to join the already large pool of uninsured immigrants.

IMPROVING IMMIGRANT WORKERS' ECONOMIC PROSPECTS

Access to the labor market remains the nation's most potent integrating mechanism. As Waldinger and Reichl note, the immigrant labor force is characterized by high employment levels, even among the low skilled. The immigrant labor force has an hourglass shape, with large shares of immigrants at the top and bottom of the skill distribution. Thirty percent of foreign-born workers have less than a high school education, while they are also as likely as natives to hold a Bachelor's degree or more (28 percent).

But while work is central to both immigration and integration, the policies and resources devoted to promoting immigrant workers' mobility are thin. Beeler and Murray describe the current system's shortcomings, setting out three complementary investment strategies (Chapter 8).

Workforce Development
The first is workforce development — aimed primarily at the lower skilled among immigrant workers. A main engine of federal investment is the ESL component of the Adult Basic Education Act, which in 2003/2004 supported language training for roughly 1.2 million of the 10 million LEP immigrant adults in the United States. According to state data and to anecdotal evidence, classes are oversubscribed; there are gaps in curricula, especially when it comes to providing language training for those who have some English skills; class levels are not carefully aligned ("articulated"); and the power of technology is not being exploited. Immigration reforms that would inject new "clients" into this system would have to come to terms with these institutional shortcomings.

Federal job training is primarily delivered through the programs funded under the Workforce Investment Act (WIA). While 20 percent of all low-wage workers in the United States are immigrants, it appears that LEP adults (at 7 percent of total WIA enrollment) may be under-enrolled in the program. Further, training programs are generally aimed at workers with education and skill levels (that is, at least a ninth grade education) that exceed those of many recent immigrants.

Of course, employers play an important role in developing the skills of their workforce. Little is known, though, about employers' practices, and even fewer reliable evaluations exist. In practice, employers often complain about the problems associated with scheduling language and skills instruction, the costs associated with the training, and the lack of employee time and interest. Moreover, employer training programs are typically targeted to the most, not the least, skilled within firms.

Making Skills and Credentials Count

One strategy for finding the skilled workers that firms need is to capitalize on the skills and knowledge that immigrants bring with them to the United States. According to one study, half of legal immigrants experience occupational downgrading in their first year.[13] Further, recent Migration Policy Institute analysis of the US Census finds that 17 percent of immigrants with a Bachelor's degree or more are low-income, i.e., are living below 200 percent of the federal poverty level, versus 8 percent of US natives. Here again, public policies and resources are thin. Verification of *educational* credentials is carried out by firms such as World Education Services (a nonprofit organization). No such nationwide organization exists when it comes to *professional* licensing, a process that is driven in part by standards that vary state by state. There may be lessons to learn from other countries here. Realizing that all net labor force growth in the future will come from immigration, Canada has instituted a new Foreign Credential Recognition Program on which it will spend $70 million in the next six years.

Supporting Immigrant Entrepreneurs

The importance of supporting entrepreneurship among immigrants is often overlooked as a workforce development strategy. Immigrants are disproportionately likely to be self-employed, and the self-employed have the highest incomes of all immigrants. Further, immigrant entrepreneurs are themselves a source of employment. In some cases, though, the jobs they create can complicate integration as they offer low wages, few benefits, and limited opportunities to learn English.

---

13 I. R. Akresh, "Occupational Mobility among Legal Immigrants to the United States," *International Migration Review* 40, no. 4, publication forthcoming.

Policies promoting entrepreneurship could include making it easier for immigrant business owners to establish credit histories and developing more uniform rules for public agencies regarding legal immigrants' eligibility for government grants, loans, and business advice.

NATURALIZATION AND CITIZENSHIP

Over the past decade there has been a striking rise in both the rate of naturalization and the absolute number of immigrants who have naturalized. Beginning in the mid-1990s, the number of naturalized citizens rose for the first time in decades, from 7 million in 1995 to 13.1 million in 2004 (Appendix III).

But despite rising numbers and rates, a large pool of immigrants — roughly 8 million in 2002 — was eligible to naturalize but had not. These "eligibles" are notable in part because 60 percent were LEP, 25 percent had less than a ninth grade education, roughly half were low income, and a disproportionate share (28 percent) was Mexican.

The number and characteristics of the eligible population are important concerns given ongoing efforts to redesign the nation's citizenship test. This effort — which parallels initiatives now taking place in Europe — is intended to standardize the test and make its content more meaningful. But the test redesign effort so far has revealed three underlying tensions:

- Asking test-takers to demonstrate an understanding of complex ideas and abstract concepts while at the same time only using the basic level of English required by the Immigration and Naturalization Act;

- Standardizing test administration across centers and officers while permitting administrators to take an individual applicant's background into account or according "due consideration" in weighing test performance; and

- Creating a more meaningful test without making it more difficult and increasing current denial rates.

If immigration reform were to lead to the admission of a larger number of workers with comparatively low educations and English language skills, the introduction of a more demanding naturalization test could have implications in two areas: the demand for civics and English classes (particularly if workers were offered a "pathway to citizenship") and the number of legal, non-citizen temporary workers with limited rights (see Chapter 5).

V. What Should A New Integration Agenda Include?

I conclude with a few thoughts on key elements of a national integration agenda and opportunities directly presented by comprehensive immigration reform. My point of departure is that — as in the past — the enterprise of integration will take place primarily at the state and local levels and will come about thanks to the efforts of employers, family, churches, public and private organizations, and of course, immigrants themselves. But given the concerns raised throughout the chapters in this volume, the laissez faire approach taken to integration in the past may leave too much to chance. The question, then, is what public policies and supports will be needed?

Balancing temporary and permanent immigration

To begin, temporary immigration should not be the primary thrust of immigration policy reform, thus allowing the reform effort to sidestep the issues surrounding economic and social integration. Many temporary immigrants come for permanent jobs in the economy and they, like the jobs, often stay. But by remaining in temporary, or falling into unauthorized status, they do so without the benefit of open access to the labor market, the rights reserved for citizens or permanent immigrants, the social safety net, and investments in human capital that can promote their integration.

Education

Perhaps the most powerful exception to the generally positive set of generational trends documented by Roger Waldinger and Renee Reichl is the low rate of college completion among both the Mexican first and second generations. In an increasingly knowledge-driven economy, this is a gap that policy will need to fill more completely with programs that focus on the completion of two-year programs at community colleges and the transition to, and completion of, four-year college education.

At the pre-kindergarten to 12 level, the rapid rise of the LEP student population, its concentration, and the persistence of limited English proficiency beyond the first to the second and even third generations have been noted. Taken together, these trends reinforce the need to sustain a focus on the "high LEP" schools that are disproportionately failing to meet standards under NCLB. They also underscore the need to preserve systems of accountability and the importance of pre-kindergarten programs that promote English language acquisition.

Workforce training and language policy

The adult basic education system's ESL programs are oversubscribed, and immigrants and LEP workers are underrepresented in the nation's workforce development programs. Employers' role in training immigrants remains understudied, and there is little systematic knowledge of promising practices. At minimum, we need a better mapping of these fragmented education and training systems. A more ambitious approach would be to develop a more deliberate national English language acquisition policy — one that might parallel the Bush Administration's recently announced initiative to promote foreign-language acquisition among US citizens. One focus would be to better integrate the country's adult literacy and workforce development systems.

Along these lines several Senate bills call for the creation of a new grant program to fund civics and integration classes. The program would be funded at least in part by a new public/private foundation that would be authorized to solicit, accept, and make charitable contributions. This idea may be a good way to put the language and civics issues on the national agenda, but public sector funding will also be required.

Access to health care

Strikingly low levels of health insurance coverage among immigrants and their families are in part the product of deliberate policy choices that excluded legal immigrants entering after 1996 from federal Medicaid and SCHIP programs for at least five years after entry. Forty percent of all legal permanent residents in the United States entered in the last ten years and fall under these restrictions. Some states have stepped in to fill the gap for children and pregnant women using their own funds, but coverage is incomplete and in danger as some states experience their own budget crises. As a result, recently arrived immigrants who are least able to obtain private insurance are excluded from coverage.

Immigration reform confronts policymakers with the dilemma of new temporary workers and legal immigrants joining the large pool of uninsured immigrants in the United States today. Several differing coverage options present themselves (see Chapter 7). They include:

- Restoring Medicaid and SCHIP to legal immigrants;

- Applying a portion of the fees collected from employers for worker visa applications to the financing of insurance costs;

- Making it easier for employers and employees to lower insurance costs by pooling risks;

- Allowing employers to "buy into" state employee health insurance plans or into state Medicaid or SCHIP coverage;

- Expanding bi-national or cross-border health insurance. Participants living in the United States now receive care at lower cost facilities in Mexico but can receive emergency care and other forms of unavailable care in the United States;

- Expanding the availability of free or reduced price primary care and pre-ventive health services at safety net primary care clinics; and

- Developing bilateral agreements with sending nations (Mexico, for exam-ple) to support primary care clinics in areas where their nationals reside.

IMPACT AID

As Deborah Garvey points out in Chapter 10, immigration reform begs the question whether policymakers should expressly take into account the poten-tial fiscal impacts of new migration flows on receiving communities. Research has found that low-skilled immigrants, whose numbers would increase substan-tially under many reform proposals, create a net fiscal strain on state and local governments due to costs of education, public benefits, and healthcare. At the same time, though, low-skilled immigrants also provide a net fiscal surplus to the federal government through payment to programs such as Social Security, raising the question whether some federal reimbursement should be made to states and localities. Further, assisting states and localities in providing educa-tional and preventive health services to new immigrants can benefit receiving communities as a whole, as well as the national economy, by creating healthier, more economically productive residents.

The last comprehensive federal impact aid program — the State Legalization Impact Assistance Grants Program (SLIAG) enacted as part of the 1986 Immigration Reform and Control Act — was deemed unsuccessful. The pro-gram's failure owed to delayed reimbursements, burdensome documentation requirements, and poor coordination between federal, state, and local govern-ment and community-based organizations.

One issue policymakers may face will be the degree to which an impact aid program is paid for out of fees collected from migrants who are adjusting status or entering as temporary workers. Neither SLIAG nor the Emergency Immigrant Education Program adopted such a fee-based approach, which obviously would increase processing costs for newcomers or their employers.

NATIONAL OFFICE FOR IMMIGRANT AND REFUGEE INTEGRATION

The importance of integration also begs the question whether a central office in the federal government should be created that would serve as a focal point for the multi-agency and cross-disciplinary issues that immigrant integration raises. The goals of a National Office on Immigrant Integration could be to: (1) establish national goals for immigrant integration and measure the degree to which they are met; (2) assess and coordinate federal policies that bear on integration; (3) serve as an intermediary with state and local governments in meeting integration goals; and (4) systematically examine current and future supply and demand for English acquisition services among migrant families, and authorize means for meeting that demand.

The proposed office could build on the Bush Administration's recently announced Task Force on Immigrant Integration. The Task Force was established by an executive order issued in June 2006. It convenes cabinet-level agencies under the direction of the DHS. The Task Force's core mission will be to "provide direction to executive departments and agencies concerning the integration into American society of America's legal immigrants, particularly through instruction in English, civics, and history." As of this writing, the scope of the Task Force's staffing, funding, and policy reach remains in the formative stages.

A national office would work closely with federal agencies helping to assess and shape policies that are likely to have substantial impacts on the integration of immigrants. It would help coordinate federal action and serve as an intermediary to state and local governments that typically are in the lead in implementing policies that promote integration.

UN MILLENIUM DEVELOPMENT GOALS

1. **Eradicate extreme poverty and hunger**

2. **Achieve universal primary education**

3. **Promote gender equality and empower women**

4. **Reduce child mortality**

5. **Improve maternal health**

6. **Combat HIV/AIDS, malaria, and other diseases**

7. **Ensure environmental sustainability**

8. **Develop a global partnership for development**

In setting national goals for immigrant integration, one model might be the United Nations' Millennium Development Goals, which establish a blueprint for meeting the needs of the world's poor.[14] The office should also identify national indicators of immigrant integration and commission research that measures their achievement. The results should be detailed in an annual Report to the President that is available as a public resource.

---

14 For more on the UN Millennium Development Goals, see http://www.un.org/millenniumgoals/.

PART I
DEFINING THE INTEGRATION VISION

CHAPTER 2

IMMIGRANT INTEGRATION — THE AMERICAN EXPERIENCE*

TAMAR JACOBY

I mmigrant integration — or absorption or assimilation — is an old and familiar story in the United States. So much so that one of our greatest historians, Oscar Handlin, began his greatest book by declaring: "Once I thought to write a history of the immigrants in America. Then I discovered that immigrants were American history and that to tell their story fully would require setting down the whole history of the United States." The immigrant experience is also an intimate story for most people in the United States. We're almost all the children of immigrants, and we all know something of "the melting pot."

Yet, for all this, it is instructive to go to Europe and compare notes with those who are now also dealing with issues of immigration and immigrant absorption. The metaphor that comes to my mind is two people commiserating outside of a clinic. Not that immigration is necessarily a complaint, and certainly not an illness. On the contrary, in the right number and under the right circumstances, immigration is a great boon to the receiving country — to its economy and its spirit. But the influx does sometimes come with some aches and pains — if only growing pains — and plainly many countries are facing those aches and pains today.

The good news is that assimilation is going pretty well these days in the United States. Whether in fact this is true is a much disputed and much monitored question — and rightly so. After all, with about a million legal and illegal immigrants coming into the country every year, if they're not assimilating, we're heading for real trouble. But most of the evidence I see supports a degree of optimism.

---

* This chapter has been adapted from a presentation at a Stockholm Network Conference in Madrid, Spain, 2002.

Obviously, the first component of absorption is economic. It's not the be-all and end-all. You can be doing all right economically and still not be fully integrated. But it's certainly the first building block. As I read the economic data, on this score, the glass is at least half full.

Most immigrants who come to America come to work. Most don't get welfare — they are not entitled to it for the first five to ten years. They know from other immigrants who have preceded them from their regions of origin whether or not work is available. Communications are very good now between American cities and the little villages of Latin America. If there aren't many jobs to be had, few immigrants make the trip. After all, if you're going to be unemployed, it's much better to unemployed at home than in the United States. It's usually a lot warmer at home and much less expensive to live, and you're usually surrounded by a network of supportive family and friends. So even though, technically, three-quarters of American immigrant visas are given out on the basis of family ties, almost every foreigner who comes to the United States gets a job — or two or three jobs — and works hard at it. Indeed, Hispanic males — and Hispanics account for about half the foreign born in the United States — have the highest labor-force participation rates of any group in the country.

Now of course it's true that many immigrants are poor and the jobs they do are often the dirtiest and most dangerous jobs going: jobs that native-born Americans don't want to do, like busboy and chambermaid and assembly-line worker in a meat-processing plant. But these people at the bottom of the economic ladder are only one component of the vast flow of immigrants that has been coming to America in recent decades. America has accepted a lot of people at the top end of the economic ladder such as nurses, engineers, and entrepreneurs. About a quarter of today's newcomers have less than nine years of schooling but another quarter have university degrees — about the same percentage as the native born. When you mix this second group's educational background with the phenomenal personal drive that most immigrants bring, it can prove an unbeatable combination. Just spend some time in Silicon Valley, where foreign-born scientists account for a third of the scientific workforce and Chinese and Indian entrepreneurs run a quarter of the high-tech companies.

The poverty and social backgrounds of many of today's newcomers are, of course, a cause for some concern. There's no question that, like many European nations, the United States today is basically a middle-class country importing a new lower class. That's the point, really, or a big part of the point: America no longer has a lower class, and it turns out that it needs one. But that doesn't necessarily mean these immigrants aren't going to be absorbed by the economy or do well for themselves by it, because generally they do. In fact, by the time the average immigrant has been in the United States for 10 or 15 years, he or she is usually making more than the average native-born American.

Which brings us to the second component of integration: How are the immigrants' children faring? This is the critical question. After all, the first generation is always transitional. They always live between two worlds, and if they arrive as adults, they never fully integrate. And to some degree, in America today, it's too soon to tell how the second generation is doing. Nevertheless, the evidence is beginning to trickle in, and to me it looks a lot more positive than negative.

Troubling signs do exist. Those who were born abroad — or whose parents were — often start at the bottom of the socioeconomic ladder. They certainly go to some of the worst schools in the country — failing, overcrowded inner-city schools, where many of the native-born students disdain learning and scorn mainstream success. And yes, some second-generation immigrant kids catch this bad attitude from their schoolmates.

But, as a group, these immigrant children come home with a superb report card. One important study conducted over the last decade in San Diego and Miami found that whatever country they come from, across the board, these students work harder than their native-born classmates. They do an average of two hours of homework a night compared with the "normal" 30 minutes. They aspire to greater achievement than American-born students. They get better grades, and they drop out far less often — between a third and half as often. The second generation is likely to outstrip their parents educationally and economically, vindicating the parents' urge to take the risk of coming to the United States to make a better life for their families.

The third key component of assimilation is the question of language. Are today's immigrants learning to speak English? This is an issue of huge concern in the United States — it is probably the greatest fear of those who worry that assimilation is not working — and there is no question, there is undoubtedly a lot more Spanish in the air today than there used to be 20 or 30 years ago. There are signs in Spanish just about everywhere you go. Politicians in heavily immigrant cities and at the federal level are falling all over themselves to learn Spanish. Even corporate America is catching the bug, spending hundreds of millions of dollars a year on advertising in Spanish and even Mandarin Chinese. So it would be easy to surmise that immigrants are not learning English, particularly not Hispanic immigrants, who often live in large enclaves of other Spanish-speaking people, where, some argue, you do not need English to get by.

But when you start to look at some real evidence, it turns out that the conventional wisdom driving people to campaign and advertise in Spanish is quite wrong. According to the Census, about 10 percent of the US population now lives in a household where Spanish is spoken. That sounds like a fairly large number but it turns out to be quite misleading, because for the Census Bureau, even one Spanish speaker — and in many cases, it's an elderly grandparent — is enough to get a family classified as Spanish-speaking. Yet within those households, 85 percent of the kids and 70 percent of the working-age adults speak English well or very well.

This has nothing to do with language classes. America doesn't provide much in the way of language classes. It's mainly about the power and reach of American pop culture. About 60 percent of today's new immigrants come to the United States speaking English well or very well — it's hard to avoid it in the world today, even in a poor village in rural Mexico. Despite the travesty that is bilingual education, virtually everyone who grows up in America eventually learns English. According to the second-generation study, by the end of high school, 98 percent of today's immigrants' children speak and understand English well or very well, and nine out of ten prefer it to their mother tongues.

There are some other important ways that people measure assimilation. Home-ownership is a good indicator that means immigrants are putting down roots and investing in them — as are citizenship and intermarriage — and on all those measures in America today the indications range from pretty good to astonishing.

Let's look first at home-ownership. True, as those who are pessimistic about assimilation are quick to tell you, many recent immigrants are anything but settled. They go back and forth to the old country. They often leave their families at home and maintain strong ties to the old world. But after a while, they settle down. They ask their families to join them or they marry someone they've met in America; and within 20 years, 60 percent of them are homeowners. And by the time they've been in the United States for 25 years, they're actually more settled than native-born Americans — a significantly higher share of them own their own homes.

Similarly, with citizenship. True, today, unlike in the past, it is possible for people from many countries to maintain dual citizenship — and with it, perhaps, troublingly dual or conflicting loyalties. True, naturalization is a slow, gradual process. Among those who arrived in the years since 1990, less than 10 percent have become citizens. But among those who have been in the United States since 1970, as many as 80 percent are naturalized. The point is clear: If you stay, you eventually join — today, as in the past, you eventually graduate from sojourner to member.

Finally — saving the most stunning numbers for last — there is the ethnic intermarriage rate. Just to give some perspective, until very recently the black-white intermarriage rate in the United States was well under 5 percent but, when it comes to US-born Asians and US-born Hispanics, between a third and a half marry someone of a different ethnicity and by the third generation, according to some demographers, the rates are over 50 percent for both groups.

Naturally, none of these measures really capture the ineffable that is the essence of integration — the sense of fully belonging in a new land and a new culture. Do today's immigrants feel they are truly Americans? Do they place their loyalty to the things we all share as a nation above their loyalties to their groups and their particular ethnicities? Well, relatively few people do, even among the native born. And the mainstream culture hardly encourages it. Many Americans themselves no longer know what it means to be American. Our schools teach at best a travesty of American history, distorted by political correctness and the excesses of multiculturalism and, even in the wake of September 11, few leaders have tried to evoke more than a fuzzy, feel-good enthusiasm for America.

So there's no question that today's immigrants are at a disadvantage compared to yesterday's when it comes to what some people call "patriotic assimilation." But this is as much the nation's fault as it is the fault of immigrants. America is full of self-styled ethnic "leaders" and ethnic-studies professors and ethnic marketers fomenting chauvinism and divisiveness — most of them second or third or fourth generation. But your average, hard-working immigrant is only baffled by identity politics. Today's migrants, like yesterday's, want to make it in America, not live apart in anger and alienation. Their children may be a different matter and we have to reach out to their children in a different way. But given half a chance, there's no one more patriotic than a new immigrant. You should have seen the flags flying in the Mexican American neighborhoods in the wake of 9/11. According to one of the largest and most comprehensive national surveys of Latinos, conducted by the *Washington Post*, 84 percent believe it is "important" or "very important" for immigrants "to change so that they blend into the larger society, as in the idea of the melting pot."

So a picture is beginning to emerge here. It's a mixed picture and, to a significant extent, the jury is still out. But whatever question marks remain, today's new American immigrants are not spawning a new "rainbow underclass." There are a lot of reasons for this but by and large, the immigrant integration story that's developing in America today is a success story. If you have any doubts, just spend some time among the Mexican American middle class in a place like Houston, Texas, or with the first-generation Chinese Americans — and there are quite a few of them — who sit on the board of overseers that runs the California state university system.

So the question is: What can be done, whether in Europe or in America, to encourage and assist immigrant integration? But before I get to that, I want to consider the parallel — or, more precisely, what is parallel and what isn't — between America and Europe. Certainly, Americans have been dealing with this for a lot longer. This does not mean that we are necessarily better at it: People tackling an issue for the first time often bring a combination of energy and ideas that's missing among people who have been grappling with a problem forever. But certainly, there are some factors that make this issue a little easier in America.

It helps that there really is no such thing as a hereditary American in the way that there are in effect hereditary Frenchmen and hereditary Germans. America has always been a place where foreigners could show up and participate — maybe not on an equal basis, but still participate — and in most cases, they eventually found they were accepted as full members.

It also helps that we don't have — and never have had — an established state religion. So neither your religion nor your ethnicity is an a priori obstacle to integration. Finally, crime is not a particular problem among American immigrants, and even in relatively sour economic times, the unemployment rate in the United States is nothing like unemployment rates in Europe.

So there are a lot of ways in which I think we have it easier. And it's quite possible that the differences between the two continents make the American experience completely irrelevant in Europe.

IMMIGRATION POLICY OUGHT TO BE BASED ON WORK

The primary criterion for whom to let in ought to be who is coming to do a job that needs doing and that native-born people don't tend to want to do. Sure, humanitarian concerns have an effect on policy. Family reunification has a place and so, of course, does helping refugees. But the main reason people move from one country to another is to improve their lot, usually economically, and the only real, enduring interest a foreign country has in accepting them is if they're going to contribute. So let's recognize this and make it the basis of policy.

Besides, the more of a premium a country can place on economic migrants — the more clearly it acknowledges those who are economic migrants and the more access it gives them to its labor markets — the better immigrant integration will work. People who work establish roots and relationships. People who work learn the language. People who work eventually better themselves. And people who work earn the respect of their fellow countrymen. Now, as I say, this is a point I spend a lot of time trying to press home, where our essentially family-driven system gets us in trouble because of the way it's out of sync with our labor needs. But if anything, the principle seems even more relevant in America than in Europe. Why not recognize that whatever the political circumstances in countries like Turkey and Afghanistan, many of the migrants from those places are coming to Europe to work and make a better life for themselves? Recognize this, let them work — and reap the rewards, as working helps them to assimilate.

TOO MUCH GOVERNMENT ASSISTANCE IS A MISTAKE

Refugees who for one reason or another can't work may need some help from the government, but this isn't true for most economic migrants — and for them, assistance can be as much a curse as a blessing. All too often, welfare discourages work and the assimilation that inevitably comes with it. In the case of government housing, whether in accommodation centers or elsewhere, the supposedly helping hand of the state encourages segregation. Too warm a welcome creates a false incentive for other would-be migrants, luring more people into the country than can productively work and integrate there. And it only leads the native born to look down on the migrants who receive it, further adding to the difficulty of assimilating.

Of course, all of this begs the question: How much is too much? And I'm not against providing some basic services — whether emergency services or other necessities, as well as any services that spur assimilation. (I'm all for better public schools, for example, and vocational apprenticeships and classes that help people learn to help themselves — teaching them financial literacy and that sort of thing. In some cases, I'm even at the generous end of the spectrum on services. I'm all for allowing even illegal immigrants' children to go to public universities, for example — a big issue in the United States right now.) But I don't think the United States made a mistake in barring immigrants from receiving welfare, and to the degree that's possible in Europe, I urge European policymakers to consider it.

Short-Sighted, Unrealistic Laws That Force Otherwise Legitimate Migrants to Live Underground Are Only Going to Slow Their Absorption

This is only common sense. The law-abiding are more likely to fit into society and be accepted there than people who live outside the law and adopt the habits of law-breakers.

The problem in the United States is that although a million immigrants come into the country each year to work, the law only recognizes two-thirds that number — and the other third are forced to sneak in and then to live like fugitives. Not only does this criminalize badly needed productive activity, it also makes an ass of the law — and creates all kinds of obstacles to assimilation. And I'm sure this must be true in Europe, too, where so many who want to work are forced to work illegally, and even those seeking asylum often start their new lives as outlaws. If they are going to come anyway, far better to recognize reality and create legitimate channels.

It Is Not a Mistake to Make Demands of Immigrants

Demands that they learn the language in their new, adopted country; demands that they learn the manners and mores; demands that they eventually become citizens. This is not racist or unduly nationalistic, although this sort of incorporation effort should be as positive as possible — a matter not of sanctions and punishment but of highlighting the allure of the new country. You ask and encourage people to learn the ways of a culture because those ways are the keys to success there. If you're going to require, say, learning the language, you ought to provide and pay for classes. (The government does not need to provide them, but it ought to create incentives so that others do.) This will only work to the degree that newcomers are also allowed to maintain some degree of attachment to the culture they come from.

Don't Ask People to Obliterate Their Old Loyalties

America does not ask immigrants to forget about their ethnicity. On the contrary, anyone who knows what makes America great knows that Italian Americans will be Italian, Jewish Americans will be Jewish — and in the 21st century, Latino Americans will be Latino. What we ask, or have asked in the past, is that people learn to balance the two sides of their identity — the ethnic side and the American side. Traditionally, what this meant for most groups was that at home and on the weekends and in your neighborhood — i.e., in private —you lived your ethnic background, or were free to. But when it came to the workday or the workplace or anything public or official, you were a citizen among citizens and you could be accepted as a full member there in the public sphere, no matter what you did or were at home.

It's true that this traditional balance is out of kilter in the United States today: Our obsessive and insistent multiculturalism has disrupted the age-old balance. We may not be requiring enough of our new immigrants today — or holding out enough in the way of a coherent idea of what it means to be American, and this is a crucial challenge for the United States going forward.

But immigrant absorption cannot work without this balance, because you can not expect people to simply give up who they are — to throw away the habits they have grown up with and the age-old loyalties that help to make them strong. But you also can't hope to assimilate them unless you permit and encourage full membership. So you have to come up with a notion of membership that allows for some kind of hyphenated existence that isn't second-class. At least that's the formula in America.

So the great question, of course, is whether any of this can work in Europe. I don't think there's any doubt that it is what has made America what it is today. From Anglo-Saxon political traditions to Jewish humor, from the German work ethic to Irish eloquence: Just about everything that makes America great was brought here by an immigrant. But Europe is a very different place, with little or no tradition of immigrant absorption and where people are already anxious that for one reason or another — globalization, modernization — the traditional fabric and character of the society is being eroded. It is easy to understand those concerns and to see why immigration poses a harder challenge in Europe.

In the long run, however, it's a challenge that cannot be avoided. For demographic reasons, because of changing labor needs, thanks to globalization and the ever-accelerating interconnectedness of the world today, immigration is Europe's future whether she likes it or not. Better to recognize it, regularize it, bring it above ground — and get on with the hard business of helping the newcomers assimilate.

CHAPTER 3

FROM IMMIGRANT TO CITIZEN*
JANET MURGUÍA AND CECILIA MUÑOZ

Perhaps the most extraordinary thing about the integration of immigrants in this nation of immigrants is just how much it is being done by the immigrants themselves, with a minimum of effort by government or society at large. Despite widespread hand-wringing that today's immigrants are not learning English or becoming "like us" as they used to, the traditional indicators — English-language acquisition, workforce participation, homeownership, military service, civic participation, and intermarriage — make it clear that immigrants continue to do what they have always done: become Americans relatively quickly. We're getting an enormous return on a tiny investment.

This pattern contrasts radically with the immigration wave of a century ago, when government and private philanthropy — through civics education, English-language outreach, and what was termed "Americanization" — smoothed the path to citizenship and full participation in US society. Ironically, those who worry most about assimilating the current wave of immigrants are doing the least to foster their integration.

The biggest worry focuses on English-language acquisition. Despite the common perception that our immigrant grandparents and great-grandparents adopted the language without much trouble and without any help, most groups followed a three-generation pattern, in which the immigrant adults learned enough English to get by, their children were bilingual with English as the dominant language, and their grandchildren, largely, spoke English only. As for today's immigrants, the vast majority of whom are Latino and Asian, there appears to be no cause for worry. According to the 2000 census, of the people who report speaking Spanish at home, 72 percent also report speaking English "well" or "very well." This proportion for speakers of Asian languages is more than 77 percent. The research on the second and third generations consistently

* This chapter is reprinted with permission from Janet Murguía and Cecilia Muñoz, "From Immigrant to Citizen," The American Prospect, Volume 16, No. 11: November 10, 2005. The American Prospect, 11 Beacon Street, Suite 1120, Boston, MA 02108. All rights reserved.

shows adherence to the three-generation pattern. For example, a recent report on language assimilation by the Lewis Mumford Center for Comparative Urban and Regional Research in Albany, New York, found that the second generation is largely bilingual; 92 percent of the Hispanics speak English "well," as do 96 percent of the Asians, though most also speak another language at home. The third generation generally speaks English only.

Despite this success, the integration of immigrants would benefit enormously from an infusion of resources. Among the unmet needs of immigrants are more English as a Second Language (ESL) programs. According to the Center for Adult English Language Acquisition, almost half of the 1.2 million adults in federally funded adult education programs are there to learn English. Waiting lists for class slots are often so long that some immigrants wait months or years before getting a space. Studies by the National Center for Education Statistics suggest a pool of three million or more adults who are interested in ESL classes but not enrolled for a variety of reasons, including the fact that the classes are oversubscribed.

Immigrant communities and their co-ethnics are attempting to fill the ESL class gap; out of more than 300 affiliates of the National Council of La Raza, more than half provide ESL classes to adults, most without public funding of any kind. This pattern is repeated across ethnic groups, church organizations, and other nonprofits, which largely attempt to meet the need with donated classroom space, volunteer teachers, and whatever curricula they can find on the Internet. Essentially, a large part of the national effort to provide English-language instruction for immigrant adults is being carried out with the educational equivalent of duct tape and string.

But English alone will not be enough to help today's immigrants integrate into American society. While America of the 19th century needed physically able immigrants, economic advancement today now requires an education. The ability of adult-education programs to go beyond basic English skills for immigrant adults, and a successful public-education system for their children, is essential for the full economic integration of today's immigrants. Similarly, we all have a stake in the extent to which immigrants — who are overrepresented among those who don't have bank accounts — develop financial literacy and the wherewithal to amass savings for their children's education or their own retirement. Recently arrived immigrants also are often working in jobs that don't provide health insurance, and are categorically ineligible for government-funded programs that can provide vital preventive care, health education, and other services important to the broader public health. Even the crises in the Gulf Coast have highlighted the failure of federal and local governments to communicate about the need to evacuate in languages that all residents could understand; neither the public nor most private relief efforts managed to communicate with all of those affected.

Finally, we need to find a way to help eligible immigrants naturalize. The United States does nothing at all to encourage or assist immigrants in taking this final step. There is no notification when an immigrant or refugee becomes eligible to naturalize, and the process is a confusing, lengthy, and expensive quagmire. The waiting period for a naturalization petition to be adjudicated is rarely less than six months, and in many parts of the country often exceeds one or even two years. At $320, not including fingerprinting and other costs, the fee is very high compared with any other government processes, like obtaining passports or driver's licenses, both of which involve much more expensive, security-conscious documents. The new agency administering the process, the bureau of Citizenship and Immigration Services in the Department of Homeland Security, has yet to improve upon the reputation of the former Immigration and Naturalization Service for lost files, delays, and other bureaucratic red tape. We'd be well served by changing the system, particularly because those who naturalize have a higher propensity to participate in the political process. In fact, Americans by choice are more likely to vote than Americans by birth.

Unfortunately, there is plenty of talk today about how to keep immigrants out, but hardly any of what to do for those who come in. The absence of anything resembling a public strategy to maximize the speed and depth of their integration is extraordinary. Think about the major policy debates of the last decade, from health care to the Social Security debate, all arguably opportunities to incorporate elements of a broader immigrant-integration strategy in which the discussion simply never happened.

In conservative circles, the discussion is largely focused on cultural issues and fears that assimilation is not taking place. Many dedicate their firepower to the subject of bilingual education, which is intended to support immigrant students in their efforts to move forward in subjects like math and science while they learn English; detractors like to mischaracterize it as a nationalistic effort by organizations like ours, the National Council of La Raza, to preserve Spanish at all costs. As contentious as this debate is, it is focused on a tiny program. In the meantime, fully two-thirds of immigrant students who need to learn English have no access to programs of any kind to help them do so. Surely we can do better for these students than an endless ideological debate about eliminating bilingual programs.

But at least conservatives are talking about *something*. The progressive movement, which once did so much to facilitate the process by which immigrants become Americans, is largely absent from the discussion. Except for ethnic organizations that directly work with immigrant constituencies, progressives tend to say the right things about immigrants and their co-ethnics without really making them a presence in their policy agendas, philanthropic strategies, or institutions.

This is in stark contrast to the progressive movement of 100 years ago, when multiple sectors of American society made extraordinary investments in the integration process, undertaking major reforms on a scale that is almost unimaginable today. These investments, which were aimed directly at immigrant integration, created at least two major American institutions: the public schools and the adult-education system. Similarly, philanthropy of the late 19th and early 20th centuries focused substantial investment in the assimilation of new immigrants, including the expansive settlement-house movement and the creation of the modern public-library system by industrialist-turned-philanthropist Andrew Carnegie. Other innovations were a little more indirect: By telling the story of immigrant living conditions in *How the Other Half Lives*, Jacob Riis inspired significant tenement reforms; 16 years later, Upton Sinclair wrote *The Jungle*, a fictional but authentic accounting of the immigrant experience in the meatpacking industry that horrified the nation and led to the enactment of major labor laws. Indeed, the history of the labor movement in the United States is deeply intertwined with our immigrant history, as is the development of major political machines in major cities. Say what you will about Tammany Hall, it encouraged citizenship and voting by giving immigrants a direct stake in the electoral process.

By contrast, immigrants and the impact of immigration rarely appear in much of the current progressive debate on social issues. The big exception to this may be some parts of the labor movement. It is no accident that, for the most part, the only unions that are growing are the ones organizing in industries populated by immigrant workers. These unions, especially the Service Employees International Union and the newly merged UNITE HERE (representing the hotel, restaurant, and garment industries), led an effort that reversed the AFL-CIO's traditionally restrictionist posture and allied it with the immigrant-rights movement. But the labor movement as a whole is still deeply ambivalent about the presence of immigrants in the workforce and the country, which may contribute to the broader progressive movement's silence on immigrant issues, including integration.

Similarly, few if any of the major voices on education policy have anything to say about the students who are either immigrants themselves or the children of immigrants still learning English (English Language Learners, or ELLs). Despite the fact that ELLs now constitute more than 10 percent of students in our schools, and more than twice that proportion in key urban areas, the public-education system is largely unresponsive, and the gap in educational outcomes between these students and their peers is not narrowing.

And these gaps are stubborn. Many a suburban school continues to be labeled "in need of improvement" because of the struggles of its ELL students (along with special-needs students). This has led to a vigorous debate about the fairness of the tests for students whose native language is not English. In some cases the discussion focuses on testing students in a language they understand in order to measure what they know (it's hard to know their capacity in math if they can't get past the instructions on the test). This discussion is inevitably controversial because it bumps up against the familiar suspicion that those seeking these assessments are really anti-English ideologues. The alternative, which is raised distressingly often, is to exempt ELL students from assessments altogether, which relieves the immediate pressure on schools and teachers but also dismantles the entire accountability structure for educating this group of students. For schools under enormous pressure from all sides, it's difficult to imagine that such a scenario would result in better outcomes for immigrant youth.

Efforts to expand the number and quality of programs to teach English language and literacy to adults are also limited to a few lonely voices in the wilderness. The notable exceptions are innovative state-level ESL and naturalization initiatives in Illinois and New York, the product of savvy and effective advocacy campaigns by immigrant coalitions. These initiatives are notable in that they are so rare. Federal resources for adult ESL education expanded briefly during the Clinton administration, but have either remained stagnant or declined ever since.

Aside from persistent advocacy from within the immigrant-rights movement itself, improvements in the naturalization process are also absent from the progressive agenda, though it must be said that when then–Vice President Al Gore proposed to facilitate the naturalization of immigrants, he was pilloried for supposedly politicizing the process. (By drafting an internal memorandum suggesting ways to streamline a badly backlogged naturalization process, the vice president became the subject of congressional inquiry and a media firestorm focused on the notion that he was "cheapening" the process in order to crank out voters who would likely cast ballots for him in 2000.) But when Republicans have taken steps to make naturalization more difficult by increasing fees, revamping the naturalization exam, and other measures, the left has been silent. The generous explanation for this silence is the fear of the kind of political reprisals faced by Gore; the more likely explanation is indifference.

Indeed, Republicans are outsmarting progressives, particularly when it comes to reaching the intrepid immigrants who have survived the naturalization process, airing campaign ads in Spanish as well as English and courting votes. This is a new phenomenon, road tested in the most recent presidential election, and right now it is more style than substance. Nonetheless, the portion of the Republican Party that is not engaged in immigrant-bashing is poised to make a serious investment in moving immigrant voters into its ranks.

The progressive movement should take note. This political transformation is not inevitable, but it is indeed possible, and it is one area of integration in which a serious investment is being made. Progressives, however, have been largely missing in action on this front, assuming that Latino and Asian immigrants and their co-ethnics are part of the "base." There are plenty of other good reasons to invest in immigrant integration; perhaps this is the one that will shake the left out of its complacency.

CHAPTER 4

TODAY'S SECOND GENERATION: GETTING AHEAD OR FALLING BEHIND?

ROGER WALDINGER AND RENEE REICHL

INTRODUCTION

The United States is once again a country of mass immigration — testimony to its undiminished capacity to provide newcomers opportunities to better their lives. Comparison to the circumstances newcomers leave behind makes it clear that arrivals from abroad generally do well for themselves by moving to the United States. Two decades of scholarship suggest, however, that while conditions for newcomers may certainly be improving, they are not at a pace needed to catch up with the native born. In the long run, however, the fate of immigrants may not be the central issue. They, after all, are a transitional generation, caught between here and there. What is more important are the prospects for integration and social and economic mobility of the *second generation* — the US-born children of immigrants.

As the fate of today's second generation is still unfolding, research has not yet produced a definitive analysis of the paths that the children of immigrants are likely to follow. The most pessimistic scenario, formulated by sociologists, is associated with the hypothesis of segmented assimilation.[1] It contends that a sizeable portion of today's second generation — especially the children of working-class immigrants — may be a "rainbow underclass" in the making, comprised of those who have failed to acquire the skills needed to move ahead and of those who are disconnected from regular participation in the labor market. The more conventional perspective posits "assimilation" of the second generation as some progress beyond their parents' socioeconomic status. This modestly optimistic view is almost surely correct, at least as concerns the great majority.

---

1   See A. Portes and R. G. Rumbaut, *Legacies: The Story of the Immigrant Second Generation* (Berkeley, CA: University of California Press, 2001).

On the other hand, relative, not absolute progress may be the more important factor: Divergence from the parental generation does not necessarily imply convergence with the dominant or majority group (i.e., native-born whites). For example, convergence may be postponed or precluded if the second generation never quite succeeds at educational catch-up and if income growth is largely concentrated among workers with the most schooling. The question of which contrast counts is also a matter of perception: The high school-educated children of barely literate dishwashers or factory workers may well outpace their parents, but be unable to attain the very middle-class American dream that teachers, media, and peers have been exhorting from day one. If over time their prospects remain bleak and they find themselves stagnating in lower socioeconomic ranks (joining historically underprivileged groups), second-generation youth may also conclude that their search for advancement has stalled and resign themselves to lower educational and occupational outcomes.

In this chapter we focus on the experience of the contemporary second generation, examining their most salient educational and labor market characteristics: What is the ethnic, national origin, and age composition of today's second generation? How does the second generation compare to first- and third- (and later) generation Americans in terms of educational attainment and attachment to the workforce? Are they becoming economically self-sufficient? Are they getting ahead or falling behind in America?

The chapter begins by depicting overall numbers and trends, comparing the characteristics of the second generation to that of the first. We then move on to our key concern: gauging progress made by US-born children of immigrants by examining key indicators regarding schooling, employment, and earnings. We pay special attention to the Mexican-origin second generation who represent a quarter of the entire second-generation population and more than a third of the second-generation children under age ten. Our goal is to examine whether the rainbow underclass hypothesis is well-founded and supported by evidence (especially in the case of the Mexican-origin second generation). The analysis involves a series of contrasts: by generation, gender, national origin, and race/ethnicity to determine whether and to what extent the second generation is diverging from their parents, their white peers (the dominant group), and African American peers (the underprivileged group).[2]

---

2   A word of caution is in order: Although we compare the generation and origin groups in terms of their educational and work characteristics, we did not test the group differences for their statistical significance. As such, our analysis provides only a descriptive portrayal of group differences.

DEFINITIONS AND DATA

The second generation is still an emerging phenomenon. It has an unusual age structure, strongly skewed toward youth and reflecting the ebbs and flows of immigration over an extended, almost century-long period. Most importantly, adult offspring of immigrant parents from the Americas and Asia remain a comparatively small group. With the exception of Mexicans, the numbers are too small for disaggregating by distinctive national origin. Consequently, we have grouped all second-generation persons into one national category, Mexicans, and three global categories: Europeans/Canadians/Australians (to be referred to as Europeans/Canadians), "other Americas" (all countries in the Western hemisphere *except* Mexico and Canada), and "Asians" (including *all* countries in Asia, whether in eastern or western Asia). While these global categories undoubtedly conceal a good deal of internal heterogeneity, further breakdowns would not yield reliable numbers; for now, this is the best that we can do.

We define the *first generation* as persons who were born abroad (i.e., our definition includes children born abroad to US citizens, persons from US outlying territories, persons who acquired US citizenship through naturalization, and non-US citizens). The *second generation* consists of persons born in the United States, with at least one foreign-born parent. Finally, the *third generation* consists of persons born in the United States to parents also born in the United States. Though we will refer to this latter group as a "third generation," in reality it is a "third-plus" generation, as many have ancestors whose residence in the United States dates back several generations. Given our interest in generational differences, we restrict our third generation to two groups of native born that comprise the great bulk of America's third generation population: whites and African Americans. Any reference to whites or African Americans only extends to third generation members of these groups.[3]

The chapter draws on a variety of statistical sources. As is well known, the great workhorse of the American statistical system — the US Census of Population — is of limited use for this purpose, as it ceased asking questions about parents' place of birth in 1970, making it impossible to track the children of immigrants once they had moved out of their parents' home. We use Census data for the 1970 results. For later years, we fall back on the Current Population Survey (CPS), which began asking respondents about their parents' nativity on a periodic basis, starting in 1979, and began doing so on a regular

---

3 In the following narrative, the terms "foreign born" and "immigrant" are used interchangeably.

basis in 1994. Reliance on CPS entails drawbacks of its own, mainly the survey's small sample size. Consequently, we have followed a now common practice of combining (or concatenating) several survey years to increase the sample size.[4]

THE NEW SECOND GENERATION COMES OF AGE: A DEMOGRAPHIC PROFILE

ORIGINS OF THE FIRST AND SECOND GENERATIONS

The shift in national origins — from Europe to other parts of the world — is perhaps the single most distinctive aspect of post-1965 US immigration. Since hitting its nadir in 1970, when the foreign born accounted for just over 5.4 percent of the US population, immigrant numbers have been steadily rising. In 2004, nearly 13 of every 100 persons living in the United States were born abroad. National origins have transformed as numbers have grown (see Table 1). Although, in 1970, the great bulk of the foreign-born population originated in Europe and Canada, the relative size of that group quickly eroded, tumbling to less than 20 percent by 2004. By the turn of the 21st century, the foreign-born mix was overwhelmingly dominated by persons of non-European origin, with Mexicans and a diverse group of immigrants from Asia each comprising roughly 30 percent.

The transformation of the second generation, however, has been a more protracted development, clearly in evidence, but far from complete. The legacy of the era of mass migration took the form of a large second generation, dominated by cohorts born roughly between 1905 and 1925, tailed by a smaller, though not insignificant group, born in the succeeding 15 years. Those immigrant offspring were later augmented by the descendants of the smaller waves of European immigrants who arrived during the 1930s, and again, in the immediate post-World War II period. In contrast, the "new immigration" from Asia and the Americas is still of quite recent vintage. Many of today's major groups are very recently arrived: For all practical purposes, Vietnamese and Central American immigration dates from the late 1970s.

Consequently, in relative size and composition, today's second generation has evolved in ways far different from that of the first wave. As of 1970, second-generation persons comprised 11.5 percent of the US population; that propor-

---

4   This report principally relies on merged data from the 1997, 1999, 2001, and 2003 CPS; as the year 2000 falls in the midpoint among these years, we will refer to this merged sample as the "2000" survey.

TABLE 1. WEIGHTED PERCENT OF FIRST AND SECOND GENERATION BY ORIGIN, 1970 TO 2004

	1970	1979	1990	2000	2004
First Generation					
Canada/Europe/Australia	68.8	48.7	33.2	20.2	17.1
Asia	9.1	21.2	23.2	26.3	28.9
Mexico	9.7	15.2	24.8	27.9	28.8
Other Americas	11.4	13.6	17.4	23.3	22.8
Africa	1.1	1.2	1.5	2.4	2.4
Total	100.0	100.0	100.0	100.0	100.0
Second Generation					
Canada/Europe/Australia	87.8	81.3	32.9	43.4	34.9
Asia	2.8	4.3	23.6	15.1	19.4
Mexico	6.9	10.2	25.5	26.1	28.5
Other Americas	2.3	3.9	16.8	14.2	15.5
Africa	0.3	0.3	1.2	1.2	1.7
Total	100.0	100.0	100.0	100.0	100.0

Sources: 1970 IPUMS; 1979 November CPS; 1989 November CPS; 1997-2003 March CPS; 2004 March CPS

tion has slightly declined over time, falling to 10.4 percent as of 2004. Thus in relative size, the two groups have flipped: Formerly less than half the size of the second generation, the foreign born are now a good deal more numerous.

Likewise, national origins have also changed, while still reflecting the impact of the immigration patterns of the first half of the 20th century. Thirty-five years ago, European origins were far more prevalent among the second generation (see Table 1). While the mix has since changed greatly, the ranks of immigrant offspring still retain a European plurality (34.9 percent). Moreover, the US-born children of the recent arrivals have only begun to make their mark: note the large proportion of the second generation with Mexican-born parents (28.5 percent), reflecting the long-standing nature of Mexican immigration to the United States, and the much smaller share maintained by very diverse Asian-origin second generation (19.4 percent). Surely, this will all shift in the years to come. Still, the nature of the demographic processes at work — having to do with mortality rates among the aging descendants of the European immigrants and fertility differentials among the new immigrants — means that the composition of the second generation will continue to look quite different from the first generation for quite some time.

In terms of national origins, Mexicans accounted for 28.8 percent of all foreign-born persons living in the United States, as of 2004. No single country of origin was remotely as numerous; Filipinos, the next largest group, made up only 4.4 percent of the foreign born. Seven of the ten largest sending countries were either in Asia (China, India, Vietnam, and Korea) or in the Americas (Cuba, Canada, and El Salvador). The national origins of the second generation, however, take a very different form. Though Mexicans predominate (accounting for 25 percent), the legacy of earlier immigrations can still be readily detected: Italy, Russia, Poland, Germany, Canada, England, and Ireland still rank among the top ten countries of origin among the second-generation population. However, if the focus is on the very young, a different profile is emerging: The national origins of second-generation children ages ten or under closely resemble the national origins of the foreign-born population. However, there is one key exception: Mexican-origin persons account for 36.5 percent of this group, as opposed to 28.8 percent among the foreign born.

DIFFERENCES IN AGE STRUCTURE BETWEEN THE FIRST AND SECOND GENERATIONS

Age structure provides another significant dimension of variation. Migration is a selective activity, most likely to be undertaken by younger adults. The age distribution of the foreign-born population highlights this propensity, as children are under-represented and adults aged 20 to 29 and 30 to 49 are over-represented among this group (see Figure 1). The age structure among the second generation takes a very different, U-shaped form, with the largest groups either younger than ten or older than 50 and a small population of prime-age adults. This distinctive U-shape reflects the discontinuities in America's migration history. The large cohort at the older end of the age structure represents the US-born children of the immigrants of the last age of mass migration. The even larger cohort at the young end of the age structure is the offspring of today's arrivals. By contrast, the cohorts of prime-age adults are persons born in the United States between the end of World War II and the very early 1980s.

Controlling for national origin provides an important refinement. The second generation with origins in Europe, Canada, or Australia is an especially old group: Almost 60 percent are 50 years of age and above. By contrast, young

FIGURE 1. PERCENT OF TOTAL POPULATION BY GENERATION AND AGE GROUP, 2000

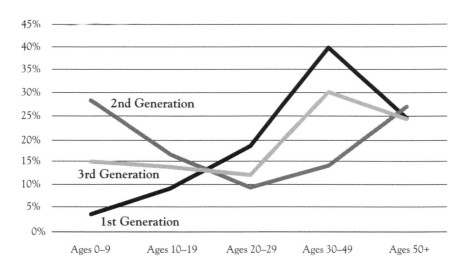

Source: Current Population Survey, March 1997-2003.

children predominate among all the other national origin categories: Among second-generation persons with origins in Mexico, elsewhere in the Americas or Asia, well over 40 percent were younger than ten years old as of 2000. About 70 percent in all three national origins categories were under age 20.

We argue that the distinctive age structure of the second generation implies that the advent of a "new" second generation has yet to yield its full effect. As of now, the institutional impact is mainly felt by the schools, especially those in the major immigrant-receiving cities, where growing immigrant numbers have produced a large population of school children of immigrant origins. In contrast, the impact on the labor market is far more modest due to the small size of the prime-age worker cohort of today's second generation.

In terms of national origin, US-born offspring of Mexican immigrants — the children of America's lowest skilled immigrants — will comprise the overwhelmingly largest group of the second generation. Other national origin groups such as Salvadorans and Dominicans that have similar social and economic characteristics will add a smaller, but still substantial component to the new second generation moving into the labor force. Though most of the new second-generation children are still in school, the base size of the population is such that small proportions translate into large numbers of second-generation persons, already either in the labor force or making the transition from school to work. Acknowledging that the future is always unpredictable, the remainder of this chapter focuses on the education and employment of youth and young adult members of the second generation. While partial, their current experience in the worlds of school and work is sufficiently extensive to offer at least a reasonable benchmark from which to make forecasts.

From School to Work

Schooling is a prerequisite for advancement in the 21st-century United States. A critical hurdle is obtaining a high school diploma, a credential which a large and rising share of prime-aged native-born adult Americans has attained. A large proportion of immigrants, however, arrive in the United States with just a few years of secondary schooling and many possess less. Thus, for immigrants' offspring to move beyond their parents, graduation from high school often represents a major leap. However, the fact that low-skilled immigrants are employed at impressively high rates may mean that a failure to complete high school may not have equally negative effects for all. To examine this crucial passage, we begin by looking at the transition from school to work.

Youth, ages 16 to 20

School enrollment is lowest among first-generation Mexicans 16-20; only 40 percent of whom are in school (see Table 2). Going to school is much more common among all other first- and second-generation groups, with rates generally hovering either around or above the level for third-generation whites and substantially above the level for African Americans. Among the second generation, enrollment rates of persons originating in Europe, "the other Americas," and especially Asia compare favorably with the pattern for third-generation whites. Not surprisingly, all groups report lower full-time enrollment rates. Relative to whites, the Asian advantage in full-time enrollment rates is even greater than for enrollment of all types; whether one focuses on general or full-time enrollment rates, African Americans appear equally (and slightly) disadvantaged.

In general, individuals who leave school early suffer a greater risk of joblessness. Among third-generation whites, 71.4 percent of males and 65.1 percent of females report having a job (see Table 2, "Youth aged 16-20" panel). Overall, employment rates for out-of-school youth from most first- and second-generation groups fall below the level enjoyed by whites; the gap, however, is modest.

Table 2. Percentage Teenagers (Ages 16 to 20) in School by Nationality and Generation, 2000

Enrollment types	All	Full-time	All	Full-time
	First Generation		**Second Generation**	
Canada/Europe/Australia	72%	69%	72%	67%
Asia	77%	73%	79%	76%
Mexico	40%	35%	64%	57%
Other Americas	61%	56%	72%	68%
	Third Generation			
Whites	66%	62%		
African Americans	62%	59%		

Source: Current Population Survey March 1997-2003.

The group least likely to be in school, immigrant Mexicans, is also the group most likely to be at work: 81.3 percent of out-of-school men in this group hold a job. By contrast, out-of-school African Americans appear the least likely to have moved from school to a job: Whether male or female, less than half of African Americans out of school hold a job. Young African Americans are particularly disadvantaged, holding jobs at less than 60 percent of the rate for out-of-school whites.

Young adults, ages 21 to 25

As compared to their younger counterparts, adults aged 21 to 25 are far less likely to be enrolled in school. In this age range, just over a quarter of third-generation whites are in school (see Table 3). At this modest level, whites are outdistanced by a number of groups: Close to half of the Asian foreign born and second generation are still in school; enrollment rates for Europeans/Canadians, both first and second generation, as well as second-generation persons with origins in the "other Americas" compare favorably with the pattern displayed by whites. As young adulthood is also the prime age for migration (especially among the low-skilled), school enrollment is rare among Mexican immigrants; by contrast, enrollment among second-generation Mexicans falls just modestly below the level for whites. While rates of full-time enrollment are lower for all groups, whites lag behind first- and second-generation persons of

TABLE 3. PERCENTAGE YOUNG ADULTS (AGES 21 TO 25) IN SCHOOL BY NATIONALITY AND GENERATION, 2000

Enrollment types	All	Full-time		All	Full-time
	First Generation			Second Generation	
Canada/Europe/Australia	34.9%	28.8%		34.0%	27.9%
Asia	44.8%	38.8%		45.3%	36.8%
Mexico	7.3%	4.7%		24.4%	15.4%
Other Americas	22.4%	16.4%		38.8%	31.4%
	Third Generation				
Whites	27.2%	21.7%			
African Americans	22.7%	17.6%			

Source: Current Population Survey March 1997-2003.

European/Canadian and Asian origin, as well as second-generation young adults of origin in the "other Americas." For Mexican immigrants, however, the full-time enrollment rate is a fifth of the white level; the Mexican second generation does much better, but in comparison to whites, only three quarters as many Mexican American young adults are studying full-time.

Although youth is a period of protracted transition from school to work, the early adult years tend to yield stable job attachment. Overall, 83 percent of out-of-school young men and 71 percent of young women in this age range are working. Among men, Mexican immigrant men work at the highest rates of all (88.6 percent) (see Table 3, "Youth aged 21-25" panel). Job-holding rates among other foreign-born and second-generation individuals do not fully match up to that of white men (86.8 percent), though the gap ranges from a percentage point for European/Canadian foreign born to 10 percentage points for the second-generation "other Americas" men. A similar pattern holds true for women, with the notable exception being Mexicans: Whether first or second generation, their employment rate lags 34 and 10 percentage points, respectively, behind the employment rates of white women (76.6 percent). That disparity notwithstanding, Mexican female employment rates rise from 42.3 percent to 66.6 percent between the first and second generations.

Although the job-holding gap among African Americans ages 16-20 narrows in the 21 to 25 age range, African Americans remain at a great disadvantage.

African American men do particularly poorly, working at rates substantially below those of all other groups. African American women, by contrast, have employment rates roughly comparable to those of immigrant women from Asia and the "other Americas," as well as second-generation Mexican women.

As noted earlier, the bleaker social science view forecasts the emergence of a rainbow underclass scenario, in which the offspring of working-class immigrants fail to acquire the skills they need to get ahead and, if they drop out of school, to barely enter the labor force. As a result, they join a population locked out of the labor force on a long-term or, perhaps, even permanent basis. The patterns reviewed above provide little support for this pessimistic assessment. The group least likely to stay in school — Mexican immigrants — are also the most likely to be at work, a pattern that persists to older ages, as we shall see below. In all likelihood, the low enrollment rates capture the behavior of both Mexican-born, but US-raised youth, as well as young Mexican immigrants, who move right from Mexico into employment in the United States. For these young newcomers, as with older immigrants from Mexico, the strength and prevalence of networks connecting veteran settlers with newcomers provide relatively easy access to US workplaces, albeit at poorly paid jobs.

By contrast, we find that second-generation Mexican youth maintain enrollment patterns fairly close to whites' levels. To be sure, the fall-off in school enrollment is greater among young Mexican adults in the college-attending ages, with the full-time enrollment rate dropping noticeably. Nonetheless, out-of-school second-generation youth of Mexican origin tend to be working; young adults in their early 20s maintain employment rates close to the white level, suggesting that difficulties in securing employment experienced by the slightly younger group (aged 16 to 20) are a transitional phenomenon. The pattern among second-generation Mexican women, who are both advancing well beyond the schooling levels of the first generation and maintaining higher employment levels, is particularly striking. Thus, there is ample evidence of integration, though the sharp drop-off in school enrollment rates among young adults suggests that, whether male or female, relatively few young second-generation Mexican adults will complete college, a factor that will surely limit their ability to catch up with whites in terms of economic rewards.

Regarding the other first- and second-generation groups, caution needs be taken given the global nature of the categories used in this chapter. However, there is certainly no support for the notion of a rainbow underclass. The data for Asians, both foreign and native born, point in the direction of a very positive outcome, a pattern consistent with the findings of other studies.[5] The chief source of concern, rather, involves African Americans, and particularly men, for whom a "youth employment crisis" identified well over two decades ago does not seem to have abated. Moreover, employment difficulties experienced in the late teenage and early adult years prove more persistent than among all other groups, a pattern evident among prime-age adults as well.

THE WORKING-AGE POPULATION

This section focuses on adults between ages 25 and 65, with a particular focus on employment, wages, and non-monetary forms of compensation. As economic attainments are likely to be influenced by the skills that workers bring to the market, we begin by examining changes in both the absolute and relative levels of their education.

EDUCATIONAL LEVELS

A paradox of the new immigration patterns is that the influx of a large group of low-skilled workers occurs just as the American economy shifts to ever higher levels of skill intensity. Less-skilled workers have seen earnings growth stagnate as demand has shifted to workers with higher levels of education. Employment in manufacturing has also eroded as low-skilled production jobs have moved overseas. In the view of many researchers, the decline of manufacturing accounts for the persistent employment problems experienced by less-skilled African American men. At the same time, components of both the native and the immigrant labor force have engaged in substantial skill upgrading. The past three decades have witnessed a large growth in the size of the college-educated domestic population; likewise, significant numbers of highly skilled immigrants have entered the US economy. How second-generation Americans fit into this evolving skills structure will determine their access to employment and the jobs and compensation they attain.

As shown in Table 4, the relative size of the less-educated labor force has been in sharp decline for over 30 years. While 48.5 percent of all adults did not possess a high school degree in 1970, by 2004, only 12.1 percent had failed to finish high school. Although these declines are found among every group, there are considerable inter-group differences in educational progress.

---

5   See M. Zhou, "Contemporary Immigration and the Dynamics of Race and Ethnicity," pp. 200-242 in N. Smelser, W. J. Wilson, and F. Mitchell, eds., *America Becoming: Racial Trends and Their Consequences*. Volume I. Commission on Behavioral and Social Sciences and Education, National Research Council. Washington DC: National Academy Press, 2001.

TABLE 4. PERCENT WITH LESS THAN HIGH SCHOOL EDUCATION. ADULTS (AGES 25 TO 65) 1970, 2004

	1970	Difference from whites (1970)	2004	Difference from whites (2004)	Percent change from 1970
First Generation					
Canada/Europe/Australia	48.8	8.7	6.1	-0.4	-88
Asia	31.5	-8.6	9.5	3.0	-70
Mexico	81.2	41.1	58.0	51.5	-28
Other Americas	48.3	8.2	26.5	20.0	-45
Second Generation					
Canada/Europe/Australia	40.2	0.1	2.9	-3.6	-93
Asia	24.6	-15.5	3.6	-2.9	-85
Mexico	69.1	29.0	16.9	10.4	-76
Other Americas	31.6	-8.5	2.4	-4.2	-93
Third Generation					
Whites	40.1	-	6.5-	-	84
African Americans	65.5	25.5	12.1	5.6	-81
Total population	48.5	8.4	12.1	5.6	-75

Sources: 1970 IPUMS; 2004 March CPS.

Among immigrants, Mexicans have consistently been the least educated. In 1970, eight out of ten adult Mexican immigrants lacked a high school degree; in 2004, the proportion fell to just under six in ten (see Table 4). This gradual decline, however, was out of line with the shifts experienced by other groups. Thus, for Mexican immigrants, the education gap with whites and other groups actually grew. A somewhat different story holds true for the second-generation Mexican adults, who in 1970 were an overwhelmingly less-educated group. However, over time, they experienced a substantial educational upgrading, as the share of the Mexican second generation without a high school degree fell from 69 to 17 percent between 1970 and 2004.

The proportion of college-educated workers grew rapidly during the same period, though the rate of growth at the high end of the educational spectrum was

TABLE 5. PERCENT WITH A COLLEGE DEGREE, ADULTS (AGES 25 TO 65) 1970, 2004

	1970	Difference from whites (1970)	2004	Difference from whites (2004)	Percent change from 1970
First Generation					
Canada/Europe/Australia	10.9	-0.9	42.2	10.5	286
Asia	35.4	23.6	51.2	19.5	45
Mexico	2.2	-9.7	5.7	-26.0	166
Other Americas	12.1	0.3	21.2	-10.5	76
Second Generation					
Canada/Europe/Australia	12.2	0.4	42.6	10.9	251
Asia	16.2	4.4	57.4	25.7	256
Mexico	3.2	-8.6	14.1	-17.6	334
Other Americas	15.1	3.3	41.3	9.6	174
Third Generation					
Whites	11.8	-	31.7	-	169
African Americans	4.7	-7.1	17.8	-13.9	277
Total population	10.2	-1.6	29.8	-2.0	192

Sources: 1970 IPUMS, 2004 March CPS.

not as sharp as the rate of decline at the low end. In 1970, a college education (or higher) was relatively rare, possessed by one in ten adults; by 2004, it had become a good deal more commonplace, with about a third completing college (see Table 5).

Whites have consistently lagged behind a number of first- and second-generation groups. In 1970, the relatively small group of Asian immigrants residing in the United States already possessed a markedly high-skilled profile; by 2004, more than half of Asian-born adults had a college diploma. Even more notable is the shift among Asian second-generation adults, who already enjoyed a slight lead over whites in 1970, but are now almost twice as likely to have earned a college degree.

Groups that lagged in 1970 have made little progress toward reducing the gap. A college education was rare among Mexican immigrants in 1970. At the time, it was almost as scarce among African Americans and second-generation Mexican adults. A college education remained highly uncommon among Mexican immigrants throughout the intervening years; as a result, Mexican immigrants were just as disadvantaged at the turn of the 21st century as they had been three decades before. Levels of college education rose more rapidly among second-generation Mexicans and African Americans. Although the increasing educational attainment of these two groups narrowed the gap, it still left them well behind whites.

To sum, we find that the educational levels of the workforce have risen sharply over the past three decades. At the same time, the ranks of the least skilled immigrants, arriving with schooling levels far below the norm for any native group, have burgeoned. As noted, one can detect a change toward a better-educated migrant flow from Mexico, but the shift is so slight that the educational attainment gap separating Mexicans from whites has actually grown.

Other groups that were highly disadvantaged in 1970 — most notably the US-born offspring of Mexican immigrants and African Americans — have made considerable strides since then, as evidenced by a sharp fall-off in the proportion of persons lacking a high school degree. That progress, however, has not matched the rate of change among whites. Thus, although only a small minority of second-generation Mexicans and African Americans possess low levels of schooling, the share of those with less than a high school degree remains disproportionately large.

A college education is far more common in 2004 than it was in 1970, a statement that holds for almost all groups except Mexican immigrants. Compared to their parents, members of Mexican second-generation are more likely to possess a college degree; however, they still lag behind whites. Low levels of college completion are likely to translate into depressed earnings capacity among the Mexican second generation, to the extent that the economy continues to pay a premium for levels of schooling including college completion.

LABOR MARKET OUTCOMES

Employment provides the best gauge for assessing the contention that the offspring of today's working-class immigrants are likely to enter the ranks of a rainbow underclass. Although there are many ways to define the "underclass," William Julius Wilson's description of a world where "work has disappeared" captures the phenomenon's central trait.[6] In this section we compare rates of current employment as an indicator of labor force attachment. The sections that follow examine other kinds of labor market outcomes, namely, groups' earnings and health and pension coverage.

EMPLOYMENT

In the years since 1970, employment trends for men and women have followed two very different paths, with job-holding rates eroding modestly among men, while increasing substantially among women. In 1970, 87 percent of adult males were employed. By 2004, only 82 percent of men were holding a job. This overall shift closely corresponds to the trend among white men and among most first- and second-generation men (see Table 6). Paradoxically, given the economy's evolving structure of skilled work, the great exception to employment decline occurs among the one group — Mexican immigrant men — that should be most at risk of job loss. While Mexican immigrant men were less likely than white men to be employed in 1970, they have consistently become more likely to hold jobs (see Table 6). US-born men of Mexican origin have seen a slight erosion in job-holding, with employment rates always remaining just a few percentage points below the white level. The most severe decline in job-holding has occurred among African American men. Already a good deal less likely than whites to be employed in 1970, barely seven out of ten African American men were employed in 2004.

For women, the story is quite different: In 1970, 46 percent of adult women were working; by 2004, the figure stood at 68 percent. Employment rose among all groups, though the increase started from disparate beginnings and changed at varying rates. The sharpest gains were made by second-generation Mexican women: 38.8 percent were employed in 1970 and 70.2 percent in 2004 — essentially equivalent to white women (70.5 percent) (see Table 6). That pattern differs from the experience of Mexican immigrant women, among whom job-holding rates rose from very low levels recorded in 1970, but at such a slow pace that they fell further behind whites, in both absolute and relative terms. Unlike their male counterparts, African American women increased job-holding rates in the years after 1970; however, the pace of change was modest, with the result that employment rates, which earlier had exceeded those of white women, subsequently slipped below the white job-holding level by 2004.

This review of employment patterns finds little support for the view that the new second generation may be a rainbow underclass in the making. The

---

6 See W. J. Wilson, *When Work Disappears: The World of the New Urban Poor*, New York: Knopf, 1996.

TABLE 6. PERCENT EMPLOYMENT AMONG ADULTS IN THE LABOR FORCE BY GENERATION AND ORIGIN (AGES 25 TO 65), 1970 TO 2004

	1970	1980	1990	2000	2004
MEN					
First Generation					
Canada/Europe/Australia	88.7	87.9	83.6	84.5	83.4
Asia	87.8	83.4	85.0	84.4	86.4
Mexico	84.9	87.9	85.4	87.6	87.3
Other Americas	89.1	88.4	81.6	85.1	84.9
Africa	84.3	92.9	82.2	85.1	84.7
Second Generation					
Canada/Europe/Australia	90.0	81.8	79.6	81.2	82.6
Asia	93.6	90.0	88.8	84.0	83.6
Mexico	86.3	85.6	78.0	80.9	81.1
Other Americas	88.6	78.6	83.3	84.7	83.6
Third Generation					
Whites	89.1	87.8	86.7	85.0	83.2
African Americans	80.3	77.8	73.7	73.3	69.7
WOMEN					
First Generation					
Canada/Europe/Australia	43.9	52.6	59.0	62.9	62.9
Asia	47.4	56.7	60.7	63.4	62.6
Mexico	30.8	38.2	42.6	47.5	45.3
Other Americas	54.6	59.8	58.2	64.3	66.0
Africa	38.9	59.2	62.5	63.2	62.5
Second Generation					
Canada/Europe/Australia	46.2	52.2	60.4	69.1	69.9
Asia	58.5	62.0	68.4	74.3	68.3
Mexico	38.8	51.5	54.4	66.7	70.2
Other Americas	54.7	55.3	60.0	75.0	84.0
Third Generation					
Whites	43.8	57.3	68.1	71.5	70.5
African Americans	52.8	58.7	62.9	68.4	67.4

Sources: 1970 IPUMS; 1979 November CPS; 1989 November CPS; 1997-2003 March CPS; 2004 March CPS.

experience of second-generation Mexican women, in particular, is at odds with the predictions of this pessimistic scenario: Labor force attachment is far stronger in the second, as opposed to the first generation, yielding strong evidence of convergence, *not* divergence, with the dominant group. The trends among Mexican men differ, in part, because employment rates among the first generation are exceptionally high, an aspect probably intrinsic to the immigrant phenomenon itself and not likely to be reproduced by those who never undergo the migration experience. That being said, the employment rate of second-generation Mexican men is close to white men and diverges widely from that of African American men, among whom there is the weakest attachment to work.

THE TERMS OF COMPENSATION: MEDIAN EARNINGS

In 2000, median earnings for third-generation white men were close to $49,000, a figure that put them above most, but not all groups of men (see Figure 2). Second-generation Europeans/Canadians reported the highest earnings of all ($59,330), followed by first-generation members of the same group, and then second- and first-generation Asians, respectively. Mexican immigrants stand at the other end of the spectrum, earning half as much as whites; African Americans, with earnings two-thirds those of whites; and immigrants from the "other Americas," reporting earnings 68 percent of the white level. Second-generation Mexican men also lagged: with earnings 76 percent those of whites, they fall at the mid-point between first-generation Mexican and white men.

With a median salary of roughly $28,000, white women earned just over half as much as white men. They earned more than all the foreign-born groups but less than second-generation European/Canadian, Asian, and "other Americas" women. As with men, Mexican immigrant women earned less than all other groups and earned slightly more than half ($14,552) that of the level of white women. As compared to their male counterparts, second-generation Mexican women and African American women experienced a much smaller earnings gap.

The source of earnings disparity cannot only be linked to differing educational levels but to earnings within major educational categories. To simplify, we limit the following discussion to the contrast among first- and second-generation Mexican workers, African Americans, and third-generation whites. Higher levels of education yield higher earnings for all groups, whether among men or women. However, the impact of education varies by level received, as college completion (or continuation beyond college) boosts earnings more sharply than any other increment in schooling. Moreover, inter-group earnings disparities vary both by education and gender. Disparities are smallest for workers with the lowest levels of education but expand with higher levels of schooling. However, inter-group differences are consistently greater among men than among women.

FIGURE 2. MEDIAN YEARLY WAGE AND SALARY INCOME ($) OF WORKERS* BY GENERATION, ORIGIN, AND GENDER, 2000

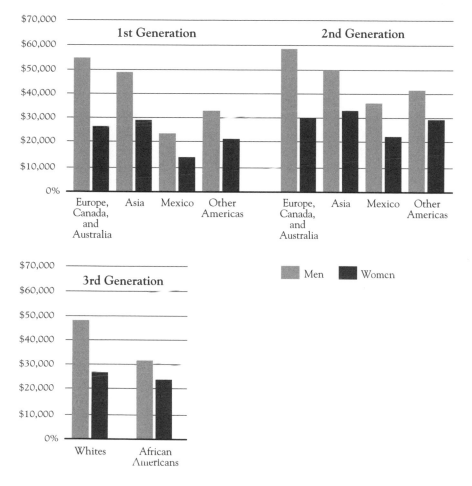

* Workers, ages 25 to 65, reporting positive wages

Source: Current Population Survey March 1997–2003.

FIGURE 3. PERCENT OF ADULTS WITH EMPLOYER-PROVIDED
HEALTHCARE COVERAGE, BY GENERATION AND ORIGIN, 2000

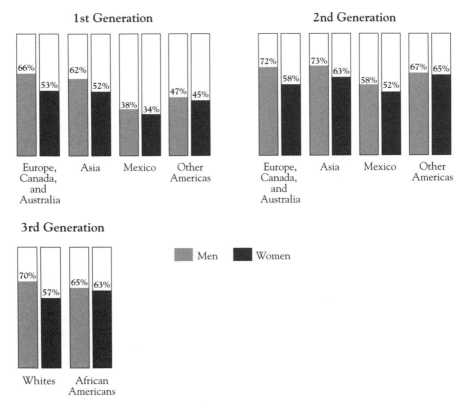

Source: Current Population Survey March 1997-2003.

Although more schooling has a positive effect on all groups, it does not affect
them uniformly. Mexican-born workers are poorly compensated for additional
skills acquired prior to migration. For Mexican immigrants, additional levels of
schooling tend to widen earnings disparities, with college completion having
only a limited positive effect. By contrast, each major increment in schooling
pushes the earnings of second-generation Mexican men upward. At all educational levels, second-generation Mexican workers earn more than their African
American counterparts, for whom college completion has a much weaker
impact for all groups except Mexican foreign-born workers.

THE TERMS OF COMPENSATION: BENEFITS

Fringe benefits — most notably pensions and health insurance — comprise a crucial dimension of job quality. In the United States, health and pension benefits are largely provided by employers.[7]

HEALTH INSURANCE

Seventy percent of white male workers receive some form of health coverage from their employer (see Figure 3). Other groups do better, most notably European/Canadian and Asian second-generation workers. Foreign-born workers, however, lag behind whites, with Mexican immigrants — only 35 percent of whom receive any form of health insurance — being the most disadvantaged. By contrast, 65 percent of African American men and close to 60 percent of second-generation Mexican men get health insurance from their employer.

Health insurance coverage is uniformly lower among women than among men for all groups but one: African American women. Close to two-thirds of African American women receive health coverage from their employers, a rate roughly equivalent to African American men and higher than white women (see Figure 3). Most second-generation women are also insured at higher rates than whites, with Mexican second-generation women being the exception. While employer-provided health coverage is much higher among second- versus first-generation Mexican women, low insurance levels for both may be related to the prevalence of employment within private households and other similar jobs.

Employer-provided health insurance usually entails partial premium coverage; only 19 percent of men and 15 percent of women workers have the entire cost paid by the employer. Among men, all immigrants (except those from Europe/Canada/Australia) are less likely than whites to receive full premiums. Mexican immigrants are particularly disadvantaged, having full premium coverage at half the rate received by whites. All second-generation groups do better than their first-generation counterparts. Thus, while second-generation Mexican men lag substantially behind whites, they do much better than Mexican-born men, enjoying full benefit coverage at roughly the rate of African American men.

---

7   Information on both health benefits and pension provision is collected in the CPS, though only from persons employed as wage and salaried workers; no comparable data are available for the self-employed. In the CPS, respondents are asked whether the employer provides a pension plan for any of the employers; those answering yes are then asked whether they are covered in the plan. Respondents are also asked whether they received health insurance, and if so, whether coverage extended to other family members and to what extent payments were made by the employer.

Table 7. Percent of Adults Included in Employer-Provided Pension Plan, by Generation and Origin, 2000

	Men	Women
First Generation		
Canada/Europe/Australia	47.2%	41.9%
Asia	43.3%	40.9%
Mexico	20.9%	19.6%
Other Americas	28.7%	29.7%
Second Generation		
Canada/Europe/Australia	58.3%	52.2%
Asia	53.6%	54.4%
Mexico	43.3%	43.9%
Other Americas	48.4%	45.5%
Third Generation		
Whites	56.4%	50.4%
African Americans	49.6%	48.1%

Source: Current Population Survey 1997-2003.

Pension benefits

Employers are more likely to provide health than pension benefits. About 58 percent of white males are covered by a pension; second-generation men of European/Canadian origin slightly exceed whites in pension coverage (see Table 7). Foreign-born men are all less likely than whites to be covered by a pension plan. Pension coverage is particularly low for Mexican immigrants — with their coverage being just over one third of the white rate. Pension coverage of US-born men of Mexican origin is twice as high as among foreign-born Mexicans, though it still lags well below the white rate.

Among women, second-generation Asian and European/Canadian workers are covered at higher rates than white women; all other groups are covered at lower rates. Mexican immigrant women are again highly disadvantaged, with just a fifth covered by an employer-provided plan.

Our review of earnings and fringe benefits indicates that low-skilled immigrant workers have surely found a place in America's economy, but they have done so at a price — namely, jobs that pay low wages and provide little in the way of non-monetary rewards. For Mexican immigrants, other factors seem to compound the disadvantages of being low skilled. Higher levels of schooling produce a smaller increase in rewards for Mexican immigrants than for other groups, although characteristics not measured here, such as English-language proficiency or years of work experience in the United States, may keep the returns on educational investment depressed.

Compared to immigrants, Mexican second-generation workers do better on several counts: They receive higher wages; they are less likely to work in the lowest paying jobs; they are more likely to hold jobs at higher ends of the earnings distribution; and their jobs are more likely to be accompanied by health and pension benefits. Additional increments in schooling yield substantial increases in earnings, in contrast to the Mexican foreign born. Still, although US-born workers of Mexican parentage are rewarded for college completion, college completion rates remain relatively low. Low completion rates are a powerful constraint on compensation, and all the more so in an era where college-educated workers are especially well-rewarded.

Another important finding is that second-generation Mexican women demonstrate the greatest inter-generational progress and convergence with the native white women. Compared to their Mexico-born counterparts, second-generation Mexican women have substantially higher earnings and health and pension coverage. Moreover, their job-holding rate is the same as that of whites.

While the prevalence of low-wage work among Mexican immigrants is troubling, the more dismaying evidence involves the levels of compensation earned by African American men, a disproportionate share of whom have no earnings at all. Though certainly better paid than Mexican immigrants, African American men still lag far behind whites. As with second-generation Mexican men, persistently low levels of education account for a good part of this gap. Nonetheless, college-educated African American men do consistently worse than their white counterparts.

CONCLUSION

Research on the "new" second generation has begun on a note of inflected pessimism. Concern for the prospects of the children of today's immigrants is certainly warranted. While low-skilled immigrants are moving to the United States in large numbers, they are entering an economy that provides little reward for workers with modest schooling, regardless of ethnicity. The cultural, linguistic, and legal challenges that the foreign born face impose a further penalty, adding to the difficulties that derive from low schooling. And although extensive migration networks connect immigrants — or at least immigrant men — to employers quickly, the social connections that generate attachment seem less able to produce the skill acquisition needed for occupational mobility. Mexican immigrants, the largest single group of poorly schooled newcomers, are members of the working poor, with limited access to jobs beyond the low-wage sector. Given these circumstances, can we expect that their US-born and US-raised children will make progress?

In the view of some researchers, the answer should be no. But this chapter finds little support for the point of view that the offspring of working-class immigrants will experience downward assimilation into a rainbow underclass. While second-generation Mexican men do not retain the extraordinary job-holding rates of the foreign-born generational groups, their employment rates approximate those of native-born whites. As the second generation is significantly better educated than the first, Mexican second-generation men find jobs associated with greater stability, significantly higher levels of pay, and much greater fringe benefit coverage.

Taking gender into account alters the picture still more. As shown in this chapter, the labor force behavior of Mexican immigrant men and women sharply diverges: Mexican immigrant women show much lower levels of labor force attachment than do their male counterparts. By contrast, the labor force behavior of US-born women of Mexican origin looks a good deal more like the pattern evident among native white women. Though a gap persists, the disparity is of greatly diminished proportions. As with their male counterparts, US-born women of Mexican parentage enjoy higher levels of schooling, which in turn generates more handsome economic rewards.

Moreover, pessimism about second-generation prospects is hard to reconcile with the socioeconomic diversity that is such a salient feature of contemporary immigration. While there are certainly large numbers of low-skilled immigrants, the situation still stands in contrast to the pattern of the last age of migration. At the turn of the 20th century, newcomers were largely concentrated at the bottom of the occupational distribution. Today, there is a substantial inflow of highly skilled immigrants, many of whom equal or exceed the attainments of native whites. The children of these immigrants are succeeding on all counts as well.

If a pessimistic assessment is not warranted, there are still ample grounds for concern. The progress of second-generation Mexican men and women exemplifies assimilation, but only if one defines it in absolute terms. Relative to the majority, that is to say, whites, a very substantial gap remains. Catching up will require continued schooling, indeed persistence through the college years; for many of the US-born offspring of Mexican immigrants, that achievement still seems far off. Enrollment patterns in the high school and college years clearly leave much to be desired. It is important to remember that second-generation Mexican drop-outs do find jobs, at rates very close to their counterparts among whites. The problem, however, is that whites are far more likely to remain enrolled; furthermore, while college completion rates have grown, the pace of change for the Mexican second generation is very modest. The consequences of the college completion gap might be different were the economy moving along a different path. But under current conditions, the best educated are the best rewarded, and to a much greater extent than was true when the offspring of the last great migration came of age. If today's second-generation adults are struggling to catch up, one also wonders how tomorrow's will manage; after all, these are the children of the immigrant working poor, for whom economic conditions certainly have not improved over the past 20 years. And their future cannot be of academic interest only, as demography ensures that the second generation will be a force not to be ignored.

PART II
THE CURRENT STATE OF RIGHTS AND SERVICES

CHAPTER 5

IMMIGRANT RIGHTS, INTEGRATION, AND THE COMMON GOOD

DONALD KERWIN

I. INTRODUCTION

The interplay between the "rights" and the "integration" of immigrants consti-
tutes a defining feature of the American experience. The United States has no
formal or coordinated immigrant integration policy, but it has nonetheless been
a nation where integration occurs. With some painful exceptions, immigrants
and their progeny have been able to become Americans. This has been due, in
part, to a constitutional framework that gives the federal government broad
power to regulate immigration, but that extends its core protections to all "persons," including noncitizens.

In recent years, the opposing sides in the immigration debate have miscon-
strued "rights" and "integration" and have pitted these concepts against each
other. Anti-immigrant groups argue that a growing litany of individual rights,
divorced from any sense of the "general welfare," threatens to balkanize the
nation. Immigrant advocates fear that notions like "assimilation" and "integration" reject the diverse cultural and social contributions of immigrants. This
paper posits a mutually re-enforcing view of "rights" and "integration" that
reflects our constitutional tradition, as well as the aspirations of immigrants. By
this view, "rights" entail civic responsibilities and further the "common good."
"Integration," in turns, demands a commitment to shared values, and an openness to the myriad contributions of immigrants.

In this chapter, the term "rights" refers to the rights guaranteed to "persons"
under the US Constitution. These "rights" can be distinguished from the
"privileges," "attributes" or "benefits" that may attach to noncitizens as
members of US society. The chapter argues that extending both "rights"
and membership privileges/attributes/benefits to noncitizens expedites
their integration.

The need to clarify the relationship between rights and integration has assumed overriding significance in recent years for two reasons. First, the US foreign-born population has grown to nearly 36 million persons.[1] These include roughly 13 million naturalized citizens, 12 million lawful permanent residents (LPRs), and 11 million undocumented persons.[2] The nation's immigrant population plays a central role in defining US institutions such as the family, the work place, schools, places of worship, and the armed forces. The success of these institutions — and the nation's welfare — will increasingly depend on the contributions of immigrants. Second, immigration and welfare reform legislation in 1996 sharply distinguished between US citizens and LPRs, making it far more difficult for immigrants and their families to integrate. The vision that underlies the 1996 legislation, subsequent federal and state legislation, and several pending "reform" proposals in Congress has been to make life so difficult for the undocumented and certain other immigrants in the United States that they will be forced to leave, and others will be deterred from coming. This chapter does not dispute the need to control US borders. It argues, however, that honoring "rights" — correctly understood — allows immigrants to integrate and to contribute fully to their adopted nation. Their integration, in turn, serves the national interest. The chapter concludes that "rights" must be incorporated into an immigrant integration agenda.

II. HISTORICAL BACKGROUND AND LEGAL FRAMEWORK

US citizenship notably, if inaccurately, has been defined as the "right to have rights."[3] In fact, constitutional rights apply not just to citizens but to "persons," a term that encompasses noncitizens. The US Constitution protects "the right of the people peaceably to assemble"; "the right of the people to be secure ... against unreasonable searches and seizures"; the right of any "person" not to be subject to double jeopardy, not to incriminate herself, not "to be deprived of life, liberty, or property, without due process of law," and not to have "property taken for public use, without just compensation"; the right to legal counsel and an impartial trial in criminal cases; the right of "any person" not to be deprived by a state of "life, liberty, or property, without due process;" and the right to "equal protection of the laws."[4] The application of these core protections to

---

1   J. Passel, "Estimates of the Size and Characteristics of the Undocumented Population" (Pew Hispanic Center, Mar. 21, 2005), p. 7 [hereinafter "Characteristics of the Undocumented"].

2   Ibid., pp. 1, 3; see also, A. Erlich and D. Dixon, "Spotlight on Naturalization Trends," Migration Information Source (*Migration Policy Institute*, Nov. 1, 2005).

3   *Perez v. Brownnell*, 356 US 44, 64 (1958) (Warren, Black, and Douglas dissenting).

4   US Const., amends. I, IV, V, VI, XIV, § 1.

noncitizens represents a fundamental form of "integration" in our constitutional system.[5]

At the same time, courts have consistently held that the political branches of the federal government enjoy "plenary" authority to regulate immigration. Not every restriction on *immigrants* implicates the federal *immigration* power that governs who can enter, who can stay, and who must leave. In addition, Congress and the Executive must exercise their authority over immigration in ways that reflect constitutional norms. Nonetheless, noncitizens have scant constitutional rights in immigration matters. Curiously, the US Constitution does not expressly delegate to Congress the power to regulate immigration.[6] Courts have instead located the federal government's power to regulate immigration in the nation's inherent power of self-determination or, put differently, as an incident of national sovereignty.

A. RIGHTS THAT APPLY TO "PERSONS"

For 120 years, US courts have recognized that noncitizens — as persons — enjoy a panoply of civil rights. In 1886, the Supreme Court in *Yick Wo v. Hopkins* invalidated a municipal ordinance that targeted Chinese aliens by making it unlawful to house a laundry business in a building not constructed of stone or brick.[7] It held that the Fourteenth Amendment applied "to all persons within the territorial jurisdiction, without regard to any differences of race, of color, or of nationality."[8] In *Wong Wing v. United States*, the Court considered the Chinese exclusion bill of 1892, which required imprisonment at hard labor of Chinese aliens prior to their deportation.[9] Citing *Yick Wo*, the court held that "all persons within the territory of the United States are entitled to the protection guaranteed" by the Fifth and Sixth Amendments, particularly the right to indictment by a grand jury and not to be "deprived of life, liberty, or property without due process of law."[10] More recently, courts have recognized

---

5   This chapter focuses on three categories of foreign-born persons: naturalized citizens, lawful permanent residents (known as "immigrants" under US law), and the undocumented. The Quota Act of 1921 (42 Stat 5) established the "immigrant" category and distinguished "immigrants" from those allowed to enter for a temporary period ("non-immigrants"). The chapter uses the term "immigrant" in its colloquial sense to refer to all foreign-born persons.

6   Congress can "regulate Commerce with foreign Nations, and among the Several States"; "establish an uniform Rule of Naturalization"; "declare War"; and make the "necessary and proper" laws to execute these powers. US Const., art. I, § 8, cls. 3, 4, 11, 18.

7   118 US 356, 6 S.Ct. 1064 (1886).

8   Ibid., p. 1070.

9   163 US 228 (1896).

10   Ibid., p. 238.

that freedom of speech and of the press extend to noncitizens;[11] that foreign corporations must receive just compensation for Fifth Amendment takings;[12] and that the undocumented must receive *Miranda* warnings prior to custodial interrogations.[13]

Education represents a core concern for immigrants who come in search of greater opportunity for themselves and their children. In *Plyler v. Doe*, the court held that undocumented children enjoy an equal protection right to free public education.[14] It reasoned that the "Fourteenth Amendment extends to anyone, citizen or stranger, who is subject to the laws of a State, and reaches into every corner of a State's territory."[15] It did not consider undocumented status a "constitutional irrelevancy," or education a "fundamental right."[16] However, it concluded that the statute imposed a "lifetime hardship on a discrete class of children not accountable for their disabling status" and would deny them "the ability to live within the structure of our civic institutions, and foreclose any realistic possibility that they will contribute in even the smallest way to the progress of our Nation."[17]

The right to pursue a livelihood also strongly resonates in the US constitutional tradition.[18] The Supreme Court has often re-enforced the comparative openness of the US labor market by invalidating alienage restrictions on employment. *Hampton v. Mow Sun Wong*, for example, involved a challenge to a federal regulation that denied competitive civil service jobs to noncitizens.[19] The court held that the regulation deprived "a discrete class of persons of an interest in liberty on a wholesale basis."[20] It found a due process viola-

---

11 *Bridges v. Wilson*, 326 US 135, 148 (1995).

12 *Russian Volunteer Fleet v. United States*, 282 US 481 (1931)

13 *United States v. Casimiro-Benitez*, 533 F.2d 1121, 1124 (9th Cir.), *cert denied*, 429 US 926 (1976); *United States v. Henry*, 604 F.2d 908, 914 (5th Cir. 1979).

14 457 US 202 (1982)

15 Ibid., p. 210, 215.

16 Ibid., p. 223.

17 Ibid.

18 See Thomas Jefferson, First Inaugural Address, Washington, D.C., March 4, 1801 ("... a wise and frugal Government, which shall restrain men from injuring one another; shall leave them otherwise free to regulate their own pursuits of industry and improvement; and shall not take from the mouth of labor the bread it has earned. This is the sum of good government, and this is necessary to close the circle of our felicities."); See also *Greene v. McElroy*, 360 US 474, 492 (1959) ("... the right to hold specific private employment and to follow a chosen profession free from unreasonable governmental interference comes within the 'liberty' and 'property' concepts of the Fifth Amendment [citations omitted].")

19 426 US 88 (1976)

20 Ibid., p. 103.

tion in the absence of any justification for the classification within the Civil Service Commission's area of authority.[21] In *Takahashi v. Fish and Game Commission*, the court held unconstitutional a California statute that denied commercial fishing licenses to noncitizens (primarily Japanese LPRs) who were ineligible for citizenship under federal law.[22] It held that the statute, in imposing "discriminatory burdens upon the entrance or residence of aliens," conflicted with the federal scheme for regulating immigration and violated the Fourteenth Amendment's protection of "all persons."[23] Likewise, in *Sugarman v. Dougall*, the court invalidated on equal protection grounds a New York state statute that limited "competitive" civil service jobs to US citizens.[24] The state argued that the positions needed to be filled by persons (citizens) with undivided loyalty to the state. The court reasoned that the New York scheme was not "precisely drawn" to meet this purpose. In particular, its "citizenship" requirement applied to relatively low-grade employees, but not to elected officials or high office holders.[25]

Conversely, the court has upheld citizenship requirements for jobs that are "bound up with the operation of the State as a governmental entity" and that are "fundamental to the definition and government of a State."[26] By this reasoning, certain government positions should be open only to those who fully identify with the polity. *Ambach v. Norwick* involved an equal protection challenge to a state statute that denied employment to elementary and secondary school teachers who were eligible for citizenship, but who did not intend to become US citizens. The court found that public school teachers performed a core government function and that the classification rationally furthered the state's educational goals.[27] The court has also upheld citizenship requirements for police[28] and probation officers.[29]

---

21 Ibid., p. 116.

22 334 US 410 (1948).

23 Ibid., pp. 419-420; See also *Truax v. Raich*, 239 US 33, 42 (1915) (An Arizona law requiring employers with more than five workers to employ at least 80 percent US citizens violates equal protection and is "tantamount to the assertion of the right to deny ... entrance and abode" in conflict with federal immigration authority.)

24 413 US 634 (1973).

25 Ibid., p. 643.

26 *Ambach v. Norwick*, 441 US 68, 73-75 (1979).

27 Ibid., pp. 79-81.

28 *Foley v. Connelie*, 435 US 291, 297 (1978) (holding that "the right to govern is reserved to citizens" and police "exercise an almost infinite variety" of public powers.)

29 *Cabell v. Chavez-Salido*, 454 US 432, 447 (1982) (A probation officer "may personify the State's sovereign powers; from the perspective of the larger community, the probation officer may symbolize the political community's control over, and thus responsibility for, those who have been found to have violated the norms of social order.")

Beyond issues relating to the hiring of immigrants, the Court has also addressed issues relating to their firing. In 2002, the Supreme Court weakened the statutory protections available to undocumented workers. In *Hoffman Plastics, Inc. v. NLRB*,[30] it held that undocumented persons who are illegally fired for union organizing cannot be awarded back pay, the strongest remedy for violations of the National Labor Relations Act (NLRA).[31]

The Constitution does not guarantee citizens (or noncitizens) a minimal standard of "social or economic" well-being.[32] However, it guards against discriminatory classifications *by states* in the provision of public benefits. In *Graham v. Richardson*, for example, the court invalidated a state statute that made welfare benefits available only to LPRs who had lived in the United States for 15 years or longer.[33] The court recognized LPRs as "persons" under the Fourteenth Amendment, characterizing them as a "prime example of a 'discrete and insular' minority" and strictly scrutinized this "inherently suspect" classification.[34] It found that the state's rationale (limiting expenses) did not justify the discriminatory classification.[35] It further held that by imposing an "auxiliary burden" on the entry and residence of select noncitizens, the state restriction conflicted with federal policy in an area of exclusive federal authority.[36] This holding, of course, did not speak to *federal* restrictions on public benefit eligibility.

B. THE PLENARY POWER OF CONGRESS AND THE EXECUTIVE TO REGULATE IMMIGRATION

While noncitizens possess rights in non-immigration matters, Congress has "plenary" authority to make laws (implemented by the executive) governing the admission and exclusion of noncitizens. The so-called plenary power doctrine has an unedifying provenance; it arose from challenges to the infamous Chinese exclusion bills of the late 19th century. In 1882, legislation suspended immigration by Chinese laborers for ten years, barred them from naturalization, and created a certificate of re-entry for those traveling outside the country. In

---

30 122 S. Ct. 1275 (2002).

31 29 USC §§ 151-169.

32 *Dandridge v. Williams*, 397 US 471, 487 (1970) ("[T]he intractable economic, social, and even philosophical problems presented by public welfare assistance programs are not the business of this Court.")

33 403 US 365 (1971).

34 Ibid., pp. 372, 376.

35 Ibid., p. 376.

36 Ibid., pp. 379-380.

1884, this certificate became the exclusive means to establish a "right of entry." In 1888, Congress barred entry to all Chinese laborers, whether or not they had obtained a certificate prior to their departure. In *Chae Chan Ping v. United States (The Chinese Exclusion Case)*, the court rejected a challenge to this legal regime, holding that the power to exclude was "an incident of every independent nation."[37] In 1892, legislation suspended Chinese immigration for another ten years and provided for the deportation of all unlawfully present Chinese laborers unless they could obtain a certificate of residence within a year, or could show that their failure to obtain a certificate had been unavoidable and that they were residents of the United States at the time of the act's passage, as attested to by at least one "credible white" witness. In *Fong Yue Ting v. United States*, the court upheld this scheme based on the "inherent and inalienable right" of a sovereign nation to regulate immigration.[38]

Roughly 60 years later, the court considered the cases of two noncitizens who had been excluded based on confidential determinations that their admission would prejudice the public interest. Ellen Knauff, the alien wife of a US citizen, had been detained for more than a year at Ellis Island after seeking admission to naturalize. The court held that her exclusion implicated a "fundamental act of sovereignty" inherent in the executive's power over foreign affairs.[39] It held that "[w]hatever the rule may be concerning deportation of persons who have gained entry into the United States, it is not within the province of any court, unless expressly authorized by law, to review the determination of the political branch of the Government to exclude a given alien" and "[w]hatever the procedure authorized by Congress, it is due process as far as an alien denied entry is concerned."[40] *Shaughnessy v. United States ex. rel. Mezei* concerned the exclusion and detention of the LPR spouse of a US citizen.[41] The court affirmed the "entry" doctrine by which constitutional rights apply to noncitizens who manage to enter the country, but not to those stopped at the border.[42]

In *Kleindienst v. Mandel*, the court considered a First Amendment challenge to the denial of admission to a Marxist author.[43] It held that the alien enjoyed "no constitutional rights of entry" and it refused to "look behind" a denial

---

37 130 US 581, 608-609 (1889).

38 149 US 698, 711 (1893).

39 *Knauff v. Shaughnessy*, 338 US 537, 542 (1950).

40 Ibid., pp. 543-544.

41 345 US 206 (1953).

42 Ibid., p. 210.

43 408 US 753 (1972).

made for a "facially legitimate and bona fide reason."[44] In *Fiallo v. Bell*, the court adopted this standard of review to reject a due process and equal protection challenge to a statute that granted special preference immigration status to the illegitimate children of US citizen and LPR mothers, but not fathers.[45] It found that the statutory distinction raised a policy issue "entrusted exclusively to the political branches."[46]

Courts have been loathe to invalidate federal classifications even when they (arguably) do not implicate the federal power to regulate immigration. In *Matthews v. Diaz*, for example, the court upheld the denial of Medicare benefits to LPRs who had lived in the United States for less than five years.[47] It recognized that even "one whose presence is unlawful, involuntary, or transitory" enjoys due process protections, but found that the statute's alienage restrictions implicated the federal authority "to regulate the conditions of entry and residence of aliens."[48] It noted that Congress "regularly makes rules that would be unacceptable if applied to citizens" and the fact "that all persons, aliens and citizens alike, are protected by the Due Process Clause does not lead to the further conclusion that all aliens enjoy all the advantages of citizenship..."[49] In its treatment of federal benefit restrictions as an acceptable "immigration" enforcement tool, the court anticipated welfare reform legislation in 1996.

C. Limits on the Plenary Power Doctrine

The federal government possesses broad authority to regulate the admission, exclusion, and removal of immigrants. However, it must exercise this power — including in its use of detention — in a way that reflects constitutional norms. In *Zadvydas v. Davis*, the court considered the situation of "lifers," noncitizen detainees who have been ordered removed (deported) but whose countries will not accept their repatriation.[50] The Immigration and Nationality Act (INA) provides that aliens ordered removed "may be detained" past 90 days if they represent a flight risk or a danger.[51] The court construed this language to allow detention for "a period reasonably necessary"

---

44 Ibid., p. 770.

45 430 US 787 (1977).

46 Ibid., p. 798.

47 426 US 67 (1976).

48 Ibid., pp. 77, 84.

49 Ibid., pp. 78-80.

50 533 US 678 (2001).

51 INA § 241(a)(6).

to execute the removal.[52] It found six months (following a removal order) to be a "presumptively reasonable period of detention."[53] Deciding the case on statutory grounds in order to avoid finding it unconstitutional,[54] the court reasoned that indefinite detention would be a constitutionally impermissible way to implement the federal government's immigration authority.[55] In *Clark v. Martinez*, the court extended this statutory interpretation to "inadmissible" persons who had not effected an "entry."[56]

III. Legislation Restricting Rights and Limiting Membership Claims

Immigrants who become citizens enjoy the full rights and responsibilities of membership in our constitutional democracy.[57] By contrast, LPRs cannot vote in federal or state elections, cannot hold certain public offices, and can be removed for a growing range of offenses. In other ways, however, LPRs have traditionally enjoyed the non-political rights (attributes/benefits) of US citizens. They have worked, attended public schools, raised families, participated in government programs, and served in the armed forces. Immigration and welfare reform legislation in 1996 altered this paradigm, making citizenship a far more significant criteria for public benefit eligibility, and benefits themselves more difficult to obtain. The legislation has particularly hurt families whose members have different immigration statuses.[58]

The Personal Responsibility and Work Opportunity Reconciliation Act of 1996 (PRWORA) sharply distinguished between US citizens and LPRs.[59] The law's scheme, which uses public benefit restrictions as a means of immigration control, has survived legal challenge. Prior to PRWORA, citizens and LPRs had mostly qualified on equal terms for federal benefits, and state attempts to restrict

---

52 533 US, p. 699.

53 Ibid., p. 701.

54 Ibid., pp. 689-690.

55 Ibid., p. 695.

56 543 US 371 (2005).

57 Two main distinctions also exist between native-born and naturalized citizens. First, under the US Constitution (art. II, § 1, cl. 5), only a "natural born" citizen can serve as president of the United States. Second, naturalized citizens can be denaturalized in limited circumstances. INA §1451.

58 More than three million US-born children live in households headed by undocumented persons. "Characteristics of the Undocumented," p. 3.

59 Pub. L. No. 104-193, 110 Stat. 2105.

eligibility had been invalidated. PRWORA limited eligibility for "federal public benefits" to US citizens and "qualified aliens," a category that includes LPRs and others.[60] It barred even "qualified aliens" from Supplemental Security Income (SSI) and food stamps, with an exception for LPRs who had completed 40 "qualifying quarters" of work for the purposes of Social Security coverage,[61] and for two other groups.[62] It gave states the option to provide Temporary Assistance to Needy Families (TANF), Medicaid, and State Children's Health Insurance Program (SCHIP) benefits to "qualified aliens."[63] Every state subsequently opted to provide TANF and (with the exception of Wyoming) Medicaid to "qualified aliens" who had arrived by PRWORA's passage.

PRWORA, however, barred even "qualified aliens" from "means-tested" federal benefits — SSI, TANF, food stamps (non-emergency), Medicaid, and SCHIP — for five years after "entry."[64] It also provided for "sponsor-to-immigrant" deeming (i.e., attribution of the sponsor's income to the immigrant for the purposes of determining benefit eligibility), which disqualifies many LPRs from these means-tested benefits after five years.[65] In addition, several states have chosen to deny TANF and Medicaid to post-enactment immigrants who have met the five-year requirement.

PRWORA barred "unqualified" immigrants (including the undocumented) from "federal public benefit" programs. The undocumented qualify only for limited emergency and public health benefits, including emergency Medicaid, non-cash disaster relief, immunizations, and school lunches.[66] PRWORA required states to enact laws if they intended to extend public benefits to the undocumented.[67]

Since passage of PRWORA, some benefits have been restored to certain groups. For example, Congress has restored: (1) SSI to most LPRs who resided

---

60 The term "qualified alien" refers to LPRs, asylees, refugees, parolees for periods of at least one year, those granted withholding of deportation, and conditional entrants. Welfare Act § 431.

61 Welfare Act § 402(a)(2)(B).

62 The two other groups of eligible non-citizens were: (1) refugees, asylees, and persons granted withholding of deportation, for the first five years after entry as a refugee or after the grant of asylum or withholding; (2) lawfully residing active duty military and veterans, as well as their spouses and unmarried, dependent children. Welfare Act §402(a)(2)(A), (C).

63 Welfare Act §402(b)(1).

64 Welfare Act §403(a).

65 Welfare Act §421(a). "Qualified aliens" exempt from the five-year bar include refugees, asylees, those granted withholding of deportation; lawfully residing veterans, active duty military, and their spouses and depend children; and Cuban and Haitian entrants. Welfare Act §§403(b), (d).

66 Welfare Act §§ 401(b)(1), 411(b).

67 Welfare Act § 411(d).

in the United States prior to PRWORA's passage;[68] (2) food stamps to immigrant children, the elderly, and the disabled who entered pre-enactment;[69] (3) food stamps to "qualified aliens" receiving disability assistance, persons who have been "qualified" for five years or more, and children.[70] Despite the ameliorating legislation, the basic architecture of PRWORA — the hard distinction between US citizens and LPRs — remains intact.

The Illegal Immigration Reform and Immigrant Responsibility Act of 1996 (the 1996 Immigration Act or IIRIRA) created a web of restrictions that inhibits the integration of large numbers of immigrants and their families.[71] Thus, the law works at cross purposes to family reunification, a defining priority of the US legal immigration system.[72] It also conflicts with jurisprudence that, in other contexts, recognizes the right to live with family.[73] Finally, IIRIRA fails to reflect the growing population of US "mixed status" families, and the deep ties to the United States that noncitizens develop over time.

The 1996 Immigration Act has undermined families in three ways.[74] First, it significantly expanded the crimes for which LPRs could be removed. At the same time, it sharply limited and, in many cases, removed discretion from immigration judges to allow removable persons to remain in the United States based on the severity of their crimes, rehabilitation, family ties, employment, and other equities. As a result, thousands of long-term LPRs have been removed for relatively minor crimes that they committed years in the past, with disastrous consequences for their families. Second, IIRIRA made it more difficult for low-income US citizens and LPRs to sponsor family members for visas. It required the petitioner/sponsor to demonstrate "the means to maintain" an income (for the family) of 125 percent of the federal poverty line and

---

68 The Balanced Budget Act of 1997, Pub. L. No. 105-33, 111 Stat. 251 (Aug. 5, 1997).

69 Agriculture Research, Extension and Education Reform Act, Pub. L. No. 105-185 (June 23, 1998), §§ 4401 (May 13, 2002). This act also extended refugee eligibility for Food Stamps from five to seven years.

70 The Farm Security and Rural Investment Act, Pub. L. No. 107-171, §4401 (May 13, 2002).

71 Pub. L. No. 104-208, 110 Stat. 3009.

72 The most common path to lawful permanent residence — responsible for 65 percent of the immigrant visas awarded — is through a qualifying relationship to a US citizen or LPR. US Department of Homeland Security, Office of Immigration Statistics, "2004 Yearbook of Immigration Statistics," Table 7, available at http://uscis.gov/graphics/shared/statistics/yearbook/.

73 Lassiter v. Department of Social Services of Durham County, North Carolina, 452 US 18, 27 (1981); see also, The Universal Declaration of Human Rights, Art. 16(3) ("The family is the natural and fundamental group unit of society and is entitled to protection by society and the State.")

74 See Catholic Legal Immigration Network, Inc., Placing Immigrants at Risk: The Impact of our Laws and Policies on American Families (2000); American Bar Association, Commission on Immigration, American Justice through Immigrants' Eyes (2004).

to maintain the immigrant at that level until he or she naturalizes or works for 40 "qualifying quarters."[75] This commitment can be legally enforced against the sponsor by the sponsored alien or the federal or state government.[76] Even with the ability to secure co-sponsors, 20 percent of US citizens and LPRs who come to charitable agencies to bring in family members cannot meet the income requirement.[77] In other cases, they must stagger the immigration of family members over many years. Third, IIRIRA created a series of multi-year and permanent bars to admission based on unlawful presence in the country, removals, misrepresentations to immigration officials, and claims (even mistaken) to citizenship. These bars make it impossible for thousands of noncitizens to gain legal status.

The 1996 Immigration Act also barred states from providing in-state tuition to in-state, undocumented residents for post-secondary education.[78] The bars have limited the opportunities of low-income students, many of whom were brought to the United States as children and who are, for all intents and purposes, Americans.

Immigrant families who are not affected by the myriad provisions in the 1996 Immigration Act still encounter multi-year backlogs in the family-based immigration system. These result from numerical caps on visas granted by qualifying relationship ("preference category") and by nationality. DHS processing periods further lengthen the backlogs. Affected families either face long-term separation or they remain together (but unsettled and insecure) in the United States. Backlogs and delays inhibit integration not only by destabilizing families, but also by delaying the naturalization process that serves as a focal point for such "integration" activities as English-language classes, civics instruction, and access to many public sector jobs.

The driving vision behind many post-1996 legislative proposals has been to make it so burdensome to remain that certain noncitizens — particularly the undocumented — will be forced to leave.[79] It has long been a crime to enter the United States illegally. However, legislation proposed in 2005, the Border

---

75 INA §§ 213A(a)(1)(A), 213A(a)(2)-(3), 213A(f)(1)(E).

76 INA § 213A(a)(1)B; see also, C. Wheeler, "Alien vs. Sponsor: Legal Enforceability of the Affidavit of Support," 10 *Bender's Immigration Bulletin* No. 23 (Dec. 1, 2005).

77 Catholic Legal Immigration Network, Inc., *The Affidavit of Support and Its Effect on Low-Income Families* (Aug. 2000), p. 13.

78 8 INA §1623(a).

79 State legislation that targets immigrants has also proliferated. N. Riccardi, "States Take on Border Issues," *Los Angeles Times* (Jan. 16, 2006).

and Immigration Enforcement Act of 2005, would make it a federal crime to be in the United States in undocumented status. Most agree that it would be preclusively expensive (by one estimate it would cost $206 billion over five years[80]) to remove the nation's 11 undocumented persons: Their removal would also impoverish millions of families and devastate the economy.[81] Criminal prosecution for illegal presence seems even less feasible. Similarly, the REAL ID Act of 2005 seeks to compel states to deny drivers' licenses to the undocumented for security reasons.[82] The law will make life harsher for the undocumented and will lead to more drivers without licenses and insurance. Further, it is unlikely that the REAL ID Act will enhance US security as it will remove noncitizens from databases used by police throughout the country and drive them further outside the government's reach.

IV. Conclusion

The US immigration debate has reached a crossroad. Immigration "reform" legislation could extend legal status to broad categories of undocumented persons, it could further push the undocumented (and other noncitizens) to the nation's margins, or it could seek to put some limited percentage of the undocumented on a path to citizenship but make life even more tenuous for others. As it stands, immigrants (including the undocumented) enjoy significant rights in non-immigration matters, including the right to secondary education. On the other hand, the undocumented cannot legally work, and large categories of LPRs can be separated from their families through deportation.

While we cannot know the final shape of immigration reform, we can at least clarify the terms of the debate and the interests at stake. Up to this point, "rights" language has not offered a productive framework for evaluating the underlying issues. To the contrary, the immigration debate exemplifies how claims of competing "rights" can stymie public discourse.[83] Advocates argue

---

80 R. Goyle and D. A. Jaegar, PhD, "Deporting the Undocumented: A Cost Assessment" (Center for American Progress, July 2005).

81 The foreign born represent 15 percent of the US workforce. US Department of Labor, Bureau of Labor Statistics, "Labor Force Characteristics of Foreign-Born Workers in 2004) (May 12, 2005). Roughly one-third of these workers — 5 percent of all US workers — do not have legal status. "Characteristics of the Undocumented," p. 4.

82 Pub. L. No. 109-13, 119 Stat. 231.

83 See M. A. Glendon, *Rights Talk* (Free Press, 1991), pp. 12, 14 (Glendon argues that in the United States "rights" tend to be formulated in absolute and individual terms, without reference to "ends" or to responsibilities.)

that US immigration laws offend the right to family reunification, to make a living, and to just working conditions. Yet many US residents, particularly in border states, maintain that migrants violate their rights to security and to property. Some employers think that their right to earn a living is compromised by immigration policies that prevent them from hiring willing (immigrant) workers. Some US citizens think that immigrant laborers undermine their right to just wages and working conditions. Many immigrants believe that they have a right to live with their families in the United States. Others think that undocumented persons, even those approved for family-based visas, violate the rights of those who obey the law by remaining outside the country until they can legally enter.

If they are to become an effective policy tool, "rights" need to be conceptualized differently. Too often, claimed "rights" mask desired social outcomes, but do not closely relate to the kind of self-evident values or "inalienable rights" such as "life, liberty, and the pursuit of happiness" that undergird our constitutional democracy.[84] Not every position claimed as a "right" amounts to one.

At the same time, extending to noncitizens certain "privileges," "attributes," or "benefits" of membership in US society contributes to their integration and to the common good. As a practical matter, for example, when immigrants can access health insurance, it benefits public health efforts, decreases the inefficient and expensive use of emergency rooms, and helps to maintain a strong workforce. Provision of certain benefits to particularly needy noncitizens — the very poor, the disabled, the elderly, the infirm — allows them simply to function, a minimal pre-condition to integration. The application of labor and workplace protection laws to immigrants prevents unscrupulous employers from using them to depress wages and standards for all workers. The education of immigrant children trains them to contribute to their adopted country. A viable path to legal status preserves families, strengthens the US workforce, decreases predation against noncitizens, and enhances security. Providing legal counsel to persons in removal proceedings furthers our nation's interest in having the best decisions made under its laws.

Rights and "benefits" also foster the participation of immigrants in mediating institutions — like families, places of worship, schools, workplaces, and labor unions — that promote their integration. These institutions impart practical

---

84 See L. Henkin, "The Idea of Rights and the United States Constitution," *The Age of Reason* (1990), pp. 83-97, reprinted in L. Henkin, G. Neuman, D. Orentlicher, D. Leebron, *Human Rights* (Foundation Press, 1999) (arguing that the Declaration of Independence sets forth the underlying "theory of American constitutionalism").

skills (language and job training) and civic values (consensus building, tolerance, and participation). They instill a sense of belonging, of support, and of the ability to influence the larger community. Conversely, the process of "integration" vindicates rights on a fundamental level. "Rights" theories typically view humans as "social" beings, whether by nature (in religious traditions) or by social necessity (in state traditions). For this reason, exclusion from institutions like family, school, the work place, or the polity offends human rights. Similarly, since human identity finds expression in culture, the "integration" process must be able to accommodate the cultural contributions of immigrants. A process that attempted to bring persons into the national community, but that denied or erased what contributed to their personhood, would necessarily violate their rights and could not be viewed as integration at all.

One might argue that rights not only allow immigrants to integrate, but in a nation created to protect them, rights are the "good" that is "common" to all of us. In *Plyler v. Doe*, the court recognized that without rights, immigrants cannot integrate or contribute fully to the common good:

> It is difficult to understand precisely what the State hopes to achieve by promoting the creation and perpetuation of a subclass of illiterates within our boundaries, surely adding to the problems and costs of unemployment, welfare, and crime. It is thus clear that whatever savings might be achieved by denying these children an education, they are wholly insubstantial in light of the costs involved to these children, the State, and the Nation.[85]

Immigrants aspire to be treated as full members of US society. For them, this means embracing US political and civic values, without forfeiting their cultural identities. It also means contributing to their adopted countries through their labor, industry, values, families, and faith. They may not use terms like rights, integration, or the common good. However, their lives and aspirations testify to the interconnectedness of these concepts. An immigrant integration agenda would do well to honor their vision.

---

85 *Plyler v. Doe*, 457 US, p. 230.

CHAPTER 6

FEDERAL SPENDING ON IMMIGRANT FAMILIES' INTEGRATION

JULIA GELATT AND MICHAEL FIX

INTRODUCTION[1]

As the country works toward a revised immigration system and public attention is increasingly drawn to immigration enforcement and entry for workers, much less interest has focused on the country's integration programs. Indeed, immigrant integration in the United States is approached in a laissez faire fashion, especially at the federal level, as most integration work falls to state and local governments or to nongovernmental social service groups.

However, several federal programs do form a patchwork system of immigrant integration services, including educational services targeted at immigrant children and families; health and education services targeted to migrant workers; and job training, health, and other services for refugees and asylees.

In this chapter we explore the limited set of federal programs and expenditures that are expressly targeted to populations wholly or largely composed of migrants and/or their families. We then briefly discuss the federal spending that takes place within the context of mainstream programs that may serve immigrants, but were not specifically created for them.[2] (An example is the Title I education program for the disadvantaged, now folded into the No Child Left Behind Act.) Despite its importance, we do not tackle private foundation spending dedicated to newcomers.

---

1 This chapter provides an update to Section VI, "What Does the Federal Government Spend on Immigrant Family Integration," pp. 43 to 52 in M. Fix, W. Zimmerman, and J. Passel, "The Integration of Immigrant Families in the United States" (Washington, DC: Urban Institute, July 2001).

2 We exclude spending on what are termed general goods such as roads, the military, and the like, despite the fact that immigrants capture a share of the benefits generated.

TABLE 1. TARGETED FEDERAL SPENDING ON IMMIGRANTS 1999 AND 2005, IN MILLIONS OF 2005 DOLLARS

	FY 1999 Spending	FY 2005 Spending	% Change 1999 to 2005
Refugee Resettlement Program	$ 545	$ 470	-13.8%
Migrant Head Start	$ 209	$ 266	27.3%
Migrant Education	$ 421	$ 390	-7.4%
Migrant Education Even Start	$ 5	$ 8	60.0%
Migrant Health	$ 92	$ 144	56.5%
NCLB Language Acquisition State Grants	-	$ 673	-
EIEP (Emergency Immigrant Education Program)	$ 176	-	-
Federal Bilingual Education	$ 273	-	-
Adult ESL*	$ 207	$ 277	33.8%
USCIS Office of Citizenship	-	$ 3	-
Emergency Health Care for Unauthorized Immigrants	-	$ 250	-
Total	**$ 1,928**	**$ 2,481**	**28.7%**

* *Note:* We assume here that expenditures on Adult ESL are proportional to shares that ESL recipients represent of total Adult Basic Education participants in the closest year for which data is available. For FY 1999, we use data from the 1997-1998 school year.

FEDERAL PROGRAMS

The major targeted immigrant policy programs are set out in Table 1. Although this list of programs is not comprehensive, it does reflect the principal congressional initiatives that have been deliberately designed to help immigrants and their communities. Viewed collectively, at least four points can be made about these targeted programs. First, they were created in an ad hoc manner over the years, and not surprisingly, they fall short of constituting a coherent integration agenda for immigrant families. Second, total funding for the programs (roughly $2.6 billion in fiscal year [FY] 2004) can be viewed as modest at best, since the 35 million immigrants in the United States now represent more than 12 percent of the nation's population. Indeed, $2.6 billion is substantially less than

Figure I. Federal Refugee Resettlement Program Spending and Refugee Admissions, FY 1984 to 2004

IN MILLIONS OF 2005 DOLLARS

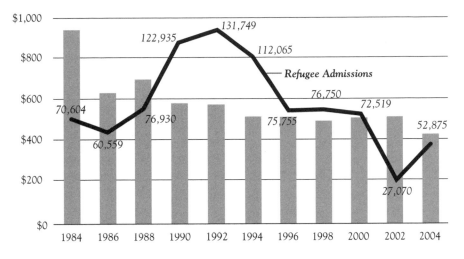

Note: Although asylees, Cuban and Haitian entrants, certain Americans, and Victims of Severe Forms of Trafficking are also eligible for assistance under the Refugee Resettlement Program, the Department of Health and Human Service reports that refugees are the main beneficiaries of the program. Therefore, we only include refugee data in our figures.

Sources: US Federal Budget, Appendix, Department of Health and Human Services, 1984-2006; Office of Refugee Resettlement, Annual Report to Congress, 2002.

the $4 billion in aid provided to states to offset service costs associated with legalizing 2.8 million immigrants following the 1986 Immigration Reform and Control Act's passage.[3] Third, while generally small in scale, spending on many of these programs has grown quite slowly, or stagnated, since 2000 after increasing in the late 1990s. Finally, a significant share of spending is directed at comparatively small migrant populations: refugees and migrant workers.

---

3   The State Legalization Impact Assistance Grant (SLIAG) program was created to help states offset the costs of providing services to immigrants newly legalized under the 1986 Immigration Reform and Control Act. The program ended in 1995, but provides some lessons for the design of impact aid programs. Strict requirements for documenting spending by individual legalized immigrants proved extremely cumbersome and led to significant delays in state reimbursement and to some unspent funds, despite continued federal deferrals.

Assistance to Refugees

The only reasonably comprehensive federal integration program is targeted at refugees and asylees found to be fleeing persecution. Funds are intended to assist with the adjustment of these persons to the United States and their settlement in new communities. The refugee resettlement program provides refugees and those granted asylum in the United States short-term cash and medical assistance, employment and other skills training, job placement, language instruction, and assistance for victims of torture. While the program is

TABLE 2. FEDERAL FUNDING FOR MIGRANT EDUCATION PROGRAMS: 1990 TO 2005

Fiscal Year	Federal Spending (millions of 2005 dollars)	Participating Students	Spending per Student (in 2005 dollars)
1990	$426	411,700	$1,036
1991	428	437,363	979
1992	434	531,841	816
1993	410	548,163	748
1994	403	609,916	660
1995	395	686,667	576
1996	384	564,048	681
1997	376	580,664	647
1998	370	621,464	595
1999	421	682,090	617
2000	407	685,536	594
2001	424	737,684	575
2002	435		
2003	424		
2004	412		
2005	390		

Note: Participant counts are unduplicated within states but are duplicated at the national level because each state counts and reports participants as they migrate across the country. Therefore, these data may represent overcounts of the number of participants receiving MEP services nationally.

Sources: CRS Report for Congress, "The Federal Migrant Education Program: An Overview"; US Department of Education budget documents (1999-2000); US Department of Education, FY 2001 Appropriations Table; US Department of Education, "Funding Status"; US Department of Education, "Title I Migrant Education Program Trends Summary Report: 1998-2001," 2004, http://www.ed.gov/rschstat/eval/disadv/migrant/final00.doc.

federally run, most services are provided by states and private voluntary resettlement agencies.

Funding:

- In constant dollars, spending on refugee resettlement has decreased over time, falling from $943 million in FY 1984 to $429 million in FY 2004, while the number of refugees has fluctuated over time with 70,604 admitted in 1984 and 52,875 in 2004. (See Figure 1)

- Spending per refugee admitted decreased greatly from the mid-1980s to mid-1990s, falling 65 percent from $13,361 in FY 1984 to $4,628 in FY 1994.

Since 1994, spending per refugee has increased, particularly as refugee admissions dropped dramatically following the terrorist attacks on September 11, 2001. Spending per refugee increased 75 percent from $4,628 in FY 1994 to $8,111 in FY 2004.

ASSISTANCE TO MIGRANT WORKERS AND THEIR FAMILIES

The set of federal programs in health, education, and workforce training directed at migrant workers and their families can be viewed as substantial elements of federal integration policy. The migrant workforce has changed in recent decades from being predominately native born to predominately foreign born. According to the most recent National Agricultural Workers' Survey (NAWS), almost four out of five of all hired agricultural workers were foreign born.[4]

MIGRANT EDUCATION

The Migrant Education Program aims to meet the educational needs of children in migrant families.[5] The program includes both education and support

---

4   US Department of Labor, Office of the Assistant Secretary for Policy, Office of Programmatic Policy, "Findings from the National Agricultural Workers Survey (NAWS) 2001 - 2002. "A Demographic and Employment Profile of United States Farm Workers." Research Report No. 9, March 2005, http://www.doleta.gov/agworker/report9/toc.cfm.

5   Migrant children are defined as "children of migratory workers who have, within the last 36 months, moved across school district boundaries in order to obtain temporary or seasonal employment in agriculture or fishing." US Department of Education, *Policy and Program Studies Service Report Highlights, Title I Migrant Education Program* (2004), http://www.ed.gov/rschstat/eval/disadv/migrant/highlights01.doc. Since the late 1980s, the program has focused attention on employees in agricultural jobs with high turnover rates. Children of immigrants who worked in industries such as meat processing with a worker turnover rater of 60 percent annually over 18 months became eligible for the Migrant Education Program. P. Martin and D. Martin, *The Endless Quest: Helping America's Farm Workers* (Boulder, CO: Westview Press, 1994).

services such as social work and health. Services are delivered by schools, school districts, and/or public or private community organizations.

Between the 1989-1990 and 2000-2001 school years, the number of students participating in Migrant Education programs grew 79 percent from 411,700 to 737,684 children. Over half of participating children in 2000-2001 were served in California, Texas, and Florida.

Funding:

■ Funding for Migrant Education has remained at approximately the same level since 1990. However, because the number of students participating in Migrant Education-funded programs has grown, spending per student fell from $1,036 in FY 1990 to $575 in FY 2001. (See Table 2)

■ Although funding was relatively steady, appropriations (in 2005 dollars) declined slowly from $426 million to $370 million between FY 1990 and 1998, then increased to above $400 million per year each year between FY 1999 and 2004.

■ Appropriations for FY 2005 were $390 million.

MIGRANT HEAD START

Migrant Head Start is a special initiative of the broader national Head Start program. Head Start is a child development program that serves pregnant women, children from birth to age five, and families, providing education, health services, and social services. The program aims to prepare low-income children for entry into school. Services are provided by public agencies, private organizations, and school systems. Eligibility for Head Start is based on income at or below the federal poverty line, while Migrant Head Start serves families that earn more than half their annual income from agricultural work and move at least once in each two-year period in search of work. Migrant Head Start concentrates on providing child care for young children, so they will not have to be cared for in the field or by siblings.

Funding:

■ Funding for Migrant Head Start increased steadily throughout the late 1990s, and into the first years of the new century. However, after FY 2002, appropriations decreased from $280 million to $266 million in FY 2005. (See Table 3)

Migrant Education Even Start

Even Start is a small, national program aimed at teaching children to read by offering reading education to both children and parents and offering parenting classes. The program provides federal funds matched by state and local dollars and often supplemented by private grants, and is run by schools and/or non-profit organizations. Migrant Even Start serves families that meet the definition of a migratory worker used for Migrant Education. Legislation mandates that Migrant Education Even Start receive a percentage set aside from the total Even Start program (along with Native American Even Start); Migrant Education Even Start has received either 3 or 3.5 percent of total funding each year since 1990.

The Even Start program as a whole was singled out by President Bush as a federal program that showed little evidence of success. A review of the program in 2003 found that Even Start parents and children performed no better than a control group. However, advocates of Even Start insist the program has been successful in preventing adults from remaining unemployed and children from

TABLE 3. FEDERAL FUNDING FOR MIGRANT AND SEASONAL HEAD START: 1995 TO 2005

Fiscal Year	Federal Spending (millions of dollars)	Federal Spending (millions of 2005 dollars)	% Change From Previous Year (using constant 2005 dollars)
1995	$139	$178	-
1996	139	173	-3%
1997	154	187	8%
1998	162	194	4%
1999	178	209	8%
2000	207	235	13%
2001	247	272	16%
2002	258	280	3%
2003	260	276	-1%
2004	265	274	-1%
2005	266	266	-3%

Source: Budget Office of the Department of Health and Human Services.

TABLE 4. FEDERAL FUNDING FOR MIGRANT EDUCATION EVEN START: 1990 TO 2004

Fiscal Year	Federal Spending (millions of 2005 dollars)	% Change From Previous Year
1994	3.6	
1995	3.8	6.9%
1996	3.8	0.0%
1997	3.8	-2.2%
1998	4.3	15.7%
1999	4.7	8.4%
2000	5.1	7.6%
2001	9.0	78.2%
2002	9.5	4.8%
2003	9.2	-3.0%
2004	8.2	-10.9%
2005	7.9	-3.7%
2006	3.6	-61.9%

Note: Numbers show the funds set aside for migrant education out of total Even Start appropriations. Migrant Education Even Start received 3 percent of Even Start appropriations FY 1990 to 2000 and FY 2006; and 3.5 percent of Even Start appropriations FY 2001 to 2005.

Source: US Federal Budget, Appendix, Department of Education, 1996-2007.

dropping out of school, and that after program revisions in 2000, Even Start has been operating much more successfully. Despite these arguments, funding for Even Start, and consequently for Migrant Even Start, was halved between FY 2005 and 2006.[6]

Funding:

- Funding for the Migrant Even Start program increased slowly throughout the late 1990s, rising from $3.6 million to $5.1 million from FY 1994 to 2000. (See Table 4)

- Appropriations jumped to $9 million in FY 2001, but fell to $8.2 million in FY 2004, and were cut to $3.6 million in FY 2005.

---

6   D. Nather, "The Perils of a Low Profile," *Congressional Quarterly*, 2005.

MIGRANT HEALTH

Under the Migrant Health program, the Department of Health and Human Services provides grants to community organizations for culturally appropriate medical care and other related services for migrant workers and their families. The migrant health program provides care regardless of immigration status.

Funding:

■ Funding for Migrant Health grew in the late 1990s and early 2000s. Appropriations grew 71 percent from FY 1998 to 2005. (See Table 5)

■ The number of migrants and dependents served by the Migrant Health program grew 25 percent from 1998 to 2004, while spending per migrant or dependent served grew 32 percent from $145 to $191.

TABLE 5. FEDERAL FUNDING FOR MIGRANT HEALTH: 1998 TO 2005

Fiscal Year	Federal Spending (millions of dollars)	Federal Spending (millions of 2005 dollars)	% Change From Previous Year	Migrants/ Dependents Served	Funding per Migrant/ Dependent Served
1998	$70	$84	-	580,423	$145
1999	79	92	10%	582,599	158
2000	87	98	7%	653,369	150
2001	100	110	12%	686,166	160
2002	114	123	12%	708,611	174
2003	125	133	8%	694,040	191
2004	134	139	4%	726,813	191
2005	144	144	4%	-	

Note: Data on Migrants and Dependents served shows calendar rather than fiscal years.

Source: Budget Office of the Department of Health and Human Services; US Department of Health and Human Services, Uniform Data System reports submitted by grantees of the Health Resources and Services Administration's Bureau of Primary Health Care, 1998-2004.

OTHER TARGETED IMMIGRANT EDUCATION PROGRAMS

THE EMERGENCY IMMIGRANT EDUCATION ACT

Prior to 2001, federal funds supported the education of immigrant and limited English proficiency (LEP) students through two programs — the Emergency Immigrant Education Program (EIEP) and the Bilingual Education Program.

EIEP was intended to help offset state and local costs incurred as a result of immigration by aiding schools with large numbers of new immigrant students. The program provided funds to school districts based on the number of foreign-born students ages 3 to 21 who had been attending US schools for three years or less. The funds supported assistance in basic educational instruction, tutoring, and mentoring/counseling for immigrant students as well as funding for staff trained in serving immigrant students and activities to increase parental involvement in a child's education.

Funding:

- Funding for EIEP declined during the 1980s and early 1990s. However, Congress nearly doubled the program's funding in FY 1997 from $61 million to $120 million. (See Table 6)

- Spending per student served by EIEP programs increased from a low of $47 per student in FY 1994 to $210 per student in FY 2000.

THE BILINGUAL EDUCATION ACT

The Bilingual Education Act (BEA) of 1968 provided funding, through competitive grants, for local school districts to help them provide bilingual education and language assistance to LEP students. The program was controversial, and the subject of long-standing debate over the appropriateness of providing instruction in languages other than English. The program's reach was relatively narrow — in FY 2001, only about 12 percent of LEP children were served by BEA-funded projects.[7]

Funding:

- Appropriations for Bilingual Education fell somewhat throughout the 1990s, but increased each year between FY 1996 and 2001. However, as

---

7   P. Osorio-O'Dea, "Bilingual Education: An Overview," Congressional Research Service Report for Congress (June 7, 2001).

TABLE 6. FEDERAL FUNDING FOR EMERGENCY IMMIGRANT EDUCATION PROGRAM (EIEP): 1985 TO 2001

School Year	Federal Spending (millions of dollars)	Federal Spending (millions of 2005 dollars)	EIEP Students*	Spending per Student
1984-1985	$30.0	$54.5	348,287	$156
1985-1986	30.0	53.5	422,549	127
1986-1987	28.7	49.3	436,612	113
1987-1988	30.0	49.5	428,688	116
1988-1989	28.7	45.2	427,870	106
1989-1990	29.6	44.2	478,172	92
1990-1991	30.1	43.2	616,604	70
1991-1992	29.3	40.8	687,334	59
1992-1993	30.0	40.5	778,508	52
1993-1994	29.4	38.7	825,968	47
1994-1995	38.9	49.9	773,976	64
1995-1996	50.0	62.2	823,149	76
1996-1997	50.0	60.8	834,876	73
1997-1998	100.0	119.8	886,196	135
1998-1999	150.0	175.8	796,254	221
1999-2000	150.0	170.1	811,154	210
2000-2001	150.0	165.4		
% Change 1984-1985 to 1999-2000		212.4%	132.9%	34.1%
% Change 1991-1992 to 1999-2000		317.1%	18.0%	253.4%

* EIEP students are foreign-born students who have attended US schools for three years or less.

Sources: US Department of Education, Biennial Report to Congress on the Emergency Immigrant Education Program, June 1999 and June 2002; US Department of Education, FY 2001 Appropriations Table.

Table 7. Federal Funding for Federal Bilingual Education: 1991 to 2001

Fiscal Year	Federal Spending (millions of dollars)	Federal Spending (millions of 2005 dollars)	Total LEP Students	Spending per LEP Student
1991	$169	$245	2,198,778	$112
1992	195	275	2,430,712	113
1993	197	269	2,735,952	98
1994	201	268	3,037,922	88
1995	157	204	3,184,696	64
1996	128	161	3,228,799	50
1997	162	199	3,452,073	58
1998	204	247	3,470,268	71
1999	230	273	3,540,673	77
2000	256	294	4,416,580	67
2001	310*	346	4,584,946	75

* estimate

Sources: US Federal Budget, Appendix, Department of Education, 1992-2002; US Department of Education, "The Growing Numbers of Limited English Proficient Students," 2002-2005.

numbers of LEP students rose substantially each year, available funds per student remained at far lower levels than in the early 1990s. (See Table 7)

No Child Left Behind Act

In 2001, the No Child Left Behind (NCLB) Act combined funding for bilingual education and Emergency Immigrant Education into a single formula grant to states for English Language Acquisition and Language Enhancement under its Title III. These grants are based on the LEP population and the number of recent immigrant students in the states. Every state receives at least $500,000 to ensure that LEP children become proficient in English, have high academic attainment, and meet the same standards as those set for all children.[8] The funding is used for English language instruction, instructional and

---

8   J. Murray, M. Fix, and W. Zimmerman, "New Directions for Newcomers: A Roadmap to No Child Left Behind and Children of Immigrants" (Washington, DC: The Migration Policy Institute, publication forthcoming).

TABLE 8. No Child Left Behind: Language Acquisition State Grants (combines former EIEP and Bilingual Education)

Year	Federal Spending (millions of dollars)	Federal Spending (millions of 2005 dollars)	LEP Students Served	Immigrant Students Served	Funding per LEP Student**
2001/02	$403	$437			
2002/03	685	727	3,649,255	753,085	$199
2003/04	685	708	4,017,504	827,638	172
2004/05	673	673			
2005/06	678*	678			
% change 2002 to 2006		55%			

* estimate
** We focus here only on LEP students because there is substantial overlap between "immigrant" and LEP students.

Source: CRS report to Congress, "Education of Limited English Proficient and Recent Immigrant Students: Provisions in the No Child Left Behind Act of 2001," April 26, 2004; US Federal Budget, Appendix, Department of Education, 2004-2007; US Department of Education, "Biennial Report to Congress on the Implementation of the State Formula Grant Program," March 15, 2005.

other services for LEP and immigrant students, family literacy and parental outreach, mentoring and counseling, and professional development of teachers and staff.

Funding:

■ FY 2002 appropriations for Language Acquisition State grants were below the $511 million appropriated for BEA and EIEP combined in FY 2001. However, appropriations increased substantially with the enactment of the No Child Left Behind Act in FY 2003 to $727 million, before dropping to $678 million for FY 2006. (See Table 8)

■ Between the 2002-2003 and 2003-2004 school years, the number of students served by Title III grants increased 12.6 percent. Spending per student decreased 13.5 percent.

ESL for Adults

Federal funding for adult English as a Second Language (ESL) instruction comes as part of the federal Adult Education program, which funds literacy (Adult Basic Education), GED preparation (Adult Secondary Education), and English instruction. In general, states may divide their federal grants among these three programs as they see fit. Enrollment numbers, however, show that between 30 and 50 percent of Adult Education students have been ESL students since the early 1990s. (See Figure 2) Since FY 1997, enrollment in ESL programs has exceeded enrollment in basic education or secondary education. Between 1993/1994 and 2003/2004, enrollment declined in adult basic education (from 1.4 to 1.2 million) and in adult secondary education (from 1.1 to 0.4 million). Enrollment remained steady at 1.1 million in ESL. Meanwhile, the number of LEP adults was growing rapidly with 54 percent growth from 12 million to 18 million between 1990 and 2000.

Figure 2. Enrollment in Adult Education Programs, in Millions: FY 1994 to 2004

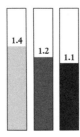 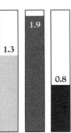 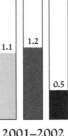 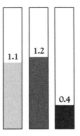

1993–1994	1997–1998	2001–2002	2003–2004
Enrollment:	*Enrollment:*	*Enrollment:*	*Enrollment:*
Total: 3.7 million	Total: 4.0 million	Total: 2.8 million	Total: 2.7 million
ESL: 1.2 million	ESL: 1.9 million	ESL: 1.2 million	ESL: 1.2 million

☐ Adult Basic Education   ■ English as a Second Language   ■ Adult Secondary Education

Sources: US Department of Education, Office of Vocational and Adult Education, "Enrollment and Participation in the State-Administered Adult Education Program."

In 1998, Congress passed legislation reauthorizing the Adult Education and Family Literacy Act (AEFLA), which mandated the Office of Vocational and Adult Education to provide formula grants to states for English Literacy (EL) and Civics Education for immigrants and other LEP populations beginning in 2000. The Civics Education program provides instruction on the rights and responsibilities of citizenship and on civic participation. Each year since 2000, appropriations legislation has earmarked a certain percentage of total adult education funds for EL/Civics education. In 2000, this portion was about 5.7 percent; ever since it has remained at about 12 percent per year. Each state's portion of that funding is based on US Citizenship and Immigration Services data on the state's share of lawful permanent resident (LPR) admissions, and on the rate of the immigrant population's growth (providing funds for "new

TABLE 9. FEDERAL FUNDING FOR ADULT EDUCATION PROGRAMS, STATE GRANTS: 1992 TO 2005

Fiscal Year	Federal Spending (millions of dollars)	Federal Spending (millions of 2005 dollars)	% Change From Previous Year
1992	$236	$332	-
1993	255	349	5%
1994	255	340	-2%
1995	252	327	-4%
1996	246	310	-5%
1997	342	421	36%
1998	345	418	-1%
1999	364	432	3%
2000	443	508	18%
2001	538	600	18%
2002	571	627	4%
2003	554	595	-5%
2004	602	630	6%
2005	569*	569	-10%

* estimate

Sources: US Federal Budget, Appendix, Department of Education, 1994-2007; US Department of Education Office of Vocational and Adult Education Division of Adult Education and Literacy, October 1999 (1992-1993).

growth" states). All states receive at least $60,000.[9] Though these funds must be used for immigrant and LEP programs, states retain discretion to allocate the remainder of their Adult Education funds according to local needs.

Funding:

- Funding for adult education remained relatively low throughout the 1990s, but increased after 2000. Funding fell by 10 percent between 2004 and 2005, however — the sharpest single year decline in any year of the program from 1992 on. (See Table 9)

- Despite a rapid rise in immigration during the decade between 1994 and 2004, the number of Adult Basic Education enrollees receiving ESL did not change.

- Adult education spending per enrolled student increased from $92 in FY 1994 to $233 in FY 2004, reflecting both declining enrollments and increased appropriations for the program.

- President Bush's budget proposal for FY 2007 would fund Adult Education at $570 million, a 10 percent decline from FY 2004 levels.

REIMBURSING HOSPITALS' COSTS OF SERVING UNDOCUMENTED IMMIGRANTS

There are essentially three existing impact aid-like programs intended to offset state and local government's immigrant-related expenditures. One is the Emergency Immigrant Education Program. Another, the State Criminal Alien Assistance Program, reimburses localities for the costs of jailing unauthorized immigrants convicted of felonies (a program that cannot be viewed as an "integration" policy). A third, comparatively new targeted federal program goes some way toward funding medical care for immigrants by reimbursing states for the emergency medical services they provide to unauthorized immigrants. Hospitals participating in Medicare are required to provide emergency medical services to everyone, regardless of ability to pay or immigration status. The Medicare Prescription Drug, Improvement, and Modernization Act of 2003 provides $250 million per year from FY 2005 to 2008 ($1 billion in total) to

---

9   US Department of Education, "Funds for State Formula-Allocated and Selected Student Aid Programs, by Program," August 2006, http://www.ed.gov/about/overview/budget/statetables/index.html.

reimburse states for uncompensated emergency care.[10] Two-thirds of the funds are distributed among all 50 states and the District of Columbia based on their estimated unauthorized immigrant population; one-third will be divided among the six states with the largest unauthorized migrant populations: California, Texas, Arizona, New York, Florida, and New Mexico.

Prior to this act, some federal funding was available to hospitals treating unauthorized immigrants, but the only funding targeted directly for care of unauthorized immigrants, provided under the 1997 Balanced Budget Act (BBA), was meager: $25 million a year from FY 1998 to 2001. According to the US General Accounting Office (GAO), in FY 2001, both the state receiving the largest BBA allotment and the state receiving the smallest BBA allotment were each only able to cover 2 percent of emergency Medicaid expenditures with BBA money.[11]

GENERAL FEDERAL SOCIAL WELFARE SPENDING REACHING IMMIGRANTS

There are many federal programs that reach substantial numbers of immigrant families, but are not directly targeted to immigrants. Broadly speaking, several government programs provide education and training, financial and medical assistance, and tax reimbursements that reach immigrant families along with great numbers of native-born residents. With the relatively substantial funding for these non-targeted social programs, targeted spending programs form only one small part of overall federal spending affecting the integration of immigrant families in the United States. While a comprehensive picture of all federal programs influencing immigrant families' integration is beyond the scope of this chapter, we highlight several important programs, and the limitations that may exist to immigrant families' access to these programs.

One important example of federal education and training reaching immigrant families is Title I education funding for the disadvantaged, now incorporated in the No Child Left Behind Act. As children of immigrant families are more likely than other US children to live in low-income households, Title I funding

---

10 We do not include this money in our overall total for integration spending because the money does not fund services for immigrant families, but instead reimburses states for services they are obligated by law to provide for all residents, regardless of cost.

11 US General Accounting Office (GAO), "Undocumented Aliens: Questions Persist about Their Impact on Hospitals' Uncompensated Care Costs," GAO-04-472, May 2004, http://www.gao.gov/new.items/d04472.pdf. The 1997 Balanced Budget Act (BBA) funds were distributed among 12 states with the highest numbers of unauthorized immigrants.

is important to many of the schools and districts serving immigrant families. In FY 2001, Title I funding was reported to have reached 1.5 million LEP students, while Bilingual Education funding reached only 400,000 LEP students.[12] Title I appropriations in FY 2004 were $18.5 billion.[13]

Title I of the Workforce Investment Act (WIA) is the principal source of US federal funding for job training. In the past, LEP adults have comprised only a small share of those receiving training: only 5.3 percent in 2003.[14] However, pending legislation could expand the program's reach to immigrants. In 2005, the House approved the Job Training Improvement Act of 2005 reauthorizing the Workforce Investment Act (WIA) and the Adult Education and Literacy Act; the Senate approved the bill in June 2006.[15] The House version would require states to develop a plan for training specific groups including LEP adults and authorize training programs that included English-language instruction. Similarly, the Senate's version would encourage services for "hard to serve groups," including LEP adults, and authorize training programs that integrate skills and English-language learning as well as funds for demonstration projects involving LEP workers.

Finally, the Earned Income Tax Credit (EITC), which reduces or eliminates the taxes that low-income working families must pay, reaches some immigrant families. However, immigrant families are less likely to have heard of or received the EITC than native families. An Urban Institute study found that 79 percent of native families had heard about the EITC in 2002, compared to 26 percent of immigrant families, and only 14 percent of immigrant families reported receiving the EITC compared to 57 percent of native families. While this gap may be inflated by the fact that immigrant families may receive the EITC without knowing the name of the program or being able to identify it in a national survey, the Urban Institute concluded that many immigrant families receiving the EITC do so only with the help of tax preparers, who often charge high fees, or offer loans with high interest rates based on anticipated refunds.[16]

---

12 Osorio-O'Dea, "Bilingual Education" (see n. 7).

13 The $412 million for Migrant Education in FY 2004 came out of this Title I funding.

14 A. Frank and E. Minoff, "Declining Share of Adults Receiving Training under WIA are Low-Income or Disadvantaged" (Washington, DC: Center for Law and Social Policy, December 14, 2005), http://www.clasp.org/publications/decline_in_wia_training.pdf.

15 United States House of Representatives, "Job Training Improvement Act of 2005," H.R. 27, 109th Cong. 2nd Sess. (2005); United States Senate, "Workforce Investment Act Amendments of 2005," S. 1021, 109th Cong. 2nd Sess. (2005).

16 R. Capps, M. Fix, E. Henderson, and J. Reardon-Anderson, "A Profile of Low-Income Working Immigrant Families," Washington, DC: Urban Institute, June 2005.

CONCLUSION

In sum, targeted federal integration programs form a fragmentary system of support for immigrant families in US communities, with refugees and asylees receiving the most comprehensive assistance. Many of the programs that do exist have seen declining funds over recent years, following a period of growth for most programs during the late 1990s and early 2000s. Further, federal spending on integration has failed to keep pace with the growing flows of new immigrants and particularly immigrant children. As the number of immigrants in the country continues to increase by between one and two million a year, the holes in support for immigrant integration threaten to allow already tough public policy challenges to grow.

While some medical coverage is targeted to the small fraction of immigrants who are in migrant worker families or are refugees, new legal immigrants remain barred from the federal Medicaid/SCHIP program for five years. More than 44 percent of non-citizen immigrants do not have health insurance, and must rely on a system of safety net clinics and hospitals, which create high costs for uncompensated health care in their communities.[17] Rather than merely reimbursing hospital for the costs of this care, policymakers could focus on ways to ensure that larger shares of immigrants have access to health insurance. This could both improve the health of immigrant communities and likely reduce overall health costs by enabling immigrants to afford primary and preventive care, making them less likely to resort to expensive visits to the emergency room.

Another example of the shortcomings of federal initiatives is the growing wait lists for Adult ESL classes. The fact that enrolment in Adult ESL classes has not increased over the past ten years obscures the fact that demand for these classes has been growing rapidly, while federal funding for adult ESL has stagnated. A study by the New York Immigration Coalition in 2001 estimated that only 5 percent of the need for English classes was being met in New York City.[18] While loud voices in national immigration debates deride immigrants for failing to learn the country's language, legislators have failed to make the necessary investments to give immigrants the means to do so.

---

17 See Chapter 7, pp. 83-106, of this volume.

18 T. Robbins, "Language Lockout: For Immigrants, Hard Work Yields Few Benefits," *The Village Voice*, September 10-16, 2003, http://www.villagevoice.com/news/0337,robbins,46891,5.html.

As the nation considers reforming its policies on immigration to the United States, the scope and depth of the federal government's responsibility for assisting immigrant families' integration is likely to become an increasingly pressing reality at state and local levels, if not within national debates. In the intermediate term, these concerns should translate into plans for an impact aid program that draws on the lessons from the 1986 Immigration and Reform Act and from other fields. (See, generally, chapter 10 of this volume).

NOTE ON DATA SOURCES

The data on funding in this chapter were taken from a variety of sources, utilizing the most accurate figures available to provide a view of funding changes over time. In some cases, these data were reported by the government department that distributes the funding to the state and local agencies serving immigrant and LEP families. In other cases, the budget data were taken from the appendices of the US federal budget. Budget data from departments reflect the amount they had available to spend, not necessarily the amount they actually spend. Data from the federal budget reflect actual obligations, or the money the agency committed to be spent on integration services. In most cases, appropriations and obligations are very similar within each fiscal year; using either metric of funding provides a picture of the general level of available funds for each integration activity.

PART III
KEY POLICY ISSUES

CHAPTER 7

Access to Health Care and Health Insurance: Immigrants and Immigration Reform

LEIGHTON KU AND

DEMETRIOS G. PAPADEMETRIOU

Introduction[1]

The high costs of health care and the erosion of health insurance coverage are two important long-term challenges that confront all Americans. But these problems are especially acute for immigrants to the United States, who have extremely low rates of health insurance coverage and poor access to health care services. (The principal focus of this chapter is those who are not naturalized and, unless otherwise stated, "immigrants" means non-citizen immigrants.) Immigrants — particularly those who have not yet become American citizens — encounter roadblocks that make it far more difficult to get either public or private health insurance and to obtain adequate access to health care.

As a result of these barriers almost half of all immigrants are uninsured, a level that falls far outside the experience of most mainstream Americans. In addition to the obvious health and humanitarian concerns associated with poor health care access, there are other economic and social reasons to be concerned. Unresolved health problems can limit immigrants' ability to maintain productive employment, particularly given that many work in physically strenuous jobs or in jobs in which there is a high incidence of occupational injuries. Because so many immigrants lack the protections of health insurance, the cost of even a single hospitalization can drive many into debt and financial insolvency. The Institute of Medicine has estimated that the societal costs of

---

1   The opinions expressed here are those of the authors and do not necessarily reflect the positions of the Center on Budget and Policy Priorities or the Migration Policy Institute. The authors thank a number of colleagues who offered helpful suggestions and constructive criticism.

uninsurance in the United States are substantial; between $65 and $130 billion per year, due to health impairments and years of productive life lost (this estimate is for all those who are uninsured, not just immigrants).[2]

Since almost half of US immigrants are uninsured, they often rely on a patchwork system of safety net clinics and hospitals for free or reduced price medical care, including state and county-owned facilities, as well as charitable and religiously affiliated facilities. Immigrants' reliance on this system leads many states and communities to be concerned about uncompensated health care costs for uninsured immigrants and the state and local fiscal burdens that result.

Immigration reform has the potential either to improve immigrants' access to medical care or to leave them with access far below the standards of most of those living in the United States. At the very least, discussion and debate about immigration reform offer opportunities to review these issues and to think about how improvements could be made. This chapter summarizes key issues and research concerning immigrants' access to health care, reviews some persistent myths that make solutions more difficult, and suggests potentially constructive solutions and ideas concerning health care access and coverage for those affected by immigration reform proposals.

IMMIGRANTS' ACCESS TO HEALTH INSURANCE AND HEALTH CARE

Census data show that immigrants are more likely to be uninsured than native-born citizens (Table 1). Overall, non-citizen immigrants are more than three times as likely to be uninsured (44 percent) as native citizens (13 percent). The percent of naturalized citizens who are uninsured (17 percent) is between that of non-citizens and native citizens. Immigrants' insurance coverage is worst when they are recent immigrants and improves as they reside in the United States for longer periods. (Similarly, incomes grow with tenure in the United States. This is partly because immigrants' employment tends to improve with time and partly because both citizens' and immigrants' incomes increase with age and greater job experience.) The main reason that immigrants are less insured than native-born citizens is that, despite their high rates of employment, fewer immigrants have employer-sponsored health insurance.

---

2 Committee on the Consequences of Uninsurance, Institute of Medicine, *Insuring America's Health: Principles and Recommendations* (Washington, DC: National Academy Press, 2004).

TABLE 1. HEALTH INSURANCE COVERAGE OF US POPULATION BY IMMIGRATION STATUES AND INCOME, 2004

	Uninsured	Employer-Sponsored Insurance	Medicaid SCHIP	Non-group & Other Private	Medicare & Other Public
All Incomes					
US-Born Citizens	13.3%	59.1%	13.0%	5.5%	9.1%
Naturalized Citizens	17.2%	54.9%	10.3%	5.4%	12.2%
Non-Citizen Immigrants	44.1%	36.5%	12.6%	4.0%	2.9%
Low-Income (Below 200% of Poverty Line)					
US-Born Citizens	22.6%	24.9%	32.5%	6.4%	13.5%
Naturalized Citizens	26.2%	26.4%	23.2%	5.6%	18.7%
Non-Citizen Immigrants	56.1%	18.1%	19.3%	3.6%	2.9%

Source: Authors' analyses of March 2005 CPS

The discrepancy between immigrants and native-born citizens persists among those with incomes below 200 percent of the poverty line (or about $33,000 per year for a family of three in 2006), a group comprised primarily of non-citizen immigrants but that also includes a small minority of native-born citizens. Among the low-income category, 56 percent of non-citizen immigrants are uninsured versus 23 percent of native-born citizens (Table 1 and Figure 1). However, reasons for the insurance gap change when one focuses on the low-income population. The primary reason for the difference in coverage between low-income immigrants and citizens is that fewer immigrants have public coverage, including Medicaid (which serves the poor) and Medicare (which serves the elderly). Low-income immigrants are also less likely to have employer-sponsored coverage and other private coverage, but the gaps are somewhat narrower.

Although Census data do not reveal whether immigrants are legal or not, it is important to recognize that these profiles are affected by the types of immigrants living and working in the United States. Analyses indicate that the proportion of new immigrants who are unauthorized has grown in recent years,

Figure 1. Distribution of Health Insurance for Immigrants and Native-Born Citizens with Incomes Below 200% of Poverty, 2004

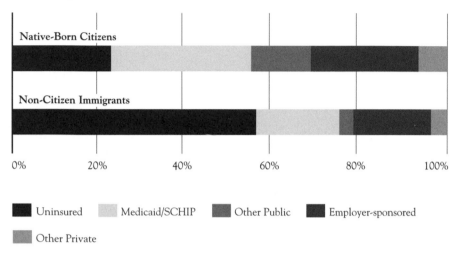

Legend:
- ■ Uninsured
- ▨ Medicaid/SCHIP
- ■ Other Public
- ■ Employer-sponsored
- ▨ Other Private

Source: Authors' analyses of March 2005 CPS

while the proportion legally admitted has fallen.[3] Unauthorized immigrants are ineligible for public benefits (except for limited Medicaid coverage for treatment of emergency medical conditions) and have greater difficulty securing private health insurance as well.

Private Health Insurance

Employer-sponsored insurance is the mainstay of health coverage for most Americans, but not for immigrants. As seen above, immigrants are much less likely to have private insurance coverage than citizens, even though immigrants have high levels of employment. Analyses of Census data have found that a key reason for this lack of coverage is that immigrant workers, particularly Latino immigrants, are less likely to be offered insurance at work than citizen workers.[4] Job-based health insurance is offered to 87 percent of white citizen

---

3   J. Passel and R. Suro, "Rise, Peak and Decline: Trends in U.S. Immigration 1992-2004" (Washington, DC: Pew Hispanic Center, September 2005).

4   C. Schur and J. Feldman, "Running in Place: How Job Characteristics, Immigrant Status, and Family Structure Keep Hispanics Uninsured" (New York City: Commonwealth Fund, May 2001).

workers, but to only 50 percent of Latino immigrant workers. However, when they are offered health insurance, comparable numbers of white citizens and Latino immigrants accept the offer and take employer-sponsored insurance (87 percent of white citizen workers and 81 percent of Latino immigrant workers). In most cases, accepting the insurance offer means that immigrant employees are also willing to bear a portion of the costs in the form of employee premiums and other cost-sharing mechanisms. The offer and acceptance rates for Latino citizen workers are about the same as those for white citizens.

Part of the reason immigrants are offered insurance at lower rates is that they frequently work in the types of industries that are less likely to offer health insurance, such as agriculture, construction, food processing, restaurant, hotel, and other service jobs. But more detailed analyses have shown that even if one statistically adjusts for differences in job type, salary level, and such, immigrants are still less likely to be offered insurance.[5]

In some cases, employers may be able to effectively treat immigrants — even legal immigrants — differently by classifying them as contract, temporary, or part-time workers, so they are not required to offer benefits. Moreover, rather than directly hiring workers (e.g., farm workers, janitorial staff, etc.), some firms instead pay contractors for labor, knowing that the contractors lower their costs by not offering benefits to their employees. A recent report found that, regardless of citizenship, contract, temporary, and part-time workers are far less likely to have employer-based insurance: 21 percent of these workers were insured, compared with 74 percent of full-time regular workers.[6]

It is not clear whether immigrants are not offered health insurance while citizen workers in the same companies are offered coverage or whether immigrants tend to work in firms that do not offer insurance, compared to citizen workers in the same types of jobs. (That is, it is not clear if immigrants are subject to some form of discrimination within firms or are offered insurance less often because they work in a segmented labor market in which some companies primarily hire immigrants while other companies of the same type primarily hire citizens.) Under federal law, employers are supposed to offer health insurance on equivalent terms to all their workers, but it is plausible that immigrants, particularly unauthorized workers or temporary visa holders, are often not offered health benefits on terms equivalent to other workers.

---

5   Ibid. Also see T. Buechmiller et al., "Immigrants and Employer-Provided Health Insurance," ERIU Working Paper #38 (Ann Arbor, MI: University of Michigan, August 2005).

6   E. Ditsler et al., "On the Fringe: The Substandard Benefits of Workers in Part-Time, Temporary, and Contract Jobs" (New York: Commonwealth Fund, December 2005).

ACCESS TO PUBLIC HEALTH INSURANCE

For most low-income people, Medicaid is the mainstay of health insurance coverage. But there are sharp legal distinctions in terms of immigrants' eligibility for Medicaid and its counterpart, State Children's Health Insurance Program (SCHIP). Undocumented immigrants and temporary visa holders (e.g., those with student or temporary work visas) are not eligible for Medicaid, except for Medicaid coverage of emergency room services. Medicaid generally does not provide coverage for non-elderly adults without dependent children in the United States, so many of the immigrant adults who come to the United States primarily to work are not eligible for regular or emergency Medicaid. Elderly immigrants, though often ineligible for Medicare because they did not work in the United States for a sufficient number of years to qualify for Social Security or Medicare, may still be eligible for Medicaid if they are poor enough and meet other eligibility criteria.

The 1996 welfare reform law prohibited most lawful permanent residents admitted after the law's enactment from receiving federal Medicaid or SCHIP coverage during their first five years in the United States (similar prohibitions also barred eligibility for other benefits such as food stamps, welfare, and supplemental security income).[7] By now, about 40 percent of lawful immigrants in the United States have entered since 1996 and have been subject to this prohibition.[8] Nonetheless, a number of states have opted to cover some of these immigrants, particularly children or pregnant women, using state funds.[9] Beginning in the late 1990s, the federal eligibility prohibition combined with fears in the immigrant community that receiving Medicaid or SCHIP could harm an immigrant's chance of getting lawful residence, remaining in the United States, or becoming naturalized, discouraged participation even among those eligible for public benefits.[10] (The federal government subsequently clarified that getting Medicaid or SCHIP benefits would not make an immigrant ineligible for permanent residency.) Nonetheless, since welfare reform's 1996 enactment, low-income immigrants have lost Medicaid coverage and are more likely to be uninsured.

---

7   S. Fremstad and L. Cox, "Covering New Americans: A Review of Federal and State Policies Related to Immigrants' Eligibility and Access to Publicly Funded Insurance" (Washington, DC: Kaiser Commission on Medicaid and the Uninsured, November 2004).

8   Estimate by J. Passel of the Pew Hispanic Center, February 2006, based on analysis of trends from recent Census data. This is a ratio of the number of non-refugee lawful permanent residents who entered after 1996 divided by the number of total lawful permanent residents in the United States.

9   Ibid.

10 M. Fix and J. Passel, "The Scope and Impact of Welfare Reform's Immigrant Provisions" (Washington, DC: The Urban Institute, January 2002).

FIGURE 2. CHANGES IN PERCENTAGE OF LOW-INCOME CHILDREN
(BELOW 200% OF POVERTY) WHO ARE UNINSURED.
1995 TO 2004

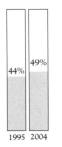

1995 2004

Immigrant Child

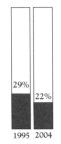

1995 2004

**Citizen Child/
Immigrant Parents**

1995 2004

**Citizen Child/
US Born Parents**

Source: Authors' analyses of March 1996 and 2005 CPS

Gaps in insurance coverage between immigrant children and citizen children widened over the past decade (Figure 2).[11] After the 1996 immigrant prohibitions, more immigrant children became uninsured. In contrast, the enactment of SCHIP in 1997 and subsequent state efforts to expand children's coverage with SCHIP and Medicaid led to higher insurance coverage of citizen children. As a result, the percentage of low-income children in native-born families who were uninsured fell from 19 percent in 1995 to 16 percent in 2004. These expansions were not felt by immigrant children, however, in part because of the immigrant exclusions; the percent of low-income immigrant children who were uninsured climbed from 44 percent to 49 percent.

Initially, immigrants' fears concerning welfare reform led to reductions in participation in Medicaid and SCHIP by US-born children whose parents were immigrants ("mixed status" families), even though the children were always eligible because they were citizens. But as Figure 2 shows, this problem has eased thanks in large measure to substantial outreach and educational efforts on the part of state and local governments and community-based organizations. The

---

11 In 2000, the Census Bureau added an additional question to verify insurance coverage; this reduced the number of people who are reported as uninsured. In order to fairly compare data before and after 2000, these analyses use the "pre-verification" versions of the insurance questions that are the same for 1995 and 2004.

coverage of children in mixed status families has improved, even though they are still more likely to be uninsured than children with native-born parents. (Note: Net insurance coverage for citizen children improved because Medicaid or SCHIP coverage increased between 1995 and 2004 and such improvements occurred despite reductions in private insurance coverage. For immigrant children, both Medicaid/SCHIP coverage and private coverage declined, which contributed to lower insurance coverage.)

THE ROLE OF IMMIGRANT SPONSORS

The 1996 prohibition on Medicaid and SCHIP coverage was based on some legislators' belief that sponsors of immigrants ought to be responsible for their health insurance coverage. Since 1997, those who sponsor immigrants must agree to be responsible for them and are informed that they may be held liable for the costs of public assistance, like Medicaid or SCHIP, if the sponsored immigrants receive benefits. Expectations that most recent immigrants could get private insurance from employers or that their sponsors would step in to provide other private coverage have proven to be unrealistic. Analyses of Census data for low-income immigrant children show that the share with private coverage (employer-sponsored or non-group) fell from 19 percent in 1995 (before the 1996 changes) to 17 percent by 2004. For low-income parents, the share with private coverage fell from 28 percent in 1995 to 25 percent by 2004. In 2004, as in 1995, immigrants were much less likely to have private insurance than native-born citizens. Combined with the loss of Medicaid coverage immigrants experienced over this period, the net result has been a substantial increase in the percentage of low-income immigrants who are uninsured.

While sponsors may be able to provide financial support in some areas, it can be quite difficult for sponsors to afford health insurance for the immigrants they have sponsored. In 2005, the price of an average employer-sponsored health insurance policy for a family was over $10,000; for an individual, the cost of such a policy was over $4,000. The prices can be even higher when insurance must be purchased on a non-group basis, as would be required for those who are not in the sponsors' immediate families.[12] Many Americans are themselves uninsured and sponsors with low and middle incomes usually cannot afford the health insurance of those they sponsor. The prohibition on Medicaid coverage for legal immigrants during their first several years in the United States effectively means that a large number of immigrants are uninsured, even if they are working and have serious health needs.

---

12 Kaiser Family Foundation and Health Research and Educational Trust, "Employer Health Benefits: 2005 Summary of Benefits" (Menlo Park: Kaiser Family Foundation, 2005).

Federal legislation that passed in early February 2006 adds a new requirement that American *citizens* applying for Medicaid must submit proof of citizenship, such as a US passport or birth certificate. This provision would not apply to immigrants applying for Medicaid, who must already submit documentation of their legal status. A recent study has estimated that the coverage of three to five million citizens on Medicaid may be jeopardized because they do not have a passport or birth certificate.[13] Although the legislation is aimed at citizens, it could have repercussions for immigrants as well if it leads many in the immigrant community (and some caseworkers) to believe that they must also show proof of citizenship to obtain coverage and that non-citizen immigrants are not eligible for Medicaid.

ACCESS TO HEALTH CARE

Because immigrants are so often uninsured, out-of-pocket health care costs are higher than those paid by the insured and immigrants are less able to get the care they need. Other factors, like language barriers, also impair immigrants' access to medical care and the quality of that which they do receive. The net result is that immigrants are much less likely to use primary and preventive medical services, hospital services, emergency medical services, and dental care than are citizens, even after controlling for the effects of race/ethnicity, income, insurance status, and health status. Low-income immigrant adults are twice as likely as low-income native citizen adults to report that they have no regular source of health care. Similarly, low-income immigrant children are four times more likely to lack a usual source of care as low-income children with native citizen parents.[14] A federal report recently concluded that racial/ethnic disparities in health care are gradually becoming narrower between African Americans and white Americans, but are widening between Latinos and white Americans.[15] The poor health care access of immigrant Latinos is a major reason for this widening gap in medical care.

What little is known about the health care access of unauthorized immigrants suggests that it is particularly poor. One broad survey of California farm workers, who are largely undocumented, found that only one-sixth were offered employer-sponsored health insurance and one-third of those receiving offers of

---

13 L. Ku et al., "Survey Indicates Budget Reconciliation Bill Jeopardizes Medicaid Coverage for 3 to 5 Million Citizens" (Washington, DC: Center on Budget and Policy Priorities, January 26, 2006).

14 L. Ku and S. Matani, "Left Out: Immigrants' Access to Health Care and Insurance," *Health Affairs* 20, no. 1 (Jan/Feb 2001): 247-56.

15 Department of Health and Human Services, 2005 *National Healthcare Disparities Report* (Rockville, MD: Agency for Healthcare Research and Quality, 2006).

coverage said they could not afford the insurance offered. Half of the males and a third of the females had not seen a physician in the past two years, even though many had occupational illnesses or chronic health problems like high blood pressure and anemia.[16] A national survey of day laborers, predominantly unauthorized, also found a high level of occupational injuries.[17] One-fifth of day laborers had suffered a work-related injury, but less than half received medical care for that injury.

Many immigrants — regardless of their legal status — experience a health care environment that is strikingly different from that seen by most Americans. They are directly exposed, without the financial buffers of insurance, to the high costs of health care, from doctor's office visits to prescription drugs to hospitalizations. As a result, immigrants are less likely to get care in private doctors' offices and are more reliant on safety net clinics or hospitals that offer free or reduced price medical care, such as state or county-owned, charitable, or religiously affiliated health care facilities.[18]

Even these facilities are not always perceived as "safe" since some public facilities inquire about immigration status, causing concerns among immigrants that they may be reported to the government. Thus, some immigrants turn to "black market" sources of health care, such as unlicensed health care providers (e.g., immigrant doctors not licensed to practice in the United States), and may purchase prescription drugs that have been smuggled into the United States and are sold without prescriptions.[19]

Because so many lack insurance and rely on safety net clinics and hospitals, the unauthorized place a greater burden of the costs of uncompensated health care in areas with high concentrations of immigrants. One study estimated that the cost of uncompensated hospital emergency care for unauthorized immigrants in southwestern border counties was about $190 million in 2000.[20] The total cost of uncompensated health care for uninsured immigrants — lawful and unauthorized — provided by hospitals, clinics, and other health care providers

---

16 D. Villarejo et al., "Suffering in Silence: A Report on the Health of California's Agricultural Workers" (Woodland Hills, CA: California Endowment, 2000).

17 A. Valenzuela et al., "On the Corner: Day Labor in the United States" (University of California at Los Angeles and University of Illinois at Chicago, January 2006).

18 Ku and Matani, "Left Out" (see n. 14).

19 L. Ku and A. Freilich, "Caring for Immigrants: Health Care Safety Nets in Los Angeles, New York, Miami and Houston" (Washington, DC: Kaiser Commission on Medicaid and the Uninsured, February 2001).

20 US-Mexico Border Counties Coalition, "Medical Emergency: Who Pays the Price for Uncompensated Emergency Medical Care Along the Southwest Border?" 2002.

across the nation is substantially higher. A large share of the costs is borne by state and local governments or charitable or religious organizations that operate the facilities. Some costs are also indirectly transferred to those with private insurance, who bear somewhat higher health care costs when hospitals or other facilities cross-subsidize their losses from uncompensated care for uninsured people by charging private health insurers more (cost-shifting).[21]

MYTHS THAT MAKE REFORMS MORE DIFFICULT

Like many topics relating to immigrants and immigration, persistent rhetoric and myths about immigrants and health abound, making informed policy choices more difficult. This section addresses three of the more common myths.

MYTH: IMMIGRANTS ARE THE MAIN REASON THE NUMBER OF UNINSURED IS GROWING

Trends reported by the Census Bureau show that the number of people who are uninsured grew by about six million between 2000 and 2004.[22] One common myth is that immigration is the main reason that the number of uninsured people is rising. A recent report, for example, stated that immigrants and their children are responsible for three-quarters of the growth in the number of uninsured.[23]

More careful analyses, however, indicate that immigrants play a much smaller role in the growth in the number of uninsured, although the relative role of immigrants depends partly on broader economic changes.[24] The analyses, summarized in Figure 3, examine changes in the number of uninsured people between 1994 and 2003, partitioning them into three periods: 1994-1998, 1998-2000, and 2000-2003. In each period, the number of uninsured non-citizen immigrants and naturalized citizens grew slightly. However, during the 1994-1998 and 2000-2003 periods, there were broad increases in the number of uninsured and the overwhelming majority of growth in the ranks of the uninsured occurred among native citizens. In the period between 1998 and 2000,

21 A. Dobson et al., "The Cost-Shift Payment Hydraulic: Foundation, History and Implications," *Health Affairs* 25, no. 1 (Jan/Feb 2006): 22-33.

22 US Census Bureau, "Income, Poverty, and Health Insurance Coverage in the United States: 2004," August 30, 2005.

23 S. Camarota, "Immigrants at Mid-Decade: A Snapshot of America's Foreign-Born Population in 2005" (Washington, DC: Center for Immigration Studies, December 2005).

24 J. Holahan and A. Cook, "Are Immigrants Responsible for Most of the Growth of the Uninsured?" (Washington, DC: Kaiser Commission on Medicaid and the Uninsured, October 2005).

FIGURE 3. CHANGES IN THE NUMBER OF NON-ELDERLY UNINSURED
BY CITIZENSHIP STATUS, 1994 TO 2003 (IN MILLIONS OF PEOPLE)

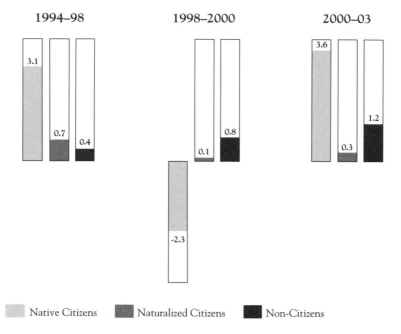

Source: Holahan and Cook, Analyses of Census data, 2005

the number of native citizens who were uninsured fell, so the increases in that period occurred among immigrants.

Immigrants, particularly recent immigrants, are more often uninsured than native citizens. Thus, growth in the number of immigrants in the United States contributes incrementally to growth in the overall number of those uninsured. Most health care analysts agree, however, that the recent growth in the number of uninsured people is primarily attributable to the erosion of employer-sponsored health insurance, which is, in turn, primarily due to the rising costs of health care. These factors affect immigrants and non-immigrants alike, but there are far more native citizens in the United States than immigrants, so changes in the status of native citizens dominate the overall insurance profile of the nation. Moreover, the disparity in changes in insurance coverage that occurred in 1998-2000 suggests that even a rising tide of increased insurance coverage may not lift immigrants' boats because they are less likely to be offered either private or public insurance coverage.

MYTH: THE HEALTH CARE COSTS OF IMMIGRANTS ARE BANKRUPTING THE SYSTEM

Persistent stories about uncompensated health care costs for immigrants have led to a perception on the part of the general public that immigrants have extraordinarily high health care costs, in part because they use emergency rooms too much.

Research demonstrates that medical expenditures for immigrants are *much lower* than for native citizens and that immigrants are *less* likely to use emergency rooms than native citizens. Figure 4 summarizes a recent national study that found per capita medical expenditures for immigrants — whether paid by insurance or out-of-pocket — were *less than half* those of native-born citizens.[25] Another study found that non-citizen immigrants were much less likely to use emergency rooms than native citizens.[26]

Both studies indicate that immigrants use less health care than native citizens, even after statistically controlling for the effects of factors like insurance coverage, race/ethnicity, income, age, gender, education, and health status.[27] Insurance coverage promotes better access to care for immigrants, just as it does for native citizens, but additional factors impede health access and utilization for immigrants, such as language barriers and perhaps a lack of familiarity with the American health care system. The health care utilization of naturalized citizens is closer to that of native citizens, suggesting that these discrepancies ease as immigrants reside in the United States for a longer period.

How can we resolve the apparent disparity between stories about high medical costs and studies showing that immigrants have low costs? The key is that, even though immigrants have relatively low per capita medical costs, immigrants are often uninsured and many of their costs are incurred as uncompensated care received at safety net facilities. Thus, in locales where immigrants are concentrated and numerous, a large share of the additional government costs for uncompensated care would be incurred for immigrants. In these locales, uncompensated care costs for uninsured immigrants can impose additional costs and burdens on safety net health care providers.

The costs of uncompensated care for uninsured immigrants may be affected in part by state policies, however. Some states, like California or New York, are

---

25 S. Mohanty et al., "Health Care Expenditures of Immigrants: A Nationally Representative Analysis," *American Journal of Public Health* 95, no. 8 (Aug 2005): 1431-1438.

26 Ku and Matani, "Left Out" (see n. 14).

27 Ibid.

FIGURE 4. AVERAGE PER CAPITA ANNUAL MEDICAL EXPENDITURES

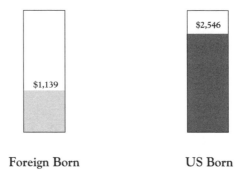

$1,139 Foreign Born

$2,546 US Born

Source: Mohanty et al., 2005, based on Medical Expenditure Panel Survey. Estimates are adjusted for differences in race, insurance, income, etc.

more generous in providing state-funded Medicaid coverage to legal immigrants than other states, like Arizona or Texas. Because of this, a greater share of the health care provided to immigrants in more restrictive states is likely to be uncompensated care for immigrants who are uninsured, while care for immigrants in more generous states is more likely to be covered by insurance.

MYTH: OFFERING HEALTH BENEFITS CREATES AN IMMIGRANT MAGNET
One factor that has discouraged some states from offering better health care to immigrants is the fear that more generous benefits will serve as a "magnet," attracting more poor and uninsured immigrants to their states.

Such a view is not supported by the research, however, which finds that people migrate for better economic prospects (i.e., a better job), to be reunited with family members, or to flee persecution in their home country, not because of perceived advantages in health benefits or social services.[28] For example, in a survey of unauthorized immigrants in California and Texas, less than half of 1 percent said they came to the United States for social services; most came for employment or family reunification.[29] Recent trends in the residential patterns of immigrants also dispel this myth. The number of immigrants has grown the

---

28 Fix and Passel, "The Scope and Impact of Welfare Reform" (see n. 10).

29 M. Berk et al., "Health Care Use Among Undocumented Latino Immigrants," *Health Affairs* 19, no. 4 (Jul/Aug 2000): 51-64.

most rapidly in states, such as southern or Rocky Mountain states, that offer less than generous Medicaid or welfare benefits, and away from more traditional immigrant strongholds, like California and New York, which have more generous immigrant benefits.[30] Immigrants moved to the non-traditional states because they found new employment opportunities, such as work in the poultry and food processing industries.

WHAT ARE POTENTIAL SOLUTIONS?

Immigration reform offers the opportunity to improve immigrants' access to health care, both because it would change the legal status of large numbers of immigrants and because it offers a window for Congress, advocates, and analysts to review other policies concerning the status of immigrants in the United States.

Some recent immigration reform proposals have included provisions to increase the number of immigrants admitted as lawful permanent residents, created new categories of temporary workers, and developed more stringent immigration enforcement mechanisms.[31] Even so, many unauthorized immigrants will remain in the United States. This section describes policy options to improve health coverage and access for immigrants falling into three categories: (1) lawful permanent residents; (2) temporary workers authorized by immigration reform; and (3) the remaining unauthorized immigrants.

Of course, we do not know what direction immigration reform will take. It is conceivable that an eventual immigration reform policy could make health access more difficult for many immigrants, for example, by making it more difficult for immigrants to gain access to public benefits, receive care at safety net facilities, or by making it illegal for health or social service providers to offer assistance to unauthorized immigrants.

Lawful Permanent Residents. As noted above, immigration reform could increase the number of lawful permanent residents admitted to the United States each year. It might also adjust immigration categories or eligibility criteria and change the proportions admitted under different categories. Three areas for reform for lawful permanent residents can be considered:

---

30 R. Capps et al., "The Dispersal of Immigrants in the 1990s" (Washington, DC: The Urban Institute, November 2002).

31 M. Rosenblum, "Comprehensive Legislation vs. Fundamental Reform: The Limits of Current Immigration Proposals," Task Force on Immigration and America's Future Policy Brief No. 13 (Washington, DC: Migration Policy Institute, January 2006).

PRIVATE HEALTH INSURANCE
To the extent that more immigrants have legal residency, they may find it easier to get better jobs. This could lead to increased offers of employer-sponsored health insurance and increased private insurance coverage.

However, as discussed above, immigrants encounter roadblocks to job-based coverage. The main reason immigrants are less insured is that fewer are offered employer-sponsored health insurance than citizen workers as they often hold low-wage, low-benefit jobs. Reducing these gaps in the availability of employer-sponsored coverage would require broad efforts to improve the job skills of immigrants (e.g., better education and training, better English skills) or to reduce health insurance costs. Both of these are laudable objectives, but would require relatively sweeping changes, which are beyond the scope of this chapter.

More specifically, the federal government and employers could more carefully investigate the reasons that offers of job-based health insurance are so low among immigrant workers and identify possible remedies to the problem. Developing remedies could require a closer look at whether employers are more likely to classify immigrants as contract, temporary, or part-time workers in order to avoid offering them health and other benefits, as well as whether immigrants are offered insurance on the same terms as citizen workers performing similar duties. The results could lead to better monitoring and enforcement of current employment and civil rights laws.

PUBLIC INSURANCE
In 1996, Congress prohibited providing Medicaid and SCHIP (and other public benefits) to recent legal immigrants. The rationale for this change was that the government should not be responsible for recent immigrants and that their needs should be met by their sponsors or by private employment. The 1996 policies have had the unfortunate effect of denying health insurance coverage to legal immigrants during their initial years in the United States when they are least likely to get jobs that offer private insurance coverage or are able to afford private coverage. The belief that immigrants' sponsors will be responsible for providing health care coverage for those they sponsor remains unproven. As noted above, the percentage of immigrants who have private insurance — whether through employment or through sponsors — has fallen since 1996. Immigrants' health insurance coverage, and thus their health care access, fell even more, in part because legal immigrants lost access to Medicaid and SCHIP. Restoring federal Medicaid and SCHIP coverage for legal immigrants could improve their ability to secure health care during their initial years in the United States.

IMPROVING LANGUAGE ACCESS IN HEALTH CARE

Language barriers make it harder for immigrants to obtain health care, even if they have insurance, and increase the risk of errors or misunderstanding because the patient and physician cannot communicate. Language barriers affect a broad spectrum of individuals who are not English proficient, including both legal immigrants and naturalized citizens. Existing federal civil rights policies require that health care providers who receive federal funds (which include the great majority of providers including virtually all hospitals and clinics) bear the responsibility of overcoming language barriers by providing bilingual services or language assistance to patients with limited English proficiency.[32] Unfortunately, these policies are not closely monitored and the lack of financial reimbursement for interpretation and language services means that health care providers have few incentives to arrange these services. Thus, language barriers remain a common and serious problem. Insurers, including federal, state, and private insurers, could reduce language barriers by paying for interpretation and taking steps needed to improve language access.[33]

Many believe that immigrants should learn English and that the acquisition of English skills is a critical part of immigrant integration and ultimately improves immigrants' economic and social opportunities. While most immigrants eventually learn English, many run into problems because of limitations in the availability in English as a Second Language classes. However, there is no reason to believe that offering language assistance in health care will discourage immigrants from learning English. The importance, complexity, and sensitivity of medical problems mean that people should be able to communicate with their doctors and other health care providers in the language with which they are most familiar.

Temporary Workers. Discussing options for the health coverage of temporary workers is thorny because there is no clear consensus on whether health care should be an important component of immigration reform. Even if people agreed that it was important, there is no consensus on the respective responsibilities of employers, employees, and governments to help finance health care for temporary workers.

Immigration reform may create a new category (or categories) of legal temporary workers, who may have fewer legal rights than lawful permanent residents, but more than those who are undocumented. Some immigration reform propos-

---

32 Presidential Executive Order 13166, "Improving Access to Services for Persons with Limited English Proficiency," *Federal Register* 65:50121, 2000.

33 L. Ku and G. Flores, "Pay Now or Pay Later: Providing Interpreter Services in Health Care," *Health Affairs* 24, no. 2 (Mar/Apr 2005): 435-444.

als offer a path to upgrade status to lawful permanent residency, while others do not; this chapter makes no assumptions about eventual legal status. Because immigration reform offers new ways for immigrants to obtain legal employment, it could help bolster their opportunities to get job-based health insurance. However, such opportunities rely on two assumptions: (1) legal status helps temporary workers secure better jobs and (2) employers offer them health benefits. If employers do not offer health insurance to these workers or if they classify them into job categories that are ineligible for health insurance (e.g., as temporary employees or contract workers), then the immigrants will not gain private insurance coverage.

Some earlier proposals for immigration reform exclude temporary workers from eligibility for public insurance, like Medicaid or SCHIP, even though, as discussed below, some government subsidy of health insurance is inevitable. If they are excluded from public coverage and are still unable to secure private coverage, then the majority of temporary workers and their families will be uninsured and experience serious problems getting care. Much of the costs of their care will inevitably be incurred as uncompensated care costs borne by state, local, and charitable organizations.

One potential policy goal could be to assure that temporary workers are treated in an even-handed fashion with respect to citizen employees and receive similar offers of private health benefits as citizen workers. The costs of such coverage would primarily be borne by employers and employees. In crafting such a policy, it will be important to ensure that employers do not classify temporary workers in job categories that make them ineligible for coverage.

Would employers and employees be willing to shoulder such costs? This would depend in large measure on how much they are expected to contribute and under what terms. Fortunately, since medical expenses for immigrants are much lower than for native-born citizens, insurance for immigrants ought to be less expensive than insurance for citizen workers.

Research shows that most immigrants take up employer-sponsored insurance if it is offered. The findings suggest that most would be willing to contribute something toward their insurance coverage if it was offered. In addition, some immigration reform proposals require that immigrants pay substantial fees for legal entry; a portion of these fees could be applied to help finance their insurance costs.

Employers will gain from an enhanced supply of legal workers, particularly as the labor market tightens due to the aging and retirement of baby boomers and, thus, may be willing to contribute payments in order to gain access to a legal supply of labor. However, if it is entirely voluntary for employers to offer health insurance and for employees to take it, current trends suggest that very low rates of coverage will result. A stronger set of requirements for employers to offer health benefits and for employees to take them may be needed to see meaningful improvement.

Mandating health benefits has advantages and disadvantages. On the one hand, it will improve immigrants' access to health care, reduce reliance on safety net providers and spare state and local governments costs that they now bear for uncompensated care. It would reduce the incentives that employers may now have to hire immigrants over citizen workers because they may not feel it necessary to offer health benefits to immigrant employees. On the other hand, such a policy would increase the cost of employing these temporary workers, which may discourage employers from hiring them. In addition, it would be challenging to monitor the implementation of new federal requirements for parity in insurance offers.

The costs could be partially mitigated by government subsidies. Some degree of government subsidy for immigrants' health coverage is inevitable. When any employer offers health insurance — whether to citizen or immigrant employees — the costs are deductible from the employer's federal and state income taxes and constitute a substantial government subsidy of private health insurance. One study estimated that the total value of federal health insurance tax deductions in 2004 equaled $189 billion, an amount greater than the federal cost of Medicaid.[34]

In the case of temporary workers, additional government subsidies for health insurance might be available from other sources. Employers and employees pay payroll taxes to support Social Security and Medicare benefits for retirement. These payroll taxes add up to a substantial amount, about 15 percent of wages. (The Social Security payroll tax is equal to 12.4 percent of an employee's wages, half withdrawn from employee pay and half matched by the employer, up to a maximum amount that is revised annually. The Medicare payroll tax is 2.9 percent of wages, half withdrawn from employee wages and half matched by the employer; there is no cap on contributions.) But if the new workers are temporary and will not collect these benefits because they are not eligible, a portion of the funds could be used to help subsidize health benefits while they

---

34 J. Sheils and R. Haught, "The Cost of Tax-Exempt Health Benefits in 2004," *Health Affairs web exclusive*, February 22, 2004.

are in the United States. (If they become permanent residents, the subsequent funds could be channeled back to the Social Security and Medicare trust funds when the legal status adjustment occurs.) The federal government could redirect a portion of the Social Security and Medicare payments from temporary workers to establish health insurance subsidies.

One idea that could make health insurance costs a little less expensive for some firms is to develop new insurance pools or products that can be offered to the temporary workers. Small companies are typically charged higher insurance premiums than larger firms because their health insurance and administrative costs are not spread over as many people (i.e., they cannot pool risks as efficiently) and because larger firms can "self-insure" and thereby avoid certain insurance costs that apply to smaller firms. To ease this problem, the federal government could help make it easier for companies to obtain lower insurance costs by pooling risks. For example, the Western Growers Association offers health insurance products for farm workers in California and Arizona. (While they provide insurance for a large number of farm workers, the great majority of farm workers are nonetheless uninsured.) Alternatively, employers could be allowed to "buy into" state employee health insurance plans or into state Medicaid or SCHIP coverage. The development of new products or pools could slightly reduce the costs of health insurance, but would not, by itself, greatly improve access unless employers and employees are willing to bear the remaining costs.

For immigrants who live close to the Mexican border, binational or cross-border health insurance may be a lower cost option. Some insurers in California (e.g., Blue Shield and the Western Growers Association) offer cross-border insurance policies through which members living in the United States receive care at lower cost facilities across the border in Mexico, but can receive emergency care in the United States or care that is not available across the border.[35] The Mexican government also arranges health insurance to let Mexican citizens or their dependents living abroad receive medical care at Mexican facilities through the Mexican Social Security Institute (IMSS) and Seguro Popular for Migrant Families.[36]

Another approach might be to expand the availability of free or reduced price primary care and preventive health services at safety net primary care clinics for temporary workers, rather than provide health insurance coverage. There

---

35 S. Skidmore, "Cross-border Health Insurance Is a Hit with Employers and Workers," *San Diego Union-Tribune*, October 16, 2005.

36 California Healthcare Foundation and California-Mexico Health Initiative, "Guide to Health Programs," Fall 2005.

are various ways to expand the availability of safety net primary care clinics. One possibility is to expand the current system of community (and migrant) health centers, targeting areas that are known to have high concentrations of temporary workers. The administration and Congress have supported expanding the community health center system and the number of sites and patients seen has grown in recent years. Of course, community health centers serve a broad range of patients and in most locales only a fraction of the new patients seen are immigrants.

Another possibility is to develop bilateral agreements for sending nations (e.g., Mexico) to support these clinics in areas where their nationals reside, whether through direct staffing or funding. It would be challenging to permit direct staffing (e.g., sending Mexican health care personnel to the United States) because foreign health care professionals are not licensed to practice in the United States and licensing requirements vary across the states. Unless they are licensed, it would be illegal for them to practice medicine in the United States. Using funds from a sending nation to pay for clinics makes this more feasible, if the sending nation is willing to provide those funds. If a new system of clinics is established, it may also be possible to give them access to lower prices for prescription drugs by letting them participate in the federal discount drug pricing program (called Section 340B). As discussed above, for workers living near the border, a cross-border or binational health coverage plan may be feasible.

Expanding the capacity of safety net clinics could improve immigrants' access to care, but would leave other needs unmet. The range of services provided at clinics varies: Some offer mental health or dental services, but many do not. Certain services are beyond the capacity of primary care clinics. For example, a clinic may be able to provide prenatal care, but not labor and delivery services, for which a hospital is normally required. Clinics can provide primary care for heart problems, but may not be able to perform more sophisticated diagnostic testing or treatment, including surgery.

Targeting of resources will also be a problem. Many temporary workers live outside the areas where these facilities are located and may continue to have problems getting care without health insurance. For example, a study of California agricultural workers found that only 7 percent of the medical care they received came from migrant health clinics.[37] It is also questionable whether new facilities will be

---

37 T. Hernandez, "The California Farm Labor Force: Findings from the National Agricultural Workers Survey, 2003-2004," report for California Program on Access to Care, University of California, November 2005.

able to limit their practices to immigrants or to temporary workers; so much of their services may go to help other needy patients. Certainly, federal community health centers cannot offer services only to immigrants and deny care to citizens.

It would also be appropriate to clarify that temporary workers count, for the period that they are authorized to be in the United States, as lawful residents. Some states impose their own residency requirements for Medicaid. Thus, immigrants with temporary visas sometimes do not count as residents, even though they legally reside in the state for several years. Additionally, because they are not "residents," they do not even qualify for emergency Medicaid coverage. Because of this, temporary workers can be at a disadvantage compared to undocumented immigrants. A simple remedy would be to clarify that temporary workers should be considered residents during their authorized period.

A final issue is that immigrants are often employed in strenuous, risky jobs. Under all states' laws, workers injured on the job — including acute injuries like a broken arm and longer-term injuries such as back strain or illnesses caused by exposure to toxic chemicals — are covered under workers' compensation for their medical testing and treatment. (Depending on the state, some workers such as independent contractors or casual workers may be excluded from workers' compensation requirements.) But data cited earlier suggests that many of these injuries go untreated. At a minimum, temporary workers authorized under the new categories should be protected by workers' compensation laws.

Unauthorized Immigrants. In spite of immigration reform efforts or changes in border security, a substantial number of unauthorized immigrants will undoubtedly remain in the United States. The system that now responds to their health care needs is at best a rudimentary patchwork. In many areas, poor unauthorized immigrants may be able to get free or reduced price health care at certain public or nonprofit clinics or hospitals, just as poor citizens or legal immigrants can get free or reduced price care. Most of the health costs are borne by state, local, and charitable safety net health care providers. The federal government subsidizes a portion of these costs through federal funding for community health centers and migrant health centers. Unauthorized immigrants may obtain Medicaid coverage for emergency medical care, including labor and delivery, but not prenatal care, if they meet other Medicaid eligibility criteria. Thus, while low-income children and parents may get Medicaid coverage for emergencies, adults without dependent children do not.

Recent legislation provided a limited amount of federal funding to help reimburse hospitals and physicians for a portion of the uncompensated health care costs of emergency care provided to unauthorized and certain other immigrants.[38] The legislation allocates $1 billion over four years for this purpose, but it is too early to know how much will be spent and whether the initiative will be effective in meeting the needs of immigrants or health care providers.

One option to consider is increasing funding to support safety net health care providers who offer services to unauthorized immigrants, perhaps through a combination of federal funds and payments from businesses that are most likely to employ the unauthorized. It would be a challenge, however, to design a simple allocation and reporting system that does not deter unauthorized immigrants from getting health care. For example, many objected to a plan to allocate $1 billion in additional funds that required determining and documenting which emergency patients were undocumented because it might intimidate some immigrants and push them away from care, rather than facilitating care.

A final issue to consider is whether legal status should be a factor in offering insurance coverage for certain groups, such as children or pregnant women. Because of the public health interest in improving their health care, some policymakers, analysts, and advocates support offering universal coverage to all low-income children or pregnant women, regardless of whether they are immigrants or citizens. Children born of pregnant immigrants will be native-born citizens and undocumented children generally did not enter the United States of their own volition and may remain here for the balance of their lives. Thus, it may be appropriate to offer children and pregnant women access to health insurance and health care on the same terms as native-born citizens. The state of Illinois and a number of counties in California have developed universal health plans for children that offer publicly funded health insurance for all low-income children, regardless of immigration status.

CONCLUSIONS

For myriad reasons, about half of all immigrants lack health insurance coverage and many experience great difficulty obtaining medical care. Because so many immigrants are uninsured, these gaps lead to human costs associated with unmet medical needs and poor health, as well as to costs for uncompensated care that end up being borne by state, local, and charitable health care providers and by cost-shifting to the privately insured. Immigration reform could improve immigrants' health access, particularly if it increases the likelihood that immigrants

---

38 Center on Medicare and Medicaid Services, "Services Furnished to Undocumented Aliens," at www.cms.hhs.gov/UndocAliens/.

are offered private employer-sponsored health insurance. To do so would require a commitment to ensure that such efforts are an integral issue in immigration reform. It is not clear if that commitment exists, however. Providing health benefits to temporary workers would create additional costs for employers, employees, and/or governments. Some may believe that adding concerns about health benefits would further complicate discussions and decisions about a number of other controversial issues in immigration reform.

If there was a consensus that the effort is worthwhile, it should be possible to design approaches that spread the costs of immigrants' health benefits across employers, employees, and governments. This would help assure that the jobs temporary workers obtain are good jobs that offer health benefits.

Immigration reform also affords policy officials the opportunity to examine health access for other immigrants, including lawful permanent residents and unauthorized immigrants. Modest changes, such as restoring access to Medicaid and SCHIP for legal immigrants and reducing language barriers to health services, could help improve the health care for those already in the United States.

As it stands, health care coverage and access for immigrants in the United States is deplorable. The debate about immigration reform presents an opportunity to ask whether we can do better.

CHAPTER 8

Improving Immigrant Workers' Economic Prospects: A Review of the Literature

Amy Beeler and Julie Murray

Introduction

Today's US economy is highly dependent on immigration, authorized and unauthorized, temporary and permanent. Immigrants contributed more than 50 percent to the nation's civilian labor force growth in the 1990s and currently comprise over 14 percent of the US labor force. They are expected to be a critical driver of labor force growth when the first wave of baby boomers starts retiring in 2008. And without the contribution of immigrant labor, the output of goods and services in the United States would be at least $1 trillion smaller than it is today and the civilian labor force would have only grown 5 percent (versus 11.5 percent) between 1990 and 2001.[1]

Nevertheless, immigrants face challenges to full incorporation in the US workforce. Many arrive with few skills and little education, requiring basic education, language training, and technical skill training. Many others come with advanced skills and require certifications and training that tap them. Still others seek to start businesses in their new communities and need assistance to fulfill that goal.

This chapter provides an overview of the literature on workforce development, skill transfer, and entrepreneurship among immigrants in the United States. It highlights key academic studies that test the effectiveness of different strategies to address these issues. Since the scientific literature in these areas is far from

---

1 National Immigration Law Center (NILC), "Facts about Immigrant Workers" (Los Angeles, CA: NILC, 2003). A. Sum, N. Fogg, I. Khatiwada, S. Palma, "Foreign Immigration and the Labor Force of the U.S.: The Contributions of New Foreign Immigration to the Growth of the Nation's Labor Force and Its Employed Population, 2000 to 2004," July 2004. Available online at http://www.nupr.neu.edu/7-04 /immigrant_04.pdf#search=%22contribution%20of%20immigration%20to%20the%20labor%20force%22.

complete, it also relies on descriptions of promising practices that have emerged in recent years.

THE IMMIGRANT WORKFORCE

In 2004, there were 21.4 million employed foreign-born workers in the United States.[2] These workers are very diverse in terms of country and region of origin. Over half are from Latin America and the Caribbean, while another quarter are from Asia. Unlike the last great wave of immigration at the turn of the 20th century, when Europeans comprised the largest regional immigrant group, workers born in Europe account for just 12 percent of today's foreign-born workers.

While immigrants are found across the employment spectrum, they are disproportionately low-wage workers, comprising 20 percent of this population. Immigrants' hourly wages are lower on average than those of natives: nearly half earn less than 200 percent of the minimum wage — as compared to one-third of native workers.[3]

An increasingly large segment of the immigrant workforce is unauthorized. Following several years of rapid growth, the number of unauthorized migrants reached an estimated 11.1 million in 2005. The unauthorized are very likely to be part of the workforce: Ninety-six percent of undocumented men were employed in the labor force — a rate higher than that for legal immigrants and native-born workers.[4]

Low wages and low educational levels are common among the unauthorized. Two-thirds of unauthorized immigrants earn less than twice the minimum wage, compared to one-third of all workers. And despite the fact that 15 percent of the unauthorized have at least a college degree and another 10 percent have some college education, they are considerably more likely than natives to have very low levels of education.[5] Unauthorized immigrants are also more likely than other immigrants to lack English proficiency.[6]

---

2 US Department of Labor Bureau of Labor Statistics, "Labor Force Characteristics of Foreign Born Workers in 2004" (Washington, DC: BLS, 2004), http://www.bls.gov/cps/.

3 R. Capps, M. Fix, J. S. Passel, J. Ost, and D. Perez-Lopez, "A Profile of the Low-Wage Immigrant Workforce," Immigrant Families and Workers Facts and Perspectives, Brief No. 4 (Washington, DC: The Urban Institute, 2003).

4 University of Illinois at Chicago, Center for Urban Economic Development study, 2002. J. Passell, "Unauthorized Migrants: Numbers and Characteristics," Background Briefing Prepared for the Migration Policy Institute's Independent Task Force on Immigration and America's Future, Pew Hispanic Center, June 14, 2005. Available online at pewhispanic.org/files/reports/46.pdf.

5 Passel, "Unauthorized Migrants," Background Briefing Prepared for the Migration Policy Institute's Independent Task Force on Immigration and America's Future (Washington, DC: Pew Hispanic Center, 2005).

6 R. Capps, L. Ku, M. Fix, et al., "How Are Immigrants Faring after Welfare Reform? Preliminary Evidence from Los Angeles and New York City" (Washington, DC: The Urban Institute, 2002).

Building Immigrants' English and Job Skills

Workers with Limited English proficiency

Due to high rates of immigration, limited English proficient (LEP) individuals have become a large and growing segment of the US workforce.[7] According to the 2000 Census, approximately 14 million, or nearly 9.5 percent, of all working-age adults in the United States either did not speak English at all or spoke it less than "very well," and 89 percent of the adult LEP population was foreign born.[8]

LEP immigrant adults tend to be relatively recent immigrants with low levels of formal education. Nearly 60 percent of LEP immigrant adults arrived in the United States in the last ten years.[9] Fifty percent report having nine or fewer years of education, and 64 percent have less than a high school degree. Only 18 percent have any post-secondary education.[10]

Limited English proficiency is associated with numerous risk factors among immigrant families. Research conducted in New York City and Los Angeles found that limited English proficient immigrant families are more likely to earn significantly lower wages, experience higher rates of unemployment, be food insecure, and live in poverty than English proficient immigrant families.[11]

Surveys and studies of this population indicate that the overwhelming majority of LEP immigrants are motivated to learn English, but due in part to limited government funding, demand far exceeds the supply of English classes.[12] Immigrants' growing numbers and their pivotal role in the economy create a compelling demographic, social, and economic imperative for providing them more opportunities to improve their English skills.

---

7   A person is "limited English proficient" if he/she reports *speaking* a language other than English at home and does not *speak* English "very well." R. Capps, M. Fix, J. S. Passel, J. Ost, and D. Perez-Lopez, "A Profile of the Low-Wage Immigrant Workforce," Immigrant Families and Workers Facts and Perspectives, Brief No. 4 (Washington, DC: The Urban Institute, 2003).

8   US Census Bureau, 2000 Supplementary Survey Summary Tables, http://factfinder.census.gov.

9   T. E. Martinez and T. Wang, "Supporting English Language Acquisition: Opportunities for Foundations to Strengthen the Social and Economic Well-Being of Immigrant Families," The Annie E. Casey Foundation and Grantmakers Concerned with Immigrants and Refugees, 2005.

10   Ibid.

11   Capps, et al., "How Are Immigrants Faring after Welfare Reform? Preliminary Evidence from Los Angeles and New York City." (see n. 6).

12   Martinez and Wang, "Supporting English Language Acquisition" (see n. 9). See also http://www.education.umn.edu/nceo/OnlinePubs/MnReport8.html.

The financial impact of limited English

English language proficiency plays an important role in increasing immigrant earnings, employment, and opportunities for advancement. After adjusting for other socioeconomic factors including education and work experience, one study found that English-speaking immigrants earned 17 percent more than non-English speaking immigrants.[13] Another study found that immigrants and refugees who are fluent in oral and written English earn about 24 percent more than those who lack fluency, regardless of their qualifications.[14] As Fremstad notes, "as much as half of the relative wage growth experienced by immigrants in the first 20 years after arrival may be attributed to gains from learning the English language."[15]

However, the extent to which improved English skills leads to better paying jobs depends in large part on one's level of education. Research shows that learning to speak English fluently results in a 76 percent jump in earnings for immigrants with more than 12 years of education, compared to only a 4 percent increase for workers with fewer than eight years of education.[16]

Thus, while learning English is important, it will not necessarily increase the earnings of less-educated immigrants, who make up the majority of the limited English-speaking adult population, if they still lack the basic literacy and math skills needed to succeed in the US workplace.[17]

Basic job skills for immigrant workers

While a segment of the immigrant workforce has high levels of education, immigrant workers are more likely than natives to have lower education levels. Thirty percent of foreign-born workers have less than a high school education,

---

13 B. Chiswick and P. W. Miller, "Language in the Immigrant Labor Market," in *Immigration, Language and Ethnicity: Canada and the United States*, ed. B. R. Chiswick (Washington, DC: American Enterprise Institute, 1992).

14 A. Gonzalez, "The Acquisition and Labor Market Value of Four English Skills: New Evidence from NALS," *Contemporary Economic Policy* 18, no. 3 (2000): 259-269.

15 S. Fremstad, "Immigrants, Persons with Limited Proficiency in English, and the TANF Program: What Do We Know?" (Washington, DC: Center on Budget and Policy Priorities, 2003).

16 M. Mora, "An Overview of the Economics of Language in the U.S. Labor Market," Presentation Notes (Denver, CO: American Economic Association Summer Minority Program, 2003), http://www.workandeconomy.org/The%20Integration%20of%20Immigrants%20in%20the%20Workplace%20Prepublication%20Release%207-31-06.pdf#search=%22%22An%20Overview%20of%20the%20Economics%20of%20Language%20in%20the%20U.S.%20Labor%20Market%22%22.

17 Martinez and Wang, "Supporting English Language Acquisition" (see n. 9).

and 18 percent have less than a ninth-grade education. These shares compare to 8 percent and 1 percent, respectively, among US-born workers.

FINDING THE BEST APPROACH TO ENGLISH-LANGUAGE ACQUISITION AND JOB TRAINING

There seems to be wide agreement that a comprehensive workforce development approach, which integrates job training (both hard and soft skills), English-language acquisition, and cultural orientation, is the most effective approach for immigrant workers in need of new skills.[18] However, despite knowledge that English-language and job-training services can make a difference for labor market success, little scientific research has been conducted on the most effective ways to deliver English-language, literacy, and job-training services to the immigrant population.[19]

One random assignment evaluation in the early 1990s measured the effectiveness of a program that served primarily Hispanic workers, many of whom were LEP. The program, the Center for Employment and Training (CET), was a six- to seven-month, full-time, comprehensive job training program that employed staff familiar with local labor markets.[20] Individuals entered job training immediately (regardless of their educational levels) and received English-language, literacy, and math instruction, which was integrated directly into training for a specific job. Importantly, the initially positive effects of participating in the CET program faded after five years for those with less than a high school diploma, signaling the need for ongoing support in English-language and literacy services.[21]

According to another 2001 survey of 11 job training programs — none of which specifically targeted LEP or immigrant workers — the most successful approach blended short-term education and training with a job search program that emphasized good jobs. For immigrants, such a "mixed approach" could include intensive English as a Second Language (ESL) courses for

---

18 Fremstad, "Immigrants, Persons with Limited Proficiency in English, and the TANF Program" (see n. 15); H. S. Wrigley, E. Richer, K. Martinson, H. Kubo, and J. Straw, "The Language of Opportunity: Expanding Employment Prospects for Adults with Limited English Skills" (Washington, DC: Center for Law and Social Policy, 2003); J. Lewis and R. Paral, "Policy Implications of Immigrant Workers and Entrepreneurs. Directions for State Policymakers" (Chicago, IL: Roosevelt University Institute for Metropolitan Affairs, 2001).

19 Wrigley et al., "The Language of Opportunity" (see n. 18).

20 Ibid.

21 Ibid.

persons with very low literacy levels, ESL in combination with employment for other LEP adults, job placement services that help immigrants find good jobs with opportunities for advancement, and job training to increase skill levels.[22]

CONSIDERING TIME CONSTRAINTS

In addition to determining a curriculum for skills education, service providers must also take into account time constraints facing immigrant workers. Less-educated LEP adults must typically go through a long, sequential educational process to improve their vocational skills. First they need to enroll in ESL courses and improve their English skills sufficiently before enrolling in GED, higher education, or job training programs. Given the financial need to work, most LEP adults do not have the time to complete this lengthy process.[23] Lewis and Paral argue that English language and vocational training need to be integrated into work, or at least accomplished at the same time.[24]

CONSIDERING NATIVE-LANGUAGE LITERACY

While traditional language acquisition programs emphasize English immersion, emerging research suggests that helping LEP individuals develop native language literacy and other related skills may facilitate English acquisition.[25] An estimated 32 percent of adults enrolled in ESL programs lack literacy skills in their native language, and research suggests that these adults are slower in learning a second language than their literate counterparts.[26] One study found that Haitian participants who received native language literacy instruction while learning English developed stronger literacy skills in English than those who only received English instruction, even though the total number of instructional hours for the two groups were equal. Another study found that immigrant adults with minimal literacy in Hmong acquired English reading skills more rapidly than those who had no Hmong literacy.[27]

---

22 Fremstad, "Immigrants, Persons with Limited Proficiency in English" (see n. 15).

23 Martinez and Wang, "Supporting English Language Acquisition" (see n. 9).

24 Lewis and Paral, "Policy Implications of Immigrant Workers" (see n. 18).

25 Wrigley et al., "The Language of Opportunity" (see n. 18).

26 Martinez and Wang, "Supporting English Language Acquisition" (see n. 9).

27 M. Burtoff, "The Haitian Creole Literacy Evaluation Study Final Report" (New York: Ford Foundation, 1985); and B. Robson, "Hmong Literacy, Formal Education, and Their Effects on Performance in an ESL Class," in The Hmong in the West: Observations and Reports, ed. B. T. Downing and D. P. Olney, 201-225, 1982, as cited in Martinez and Wang, "Supporting English Language Acquisition" (see n. 23).

Vocational English as a Second Language (VESL)

Programs that teach both English and workplace skills are collectively known as Vocational English as a Second Language (VESL) courses. To make this approach work for immigrants who speak little English, language instruction is tied to training in particular occupations and incorporates workplace communication skills as well as job-specific language needed for training, certification, and testing like the CET program. Successful initiatives included staff with extensive knowledge of the local labor market.[28]

Many VESL programs teach participants about job search and interview skills, customs and norms in the US workplace, and ways to communicate effectively with co-workers. These programs provide orientation and training; some offer instruction in basic computer software programs.

In recent years, a growing number of community colleges, unions, and community-based organizations have begun to offer occupation-specific VESL courses. The goals of instruction have varied from teaching English vocabulary commonly used in construction, nursing, or childcare jobs to training for entrance examinations or certification in specific occupations.[29]

While some employers balk at offering ESL training to immigrant workers, citing scheduling issues, cost, a perceived lack of benefit to companies, and a sense that teaching employees English is not their responsibility,[30] others clearly see this kind of training as valuable for employees and have implemented programs. For example, one recent survey of manufacturing employers found that a majority of survey respondents provided specialized on-the-job resources for their immigrant workers, including job-related training material, ESL classes, bilingual training, and job-specific English instruction.[31]

The benefits of improved language skills are felt by both the employer and learner. The final report to the Department of Education on the National

---

28 Ibid.

29 AFL-CIO Working for America Institute, "Getting to Work: A Report on How Workers with Limited English Skills Can Prepare for Good Jobs" (Washington, DC: AFL-CIO, 2004).

30 M. Burt, "Issues with Outcomes in Workplace ESL Programs, National Center for ESL Literacy Education," Submitted to US Department of Education, Office of Adult and Vocational Education and The Institute for Work and the Economy, January 6, 2004.

31 National Association of Manufacturers and the Center for Workforce Success, "Closing the Immigrant Skills Gap: A Report on Challenges and Opportunities Facing the Manufacturing Sector" (Washington, DC: Center for Workforce Success, 2004). It should be noted, though, that the survey had a low response rate, calling into question the generalizability of its results.

Workplace Literacy Program — a now-defunct federal program that integrated job training with language acquisition — found that after employees participated, employers reported fewer attendance problems, better production, increased job retention, and increased quality control. Employees reported improvements in job security and more opportunities for job advancement.[32]

FEDERAL POLICIES REGARDING IMMIGRANTS' WORKFORCE DEVELOPMENT

THE WORKFORCE INVESTMENT ACT (WIA)

The Workforce Investment Act (WIA), which replaced the Job Training Partnership Act (JTPA) in 1998, provides federal funding for workforce development and adult education, including ESL, nationwide.

WIA'S JOB TRAINING AND PLACEMENT: ACCESSIBILITY TO IMMIGRANTS

The act's Title I provides for a variety of services, such as résumé preparation, career counseling, and job readiness training and placement for low-skilled, poor, or unemployed workers. Despite low educational levels on average, LEP workers are arguably under-represented among recipients of Title I services, comprising only 7 percent of participants in 2000 while being over-represented among low-wage workers overall.[33] One reason for this under-representation is that 40 percent of low-wage immigrant workers are undocumented and hence ineligible for WIA job training services.[34]

While many other immigrants and LEP individuals are eligible for WIA job training services, these populations often encounter barriers to participation. According to one study, many job training and placement programs are not accessible to, or do not meet the unique needs of, immigrant and other limited-English workers. One-stop centers — sites that provide job search services and avenues to job training and education — and other publicly funded programs often have difficulty providing basic language access and culturally differentiated services.[35] LEP individuals face challenges due to a short sup-

---

32 NILC, "Facts About Immigrant Workers" (see n. 1).

33 Regarding the share of WIA Title I participants who are LEP, see Wrigley et al., "The Language of Opportunity" (see n. 18).

34 Capps et al., "A Profile of the Low-Wage Immigrant Workforce" (see n. 3).

35 T. Moran and D. Petsod, "Newcomers in the American Workplace: Improving Employment Outcomes for Low-Wage Immigrants and Refugees" (Sepastopol, CA: Grantmakers Concerned with Immigrants and Refugees and Neighborhood Funders Groups, 2004).

ply of translators at service centers.[36] Training providers who want to offer programs that integrate vocational training and language acquisition also face obstacles due to the lack of coordination between the workforce development system and the adult education system.[37]

In some cases, programs' minimum standards may also effectively exclude immigrants with limited English proficiency. For example, some one-stop centers provide training services to the individuals most likely to get a job, thereby overlooking the most hard-to-serve populations, including LEP workers. Similarly, some training providers exclude LEP persons by imposing minimum participation requirements (an eighth-grade reading level, e.g.) that many LEP workers cannot meet.[38]

ESL CLASSES FUNDED UNDER WIA'S ADULT BASIC EDUCATION PROVISION

In addition to job training services, through its Title II, WIA also provides the central federal funding stream for adult education and family literacy services for adults lacking basic skills, including English proficiency. Nearly 1.1 million adults were served in ESL classes in 2000 funded under Title II — or approximately 13 percent of the nation's LEP adults.[39]

There is some evidence, though, that ESL classes provided through WIA, in addition to those funded by the states, are oversubscribed. In light of limited state and federal funding, the demand for such classes outstrips the supply.[40] For example, in 2005, the Massachusetts Department of Education reported that more than 18,000 residents were on waiting lists for ESL classes; the average wait is six months to two years.[41] Unfortunately, federal and state funding for English acquisition programs has not kept pace with the growth of the LEP population. Many of these programs continue to teach immigrants only basic skills, or what some have characterized as "survival English," often with the goal of quickly pushing participants into — if not preparing them for — the workforce.

36 AFL-CIO, "Getting to Work" (see n. 29).

37 NILC, "Facts about Immigrant Workers" (see n. 1).

38 Ibid.

39 Wrigley et al., "The Language of Opportunity" (see n. 18).

40 Ibid.

41 Martinez and Wang, "Supporting English Language Acquisition" (see n. 9).

MAKING SKILLS AND CREDENTIALS COUNT IN THE UNITED STATES

THE CHALLENGES OF TRANSFERRING SKILLS AND CREDENTIALS

Some new immigrant workers do not need basic English instruction or job training. They enter the United States with substantial skills — education, experience, and credentials — from their home countries and may just have difficulty transferring these skills to the US workforce. For example, data from 2001 indicate that 42 percent of current immigrants enter the United States with 12 or more years of formal education.[42]

Evidence in the United States and abroad indicates that immigrants pay a penalty when their skills do not transfer to their new home countries. Recent US research found that 50 percent of legal immigrants experienced occupational downgrading in their first year in the country, meaning that they worked in jobs requiring lower skills than those they had abroad.[43]

There are various reasons why immigrants cannot easily transfer their skills after migration. Anecdotal evidence indicates that immigrants lack networks through which they may be made aware of openings for jobs that require substantial skills; they may be unfamiliar with US job search techniques; and they may need to update existing skills or certify, re-certify, or gain licensure or credentials.[44] Indeed, attaining accreditation in certain states can be so arduous that immigrants travel to neighboring states to acquire accreditation.[45]

A Canadian study leads to similar conclusions, finding that immigrants lack information about how to access a profession or trade, meet licensing standards and requirements, and obtain recognition of foreign academic credentials and work experience.[46] In order to make an accurate assessment of an individual's prior training, employers and regulatory bodies need considerable expertise in comparative education and a familiarity with international educational sys-

---

42 I. Light, "Immigrant Neighborhoods as Centers of Commerce," Presented to the Illinois Immigration Policy Project (Chicago: Roosevelt University Institute for Metropolitan Affairs, 2001).

43 I. R. Akresh, "Occupational Mobility among Legal Immigrants to the United States," *International Migration Review* 40, no. 4, publication forthcoming.

44 Available at Upwardly Global Web site, http://www.upwardlyglobal.org/about/faqs.php.

45 A. Morse, Program Director for the Immigrant Policy Project at the National Conference of State Legislatures, presentation at Institute for Work and the Economy conference, Chicago, April 17, 2006.

46 A. Brouwer, "Immigrants Need Not Apply" (Ottawa: Caledon Institute of Social Policy, 1999).

tems. Shortcomings in each area are frequently cited by Canadian licensing bodies as reasons for not evaluating prior learning.[47]

CREDENTIALING PROGRAMS IN THE UNITED STATES

There is no formal public system in the United States for employers or educational bodies for converting prior learning or foreign credentials. Some nongovernmental programs do exist in the United States that assist immigrants seeking accreditation. For example, World Education Services (WES) — a nonprofit established in 1974 — maintains a comprehensive database of world universities. For a fee of $100 to $200, WES will evaluate a degree from any country in the world and convert it to its US or Canadian equivalent. In 2004, WES reported processing more than 50,000 evaluations from more than 150 countries, providing this information to 2,300 higher education institutions in the United States and Canada.[48]

There are no organizations that focus on re-licensing issues in a similarly comprehensive way, although some do focus on specific fields. For example, the Education Commission for Foreign Medical Graduates assesses the readiness of foreign-trained medical graduates to enter the medical field in the United States.[49]

THE CANADIAN FOREIGN CREDENTIAL PROGRAM: A MODEL

An ongoing effort in Canada to create a national system for helping immigrants transfer skills or credentials may provide a model for US policymakers. Facing a situation where virtually all net labor force growth will come from immigration by the middle of the next decade, the Canadian government is taking a proactive approach toward ensuring internationally trained workers can fully participate in the labor market. The government of Canada is working with provincial/territorial governments, licensing and regulatory bodies, sector councils, employers, and many other groups to accelerate the integration of internationally trained workers into the workforce and society. The government has instituted a new Foreign Credential Recognition (FCR) program and is providing $68 million over six years to implement it.[50]

---

47 Ibid.

48 Available online at http://www.wes.org.

49 Available online at http://www.ecfmg.org.

50 Human Resources and Skills Development Canada, http://www.hrsdc.gc.ca/en/ws/programs/fcr/backgrounder_fcr.pdf.

Supporting Immigrant Entrepreneurs

The self-employed immigrant entrepreneur

In addition to being traditional employees, immigrants comprise a disproportionate share of the self-employed in the United States. In every US census from 1880 to 1990, immigrants have been more likely to be self-employed than natives.[51] As entrepreneurs, immigrants may make important contributions to the economy while ensuring their own self-sufficiency. In the case of Illinois, a traditional immigrant receiving state, Lewis and Paral found that entrepreneurship was a key factor in the economic development of immigrants and their communities. The number of Asian-owned businesses in Illinois grew by 353 percent between 1982 and 1997, and the number of Latino-owned businesses increased by 528 percent. By 1997, there were approximately 37,000 Asian-owned and 31,000 Latino-owned businesses in the state.[52]

There is great variation in self-employment rates of different immigrant and ethnic groups. Researchers disagree about the reason for this variation, with some contending that it is the result of human or financial capital of individual immigrants, and others suggesting that immigrant communities are themselves differential sources of entrepreneurial energy.[53] Entrepreneurship may be difficult to measure as some ethnic groups are more likely to begin and sustain their businesses in the informal sector.

How immigrant businesses promote integration

Immigrant-owned businesses present a variety of potential benefits to immigrant entrepreneurs themselves and to their employees. Immigrant business owners may find that self-employment is a more profitable endeavor than other forms of work. Evidence in the 1990s, for example, indicated that self-employed immigrants had incomes that were substantially higher than all other groups of immigrant workers and equal to incomes of US-born entrepreneurs.[54]

In addition, immigrant entrepreneurs can create employment opportunities for vulnerable immigrants seeking work. Light claims that the income derived

---

51 D. Aronson, "Immigrant Entrepreneurs," *Research Perspectives on Migration* 1, no. 2 (Washington, DC: Carnegie Endowment for International Peace, 1997).

52 Lewis and Paral, "Policy Implications of Immigrant Workers" (see n. 18).

53 Aronson, "Immigrant Entrepreneurs" (see n. 54).

54 M. Fix and J. S. Passel, *Immigration and Immigrants: Setting the Record Straight* (Washington, DC: The Urban Institute, 1994).

SPOTLIGHT ON EMPLOYING SKILLED IMMIGRANTS: UPWARDLY GLOBAL

Upwardly Global is a nonprofit organization based in San Francisco that works with skilled legal immigrants and employers. It offers services to job-seekers that include help with writing résumés, sharpening interviewing skills, and developing professional networks. Upwardly Global also works with employers to match positions with skilled immigrants and evaluate foreign credentials.

According to Upwardly Global, employers may lack the resources and knowledge to hire immigrants. Examples of barriers in the path of qualified immigrants seeking work include:

- Employers who overemphasize the importance of English (e.g., requiring flawless grammar for an accounting position);

- Recruiters who pass over a résumé because of a foreign sounding name;

- Interviewers who insist on conducting a phone screening (which could handicap non-native English speakers);

- Employers who consider foreign universities and degrees to be invalid or inferior;

- Employers who do not have the capacity to verify foreign credentials;

- Employers who will not hire someone who does not have US work experience; and

- Companies that advertise that only permanent residents or US citizens need apply (there are many immigrants or refugees who are work-authorized, but not technically permanent residents).

Source: Upwardly Global Web site, available at www.upwardlyglobal.org

from "ethnic economies" — in which ethnic entrepreneurs hire co-ethnics —
is "especially valuable for those otherwise most disadvantaged in the general
labor market by dint of low education, poor health, lack of English-language
skill, lack of child care, exclusion from mainstream social networks, ethno-
religious discrimination, or racism."[55]

Ethnic economies strengthen the human capital of immigrants and low-income
ethnic minorities in two ways. First, they have the capacity to educate future
ethnic entrepreneurs,[56] teaching them their trade and how to start and run a
business. Second, ethnic economies offer a second-tier labor market in which
co-ethnics disadvantaged in the general labor market can acquire employment
skills. Once these skills are acquired, immigrant workers can find employment
in the mainstream economy, presumably at higher wages.

ENTREPRENEURS, ETHNIC ECONOMIES, AND INTEGRATION CONCERNS

Some researchers have suggested that ethnic economies may be a sign of underlying discrimination in the work force. Immigrants who anticipate discrimination in the labor market may turn to their own businesses as an alternate form
of work.[57] One study found that a substantial number of Korean, Middle
Eastern, or South Asian business owners in Chicago started their own businesses, at least in part, because they felt disadvantaged in the US labor market.[58]

Ethnic economies can potentially have negative effects on the mobility of
immigrant workers within them. Martinez and Wang argue that wages paid in
immigrant neighborhoods were relatively low, reflecting the constant stream of
newcomers competing for entry-level or low-skill jobs. One study of Mexican
entrepreneurs in the United States found that a concentration of self-employed
Mexican immigrants had a negative effect on the earnings of Mexican immigrants overall in small ethnic labor markets.[59]

English skills are in less demand by employers whose businesses either serve a
non-English speaking population or are in industries that rely on low-wage
labor (e.g., janitorial, food service, gardening, or residential construction).

---

55 Light, "Immigrant Neighborhoods" (see n. 45).

56 R. Raijman and M. Tienda, "Immigrants' Pathways to Business Ownership: A Comparative Ethnic
    Perspective," *International Migration Review* 34, no. 3 (2000): 682-706.

57 I. Light, *Ethnic Enterprise in America* (Berkeley, University of California Press, 1972).

58 Raijman and Tienda, "Immigrants' Pathways to Business Ownership" (see n. 59).

59 D. Spencer and F. D. Bean, "Self-Employment Concentration and Earnings among Mexican Immigrants in
    the U.S.," *Social Forces* 77 (1999): 1021-1047.

Lower demand reduces the need to learn English, which could affect immigrants' economic mobility and social integration outside of the enclave. In sum, under some scenarios, immigrant entrepreneurship and ethnic enclaves signal negative, not positive integration.

FINANCIAL SUPPORT FOR IMMIGRANT ENTREPRENEURS

If we concede that on balance entrepreneurship promotes integration and mobility, what public policies advance business formation?

Federal agencies provide a wide range of benefits to many immigrant business owners through technical assistance, microenterprise loans, and the award of government contracts. Nearly every federal department or agency has some form of assistance for minority or other historically disadvantaged business owners, which would often include immigrant groups. For example, the Minority Business Development Agency, part of the Department of Commerce, provides personalized assistance — such as help in writing business plans, marketing, management and technical matters, and financial planning — to socially and economically disadvantaged groups.

However, there is some evidence that standards for non-citizen access to these services are not consistent across the federal government. For example, the Small Business Administration's (SBA) designation of minority-owned businesses, needed to obtain SBA benefits, is not available to legal non-citizen business owners.[60] By way of contrast, a designation as a minority business by the Department of Transportation is available to both citizens and legal permanent residents.[61]

Beyond government benefits, immigrant communities themselves have historically been sources of capital for entrepreneurship. One strategy has been to rely on informal mechanisms, commonly known as Rotating Savings and Credit Associations (ROSCAs), to finance business undertaking. With minimal documentation, a small group of investors agrees to pool financial resources, loan them to a member of the group, collect the loan with interest, and then share it with another member, so that use of the capital rotates among the membership.[62] These systems can be an effective means of providing capital for small business projects. However, they often do not generate

---

60 See Small Business Administration Web site: http://www.sba.gov/sdb/sbadot.html.

61 See, e.g., Department of Transportation application for designation: http://osdbuweb.dot.gov/documents/doc/dbe/Final%20 Application.DOC.

62 Lewis and Paral, "Policy Implications of Immigrant Workers" (see n. 18).

the kind of records needed to document credit history for larger, longer-term loans from formal financial institutions.[63]

Lewis and Paral propose that a review should be undertaken of ROSCAs' place within American banking laws to determine whether they should be legally enforceable and insurable, whether licensure could be helpful, and how and whether they should be taxed. Additionally, they argue for developing ways to document ROSCA transactions so the loans can be used to establish credit history.[64]

Due to the often informal nature of immigrant businesses, further outreach could be undertaken to provide additional information about how to establish a business, how to obtain necessary financing, and how to arrange for legal transactions.[65] States can work further to provide additional technical assistance to immigrant-owned businesses, in, for example, zoning, licensing, marketing, and financing.[66]

CONCLUSION

US policymakers have an opportunity to invest more in immigrant workers in coming years. Potential changes to WIA could have large impacts on immigrant workers. One proposed WIA bill encourages services for hard-to-serve groups, provides new incentives to serve LEPs, and explicitly authorizes training programs that integrate vocational skills and English-language learning. It provides at least ten grants for demonstrations of integrated occupational and language acquisition programs.

In addition to skill-building, policymakers could also opt to take up the issue of credentialing among more highly skilled workers. Examples from the Canadian government and US nongovernmental actors may offer lessons regarding a larger role for the public sector in either the regulation or standardization of credentialing.

In the area of entrepreneurship, the process for determining recipient eligibility accompanies the seemingly wide array of government services for business own-

---

63 Ibid.

64 Ibid.

65 M. Tienda, "Comparative Perspectives on Ethnic and Immigrant Entrepreneurship and Business Development in Chicago" (Chicago: Roosevelt University Institute for Metropolitan Affairs, 2001).

66 Lewis and Paral, "Policy Implications of Immigrant Workers" (see n. 18).

ers and varies in illogical ways across agencies. Differences in non-citizen eligibility may decrease access to capital, technical assistance, and the like for many immigrant entrepreneurs, suggesting that legal non-citizen firms be more broadly eligible for federal contracts and assistance.

One clear implication of this literature review is that more quality research is needed to determine how best to train immigrant workers. In particular, more could be done to study *employers'* role in building immigrants' skills, why employers do or do not offer ESL or job-training services, and the costs and benefits that accrue to employers that offer worker development programs. The field also needs a more systematic understanding of the approaches that promote language acquisition among workers.

A final point is that workforce development for immigrants — whether it includes basic English or job skills, credentialing, or services for entrepreneurs — will not automatically lead to workforce integration. Many factors will likely have more far-reaching effects on incorporation than training or skills. The large population of unauthorized and temporary workers already in the United States raises questions about whether and how these workers should become a permanent part of the workforce. Proposals for a new, large-scale temporary worker program lend even greater importance to these questions. And the anticipation of disproportionate growth in low-wage, low-skilled work in the US economy in coming years calls into question whether English skills and vocational training for the least skilled immigrant workers will be sufficient to promote future economic mobility.

CHAPTER 9

EDUCATING THE CHILDREN OF IMMIGRANTS

JULIE MURRAY, JEANNE BATALOVA, AND MICHAEL FIX[*]

INTRODUCTION

The demographics of US elementary and secondary schools are changing rapidly as a result of record-high immigration, increasing diversity in terms of immigrants' origins and native languages, and immigrants' expanding geographic dispersal throughout the United States. Sustained high levels of immigration have also led to a rapid increase in the number of children with immigrant parents. By 2000, immigrants represented one in nine of all US residents, but their children represented one in five of all children under age 18. Many of these children do not speak English well, have low-educated parents, and live in poor families. Meeting their linguistic and academic needs presents a challenge to educators nationwide.

This chapter begins with a description of the demographic challenges that US schools face when serving children of immigrants, particularly those who do not speak English very well, whom we refer to here as limited English proficient (LEP) students (see Box 1). It also provides a description of the academic achievements of children of immigrants and LEP students and a brief history of education mechanisms developed to foster the integration of immigrant families. Finally, this chapter describes five persistent policy and practice issues relating to the children of immigrants in US schools, with special attention devoted to the federal education legislation, the No Child Left Behind (NCLB) Act, and other policies that may significantly impact this population.

---

* The authors would like to thank Mary Helen Ybarra Johnson for her helpful assistance on this project.

DEMOGRAPHIC CHALLENGES OF NEW IMMIGRATION

ABSOLUTE AND RELATIVE GROWTH OF CHILDREN OF IMMIGRANTS

The 1990s was a decade of record-high immigration: Between 14 and 16 million immigrants entered the United States, up from 10 million in the 1980s and 7 million in the 1970s. By 2005, the US foreign-born population had reached 35 million, or 12.1 percent of the total population.[1] Following overall immigration patterns, the share of children of immigrants among the school-age population increased rapidly, from 6 percent in 1970 to 19 percent in 2000.[2]

BOX 1. DEFINITIONS OF CHILDREN OF IMMIGRANTS AND LIMITED ENGLISH PROFICIENT CHILDREN

DEFINING THE POPULATION OF INTEREST

Children of immigrants or *children in immigrant families* are defined as those with at least one parent born outside the United States. The children may have been born abroad (in which case we refer to them as first generation) or in the United States (which we term second generation).*

Limited English Proficient (LEP). In all households where a language other than English is spoken, the US Census Bureau asks if members of the household speak English "very well," "well," "not well," or "not at all." The Census Bureau measures only spoken English proficiency. Using the census's definition, we consider all persons speaking English less than "very well" as limited English proficient.

* Following the definition used by the US Census Bureau, we do not consider children with parents born in Puerto Rico or other US territories to be the children of immigrants.

---

1   Current Population Survey 2005 estimates.

2   Our profile of demographic and socioeconomic characteristics of the children of immigrants and LEP children draws on analysis from the Urban Institute, as well as our own calculations. The data come from the US Census 2000, 1 percent Public Use Microdata Samples (PUMS). The sample is limited to children aged 3 to 21 (and 5 to 21 for LEP children). The information about grade-level completion and enrollment figures from the census is used to categorize the children into two groups: pre-kindergarten through 5th grade and 6th through 12th grade.

FIGURE 1. STATES WITH MORE THAN 100 PERCENT INCREASE IN THE NUMBER OF CHILDREN OF IMMIGRANTS IN PRE-KINDERGARTEN TO 12TH GRADE BETWEEN 1990 AND 2000

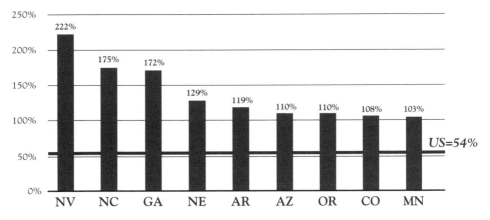

Source: Authors' calculations of Urban Institute data; R. Capps, et al. *The New Demography of America's Schools: Immigration and the No Child Left Behind Act* (Washington, DC: The Urban Institute, 2005).

INCREASING GEOGRAPHIC DISPERSAL

The 1990s also witnessed increasing geographic dispersal of immigrants. Unlike immigrants before them, post-1990 immigrants passed by traditional gateway states and cities in favor of other destinations. For example, North Carolina, Georgia, and Nevada experienced more than a 200 percent increase in their foreign-born population between 1990 and 2000. And while it is true that the absolute numbers of children of immigrants in the so-called new growth states are still small compared to those in more traditional receiving states (California, Texas, New York, New Jersey, Florida, and Illinois), the growth is quite rapid (see Figure 1). Fast growth raises important questions about whether these states have the resources and infrastructure to accommodate the children of immigrants and to ensure that the children have adequate academic and language instruction.

THE FOREIGN-BORN CHILDREN OF IMMIGRANTS

Overall, 75 percent of school-age children of immigrants were born in the United States. The remaining share of the children of immigrants who are foreign born is lowest in pre-kindergarten (one in eight) and highest in grades 6 through 12 (one in three). The reason for this pattern is straightforward: Older

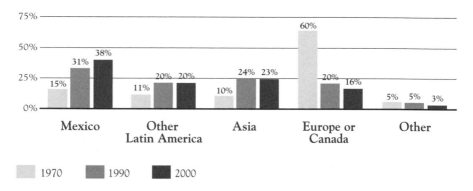

Source: 1 percent Integration Public Use Microdata Series (IPUMS), 1970, 1990, and 2000. Urban Institute tabulations.

children have lived longer and therefore had more opportunity to enter the United States. Secondary schools may find this group of students especially challenging since many immigrant children arrive with limited English proficiency and little formal schooling from their countries of origin. In addition, these late entrants will have fewer years to learn English in US schools than the children of immigrants who enter the schools at earlier ages.

THE DIVERSE ORIGIN OF IMMIGRANT CHILDREN

One of the most salient characteristics of post-1965 immigration is the dramatic shift away from Europe toward Asia and Latin America as major sources of new immigrants. Therefore, it is not surprising that today's immigrant children are more likely to be from Mexico and other Latin American and Asian countries than they were in 1970. In contrast, the proportion of children from Europe and Canada has declined (see Figure 2).

THE CHILDREN OF UNDOCUMENTED MIGRANTS

According to Urban Institute estimates using 2003 data, almost 4.6 million children have one or more undocumented parents. They constitute about 27 percent of all children of immigrants and 5 percent of all children in the United States. An overwhelming majority of these children (3 million) are US citizens, although a sizable minority are themselves undocumented. The Urban

Institute estimates that approximately 65,000 undocumented adolescents graduate each year from US high schools.[3]

LIMITED ENGLISH PROFICIENT CHILDREN

LEP CHILDREN: NUMBERS, GROWTH, AND CONCENTRATION

According to the Department of Education, about 49.6 million K-12 students were enrolled in American schools in the 2003-2004 academic year. Ten percent of these students were identified as LEP students.[4]

California, with its 1.6 million LEP students, accounted for almost a third of all LEP students in the nation. The states with the next-largest LEP student populations were other traditional immigrant-receiving states such as Texas, Florida, New York, and Illinois.

Figure 3 demonstrates the impressive growth of LEP enrollment between 1993-1994 and 2003-2004 that occurred alongside a modest increase in the total K-12 enrollment. As the figure shows, the total K-12 enrollment in the United States grew 9 percent from 45.4 million to 49.6 million during that time. In contrast, the LEP enrollment increased by 65 percent from 3 million to 5 million students.

As in the case of the children of immigrants, states with the fastest-growing LEP populations are not the same states that have the largest absolute numbers of LEP students. For example, between 1993-1994 and 2003-2004, LEP enrollment grew more than 400 percent in South Carolina, North Carolina, Tennessee, and Indiana, which only recently experienced an increase in their immigrant populations (see Figure 4). In contrast, traditional immigrant receiving states experienced either much lower growth (California and New Jersey, e.g.) or declines (New York, e.g.) in their LEP populations.

LEP students are highly concentrated in relatively few school districts. In the 2003-2004 school year, 29 school districts, each with at least 10,000 LEP students, accounted for 25 percent of the nation's total LEP population. Thirteen

---

3   J. S. Passel, "Further Demographic Information Relating to the DREAM Act," Memorandum from the Urban Institute to the National Immigration Law Center, 2003. Available online at http://www.nilc.org/immlawpolicy/DREAM/DREAM_Demographics.pdf.

4   Note that the Department of Education compiles LEP data received from state and local educational agencies. Many states and districts rely on their own definitions of this population using assessment results from reading, writing, listening, and speaking tests.

Figure 3. Rate of total K-12 and LEP enrollment growth: United States, 1993-1994 to 2003-2004

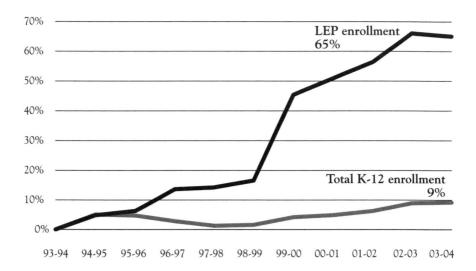

Source: US Department of Education, National Clearinghouse for English Language Acquisition & Language Instruction Educational Programs (NCELA), National and Regional Numbers and Statistics

of these districts were in California. The top five school districts in terms of number of LEP students were Los Angeles, New York City, Chicago, Houston, and Miami-Dade County.[5]

Within school districts, LEP students are also largely concentrated in a small number of schools. An Urban Institute study, which examined the 1999-2000 Schools and Staffing Survey data on elementary schools, found that almost 70 percent of the LEP elementary-level students were enrolled in 10 percent of elementary schools.[6] The study also reported that high-LEP schools, defined as those in which LEP students made up a quarter or more of all enrolled students, tended to have large student populations, to be located in urban areas, and to have difficulties filling teacher vacancies. The students in the high-LEP schools tended to be from minority and economically disadvantaged families.

---

5   See NCELA data on school districts, available at http://www.ncela.gwu.edu/expert/faq/02districts.htm.

6   C. Cosentino de Cohen, B. Chu Clewell, and N. Deterding, *Who's Left Behind?: Immigrant Children in High and Low LEP Schools* (Washington, DC: The Urban Institute, 2005).

FIGURE 4. RATE OF TOTAL K-12 AND LEP ENROLLMENT GROWTH: NORTH CAROLINA AND CALIFORNIA, 1993-1994 TO 2003-2004

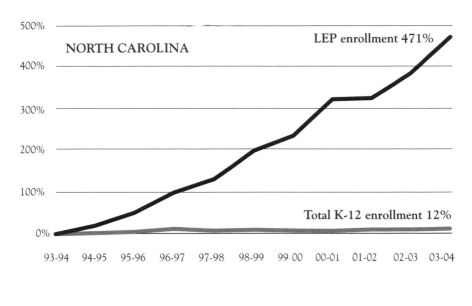

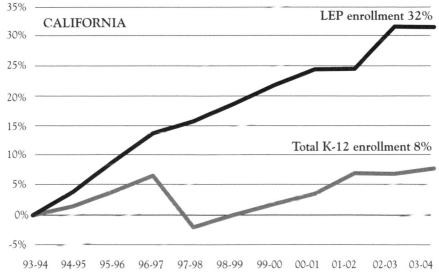

Note: ELL refers to English Language Learners, a term preferred by many researchers over LEP. In this chapter, we primarily used the term LEP, to follow the language in NCLB.

Source: US Department of Education, National Clearinghouse for English Language Acquisition & Language Instruction Educational Programs (NCELA), National and Regional Numbers and Statistics.

The report maintains that the high concentration and segregation of LEP children at the state, district, and school level has both positive and negative implications for students' learning of English and academic subjects:

> On the positive side, the density of LEP enrollment makes the provision of specialized services more cost-effective and a higher priority. It is often easier to justify expenditures for special programs when a large proportion of the student body will benefit. On the negative side, the segregation of LEP students results in their isolation from the educational mainstream and the loss of the benefits of interacting with English-speaking classmates.[7]

THE NATIVE LANGUAGES OF LEP STUDENTS

LEP students speak over 100 native languages. However, the lion's share of LEP students — 79 percent — speak Spanish as their native language. The next most commonly reported native languages are Vietnamese and Hmong, accounting for only approximately 2 percent of LEP students each.[8]

LEP STUDENTS: DEMOGRAPHIC AND SOCIOECONOMIC CHARACTERISTICS[9]

Populations of the children of immigrants and LEP children are neither identical nor mutually exclusive (see Figure 5). Of 54 million total children in the United States, children who are both LEP and born to immigrant parents constitute about 4.9 percent. Children of immigrants who are not LEP make up an additional 13.8 percent of the child population, whereas LEP children with US-born parents represent another 1.5 percent.

GENERATION
LEP children represent about 6.4 percent of all children, and most LEP students are not foreign born (see Figure 6). In fact, three-quarters of LEP elementary school students and over one-half of LEP secondary school students were

---

7 Ibid.

8 See NCELA 2001 data on the most common languages for LEP students, available at http://www.ncela.gwu.edu/expert/faq/05toplangs.htm.

9 Since the US Department of Education data provide neither a distinction between children of immigrants and LEP children nor information on the characteristics of these populations, we turn to the Census data to describe demographic and socioeconomic profile of LEP children. Note that due to the differences in data collection and years for which the data are reported, the absolute numbers of LEP children reported by the US Department of Education and Census are not the same.

FIGURE 5. CHILDREN OF IMMIGRANTS AND LEP CHILDREN AS A PERCENT OF THE TOTAL NUMBER OF CHILDREN, 2000

ALL CHILDREN AGE 5-21 (54 MILLION)

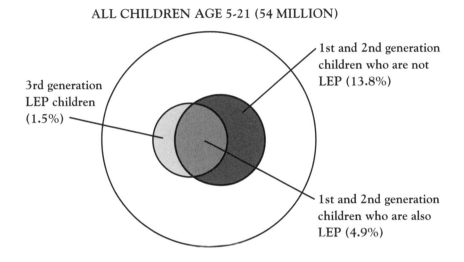

3rd generation
LEP children
(1.5%)

1st and 2nd generation
children who are not
LEP (13.8%)

1st and 2nd generation
children who are also
LEP (4.9%)

Notes: 1st generation = children born abroad; 2nd generation = US-born children with at least one foreign-born parent; 3rd generation plus = US-born children with US-born parents

Source: Authors' calculations based on the 2000 Census data

born and likely raised in the United States. Many have US-born parents. The large share of secondary school LEP students who are US-born is surprising; clearly, many LEP children are still not proficient in English even after seven or more years in US schools.

Nevertheless, over time children are learning English as illustrated by the decline in the proportion of LEP students from 10 percent in kindergarten to 6 percent in the 6th to 12th grade group (see Figure 7).

LINGUISTIC ISOLATION AT HOME
In 2000, about six in seven LEP students at the elementary level lived in linguistically isolated households (those in which everyone over age 14 is also LEP) (see Figure 7). The share of linguistically isolated children was highest in kindergarten (8 percent) and substantially lower in secondary school (4 percent), following the pattern for children's English proficiency. High levels of linguistic isolation present a challenge to involving limited-English speaking families in their children's education.

FIGURE 6. SHARE OF LEP STUDENTS BY GENERATION, 2000: GRADES PRE-KINDERGARTEN TO 5 AND 6 TO 12

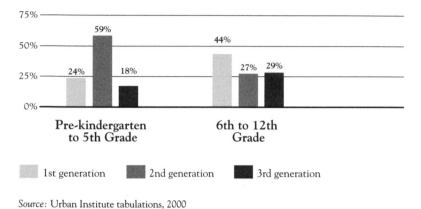

Source: Urban Institute tabulations, 2000

FIGURE 7. LIMITED ENGLISH PROFICIENT AND LINGUISTICALLY ISOLATED CHILDREN BY GRADE LEVEL, 2000 (PERCENT)

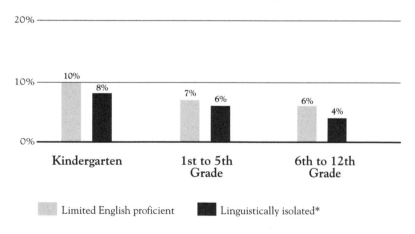

* Students living in households in which all persons age 14 and older are LEP.

Source: 1 percent PUMS, 2000. Urban Institute tabulations; Randy Capps, et al. *The New Demography of America's Schools: Immigration and the No Child Left Behind Act.* (Washington, DC: The Urban Institute, 2005).

PARENTAL INCOME AND EDUCATION

There is a considerable overlap among low-income students and limited English proficient students. In 2000, about two-thirds of LEP children were low-income, compared to only about one-third of English proficient children. This finding is consistent with previous research showing a high correlation between limited English proficiency and poverty along with other hardship measures.[10]

In terms of parental education, in 2000, almost half of LEP children in elementary school had parents with less than a high school degree, and a quarter had parents with less than a 9th grade education (see Figure 8). Only 11 percent of English proficient children had parents without a high school degree, and just 2 percent had parents who had not completed the 9th grade. In secondary school, a lower share of LEP children had parents without a high school degree (35 percent), but this was still several times the share for children of natives.

As this section shows, LEP students, many of whom are children of immigrants, are likely to live in poor families and have parents with little education, which are known risk factors for students' academic achievement.

FIGURE 8. PERCENT OF ENGLISH PROFICIENT (NON-LEP) AND LEP STUDENTS BY PARENTAL EDUCATION AND GRADE LEVEL, 2000

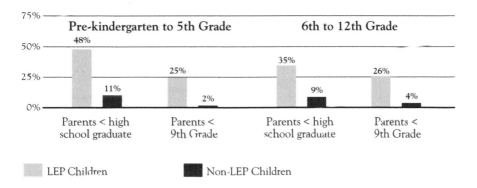

Source: 1 percent PUMS, 2000. Urban Institute tabulations; R. Capps, et al. *The New Demography of America's Schools: Immigration and the No Child Left Behind Act.* (Washington, DC: The Urban Institute, 2005).

10 R. Capps, L. Ku, M. Fix, C. Furgiuele, J. S. Passel, R. Ramchand, S. McNiven, and D. Perez-Lopez, *How Are Immigrants Faring after Welfare Reform? Preliminary Evidence from Los Angeles and New York City—Final Report* (Washington, DC: The Urban Institute, 2002).

ACADEMIC ACHIEVEMENT OF CHILDREN OF IMMIGRANTS

Clearly, the children of immigrants, particularly those who are LEP, face many barriers to academic success in US schools. Despite these challenges, though, the existing literature suggests that children of immigrants overall are adapting well to the US educational system, often outperforming even children with US-born parents.[11]

The academic achievement of children of immigrants — as measured by grade point averages (GPAs), test scores, and school enrollment rates — varies by time spent in the United States. In one study, US-born children of immigrants outperformed their foreign-born peers, particularly those who had been in the United States nine years or less, on reading and math tests. However, the foreign-born students' GPAs in this study fell as time spent in the United States increased, suggesting that acculturation actually exerted downward pressure on grades.[12] Another recent study reported that US-born children of immigrants demonstrate significant intergenerational progress in terms of enrollment in high school and college.[13]

There are also major variations among immigrant groups in terms of how well students are doing in school. Studies find that, on average, students of Asian and European-descent (especially recent arrivals) are doing as well or often better than their native-born peers. In contrast, children of immigrants from Latin America and the Caribbean are more likely to have lower GPAs and higher dropout rates.

Further consideration of national origin diversity among immigrant groups allows for a more refined picture of group differences in student achievement. For example, in their study of US- and foreign-born children of immigrants in Miami and San Diego, Portes and Rumbaut found that students of Chinese and Korean origin were among the top-performing groups on math and reading tests. In contrast, Laotian and Cambodian students lagged behind all other

---

11 A. Portes and R. Rumbaut, *Legacies: The Story of Immigrant Second Generation* (Berkeley, CA: University of California Press, 2001); See also C. Suarez and M. Suarez-Orozco, *Children of Immigrants* (Cambridge, MA: Harvard University Press, 2001); N. Foner, *From Ellis Island to JFK: New York's Two Great Waves of Immigration*, Chapter 7 (New Haven: Yale University Press, 2000).

12 Portes and Rumbaut, *Legacies*.

13 R. Waldinger and R. Reichl, "Today's Second Generation: Getting Ahead or Falling Behind?" in *Securing the Future: US Immigrant Integration Policy*, ed. Michael Fix. Note that school enrollment, which is highlighted here, is only one of several different commonly used academic achievement measures; others include dropout rates and school completion rates. Importantly, if young immigrants come to the United States to work and never enroll in school, they would not be captured in traditional dropout rates.

children of immigrants except for those of Mexican origin. The authors found that parents' social and economic capital played a role in these populations' trailing scores.

PERSISTING GAPS IN LEP ACADEMIC ACHIEVEMENT

While the children of immigrants, on the whole, are doing well given the challenges they face, LEP students persistently lag behind their non-LEP peers. One indicator of LEP student achievement is students' progress in reading and math when analyzed over time and in comparison to non-LEP students. The most recent data on LEP achievement are provided by results from the 2005 National Assessment of Educational Progress (NAEP). Often called "The Nation's Report Card," NAEP is the only nationally representative and continuing assessment of what students in US schools should know and can do in various subject areas.[14]

ACHIEVEMENT RESULTS FROM NAEP DATA

Figures 9 and 10 indicate that although 4th and 8th grade LEP students had higher average scores on math tests in 2005 than in any previous year, the historical achievement gap between LEP and non-LEP students persisted. For the first time, the 2005 NAEP distinguished between current and former LEP students (those who completed language instruction programs) and found that former LEP students were doing much better than their LEP peers and in some cases received the same score as non-LEP students (4th grade). NAEP data also indicate that whereas only 6 percent of LEP 8th graders scored at proficient or above level on math, 24 percent of former LEP students did so (compared to 31 percent of non-LEP students). These findings of remarkable progress of former LEP students at the national level (NAEP) dovetails with earlier research findings of adolescents' test scores on state achievement tests in California and Colorado.[15] In both states, 8th grade students who have reached English

---

14 NCLB requires states that receive Title I funding to take part in the NAEP (Title I is a federal funding stream used by all states that is directed at low-income children and the schools that serve them.) States must participate in the NAEP math and reading evaluation of 4th and 8th graders. The closely monitored and standardized administration of the same tests with the same proficiency thresholds make cross-state comparisons of students' educational outcomes possible. Instead, the results are only suggestive of achievement patterns of LEP students.

15 J. Batalova, M. Fix, and J. Murray, *Adolescent English Language Learners: Their Demographic Profile and Literacy Achievements.* A Report to the Carnegie Corporation of New York (Washington, DC: Migration Policy Institute, forthcoming).

FIGURE 9. AVERAGE SCORES OF 4TH GRADERS IN MATH BY ENGLISH LANGUAGE PROFICIENCY: NAEP, 1996 TO 2005

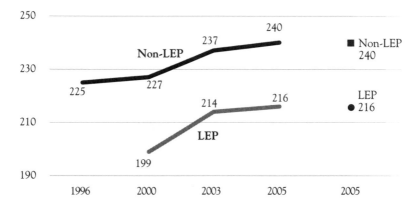

Notes: The average scores in 2005 are significantly higher than those in 1996, 2000, and 2003 for both non-LEP and LEP subgroups.

Source: US Department of Education, Institute of Education Sciences, National Center for Education Statistics, National Assessment of Educational Progress (NAEP), 2005 Mathematics Assessment, 4th grade.

FIGURE 10. AVERAGE SCORES OF 8TH GRADERS IN MATH BY ENGLISH LANGUAGE PROFICIENCY: NAEP, 1996 TO 2005

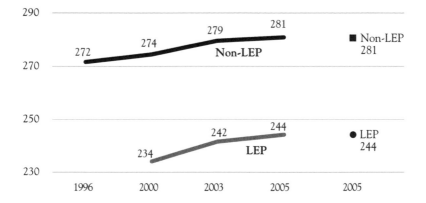

Notes: The average scores in 2005 are significantly higher than those in 1996, 2000, and 2003 for both non-LEP and LEP subgroups.

Source: US Department of Education, Institute of Education Sciences, National Center for Education Statistics, National Assessment of Educational Progress (NAEP), 2005 Mathematics Assessment, 8th grade.

proficiency after receiving language development services scored much better on state math tests than their LEP counterparts. Moreover, in California, the gap between former LEP students and non-LEP students was very small.

NAEP data allow for similar comparisons on the reading assessment. Although the data also demonstrate a gap in reading test scores between LEP and non-LEP students, we find this comparison less indicative of purely academic achievement because LEP students, by definition, are not proficient in English.

THE EVOLUTION OF THE EDUCATION OF THE CHILDREN OF IMMIGRANTS

Education in the United States has not only been a mechanism for but a marker of immigrant integration.[16] In the last 100 years, the United States has absorbed two great waves of immigration: one at the turn of the 20th century, comprised mainly of Europeans, and another since 1965, comprised increasingly of Asians and Latin Americans.

There are striking similarities between the contexts in which children of today's immigrants and children of the early 20th-century immigrants encountered the American educational system. As now, education at the turn of the 20th century was linked to social and economic mobility; a significant portion of arriving immigrants did not speak English; and many schools, especially those in urban areas, were overcrowded and lacked resources and qualified staff.

However, there are substantial differences between the two periods that underline the critical importance of schooling for the social and economic mobility of children of contemporary immigrants.

EDUCATION IS NO LONGER A LUXURY, BUT A NECESSITY

One important difference is that the US economy now requires higher levels of education from workers. In the early 20th century, having a high school diploma was a luxury: children's income contributions toward family expenses were a norm and necessity. Until the 1970s, there were well-paid manufacturing jobs that immigrants could take and thus join the ranks of blue-collar workers who achieved a middle-class lifestyle without significant formal education.

---

16 B. Weiss, *American Education and the European Immigrant, 1840-1940*, Introduction (Chicago, IL: University of Illinois Press, 1982).

Today, the knowledge-based American economy is predicted to generate jobs that rely on a skilled and educated workforce.[17] As numerous studies show, the average premium on high-level education paid by the labor market has grown dramatically. Regardless of one's gender, full-time workers with a Bachelor's or higher degree are paid almost twice as much as those with a high school diploma.[18] And, of course, the corollary of this wage premium is the penalty imposed on those who fail to complete high school.

THE CHANGING ROLE OF THE FEDERAL GOVERNMENT IN THE EDUCATION OF CHILDREN OF IMMIGRANTS

At the time of the previous wave of immigration, there was no legal recognition that children of immigrants had a "right" to an education. Since the 1960s, the ways in which children of immigrants are instructed and welcomed into US schools have changed dramatically. Until the 1960s, the most popular method of language instruction was English immersion or a "sink-or-swim" approach. Moreover, students were not allowed to move to the next grade until their English was sufficient to advance in academic subjects. With passage of the Bilingual Education Act in 1968 Congress established a federal policy of bilingual education for economically disadvantaged language LEP students; allocated funds for innovative programs; and recognized the unique educational disadvantages faced by non-English speaking students. In 1974, the US Supreme Court ruled that "school districts must take 'affirmative steps' to overcome educational barriers faced by non-English speakers."[19] Congress eventually voted to expand eligibility for bilingual programs from students of "limited English speaking ability" to those of "limited English proficiency" (1978); and support family English literacy programs.

As a result of these and other federal and state efforts, today's educational system offers a wide range of programs to accommodate different levels of academic preparation and knowledge of English among the children of immigrants.[20]

---

17 Bureau of Labor Statistics, "Table 3b. The 10 fastest growing occupations, 2002-12." US Department of Labor, 2004, http://www.bls.gov/news.release/ecopro.toc.htm.

18 M. W. Horrigan, "Employment Projections to 2012: Concepts and Context," *Monthly Labor Review* 127, no. 2 (Feb 2004): 80-105.

19 For a brief review of federal policies and laws with regard to language minority students refer to NCELA, FAQ#3 History available at http://www.ncela.gwu.edu/expert/faq/03history.htm. See also G. Stewner-Manzanares, *The Bilingual Education Act: Twenty Years Later*, NCBE, Number 6, 1988, http://www.ncela.gwu.edu/pubs/classics/focus/06bea.htm.

20 Ibid.

No Child Left Behind: landmark education legislation

The No Child Left Behind (NCLB) Act, signed into law in early 2002, is the subject of the most recent chapter in the story of US education and children of immigrants. The act reauthorizes a long-standing federal education law and funding stream targeted to low-income students and the schools that serve them (Title I). NCLB holds all states, districts, and schools responsible for improving student academic achievement, as measured by regular state standardized tests in reading and math. Most notably, student improvement must occur among historically vulnerable subgroups: major racial and ethnic minority groups, disabled students, and students with limited English proficiency, categories that include many children of immigrants. Schools and districts that do not show sufficient progress toward meeting these standards face tough federal sanctions. After several years they may be forced to fire staff, reorganize curricula, or even close. By 2014, NCLB requires that all students be proficient in reading and math. For the first time, the law also requires that districts demonstrate that they are teaching English to LEP students by administering annual English proficiency tests.

Within NCLB's text lay the most sweeping changes to federal education policy — and arguably federal immigrant integration policy — in decades.

Current policy and its impact on children of immigrants and LEP students

NCLB made the integration of historically marginalized groups, including the children of immigrants, a priority. However, many challenges remain for serving the children of immigrants and LEP students, not just in the implementation of NCLB but also in other areas of education policy and practice. We describe below five important policy issues: 1) assessing the academic progress of LEP students; 2) closing the linguistic gap; 3) expanding immigrant parent involvement; 4) attracting qualified bilingual or English as a Second Language (ESL) teachers; 5) and meeting the needs of immigrant adolescents. We also highlight three local practices developed in response to some national policy concerns surrounding the education of children of immigrants.

Assessing the academic progress of LEP students

Prior to NCLB, LEP students were often excluded from the standardized state tests used to spur schools' accountability.[21] NCLB clearly changed this pattern

---

21 See, for example, Council of the Great City Schools (CGCS), "Educating English Language Learners in the Nation's Urban Schools," 2001. This study, done prior to the introduction of NCLB, found that only half of the nation's largest urban districts, where most LEPs are concentrated, included the results of LEP students on statewide assessments in district results.

of exclusion by requiring that schools and districts assess and report LEP progress annually in reading and math.[22] Now the LEP students as a group must make adequate yearly progress, working toward the law's controversial goal of attaining 100 percent student proficiency in reading and math by 2014.

Implementing these new requirements is tough. First, current LEP students will eventually learn English and exit LEP status, while new LEP students will come to the United States and enroll. In this sense, the LEP subgroup is expected to change over time, distinguishing it from the other "protected" groups under NCLB, which are based on race or physical disability, for example. While NCLB holds schools responsible for LEP students as a group, the group consistently loses higher-performing students as they learn English while absorbing new members who are not proficient in English.

The US Department of Education has recognized the problem and now permits school districts to include former LEP students in the LEP subgroup for two years after they attain English proficiency.[23] Theoretically, these former LEP students will do better on standardized academic assessments, raising the overall performance of the LEP subgroup as a whole, allowing the schools they attend to avoid sanctions.

However, this temporary "fix" fails to sidestep a much larger policy challenge: having a group defined by its very lack of skills attain full proficiency. Some have suggested that assessing and rewarding the longitudinal progress of individual students rather than entire groups like LEP students would be a better measure of progress under NCLB. This approach to assessment could also mitigate the impact of the evaluation problems associated with the LEP subgroup's ever-changing composition, since it bases progress on an individual child's performance. In 2005 Education Secretary Margaret Spellings authorized pilot programs using longitudinal assessments of individual students. Nonetheless, the goal of 100 percent academic proficiency by 2014 for all students, including LEP students, has been maintained.[24]

Additionally, it is difficult to disentangle a LEP student's academic knowledge from his or her language skills when academic assessments are written in

---

22 NCLB's predecessor, the Improving America's Schools Act of 1994, also required states to include LEP students in assessments and report their results separately as a subgroup. However, it lacked the tough accountability mechanisms of NCLB, and many states never complied with this earlier law. See Citizens Commission on Civil Rights, *Closing the Deal: A Preliminary Report on State Compliance with Final Assessment & Accountability Requirements Under the Improving America's Schools Act of 1994*, March 1, 2001.

23 See US Department of Education, Letters from Secretary Rod Paige, June 24, 2004.

24 US Department of Education, *No Child Left Behind: A Road Map for State Implementation*, 2005.

English. NCLB directs states, to the extent practicable, to test LEP students in a language and form that are most likely to yield valid and reliable results of what the student knows and can do. Thus, LEP students could receive the same tests in English as their peers, tests with simplified English or other accommodations (such as extra time or a dictionary), or tests in their native languages. Currently ten states use some native language testing to assess LEP students under NCLB.[25] The types of other accommodations available to LEP students vary widely by state.[26]

The research base, however, is thin on approaches that yield valid and reliable results among LEP students. Research indicates that children do best when tests use the language in which the students are taught.[27] Nationwide, well over half of all LEP students receive either no services targeted to LEP students or services that are almost entirely in English, suggesting that native-language testing would not be appropriate for the vast majority of LEP students.[28] However, with states now responsible for the progress of LEP students, state evaluations of the effectiveness of their other testing accommodations for tests in English and whether they give LEP students an unfair advantage over native English-speaking peers are crucial.[29]

CLOSING THE LINGUISTIC GAP

Many approaches to teaching English exist, ranging from English-only instruction in mainstream classrooms to programs that emphasize building both a child's native language and English skills simultaneously. These approaches may even vary for different age groups and depend on the number of students in a given school who speak a shared language. For example, elementary schools with large numbers of Spanish-speaking students may opt for bilingual programs, while high schools, where LEP students are comparatively fewer, may use traditional English as a Second Language pull-out instruction with students

25 M. A. Zehr, "Wary Districts Shift or Forgo Federal Funds," *Education Week*, September 14, 2004.

26 US Department of Education, *Biennial Evaluation Report to Congress on the Implementation of the State Formula Grant Program 2002-2004*, English Language Acquisition, Language Enhancement and Academic Achievement Act (ESEA, Title III, Pt. A) Washington, DC, 2005.

27 See J. Abedi, C. Lord, and C. Hofstetter, "Impact of Selected Background Variables on Students' NAEP Math Performance," *Center for the Study of Evaluation Technical Report 478* (Los Angeles, CA: UCLA National Center for Research on Evaluation, Standards, and Student Testing, 1998).

28 Data on LEP services from A. M. Zehler, H. L. Fleishman, P. J. Hopstock, T. G. Stephenson, M. L. Pendzick, and S. Sapru, *Descriptive Study of Services to LEP Students and LEP Students with Disabilities, Research Report Volume 1* (Arlington, VA: Development Associates, Inc., 2003).

29 J. Abedi and R. Dietel, *Challenges in the No Child Left Behind Act for English Language Learners*, National Center for Research on Evaluation, Standards, and Student Testing (CRESST)/UCLA, 2004.

Box 2. Instructional approaches for LEP students in the nation's urban districts

Program names	Languages of Instruction	Languages of content instruction	Languages Arts instruction
Dual Language, Two way, Bilingual immersion	English and the native language	English and the native language	English and the native language
Developmental, Late exit	English and the native language	English and the native language; instruction through English increases as students gain proficiency	English and the native language
Transitional, Early exit	English only	English and the native language; quick progression to all or most instruction through English	English, native language used to assist transition to English
Sheltered, SDAIE, Content-based ESL	English only	English adapted to students' proficiency level	English in a classroom with native English speakers and ELLs
Pullout ESL, Self Contained ESL	English only	English adapted to students' proficiency level	English in a classroom with all ELLs
English Only (no language support)	English only	English	English

Note: ELL refers to English Language Learners, a term preferred by many researchers over LEP. In this paper we primarily use the term LEP to follow the language in NCLB.

Chart reprinted with permission: Beth Antuñez, "English Language Learners in the Great City Schools: Survey Results on Students, Languages, and Programs" (Washington, DC: Council of the Great City Schools 2003), 12.

who speak less common languages, such as Urdu or Portuguese (see Box 2 for an overview of programs for LEP students in urban districts).[30] As detailed early in this paper, children of immigrants speak more than 100 languages, creating a need for a variety of instructional approaches.

Pre-kindergarten programs, which many states have expanded in recent years, may provide a promising avenue for early English acquisition among young children of immigrants. Research indicates that there are some effective pre-kindergarten models with positive impacts on child academic outcomes, including bilingual pre-kindergarten targeted to LEP children.[31] One recent study in Oklahoma found that Hispanic children had the largest gains of any group in the state's universal pre-kindergarten program.[32] Children of immigrants are currently underrepresented in the nation's pre-kindergarten programs though, suggesting a need for greater outreach.[33]

Schools now face tougher challenges when students enter kindergarten or later grades without English proficiency. In an unprecedented move, NCLB requires states to develop English language proficiency standards, assessments, and measurable objectives by which they can gauge LEP progress.[34] States must demonstrate an annual increase in the number or percentage of children *who make progress in learning English* and an annual increase in the number or percentage of children who *attain English proficiency* by the end of each school year. Spoken English proficiency takes an average of three to five years to develop, while academic English proficiency, which is needed for academic content tests under NCLB, typically takes five to seven years.[35]

---

30 Data on LEP students in secondary schools from R. Capps, M. Fix, J. Murray, et al., *The New Demography of America's Schools: Immigration and the No Child Left Behind Act* (Washington, DC: The Urban Institute, 2005).

31 See, e.g., W. S. Barnett, "Long-Term Effects of Early Childhood Programs on Cognitive and School Outcomes," *The Future of Children* 5, no. 3 (1995) for information on the long-term effects of some early childhood programs; see J. L. Rodríquez, R. M. Díaz, D. Duran, and L. Espinosa, "The Impact of Bilingual Preschool Education on the Language Development of Spanish-Speaking Children," *Early Childhood Research Quarterly* 10 (1995): 475-490 and A. Winsler, R. M. Díaz, L. Espinosa, and J. L. Rodríguez, "When Learning a Second Language Does Not Mean Losing the First: Bilingual Language Development in Low-Income, Spanish-Speaking Children Attending Bilingual Preschool," *Child Development* 70, no. 2 (1999): 349-362 for descriptions of small-scale evaluations of bilingual pre-kindergarten programs.

32 W. Gormley and D. Phillips, "The Effects of Universal Pre-K in Oklahoma: Research Highlights and Policy Implications" (Washington, DC: Georgetown Public Policy Institute, 2003).

33 Capps et al., *The New Demography of America's Schools* (see n. 30).

34 US Department of Education, *Biennial Evaluation Report to Congress*, 2005 (see n. 26).

35 K. Hakuta, Y. G. Butler, and D. Witt, *How Long Does It Take English Learners to Attain Proficiency?* Policy Report 2000-1. The University of California Linguistic Minority Research Institute, 2000.

States are making some progress in attaining these goals. In its recent report to Congress, the Department of Education found that 33 of 42 states reporting results met their targets for English acquisition *progress*, while 41 of 45 reporting met at least some targets for students' *attainment* of English proficiency.[36]

NCLB's accountability provisions for English-language proficiency are not as stringent as those for meeting academic content standards in reading and math. They do not establish any national proficiency goals like NCLB's controversial mandate that schools meet 100 percent student proficiency in reading and math by 2014. Accountability provisions for English proficiency also apply primarily at the district rather than school level, and they do not trigger interventions such as school restructuring, school choice, or supplemental services.[37]

EXPANDING IMMIGRANT PARENT INVOLVEMENT

A long line of research has established positive academic benefits to children when their parents are involved in their educations, either in the home or school setting.[38] Nevertheless, researchers have identified a variety of barriers to involving immigrant and LEP parents, including language barriers, limited understanding of the US school system, or culturally reinforced deference to school administrators.[39]

Under NCLB, parents of LEP students must be notified that their child is LEP, of the options for instruction and instructional goals, the requirements to exit LEP status, the expected rate of English mastery, and of their right to refuse language instruction. NCLB also emphasizes that schools and districts should, "to the extent practicable," communicate with all parents in a language that they can understand and involve them in plans for school improvement if needed.

---

36 US Department of Education, *Biennial Evaluation Report to Congress on the Implementation of the State Formula Grant Program 2002-2004*, English Language Acquisition, Language Enhancement and Academic Achievement Act (ESEA, Title III, Pt. A) Washington, DC, 2005.

37 Center on Education Policy, *From the Capital to the Classroom: Year 3 of the No Child Left Behind Act*, 2005. Application of English-proficiency accountability mechanisms at the district level is due in large part to the funding stream of Title III, which is directed toward LEP students. Title III, unlike Title I, goes to states and is then given to districts or district consortia; individuals schools are not direct recipients of the funding. However, if one or a small number of schools in a district cause the district to fall short of its English-proficiency goals, a district may specify changes in select schools in the improvement plan it creates as required by NCLB.

38 S. Carter, *The Impact of Parent/Family Involvement on Student Outcomes: An Annotated Bibliography of Research from the Past Decade* (Eugene, OR: Consortium for Appropriate Dispute Resolution in Special Education, 2002).

39 See A. B. Bermúdez and J. A. Márquez, "An Examination of a Four-Way Collaborative to Increase Parental Involvement in the Schools," *The Journal of Educational Issues of Language Minority Students* 16 (Summer 1996) for a short review of this literature.

Interacting with parents forces schools to contend with many parents' low educational levels, linguistic isolation, and irregular or heavy work hours. Finding translators for parents may be particularly difficult in new gateway immigrant communities going through rapid demographic change or in schools where many different languages are spoken. In response to these challenges, some districts and schools have created innovative partnerships with immigrant or other community-based organizations to expand outreach to parents and prepare them to take an active role in their child's learning.

ATTRACTING QUALIFIED BILINGUAL OR ESL TEACHERS

NCLB responded to a concern that teachers in our nation's schools were not adequately prepared to teach the classes to which they were assigned. High-

---

BOX 3. SPOTLIGHT ON MEANINGFUL PARENTAL INVOLVEMENT: THE PARENT INSTITUTE FOR QUALITY EDUCATION, STATE OF CALIFORNIA

The Parent Institute for Quality Education (PIQE) has worked with over 1,200 California schools to engage immigrant parents more fully in their children's education. The Institute offers a nine-week training course for low-income or immigrant parents on parental involvement in schools. The course has been offered in 14 languages thus far and covers navigation of the school system, ways to support learning at home, and college preparation. Since 1987, more than 335,000 parents have successfully graduated from the ten PIQE program sites in California. A study analyzing long-term outcomes for children whose parents attended the San Diego program found that PIQE children had a dropout rate of just 7 percent, compared to the county average of 41 percent. Students whose parents participated in the program also had a higher level of college attendance. Overall, the number of students attending college exceeded the county average (79 to 52 percent, respectively). While these findings may be influenced by selection bias — i.e., parents who enroll in the program may be more likely to send their children to college or keep them in high school — they provide at least a suggestion that the program may have a positive impact on students.

Sources: Garza and Osterling, "Strengthening Latino Parental Involvement, Forming Community Based Organizations/School Partnership," *National Association of Bilingual Educators (NABE) Journal of Research and Practice* 2, no. 1 (Winter 2004): 270-284; Sahafi and Vidano, "Parent Institute for Quality Education," *Organization Special Report on PIQE's Performance Evaluation*, December 2004; PIQE Website: http://www.piqe.org/.

Box 4. Spotlight on Teacher recruitment: The PAR²A Center, University of Colorado at Denver

The PAR²A Center was created in 1994 to serve as a resource and research center for the training of paraeducators wishing to become teachers. The Center has worked in collaboration with area community colleges and school districts to create effective training programs for paraeducators specializing in bilingual and special education. Currently, the Center offers several projects in its Career Ladders program that help transition paraeducators into professional teaching positions. The Collaborative Bilingual Education Teacher Training project (C-BETT II), for example, supports a cohort of 32 participants who are pursuing their Bachelor's degree and teaching license in elementary or secondary bilingual education. Participants wishing to pursue graduate study in the field also have the option of enrolling in the Master's program at the University of Colorado at Denver. The Center has created a mentoring program for participants in the C-BETT II program that lasts through their first years as new teachers.

Source: The PAR²A Center Web site: http://www.paracenter.org

LEP schools in particular are more likely to have trouble filling teaching vacancies and to have teachers with provisional credentials. One 2001 study found that one of five teachers of LEP students in the nation's urban school districts held provisional or emergency teaching credentials.[40] In Texas, 48 percent of elementary and 40 percent of secondary bilingual/ESL teachers hired in 2000-2001 did not hold full certification.[41]

In 2002, NCLB required that all teachers, including bilingual and ESL teachers, have full state certification, hold at least a Bachelor's degree, and show mastery of the subjects they teach. Teachers can demonstrate mastery through an academic major, graduate degree, additional coursework, or passage of state subject tests.

Even before NCLB, research indicated a shortage of bilingual and ESL teachers in critical high-immigrant areas; new evidence suggests that this problem con-

---

40 Council of the Great City Schools, *Educating English Language Learners in the Nation's Urban Schools* (Washington, DC: CGCS, 2001).

41 Institute for School-University Partnerships, "Teacher Demand Study 2000-2001," Texas A&M University System, 2001.

tinues. More than 60 percent of the nation's urban districts, where most children of immigrants reside, reported a shortage of LEP teachers in 2001, roughly coinciding with NCLB's introduction.[42] Several years later, in a study assessing NCLB's third year of implementation, districts cited finding qualified teachers as their greatest challenge in serving the LEP population.[43]

The need for teachers of the LEP population is not likely to decline any time soon. Estimates indicate that children of immigrants will comprise 30 percent of all students in our nation's schools by 2015.[44] Schools, districts, and states must continue to search for ways to grow the number of highly qualified bilingual and ESL teachers — encouraging the promotion of promising bilingual paraprofessionals, for example.[45]

MEETING THE NEEDS OF IMMIGRANT ADOLESCENTS

About one-third of the adolescent children of immigrants were born abroad, and immigrant adolescents are uniquely at-risk in the educational system.[46] Many may not have arrived in the United States until secondary school, where fewer instructional options exist for students who do not speak English. Others may not have received sufficient academic preparation in their home countries to prepare them for middle and high school classes in the United States. And, as detailed earlier in this chapter, immigrant adolescents are also more likely than US-born students to drop out of high school.[47]

In response to these risks, schools, districts, and states have experimented with new ways to educate and engage immigrant adolescents. Two types of initiatives in particular have received particular attention.

First, some districts have chosen to create what are called "newcomer schools," schools that exclusively serve recently arrived immigrant students. In addition to

---

42 CGCS, *Educating English Language Learners* (see n. 40).

43 Center on Education Policy, From the *Capital to the Classroom: Year 3 of the No Child Left Behind Act*, 2005.

44 M. Fix and J. S. Passel, *US Immigration: Trends and Implications for Schools*, National Association of Bilingual Education (NABE) Presentation, 2003.

45 See B. C. Clewell and A. M. Villegas, *Evaluation of the DeWitt Wallace-Reader's Digest Fund's Pathways to Teaching Careers Program* (Washington, DC: The Urban Institute, 2001) for an example of a program that was successful in recruiting new racial and ethnic minority teachers among the paraprofessional / teacher aide population.

46 Capps et al., *The New Demography of America's Schools* (see n. 30), with regard to the share of adolescent children of immigrants who are themselves foreign born.

47 J. R. de Velasco, M. Fix, and B. C. Clewell, *Overlooked and Underserved: Immigrant Students in US Secondary Schools* (Washington, DC: The Urban Institute, 2000).

Box 5. Spotlight on Immigrant Adolescents: Belmont Newcomer Center, Los Angeles, California

The Belmont Newcomer Center opened in 1989 to serve newly arrived immigrant students at Belmont High School and those from surrounding Los Angeles area schools. The Center aims to smooth the transition of these students into American culture while preparing them academically for mainstream high schools. There are two different models utilized at the Center, and students are assigned to one on the basis of their native language. The first is an Alternative Bilingual Program that offers 9th to 11th grade coursework in Spanish or Mandarin in addition to English. The second option (for speakers of languages other than Spanish or Mandarin) is the Structured English Immersion program, which offers English instruction to classes of all LEP students for the full high school curriculum. Approximately 450 students are enrolled at a time, with an average of 180 students graduating each year. By working with community organizations, the Belmont Center has also been able to provide students with better access to student and family services, such as counseling. Belmont retains a high number of bilingual and multilingual staff, many of whom previously attended the school.

Source: Spaulding et al., *Immigrant Students and Secondary School Reform: Compendium of Best Practices*, Council of Chief State School Officers, January 2004; Center for Applied Linguistics, Newcomer Database, http://www.cal.org/newcomerdb.

language instruction and academic courses targeted to LEP students, newcomer schools offer a unique and sheltered transition to the US school system. Most educate adolescents and their families about US schools, and they may provide follow-up evaluations once a student moves to a regular instructional school.[48]

Second, in recent years immigrant leaders have advocated for fee changes in higher education that might encourage undocumented immigrant adolescents to stay in school and pursue a university degree. Because undocumented immigrants are not legally present, most states consider them "out-of-state residents" when assigning their university tuition fees, even if the students have been residents for many years. Currently ten states grant undocumented youth in-state tuition rates.[49] Proposed federal legislation (called the DREAM Act) would

---

48 D. Short, *Secondary Newcomer Programs: Helping Recent Immigrants Prepare for School Success.* CAL Digest — March 1998 (Washington, DC: Center for Applied Linguistics, 1998).

49 National Immigration Law Center, "Basic Facts about In-State Tuition for Undocumented Immigrant Students," 2006, www.nilc.org/immlawpolicy/DREAM/in-state_tuition_basicfacts_041706_ rev.pdf.

make legal resident status available nationwide to undocumented youth who arrived in the United States before age 16, have been in the United States for at least five years, have graduated from high school, and are of good moral character. The bill, which has been pending before Congress since 2001, was incorporated into the comprehensive migration reform bill known as the McCain – Kennedy bill. MPI estimates that as of 2006, 360,000 undocumented students would become eligible for legal status if the law were passed.[50]

CONCLUSION

Several factors — the changing demographics of US schools, NCLB's motivating force, and innovative practices at the local level — all make today's educational environment one of unusual opportunity for the integration of the children of immigrants. The sheer number of children of immigrants and their expanding reach to new-growth destinations are bringing this population into the US mainstream.

But while some children of immigrants do very well in US schools, research also indicates that many are struggling, particularly those who do not speak English well. The spirit, if not the precise text, of No Child Left Behind recognizes that there is room for improvement in the education of the children of immigrants and demands more from schools and districts serving LEP and minority students.

The law is due for reauthorization in 2007, and policymakers are already proposing a variety of changes, including changes in the state testing and accountability mechanisms for LEP students.[51] The process will likely pit those who think the current law's requirements are unworkable in practice and that the law will undermine public schools against advocates who fear changes will weaken NCLB's high expectations for students who have been historically overlooked. Any attempts to weaken the accountability provisions will be met with resistance. Several civil rights groups recently sided with the federal government in a lawsuit it faces from the State of Connecticut. In the suit, Connecticut asserts that NCLB is an unfunded mandate and therefore is not enforceable.[52]

---

50 J. Batalova and M. Fix, "New Estimates of Unauthorized Youth Eligible for Legal Status under the DREAM Act," Backgrounder (Washington, DC: Migration Policy Institute, 2006), available online at: http://www.migrationpolicy.org/pubs/Backgrounder1_Dream_Act.pdf.

51 M. R. Davis, "Political Shifts Cloud Outlook for Renewal of Federal Education Law," *Education Week* 25, no. 15 (December 2005): S4-S5.

52 A. Salzman, "NAACP Challenges Education Lawsuit in Connecticut," *The New York Times*, January 31, 2006, Section B3.

In addition to upcoming policy decisions on NCLB, comprehensive reform of immigration policy could have far-reaching effects on US schools. Take, for example, legislative proposals for a new temporary worker program that would also allow immigrant workers to bring their families with them. The resulting flow of students could place a new burden on schools and districts in places where temporary workers are concentrated. It is unclear how willing US tax-payers would be to provide for the education of many children they see as "temporary" residents. Other proposals would clear backlogs of immediate family members of legal permanent residents or dramatically expand the num-bers of green cards granted for employment-related purposes.

CHAPTER 10

Designing an Impact Aid Program for Immigrant Settlement

DEBORAH L. GARVEY*

Introduction

As debate over immigration policy has evolved, two legislative paths have emerged. One calls for "enforcement only" strategies — including expanded border and workplace regulation. A second path embodied in the popularly known McCain – Kennedy bill (S2611) would create, alongside expanded enforcement, an earned legalization program leading to citizenship, a limited guest worker program, and a substantial increase in the number of green cards issued to both low- and high-skilled workers.

The reform debate has focused little attention on the potentially negative short-term fiscal impacts faced by state and local governments that receive the nation's newcomers, and provide little, if any, funding for programs to foster immigrants' successful integration into the social fabric.

This chapter assesses the likely fiscal impacts of immigration reform proposals on state and local governments, provides a rationale for federal intergovernmental aid in the context of immigration reform, outlines past federal reimbursement programs designed to offset state and local costs, and provides recommendations for policymakers on the design and implementation of a federal "impact aid" program to mitigate costs incurred by communities that receive the nation's newcomers.

* I gratefully acknowledge the invaluable assistance of Julia Gelatt and Mark Litchman in identifying and gathering background research for this chapter.

THE FISCAL IMPACTS OF IMMIGRANTS

The foreign born are not evenly distributed nationwide, but rather, are concentrated in the traditional gateway states of California, New York, Texas, Illinois, and Florida, and are a rapidly growing presence in the new immigrant gateways such as North Carolina, Georgia, and Nevada. Both immigrants and nonimmigrants tend to be highly concentrated even within these states, as they cluster in select employment-rich urban or rural areas.[1] Those arriving under the immigration reform proposals are likely to follow in the footsteps of other recent arrivals and replicate recent geographical settlement patterns. Thus, the "fiscal impact" of these new arrivals will very much be a local phenomenon, felt by receiving states and more acutely, by particular local communities.

Fiscal impacts can be viewed as the difference between an individual's receipt of government expenditures on public goods, public services, and transfer payments, and his or her tax payments to government entities at each jurisdictional level. If fiscal costs exceed revenues, the individual is a net fiscal burden to other taxpayers. Conversely, if fiscal costs are less than revenues, the individual is a net fiscal asset to other taxpayers. Fiscal impacts can be measured using an individual's lifetime perspective or a short-run, annual budgetary perspective. Since immigrant settlement is a local phenomenon, and state and local governments are legally bound to balance their annual budgets while facing constraints in their ability to raise revenues, a short-run measure of fiscal impacts may be more relevant for informing federal immigration policy.

In 1997, The National Research Council (NRC) estimated that the net annual fiscal impacts of foreign-headed households varied substantially by state.[2] As shown in Table 1, immigrants in New Jersey imposed a modest negative fiscal burden of $1,850 (or $290 in additional taxes required per native household to offset immigrants' fiscal costs), but a substantially higher fiscal deficit of $4,311 in California ($1,466 additional taxes per native household). Local fiscal burdens are proportionately higher in states like New Jersey where public education is primarily locally funded; local burdens are lower in California since

---

1   R. Capps, M. Fix, and J. S. Passel, 2002, *The Dispersal of Immigrants in the 1990s*, Washington, DC: The Urban Institute.

2   J. P. Smith and B. Edmonston, eds., 1997, *The New Americans: Economic, Demographic, and Fiscal Effects of Immigration*, Panel on the Demographic and Economic Impacts of Immigration, The National Research Council, Washington, DC: National Academy Press. Immigrants tend to be net fiscal assets to the federal government, as discussed in the NRC report and in A. L. Gustman and T. L. Stenmeier, 2000, "Social Security Benefits of Immigrants and U.S. Born," in *Issues in the Economics of Immigration*, G. J. Borjas, ed., pp. 309-351, Chicago: University of Chicago Press for the National Bureau of Economic Research.

public schools are primarily funded by the state. Garvey et al. (2002)[3] show that fiscal impacts are determined by the education level of the householder, family size, and household location. The different levels of expenditures for native born and immigrant residents are principally driven by immigrant families' higher education costs (owing in part to their larger families) and by lower local property and state income taxes paid by less-educated, lower income immigrant householders. In short, less-skilled foreign born generally impose higher short-term fiscal burdens on state and local governments than their higher-skilled native or immigrant counterparts.

While many state and local policies have changed since the 1990s when the NRC estimates were calculated (one example is welfare reform's bars on legal immigrants' use of public benefits), these figures do provide a rough idea of the range and magnitude of annual fiscal costs of state and locally provided education and public goods and services made available to new arrivals under most "comprehensive" immigration reform proposals. If the number of less-skilled, legally present immigrants were to rise significantly, then the net fiscal burdens of the newly arriving households would likely move closer to the extreme case of California, with a high proportion of unauthorized migrants and less-skilled immigrants.

TABLE 1. NET ANNUAL LOCAL AND STATE FISCAL BURDENS, SELECTED STATES (2005 DOLLARS)

State	Average Fiscal Deficit of an Immigrant Household	Taxes Required per Native Household to Offset Immigrant Fiscal Deficit
California		
Local	$1,034	$352
State	3,276	1,114
Total	4,311	1,466
New Jersey		
Local	$1,148	$179
State	700	110
Total	1,847	289

Note: Totals may not sum exactly due to rounding.

Source: Smith and Edmonston (1997).

---

3 D. L. Garvey, T. J. Espenshade, and J. M. Scully, 2002, "Are Immigrants a Drain on the Public Fiscal State and Local Impacts in New Jersey?", Social Science Quarterly 83(2):537-553.

The potential state and local fiscal burden may exceed the NRC estimates in one important area: public assistance receipt. In the current era of welfare reform, nonimmigrants and even LPRs, particularly working-age adults, face restricted access to federally funded public welfare benefits such as Temporary Assistance for Needy Families (TANF), food stamps, the State Child Health Insurance Program (SCHIP), and Medicaid. By shifting the burden of providing a safety net to state and local governments, welfare reform's bars may increase outlays of communities that choose to extend benefits to recently arrived legal immigrants.[4]

RATIONALE FOR FEDERAL INTERGOVERNMENTAL AID

Since immigrants and nonimmigrants cluster in certain states and localities, areas of new foreign-born settlement may experience disproportionately adverse fiscal impacts, at least in the short run, arising from the need to provide education, emergency health, and selected state-funded health and social services to their new temporary workers and LPRs in the face of limited policy levers to increase tax revenues. Local governments are particularly constrained in the short run from raising taxes. The single most important local tax, the property tax, has a relatively fixed tax base in the short run, and most local governments are legally prohibited from imposing sales taxes. State governments frequently face intense political pressure or constitutional tax limitations that restrict their ability to increase broad-based sales and income taxes. Despite these potentially significant fiscal needs and binding tax constraints facing state and local governments, the state and local fiscal impacts of changes to the LPR and nonimmigrant visa admissions systems have not been subject to much legislative attention or debate.[5]

Beyond state and local government needs, there is also a revenue rationale for increasing federal intergovernmental aid: the windfall the federal tax system

---

4   For a description of state-level immigrant welfare policies, see W. N. Zimmermann and K. C. Tumlin, 1999, *Patchwork Policies: State Assistance for Immigrants under Welfare Reform*, Washington, DC: The Urban Institute.

5   Take, for example, a 2006 document issued by the National Conference of State Legislatures. It reads: "State governments also fund and provide critical English-language instruction and public education to newcomers that is essential for promoting public safety, reducing community tensions, and integrating newcomers into our communities, including those who might be here on a temporary basis. Most immigration reform proposals in Congress would impose significant cost-shifts to state and local government. NCSL urges Congress to include in immigration reform a funding stream to address the entire fiscal impacts on state governments of any guestworker program, earned legalization, and/or increases in the number of immigrants." NCSL, "Immigration," 2006.

obtains from the new immigration. Accumulating research suggests that immigrants and temporary or nonimmigrant workers are net contributors to the federal tax system. These individuals have relatively high labor force participation rates and thus pay federal income and social security taxes. In particular, new arrivals are net fiscal assets in relation to the social security system: Immigrants' social security taxes subsidize native-born social security benefit receipt, since estimates suggest at least a third of the foreign born return to their countries of origin and never claim social security benefits.[6]

The Use of Federal Impact Aid in Other Policy Areas

There are policy precedents outside of the immigration field for intergovernmental aid programs that reimburse states and localities for fiscal burdens imposed by federal government policies. The most important, in terms of expenditures, longevity, and individuals affected, is the Federal Impact Aid program administered by the Department of Education.[7] (The much smaller Department of Defense Supplement to Impact Aid is not discussed here.) For over 50 years, the Impact Aid program has provided federal funds to reimburse local public school districts that educate federally connected students (military or civilian federal employees, Native Americans, and residents of federal public housing). Funds are distributed to compensate districts for the additional fiscal burden imposed by the presence of federally connected children in the school district and reduced property tax base arising from the tax-exempt status of federal property. Over $1.2 billion in Impact Aid was distributed in FY 2004 to over 1,400 school districts that enroll 1.2 million eligible children (see the first three columns of Table 2). Only Title I compensatory education and special education receive a larger share of federal spending on elementary and secondary education.

While this impact aid program provides an important precedent for federal reimbursement, the complex funding formula it adopts creates several perverse incentives and funding inequities that make it a poor model for an immigrant intergovernmental aid program. Because Congress does not usually allocate sufficient funding to cover reimbursement for all eligible school districts, a special formula is triggered that provides higher per-pupil reimbursement to districts with larger percentages of federally connected students and to districts in states

---

6   R. Lee and T. Miller, 2000, "Immigration, Social Security, and Broader Fiscal Impacts," *American Economic Review* 90 (2):350-54.

7   R. Buddin, B. Gill, and R. W. Zimmer, 2004, "Examining Federal Impact Aid's Reimbursement for Local School Districts," *Contemporary Economic Policy* 220(4): 534-43.

with above-average per-pupil expenditures — irrespective of local expenditure effort. Federal reimbursement falls when districts increase local spending, all else being equal.

Under the program's odd funding formula, the amount of Impact Aid a district receives is disconnected from the costs of educating federally connected students.[8] Districts with the same number of eligible pupils receive widely differing reimbursements depending on their size, state expenditure levels, and locally financed education spending. Impact Aid's incentives cause two kinds of distortions at the district level that lead to inefficiencies. First, small districts receive higher per-pupil reimbursement than larger districts with the same number of eligible students. As a consequence, small districts with large proportions of federally connected children have no incentive to consolidate into a larger district to achieve economies of scale, since their Impact Aid payments will fall. Second, districts with large proportions of military students are discouraged by the Impact Aid formula from increasing locally financed education spending.

IMPACT AID PROGRAMS IN THE CONTEXT OF IMMIGRATION POLICY

There are several precedents for federal intergovernmental impact aid to help offset state and local costs associated with immigration. Specifically, intergovernmental aid has focused in the past on compensating states and localities for the costs of educating foreign-born children, providing emergency health care to unauthorized migrants, and incarcerating unauthorized criminal migrants.

THE STATE LEGALIZATION IMPACT ASSISTANCE GRANTS (SLIAG)
The SLIAG program was the largest federal impact aid program.[9] The $4 billion program, one of the provisions of the 1986 Immigrant Reform and Control Act (IRCA), compensated states and localities for the costs of providing public welfare benefits, public health, and education services to the roughly 2.8 million formerly undocumented migrants who legalized under IRCA. Newly authorized aliens were denied access to federal welfare benefits during a five-year exclusion period. SLIAG thus compensated states and localities for the

---

8   R. W. Zimmer, R. Buddin, and B. Gill, 2002, "Distribution Effects and Distorted Incentives; A Case Study of the Funding Formulas of the Federal Impact Aid Program," *Journal of Education Finance* 27(4), 939-963.

9   This description of the SLIAG program is derived from L. C. Liu, 1991, *IRCA's State Legalization Impact Assistance Grants (SLIAG): Early Implementation*, RAND Note N-3270-FF, Santa Monica, CA: The RAND Corporation.

welfare expenditures (cash benefits, health care, emergency medical care, and food stamps), public health costs (e.g., immunizations and preventive health screenings), and selected adult education costs (e.g., instruction in basic English, American history, civics, and citizenship preparation) provided during legalizing immigrants' five-year exclusion from federal benefits.

SLIAG represented the first comprehensive federal response to the short-run fiscal burden imposed on state and local governments by immigration policies that sharply increased the number of less-skilled LPRs by adjusting their status. SLIAG's appropriations were over $1,500 (in 2005 dollars) per eligible authorized immigrant. Despite its good intentions, the program aroused bitter feelings among state and local officials who complained that program funds were insufficient. Reimbursement was delayed by the sheer magnitude of the program and breadth of covered services, slow issuance of regulations, complex program definition, and cost documentation requirements. Delays also arose from the need to coordinate across three levels of government and with community agencies. Indeed, nearly a quarter of the appropriated funds were still owed at the start of the seventh and final year of the program in FY 1994.

The SLIAG experience sounds a cautionary note regarding the design of complex intergovernmental aid programs. While state and local governments were reimbursed on the basis of the proven costs of providing services, agencies were burdened with strict requirements for attributing costs specifically to legalized immigrants, which substantially delayed reimbursements.[10] In addition, SLIAG severely restricted reimbursement of administrative and facilities' costs uniquely associated with provision of citizenship and language education services to the new LPRs.

THE EMERGENCY IMMIGRANT EDUCATION PROGRAM (EIEP)
EIEP was first authorized in 1984 and is the only federal program that targets monies based on the number of immigrant students rather than the number of English language learners (ELLs). The EIEP was specifically designed to offset the additional state and local educational costs incurred in educating recent immigrant students, defined as those who have been in US schools fewer than three years. The program funds supplementary educational instructional expenditures, tutoring, family literacy, and parental outreach.[11] Funding for the EIEP can only be separately identified through 2001, since the EIEP program and

10 Liu, *IRCA's State Legalization Impact Assistance Grants (SLIAG)*.

11 For more information on the targeted nature of EIEP, see A. I. Gershberg, A. Danenberg, and P. Sanchez, 2004, *Beyond "Bilingual" Education: New Immigrants and Public School Policies in California*, Washington, DC: Urban Institute Press.

Table 2. Expenditures on Federal Impact Aid and No Child Left Behind Language Acquisition State Grants

| | Impact Aid | | NCLB Title III | |
| | Appropriations (millions of | Appropriations (millions of | Appropriations (millions of | Appropriations (millions of |
Year	dollars)	2005 dollars)	dollars)	2005 dollars)
2002	$1,144	$1,242	$403	$437
2003	1,188	1,261	685	727
2004	1,230	1,272	685	708
2005	1,230*	1,230*	683*	683

* estimates

Note: NCLB spending combines former Emergency Immigrant Education Program (EIEP) and Bilingual Education funding.

Sources: CRS Reports to Congress, "K-12 Education Programs: Appropriations and Summary," September 30, 2004, and "Education of Limited English Proficient and Recent Immigrant Students: Provisions in the No Child Left Behind Act of 2001," April 26, 2004.

bilingual education are now part of Title III (Language Instruction for Limited English Proficient and Immigrant Students) of the No Child Left Behind Act. Although EIEP funding more than tripled from 1996 to 2001, it does not appear to have risen beyond $210 per eligible student, a small sum of average per-pupil spending.[12]

It is instructive to compare EIEP and bilingual education expenditures, the only two major federal impact aid programs directed to immigrant students and ELLs, respectively, with those of the Federal Impact Aid program. Recall that 2004 Impact Aid expenditures (Table 2) were approximately $1,000 per eligible child. By contrast, English language acquisition expenditures under Title III of NCLB (rightmost column of Table 2) were approximately $136 per English language learner (ELL), an order of magnitude lower. Per-pupil expenditures are likely to deteriorate in coming years, as the ELL population —

---

12 M. Fix, W. Zimmermann, and J. S. Passel, 2001, *The Integration of Immigrant Families in the United States*, Washington, DC: The Urban Institute

which has more than doubled since 1991 — continues to experience large growth.

COMPENSATING FOR HEALTH CARE PROVIDED TO THE UNAUTHORIZED

A third source of federal impact aid to offset fiscal costs of immigrants is a set of federal programs that compensates hospitals and other medical service providers for emergency medical services delivered to unauthorized migrants and certain other nonimmigrants.[13] The Medicare Prescription Drug, Improvement, and Modernization Act of 2003 provides $250 million per year for FY 2005 to 2008. The design of the reimbursement scheme targets states and local communities with the largest unauthorized populations: Two-thirds of the aid is divided among states based on their relative share of the unauthorized population, while the remaining third is allocated among the six states with the largest number of unauthorized migrant apprehensions. Since apprehensions disproportionately occur at the US-Mexico border, border states will get a higher share of reimbursement for emergency care, even if unauthorized migrants disperse away from traditional receiving states.

THE STATE CRIMINAL ALIEN ASSISTANCE PROGRAM (SCAAP)

SCAAP is another example of intergovernmental impact aid to offset immigration-related burdens on state and local coffers. SCAAP was created in 1995 as a political response to state lawsuits demanding reimbursement for the costs of incarcerating migrants. Program spending quadrupled from $165 million in FY 1995 to $686 million in FY 1999 before declining by over half to $305 million in FY 2005 (all figures are in 2005 dollars). To put this figure in context, federal reimbursements to offset state and local incarceration costs under SCAAP were over $2,300 per prisoner in FY 1998, nearly ten times the rate of federal per-pupil spending on EIEP and bilingual education programs ($246 in FY 1999). Although President Bush eliminated SCAAP from his FY 2007 budget proposal, the House has approved a bill calling for appropriations of $405 million for the program for FY 2007, and the Senate Appropriations Committee has called for $100 million.[14]

---

13 For more information on federal spending programs targeted to immigrants, see J. Gelatt and M. Fix, 2006, *Targeted Federal Spending on the Integration of Immigrant Families*, Background Paper Prepared for the Independent Task Force on Immigration and America's Future, Washington, DC: Migration Policy Institute. See, also, chapter 6 of this volume, pp. 61-80.

14 United States House of Representatives, "Science, State, Justice, Commerce, and Related Agencies Appropriations Act, 2007," H.R. 5672, 109th Cong. 2nd Sess. (2006); United States Senate, "Science, State, Justice, Commerce, and Related Agencies Appropriations Act, 2007," H.R. 5672, 109th Cong. 2nd Sess. (2006).

POLICY RECOMMENDATIONS FOR DESIGNING AN IMMIGRANT "IMPACT AID" POLICY

Three economic questions must be carefully considered when designing an immigrant "impact aid" policy: First, what is the program's proper scope? Second, given scarce federal resources, how should an impact aid program be targeted? Finally, given the stated goals of impact aid, which funding mechanisms will efficiently transfer federal reimbursements to state and local coffers while minimizing distorting incentives to state and local governments, and the new arrivals themselves?

The types of state and local expenditures immigrant impact aid should address is a normative question that positive economic arguments alone cannot satisfactorily answer. However, if federal policymakers want to reduce the likely short-run fiscal distress on states and localities caused by the arrival of new less-skilled LPRs and guest workers with immigration reform, then compensating lower levels of government for the additional expenditures they incur as a result of federal policies is a sound fiscal policy goal.

From a fiscal balance perspective, it is useful to first consider compensating education service costs, since these are the single largest category of local and state spending on immigrants.[15] Investment in children's educational attainment not only increases their human capital, but promotes their successful integration into American society. Basic adult education programs will boost the human capital of the lowest-skilled adult immigrants, which will in turn raise wages for immigrants and their families, generate higher tax revenues for all levels of government, and reduce public welfare expenditures.

Federal impact aid should also be directed to community institutions providing basic, preventive health care to low-income, uninsured foreign born and their families. Lower income immigrants have the highest rates of noninsurance, less access to basic health care services, worse health outcomes, and are more likely to seek relatively expensive emergency care only when seriously ill.[16] Evidence strongly suggests that access to preventive care is not only a cost-effective use

---

15 For a demographic and socioeconomic profile of the increasing numbers of immigrant youth in US schools and their educational needs, see R. Capps, M. Fix, J. Murray, J. Ost, J. S. Passel, and S. Herwantoro, 2005, *The New Demography of America's Schools: Immigration and the No Child Left Behind Act*, Washington, DC: The Urban Institute.

16 E. A. Marcelli, 2003. "Access to Health Insurance and Medical Care among Unauthorized Mexican Immigrants to California," presented at the 25th Annual Research Conference of the Association of Public Policy and Management, November 6-8, in Washington, DC.

of scarce health-care dollars, but also improves individual and family well-being and labor market attachment of adults.

The final Gordian knot to be cut is to decide how to devise a reimbursement mechanism that compensates state and local governments for the actual cost of providing services without encouraging government entities to "game the system" by misclassifying individuals as in need of compensated services or relabeling expenditures so they fall into a compensated category. In the case of ELLs, for example, these incentives are minimized by rewarding schools for their students' growth in English language proficiency. Education economists who specialize in cost analysis have developed tools to assess the benchmark cost of achieving a particular desired educational outcome, given student characteristics. Such information can be combined with information on overall school district costs to determine an adequate level of funding. If federal aid is insufficient to reimburse all costs for a particular program, a pro-rata allocation is a simple way to avoid the perverse incentives and inequitable distribution of federal funds that appear to occur under the Federal Impact Aid program.

Concluding Observations

An important lesson to be drawn from the SLIAG program is that the success of a comprehensive federal impact aid policy is not simply a matter of properly designing a reimbursement scheme to compensate state and local governments for the education, health, and other fiscal costs associated with immigration or legalization. Understanding how bureaucracies operate and promoting interagency communication between all levels of government and with community service providers are critical prerequisites to ensuring effective implementation of a complex aid scheme.

The immigrant impact aid policies discussed here do not, for the most part, reach the funding of active settlement programs that encourage immigrants' successful integration into the fabric of American society. Citizenship preparation, civic engagement, and "newcomer" orientation programs that foster immigrant settlement, political engagement, knowledge of American social institutions, and social integration tend to be funded by state and local governments on an ad hoc basis and provided by local nonprofit agencies.

Current federal policy provides little funding for such activities, and state and local governments will be fiscally constrained from increasing their funding of seemingly optional programs. Policymakers would be well-advised to consider federal funding of active integration programs, and not just simply compensate state and local governments for the fiscal costs associated with new arrivals under immigration reform. American society would be better off knowing which newcomer programs are cost-effective and fund those with the greatest impact in order to promote the integration of our many new, likely permanent, foreign-born residents.

MAJOR LEGISLATIVE MILESTONES IN US IMMIGRATION HISTORY

CHINESE EXCLUSION ACT OF 1882
- Suspends immigration of Chinese laborers for ten years.
- Bars Chinese naturalization.
- Provides for the deportation of Chinese illegally in the United States.

IMMIGRATION ACT OF 1891
- First comprehensive law for national control of immigration.
- Establishes Bureau of Immigration under Treasury.
- Directs deportation of aliens unlawfully in country.

IMMIGRATION AND NATURALIZATION ACT OF 1924
- Imposes first permanent numerical limit on immigration.
- Establishes the national origins quota system, which resulted in biased admissions favoring northern and western Europeans.

IMMIGRATION AND NATURALIZATION ACT OF JUNE 27, 1952
- Continues national origins quotas.
- Establishes quota for skilled aliens whose services are urgently needed.

IMMIGRATION AND NATIONALITY ACT AMENDMENTS OF OCTOBER 3, 1965
- Repeals national origins quotas.
- Establishes seven-category preference system based on family unification and skills.
- Sets 20,000 per country limit for immigration from the Eastern Hemisphere.
- Imposes ceiling on immigration from Western Hemisphere for first time.

IMMIGRATION AND NATIONALITY ACT AMENDMENTS OF 1976
- Extends 20,000 per country limits to immigration from the Western Hemisphere.

REFUGEE ACT OF 1980

■ Sets up first permanent and systematic procedure for admitting refugees.
■ Removes refugees as a category from preference system.
■ Defines refugee according to international, versus ideological, standards.
■ Establishes process of domestic resettlement.
■ Codifies asylum status.

IMMIGRATION REFORM AND CONTROL ACT OF 1986

■ Institutes employer sanctions for knowingly hiring illegal aliens.
■ Creates legalization programs.
■ Increases border enforcement.
■ Creates $4 Billion State Legalization Impact Assistance Grant Program.

IMMIGRATION ACT OF 1990

■ Increases legal immigration ceilings by 40 percent and triples employment-based immigration.
■ Creates diversity admissions category.
■ Establishes temporary protected status for those in the United States jeopardized by armed conflict or natural disasters in their native countries.

ILLEGAL IMMIGRATION REFORM AND IMMIGRANT RESPONSIBILITY ACT OF 1996

■ Increases penalties for alien smuggling and document fraud.
■ Provides for expedited removal of inadmissible aliens.
■ Bars unlawfully present immigrants from re-entry for longer periods of time.
■ Sets income requirements for immigrant sponsors at 125 percent of federal poverty level.

This chart has been updated since its original publication in *Setting the Record Straight*, by M. E. Fix and J. S. Passel (Washington, DC: The Urban Institute, 1994). It is reprinted here with permission from The Urban Institute.

Access to Health Care after Immigration Reform: Lessons from New York

Adam Gurvitch

Immigration reform could affect millions of American workers, public and private health care providers, insurers, and public health. Among other things, reform could create new categories of temporary workers, increase the number of lawful permanent residents, and change the treatment of unauthorized residents. This appendix focuses on access to health care and presents the author's practical considerations for policymakers who must plan for the consequences of reforms at state and local levels. Examples from the state of New York are used to illustrate how options for immigrants' health care access might be implemented.

Guiding Principles

Whatever approach is chosen to provide health care access for participants in an immigration reform program, the following principles should guide reform:

- Do not add to the ranks of the uninsured.

- Favor the simplest, least costly administrative structures.

- Consider the interests of both healthy individuals and those who have medical needs.

- Do not weaken employer-based health insurance coverage.

- Strengthen the health care safety net for everyone in the community.

Key Design Elements

In thinking about how to structure access to health care at the local level for temporary workers and other individuals who participate in an immigration reform program, the following considerations are important:

STAKEHOLDER INVESTMENT

Employer and employee assessments or contributions are assumed to be the primary source of funding for access to health care when discussing policy options. Immigration reform that is designed to benefit employers and workers should come with the expectation that each will contribute to ensuring adequate access to health care. Employers that provide health insurance benefits to workers who benefit from immigration reform could be granted an offset or credit against the employer's assessed cost of participating in the immigration program (payment of fees, for example).

FAIRNESS IN TAXATION

Workers who reside in the United States and pay federal income taxes should be able to obtain federal means-tested public benefits on the same basis as any other American if they fall on hard times. This basic fairness is especially relevant when faced with urgently needed, expensive medical care.[1]

ACCESS TO EMERGENCY CARE

Emergency medical transportation and emergency health care are generally extended to all persons in the United States experiencing an emergency medical condition, upholding our long-standing respect for basic human decency; immigration reform should retain this commitment to all US residents.[2]

STOP-LOSS PROTECTION FOR CATASTROPHIC CARE

Medical care is extremely expensive for the vast majority of Americans and is distinct in nature from other types of expenses and debts because medical care is often incurred involuntarily. US citizens gain access to Medicaid if they have limited income and exhaust their disposable resources.[3] Migrants admitted

---

1   For a description of the restrictions currently imposed on legal immigrants' access to Medicaid and the State Children's Health Insurance Program (SCHIP), see the US Department of Health and Human Services, Centers for Medicare and Medicaid Services (CMS) Web site: http://www.cms.hhs.gov/MedicaidEligibility/05_Immigrants.asp#TopOfPage.

2   42 U.S.C. § 1395dd. US Department of Health and Human Services, Centers for Medicare and Medicaid Services (CMS) Emergency Medical Treatment and Labor Act (EMTALA) Web site: http://www.cms.hhs.gov/EMTALA.

3   US Department of Health and Human Services, Centers for Medicare and Medicaid Services (CMS) Web site: http://www.cms.hhs.gov/home/medicaid.asp. See also, "The Medicaid Program At a Glance" (Washington, DC: Kaiser Commission on Medicaid and the Uninsured, Henry J. Kaiser Family Foundation, 2005), http://www.kff.org/medicaid/upload/The-Medicaid-Program-at-a-Glance-Fact-Sheet.pdf.

under immigration reform will need some form of stop-loss protection against catastrophic medical costs; options include Medicaid,[4] Medicare, or restricted scope Medical Assistance for an emergency medical condition ("emergency Medicaid").[5] This protection will also ensure that safety net health providers are reimbursed, at least in part, for the costs of treating low-income patients.

RESIDENCY
Participants in immigration reform should be treated at least as favorably as H-1 visa holders for the purposes of participating in programs and services that currently impose a state or local residency requirement. Examples of programs that require proof of residency but not legal status include public health services, federally qualified health centers, hospital reimbursement for the treatment of an emergency medical condition through "emergency Medicaid," and, in states such as New York, free or subsidized insurance for children, pregnant women, and individuals living with HIV and AIDS.[6]

PUBLIC NOTICE
The nation's experience with the recent drug reimbursement or Medicare Part D program clearly demonstrates how important it will be for the government to provide clear instructions about health programs to participants in immigration reform. Clear communications will be vital to addressing concerns and misconceptions that lead many foreign-born individuals to avoid using health programs.[7]

POLICY OPTIONS

Access to health care is important to workers, employers, and communities alike. Public health is safeguarded only when all members of a community are willing to come forward for screening and treatment in the event of an epidemic or biological or chemical exposure. Employers experience workers' illness,

---

4   The federal Medicaid program's medically needy (MN) option allows states to extend Medicaid eligibility to persons whose income and/or resources are above the eligibility level set by their state. Persons may qualify immediately or may "spend down" by incurring medical expenses that reduce their income to or below their state's MN income level. Thirty-five states have adopted the medically needy option, and the remaining states have Medicaid for people who are "near poor." More information can be found at: http://www.cms.hhs.gov/MedicaidGenInfo/03_TechnicalSummary.asp#TopOfPage.

5   J. Perkins, "Medicaid Coverage of Emergency Medical Conditions," Clearinghouse Review Journal of Poverty Law and Policy 384 (Sept/Oct 2004).

6   New York State, Department of Health — Medical Assistance Program: GIS 04 MA/003 Attachment 1, 2004.

7   T. Bauer, J. Bergman, C. Hill, J. Fuld, and L. Weiss, "Access to Health Insurance and Health Care for Children in Immigrant Families" (New York: The New York Academy of Medicine, publication forthcoming).

injury, and disability as lost productivity and increased training and recruitment costs. US residents who cannot afford health care avoid seeking it until faced with an emergency, resulting in a less healthy, less effective population.

This paper presents five alternatives for achieving varying levels of access to health care under immigration reform, with the goals of maintaining a healthy workforce and protecting public health and the financial soundness of the US health care system.

OPTION ONE: INSURANCE BUY-IN

Individuals who participate in an immigration reform program would be allowed or required to enroll in one of the following existing health coverage programs by paying a group-rated premium: employer-based insurance, state employee health insurance plans, Medicaid, or Medicare.

Under the health insurance buy-in option, both employers and participants in immigration reform would be assessed a fee or would pay a "premium," with additional contributions required on behalf of any dependents. Employers' contributions would receive the same favorable federal and state tax treatment currently in place, constituting a government subsidy of health benefits provided by private-sector employers.

An insurance buy-in is an attractive option for providing affordable access to a full range of health services, and can potentially strengthen the public and private insurance systems. Temporary workers and other participants in immigration reform will presumably be required to pass a medical screening prior to obtaining permission from the federal government to reside and work in the United States. By definition, this population will generally be in better health and less likely than US-born citizens to be disabled, chronically and persistently ill, impaired, unable to work, or elderly.[8] It is axiomatic that 20 percent of the population generates 80 percent of all health care expenses in the United States. Adding a large number of healthy individuals to the existing population of an insurance pool would favorably distribute risks and contain the cost of insurance premiums, while promoting solvency.

> *New York State's Child Health Plus program provides an example of a successful insurance buy-in model; the program provides coverage for preventive, primary, and emergency services to any uninsured New York State resident*

---

8   T. Norgren, "Mexicans in New York City: Demographics and Health of the City's Fastest Growing Hispanic Group" (New York: Medical and Health Research Association of New York City, publication forthcoming).

younger than 19.[9] The program allows families that earn too much to qualify for children's Medicaid to purchase group-rated insurance coverage for uninsured children through the state's Child Health Plus program.

Monthly insurance premiums in the Child Health Plus program vary by family income, with the highest monthly premium set at roughly $150 for a quality insurance plan with modest co-pays; a level more affordable than health plans with comparable benefits available for the same population through the private insurance market. Enrollment in the program has been high among low- and middle-income families that do not receive health coverage through their employers. The Child Health Plus buy-in program essentially provides universal health coverage to uninsured New Yorkers through age 18, regardless of immigration status. The program consistently receives bi-partisan political support throughout New York state.

While the United States spends more per capita on health care than any other country, many US residents are unable to access care, and for many who do, the financial consequences can be devastating: Medical debt is a leading cause of bankruptcy and homelessness in the United States.[10] Many people who work find it difficult or impossible to receive adequate medical care without health insurance; this is true not only for life-saving treatments but also for the routine management of chronic conditions.

While immigrants are as likely to be employed as native-born citizens, immigrants are three times as likely to lack insurance, and immigrant workers are much less likely than native-born workers to receive health insurance coverage through their employers.[11] Immigrants work the most dangerous jobs, with the fewest workplace protections, for the lowest wages in the labor market.[12] Many immigrant New Yorkers become at-risk for health problems when they enter the workforce; immigrants account for nearly 40 percent of workplace deaths in New York state.[13]

---

9   Information about New York State's Child Health Plus program can be found at the New York City Web site: http://www.nyc.gov/html/hia/html/public_insurance/children.shtml.

10 The Access Project, "Home Sick," 2005, http://www.accessproject.org/medical.html.

11 R. Capps, M. Fix, J. Passel, J. Ost, and D. Perez-Lopez, "A Profile of the Low-Wage Immigrant Workforce" (Washington, DC: The Urban Institute, 2003); M. Fix and R. Capps, "Immigrant Well-Being in New York and Los Angeles" (Washington, DC: The Urban Institute, 2002).

12 S. Richardson, "Fatal Work Injuries Among Foreign-Born Hispanic Workers," US Department of Labor, Bureau of Labor Statistics, *Monthly Labor Review* (October 2005), http://www.bls.gov/opub/mlr/2005/10/ressum.pdf.

13 According to the US Bureau of Labor Statistics, 39 percent of fatal occupational injuries in New York State in 2000, and 67 percent of fatal occupational injuries in New York City were immigrant workers. See New York State Trial Lawyers Association, "New York's "Scaffold Law": An Essential Protection for Immigrant Construction Workers," 2004.

Most legal immigrants arriving in the United States since August 22, 1996, are categorically barred for five years from receiving federal means-tested public benefits, including the Medicaid and SCHIP health programs.[14] These bars remain in place despite the fact that these individuals — lawful permanent residents — are authorized to work and required to pay taxes that directly subsidize others' health benefits. Immigration reform, whether in the form of a temporary worker program, earned legalization program, or a broad expansion in permanent visas, will achieve greater legitimacy if it corrects the failure of earlier policies that prevent legal immigrants from accessing safety net supports during times of hardship.

Many New Yorkers, including hundreds of thousands of immigrants, earn too much to qualify for public coverage, too little to afford private coverage, and lack affordable coverage through their employers.[15] Any proposal aimed at ensuring access to affordable health care for the participants in immigration reform must also take into account the situation facing other uninsured Americans, including the US-born. That said, foreign-born residents who are permitted to live and work in the United States must have access to affordable health care in order to avoid circumstances of extreme inequity and exploitation.

A basic assumption is that the immigration reform programs will be designed with the rights of all workers in mind and will not undermine working conditions for any segment of the workforce — newly minted or well-established. It is crucial to ensure that employers who already provide health insurance benefits maintain that effort.

ADVANTAGES OF THE INSURANCE BUY-IN

- The option would subsidize US-born individuals who are insured by adding significantly younger and healthier participants to existing insurance pools.

- It would utilize existing infrastructure and administrative mechanisms and achieve savings through economies of scale.

- Cost-effective preventive and primary care could be accessed, as well as emergency and specialty care. Access to comprehensive care would be possible, depending on the design of the insurance products.

---

14 US Department of Health and Human Services website, "Summary of Immigrant Eligibility Restrictions Under Current Law as of 10/04/2004": http://aspe.hhs.gov/hsp/immigration/restrictions-sum.htm.

15 E. Hubert, D. Holahan, and A. Cook, "Health Insurance Coverage in New York, 2002-2003" (New York: United Hospital Fund, 2005).

- Health providers could adapt their existing billing and claims systems, and new administrative and information technology requirements would be minimized.

- Participants could access care through outpatient and clinical settings, rather than relying on much more costly emergency care.

- Health coverage would be portable: Individuals could avoid becoming uninsured if they change jobs or move to a different community.

- The insurance buy-in option would build on programs that work well for people, including individuals who have high needs for health care.

- It would help shore up Medicaid, Medicare, employer-based, and private insurance pools.

CONCERNS

- Many current US citizens and lawful permanent residents ("green card" holders) are not provided with insurance buy-in options,[16] therefore a tough political case would have to be made as to why employers of these new segments of the workforce are held to higher standards for subsidizing their employees' health benefits.

- A significant proportion of immigrants have difficulty navigating managed care, and they consequently under-utilize health care that is delivered in this way.[17]

OPTION TWO: SAFETY NET "MEDICAL HOME"

Participants in immigration reform programs who do not receive insurance through their employers would be matched with safety net health care providers, and a paying relationship would be established according to the providers' prevailing fees for uninsured patients. Participants would be encouraged or required to obtain a clinic card and receive an initial health screening.

---

16 A. Safir and H. Leibovitz, "State Profile of New York - Data from the 2002 National Survey of America's Families" (Washington, DC: The Urban Institute, 2004).

17 New York Community Service Society, "Low Income Consumers' Experiences: Results from a Citywide Survey of Managed Care Consumers in Medicaid, Child Health Plus, and Family Health Plus," 2005.

The safety net provider would help to enroll participants into any public insurance programs for which the immigrant qualifies, and those who did not obtain coverage would be charged on the same discounted basis as any other current member of the community, including US citizens and lawful permanent residents.[18] A mechanism would be established to bring employers into the finance system.

> *New York City's Health and Hospitals Corporation (HHC, the public health care system) represents a model for providing insurance screening and financial assistance based on patients' income, regardless of immigration status. The HHC Options program enables current and prospective patients who are uninsured to establish fee reductions from health safety net providers and to have pharmacies reduce or waive the cost of medications.[19] The program enables New Yorkers to access care in the most cost-effective clinical settings, rather than delaying care out of fear of financial consequences and then relying on much more costly emergency care. HHC finds that its generous financial assistance program provides an incentive for patients to cooperate with the hospital's financial counselors, which enables the hospital system to optimize patients' enrollment in insurance programs and maximize reimbursements to the hospital.*

Federally qualified community health centers (FQHCs), FQHC look-alikes, rural and migrant health centers, and public and private hospitals and clinics comprise a health care safety net in the communities where participants in immigration reform are likely to be concentrated.[20] The Bush Administration has expressed a strong commitment to increasing funding for FQHCs and to ensuring that one is open in most counties.

The immigration reform population (guest workers, legalizing immigrants, e.g.) would not have special rights, just the same rights all others currently share.

The rationale for putting uninsured participants into contact with safety net health care providers is the strong desirability of establishing a "medical home."[21] Making the match with a safety net provider and establishing a "med-

---

18 Participants in an immigration reform program who meet some definition of "high-income," and whose employers do not provide health benefits, could be mandated to purchase private insurance or buy-in to group coverage as a condition of residing in the United States.

19 New York City Health and Hospitals Corporation — HHC Options Web site: http://www.nyc.gov/html/hhc/html/community/hhc_options.shtml.

20 US Department of Health and Human Services, Centers for Medicare and Medicaid Services (CMS) FQHC Web site: http://www.cms.hhs.gov/center/fqhc.asp.

21 For a description of the concept of "medical home," see the American Academy of Pediatrics Web site: http://www.medicalhomeinfo.org.

ical home" would ensure that uninsured participants would not be deterred from seeking needed medical care due to fear of devastating medical debt or immigration-related concerns. Currently, too few immigrants in New York City understand the options for affordable care available through the health care safety net, and they delay care until their conditions become serious, resulting in poorer health and more costly care down the line.[22]

The health care safety net is already burdened by the uncompensated and under-compensated care it provides — a burden that is partially explained by the system's failure to proactively undertake patient education and outreach about the availability of reduced-cost care, outpatient services, and public coverage.[23] Uninsured US residents, and immigrants in particular, often receive the full bill for services, when in actuality there are reductions that could be applied, or coverage for which people are eligible but not enrolled. This confusion results in large numbers of uninsured residents who are unable or afraid to seek health care.

ADVANTAGES OF THE SAFETY NET "MEDICAL HOME"

■ Establishing a "medical home" would greatly increase the likelihood that health care would be obtained in a timely and cost-effective way through preventive and primary care.

■ Health providers could adapt their existing billing and claims systems.

■ Participants could obtain care through outpatient and clinical settings, rather than relying on much more costly emergency care.

■ This option would make it more likely that participants could receive culturally competent, linguistically accessible services regardless of their ability to pay, and further, that low-cost payment options would be available, such as sliding-scale fee reductions.

■ It would provide access to comprehensive care in most regions in the United States.

---

22 M. Doty, J. Edwards, and A. Holmgren, "Seeing Red: Americans Driven into Debt by Medical Bills" (New York: The Commonwealth Fund, 2005).

23 E. Benjamin et al., "State Secret: How Government Fails to Ensure that Uninsured and Underinsured Patients Have Access to State Charity Care Funds" (New York: The Legal Aid Society — Health Law Unit, 2004). See also, "Hospital Free Care: Can New Yorkers Access Hospital Services Paid for by Our Tax Dollars?" (New York: Public Policy and Education Fund of New York, 2003).

- It would strategically utilize existing capacity in the health care system.

CONCERNS

- This option would require matching individuals with medical providers directly, which could involve additional administrative complexity and resources.

- FQHCs and rural and migrant health centers provide preventive and primary care services, but may not provide vision or dental care, and generally do not provide emergency or acute care. However, in many areas of the United States these clinics are the only available source of care to uninsured individuals. Some form of wrap-around coverage might be necessary to reimburse providers for catastrophic health care expenses; the federal government's "emergency Medicaid" program currently serves this function.

- Patients' advocates distrust proposals that appear to channel individuals into the public health care system, fearing a two-tiered system. However, the reality for most uninsured US residents is that private health care is unaffordable and inaccessible. This population ultimately ends up receiving care from public providers, if it receives care at all. Assignment to a "medical home" would not preclude the participation of private providers or limit participants' freedom to seek care.

- It would lack portability — an individual who relocated would need to be financially screened again and establish a relationship with a new provider.

- The health care safety net in many areas of the country is over-burdened and could ill afford to take on large additional numbers of uninsured patients.[24]

OPTION THREE: PRE-PAID MEDICAL CARE

Option Three would be the same as Option Two, with the addition of an annual assessment — for instance $500 to $1,000 — paid into a pool by employers and workers. The pool could allocate this money to the local FQHC or other comparable safety net health care provider. As above, participants would make contact with their "medical home" — an outpatient clinic — and receive a

---

24 The reimbursement rates that hospitals and clinics receive from Medicaid and Medicare for providing many outpatient services have lagged behind medical inflation for decades, resulting in fundamental structural deficiencies.

medical exam and needed care. Payment would occur either by redeeming a coupon or through a pre-paid clinic card provided to participants in an immigration reform program.

The medical fees would be determined on a sliding-scale basis, as is currently the case for any other low- or moderate-income patient, and the provider would draw down from the pre-paid assessment. If a participant required more care during the period than the pre-paid assessment covered, he or she could then pay the provider's prevailing sliding-scale charges out of pocket, like anyone else. If, at the end of the year, the participant had not utilized care in the amount of the pre-paid assessment, the remainder could revert to the safety net provider or be rolled over into a future period.

Pre-paid medical care would not constitute insurance coverage; instead it would establish a financial relationship directly between the patient and the health provider. Under this option, the individual would be asked to pay a sliding-scale rate to the health provider for any medical care used in excess of the pre-paid amount. This option would allow decisions about what medical care was needed to be made by health care providers, rather than by managed care administrators, whose profit motives and duties to shareholders can be at odds with the fundamental aim of providing appropriate medical care to patients.

In addition to the advantages and concerns set out under Option Two, "Safety Net Medical Home," this option would require making direct transfers of employee and employer assessments to medical providers, which would involve additional administrative complexity.

OPTION FOUR: NEWLY CREATED INSURANCE PROGRAM

With government assistance, small businesses and other employers that do not currently provide employee health benefits could join together to form newly created health insurance programs for pooled employees. Participants in an immigration reform program could be encouraged or required to enroll, and group-rated premiums would be paid by assessments or contributions from employees and employers. These new insurance products could also be opened up to other uninsured US residents, including workers who are classified by employers as temporary, contingent, or part-time employees, who do not receive prevailing benefits, and who cannot afford to pay out-of-pocket for healthcare.

New York State offers small employers, sole proprietors, and uninsured working individuals the opportunity to purchase health insurance coverage through the Healthy NY program. These health benefits are made more affordable through state subsidies. Healthy NY includes inpatient and outpatient hospital services, physician services, maternity care, preventative health services, diagnostic and X-ray services, and emergency services. Participants may choose a benefit package with a limited prescription drug benefit or a benefit package without a prescription drug benefit.[25] Participation in Healthy NY has lagged behind expectations, largely due to the high cost of the program's premiums.

The success of a newly created insurance program would depend on its ability to offer affordable group-rated premiums and a competitive benefits package. Such a program would be unlikely to attract many participants if it presented only small reductions in cost compared to individual insurance coverage on the private market, which is currently well out of reach for many US residents. However, very significant reductions in cost could be achieved if the government permitted small businesses, sole proprietors, and others to pool their employees and to purchase group-rated insurance. These pools would essentially replicate the conditions that have enabled large employers to successfully provide employee health benefits. This approach to creating a new insurance program would share many advantages and concerns with Option One, "New Insurance Buy-In."

OPTION FIVE: ANNUAL MEDICAL SCREENING

Temporary workers and other participants in an immigration reform program would receive an initial health screening and periodic screenings thereafter from a safety net health care provider such as a hospital, FQHC, FQHC look-alike, rural or migrant health clinic, or private provider that wishes to participate. Assuming that immigration reform will contain some sort of required screening for transmissible diseases, this could be accomplished along with a thorough check-up.

New York State's Bureau of Refugee and Immigrant Affairs subsidizes medical screenings for newly arrived refugees in the communities where they are resettled.[26] Through the Refugee Health Screening program, refugees receive free medical screening for contagious diseases during their first few months in the country from designated clinics. The limitation of this screening program is that if health conditions other than contagious diseases are detected there is

---

25 New York State — Healthy NY Web site: http://www.ins.state.ny.us/website2/hny/english/hny.htm.

26 New York State, Office of Temporary and Disability Assistance, Bureau of Refugee and Immigrant Affairs Web site: http://www.otda.state.ny.us/otda/bria/bria_prog_default.htm.

no payment system in place and many providers refuse to treat uninsured patients, including those seen through the Refugee Health Screening program.[27]

The idea behind the medical screening option is to track "fitness to work" and make a linkage to an appropriate, affordable source of health care other than the emergency room.[28] Pre-paid clinic cards or some other payment mechanism would be used. If the individual needed ongoing care, for example to manage a chronic condition such as diabetes or asthma, he or she would work out a sliding-scale fee or payment plan with a safety net provider, like any other patient (as in Option Two).

ADVANTAGES OF THE ANNUAL MEDICAL SCREENING

■ An annual medical screening would assure that participants' basic health status was monitored.

■ This option would establish a link between participants and primary care providers. However, some providers may not be willing to treat patients beyond administering the health screening.

■ The screening could be paired with more comprehensive wrap-around health benefits, such as employer-sponsored insurance, buy-in options, or "emergency Medicaid."

■ The government's Refugee Medical Screening program already exists, and that program's clinic reimbursement system might provide a model.

■ This option would enable public health surveillance and monitoring.

CONCERNS

■ While the screenings could identify problems, this option would not provide for treatment, medication, or follow-up care. The participant would essentially remain uninsured, making this option limited in its usefulness, unless paired with other health access options.

---

27 Refugees are also eligible to enroll for eight months in the government's Refugee Medical Assistance (RMA) program, which reimburses health providers for services received by participating refugees; however, some refugees themselves may be unaware of this program and, in practice, health providers sometimes fail to assist refugees in applying for the RMA benefits.

28 The Access Project, "Paying for Health Care When You're Uninsured: How Much Support Does the Safety Net Offer?" 2003.

Addressing Obstacles to Health Care

The existing disparity in access to health care faced by immigrants in the United States is striking. Apart from the obvious consequences of being categorically barred from public insurance programs, having low rates of health insurance and low incomes, legal immigrants are confronted with a distinct set of concerns.[29] Immigration laws and policies are continually evolving, and the rules about immigrants' rights to government programs and services have changed significantly in recent years.[30]

The foreign born in the United States under-utilize medical care in part as a result of the chilling effect of government policies aimed at legal immigrants (not those who are unauthorized), including public charge, sponsor liability, and immigration-related restrictions on eligibility for government programs.[31] Legal immigrants receive conflicting messages about their rights to health care and their risks from using programs and services, with different perspectives and sometimes misleading advice being offered by government, lawyers, and health care providers.[32] In this complex information environment where much is at stake, many legal immigrants avoid enrolling in public programs or accessing health care due to a belief that doing so will interfere with their ability to sponsor and reunite with close family members such as spouses, children, and parents who live abroad.[33] For low-income newcomers, the health care system is nearly impossible to navigate without orientation or assistance.

The financial hardship experienced by uninsured and underinsured immigrants who use the health care system feeds negative word-of-mouth and further contributes to under-utilization of health care and reliance on more costly emer-

---

29 Norgren, "Mexicans In New York City" (see n. 8); T. Broder, "Immigrant Eligibility for Public Benefits," in *Immigration and Nationality Law Handbook*, 759 (Washington, DC: American Immigration Lawyers Association, 2005-2006 edition, updated March 2005), http://www.nilc.org/immspbs/index.htm#immelig.

30 R. Capps, R. Koralek, K. Lotspeich, M. Fix, P. Holcomb, and J. Reardon-Anderson, "Assessing Implementation of the 2002 Farm Bill's Legal Immigrant Food Stamp Restorations: Final Report to the United States Department of Agriculture Food and Nutrition Science" (Washington, DC: The Urban Institute, 2004).

31 S. Mohanty et al., "Health Care Expenditures of Immigrants: A Nationally Representative Analysis," *American Journal of Public Health* 95, no. 8 (Aug 2005): 1431-1438; Bauer et al., "Access to Health Insurance and Health Care" (see n. 7).

32 An example of misleading information provided by the US government to immigrants was retrieved on February 11, 2006, from the Web site of the US Department of Health and Human Services, Centers for Medicare and Medicaid Services (CMS): "Your child may be eligible for coverage if he or she is a US citizen or a lawfully admitted immigrant, even if you are not (*however, there is a 5-year limit that applies to lawful permanent residents*)." [Emphasis added] There has never been a five-year limit on eligibility.

33 Children's Defense Fund, "Health Insurance in New York City: Is It Working for Immigrant Families?" 2003.

gency room care.[34] Linguistic isolation compounds the challenge.[35] Millions of newcomers are not able to explain their symptoms or understand a medical diagnosis using English. They are also unable to navigate the hospital registration and billing systems and health coverage enrollment processes in English. Government will face a tough challenge to explain the rights and process at all levels for obtaining health care and insurance, or payment options, under immigration reform.

34 Bauer et al., "Access to Health Insurance and Health Care" (see n. 7).

35 R. Capps, L. Ku, M. Fix, et al., "How Are Immigrants Faring after Welfare Reform? Preliminary Evidence from Los Angeles and New York City" (Washington, DC: The Urban Institute, 2002).

APPENDIX III

NEW AMERICANS: SELECTED FACTS ON NATURALIZATION AND BIRTHRIGHT CITIZENSHIP

MARY HELEN YBARRA JOHNSON,

MICHAEL FIX, AND JULIE MURRAY

THE CITIZENSHIP TEST CIRCA 2006

The Immigration and Naturalization Act of 1952 requires the testing of individuals seeking US citizenship on English-language ability and knowledge and understanding of US history and government. The current test is given in a principally oral, rather than written, format. Applicants' language skills are evaluated during the course of the oral test on US history and government, to ensure that they have at least an elementary level of English, though no standardized measure exists to independently evaluate English language ability. A review of the testing process performed by Coopers and Lybrand in 1997 found no standard test content and that testing instruments and scoring systems often varied across testing sites.[1] Given the subjective nature of the test, immigration officials are allowed to exercise "due consideration," or make allowances in certain cases based on an individual's education, age, background, and length of time in the United States. The 1997 study also found the extent of due consideration granted to be highly variable across testing sites.

REVISITING THE SYSTEM

The United States is in the process of revising the content and purpose of its citizenship exam. It is not the only country considering a revision; there have

---

1 Department of Homeland Security, Office of the Inspector General, Letter Report: Citizenship Test Redesign, 2005.

been new initiatives in several European countries (Britain, the Netherlands, and Germany) to create citizenship exams that cover content beyond basic historical facts and that capture whether applicants share what are deemed to be core national values.[2]

NATURALIZATION TRENDS 1990 TO THE PRESENT

In 2004, approximately 38 percent of the foreign-born population (13.1 million persons) were naturalized citizens.[3] The rate of naturalization among the foreign-born population has been steadily increasing since the early 1990s. Between 1994 and 2004, rates of naturalization increased by 232 percent over the previous decade.[4] This trend has held steady even in the face of record increases in immigration levels during the past two decades. A portion of the rise in naturalizations since 1994 can be attributed to the 1986 Immigration Reform and Control Act (IRCA), which granted legal status to 2.7 million unauthorized immigrants, thereby increasing the number of eligible applicants.[5] Other factors that played a role in rising naturalizations include the exclusion of non-citizens from certain public benefits by reforms introduced in 1996 and other heightened restrictions (expanding categories for deportable offenses, e.g.) for the non-naturalized population.

NATURALIZATION BACKLOGS

Between 1997 and 2001, the federal government reported that the average processing time for US naturalization applications decreased from two years to between six and nine months. Applications are processed regionally however, and there were still significant variations in processing times due to existing backlogs. As of January 2006, district offices in Orlando, FL, and Charlotte, NC, were processing naturalization applications that were submitted in December 2004, while offices in Providence, RI, and Cincinnati, OH, were processing applications submitted as recently as October 2005.[6] US Citizenship and Immigration Services

---

2   Pilot tests have been introduced in the Netherlands and in Germany that attempt to test the values of applicants from certain countries or religious backgrounds against a set of "national values." As an example, the Baden-Württemberg region of Germany has begun asking Muslims from Islamic countries an additional set of questions to elicit their beliefs on a range of domestic issues including women's rights and religious freedom, to determine whether they should be granted citizenship. See E. Rothstein, "Refining the Tests that Confer Citizenship," *The New York Times*, January 23, 2006.

3   A. Erlich and D. Dixon, "Spotlight on Naturalization Trends," Migration Information Source (Washington, DC: Migration Policy Institute, November 1, 2005).

4   Ibid.

5   Ibid.

6   US Citizenship and Immigration Services Web site, https://egov.immigration.gov/cris/jsps/ptimes.jsp.

Figure 1. The Naturalized Speak Better English, Have More Education, and Higher Incomes

Percent of Ages 25 and over

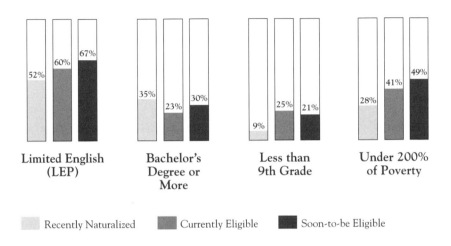

Limited English (LEP)	Bachelor's Degree or More	Less than 9th Grade	Under 200% of Poverty
52% / 60% / 67%	35% / 23% / 30%	9% / 25% / 21%	28% / 41% / 49%

Recently Naturalized   Currently Eligible   Soon-to-be Eligible

Source: Urban Institute estimates are based on Census and CPS data. M. Fix, J. Passel, and K. Sucher, "Trends in Naturalization," Immigrant Families and Workers, Brief No. 3 (Washington, DC: The Urban Institute, September 2003).

(USCIS) has been working to eliminate the backlog of applications to ensure a six-month processing time for all applications.

Characteristics of Naturalized and "Eligible" Populations

Despite a high percentage of applicants who are granted citizenship (84 percent of all 2004 applicants received citizenship), there still remain a significant number of eligible persons who do not apply for naturalization. These include green card holders in the United States for five years or more or legal permanent residents married to US citizens in the United States for at least three years. This eligible population differs from the recently naturalized population in its English-language skills, education levels, countries of origin, income, immigration status, and settlement location in the United States. In many cases, its members face educational and linguistic barriers to naturalization.

- **A significant portion of the eligible population is limited English proficient.** Sixty percent of immigrants who were eligible to naturalize in 2000-

2001 were estimated to be limited English proficient (LEP). Additionally, 40 percent of the eligible population for this period indicated that they speak English either "not well" or "not at all."

■ **Individuals with low levels of education naturalize at lower rates.**[7] In 2000-2001, the portions of the eligible population that possessed less than a ninth-grade education or possessed at least a bachelor's degree were roughly equal (25 percent and 23 percent, respectively). Thirty-five percent of the recently naturalized population was made up of college graduates versus only 9 percent with a ninth-grade education or less.

■ **Rates of naturalization vary according to national origin.** Although Mexican immigrants make up the largest portion of the population that is eligible to naturalize, as a group they have not naturalized at a proportional rate. In 2001, Mexican immigrants made up 28 percent of the total eligible population but only 9 percent of naturalized citizens.

■ **The eligible population also has lower income levels than those who have recently naturalized.** In 2000-2001, 41 percent of eligible immigrants had incomes under 200 percent of the federal poverty level and 17 percent were under the federal poverty level. In contrast, only 28 percent of recently naturalized citizens had incomes below 200 percent of the poverty level and 11 percent had incomes under the federal poverty level for this period.[8]

■ **Refugees are *more* likely to naturalize than the rest of the eligible population.** During 2000-2001, refugees made up 14 percent of the eligible population but made up a significantly higher portion — 24 percent — of the recently naturalized population. Thus, refugees are 1.5 times more likely to naturalize than the non-refugee eligible population. This phenomenon may be in part due to ongoing conflict in their home countries that precludes any possibility of future return and to the variety of immigration-related programs and services (both public and private) that are available exclusively to refugee communities.[9]

---

7   M. Fix, J. Passel, and K. Sucher, "Trends in Naturalization," Immigrant Families and Workers, Brief No. 3 (Washington, DC: The Urban Institute, September 2003).

8   Ibid.

9   Ibid.

CURRENT FEDERAL POLICY ISSUES

REDESIGNING THE CITIZENSHIP TEST

Despite demonstrated governmental interest in reforming the citizenship test, the redesign and the form it will take are currently uncertain. In December 2000, the Immigration and Naturalization Service (INS) began a formal test redesign initiative. The redesign has been aimed at improving both the content and administration of the test. Its main goals have been to (1) ensure that the test is administered in a standardized way across sites; (2) make the test a better, more meaningful gauge of the applicant's understanding of US history and civics; and (3) be fair and reliable. But achieving these multiple goals creates three basic tensions:

One tension is using simple English to test abstract concepts and ideas from US history and civics. The new test will need to evaluate applicants' understanding of complex ideas and concepts while using only the basic level of English required by the Immigration and Naturalization Act.[10] A second is balancing "due consideration" for individual cases with promoting standardization, A principal goal for the redesign process is the standardization of the exam across all testing centers. However, current regulations also dictate that test administrators should exercise "due consideration" and weigh test performance against an applicant's personal background.[11] A third is to create a meaningful test without affecting difficulty or increasing failure rates. USCIS has indicated that any changes that aim to make the citizenship exam a more meaningful tool will need to do so without affecting the current level of difficulty.[12]

In late 2006, the USCIS released new proposed questions for the citizenship test that will be pilot tested in selected sites. A new test is scheduled to be introduced in 2008.

---

10 Department of Homeland Security, "Letter Report" (see n. 1).

11 Ibid.

12 Ibid.

About the Editor and Contributors

Michael Fix is Vice President and Director of Studies at MPI. He co-directs MPI's National Center on Immigrant Immigration Policy. His work focuses on immigrant integration, immigrant children and families, the education of immigrant students, and the effect of welfare reform on immigrants.

Jeanne Batalova is a Policy Analyst at the Migration Policy Institute.

Amy Beeler is Research Director at the Institute for Work and the Economy at Northern Illinois University.

Deborah Garvey is a Lecturer at the Department of Economics, Santa Clara University.

Julia Gelatt is a Research Assistant at the Migration Policy Institute.

Adam Gurvitch is the Director of Health Advocacy at the New York Immigration Coalition.

Tamar Jacoby is a Senior Fellow at The Manhattan Institute.

Mary Helen Ybarra Johnson was a research intern at the Migration Policy Institute.

Donald Kerwin is Executive Director of the Catholic Legal Immigration Network, Inc.

Leighton Ku is a Senior Fellow at the Center on Budget and Policy Priorities.

Cecilia Muñoz is the Vice President of the National Council of La Raza's Office of Research, Advocacy, and Legislation.

Janet Murguía is the President and CEO of the National Council of La Raza.

Julie Murray was an Associate Policy Analyst at the Migration Policy Institute.

Demetrios G. Papademetriou is the President and Co-Founder of the Migration Policy Institute.

Renee Reichl is a graduate student at the Department of Sociology at the University of California, Los Angeles.

Roger Waldinger is a Professor in the Department of Sociology at the University of California, Los Angeles.

About the Migration Policy Institute (MPI)

The Migration Policy Institute (MPI) is an independent, nonpartisan, non-profit think tank dedicated to the study of the movement of people worldwide. The institute provides analysis, development, and evaluation of migration and refugee policies at the local, national, and international levels. It aims to meet the rising demand for pragmatic responses to the challenges and opportunities that migration presents in an ever more integrated world. MPI also produces the Migration Information Source, an online journal with current migration data and analysis at www.migrationinformation.org.

MPI's National Center on Immigrant Integration Policy

In February 2007, MPI launched the National Center on Immigrant Integration Policy. The Center, co-directed by Michael Fix and Margie McHugh, is a crossroads for elected officials, grassroots leaders, universities, think tanks, local service providers, state and local agency managers, and others who seek to understand and respond to the challenges and opportunities created by today's high rates of immigration. The Center provides key services, including research, policy design, leadership development, technical assistance and training for government officials and community leaders, and an electronic resource center on immigrant integration issues with a special focus on state and local policies and data.

The Independent Task Force on Immigration and America's Future

The Task Force, a distinguished bipartisan panel of leaders and experts from key sectors concerned with migration, was convened by MPI in cooperation with the Manhattan Institute and the Division of United States Studies and the Mexico Institute at the Woodrow Wilson International Center for Scholars. The Task Force's purpose was to carefully evaluate the economic, social, and demographic factors driving today's large-scale immigration to the United States, legal and illegal. Based on this analysis, the Task Force recommends that to harness the benefits of immigration and advance US national interests in the 21st century, the United States needs a new immigration policy and system. Its work has culminated in the recent publication, *Immigration and America's Future: A New Chapter*.

About MPI's Recent Publication

IMMIGRATION AND AMERICA'S FUTURE: A NEW CHAPTER
SEPTEMBER 2006
For information on the Task Force, please visit www.migrationpolicy.org. The full report can be purchased online for $14.95, plus shipping, for global delivery (Visa and Mastercard only). The Executive Summary is available online in both English and Spanish.

Order online: www.migrationpolicy.org
Order by phone: 202-266-1908
Order by fax: 202-266-1900
For questions, please call 202-266-1908 or e-mail info@migrationpolicy.org.

Supporting Task Force Publications, by Topic

OVERVIEW
Independent Task Force on Immigration and America's Future: The Roadmap
By Michael Fix, Doris Meissner, and Demetrios G. Papademetriou, Migration Policy Institute

Reflections on Restoring Integrity to the United States Immigration System: A Personal Vision
By Demetrios G. Papademetriou, Migration Policy Institute

THE UNAUTHORIZED POPULATION
Unauthorized Migrants: Numbers and Characteristics
Report by Jeffrey S. Passel, Pew Hispanic Center

Twilight Statuses: A Closer Examination of the Unauthorized Population
By David A. Martin, Migration Policy Institute and University of Virginia School of Law
Lessons from the Immigration Reform and Control Act of 1986
By Betsy Cooper and Kevin O'Neil, Migration Policy Institute

The "Regularization" Option in Managing Illegal Migration More
Effectively: A Comparative Perspective
By Demetrios G. Papademetriou, Migration Policy Institute

MEETING NATIONAL SECURITY AND IMMIGRATION
ENFORCEMENT IMPERATIVES
Immigration Enforcement at the Worksite: Making it Work
By Marc R. Rosenblum, Migration Policy Institute

US Border Enforcement: From Horseback to High-Tech
By Deborah W. Meyers, Migration Policy Institute

Eligible to Work: Experiments in Verifying Work Authorization
By Kevin Jernegan, Migration Policy Institute

An Idea Whose Time Has Finally Come?
The Case for Employment Verification
By Tamar Jacoby, Manhattan Institute

Immigration Facts: Immigration Enforcement Spending Since IRCA
By David Dixon and Julia Gelatt, Migration Policy Institute

Documentation Provisions of the Real ID Act
By Kevin Jernegan, Migration Policy Institute

Countering Terrorist Mobility: Shaping an Operational Strategy
Report by Susan Ginsburg, Migration Policy Institute

Immigration Enforcement: Beyond the Border and the Workplace
By David A. Martin, Migration Policy Institute and University of Virginia
School of Law

IMMIGRATION AND THE US LABOR MARKET
Temporary Worker Programs: A Patchwork Policy Response
By Deborah W. Meyers, Migration Policy Institute

"Comprehensive" Legislation vs. Fundamental Reform:
The Limits of Current Immigration Proposals
By Marc R. Rosenblum, Migration Policy Institute

The Growing Connection Between Temporary and Permanent
Immigration Systems
By Jeanne Batalova, Migration Policy Institute

US Employment-Based Admissions: Permanent and Temporary
By Susan Martin, Institute for the Study of International Migration,
Georgetown University

The Contributions of High-Skilled Immigrants
By Neeraj Kaushal, Columbia University, and Michael Fix, Migration Policy Institute

Immigrants and Labor Force Trends: The Future, Past, and Present
By B. Lindsay Lowell, Institute for the Study of International Migration, Georgetown University; Julia Gelatt, and Jeanne Batalova, Migration Policy Institute

**The Impact of Immigration on Native Workers:
A Fresh Look at the Evidence**
By Julie Murray, Jeanne Batalova, and Michael Fix, Migration Policy Institute

All of these publications can be downloaded as PDFs at http://www.migrationpolicy.org/ITFIAF/publications.php.

They can also be purchased through MPI's online bookstore at www.migrationpolicy.org.

ACKNOWLEDGMENTS

Thanks go the following organizations and foundations:

Carnegie Corporation of New York
Charles Evans Hughes Memorial Foundation
Evelyn and Walter Haas, Jr. Fund
Ford Foundation
Haas Foundation
JEHT Foundation
JM Kaplan Fund
Manhattan Institute
Open Society Institute
Woodrow Wilson International Center for Scholars

Michael Fix would like to thank Julia Gelatt, Julie Murray, and Meg Weaver who were instrumental in pulling this volume together. He would also like to thank Doris Meissner, Director of the Independent Task Force on Immigration and America's Future and Senior Fellow at MPI, and Demetri Papademetriou, President of MPI, for their guidance and support.